ARCHBISHOP

Also By Michele Guinness

Chosen
The Heavenly Party
Woman, the Full Story
The Guinness Spirit
Tapestry of Voices
Promised Land
Autumn Leave
Made for Each Other
Is God Good for Women?
The Word of the Wives (with Abby Guinness)

Michele Guinness

ARCHBISHOP

A NOVEL

HODDER

Unless indicated otherwise, Scripture quotations are taken from the
Holy Bible, New International Version (Anglicised edition).
Copyright © 1979, 1984, 2011 by Biblica (formerly International Bible Society).
Used by permission. All rights reserved.

First published in Great Britain in 2014 by Hodder & Stoughton
An Hachette UK company

This paperback edition first published in 2015

1

A CIP catalogue record for this title is available from the British Library

ISBN 978 1 444 75337 0
eBook ISBN 978 1444 75338 7

Typeset in Sabon MT by Hewer Text UK Ltd, Edinburgh

Printed and bound in the UK by Clays Ltd, St Ives plc

Hodder & Stoughton policy is to use papers that are natural, renewable and
recyclable products and made from wood grown in sustainable forests. The logging
and manufacturing processes are expected to conform to the environmental
regulations of the country of origin.

Hodder & Stoughton Ltd
338 Euston Road
London NW1 3BH

www.hodderfaith.com

CONTENTS

Acknowledgements   vi

Prologue: 5 December 2019   1

Part One: 2020   21

Part Two: 2020–21   173

Part Three: 2022–24   327

Part Four: February–April 2024   501

Victoria Burnham-Woods – CV   545

Sources   547

ACKNOWLEDGEMENTS

This book has been a long time in the making. I first had the idea of creating a female Archbishop of Canterbury over twenty years ago, before women were even able to be vicars in the Church of England, and I am immensely grateful to all those who encouraged me to run with it, even though, overwhelmed by the work involved, I put it and them off for so long.

Finally, though, Vicky has taken on flesh and blood, and truly insinuated herself into my life, largely thanks to the many wonderful women ministers who have shared their joys and frustrations with me over the years. Pieces of what each of you has told me have metamorphosed into the composite whole that is Vicky. I even had some notes in my possession that I had made way back in the mid-1980s during a conversation with the late Revd Mo Witcombe, whose untimely death robbed the church of one of its best and brightest.

Never in the history of acknowledgments, however, have so many wished to remain anonymous. They know who they are, and I know where they live, and am hugely indebted to them for their insights and for their so generously helping me find my way through the complex machinery of the Church of England. And in this I include the church press officer who threw me out of the punters' tearoom at Church House for being a journalist, when I went to General Synod many years ago as part of my research.

Amongst the folk I can thank by name are Ian Metcalfe at Hodder & Stoughton, for his guidance, perceptiveness, and finesse with the editorial pen (or should I say cursor?); my daughter, Abby, who critiqued the manuscript in her usual forthright, invaluable manner; Sarah Guinness and Agi Gilbert who read the manuscript and gave vital encouragement; Bernie Wilkins, David Lewis, Richard Farnell, Jane Banner-Martin and Sandra Pedder for some original ideas, and particularly, Judith Rose Gwyer, former Archdeacon of Tonbridge, and first archdeacon in the church, for her time and hospitality.

I am overawed by the work of XLP and The Message Trust and the entrepreneurial skills that led their founders to put their vision into such effective action to enable young people to fulfil their great potential. I hope they, and the hundreds of other remarkable faith-based charities that seek the best for the people they serve will find a much-deserved (but very inadequate), tribute here to all they do. Thank you too to the folk at St Mark's, Gillingham who have put up with my angst and my moaning, not to mention my near invisibility over the past two years. They released me to write, and cheered me on from the sidelines – and I want them to know how much that has meant to me.

My husband always says, 'Don't bother acknowledging me,' and that says everything about him. He has put up with my endless questions and doubts, and my reading of excerpts at breakfast, lunch, dinner and last thing at night – all with very little complaint, considering. If he hadn't got ordained there would have been no book.

The novel was all but written before Rowan Williams announced his resignation. Any resemblance of the characters in it to persons living or dead, or to their views is purely coincidental. They are all figments of my imagination. Not so, many of the situations in which they find themselves. But truth is always stranger than fiction.

For Sarah, ordained 2014.
Become whatever you are called to be.

PROLOGUE

5 DECEMBER 2019

In 2019, the position of Archbishop of Canterbury was suddenly and unforeseeably made vacant by the premature and inconvenient decease of the previous incumbent, whose body had been found, alone, in a rather depressing bedroom of a third-rate hotel in Bognor Regis, clutching an item of ladies' underwear that did not belong to his wife. Initially, the screaming headlines said only that he had had a massive coronary, admiring his frugality at not opting for a palatial, five-star resting place when the job required an overnight stay. And then, presumably via an anonymous member of staff at Lambeth Palace, the truth was exposed, including the fact that neither his wife, nor his secretary, nor indeed any of the usual suspects knew what he was doing in Bognor Regis or why. The populace's rabid hunger for salacious speculation and conspiracy theories and the embarrassment of the church, already reeling after a barrage of accusations of incompetence that accompanied the now-deceased Archbishop's short-lived attempt to unite a deeply divided church, made it imperative that a successor be found as swiftly as possible.

In the great British pecking order, the Archbishop of Canterbury is second only in status to the monarch. The Prime Minister must be content with taking third place, though few of them have been, or are.

In fact, for hundreds of years, in his or her capacity as advisor to the Crown, the Prime Minister would simply pick an archbishop. The church, understandably aggrieved at this *ad hoc* intervention in its affairs and the political bias that went with it, negotiated a system whereby all archbishops and senior bishops were selected from two names presented to the Prime Minister – a preferred choice and a back-up. Margaret Thatcher, however, had the gall to turn a formality into reality by overruling the church on no less than three occasions that included opting for a second-best candidate for Archbishop of Canterbury when the church's favourite was too left-wing for her fancy. High-handedness is not a uniquely Tory trait, however. In 1997 it was alleged that Tony Blair rejected both nominees for one particular episcopal vacancy. Probably because they weren't left-wing enough.

In 2007 Prime Minister Gordon Brown, keen perhaps to score points over his predecessors, decided that there should be no more meddling of government officials in something they knew nothing about. (Not that it ever prevented them in other areas.) In advising the Queen on her royal prerogative of choosing senior ecclesiastical posts, her 'prime ministerial advisor' would encourage her to follow the recommendations of the church. In effect, he was now relegated to messenger boy, conveying the name of the church's first choice to the monarch, the runner-up only a back-up should the church's preferred option be disqualified or die during the proceedings.

Following the demise of the Archbishop in 2019, the then Labour PM invited his old chum, Lord Gordon Fairfax, to chair the secretive Crown Nominations Commission responsible for the appointment of a successor. The only vague prerequisite for this particular role was that its holder should be an 'actual communicant lay member of the Church of England'. It is fair to say that Gordon did grace his 'local' with his presence at Christmas and at Easter – if he hadn't more pressing commitments. Mostly, he encouraged his wife to be 'communicant' on his behalf, in the belief that women were more naturally inclined to sing the praises of a male Saviour's abiding love and gentle touch. Fairfax believed that the real interests of Anglicanism were best served by faith in moderate socialism, and that therefore he was more than amply qualified for this important task.

Reading up on his duties, Gordon came across an internet description of the Commission's performance that suggested that the appointing of an Archbishop of Canterbury was a tortuous and impenetrable process, 'reflecting the church's traditional tendency towards compromise and *ad hoc* solutions'. He couldn't resist a wry smile. A fairly apt description of most of the workings of the Church of England, he suspected.

In late middle age, he appeared an unassuming kind of man, white-haired, of average height and build, who nonetheless managed to exude the quiet authority and latent power of a highly successful businessman. The former chief of his own international computer manufacturing business, he had worked hard to achieve its reputation for efficiency and delivery. 'On a par with Swiss trains,' he would boast proudly to his dedicated staff, believing his achievements well deserved the peerage he had acquired.

His daily dealings involved making a raft of swift, well-advised but lone judgements, and his instinct rarely let him down. Then why, he asked himself, had he ever agreed to let eleven apparently randomly selected, distinctly odd-ball Commission members be inflicted on his sound judgement and good sense? For twelve people consensus was well-nigh impossible. For twelve Anglicans it was as feasible as a group-swim across the Thames. But he had been allured by some vague altruistic notion of serving his country, and his church. And helping the PM out of a fix.

Six members of General Synod (the Church of England's national assembly) – three clergy and three lay – plus four representatives of the Diocese of Canterbury's 'Statement of Needs' committee (that matched the demands of the local diocese to a pre-planned identikit of their prospective bishop) constituted the Commission, along with Ryan Talbot, the new Archbishop of York – the youngest ever, at forty-two. Gordon recognised his type: a bright, bushy-tailed, disingenuous young whipper-snapper, opinionated enough to be intensely annoying at times, but with sufficient flashes of candour, humility and genius to redeem his other weaknesses.

The Commission had already met on several occasions for several days at a time, secreted away in clandestine venues closeted from the world. All very cloak and dagger, possibly more MI5 than Church of England. It might have been entertaining if it hadn't been so darned frustrating. A suitable archbishop was becoming increasingly hard to find. Given the acrimonious divisions in what was once known as the worldwide Anglican Communion, but was now more of a nominal umbrella for groups of churches across the globe with very differing views, only an outstanding leader with the qualities of the Archangel Gabriel could keep the umbrella from folding inside out and smashing the spokes in the first puff of wind.

From a shortlist of twelve names they had eventually come up with a preferred choice. But before any white smoke issued from the Sistine Chapel, before the name even reached the Prime Minister's desk, the unfortunate candidate failed his medical when he couldn't remember the Prime Minister's name, and was discovered to have symptoms of early Alzheimer's Disease. The second, reserve choice withdrew when his eldest son was excluded from boarding school for possessing and dealing class-two drugs. And so it was back to the drawing board.

'Well, here we are again,' Gordon said to the dozen, 'the select few, gathered once more in some half-forgotten diocesan retreat house, for one of the Church of England's special mini-breaks. Try to see it constructively, as the chance to get away from your . . . from our more mundane lives, while performing a sacred service to our beloved Queen and country. This unremarkable meeting-room will no doubt be as familiar to us as our own bedrooms by the end of the next few days.'

Stifling a yawn, Catherine Cole followed his glance around the walls. Bare and soulless. Not a picture to attract the eye or distract the mind. Displaying those two hallmarks of the Anglican establishment – dullness and boredom – both of which were in store for her today, of that she had no doubt; unless, of course, someone decided to play dirty tricks. One could but hope.

'This is ridiculous,' she muttered, glancing around the table over the top of her small, owlish spectacles, barely disguising the distaste that forced down the corners of her mouth. An academic specialising in nineteenth-century feminist literature, she sported a swinging, shoulder-length, grey bob, incongruous, framing such a wizened face. 'We've already dismissed the remaining ten candidates, so where do we go from here?'

'Have we? Dismissed them all? I wasn't aware of it,' boomed a bulky man with unruly eyebrows. The shapeless grey moustache drooped over a mouth that sounded full of marbles, lifted just enough to reveal a set of discoloured, uneven teeth. He held up Canterbury's 'Statement of Needs' paper and waved it at Catherine. 'This is our diocesan bishop we're talking about, remember. Ours.'

Colonel Frank Hardiman, carrying his rank around in retirement like a comfort blanket, Gordon said to himself. 'As ever.'

'Oh, for goodness' sake, Frank,' Catherine snapped, 'let's not go over that again. When it comes to choosing the archbishop, the needs and wishes of the Canterbury diocese are of lesser importance and must therefore be subsumed to the needs of the international Anglican Church.'

'What's left of it,' murmured Brian Dimmock, before Frank could summon up an apt retort.

The Revd Brian was one of the clergy trio, two men and a woman, elected by their respective lobbies in Synod. Catherine threw him a withering look.

'Okay, Brian, if you want to split hairs, the Anglican Co-op, or whatever it now is.'

'The International Anglican Alliance,' Fairfax murmured.

'I was being facetious, Gordon,' Catherine explained wearily.

'Believe what you want, do what you want and still call yourself an Anglican,' Brian Dimmock said wryly, 'as long as you give a nodding acknowledgement of the leadership of Canterbury and purport to be in community, if not unity. Actually,' he added, with a conciliatory nod in Catherine's direction, 'on this occasion, I agree with my esteemed colleague. We started the process with twelve names, then shortlisted six, two of which received by far the most favourable tweets in our nationwide consultation with the great British public. But all of them are now out of the running – our two final choices that fell by the way, the two that failed the psychometric test, and the two who said publicly they wouldn't want such a poisoned chalice. That leaves the original six we didn't shortlist. So why did we rule them out in the first place? No fire, no passion, no obvious vision or ability to share it if they had one, that's why. All safe, don't-rock-the boat choices. Most of them without a tweet in support of their name. If these six are all the Church of England can come up with, it's a poor show. Can't we be just a little more radical – for once?'

Catherine rewarded him with a look that bordered on appreciation. There was more to this often cynical, rather jaded vicar than his chinless, dishevelled appearance at first suggested.

'Well, I don't see why we're not employing the same methods for this post as we now do for any other bishop,' piped up another of the four representatives of the Canterbury Diocese – a diminutive man, whose hands, constantly fiddling with a pencil, were hidden by several extraneous inches of jacket sleeve. His small, round head, topped with a wig-like mop of copious black hair, suddenly poked out from around Frank's cumbrous frame. 'Advertising and interviewing is much fairer than this antiquated word-of-mouth nonsense.'

'We went through this last time, Clive,' Catherine said slowly, as if she were addressing one of her less able students. 'We can't. And you know that only the status-mad and power-crazed would apply. Who in their right mind would ever want a job like this?'

'Ah, yes, of course,' Clive Marshall conceded, 'especially after the sad demise of our last, much-loved incumbent. Hide of a rhinoceros and constitution of an ox, eh? A pity we didn't listen to one of his more recent predecessors.'

'Whoever we choose will be subject to even more thorough screening,' Gordon announced. 'We can't afford a repeat of the last calamity.'

An abrupt, uncomfortable silence halted the deliberations.

'Mr Pargetter,' he snapped, turning to an earnest-looking, wiry-haired man in his early forties, wearing a pin-striped suit, who appeared to spend most of his time straightening his tie, or pushing his glasses back up his nose, and never seemed entirely comfortable with the proceedings, 'I think we may need your help.'

In another life, or that was how it seemed to him now, before he was head-hunted to be the Archbishop's Appointments' Advisor, David Pargetter had been a senior executive in HR for Marks and Spencer. It had been a good company to work for – twenty per cent discount on all purchases, an annual bonus scheme, discounts on holiday and health club membership, and an exceptionally good pension. Not like the Church of England. No bonuses or discounts, no perks after his nosedive into what he now termed, amusingly he thought, the turbulent waters of 'the cold sees', his little play on the old English name for a diocese. Sometimes, he couldn't even remember what had pushed him, except for the kudos of serving the Archbishop, and a passing, rather noble desire to serve his church. But that might instead have been indigestion, since it wore off in the stark reality of his first week at work.

Still, the job had its moments. An occasional compensation. Like contributing to the choice of successor on his boss's throne. Pargetter would never have called himself a perverse kind of man. Nor even a mischief maker. He had certainly never acted out of his normal, cautious character before. But in the years that followed, throughout the multifarious and monumental consequences of the one little sentence he was about to utter, he had no idea what had provoked him into saying it.

'There is always a wild card.'

Every head around the table turned in unison in his direction, the faces a daunting mix of surprise and newly awakened expectation. It threw him momentarily. He cleared his throat loudly.

'But I'm not sure how good an idea that might be,' he faltered.

For goodness' sake, he didn't even like, let alone seriously rate the suggestion he had been about to make. Reason whispered, 'Time for a little back-pedalling, old chap – for all you're worth,' while another, more impish voice urged him on what he suspected might be a foolish, even dangerous course. 'It's said now. And what's to lose?'

'Come along,' flashed Catherine, 'don't keep us in suspense. God knows we've wasted enough time already.'

'Yes,' muttered Gordon, feeling somewhat out-chaired, as usual, by that grating little woman, and irritable because of it. 'Whatever you have up your sleeve, Mr Pargetter, we'd like to be party to it.'

The advisor thumbed slowly through his papers, beginning to appreciate the sense of power his procrastination had lent him, and slowly drew out a file.

'Ah, here it is. The current Bishop of Larchester.'

In the hush that ensued, Pargetter took the time to monitor the group's responses carefully, enjoying the raising of the eyebrows, the widening of the eyes, the opening of the mouths in complete and utter astonishment that indicated the exact moment when each one grasped the implications of his suggestion.

'Did you say wild card – or joker?' blustered Frank Hardiman, his moustache twitching as if it had a life of its own. 'No, no, no, no, no. The church isn't ready for this. Is it, Clive?'

'I . . . er . . .'

'Say something, man.'

'Ah, that turbulent priest,' jumped in the female vicar, whose arms were stretched to their limit across her ample girth, only just allowing her to fold her hands across it.

'At last, she speaks,' Gordon said to himself.

'Now that would be an interesting appointment.'

'And, as I already said at the very beginning of this process, why not a woman?' Catherine Cole interrupted, looking round the table with a fiendish smile. 'We would be making history.'

'Why not indeed?' Gordon said quickly, fearful that if he did not take immediate control the meeting would descend into a feminist squabble. Besides, the more he thought about it, the more he warmed to the idea of being cutting-edge. He rarely agreed with Catherine, but going down in history would more than make up for the unpaid hours spent on such a mind-numbing exercise. And he had the feeling that the PM would be rather pleased.

'The Commission is not discriminatory, is it?' he asked, looking round the table affably. 'The government certainly wouldn't expect us to be. After all, it is a number of years since women were admitted to the episcopacy. This was bound to happen at some point. We're simply doing it sooner rather than later.'

'Ahead of ourselves, are we? That must be a first.'

'Sarcasm is the lowest form of wit, Brian,' Catherine reminded him.

'Let's not forget that Canada, the USA, and Australia have all had women primates already,' Brian continued, 'some better than others. I don't have a problem with it.'

The female vicar nodded enthusiastically, rocking slightly as if she were sprung-loaded, her many chins oscillating. 'Primate,' she chortled, 'let's not monkey around.' No one so much as smiled. She cleared her throat and sank back into silence.

The third member of the clergy team, a cathedral dean whose pinched little mouth turned down at the corners as if he were a martyr to permanent indigestion, simply said, 'No.'

'No, you don't have a problem, Julian, or no, you don't agree with the possibility?' asked Gordon with some exasperation.

'No, I don't like the woman.'

'What have you got against her?' Catherine asked, turning to the Dean with surprise.

'Shows scant wegard for convention and twadition.'

Gordon noticed he said, 'wegard' and 'twadition', the inability to roll the 'r's a speech impediment he always found contrived and grating.

'All in the name of modernisation,' Dean Julian Riley continued smoothly, in response to the puzzled expressions.

'For example?' Catherine asked sharply.

The Dean studied her over his half-moon spectacles, sniffed lengthily and addressed his response to the chairman.

'For example? Permitting three members of the laity to preside at Holy Communion, contrary to canon law. "No person shall consecrate and administer the holy sacrament of the Lord's Supper unless ordained priest by episcopal ordination." Canon B12.'

'We all remember the incident, of course,' Brian intervened, before the Dean could fire any further Anglican canonry at them. 'Some of the clergy in her diocese were up in arms. The press made its usual song and dance about it. But as I remember, she was able to show quite clearly that authorising lay people to share unconsecrated bread and wine in a Sunday service of the Word does not officially constitute a Holy Communion. There was therefore no charge of dereliction of duty to answer.

'What's more,' he continued, before the Dean could intervene, 'she did it because a large number of rural parishes were without a vicar, and the clergy in her diocese were heartily sick of chasing from church to church every Sunday like blue-arsed flies, driving a sixty-mile round trip and more, when there were lay readers perfectly capable of administering bread and wine.'

The Dean's mouth fell open in astonishment; whether at the theology or the language, none of the gathering was entirely sure.

'And,' Brian added as a final parry, 'the congregations in question were grateful to have a service that was the nearest thing to the Holy Communion they couldn't have due to a shortage of clergy.'

'The thin end of a very big wedge,' spluttered the Dean. 'If we divest the clergy of this sacred task, what makes the priestly calling distinctive?'

'The alternative in the current situation is that some churches won't have Communion at all,' Brian replied.

'We're not here to debate church policy,' Gordon intervened swiftly, as he saw the discussion descending into liturgical one-upmanship. 'Nor to play bait-the-dean,' he added to himself.

'And anyway,' Catherine added, 'as Archbishop her wings would be clipped. There can be no policy changes without the say-so of the House of Bishops and General Synod. That's why there are so few policy changes at all.'

'She's still too wadical and gimmicky for my liking,' muttered the Dean.

Looking around the group, Gordon observed, to his surprise, that apart from the Dean and Frank Hardiman, there was only one other obvious dissenter – a lay Synod member. He invited her response.

'I'm not exactly opposed,' Dorothy Cardle explained in a gentle, measured way, with the slightest hint of a tremor as she spoke. She was an elderly woman with shrewd, lively eyes in a face mottled with age, and fluffy white hair that regularly escaped its chignon and had to be repinned into place. 'I agree with Frank, that I'm not sure the church is ready for it. There was a great deal of pain when women were made bishops. The alternative measures for the disaffected have gone a long way to preventing major schism. But we're losing enough of our members as it is, without pushing them out of the nest. I wonder whether a woman Archbishop might not be seen as deliberate provocation? And not just here in the UK, but especially by our African brothers and sisters, who are very much opposed to female bishops, let alone one in such a key leadership role.'

'It's an issue the church will have to face at some point,' Gordon said quietly.

'And she is very high profile, is she not?' Dorothy continued. 'I mean, there are few bishops so regularly asked to comment on national and international affairs.'

'Yes, indeed,' David Pargetter concurred. 'Being the first female diocesan bishop was bound to make her the centre of media attention. But Bishop Vicky first caught the public's eye over twenty years ago when she was a curate, with one of the first "Fresh Expressions", as they were called – new church communities that have developed within the Church of England in areas where traditional church has become largely irrelevant to much of the population. Since then, she has maintained a reputation for outspokenness on a raft of issues – social justice, inadequate health care, inequalities in education, environmental issues, such as the church's urgent need to sell off its energy-consuming buildings and modernise, and,' he nodded vaguely in the direction of the Dean, who winced visibly, 'the unfair differentials in clergy pay.'

'A card-carrying socialist?' Frank expostulated loudly.

Clive looked up in alarm.

'Left of centre, certainly, but not a member of any political party,'

Pargetter reassured him. 'In her university days, she made quite a name for herself as a radical in the Durham Union Society, the university's formidable debating society – which, I must say, was more than justified, judging by her later performances in General Synod.'

'A gifted speaker, certainly,' Dorothy admitted, 'quite compelling, though I have only heard her the once. Carried me along on a wave of energy and passion. Though I can't say I'm altogether happy with her near-celebrity status.' She sighed heavily. 'But perhaps that's what we need these days? When the euro collapsed, her predecessor, sadly, appeared to have little to offer the nation in the way of hope and consolation. She, I suspect, would have had a great deal more to say.'

'We said from the start that we needed the Archangel Gabriel,' said Catherine. 'Well, it seems we may have got him – in female form. Wasn't it Archbishop Randall Davidson who said, "The post of Archbishop of Canterbury is impossible for any one man to do, but only one man can do it"? Maybe a woman would do it even better.'

Frank tutted loudly and shook his head. 'I didn't think we were considering a woman just yet. Too inexperienced – only made bishops a few years ago – but if we are, I think we still need a bit more on this paragon.'

He turned to Pargetter, narrowing his eyes. 'I have the feeling there are things you haven't told us – yet.'

'Hadn't you better tell us about her theology and churchmanship?' demanded Dean Riley. 'I have met the good lady before, but many of my colleagues here haven't.'

He said 'feology' in his parsonical, southern-counties drawl. Gordon shuddered the way he did when he heard a fingernail scraped down a blackboard. He noticed that the continuous white ring of the Dean's dog collar wobbled around his scrawny neck, making his head appear detached from the rest of his body.

'I hear your reluctance, you three,' Gordon said, 'but I think we ought to hear more about the bishop before we make up our minds. Mr Pargetter?'

David Pargetter, who had just taken out a large red-and-white spotted handkerchief and was on the point of using it, gave his nose a perfunctory dab, returned the spots to his pocket and gave a peremptory cough. 'The Right Reverend Victoria Burnham-Woods. Born in Harrogate. Daughter of a men's outfitter and a primary school head teacher, privately educated, excelled academically – a first in theology from Durham, followed by a PhD in mission and culture during her training at St Christopher's. Ordained at the age of twenty-seven. Exceptional curacy, where she planted a much-publicised, highly successful community church in a virtually derelict building in an urban priority area. Dedicated parish priest, and Diocesan Director for Women. Excellent record as an archdeacon, first-rate trouble-shooter and committee chair, respected by the clergy for her pastoral care. First woman diocesan bishop, and outstanding so far – turned around the finances of a near-bankrupt diocese, encouraged the planting of several modernist "emerging" churches, as they're called, that have generated a significant rise in church attendance, supported countless initiatives amongst youth and children, and seen a sharp rise of vocations to the priesthood.'

'Background and spirituality,' urged the Dean.

Pargetter tugged at his collar and continued. 'Raised in an Anglo-catholic environment, though now more evangelical by preference, so open to other spiritualities and comfortable with the widest possible range of Anglican tradition, as you would expect of a bishop,' continued the church's HR advisor, straightening his tie. 'Conservative in matters of morality. Adheres firmly to the concept of monogamous, heterosexual marriage, and not sympathetic to clergy wishing to conduct gay marriages, or to non-celibate clergy civil partnerships.'

Catherine tutted loudly.

'Though she does claim to accept at face value the say-so of celibate gay clergy, on the basis that it cannot, nor should it, be policed. Refused to perform the gay marriage of a close friend.'

'Can we, these days, appoint an archbishop opposed to government legislation?' asked Dean Riley, his head on one side like a robin watching for a worm.

Pargetter turned questioningly to a man in a dark suit who had remained silent throughout the proceedings, sitting a little outside of the circle. The Prime Minister's Appointments' Secretary was present in an advisory capacity, and only participated if needed. He merely nodded.

'Disappointing,' conceded Catherine. 'I had hoped for a little less prejudice these days, but we can't have everything.'

'Her conservatism may of course go some way to mollifying our African brethren,' Pargetter said, looking pointedly at Brian, 'who, as you're probably aware, now constitute seventy-five per cent of the Anglican Alliance.'

'Ah, clever,' Catherine said, smiling meaningfully around the table, 'an ecclesiastical card game. Reassure them with a round of traditional moral values, then play our trump?'

Dean Riley, however, had manifestly found his worm.

'And what does the press make of her moral scruples?' he pursued.

Pargetter said, 'The broadsheets find it incomprehensible in some-one who is, in most other respects, a forward-thinker. The tabloids, on the other hand, whilst deploring bigotry, have a grudging admiration for church leaders who take a moral stand. Which means the press are hoisted on the petard of their own double standards, as ever, and we can have little certainty about how they will react. The locals in the Larchester diocese are protective and proud of her, and in her defence, make much of her attendance at the wedding of the gay friend she refused to marry.'

'Proof of her lack of homophobia?' asked Dorothy, mildly.

'Indeed,' replied Pargetter, bowing slightly to her age and wisdom.

'It's the way she dresses,' Frank announced suddenly, before anyone else had the chance to comment. 'For all her moral principles when it comes to everyone else, she is hardly conventional. Wearing those . . . lacy . . .'

'Fishnet tights?' Catherine suggested helpfully. 'Don't you find them attractive, Frank?'

'Wasn't a newspaper didn't remark on it,' he said, carefully ignoring her. 'Not enough dignity or gravitas for a bishop, let alone an archbishop, if you ask me.'

'She was going out somewhere for the evening – on a day off,' Brian said, holding out the palms of his hands in exasperation. 'For goodness' sake, Frank, the photographer probably had a telephoto lens. It was an invasion of her privacy. We can't blame her for that.'

'It isn't proper behaviour for a bishop under any circumstance,' he huffed, then added for good measure, '*Good Housekeeping* ran a feature on what she likes to cook. I ask you!'

'Since when do you read *Good Housekeeping*, Frank?' asked the woman vicar.

'The wife gets it,' he blustered.

'Well, it worries me too, Frank,' Dorothy said. 'I can't say exactly why. But when someone is pursued that much by the media, it bodes ill.'

'What we need is someone who will sort this organisation out,' Frank insisted, 'get it ship-shape – bums on pews and money in the coffers. Call me old-fashioned, but that's a man's job.'

'But that's exactly what she appears to do, Frank,' nodded Clive, smil-ing beatifically.

Frank did a double-take and stared at him, as if he had just material-ised from nowhere.

'You want this woman?'

'I . . . er . . . she seems to be exactly what we want,' Clive thumbed quickly through the Statement of Needs, then pointed at one particular page, 'according to our list of requirements.'

'Have you the same list as me, man?' Frank roared, shaking his papers in Clive's face.

The little man blinked back at him impassively.

'Come on, Frank,' Brian said soothingly. 'Bishop Vicky is the obvious choice. If she has all the qualities you outlined in your Statement of Needs – a first-class communicator and priest, an ability to grow the church and its finances – what more do you want? She is the right man for the job. The only thing she doesn't have can't be mentioned in polite conversation.'

'If you're talking about balls, she doesn't appear to be lacking in that department either,' Catherine said, defying any disapproval with her eyes.

'Catherine,' Gordon sighed, 'we don't all share your love of the vernacular.'

She had in fact jolted the chairman back from a moment of distracted desperation, of wondering whether such a disparate group could ever find consensus on where Canterbury was, let alone appoint its Archbishop.

'I have to say I'm inclined to agree with you, Frank,' he conceded, 'that we need someone with outstanding management skills. Ms Burnham-Woods certainly appears to be that.'

'But the Archbishop is not a conventional chief executive of a public company,' Brian intervened. 'The core roles are as pastor and leader. And she appears to be that too.'

'He is the voice and face of the church,' Gordon added.

'He?' asked Catherine Cole, and Gordon ruefully admitted to himself that he deserved to be picked up on such a *faux pas*. 'In fact, we've already heard that this woman has put her diocese back on its feet, Frank,' she continued. 'You can psychometric test her if you want, but personally, I think she has a thoroughly good pedigree, a great deal better than any we've heard so far.'

She turned to David Pargetter. 'No skeletons in the cupboard? No nasties in the attic? We can live with the fishnet tights. But no pornography, or drugs or drink in the family, no closet affairs or early dementia? Bearing in mind that we're two bishops down. At least their names hadn't reached the PM's desk. Egg all over our faces. Might a woman be a safer bet?'

'As you've discovered,' said David Pargetter, bowing to her slightly, 'unlike our founder, we are not omniscient.' He allowed himself an appreciative smile at his own little joke. 'There was some suggestion a few months ago of . . . an unfortunate adolescent liaison, but the *Mail* retracted it with a full apology.'

'And it won't come back to bite us on our bottoms?'

'Catherine!' said Dorothy mildly. 'Such a turn of phrase.'

'Oh get real, Dorothy. Titillation is what the media wants.'

'The *Mail* only apologises when a serious threat of a successful libel is held to its throat. So it's unlikely. But I can't be categorical, of course.'

'And the spouse?' asked Dorothy. 'Would she have his full support? It's a lot to ask of a man.' Before Gordon could intervene, she added, 'It's a lot to ask of any spouse, male or female.'

Pargetter pushed his glasses up his nose, and consulted his notes again, taking his time. 'Consultant general surgeon in one of the London hospitals, well thought of generally, though some local, and indeed national, press a few years ago over a child that died on the operating table. A verdict of accidental death was recorded at the inquest and no further action taken. There has never been any indication that he does not support his wife's career – though, it must be said, he is rarely at her side. They have one daughter, married to an American, living in the USA.'

He looked up, waiting for further questions, but there were none. The woman vicar broke the silence.

'Can't blame him for not wanting to be her consort. So boring for a man. My husband . . .'

'Vicky would certainly be a very interesting compromise,' interrupted the Archbishop of York, in what he manifestly saw as the voice of reason and plausibility.

At last, he shows his hand, Gordon said to himself. He suspected the Archbishop had spent the whole time trying to decide whether, firstly, he could work under a woman, and secondly, whether her appointment would be personally advantageous. Hitherto, the Archbishop's preferences for the post had all been men of a certain age – men who would retire within the next seven years or so, leaving the way clear for him to become the next head honcho.

'I don't think we're talking about a compromise, Archbishop,' Gordon demurred.

'Well, an interesting option, then. A risky, radical appointment, perhaps. Let's remember that when it comes to ceremonial precedence she would trump the Prime Minister, in recognition of the fact that the Archbishop crowns the monarch and is her chaplain. We want no embarrassment to the Queen. At her age, working as hard as she still does, she deserves a peaceful life.'

'Thank you, Archbishop,' said Gordon, 'but the Queen is a tough old boot and doesn't need our condescension.'

'The new Archbishop will almost certainly have a state funeral to do,' he countered.

'And Her Majesty won't be around to see it,' Gordon flashed. 'We've heard your misgivings. Just tell us your feelings. You would have to work closely with the lady in question.'

The Archbishop squirmed like a lobster dropped into a pan of boiling water. There was a pause, a look of uncertainty on his face which gave way to an intense concentration, that broke into a seraphic smile just as Gordon's patience ran out.

'In favour, generally. After all, if we are making a big mistake, at fifty-five, Vicky Burnham-Woods is not likely to continue long in the job. Women do tend to have other priorities – like family and friends – and retire early.'

Extraordinary how guileless the man appeared to be, Gordon thought, his mouth a window to his inner world. Irresistible boyish charm, the papers called it, though Gordon couldn't see it.

'Remember Margaret Thatcher,' he warned. 'She had to be forcibly removed from power.'

'There's no one less like Mrs Thatcher,' the Archbishop beamed. 'Vicky doesn't strike me as someone who feeds on power.'

'So, she sounds the perfect candidate,' Gordon said with finality, before Frank could interrupt. 'A good time to break for lunch. A full stomach might help future deliberations.'

Triangular sandwiches, crisps and pieces of fruit were rolled in on a trolley. Abstemious Anglican food, Gordon reflected. Not even a decent, filling meal. Though he had heard that in days gone by a previous Archbishop of York would host such occasions *chez soi*, and had a reputation as an excellent cook.

At the opening of the afternoon session, he decided to share his own perspective. 'As I see it, the church is in a parlous state. The pews have been emptying over a number of years and the average age of many congregations is over seventy. It faces major financial difficulties and a severe shortage of clergy. But outside the church there is an immense, untapped interest in religious and spiritual matters. The country needs more than an academic with a fine mind. It needs someone with a popular touch, who can communicate profound concepts to the man and woman on the street. Whatever you think of her unorthodox methods, Vicky Burnham-Woods is a colourful figure, who has more than proved herself capable of senior leadership, transforming her own diocese, and making faith exciting for the masses. Despite receiving her fair share of support in the national consultation process, we dismissed her when we shortlisted . . .'

'Because we were told there were serious doubts about her Anglican orthodoxy,' Catherine interrupted, 'now unfounded, I gather,' she added, looking knowingly at Brian, who nodded enthusiastically, one eye on the Dean.

'Well,' Gordon concluded, 'it would certainly be interesting to be responsible for appointing the first woman Archbishop of Canterbury.'

Frank Hardiman suddenly let out a long, low groan. It unnerved Gordon and he was trying to recall what he might have said that could have been so offensive, when he realised that the man was attempting to stand, clutching his stomach.

'Frank isn't well,' Dorothy whispered to him.

That much was now obvious to Gordon, but to what extent?

'Fine, I'm fine,' Frank stammered. 'Just need to be excused a moment.' He made a dash for the door.

Gordon sent Brian Dimmock after him to see if he needed any help. Meanwhile, the Archbishop and the Dean simultaneously excused themselves as well.

'I think there's another Gents' toilets near the reception,' said the Archbishop loudly, nodding meaningfully at his colleague as they left the room.

'A sudden problem with the bowels?' Catherine asked, voicing the concerns of the Commission's remaining members. 'Anyone else about to succumb to it?'

They all shook their heads, and sat, doodling on their papers, checking their gadgetry for messages, and sighing loudly as they waited for the outcome of the sudden exodus.

The Archbishop and the Dean arrived back smiling a short while later, very hail-fellow-well-met, as if they had just spent the evening at the pub together and were about to go home arm in arm, singing. The Archbishop was quick to pick up the enquiring looks and insisted that both his and the Dean's internal workings were fine, absolutely fine, never better in fact. Though what passed between them during that short, un-tabled break, the gathered members would never know. Gordon would sometimes ask himself in years to come, because from that moment, the voting pattern seemed to undergo a subtle change. If not wildly in favour of Vicky Burnham-Woods' appointment, the Dean ceased to show any resistance to the idea either.

'We don't have to wait for Frank, do we?' Brian Dimmock asked as he came back into the room.

Gordon raised his eyebrows.

'A severe case of the squits, I'm afraid. Definitely won't be able to leave the throne room for some time. I managed to get him some Imodium from the staff and left him to it for now. I think he'd rather be alone.'

'Food poisoning?' Gordon asked. 'Didn't we all eat the same lunch?'

'A bit soon, isn't it?' Catherine asked. 'I'll take a bet it's the dreaded heave-ho virus. In which case, a nice little bonus to take home with us. We'd better get on with the voting now.'

'Could we vote for him by proxy?' Dorothy suggested.

'Er, I don't think that's allowed,' Gordon said, rapidly thumbing his way through the instructions booklet. He looked from David Pargetter to the Prime Minister's Appointments' Secretary for guidance. Both shrugged.

'Oh for goodness' sake, can't we just get on with it?' Catherine pleaded. 'I could be home tonight, in my favourite armchair, watching a movie, with a cold, crisp Chardonnay at my side and my cat on my knee.'

'I don't see any reason why not,' Gordon agreed, throwing the instructions booklet onto the table. The thought of being liberated from Broadmoor had an irresistible attraction. It could be days before Frank was well and he couldn't face chairing yet another gathering.

'Illness can be . . .' The word 'serendipitous' was on the tip of his tongue, but he managed a recall just in time, and said, 'cannot be helped.'

When it was all done with, the Prime Minister's Appointments' Secretary, who was responsible for advising the candidate of the Commission's decision, suddenly announced, 'She'll want to know if you were unanimous.'

Everyone looked at him in surprise. A non-voting member of the committee, a man with no voice, Gerard Lancaster had remained a shadow on the wall throughout the entire procedure.

'Then tell her that it was,' said Gordon. 'Ten in favour, one abstention and one too ill to vote is near enough.'

'She'll ask if she was your first choice. She may never accept the post if she thinks it was hers by default.'

'Then do what civil servants do,' suggested Catherine. 'Lie through your teeth.'

'Let's be honest, she was our first choice. This time round,' Gordon said affably. 'The appointment can't help but be controversial, so there's no point in trying to disguise the fact that we've had a lengthy, animated and interesting debate. But in the end, those present today were of one mind. She doesn't need to know any more than that. It certainly mustn't get out that our two previous choices came to nought. Secrecy is the very basis of the Commission.'

The secretary nodded, buttoned himself into a large, black cashmere greatcoat, and backed silently out of the room.

'I wouldn't like to be in his moccasins,' Brian commented as the door closed with barely a click. 'Better go and see how Frank is getting on.'

'Of course,' Gordon said, beaming at the group with genuine satisfaction at the result and more than just a little relief that it was over, 'but before you go, a heartfelt thank-you to each of you for your time and patience. It appears we have the privilege of making history. And whether that is a good thing, only history itself will tell. Well done, one and all.'

'And best of luck, Vicky,' said Brian Dimmock, toasting her with the last of his water.

FEBRUARY 2024

From:	rtrevvicky@cmail.co.uk
Sent:	Feb 14th 2024
To:	alice.peterson@earthlink.net
Subject:	Tomorrow's vote

My Darling

4 am. I can't sleep. 11 pm in Boston, so we could have videolinked, but I don't want to risk getting you up. So a quick email instead – just to reassure you again that I'm absolutely fine. My eyelids feel as if they're lined with sand. My back's still a little red and sore, but the doctors say that's to be expected and a small price to pay. Otherwise I'm perfectly calm, and just about ready for whatever tomorrow holds.

A few years ago I learnt from one of my staff, when I was forced into letting him go, that in every situation, however unjust or hard to bear, we have a choice. We can receive it from the hands of human beings, rail against them and seek revenge. Or, we can receive it from the hand of God, and believe it's part of his plan for us. I prefer the latter option. Bitterness only destroys us in the end. Whatever tomorrow's outcome, it will be for the best.

And I count my blessings – you and Dirk, and your two lovely boys. What a comfort you all are. Too far away to touch and feel and hold, yet thanks to the wonder of the technology I often curse, neighbours on the planet and near enough to see face to face. After the great missionary, Amy Carmichael, left for India, her mother never saw her again. That's far worse than anything I'm having to face. Thank the Lord we don't live in 1895.

You should see the mounds of letters and cards stacked up on the dresser. More than at Christmas, and that doesn't include the emails and texts. Hundreds of expressions of love and support, from ordinary men and women, church-going and not, full of faith and without any. That sustains me. I am so grateful for them all.

I keep thinking back to my ordination. Had I known what lay ahead, would I have gone through with it? I nearly bottled out on the day. But even then, deep down, I knew my destiny was inescapable. Even though I could have had no idea of what was to come, those vows were always going to lead me to this moment. And yes, I would make them again for the privilege of being drawn into so many hearts and lives, and, perhaps, being able to make a small difference.

I know that my work has meant huge sacrifices for my loved ones. I wasn't always there for you when I should have been. I certainly haven't always been what a wife should be to your father, and we both paid the price for that. But I want you to know that no matter where I was, every breath I breathed was a prayer for you. I love you more than life itself and always will. You are the best, the most creative thing I ever achieved, and if existence had offered me no other satisfaction, what you are today would have been more than enough for me.

We can't change the past, and the future is out of our hands. All we have is now, this moment, to be lived as fully as we know how. So I shall go and get some fresh air, then shower and put on the Polyfilla, so that I feel ready for the occasion. I have been hanging onto a wonderful saying of Eleanor Roosevelt's. 'No one can make you feel small without your permission.' With my hand in God's and my head up, I shall walk forward, without fear, into the unknown. Who knows, maybe this will be our chance to spend that time together I've always promised you and longed for.

Sleep well, beloved daughter. There will be joy in the morning.

PART ONE

2020

Encryptogram user z3qa | to user bx4sw

It's been leaked! That woman – Ab of C. Deeply shocked. Is
it true?

Thought we agreed – no place for women in the Palace.
Thinks she's Joan of Arc, ranting, raving, rousing the rabble.
'Our Lady of the Lame Dogs and Lost Causes.'

Don't object to powerful women. Bedded a few in my
time. But this one . . . a can of worms. All pouts and
petticoats. Marches, protests, demonstrations. Keep religion
out of politics, for God's sake.

I worry for the church – and the country. If you agree, let's
meet. Somewhere discreet. Devise a plan – damage
limitation.

So many better candidates. This may be the time for such
a man as you.

ONE

JANUARY 2020

'I have the PM's Secretary for Senior Appointments on the phone, Bishop,' Marissa announced breathily from the study doorway, lingering just a little too long to disguise the curiosity beneath her usual veil of quiet professionalism.

'Thanks, Marissa,' Vicky replied. 'Just wanting my advice on some appointment or other, no doubt.'

'Of course,' Marissa acknowledged, with a short smile of relief. 'Probably wanting to make another woman bishop, and needing you to show her the ropes.'

'Probably,' Vicky agreed, resisting a further response to her secretary's attempt to explain the call, as bewildered by it as she was. It was on the tip of her tongue to joke, 'Don't worry. It won't be Canterbury. I've only been here four years.'

But something stopped her – a sudden, stomach-lurching disquiet.

She watched the door close, waited for Marissa's quiet footfall to recede down the corridor, closed her eyes in a moment's desperate prayer, then picked up the phone.

'Gerard. How are you? How's the PM?'

'I need to see you urgently, Bishop,' he said without preamble. 'Can I come later today? Or tomorrow.'

A man whose social graces appeared to have undergone surgical removal, she said to herself, wrestling with a growing sense of foreboding.

'Gerard, I'm a bishop. My diary is full of unmovables and unchange-ables. Confirmations, lectures, sermons . . .'

'I appreciate that, Bishop. What can you cancel most easily?'

Vicky picked up her e-phone and flashed quickly through her diary. Even the most recent bookings had been in for months. Nothing could be cancelled without causing dismay to a significant number of people. But she had, in fact, kept a slot free the following afternoon for reading, reflection, sermon preparation, and a visit from the hairdresser. Rare luxuries.

'Later tomorrow afternoon?' she sighed.

'Tomorrow afternoon would be excellent, Bishop. Er, given your high profile, I'd prefer it if there were no prying eyes. Can you encourage your staff to go home early without arousing their suspicions?'

'How very cloak and dagger, Gerard,' she laughed, and it jarred, sounding slightly shrill. 'Come at 5 p.m. I can guarantee that at that time on a Friday my staff will all be enjoying the beginning of a weekend off. It's my policy.'

'Perfect.'

For the intervening hours Vicky picked at the Appointments' Secretary's motives as if they were scabs on a new tattoo. What could be so important that it would bring him to her late on a Friday afternoon, when most sensible non-clergy were heading for home and a two-day break? She told herself repeatedly that it wouldn't, couldn't be Canterbury. But where else was there an urgent vacancy? The previous incumbent had hardly been the church's most exciting offering, but he had seemed a gentle, thoughtful, godly man – too sensitive, if anything; hardly the sort of man to have a secretive other life. She had loved and felt for him. Never envied him his impossible task, not for a moment. Grieved over his lonely, indecorous end.

No. They wouldn't appoint a woman to the post. It was too soon. It would ruffle too many feathers, put a fraught, dismembered church at greater risk of final schism. It had been demanding enough for her African brother bishops to accept her as an equal. Their reaction if a woman was appointed to the church's most senior leadership role didn't bear thinking about. Did Gerard want her advice on the appointment of another female bishop? He had never sought her opinion before. Perhaps the PM wanted to sound her out on issues around urban deprivation, one of her ecclesiastical specialities, as recognised by the press, if not her fellow bishops, who resented having their efforts at diocesan regeneration passed over.

Everything the first female bishop did was always going to be big news, she reassured 'the boys', as she referred to them (though she still groused to her husband about their petty jealousies).

But if that was what the PM wanted, why did he not speak to her himself?

'It must be Canterbury,' Kelvin teased her. Inevitably, Marissa had told her chaplain about the call.

'Don't say so, not even in jest, Kelvin. My blood runs cold at the thought. I'm only just getting the hang of being a bishop.'

Her relationship with Kelvin was close – closer, she suspected, than most bishops with their chaplains. In many ways he was more like the younger brother she had never had. Was that a female propensity, to dispense with the professional formalities in favour of friendship? Was it wise? But she could never look at his vulnerable, scarred and shaven head, his gold earrings and midnight shadow, without feeling a surge of wonder and thankfulness that strong partnerships, both personal and professional, could sprout from the most unlikely beginnings. For her, Kelvin was the personification of reparation, of hope in every broken relationship.

He had been reluctant to apply for the chaplain's post.

'Bishop's poodle? Not on your life, Vicky.'

'Would I have asked you to apply if I'd wanted a pet?'

'Church Scrapes the Barrel,' had been the unforgiving headline in the press. 'Is our new bishop so strapped for talented clergy that she needs to appoint a chaplain with a criminal record?' Vicky had been furious on Kelvin's behalf and had her press officer, a former *Daily Express* hack called Mike Barnes, send off a strong response. 'Kelvin Craddock has been vicar of some of the most difficult urban parishes in the country and proved himself to be a resourceful, loving and outstanding priest. This is a man re-born, whose past was redeemed by the transforming love of Christ, and who knows enough of the power of forgiveness and restoration to share it wherever he happens to be.'

'Holy mackerel, I've turned into Saint Paul,' he'd said with a broad grin when he saw it.

'I wish,' Vicky replied.

Theirs had been an unusually comfortable working partnership, and he would be loath to let her go, even for Canterbury.

'Does the Archbishop still have to wear a frock coat and tights for state banquets?'

'I think, at least I hope, that tradition died a short while back.'

'A pity. You'd look a great deal sexier than the men. Far better legs, if I may say so.'

'You may not,' she said tartly, hiding her smile. Give a man an inch . . .

Gerard Lancaster rang the bell of Bishop's House at 5 p.m. on the dot. From an upstairs window Vicky had watched his bulky, black figure emerge from the car and lumber towards the house. The Appointments'

Secretary was a broad-shouldered man, covered, almost from head to toe, in an over-large cashmere coat that looked more like it was wearing him than the other way round. He stood on the doorstep, looking around furtively. She was tempted to demand, 'Password?' as she opened the door to him, but thought better of it and offered to take his coat instead. He refused politely.

'Ready for a quick getaway?' she teased.

'Heavy,' he explained.

'Ah,' she said.

He followed her into the sitting room, but before she had time to offer him tea, he delved into his briefcase and handed her a letter. Then he removed his coat, laid it carefully over the arm of the settee and sat down next to it. She sat down opposite him, gingerly fingering the letter which had carried in the cold from outside, hardly breathing. A wave of intense heat rose from the base of her spine to her hairline, depositing beads of sweat in every nook and cranny of her body on its way. The joys of the menopause, she said to herself, and went on sitting stock-still, Lancaster's eyes focused on the letter, willing her to open it.

She postponed the moment for as long as she could, knowing instinctively that once she did, her life would never be the same again. The clock ticked, her heart raced, and the Secretary's stomach made a slight, low gurgling sound, but his eyes never left the envelope in her lap. Unless she meant to keep him in her sitting room as a permanent fixture, she had no choice but to read its contents.

The letter, of course, as she had expected it must, said exactly what she had desperately hoped, to the very last second, it did not. She was aware that her hands had begun to tremble a little, and could barely bring herself to speak.

'Is this some kind of joke?'

'I assure you that it isn't.'

'Then I'm being used to make a point?'

'To break new ground? Don't you think it's about time?'

'A test case? Don't you think the risk is too great? Women were only admitted to the highest offices of the church five years ago. I've been Bishop of Larchester for four of them and preventing schism in the diocese has taken every wile known to woman. How would an appointment like this serve the unity of the church?'

He looked at her intently, blinking from time to time through his heavy, black-rimmed spectacles. Did he deliberately withhold all sign of feeling, or was he genuinely free of what he no doubt saw as human weakness? Whichever, his coolness aggravated her beyond measure. She needed a foil, someone who would thrust and parry with her, not a stuffed dummy of a civil servant.

'You really don't know what you're asking of me, do you?'

He raised his eyebrows, but said nothing.

'To leave behind all I've worked and fought for, a diocese I've come to love, where the churches are pulling together at last to make a real difference to their communities. To be what? A lamb thrown to the wolves. Torn limb from limb, simply to make the point that a woman isn't up to the job. And then it will be years before another woman is appointed to the post. No, no, no,' she said, jumping to her feet and walking over to the dresser so that she could steady herself without having to face him, 'this is totally counter-productive.'

'I assure you there was no tokenism in the decision, no sense in which it was a gesture to prove the church's even-handedness in matters of gender. Your predecessor, whose unfortunate demise we sadly lament, did not have time or, some might say, the ability to pull the church out of its despondency and gloom. While the Commission felt that in this difficult time in the life of the nation, with the economy still severely stretched after the collapse of the euro, you have shown yourself perfectly able to confound your detractors, pulling the churches together, as you so rightly say, and bringing a glimmer or two of . . . hope, dare we say, to your kingdom here. Why should that not work on a broader canvas?'

She turned to face him.

'And the Commission believes I'm capable of doing so?'

'The Commission kept to the agreed profile stating what was required: a charismatic leader, theologically well grounded but not an academic, profound but with the communication skills to appeal to the masses, someone who could show sensitivity and compassion, yet hold their own in the political and international scene, prepared to stand for what they believe in, in these rather troubled times. And, perhaps, someone . . . a little different.'

'And I came to mind?' she asked, shaking her head in disbelief.

The Secretary made a rather lop-sided attempt at a smile of acknowledgement.

'I rather doubt it,' she said. 'But let me ask you, was I the Commission's first choice? It's only fair that I should know. When, not if, the going gets tough, I shall need that certainty to fall back on.'

The Secretary took off his glasses, delved into his coat pocket to retrieve an immaculately pressed white handkerchief, shook it out and began to wipe them. Playing for time, Vicky suspected. The response was taking him a while to frame.

'You were, eventually, the unanimous choice,' he said, putting his glasses on and the handkerchief back in his coat pocket, allowing his unblinking, almost expressionless stare to rest upon her once more. She found it disarming.

'Eventually.' What did that mean? It sounded like a dodge, but Vicky decided that pushing him wouldn't elicit a more satisfactory explanation. The Commission was more secretive than the College of Cardinals electing the Pope.

'And my more . . . conservative views?' she tried instead. 'They're hardly going to go down well with the government, let alone the large group of anti-discriminationalists in the church.'

'On sexuality issues?'

'What else? It's fairly public that I support traditional marriage as the historic bedrock of society, that I won't therefore perform gay marriages, or encourage the clergy to do so. If the press has any grouse against me, it's that.'

'But you have attended a gay marriage.'

The Secretary was certainly well briefed.

'And you support the right of gay couples to adopt.'

'I supported the right of every child in care to a decent home.'

'The *Mail* and *Express* are currently spearheading a backlash on morality issues, deploring the Scandinavian laxity that allows three or more parties to a marriage. A little traditionalism might not hurt.'

He inclined his head to one side, as the family pet dog had done when she was a child, waiting for her response.

'And besides,' he added, 'the PM knows that from a political perspective, you are on his side.'

'If I accept the post, I shan't be on anyone's side but God's.'

She realised it sounded pompous the moment it left her lips.

'Forgive me. I'm finding this all very difficult.'

The Secretary quickly changed tack.

'If it would help, let me assure you that the job specification required someone with a more traditional lifestyle than some of the American bishops we've seen.'

'No dope-smoking whisky-swillers on their third marriage, then?'

He gave the merest nod and Vicky returned to the armchair and slumped into it. She resisted the temptation to say anything more risqué and simply said, 'Lady Fisher, wife of a previous Archbishop of Canterbury, when addressing the girls of Wycombe Abbey School, was asked by one earnest pupil if she had ever considered divorce. She replied, "Divorce, never, but murder often."'

Gerard Lancaster's mouth twitched gratifyingly at the corners, the closest to a smile that he could manage. But Vicky added, without looking at him, 'I suspect that's true of many clergy marriages, where the partner is subsumed by the church.'

For even before she finished telling the anecdote, she knew with a sinking heart that if she accepted the PM's offer, Tom would most certainly share Lady Fisher's sentiments.

'How can the Commission be sure that my marriage would survive such a challenge?' she asked.

'It can't, of course,' the Secretary admitted. 'That's for you to consider. But your husband appears to have supported your ministry so far.'

'And the Commission would know, obviously, given that nothing is sacrosanct in church politics?'

Lancaster, with the wisdom of the Whitehall bureaucrat, remained silent.

'Frankly, it would be very hard on Tom,' she said.

He nodded respectfully, and changed the subject.

'What we do know is that you already have a reputation for being inspirational and motivational in difficult times, for managing change effectively, and for expressing a deep sense of compassion for the general populace. And, if I may add, that you have managed to remain very much yourself despite senior office.'

'And why is that so important to the powers that be?"

Vicky noticed that the Secretary squirmed. But she needed to know exactly what was expected of her, and she wasn't going to let him off the hook. She began to feel almost sorry for him.

'Your – your more earthy approach, for example.'

'My sense of humour?' she quizzed.

He nodded.

'We wouldn't want you to feel you have to emulate anyone else.'

'A man, for example?'

'Quite so,' he agreed. 'You would bring your unique gifts and talents to the job, I have no doubt. Don't deceive yourself that the Commission can't see that behind that, er . . . warm and approachable exterior, there lurks, if I may say so, an extremely able, even shrewd operator with a fine mind for theology.'

Vicky couldn't resist a chortle at the flow of flattery that spilled, somewhat self-consciously, from the Secretary's lips. It was borrowed, of that she was sure. He looked at her quizzically.

'I always thought that when they did appoint a woman to the post for the first time, she would have to be a cross between the Virgin Mary and a jolly headmistress, with a strong touch of the Machiavelli. It sounds as if I wasn't far wrong. Though whether I actually fit the identikit is another matter.'

Gerard Lancaster pulled himself up defensively.

'Anti-church prejudice is now deeply ingrained in the British psyche. The church is stereotyped in the press as wishy-washy and out of touch. The Commission, therefore, deploring its reputation for compromise, opted for popular appeal, choosing a woman who is anything but wishy-washy or out of touch.'

And with that he got up to go, heaved on the coat and headed for the door.

'You know I can't give you an answer without some serious prayer? I need to consult my husband, as well as God, though in this instance it may amount to the same thing. Only God knows if both will be of the same mind.'

He managed a genuine, albeit deferential smile, at last.

'I can only give you twenty-four hours, I'm afraid. Can't risk any leaks, you understand.'

She nodded dumbly, sick at the thought of the anguish the next few hours would bring.

'Then we'll just have to hope that God speaks soon.'

'Of course. But the PM very much hopes you'll say yes.'

Vicky smiled, reluctantly.

'And the PM is the highest authority?'

He nodded, apparently oblivious of her humour this time, and within seconds, the strange black figure had disappeared into his car and driven away. All he needed were horns and a tail. 'It's just not possible,' she whispered, as she stood at the door, gazing at the space where his car had been. 'I never asked for this.'

Or had she? She had made her own contribution to the cracks in the stained-glass ceiling, until, now, it was finally smashed apart.

1992

A raw curate, but with aspirations to become a vicar as soon as it was made possible, Vicky had watched the vote to admit women to the priesthood on the television twenty-eight years earlier, standing up ironing Tom's shirts. She had to have something to do as she watched the faces of the men and women who held her future in their hands, then waited for the results. It was such a close-run thing, no one could tell which way it was going to go. The debate had lasted five and a half hours. In the end, it resorted to a typically fudged fall-back. Any parish that wouldn't accept the ministry of a woman priest could legally refuse to have one. They could also refuse the ministrations of their local bishop if he had 'soiled' his hands by laying them on a woman's head to make her a priest, in favour of visiting or 'flying' bishops. Still, she would be one of the first women priests.

The motion was carried by two votes. Vicky, unaware that she had been hyper-ventilating, found that she needed to sit down. She wept, first with stunned gratitude, and then with the sheer joy of it, until the smell of burning snapped her abruptly back into the present. There was a brown, iron-shaped mark on the front of one of Tom's favourite shirts.

When the time came to vote for women bishops, after more than twenty years of synodical wrangling, Vicky was an archdeacon and full Synod member, present at the first fiasco, when the motion was defeated, and then at the second attempt, when the last bastion of professional gender inequality in the UK finally fell. It was nerve-wracking to sit, voting handset at the ready, waiting and wondering whether thousands of years of tradition were indeed to be overturned at last, after so many thwarted hopes and dreams.

The result came virtually instantly, but it was still the longest minute in Vicky's memory, every eked-out second echoing with the jarring sounds of coughing, throat-clearing, chair-squeaking, pen-fiddling, and unrestrained shuffling.

There was no victory cheer when the result was announced, just pure and simple relief. A few tears quickly checked or wiped surreptitiously away. The occasional smile of complicity caught and shared. And the same dignified silence that accompanied the moment when women won their priesting, in respect for those who would find it a bitter pill to swallow.

Vicky headed out of Church House into the crowds of Westminster, desperate for a celebratory drink, but the media cut off her exit, demanding that she analyse her emotions before she had had a chance to register them, let alone articulate them sensibly. A Church House press officer materialised at her side, press statement in hand, and after allowing her a swift expression of joy for the satisfied and sorrow for the dismayed, shepherded her out onto the street.

The phone calls continued throughout the train journey home and well into the evening.

'Are you going to be the first woman to benefit from today's vote?'

'I very much doubt it. I'm far too outspoken.'

An irate Tom, in his chef's apron, stirring a bubbling concoction on the Aga in the kitchen, barely looked up when she came in. The room was full of steam. She walked over to him and turned on the cooker hood.

'The phone's been ringing off the hook. If they haven't got the sense to know what time it is, they don't deserve a response,' he snapped, as her mobile cut him off. He removed a casserole with an oven-gloved hand, placed it on the table with a meaningful thud, removed its lid, and sat down noisily. She nodded, brought the conversation to a swift close, and joined him. When the landline rang he fastened her to the chair with a look.

'Honestly,' he complained later, propped up against the pillows, reading, as she performed her nightly cleansing ritual.

'Honestly what, Darling?' she asked as she got into bed next to him.

He removed his glasses and put them into their case with a resounding snap.

'Honestly, I'd like to throttle all of them, because they've stolen our life together.'

'This is a rather unique and special occasion.'

'Aren't they all?'

Tom lay down vigorously, the mattress rocking as he heaved the quilt over his recumbent frame, and switched off his bedside lamp. Vicky didn't know whether to feel seasick or heartsick.

Jenny James rang the following morning. 'I still can't believe the brass doors have yielded. How long before it's Bishop Vicky, then?'

'Don't you start. And anyway, what about you? You've fought for it much harder than I have.'

'I'm not an archdeacon. Mercifully.'

'You do realise that there are only two archbishops, forty-two diocesan bishops, sixty-eight suffragan bishops . . .'

'And a partridge in a pear tree. Actually, more than one partridge amongst that lot, I reckon.'

'Let's get real, Jenny. With such a flat organisation, how many of us are going to be bishops? Just take a look at the government – just a tiny percentage of women in the cabinet after all these years.'

'The church will create a token woman bishop quickly. And my money's on you.'

'You're incorrigible. I wouldn't rush to Ladbroke's if I were you.'

'But you are high profile.'

'And that will count against me.'

'You mark my words . . .'

As she put the phone down, Vicky considered whether her Uriah Heep humility wasn't a little disingenuous. People so often protested their disinterest in the very thing they wanted the most. Politicians relentlessly resisted any suggestion of ladder-climbing, when it was manifestly obvious they'd kill to be the PM. Her male colleagues rarely said they intended becoming a bishop, when it was flagrantly obvious they did. Career clergy. There were plenty of them. What they feared most was setting out their stall in public, only to have the goodies snatched away, leaving all and sundry to titter at the comeuppance of an ambitious fool. But she genuinely hadn't supported a woman's right to be a bishop with a view to becoming one herself. Or so she thought, until, a year or so before the vote, when she was summoned to meet the new Archbishop's Advisor for Appointments, he or she who screened all candidates for possible promotion, and secreted their findings in the golden files. The curriculum vitae of many able clergy were lost in there somewhere, and few ever heard anything more.

David Pargetter, the church's (only) senior executive in HR, didn't appear comfortable with his role in the church. When he wasn't rearranging his tie, he fiddled with his silver tiepin, taking some reassurance from rubbing the pad of his forefinger backwards and forwards over the cross engraved on its front. 'At least he has the courage to wear one,' Vicky thought to herself, though he was hardly going to be sacked for it by his employers. His predecessor, a woman who had trained her in the finer points of archdeaconry, had made no bones about the fact that she was consciously preparing a generation of women leaders, fully equipped and ready to move into the episcopal hierarchy when the time came. Pargetter had no doubt received the same commission from the highest levels, sympathetic as they were to the cause. But if he had, there was little sign of it.

Her career thus far was neatly laid out on the table between them, reduced to two sheets of A4.

'Mmm,' he said, pen in one hand, studying the paperwork as if he were about to award her marks out of ten. 'Thanks for coming in today. I expect you know what it's about. You obviously have friends in high places. Frankly, I don't doubt your pastoral skills, but what we're looking for today are bishops with know-how in strategy, financial stability, change and stakeholder management, conflict resolution and marketing.'

'CEOs?'

He looked up at her, startled, eyes blinking like an alligator's, magnified behind the thickness of the lenses of his rimless spectacles.

'Something like that.'

'So why summon me if you don't think I fit your identikit?'

He flicked through the papers in front of him again, looking for an answer.

'Because actually, I have had a significant amount of experience in all of them, at every stage of my career, as vicar and archdeacon, even as a curate, in the community centre I ran in an area of high urban deprivation. Not to mention mission, which seems to have dropped off your list.'

He tucked the ends of his tie into his shirt front, wriggled in his chair and coughed.

'But no experience of civic functions.'

Vicky was totally exasperated. How had someone with so little awareness of what the job entailed been given such power in deciding the future leadership of the Church of England?

'Mr Pargetter, I'm getting the impression that you seem to be under some illusion that women can be so pastorally-minded, we aren't up to the rough and tumble of leadership. If that's the case, it would constitute an effective and worrying barrier to our promotion. I'm an archdeacon, Mr Pargetter. I regularly preach in the cathedral at civic services.'

'Ah, yes, of course. And as I said, you have been noticed in high places.'

She was wearing a snug, knee-length skirt.

'And was that,' she asked, folding one leg carefully over the other, 'because of my ability and spirituality, or because of my feminine charms?'

Blow it, she said to herself as she left one of the Church of England's top bureaucrats looking nonplussed and awkward, that's the end of my chances. But maybe she had made a point. And did she want to be a bishop anyway, a manager rather than a priest, a purveyor of Anglican liturgy and rituals, rather than a pastor, when what she really loved was the work on the ground? In the end she had to believe that these matters were in God's hands, but with men like David Pargetter in the seat of power, that wasn't easy to credit.

So when it was announced that Wendy Thornham was to be the first woman bishop – a suffragan, so the junior version, but a bishop nonetheless – it was no surprise. Wendy was efficient and pleasant, had been a cathedral dean for some years and would do an excellent job. And she had a surfeit of experience of civic services. If not the legs. Enough of the cattiness and vanity, Vicky had commanded herself. You have no aspirations in that department, remember?

TWO

> God does not become a religion, so that man participates in
> him by corresponding religious thoughts and feelings. God
> does not become a law, so that man participates in him
> through obedience to a law. God does not become an ideal,
> so that man achieves community with him through constant
> striving. He humbles himself and takes upon himself the
> eternal death of the godless and the godforsaken, so that all
> the godless and the godforsaken can experience communion
> with him.
>
> JÜRGEN MOLTMANN

JANUARY 2020

Vicky closed the front door, and went back into the sitting room. She
tried to tell herself that the spectral Secretary and her bizarre conversation with him were an illusion, a bad dream. But the letter still lay on the
coffee table and there was a large bottom-shaped well in the seat of her
feather-filled settee. Not the fabrication of an overwrought imagination,
then. Too dazed to bother with closing the curtains or switching on a
lamp, she plumped up the settee, then snuggled into it in front of the fire,
tucking her feet beneath her and clutching a cushion to her chest for
comfort. Had the flames been real rather than gas, she might have been
tempted to throw the letter onto them.

She wasn't taken in by the compliments that slid smoothly from
Gerard's mouth like a slick of chocolate. Rather, she was filled with blazing indignation that she had been singled out to be the sacrificial lamb on
the altar of establishing a precedent. Wasn't being Bishop of Larchester
pioneering enough? The first female diocesan. It was certainly fulfilling
enough to use up whatever ambition had been lurking unnoticed in her
subconscious through all those years of fighting for the right, when she
had protested her personal indifference so loudly.

After four years she was beginning to feel she had the measure of
running a diocese. The wheels were turning as smoothly as they could in
a Church of England beleaguered by rising costs and falling giving. The

latest generation of churchgoers, raised in a thriving, me-centred Britain, didn't take well to the ongoing austerity of personal and national debt, inflation and a devalued pound. They didn't give like their parents. There had been swingeing cuts, staff not replaced when they left, clergy worked almost into the ground with four, five, even six parishes, buildings crumbling into dereliction and sold off. But Ralph had prevented them going bankrupt like the Mirbury Diocese, with clergy going unpaid and dependent on income support. Her wizard of a new diocesan secretary, a qualified economist with abilities way beyond those the Church of England could normally hope to attract, had waved a magic wand over the budget, somehow turning it into a piggy bank with at least some savings inside.

There were the usual problems – the barrage of complaints about closing down services that had only two people in attendance, the occasional renegade priest who had convinced himself that God meant him to run off with the churchwarden's wife, congregations who resented sharing their vicar, or being conjoined to parishes with whose members, they stalwartly declared, they had absolutely nothing in common. Nothing but their faith, or even, for crying out loud, their common humanity, Vicky thought. It was vital as an object lesson in Christian charity to try and force them into the unity and community of the saints, even if it meant knocking their heads together.

The positives far outweighed the problems. The policy of closing vast, uneconomic, often unlovely Victorian buildings, requiring a lengthy, tortuous battle with the local council and preservation societies, had at last enabled the diocese to fulfil its legal obligations to conserve energy in these straitened times. It also released enough funding to support pioneer ministers who built new congregations, meeting in homes, coffee shops, pubs and community centres. Some were growing so rapidly that members virtually sat on each other's laps. Many had divided, starting new groups in a network which now spread from one end of the diocese to the other.

It cheered her enormously to see the way some churches now served their local community in whatever way was relevant to its needs, with playgroups, toddler and after-school clubs, food, furniture and clothing banks, benefits and budgeting advice, credit unions and even healthcare. Not surprisingly, local councils had increasingly outsourced responsibility for welfare assistance for those in crisis, whose benefits had not yet come through, to faith groups. Some councils had handed over their entire budget. Why reinvent the wheel when these Christians were such ready, responsive and willing volunteers, when they were already doing what needed to be done? There were issues at stake that she hadn't managed to raise with the churches yet – how far faith-based charities were still morally free to share that faith, how far they were unwittingly shielding the government from a massive shortfall in its responsibility, given that resources were increasingly inadequate. But overall, she felt they maintained a good balance of appropriate caring and sharing.

What really exercised her mind, though, was one particular group of people who had fallen foul of heartless exploitation and could only be offered the most perfunctory of help – several hundred men, women and children in the poorest part of her diocese who had lived in low-rent accommodation on shorthold tenancies and had now been made home-less when their landlords sold out en masse to developers. How could she abandon them? A.T. Developments, in conjunction with a Rio de Janeiro-based company – the Brazilian Leisure and Entertainment Organisation, or BLEO – had managed to get planning permission to turn the Wooten Grange estate into a multi-billion-pound investment in 7,500 exclusive new homes and a commercial and retail development of millions of square feet for offices, a hotel, a multiplex cinema, a shopping mall and a casino.

She had protested loudly, writing to the local mayor, the Prime Minister and every government official in between, expressing her 'grave concerns about their policy of relaxing planning legislation to allow overseas companies with no experience of delivering these projects to invest in land and property – all in the name of "the national interest". How can it be in the interests of poorer neighbourhoods to build housing unavail-able to them, leisure facilities they could not afford, and fast-food outlets and casinos that will surely prove detrimental to their health and well-being?'

What was more, the legal obligation to provide social housing was a farce. The government might well argue that in the long run many more homes would be built, but while the eviction notices and thuggish bailiffs had arrived right on time, no affordable housing had materialised to date. An already stretched social services department struggled to provide even basic accommodation in multiple-occupancy houses with shared bath-rooms and kitchens. When Vicky visited one such dwelling she was appalled at the conditions – the damp, the squalor, the suffocating lack of space. The shared kitchen was locked at 8 p.m., the occupants told her, and the cooker was broken anyway. The heating ran for two hours morn-ing and evening if they were lucky – unless, of course, inspectors were doing their rounds. There was no garden. Incensed, Vicky had told the press, 'No child in this civilised country of ours should have to grow up like this.'

In the eyes of the media she had become the opposition's figure-head, a feisty female bishop fighting the giants of 'developmental greed'. She had led a protest march of 4,000 to 10 Downing Street with a petition for reasonably priced housing, and jobs for local people rather than the migrant workers bussed in by the elusive companies behind the development. She never could get to the bottom of where they had come from, nor find her way to the top to protest. She was even compared once or twice to 'Red Ellen', the campaigning MP Ellen Wilkerson who embarrassed the government by leading a march of 200 unemployed workers all the way from Jarrow to Downing Street to petition for jobs in the recession of 1936. How could she abandon the people who had come to depend upon her in this cruel recession of 2019? And what about her team, who had rallied round her, given her hours of their own time in providing the vital administrative support she needed? They all worked together so well. And despite Tom's initial misgivings, Ralph had fitted in fine. He was courteous, amena-ble and well liked.

'With his looks, what's not to like?' Tom had commented wryly when she said so. She kept quiet about the rumour that the predominantly female administrative offices of the diocese, based at Larchester Cathedral, ground to a halt every time he walked in.

Sitting in her study, she was gratified to hear Kelvin and Marissa's voices raised in laughter. The sound of her secretary's high-pitched laugh always brought back Vicky's memories of her as she was when Vicky first arrived – lips pulled tight into a default position of permanent disap-proval more effective than words could ever be. Unsatisfactorily single, Marissa was a woman who would have laid down her life for any male boss she served. She had never expected to work for a woman, and she wasn't planning to like it.

The expression on her face the day that Vicky had first tried on the episcopal regalia! The suffragan bishop, Martin Cunningham, a kindly, rotund little man with twinkling eyes and a bald pate encircled by tight grey curls, had offered her a crash revision course in the rites and rituals of high church ceremonial so that she could please everyone's liturgical preferences. The Church of England was a huge umbrella, covering every tradition from a catholicism that was 'higher' than Roman Catholicism, to an evangelicalism that was more charismatic than the Pentecostals, or more conservative than the Strict and Particular Baptists. Some of the Anglo-catholics and evangelicals remained implacably opposed to women bishops, so wouldn't let her near their churches anyway. The rest all had their own traditions and she would be expected to observe them.

'Let's have a look at the uniform first,' she had said, taking down the cope that had been made for her predecessor but one. She refused to splash out a vast amount of diocesan money on a new one. It was immediately evident that he had been a larger, rather different shape.

Martin moved gingerly around her, straightening it.

'You don't have to pussyfoot,' she said, as he fiddled with the clasp.

'It's called a morse, by the way. Beautiful, isn't it?'

She fidgeted with impatience.

'With respect,' he said, 'I'm not sure how it should hang. I've never dressed a woman in a cape before.'

'The only difference from a man are these things that stick out at the front.'

'Yes,' he admitted, slightly embarrassed. 'But they don't really show.'

'Tell you what, I'll hunch my shoulders and they won't show at all.'

She ambled around like the hunchback of Notre Dame, dragging the over-large cope in her wake.

'See? No boobies,' she said, and they were both roaring with laughter as Marissa Schofield appeared at the door, a tray of coffee and biscuits in her hands, and a face like a child who has just taken her first bite of a mushroom.

'You look splendid, Bishop,' she had said enthusiastically, depositing the tray onto a nearby table and tugging down her cashmere cardi. She was a woman in her early forties, silver hair tucked neatly behind ears that displayed tiny pearl earrings, glasses swinging from a chain around her neck. Utterly conservative but for the red patent shoes with their four-inch heels.

'A shoe fetish?' Vicky whispered, as she clacked her way back down the corridor of Bishop's House.

Martin giggled.

'Be warned. She doesn't suffer fools gladly. And a fool is anyone who says no to her. They say she's a treasure, really – but no one knows where it's buried.'

Marissa had remained po-faced for months, resentful of Vicky's appointment, shocked by her apparent lack of formality and her inability to accept the diary priorities her secretary suggested. Her crimson lipstick stretched into two thin lines, occasionally leaving some of it smeared onto her front teeth. But finally, just when she needed it most, Vicky struck gold.

'Marissa, could I see you in my study a moment?' she had said, that fateful day as she swept in from the hospital through the office.

Marissa had patted her waves into place and followed, looking mutinous. She stood just inside the room, hands folded defensively. Vicky suddenly realised she was expecting a reprimand, and could have kicked herself for not realising how insecure the woman was.

'Marissa, come over here and sit with me,' she said, pointing to the settee.

Marissa sat down primly at the opposite end, head high, refusing eye contact.

'The thing is,' Vicky confided, 'and here I need your absolute discretion – I'm going to have to rely on your ingenuity in a way no bishop has ever done before. But getting to know you these last few months, seeing your efficiency and the care you invest in your work, I feel confident that I can depend on you entirely.'

Even as she spoke, Marissa was transfigured in front of her, the sun melting the snow as defiance metamorphosed into a concerned, devoted allegiance. And that, miraculously, was how it had remained. They were bound together in so many ways, she, Marissa, Kelvin, Mike Barnes and Ralph. The thought of leaving them now almost broke her heart.

Why, when all was going so well, must her world be torn apart? Now – with the country in financial and moral meltdown, and the church and state at loggerheads over both issues. She had begun to see Larchester as the winding, if slightly uphill, road to a peaceful retirement, when she and Tom would grow old together, pottering around their garden, enjoying the luxury of time that their respective careers had so far denied them. But instead, she had been handed a potentially ignominious end to a reasonably satisfactory ministry.

'The day the ceiling fell in.' That was how the previous Archbishop referred to receiving the letter, openly lamenting the lack of privacy and peace. Life was the job and the job was life. A life, in his case, cruelly cut short. Who would opt for that?

She had no idea what to say to Tom, where to begin. How did anyone give their spouse the kind of news that would turn his world upside down, when he had only just acclimatised to becoming Mr Bishop? But she couldn't see how she could function without him – not just because being happily married was part of the job spec, but because she relied on him to be there for her in those moments of self-doubt no one else saw. She was grounded by his no-nonsense realism, the sarcasm that made her laugh at her own and everyone else's foibles. She needed his world, the singular view of the NHS that he brought her, as a reminder that there was life outside the church, and that every institution had its idiosyncrasies. Most of all she needed his arms to hold and comfort her and drive away the lurking demons that tell a woman of a certain age that she might no longer be sexually attractive. But he had to have a choice. She owed him that. If Tom said no, it was no.

Yet, how could she refuse? Who, in her shoes, wouldn't be enticed by the privilege of representing church to the nation and nation to the church, of having a place in the affairs of government at such a crucial time, of exercising leadership in an organisation yet to fulfil its true potential? She had always fought for the impossible. To become a priest before she could. To see women in the most senior posts in the church. To fight the injustice of financial inequalities, to bring faith back to the centre of national life, to bring hope to a world that had so little. If that was the voice of God, and her calling, who was she to say no?

1978

Vicky was thirteen when she announced she was going to be a vicar. It was 1978, the same year the first private motion to allow women into the priesthood was defeated in General Synod. As the result of the vote was announced, the silent gathering was electrified by a lone female voice ringing out from the spectators' gallery: 'We asked for bread and you gave us a stone.'

Many years later, when Vicky made the connection, she couldn't help but smile. She too had been handed a stone.

'Indeed?' her mother had said, without so much as looking up from the pile of dog-eared exercise books she was marking. 'That's the one thing you certainly can't be, Victoria. Women do not become vicars.'

She waited and watched her mother's face, fascinated by the tiny ridges of foundation that had gathered in the grooves, like rivulets in the sand when the tide goes out. But Audrey Burnham refused to be distracted from her ticks, crossings-out and comments.

'Why not?' Vicky asked, placing herself between her mother and the light from the dining-room window. She felt entitled to a reasonable explanation. Audrey had no choice but to look up from her work.

'Vicky,' she said crossly, 'the church has decided that it's a calling only men can fulfil. It's not ours to question. And I sincerely hope it stays that way – in my lifetime, at least.'

Then she tutted and slapped a red cross on yet another piece of homework that fell short of the mark.

Vicky was forced to admit that she had never come across a woman vicar. But then, she had never seen a woman doctor or dentist either, though she knew they existed. The school bus driver was a woman. The milkman was a woman. It occurred to her years later that, had she been clairvoyant, she could have told her mother that within a year the country would have its first female Prime Minister. She might also have argued that to accommodate her mother's career, her own family's domestic arrangements had been skewed in favour of the woman.

But that was the only way in which her family was unusual for its time. Otherwise, they lived a fairly traditional, unremarkable, middle-class existence, behind a tall privet hedge and the fancy lace curtains of a gracious, three-storey Edwardian town house, like so many built around the spacious, landscaped parks of bourgeois, booming Harrogate.

The historic spa town had been a mecca for the gentry, who came to take the famous waters. Once, at the Pump Room, she was dared to drink. Vicky could never resist a challenge – especially from the boys – so she scooped up a mouthful and swallowed, smiling defiantly so that they wouldn't see how near she was to gagging. The vile smell of rotten eggs remained in her nostrils for the rest of the day. But it was a small price to pay for victory.

With its Victorian elegance, gracious streets, exclusive gown shops and tea rooms, the town was the epitome of gentility, a haven for the respectably retired; all of which, for Vicky, meant stuffy and narrow. She couldn't understand why anyone would want to live in Harrogate when they could live in Leeds with its fantastic shopping and cinemas.

Her mother, desperate to get out of a working-class Leeds ghetto, had been delighted to land her first teaching job in a primary school in a more 'socially superior' part of Yorkshire. She had lived in a tiny bedsit above Cyril Burnham's tailoring business. Their first meeting was on the Saturday morning she had marched into the shop in dressing gown and slippers and accused him of stealing her daily delivery of a pint of milk while she was having a long lie-in. He stalwartly defended himself against this virago, assuring her he would never do such a thing, until one of his seamstresses approached him sheepishly, bottle in hand and said, 'It was me, Mr Burnham. I saw it on the doorstep when I arrived and assumed it was ours.' At which point, what else could the poor man do to placate his offended tenant but offer her dinner?

Vicky's father, a gentleman's outfitter, had inherited a shop that offered a discerning clientele the high standards of quality and service they could expect from a traditional family business. But even in Harrogate, with its elderly populace, old-style tailoring was giving way to the demand for cheaper, off-the-peg men's fashion. A Menswear Association Trade Fair at the National Exhibition Centre provoked a flurry of media interest by introducing male models to the catwalk – in cutting-edge suits.

Cyril Burnham was shrewd enough to know when he was beaten, and sold his prime site to a thrusting new fashion chain for more than enough money to allow him to retire comfortably at fifty-five. He called the incomers 'the McDonalds of men's fashion', after the new-fangled American fast-food outlets that were slowly encroaching from the south.

Other than financial, the benefits of the sell-out were hard to see. At work Vicky's father had had his manager, staff and clients for company. At home all he had was Rex, the family's little white Jack Russell. Audrey Burnham never took her nose out of her marking, and Vicky was at school, playing netball, hockey, lacrosse and tennis, when she wasn't involved in drama productions or speaking in the debating society, or at piano lessons, or revising for the never-ending stream of exams. Cyril Burnham had exchanged his tape measure for a dog lead. Like many men, outside of the workplace, uninspired by football, unused to the local pub, he had no idea how or where to find the companionship he had lost.

In the winter, when Vicky's commitments finished after the end of school hours, he and Rex were at the school gate waiting for her. Mostly they would walk home through the parks in silence, but occasionally he would ask her about her studies.

'Never take education for granted, Vicky. I went into the shop at fifteen. No choice. I'm a self-taught man and proud of it. But you, with the private education we've given you, the sky's the limit.'

The sky on clear nights, iridescent with a furry mass of speckles, was her father's favourite preoccupation. As they lingered while Rex decorated every one of the trees on their route home, he would stand looking up, pointing out the stars, planets and galaxies.

'Do you know them all, Dad?' she asked him once.

He guffawed loudly.

'How could I possibly, Vicky? There are billions, even zillions of them, near and light years away, filling every space in the entire universe. Think massive and it still isn't enough.'

'Wow,' she said, gazing up in awe. 'And God made all that.'

'If you say so.'

'He must have, mustn't he? How else did it happen?'

'Science might tell us one of these days – maybe sooner than we think.'

'But how were people made, then? Science can't tell us that. Can it?'

'Just over twenty years ago scientists discovered something called DNA – the cells that make us uniquely us. It could eventually transform our understanding of what it means to be human.'

'But it still doesn't explain how we got here in the first place.'

Her father simply shrugged and tugged at Rex's lead.

Had it not been for Cyril, the contents of Vicky's daily lunch box would have been cream crackers and cheese spread. Audrey was simply not interested in the trivial details of running a home. Fifteen years younger than her husband, and with a headship in her sights, she had far more pressing concerns than cookery. The demands of her career turned Cyril into an early house-husband. He moved around the kitchen quietly, constructing simple meals of meat and two veg. As old-fashioned as his family trade, he inhabited a world where spaghetti still came out of tins and couldn't be counted as real food.

No approach to his wife, evenings or weekends, verbal or physical, however concerned or gentle, could tempt her away from the dining-room table. Hour after hour she remained at her post, bent and unyielding, the work only more demanding when the coveted headship was achieved, replaced by syllabus schemes, agendas, rotas and references. She allowed herself only two distractions: a weekly card game with her colleagues, and the Sunday morning service at St Matthew's, a vast barn of a place on the catholic wing of the Anglican spectrum. Vicky accompanied her, reluctantly paraded in her Sunday best.

'No child of mine will grow up an atheist,' Audrey insisted, with a withering look in her husband's direction. Cyril simply smiled and stayed at home to make the Sunday roast.

The church was a freezing mausoleum. Such was the whirr and clunk of the radiators that Father Joe set them to come on only after his sermon. The congregation prayed it wouldn't be long in coming, and that it would be short when it finally did. By which time, some of the more elderly in the congregation, parcelled in layers of thermals and old furs, were nonetheless in the early throes of hypothermia. The toilets were so cold, especially on choir practice night when cost savings meant no heating in the church at all, that Vicky feared her wee would solidify into one long icicle before she had finished.

Sunday School was an affliction. Seven or so children huddled around a single paraffin heater in a dismal vestry, the walls patterned with mildew, for instruction from an elderly spinster, born, she loved to tell them, on the last day of the last century. She was a paid-up member of the Society for Sacramental Mission and saw it as her duty to inculcate in her tiny flock of unappreciative little heathens a knowledge of the great liturgies and catechisms of the church. Vicky loathed learning by rote. The many questions that clattered around her head were never addressed by colouring in pictures of a vapid-looking Jesus with long, blond curls. A mannequin, like the dummies in her father's shop.

Eventually, she abandoned children's instruction and, when she wasn't singing in the choir, joined her mother in the pew. The colourful vestments, the smell of incense and wine, the drama of the processions, the flickering candlelight, the echoing sound of glorious harmonies rising from the choir and reverberating around the building, the whole gamut of catholic ceremonial, fed an imagination hungry for spiritual sensation.

Father Joe, seeing a lone child in his congregation, asked her why she wasn't in Sunday School.

'Bored,' her long-suffering mother interjected.

'Is this true, Vicky?'

She nodded. He went to the vestry, and brought back a copy of *The Lion, the Witch and the Wardrobe.*

'Read this if you're ever bored in services. Aslan now, he is a symbol of our Lord, overcoming the evil and injustice in the world with self-sacrificial love.'

Vicky devoured the book, then re-read it several times. This Aslan Jesus was so much more appealing than any of the pictures she had ever seen of him. A tough lion, not a tame one, because that's what it took to lay down your life and liberate the land of Narnia. She fancied herself a Susan or a Lucy. Having found the source of all goodness, what else would she want to do but follow him?

Watching white-haired, weather-beaten Father Joe stooping to welcome his flock, each by name, at the church door every Sunday morning, or powerfully filling his pulpit, the boom of his voice echoing around the great silent vaults as he drew his congregation into the great Gospel stories, it seemed to Vicky that his must be the best job in the world. The feeling grew on her.

She didn't mention it again at home. Her parents never discussed religion. Religion was filed in the family archives under 'strictly private', along with sex, money and women's health. In fact, her parents discussed increasingly little. Mealtimes consisted of, 'Could you pass the jam, please?' from her father and, 'Don't slouch, Victoria. It's unladylike,' from her mother.

In her early teens, Vicky became aware that her parents' relationship wasn't all it might have been. She sensed, more than understood, that a lifetime in a quiet tailor's shop, of saying, 'Could you lift your arm, sir?'

combined with her mother's constant brush-offs, had robbed her father of the memory, if not the will, to express his feelings. She suspected that he was also irritated by some of her mother's affectations.

Audrey had developed a slight drawl. She had also taken to carrying a little lace hanky tucked into her watch strap. It reeked of 'Ô de Lancôme', and she would take it out and dab her mouth with it if anyone happened to call, as Father Joe did from time to time. Even so, there was another, faint, underlying smell about her that Vicky couldn't identify and didn't particularly like.

At times, too, she seemed unsteady on her feet, swaying around the house, crashing in a very unladylike manner into various bits of furniture. Cyril removed them, and anything else that might be an obstacle in her path.

'Clumsy these days, your mother, Vicky. We never needed this occasional table anyway. Well, only occasionally.'

'If that was a joke, Dad, it wasn't funny.'

He nodded in agreement and sighed as he removed the pieces of jagged wood.

'I'll walk the dog, then.'

He did little else, and was often gone for hours. Vicky wondered what he found to do with himself.

School provided a parallel universe full of jolly, boisterous girls, who were largely loyal and fair, who fell out with each other and made it up as fast, who formed devoted, committed friendships that lasted a lifetime. Harrogate Ladies College, an Anglican foundation with committed chaplains who did what they could to make chapel worship stimulating, encouraged intellectual curiosity, creativity, independent thinking and fairness. 'Can-do' might as well have been the school's motto. There was nothing a woman couldn't achieve, no mountain they couldn't conquer, no glass ceiling they couldn't shatter, no influential position denied them, especially once a grocer's daughter became the most powerful person in the country. The only thing women couldn't do – and in that, Vicky discovered, her mother was right – was become a vicar.

'Why? What difference would it make?' she asked, during an RE lesson on the beliefs of the Church of England, when in every picture in every textbook, the minister was male. Even their school chaplain, in an all-girls school, was male.

Bev Aldridge raised a hand.

'They wear a dress anyway, Miss Johnson.'

'Thank you, Beverley. Evangelical Anglicans base their argument on a verse in the New Testament that says women shouldn't be allowed to preach or have authority over men. The more high church wing of the church holds the view that since Jesus was male, church tradition dictates that his successors must be men too.'

Bev Aldridge waved a hand again.

'But if Jesus was God, Miss Johnson, is God a man?'

One or two girls began to titter.

'No, Beverley. God is neither male nor female.'

'So will the church ever change its mind and let women become priests?' Vicky persisted.

'Shush, girls. I can't really say, Vicky. But there is a small, but vociferous lobby fighting for it, so I imagine there must be a chance.'

Vicky sat down, smiling to herself. A fight? No, she wasn't afraid of that, as long as victory was at least a possibility.

In the late seventies, though, before the rise of Thatcher, even school couldn't be relied upon as an escape from the dispiriting environment of Vicky's home life. In fact, all of life seemed to be dictated by powers outside of her control. Ambulance drivers, miners, nurses, gravediggers, the bin men, there was always someone threatening to rob her of her education for the sake of higher pay. They couldn't even watch the new colour TV her father had bought. The pleasure of it would have more than made up for her mother's tight-lipped, stony silence about it, had the miners allowed them to watch it.

Her parents were annoyingly unmoved and stoical in the face of such massive inconvenience. The power cuts barely appeared to affect their humdrum lives – even in the bitter early months of 1979, when it was so cold that the entire country came to a standstill. Water froze, pipes burst, oil ran out and the school was closed to all except boarders.

Then came the blizzards. Vicky felt marooned on an iceberg, cut off from all that made existence bearable.

'Stop pacing the floor like an animal in the zoo, Vicky, and get on with your homework,' Audrey instructed, as she worked on as usual, by candlelight, wrapped in a sleeping bag and wearing fingerless gloves, immune to the cold and insensible as to whether her own school would be open or closed the next day. 'Those of us who lived through the last war will not give way to tyranny, be it Hitler, or the miners.'

Enter Mrs Thatcher and common sense, according to the Burnhams, for once in total agreement. As long as school re-opened, Vicky couldn't have cared if the wicked witch of Narnia had been elected to power. One day, she might argue that she had.

* * *

Audrey had never keen on Bev Aldridge and Mandy Jacobson, Vicky's closest friends. Vicky was regularly subjected to a discourse about their lack of suitability.

'Is it because Mandy's Jewish and Bev's Irish?'

'Don't be ridiculous, Vicky,' Audrey snapped.

'Well, you're forever moaning about the way the country's being taken over by coloured people.'

'That's different. Your friends are just not the quiet, refined sort of girls I would have expected you to chum up with at a school as expensive as yours.'

Mandy's father was a furrier, Bev's owned a textile factory, so both girls' families had benefited from Harrogate's lucrative clothing industry.

'Like us,' Vicky pointed out to her mother. But it didn't go down well.

Quiet they were not, that much she had to concede. Mandy – dark, petite and vivacious, with a wide, impish grin and exotic, brown eyes – came from a formidable Jewish family where everyone talked at once. She waved her hands to explain what she meant and was forever being cautioned by teachers to think before she spoke.

Big Bev, with long Titian locks and milky complexion, was one of a large, lippy, Protestant Irish brood, 'driven back to England', she once announced loudly in class, by 'sectarian eejits'. Her aggression on the sports field and outspokenness everywhere else repeatedly got her into trouble, but she appeared impervious to it. Anyone who crossed her was an 'eejit'. It was as simple as that. But she was clever enough to avoid the kind of insolence that might have threatened her education. She wanted to be a doctor, an ambition that eventually forced her into toeing the line, hard for her though it was.

Mandy had two brothers, Bev three, and from Vicky's perspective, they had the kind of family life she had always wanted and never had – gregarious, argumentative and affectionate. She stayed with one or the other whenever she could. But on evenings alone at home, wrapped in rugs against the glacial drafts that seeped into the house through gaps under doors and windows, when heat was denied by order of the government, her imagination taunted her with the fun-filled home life that she was missing out on, and she wondered why God had denied her that kind of happiness. It seemed so unfair.

At sixteen, the girls found themselves on the college team for the annual inter-schools quiz. Round three was hosted by an exclusive private school for boys. As they climbed the broad stone stairs of the ancient academic institution, a boy, on his way down, pointed at Mandy and shouted to his peers, 'Look at that ugly Yid!'

Vicky stopped dead, waited for him to draw level with her, then grasped his arm and shouted loudly, 'What did you just say?' He grinned slyly, and tried to shrug her off, but she held him in a vice, and yelled, 'Tell everyone what you've just called my friend.' The traffic on the stairs came to a sudden, silent halt. 'Don't, Vicky,' Mandy begged, tugging ineffectively at her free arm. The boy coloured, wriggled ineffectually for a few seconds until he eventually managed to wrench himself free, straightened his jacket, then continued his way nonchalantly down the stairs, laughing with his friends. Vicky distinctly heard the word 'Yid-lover'.

She removed her schoolbag from her shoulder and with as much force as she could muster, launched it at his back. It must have been heavier than she realised: hitting him with a loud thwack, the bag toppled the boy, and she heard bone meet stone with a resounding crack as he landed, head-first, at the foot of the stairs. She turned swiftly, ran up to Mandy and Bev, grabbed their arms, and they continued on their way, before the crowd that gathered around him had time to process what had happened.

'Vicky!' Mandy whispered, wide-eyed. 'What have you done?'

'He had it coming, the eejit,' Bev giggled.

Vicky shrugged. 'No one is rude to my friends,' she declared, as they arrived at the hall and her knees began to knock.

It was no surprise to be summoned before the headmistress the following morning.

'Vicky, this is a very serious incident. The boy was taken to hospital with severe concussion. Thankfully, it isn't a great deal worse.'

'Were you told what he said to Mandy, Mrs Lawrence?'

'I was, and it's totally unacceptable. But there are ways of dealing with it that use brain rather than brawn.'

'It made me so angry, Mrs Lawrence.'

'And your defence of your friend does you credit. The young man's behaviour should not go unchallenged. But I cannot have my girls lashing out. Aggression never achieves anything. The boy will be dealt with appropriately – with due punishment, and by having the offensiveness of anti-Semitism spelt out to him.'

'I'm sorry, Mrs Lawrence, I didn't think.'

'You have a very good brain, Vicky. Use it properly. This school encourages leadership, but good leaders know how to channel their innate sense of justice into the means to achieve the necessary change. For a start, they act co-operatively, not unilaterally. Now, go and tell Mandy to come and have a word with me.'

'It was all my fault, Mrs Lawrence. Mandy didn't do anything.'

'Which is why I think she might need some extra support. Don't you?'

'No punishment,' Vicky said to her parents, who had been informed of the incident.

'Scared to lose the Jewish fees,' her mother had replied.

'That's not true,' Vicky countered.

But Audrey merely snorted, reducing Vicky to the helpless fury she so often felt at her mother's pronouncements.

When Father Joe retired and was replaced by a young, fresh-faced minister who wanted to be known simply as Pete, Audrey wrapped her prayer book in her disgust and took them both home. Pete was married with three children and one on the way, demonstrating, she maintained, lips pursed, a certain lack of restraint for a man in his position. More to the point, he introduced songs written in the current century, started a child-friendly service once a month, and read the eucharistic prayers with meaning, not in the monotone Father Joe had preferred in order not to detract from the mystical transfer of bread and wine to body and blood. Vicky had always watched the elements like a hawk, hoping to see some Tommy Cooper-style magic trick, but as far as she could see, they never became anything other than bread and wine.

She suspected her mother had been looking for an excuse to stop going to church for some time. Her speech, especially at weekends, was becoming ever more slurred. Her eyelids drooped. At times she could barely open them, and when she did, her eyes were glazed, unable to focus.

'I get so tired these days – the responsibilities at work. You do understand?' she asked Vicky. When she lost her balance, it was, 'My legs are not what they were.'

When Vicky nodded, Audrey would pat her hand absent-mindedly and say, 'Good girl.'

'You will go to the doctor's, Mum, won't you?'

'I will, won't I, Cyril? Next week.'

'Of course we will, Audrey,' he would say, offering her his arm, giving Vicky a knowing little wink.

Although Vicky kept up her church attendance, and babysat regularly for Pete and his wife, Paula, she increasingly wondered whether her father wasn't right. The universe had simply exploded into being. There was no meaning in anything. Exams would lead to university, which would lead to work, to earn money to eat and drink, to work and end up like her parents. So when she discovered The Connexion, that prided itself in offering a clubbing experience that put the Leeds and Manchester alternatives in the shade, she transferred her worship to the gods of entertainment – Madonna, Michael Jackson, David Bowie, Depeche Mode, and Duran Duran. The louder the music, the better to fill her head with a noise that drummed out the voices telling her that life was a lottery and she had drawn a bum number.

The girl trio loved making an entrance through the double doors – Bev swinging an off-centre, ginger pony tail, her tiny scarlet hot pants exposing a pair of long, lovely legs; Mandy, hair crimped into a halo around her face, in boiled, second-skin jeans, and an oversized, off-the-shoulder T-shirt; and Vicky, a Madonna wannabe, with bleached hair, bracelets up her arms, fishnet gloves and a large, last-tribute-to-religion cross dangling from one ear. The ugly duckling had morphed, she told her newly-blonde reflection in the mirror, if not exactly into a swan, then into a passable imitation of one.

The Connexion was a draughty gin palace, all red velvet and mirrors, brass and tat, with black plastic seating that attached itself to the nether regions after a sweaty bout of dancing, and farted like a whoopee cushion when they got up. They jiggled and wiggled around their handbags, ogled the dishy DJs spinning the records on their forefingers like plates on a stick, tucked into chunks of greasy pizza, and snogged spotty youths in darkened corners.

'No more of that for me,' Bev announced one night.

'Why not?' Mandy asked.

She started to sing, 'What do you get when you kiss a girl? Germs enough to catch pneumonia.' Then, 'Snogging's boring. Why would you want a mouthful of what someone else has just swallowed – onions, garlic, curry or beer – when you can have a bar of chocolate?'

When Vicky agreed, Mandy's mouth fell open.

'I can't believe you two. There's some great guys here. You're not dykes, are you?'

'I'm up for it,' Bev grinned, picking the cocktail stick out of her Babycham and sucking the glacé cherry off its end. 'Vicky's more attractive than any of the men here, that's for sure.'

They both laughed and went back to the dance floor . . .

Recreational drug use was commonplace at The Connexion. Bev tried a pill or two, but said that for her money, the club's legendary vodka punch gave her just as good a hit.

'Try it,' she urged Vicky.

Vicky recognised the smell of it, and had to stop herself from gagging. The slightest whiff of alcohol, or Ô de Lancôme, for that matter, made her nauseous these days.

'Chicken,' Bev chanted.

She shook her head. There was no way she could explain. Mandy came to her rescue.

'The only high I need I get from shopping.'

'I've never seen anyone shop like you,' Bev agreed. 'You're the only person I know who buys knickers to match her outfit.'

Mandy grinned. 'How does a Jewish princess commit suicide?'

They waited.

'Piles all her clothes on her bed and jumps off the top.'

'Ha-ha! Leave us the lot in your will if you do,' Bev said.

'Don't be daft, Bev,' Vicky laughed, 'we couldn't get Mandy's tops over our heads. And her skirts would only do as belts.'

In the end, it was Mandy who brought their fling with night life to a sudden halt. She had squandered her virginity on one of the DJs, an older man who liked his schoolgirls pure and pristine, and ditched her for an unused model when Mandy thought she might be pregnant.

'You're not on the pill, eejit?' Bev snapped at her, when she told them.

'I didn't know how to get it,' she replied, tearfully. 'Our doctor's a member of our synagogue.'

She wasn't, in fact, pregnant, but by the time she found out, her anxieties had alerted her parents. She cracked under their prolonged, intensive interrogation, and was denied all non-kosher social contact forthwith. Including Bev and Vicky.

Bev had decided in any case that the time had come to knuckle down to her studies, if the granddaughter of a gravedigger Irish navvy was going to be the first in her family to study medicine. And for Vicky the attractions of clubbing, apart from the synchronised throb of the dance, were beginning to pall. Booze sickened her, drugs worried her, and she wasn't in any hurry to lose her virginity, seeing as the freedoms bestowed by the pill were being undermined by a frightening new virus called AIDS. Why seek amnesia for a night, only to wake in the morning to worse problems than the ones you were running from the night before?

Her epiphany occurred unexpectedly during one particular chapel service which wakened something dormant deep inside her. The preacher, Sister Phoebe, was a dynamic young Indian nun in a sari, who spent her days rescuing baby girls from dustbins, then educating them and finding them suitable husbands so that they could escape their destiny as untouchables, and fulfil their potential as Christian women.

'Pen,' she mouthed at Bev, then snatched up one of the prayer books, and tore a blank page out, while an open-mouthed Bev handed over her biro. She jotted down the gist of Sister Phoebe's words, then folded the paper and tucked it into her pocket. Years later they were still in her Bible, so crumpled and worn they were barely legible: 'No one is too small, too poor, or too insignificant to be cared for by the Father. But the only way he has of showing them his love is through our eyes, our feet, and our hands. Some of you here today will be called to live sacrificially. At present you are too young to know what that means. But wait and watch, and don't walk away from your destiny when it calls you.'

Later, sharing peanut butter sandwiches and crisps in the sixth form common room, Vicky said to Bev, 'What did you make of that?'

'Yuk, cheese and onion,' Mandy moaned. 'What have you got, Bev? Barbecue? Swop?'

'Are barbecue kosher?' Bev asked her.

'What the eye doesn't see . . .'

'Never mind the crisps,' Vicky interjected. 'Does anyone care about the country? Thatcher's taking away the dignity of the working classes – the men and women who made Britain great. She doesn't give a monkey's fart about what actually happens to a man when he's unemployed.'

'Give us a break, Vick,' Mandy groaned, biting into an apple. 'Since you started watching *Boys from the Blackstuff*, we have to sit and listen to you every dinner hour rabbiting on about the oppression of the poor. It's only television, for goodness' sake!'

'You just don't get it, do you?' Vicky snapped back. 'What's going on in Liverpool isn't just TV. It's real. Just because we're too sheltered to see it doesn't mean it isn't happening.'

'And what are you going to do about it – go up there every weekend and run a soup kitchen, Mother Teresa?'

'I don't know yet,' Vicky said, aggravated by Mandy's sarcasm, but forgiving her on the grounds that Mandy was excused chapel and hadn't heard Sister Phoebe. 'But I am going to do something.'

'What do you need me to do?' she asked Pete, after a Sunday service.

Pete and Paula seemed to be the only people in her orbit who thought the Archbishop of Canterbury was right to refuse Margaret Thatcher a victory service after the Falklands War, holding out for a commemoration of all who died on both sides.

Pete raised his eyebrows in surprise.

'Since you're asking, we're desperate for a Sunday School teacher.'

Vicky couldn't disguise her disappointment.

'What do you want to do?' Pete asked her.

She coloured and muttered, 'I want to change the world, that's what I want to do.'

'In that case, Sunday School is the best place to start. You'll have the potential to change those little lives forever.'

There were six five-to-eight-year-olds in her class – Emma, Lucy, Charlotte, Graham, William and Ben. Each had their own little charms and foibles, and before she knew it, they had wormed their way into her heart in a way she had never anticipated. They met in the redecorated vestry, still fiendishly draughty and cold, even with a proper radiator. But there was no mindless colouring-in for her class. There was drinking chocolate and the best biscuits she could afford. She got Paula to show her how to make a chocolate cake for their birthdays. She told them stories, invited discussion, encouraged questions. Questions that often made her laugh – 'What did Jonah look like when the fish sicked him up?' – or stretched her to the limit – 'What happened to all the people who weren't in Noah's ark?'

Ben was the clown of the class, forever falling off his chair or doing passable imitations of the verger, who had a slight tick. Ben was convinced the words of the Eucharist were not 'Thanks be to God', but 'Thanks Peter God', since the vicar was called Pete and thus the closest they could expect to the real thing.

'How did Jesus go up into heaven?' Lucy asked.

'In an aeroplane, silly,' answered Ben.

'That child thinks laterally!' said one of the other Sunday School teachers. But Vicky saw that Ben's answers were just obvious, while the teachers, with their pre-conceived spirituality, were the ones who asked the lateral questions. The children's extempore prayers for each other, for their parents, for her, brought a lump to her throat and made her wonder how anyone could doubt that children could be full members of a church. Their simple, trusting faith put adults to shame. Put her to shame.

Reading them *The Lion, the Witch and the Wardrobe*, the book she had come to love years before, she realised with a certain shock that she had never been a faithful follower of Aslan, like Susan or Lucy. She was more like the rebellious and wilful Edmund, who cost the lion his life. She said so to Paula one evening when she arrived to babysit at the vicarage. Paula, wrapping a rogue lock of long brown hair behind her ear as she stooped to pick up the detritus of playthings left strewn across the floor, expertly slotting the pieces of a postbox toy into the correct holes, then piling them all into a large pine box in the corner, looked up at her, and said, 'A teacher can't lead someone somewhere she isn't going herself.'

'Then what do I need to do?'

'Oof,' she groaned, 'I can see that Pete's preaching these past couple of years has really been getting through.'

'Sorry.'

'No need to apologise. It just goes to prove that God chooses his moment. Just tell him that you want to know him and follow him, and let's see how your future pans out by the time Pete and I come home from *Back to the Future*.'

Vicky sat for some time after they had gone, enjoying the tranquillity of the house, the soft, even breathing from the children upstairs, the sporadic rumbling of the boiler, the contented murmurings of the cat stretched out in front of the fire. She picked up Paula's Bible from the coffee table and thumbed through it. It was filled with red underlining and scribbles, and she marvelled that anyone should get so much out of it. And then she asked herself, not so much whether it was factual, for that hardly seemed to matter, but whether it was *relevant*. What use was it to believe that God had made the world, that he loved it, that he sent his only Son to sacrifice himself for it, if it made no difference to how she lived? An undefinable something was missing. That familiarity with God that Paula seemed to have, the intimacy that inspired Sister Phoebe. And that she needed.

Feeling a little silly, she knelt down on the carpet and asked that, if it were possible, she might know the God of Paula and Phoebe as they did. And from the Bible's open page where she had left it on the coffee table, rose up one verse, inescapable, highlighted in yellow. 'I have come that you may have life, life in all its fullness.'

Life! The more she watched her parents drowning in the consequences of her mother's need for alcohol, the more she yearned for life. Fullness of life. She held out her hands – she wasn't sure why – and waited. And then she felt it – a presence whose warmth suffused her whole being, so near she could almost reach out and touch him. In her mind she saw him place a large key onto her open palms, almost felt the coldness of it.

The key to life.

There were no angel voices in the room, no illuminated letters on the ceiling, but she knew that though nothing around her was different, everything inside her had changed. 'Got it,' she said, folding a hand around the imaginary key, then went up to check on the children. 'Now I am a true follower of Aslan,' she whispered to them, as she straightened their sheets and duvets and kissed them on their foreheads. 'I have the key to the door, though where my own personal wardrobe to Narnia may be, only God knows.'

JANUARY 2020

She heard the roar of the car engine on the drive. It came to an abrupt halt outside the house. A door slammed shut. And then the key was turning in the lock. The cloakroom door was almost wrenched off its hinges. She checked her watch. Tom was late. And not in the best of moods.

THREE

*God became man that dehumanized men might become true
men. We become true men in the community of the incarnate,
the suffering and loving, the human God.*

JÜRGEN MOLTMANN

JANUARY 2020

Tom strode into the room, went straight to the standard lamp and switched it on. He gave a start as he turned and saw her, huddled on the settee.

'What are you doing, sitting in the dark?'

When he got no reply, he walked over to the dresser, took out a glass and a bottle of gin.

'Where's the tonic?'

'Two inches to the left of your right hand.'

'Ice?'

'In the thermos. In front of you. Lemon's in the fridge, though.'

'Can't be bothered. Want one?'

'Just tonic, thanks.'

He walked across the room, handed her a glass, then sat down heavily in the armchair opposite, crossing his long legs and resting the drink on the arm of his chair.

'Strangulated hernia. Not one of the most exciting reasons to be held up, but can't be helped. Can cause a whole lot of bother. More complicated than we thought.'

He took a long, slow swallow of his gin, leant back against the chair, then said, 'Okay, what have I done?'

Vicky looked puzzled.

'The silent treatment.'

'Oh, sorry. It's not you,' she said, smiling encouragingly. A bad start. Why must men always assume that any problem a woman has is always something to do with them? 'I have a lot to think about.'

'I expected to find you out and dinner in the microwave.'

'You know I try and keep Friday evenings free. For us.'

'Really?'

'Sorry, I know I haven't been too good at it.'

He gave a short snort.

'So?'

She handed him the letter that had been lying on her lap. Tom scanned it, took a long, noisy gulp of his gin, and said, 'God!'

'Yes, we really are going to need his help with this one. Or we're scuppered.'

She was aware of twisting the tumbler round and round in her hands, of the small comfort of rubbing the criss-cross indentations of the cut glass with her finger pads. She could barely bring herself to look at Tom's face, waxen in the lamplight, his eyes two hollow caverns, blank and fixed on a space behind her right ear. She saw that he was tired and felt a twinge of conscience that she was often so taken up with her own pressures that she rarely considered his.

He shook himself, ran his hand through his hair, the way he always did when he was baffled, or distressed.

'I suppose we'll have to give up the jolly house then?' he said, looking around the room appreciatively. 'Shame. This was one of the better ones, more gracious than any we had before. Almost what I might have chosen for myself.'

'There's a three-bedroom flat in Lambeth Palace, and some kind of accommodation in the Old Palace in Canterbury – a more rambling, homely sort of place, I gather. Grade 1 listed and whatnot.'

He held up his glass and swung it thoughtfully between his forefinger and thumb, as if mesmerised by the swaying liquid that glittered in the lamplight.

'I've been thinking of buying a place of my own anyway. Somewhere nearer the hospital.'

Vicky felt a sudden crack of pain, as if she had been slapped across the face.

'But if we lived at Lambeth Palace there would be no more commutes, Tom. You'd be so much nearer.'

He looked up at her sharply, then shook his head slowly.

'And totally subsumed in your world. Get real, Vicky – a man needs his own space. Not a hutch for a domestic pet in a public monument.'

She felt her eyes begin to swim and used every ounce of concentration she possessed to fight back the tears. Tears could be so manipulative, and she didn't want him to see how much he had upset her, or to pressurise him into a decision he might later regret. She had so hoped that their past difficulties were resolved, and gone forever. She said, as evenly as she could, 'Tom, I've never expected you to conform to any role my job might require of you.'

He smiled, and shook his head.

'What an innocent you are. To the patients who read the local rags, I'm the Bishop's husband. Sometimes, the Bishop's poor husband.'

'That's them. Not me.'

He waved a hand dismissively.

'Does it matter?'

'Tom, if you feel you can't live with the Archbishop of Canterbury, then I won't accept the post. I can't. You matter so much more to me than that.'

'But you can't turn it down though, Vicky, can you?'

'Don't say it like that, Tom. I never asked for it. Never expected it. Do you think I don't know that it's a poisoned chalice? Especially for the first woman. Prototypes are rarely a success. Tell me to say no and I will.'

'If you're looking for an excuse to turn it down, don't let it be me,' he said, holding up his hands.

He saw her stricken expression and put his glass down on the coffee table. Then he got up and walked over to her, removed the glass from her hand and sat down next to her on the settee. He pulled her into his arms and sat holding her for a while. Then he whispered into her hair, 'I said when we married that I would never come between you and whatever God calls you to do. But that didn't mean I wouldn't find it bloody difficult. I know you, you see. I know how seriously you take that blessed calling of yours. You'll do what you have to do. No matter how terrifying the prospect.'

Vicky couldn't keep the tears in check any longer.

'I'm prepared to make sacrifices – but not you,' she wept. 'I'm not asking you to be a Prince Philip, at my side on every occasion. It would make you less than the man I love. I just need to know you'll be there to come home to.'

He held her by the shoulders and looked into her eyes with a tenderness that wrenched at her insides.

'You think I didn't know you'd go far? Not quite this far, admittedly. But Vicky, you must do what your heart tells you. And leave me to cope with it in my own way. That's all I ask. I don't enjoy the public attention, you know that. I need my space. My life.'

'What about *our* life?'

'When you're hardly ever there already? Our life might have to go on hold for a while – except for planned trysts and holidays. And if the

Archbishop's husband is allowed his conjugal rights from time to time. On high feasts and holy days. Oh sorry – that's when you're working.'

She managed a weak smile.

'That's my girl,' he said, taking a handkerchief from his trouser pocket and carefully mopping the tears on her cheeks with it.

'Oh Tom, my heart sinks at the thought of what this job entails.'

'We've had to live fairly separate lives. That's the cost of two demanding careers. Not ideal, but we've managed so far.'

'And the media? There'll be no such thing as "your space" as far as they're concerned.'

'Then I'll have to show them that there is.'

She let out a long, low breath.

'I don't want to be sceptical, Tom, but crucifixion by media seems to be the lot of Archbishops of Canterbury, if recent history is anything to go by. Using a spouse as the means of knocking in a nail or two is par for the course.'

' "Take up your cross and follow me." Isn't that the ultimate calling of every Christian? Tom Woods included?'

'But I've asked so much of you already, my darling,' she said, taking his hand.

'Where you go, I'll go; your God will be my God, and your people, my people. That was the commitment I made the day I took on an aspiring woman vicar, and I've stood by it so far. To the best of my ability, anyway.'

He tucked the handkerchief into his trouser pocket, and handed her back her glass of tonic. She took it and said, 'How I wish that we could let this cup pass us by.'

'So do I,' he murmured. 'But what was it Jesus said the night before the crucifixion? "Not my will, but yours." Isn't that what a calling is all about?'

'Jesus struggled with it all night. I'd better decamp to one of the spare rooms so as not to disturb your beauty sleep.'

'Thank you, Darling, much appreciated,' he said, patting her knee. 'I have a complex piece of colorectal surgery tomorrow. Needs absolute precision.'

'I understand entirely,' she said, leaning over and kissing him gently on the mouth. 'My life isn't actually at stake, but your patient's certainly is.'

To be married to the first female Archbishop of Canterbury required an exceptional sort of a man, she ruminated as she headed upstairs with a heavy heart. Tom was certainly tough, resourceful and shrewd, a dedicated doctor, but did he have the inner reserves, both spiritual and mental, for a challenge like this? She wasn't sure. Their union had been so unlikely from the start.

1982

As trainee vicars, students took on various short placements in communities where they might serve as chaplains. Vicky found herself working as an auxiliary nurse on a geriatric ward of the local hospital for six weeks. She fetched and carried, fed the patients, helped with bed baths, emptied bed pans, cleaned false teeth. She realised, of course, bright young theology graduate that she was, that it was essential that each set should be placed in its named tub. So she balanced the trayful on the bath rack, and swallowing the urge to retch, began to scrub, one set at a time. Disaster struck as she turned for more dentifrice and the rack tipped over, teeth and tubs landing in a jumbled mound in the bath. Fitting each patient with the right pair the following day proved a challenge for the Ward Sister, who, judging by her face, was glad Vicky was training for the church, not the NHS.

The dedication of some of the staff was impressive. Others, she noticed regretfully, had little patience and scant regard for the dignity of those in their care. She mentioned it to Bob, the head chaplain, who was master of his masonic lodge, and saw no conflict of interest in worshipping God by day and Jahbulon by night. He merely shrugged.

'That's the NHS culture for you. Nurses arrive here bright-eyed and bushy-tailed, but good intentions are soon whittled away by the constant drip-drip of the disenchantment of some of the older staff. It's called enculturalisation. Every institution suffers from it.'

'Even the Church of England?'

'Think about it, Vicky.'

'Disillusionment? Boredom?'

'Uncaring, unprofessional behaviour? Easy to fall into. Just remember that in the years to come.'

Shortly before Christmas Bob asked whether she would be willing to help out at the junior doctors' bash, as it clashed with a party at the lodge. She said she'd be delighted. He said she wouldn't be – for long.

'Why? What do they get up to?'

'Ah,' he said, looking at the ground, 'it gets a little . . . how shall I put it . . . rowdy. Some of the Christian medical students have taken it upon themselves to . . . be available.'

'Come on, Bob, what does being "available" entail?'

He still couldn't look at her.

'They, er, empty the sick buckets, mop the floors and loos, and get the revellers in a fit enough state to go home.'

'Well, then. How can I resist an offer like that?'

It was worse, far worse than she anticipated – a Bacchanalian nightmare. Smashed out of their heads, some of the country's brightest future doctors, male and female, stripped to their underwear, climbed onto the tables, and, singing a selection of lewd and bawdy songs, openly and explicitly fondled each other's bodies. Or dared each other to knock back the contents of the jugs of beer which they then vomited back into bright-red buckets, strategically placed for that purpose, before starting all over again.

An army of medical students from the Sheffield University Christian Union, stationed at the four corners of the room in rubber gloves and luminous tabards with 'steward' on the back, moved quietly and efficiently round the room, clearing away the buckets, replacing them with clean receptacles, and mopping the floor with enough disinfectant to mask at least some of the acrid smell.

A young woman, seeing Vicky's overalls, tottered over to her on near stilts. She was wearing a minimal number, more bathing costume than dress, and trilled, with a dismissive wave of her hand, 'You people are fantastic. If we throw up, you just clean up the mess.'

Vicky was tempted to slap her face and see how Christian she found that.

'Don't mention it,' she replied curtly, with a tight smile. 'Think of it as an act of service or charity like . . . working in a hostel for alcoholics and down-and-outs.'

The woman swayed, blinked for a moment or two at the obvious sarcasm in Vicky's voice, but before she could respond, her partner had staggered over to her, pawed her for a while, then slunk slowly down her body, until he lay, in an unmoving heap, at her feet.

'Tom, Tom, wake up,' she screamed, tugging at his arms ineffectually. 'Help me, somebody, I've got to get him up. He has a viva tomorrow. He failed the last one.'

Vicky took a quick look round and saw that she was the only 'somebody' in sight, so she turned him over, grabbed him from behind under the arms, and heaved him across the room, away from the danger of being skewered by a five-inch heel.

'A pity your Tom didn't think of that sooner,' she gasped, laying him down in a quiet corner. 'Go and get some of his mates.'

The girl staggered off, whimpering.

As she waited glumly for help to arrive, Vicky bent down to take a closer look at the prostrate figure on the floor, and check he was still breathing. For one short moment he opened the most stunning pair of grey-green eyes she had ever seen, looked straight up at her and said, 'Wow, you have the face of an angel,' before passing out again.

Two would-be doctors in a marginally better state than their friend eventually helped her manhandle the dead weight out to a taxi, as he slurred a, 'Sorry, sorry, sorry, not usually this bad,' with the girlfriend snivelling and lurching along behind. They hoisted him in, shoved the girlfriend after him, slammed the door behind them – and that, Vicky sincerely hoped, was the last she would see of him. All she wanted to do now was go home and shower away the sight, feel and smell of him.

A dozen red roses arrived at Vicky's college room the following day. Attached was a card that said, 'Please forgive me. Let me buy my angel dinner.'

She tossed it in the general direction of the rubbish bin. The cheek of the man!

She married Tom Woods six months later.

JANUARY 2020

That was perhaps the longest night she had ever gone through. Her alarm clock seemed to stretch every minute of darkness out to infinity. She tossed and turned, hovered for odd moments on the edge of sleep, a short release from the panic that churned her stomach – but at the next moment panic jolted her awake again. The media attention on the first woman bishop had been intrusive enough. Her clothes, her make-up, her jewellery, even the small mole on her cheek, had all been subject to comment in a way no man would ever have to endure. As Archbishop, she would be lifted onto a pedestal, from whence she would no doubt be cast down, like Jezebel thrown to the dogs, the moment she failed to fulfil the expectations and projections of every bishop, clergyman and -woman, the public, the press, Uncle Tom Cobley and all. In fact, everyone for whom she wasn't already anathema by dint of her gender.

If the fear of public censure didn't reduce her to helplessness, the enormity of the task did. To bring together the disparate pieces of a deeply divided church still wrangling endlessly over the same bones of contention: women in leadership, and gay marriage. To rescue an institution drowning amidst its financial obligations, with money-guzzling buildings that were either surplus to requirements or at least cost more to keep than any congregation could afford. To support a million or so people giving endless hours of voluntary work to the country, yet becoming ever more maligned and marginalised in an increasingly secular state.

A barrage of questions besieged her and left her feeling more bewildered and alone than she had ever done in her entire life. Did the invitation constitute a call? Why was she chosen? Wouldn't others do a better job? Did the Commission just think appointing a woman would be a timely and necessary gesture? What reason could she give for refusing such an honour? Could she excuse herself because of family commitments? The need for privacy? That would make her exactly the weak and feeble stereotype that antagonists to women's leadership expected.

On the other hand, if she accepted, how could she know for sure that it wasn't simply out of vanity, a desire for power, status, kudos? Sorting through her motives felt like looking for bugs in a home-grown cabbage. Were there enough bugs in there to justify binning the entire vegetable?

The real sticking point, though, was whether the Church of England was ready to have a woman at its helm. The long journey from deaconess and parish worker to deacon, priest, archdeacon, dean and finally, bishop, had been extremely painful for many. And no matter how egalitarian or psychologically prepared the rest thought they were, a good few would inevitably resent having a woman at the top for the first time.

Then there was the Anglican Church worldwide, and the risk to its precarious unity her leadership might pose. The belligerent North American members, who had already had a woman at their head, disastrous to harmonious relations as she had been, had taken their toys home some time ago over the decision not to license openly practising gay priests. The appointment of a theologically conservative archbishop would worsen that breach. Meanwhile the mighty majority African church, which would be delighted to have a leader with traditional views on sexuality, would never agree to having a woman at the head. But the Commission must have taken soundings, surely? Perhaps her traditional interpretation of the biblical texts would be a trade-off for her lack of a male appendage?

At around 3 a.m. she tiptoed down the corridor to their bedroom to see if Tom was awake, craving the warmth of his physical presence, to calm her body, if not her mind. But as she approached the bed, there wasn't the slightest disruption to the even, steady breathing. She was tempted to creep into bed next to him anyway, but it would have been selfish to risk waking him and jeopardise his concentration powers for the following day.

'Oh Donald, how I wish you were still here,' she said to herself, as she trudged back to her cold, temporary bed and pulled up the covers again. There was barely a day she didn't miss the soft Scottish burr that had purveyed so much wise counsel and loving encouragement to her over the years. What would you have said, she asked the ceiling. Probably told me to stop being such a wuss and get on with it.

1983

Donald Williams, her tutor at Durham University, was an exceedingly tall, gangly Scot with sloping shoulders, whose suits, in order to reach the end of his legs and arms, bagged at the crotch and bunched atrociously across his back. Vicky's father would have been appalled. 'So much for made-to-measure.' She had to banish the sound of his tutting from her head during Donald's stimulating seminars, filled as they were with inspirational little titbits, missed by many undergraduates too sluggish, intellectually and spiritually, to appreciate them.

It was rumoured that he had intended joining a monastic order, until romance redirected his path into both marriage and academia. It riled his students that as a member of the Franciscans' non-monastic order, he was regularly unavailable for an hour or two at midday, spent in the cathedral or some college chapel, on a park or riverside bench, wherever it took his fancy to say the daily office. With his mass of whitening hair hanging untidily round his face and over his collar, and the pair of penetrating blue eyes that peered out through it, he reminded Vicky of the Dulux dog.

He had called her back into his study after one particular tutorial, when she had held forth on the unreliability of the conflicting stories in the Gospels, and motioned her to sit. He offered her a cup of tea and she nodded. Sinking slowly into the battered armchair next to hers, limbs extended and almost filling the room, he studied her in silence, a disconcerting smile on his face as he decided how to frame a question that would be neither intrusive nor offensive. It should have felt uncomfortable, but there was such a stillness about the man that his presence was quietly reassuring instead.

Breathing in deeply through his nose, he said at last, 'Vicky, you're a first-rate student, one my colleagues would die for. I can't fault the quality of your work, but . . .'

He paused to let the perceptive blue eyes rest on her face, while he chose his next phrase carefully, 'I get the impression that it may be at the cost of your overall well-being.'

'I don't know what you mean,' she said, folding her arms across her chest defensively. 'I love the work.'

'I don't doubt that,' he replied gently, resting his head on the back of his chair, but never taking his eyes off her, 'but beware. The lure and demands of academia, especially in a discipline as soul-searching as theology, can be a Medusa that turns its victims into very stones, much like these ancient buildings.' He smiled broadly, the way he often did when he was in a slightly provocative or teasing mood. 'Take a closer look at one or two of the carvings on the way out and you'll probably catch an impression of the faces of bygone lecturers – some of them my former colleagues. I'm probably halfway there myself.'

'You think I've . . . lost something?' Vicky muttered, appalled that it was so obvious, that she hadn't earned her tutor's highest opinion.

'Have you?' he probed gently.

A hard, unwelcome lump formed in her gullet. She could say nothing for a while, then ventured a 'Maybe. What am I getting wrong?'

'No, no, no, girl. It's not about blame or brow-beating ourselves. I'm wondering whether this environment is enabling you to thrive, or whether it's failing you in some way. When you first arrived in these hallowed portals not so long ago, there was such a spark about you. You wanted to study because you wanted to learn the nature of God and understand the human soul. Now it seems you want to know only for the sake of knowing. It's as if a light has been switched off inside.'

Involuntarily, she crossed her legs as well as her arms. He studied her for a while.

'And there you are, curled up like a hedgehog. What are you protecting yourself from?'

She had had no intention of sharing her innermost thoughts and feelings with anyone, of having them mocked, trampled on, but there was something about the man that drew them out of her. Like poison from a wound. She unfolded her arms.

'I . . . I wanted to be a vicar.'

'I remember. I was struck by that. How could I not be when there's so little chance of it for a woman? "A spunky character," I said to myself.'

He watched her carefully.

'And you don't any longer?'

'I . . . I think I may have been a little naive. I thought that studying theology would give me a firm foundation for my faith. Instead, the literary criticism that challenges the authenticity of the biblical texts seems to undermine my personal beliefs.'

Donald leant forward, almost conspiratorially, and said quietly, 'Maybe it's not about needing to know whether the texts are true in the literal sense, but whether they're real. Do they impact your life? That's what makes them eternally inspirational.'

'I'm not sure. I'm not sure about anything any more. I have no role models. The only deaconess I've ever met taught us RE for a term. That was as long as she lasted. She wore a shapeless uniform and a nun-like wimple, and had a facial twitch. When she played in school concerts, her legs akimbo around her cello, the smirks and sniggers sabotaged the performance. I was mortified for her, but couldn't stop myself joining in.'

'And you're terrified you might end up like her? Now, what do you think are the chances?'

'It's not just that,' she said shortly. 'All the philosophical theory is making me question all my certainties. I don't know what truth is any more. If I ever did. How can someone who doesn't know truth help others to find it?'

Donald continued to study her, barely moving, head on one side. She noticed the large brown freckles on the backs of his hands, as they rested on the arms of his chair. Liver spots. Her father had them. A sign of sun damage, of ageing. The slow disintegration of the skin. She shook herself. This was her tutor, not her father.

'I'd be very sad,' he said thoughtfully, 'if the study we offered you here had no application to the calling you so clearly felt, if it destroyed your dreams this quickly.'

'Maybe they needed to be destroyed. Maybe they were simply the fantasy of an over-vivid childish imagination.'

He said nothing. What could he say? Vicky thought to herself. How could he tell her whether she had a calling? But then he broke into the silence and said firmly, 'Assurance of faith based solely on a conglomeration of assertions or intellectual beliefs rarely survives. A more solid base is needed.'

'But how do I find that solid base?' she shouted, and a near-despair she didn't know had been lurking inside, rose up into her throat, threatening to choke her as she gave voice to it. I'm not going to cry, I won't cry, she instructed herself.

Donald didn't move a muscle. He sat with his elbows resting on the chair arms, chin balanced on his threaded fingers, thinking. If he was aware of her outburst, he didn't show it. She could barely keep the anguish out of her voice.

'Where did you find a solid base?'

Looking up at her, he said, as if it were the most obvious thing in the world, 'In prayer. In the daily, ongoing friendship I have with my Father in heaven, with the Son, who stands by me in all of life's vicissitudes, and with the Spirit who inspires and comforts me, and encourages me upwards and onwards. That's truth, Vicky. That's real. That relationship with the divine Trinity. Oh, theological study is fascinating enough. Every scholar with a different opinion. Some with faith, some in unbelief. Some with common sense, some with nonsense. Some to stir us, some to test us. All good stuff, some of it great stuff – but don't confuse it with the basis of faith. That is intensely personal – though its outworking must be public, of course. Which is why you want to serve the church.'

He got up suddenly from his chair and motioned her to the door. She was reluctant to go. There was so much more she wanted to ask. 'Vicky,' he said gently, 'I'm not going anywhere. And my door is open whenever I'm here. Meanwhile, get yourself a copy of *The Wounded Healer* by Henri Nouwen – a great priest to have alongside you at times of overwhelming doubt. And it isn't wrong to doubt. Nouwen had plenty. We all do. It's what you do with it that counts. Let it lead you into truth, not drive you further into the arid desert of purely intellectual theology. Faith lives in our eyes, not our minds. We see, then we love.'

She nodded uncertainly, as he reached for the door handle.

'And by the way,' he added, as she was about to leave, 'get out a bit more.'

'Get a life?' she asked.

'You're a student, girl, in one of England's most beautiful cities. Enjoy. It's what students do.'

He nodded, beaming broadly as she set off down the corridor, aware of his X-ray eyes burning into her back.

'Ach,' he called out after her, and she turned, expecting some great final words of wisdom. 'And I never even got you that cup of tea. A fine one I am to talk. Next time.'

Durham, city of deep valleys and steep climbs, of winding cobbled streets, arched stone bridges and quaint little passageways, of ancient market places and churches, magnificent panoramas and shambling old colleges.

And towering over it all, particularly the young students scuttling along its timeworn alleys to lectures and seminars, its magnificent castle and cathedral, built on either side of Palace Green on a raised peninsula, bounded on three sides by the River Wear as it meandered in a deep U-bend on its winding journey north. For more than ten centuries their ancient parapets had dominated the skyline, resolutely resisting the fierce blast of a biting, corrosive east wind. On certain days, they emerged fairy-tale-like out of the dense mists that rolled in from the North Sea, enveloping the rest of the city in a giant, insulating fleece. They stood as a visible symbol of the ultimate triumph of history and tradition in this city of historic pilgrimage. And here she was, an undergraduate pilgrim in pursuit of her own calling and destiny.

The Department of Theology and Religion was founded in 1832, and there wasn't a day of her three undergraduate years when she didn't walk in or out of Abbey House, the Department's fine Georgian home adjacent to the cathedral, feeling positively Lilliputian as she stood in the shadow of such a commanding edifice, overawed by the privilege of studying in such stunning surroundings.

The curriculum, consisting of historical and systematic theology, biblical studies, philosophy and ethics, the sociology and anthropology of religion, ecclesiology, mission, spirituality and mysticism, stretched her brain to capacity. And then there was the confusion of biblical and ancient languages she could pursue, vital for the study of original texts – Greek, Hebrew, Aramaic, Syriac, Babylonian, or possibly Egyptian hieroglyphics?

The usual new student distractions took the edge off her disorientation in those first, bewildering weeks – shopping for stationery, lampshades and posters, the late-night coffees that lingered on into the early hours, the breath-taking riverside walks and boat trips, as the soaring walls of trees that dominated both banks of the Wear turned a glorious burnished bronze and burgundy, reflected back in the mirror calm of the water.

They were an amorphous group of adolescents, thrown together by academic expectation and ambition, catapulted into the world of adults, grappling with homesickness, the rudiments of survival and the ground rules of basic relationships. They sniffed around each other like dogs, scenting potentially stimulating friendships as they worked out each other's interests in sport or music, defined their likes and dislikes, told tales of home and put the world to rights.

'Theology! Why theology?' A simple enough question. The answer was anything but.

'A vicar. You want to be a vicar?' Melanie, who had been dunking a single tea-bag into a row of mugs filled with boiling water, turned to stare at Vicky, her voice, rising a decibel in disbelief, suddenly dominating all the other chatter in the student room. Vicky found herself the centre of an uncomfortable silence.

'Well, I didn't think women were vicars,' Melanie proffered. 'Round our way they're not, any road.'

'They're not. Not down anybody's road,' Melissa assured her.

It seemed incongruous that the room-mates were such inseparable chums, the oddest pairing of opposites in college. Melanie, the farmer's daughter from Grimsby, rosy-faced, big-boned, galumphing, with a heart in full proportion to her size, and Melissa, the self-contained daughter of a Winchester insurance broker, her vowels as clipped as Melanie's were flat.

Melissa sat in the one armchair, not on the bed, her legs, carefully and elegantly crossed, hugging a mug of coffee to her chest with well-manicured hands.

'Well, I admire you, Vicky,' she said, pushing her diamante-trimmed spectacles up onto the bridge of her nose with the back of her hand. 'It's brave to fight for what you believe in. There are no other jobs currently closed to women and a stand must be taken. All power to your elbow.'

'Too right,' agreed Melanie, waving a saturated tea-bag suspended on a teaspoon in Vicky's direction.

'Well, I don't see how we can overrule two thousand years of history, and verses in the Bible that forbid a woman preaching or having authority over men, just because our culture has changed,' a young man with a pitted face piped up from the corner. 'We can't always have what we want in this world.'

Melissa stared at him, eyes wide in disbelief behind the black-rimmed spectacles. 'Paul,' she snapped, 'don't tell me you've brought those archaic misogynist views to university with you?'

'They're not misogynist,' he countered, holding up a large pair of hands in self-defence, 'I'm just explaining why some of us have a problem with the idea of women vicars.'

The argument between the two continued for some time, becoming increasingly acerbic, while the rest looked on, largely uncomprehending spectators at an impromptu boxing match. Under normal circumstances Vicky would have taken on any detractor, but here amongst her peer group, where her instincts were to side with the feminist rather than the fellow Christian, she felt uncomfortable. She didn't want admiration, attention, censure or even discussion. She didn't want to be labelled a theological blue stocking, a feminist, or a religious nut either. Nor was she all that sure her calling was going to last the course, so she decided there and then to keep her aspirations to herself hereafter, lest it become the acrylic label on the back of the neck that chafed and irritated until it got on everyone's nerves.

But with Donald's guidance she managed to discover the place where her faith had hidden itself. There it was, to her surprise, lurking in a secret corner of her being – a seedling just waiting to be properly planted and fed with the spiritual disciplines that her tutor lived. Enough to sustain a future career in the church one day? She hoped so, but she was a little less presumptuous about that now.

As for getting out a bit more, she let Melissa persuade her that the Durham Union Society, Durham University's celebrated, 3,000-strong debating society, was just the place for someone with her 'inclinations'.

'Inclinations?' Vicky asked quizzically.

'In 1914 it pushed for women to have the vote – fourteen years before universal suffrage. I thought that would cheer you.'

Vicky wasn't entirely happy about becoming Melissa's feminist cause, but the society had a certain appeal. MPs, academics, journalists, diplomats and leading think-tank members would take to the floor each week and pit their wits against each other in the grand setting of the Palace Green Debating Chamber. It was an unparalleled opportunity to sit at the feet of some of the nation's finest orators, to listen, watch and learn.

Afterwards, there was a chance to engage with speakers informally at 24, DUS's illustrious bar and beer garden on North Bailey. It was renowned for its cocktails, shooters and quality beers, and more or less ruled over at the time by the infamous Etonian twins, Ralph Cooper and Mark Bradley-Hind, born, according to Melissa, with a silver spoon in their mouths and a billiards cue in their hands.

'Do those boys ever do any work?' she whispered one evening, perched compactly on a bar stool, as she sipped her New Orleans Fizz, watching them out of the corner of her eye. Vicky didn't know and didn't particularly care. Barely threw them a glance. As far as she was concerned, the final-year students were an arrogant pair of knob heads; thankfully, well out of her social circle.

What really mattered was having the chance to chat to people like Shirley Williams, founder of the new Social Democratic Party. There were comparatively few women speakers at DUS, and Vicky had found herself on her feet, passionately supporting the MP, who was defending the motion, 'Politics and Religion: Can They Ever Go Together?' After it was over, she had edged her way towards Ms Williams, watching for a break in the queue of admirers, and when she saw that she had caught the MP's eye, hoping she didn't sound too sycophantic, said how much she admired her. The MP had responded with genuine warmth and pleasure, laughter lines crinkling the outer corners of her eyes.

'And you, I see, have quite a way with words,' Shirley Williams said to her in that matter-of-fact way she had. 'Don't waste it, will you?'

For reasons she couldn't fathom, Vicky found herself blurting out her intention to be ordained one day. Ms Williams told her that when she was seven years old she had informed the first female MP, Nancy Astor, that she wanted to go into government. Lady Astor had told her she didn't stand a chance – on account of her hair.

'Can you believe anything so stupid?' she guffawed. 'Thank God, I never let her silly words deter me, and nor must you allow any institutional nonsense to hold you back.'

She paused, her head on one side like a mother bird, then added, 'I have had my fair share of venom, and so will you. Always remember: it's their problem, not yours.'

She gave Vicky a reassuring pat on the arm, and moved on.

A few days later, on their way to 24, as they sauntered down Owengate, an alleyway only just wide enough for the two of them, she and Melissa were squeezed on either side into an uncomfortable sandwich filling by Tweedledum and Tweedledee themselves.

'Impressive performance, eh, Ralph?'

'Interesting,' Ralph agreed.

'The girl deserves a drink, don't you think?'

'Oh, I definitely think so.'

That evening they were the centre of attention at the club, as Ralph and Mark's latest interests inevitably were, Melissa simpering, and Vicky decidedly frosty. In the end the young men's good-natured banter and merciless teasing of each other began to melt the ice. How could a girl not enjoy the attentions of two such heart-stoppingly good-looking men? Mark, final-year politics, handsome in that blond, quintessentially English way with dazzling white teeth, a hint of a dimple and a frond of unruly hair that had to be swept periodically out of a pair of velvety brown eyes and returned to its place with a long, slow sweep of the arm. Ralph, final-year economics, was more of the Greek god, swarthy and muscular, with a high forehead and powerful, square jaw, smudged with midnight shadow. A first-class rugby player, he was as sturdy and rugged as an old British oak. Which did she find more attractive? It was hard to say.

From then on, the two boys defined the social side of her university years; but there were other, more important contributory factors to the woman she would become. Halfway through her second year, she caught her tutor staring at her reddened, blistered hands. The old owl never missed a trick.

'I saw a poster in the Union asking for girls willing to support the Women Against Pit Closures,' she explained, 'and decided it was time to put the rest of me where my mouth was.'

'Which was where?' Donald quizzed.

'In one of the bigger pit villages. We were bussed out to a community centre and made to wear vile green pinnies and caps that looked like hospital scrubs. Then I was given a mountain of enormous, food-encrusted tureens to clean.'

She looked at her tutor ruefully and he laughed out loud.

'Grass-roots socialism, then.'

'More than tea and sympathy, anyway,' Vicky admitted. 'I did eventually get a chance to serve food in the canteen. There was an amazing woman called Stella in charge. She'd got up at 3.30 every morning for months, co-ordinating the feeding of hundreds of demoralised, hungry people, cooking in conditions never intended for that purpose, without raising her voice, or snapping anyone's head off. The team worked like a conveyor belt in a factory, and never once questioned her judgement or balked at anything she asked them to do. The customers loved her. She had a word of encouragement for each of them as she ladled the food onto their plates.'

'One in a million?' Donald agreed. 'Maybe – but I have to hand it to you, too, Vicky – you're not one for shirking the tough calls.'

'You were the one who introduced me to Henri Nouwen, remember; all his darned stuff on practical servanthood. He left his monastery to work in a home for people with special needs.'

Donald gave her a short smile of acknowledgement.

'And so you throw yourself in at the deep end too?'

'Why bother reading his books, or anyone else's, if all we do is assent with our minds, but don't let them change the way we live?'

Donald laughed again and shook his head.

'Hitting me with my own words. Dearie me, you're a case, that you are, Vicky Burnham,' he said, fastening on her working woman's hands once more. 'I'll have to take care with the food I suggest for your mind, or no worthy cause will be safe from your ministrations.'

He weighed her up for a moment.

'You know, I admire you, I really do,' he said, ignoring her protest of modesty. 'You bite life off in chunks and don't stop to spit out the unpalatable bits.'

Then he got up, wandered slowly around his desk to the high wall of books behind it, laid his hands on the two he was looking for and announced, as he sauntered back, 'I think it's time I introduced you to a new friend. What do you know about Jürgen Moltmann?'

'You mention him in your lectures from time to time. I've read some of his comments on the texts I've been studying in eschatology. A bit dense and hard to follow. Hard work, I'd say.'

'Well, he requires effort, but he's well worth it. I think you might come to like him. In fact, I'd go so far as to say that Moltmann could well be your guiding theologian of choice. He seems to encapsulate so many of the truths that are precious to you.'

He thumbed through one of the books, shook it and, picking up the scrappy piece of paper that fell out onto the floor, said, 'Let me read you what he says.'

With every righteous action, we prepare the way for the New Earth on which righteousness will dwell. And bringing justice to those who suffer violence means to bring the light of God's future to them.

He handed Vicky the piece of paper.

'Good, eh? Apposite?'

She studied it in silence for some time.

'Let me tell you a little bit more about him. In July 1943, Moltmann was a German air force auxiliary in a battery in the centre of Hamburg. During Operation Gomorrah, the firestorm let loose by the Royal Air Force that almost destroyed the entire city, the friend standing next to him at the firing predictor was ripped to shreds. But he survived unscathed. He was not a religious man, but he cried out the inevitable, "Why am I not dead too?"

'Later, in a Scottish prisoner-of-war camp, a chaplain gave him a New Testament to read. It transformed his life, and ultimately made a great theologian of him. The pictures of the Nazi death camps he and his fellow POWs were shown filled him with intense shame. He knew that what a demoralised, post-war Germany needed most was a theology of hope. For him, that was enshrined in a vision of the coming kingdom of God, when Christ will reign forever over his renewed creation. Hope in a glorious eternal future enables the believer to live a life of love, to work for the greater good now as a demonstration of the glorious future that is to come, knowing that "a passion for the possible cannot be disappointed".'

Donald rested his hands on his stomach as if he had just eaten a large, satisfying meal. Then he picked up the books that were lying in his lap and handed them to her tenderly, as if they were treasured family heirlooms. 'So then: go, Vicky, imbibe, chew, swallow and digest. May Moltmann feed and nourish your spirit as he has mine.'

By the time she graduated, there was little Vicky didn't know about Moltmann. Donald was so right. She was excited and overwhelmed by Moltmann's vision of communities, working together to bring love and joy to their broken neighbourhoods, motivated by the hope of a just and glorious eternity that could begin in the here and now.

JANUARY 2020

As the pale grey light of morning began to filter into the room through a gap in the curtains, Vicky finally got out of bed, wrapped herself in her towelling robe, and went to the chapel. A grandiose title, she always thought, for what was in fact a small, whitewashed room, its simple table covered in a lace cloth, its large candle, a couple of softly upholstered chairs, colourful cushions, a kneeling stool, a contemporary stained-glass window in blocks of colour depicting the Trinity, and a small pine cupboard for her Bible, prayer book and various other books of daily devotions. This was where she came every morning for forty-five minutes of reading, reflection and prayer, the spiritual sustenance that was as necessary to her survival as breakfast, lunch and dinner. She loved this room. The rich golden carpet seemed to emulate the glow of sunshine on the whitewashed walls, whatever the weather.

She retrieved the Bible from the cupboard and as she carried it to her favourite chair, a crumpled, wrinkled piece of paper fell to the floor. She had forgotten that she had put it in this Bible; she knew by heart every word written there. 'Some of you here today will be called to live sacrificially. At present you are too young to know what that means. But wait and watch, and don't walk away from your destiny when it calls you.'

She sat for a while, stroking the scrap of paper as it lay on her Bible, carefully ironing out Sister Phoebe's words with her hand. Then she got up slowly, stripped off her robe and lay face down upon it, shocked at first at the cold penetrating her nightdress in the early morning chill. Every part of her screamed out silently, 'I don't want this, I can't do it, I can't. I don't have what it takes. It needs more than any human being is capable of giving, let alone me.'

She remained prostrate for a long time, in a place between slumber and wakefulness, where praying and dreaming were so intermingled she had no idea, later, whether she had imagined the encounter or lived it. Except that she remembered that her feet had been freezing, and afterwards, to her surprise, they were as warm as if she had been wearing bed socks. But perhaps the central heating had come on.

As she lay there, desperate for some divine intervention or revelation that would show her what to do, she became aware of a firm, yet gentle touch on her back. The warmth of it penetrated her skin, radiated heat through the whole of her being, flooding her with such an overwhelming sense of peace that she feared to move a fraction of an inch or even breathe, lest the sensation vanish as quickly as it had come. And then it seemed as if she had been lifted up and placed firmly on her feet in front of a massive wooden cross that dwarfed and overshadowed her. And a voice spoke, in that loving Scottish lilt she knew so well, and said, 'Look, Vicky, this one is yours. The one you said you would carry to the ends of the earth. You have come to the end of the earth, to the place where heaven begins, for crucifixion gives way to resurrection, as surely as death is trumped by hope. Go and remind my beloved that the kingdom is here, near, among them. Inspire them with new hope, for that which they currently have is too weak and pitiful a thing to embrace and transform the thoughts and actions of men.'

She recognised those last words. Moltmann, who had sought to re-inspire his countrymen after the destruction of their land and the ignominious defeat of their delusional ideologies. Words for a church that had lost sight of its life-changing, life-giving ideology. Healing words. Hopeful words. Visionary words. A commission to share them, to embrace the awesome responsibility offered to her.

'Then, O God,' she whispered, finally, 'let it be to me according to your will. Only grant me, like the great, martyred apostles, the grace to endure the cost of it with dignity, integrity and courage, whatever may befall.'

The sun's rays were streaming through the coloured panes of the chapel window, streaking the walls and table with crimson and jade, when she eventually struggled up and looked at the clock. Eight thirty. She had been on the floor for over two hours. She staggered to her feet and along the corridor to the bathroom mirror, where she saw that the carpet had left an imprint on her cheek, palms and the tops of her feet. Stigmata, she said to herself, running a finger down her face and laughing at herself. The presumption of the woman!

FOUR

Those who hope in Christ can no longer put up with reality as it is, but begin to suffer under it, to contradict it. Peace with God means conflict with the world, for the goad of the promised future stabs inexorably into the flesh of every unfulfilled present.

JÜRGEN MOLTMANN

JANUARY 2020

Gerard Lancaster expressed a profound satisfaction at Vicky's acceptance of the invitation, even if it didn't register on the face that stared at her from the e-phone. She detected, from his formal manner, that he wasn't very comfortable with these long-distance yet face-to-face conversations.

'The Prime Minister can see you on Tuesday morning. Would that suit you, Bishop?'

'That soon?' she asked, shocked at the speed of it all.

'We must proceed swiftly, as I said, to reduce the risk of a leak before the official announcement.'

'Ah,' she murmured, though she had never really understood the need for all the secrecy around an appointment that had such little significance for the country, except of course for the betting shops.

'Who can I tell?'

'Absolutely no one, I'm afraid.'

On Monday afternoon Gerard rang back on her private line.

'The announcement of a cabinet reshuffle is scheduled for tomorrow morning, Bishop, which means the press will be camped outside Number 10. We can't afford to risk alerting their suspicions. Could you go to Number 11 instead? Mufti – no purple and no clerical collar.'

'Should I wear sunglasses too? And a hat with the brim pulled down?'

'Sorry?'

'Nothing, nothing.'

The following day the press were far too engrossed in their own agenda to notice the ordinary middle-aged woman in the smart navy suit who rang the bell at 11, Downing Street. History was in the making several yards from their noses. And they missed it.

Vicky had hoped that Tom would accompany her for moral support, as the wives of previous archbishops had, but he didn't think it sufficient reason to disrupt a busy theatre list.

'I told you I wouldn't play the escort, Vick, so let's start as we mean to continue.'

'Don't you want to see the inside of Number 10?'

'Not particularly. Besides, I'd probably embarrass you by saying something rude about NHS funding.'

'You can say what you like, Tom. It wouldn't embarrass me.'

The door opened and when she had passed him, Gerard Lancaster looked out to the left and the right to ensure she hadn't been noticed. Satisfied, he closed the door and escorted her through a labyrinth of corridors to Number 10, leaving her in a tiny office with instructions to don the episcopal shirt and clerical collar. He gave her just long enough. No time to touch up the hair or make-up, or check the tights for snags. No mirror, for that matter.

'The PM will see you in the terracotta room,' he said. 'That's his normal place for the more informal chats.'

She was ushered into a larger, lighter room than she expected, a little too orange for her liking, a colour which didn't do a great deal for the emerald furnishings. The chandelier, however, hanging from an ornate ceiling rose, was impressive. Gerard followed her gaze.

'Not original, I'm afraid. But imposing repro all the same. Added during Mrs Thatcher's renovation to give the rooms a more stately feel.'

'And the paintings?'

'Original. On loan from the Government Art Collection. The Prime Minister shouldn't be long.'

He inclined his head and left her to wait.

There is a limit to how long anyone can study paintings, and after twenty minutes or so, just as Vicky was beginning to wonder where she might find the nearest loo, and whether it would be acceptable protocol to be out of the room when the PM arrived, the door opened and in he rushed, fastening his jacket button, smoothing down an unruly mass of brown hair, a rather dishevelled picture of anxiety and penitence. So this was Liam Cavendish.

'So, so sorry to keep you waiting, Bishop,' he apologised, waving her to one uncomfortable-looking chaise longue while he perched on the other facing her.

She noticed droplets of sweat glistening on his brow. He loosened his tie slightly.

'A bit of a crisis, as you probably realise. Not the best day for a chat. But I am very glad that you've accepted the appointment. Imaginative for once. Not the usual Church of England compromise – let's keep everyone happy and end up pleasing no one. I like the idea of making history. If the Conservatives had the first female Prime Minister, we at least shall give the country its first female Archbishop of Canterbury. Not quite in the same league, of course, but better than nothing.'

She waited for him to draw breath. He was wound up like a spring.

'Not everyone will be pleased, of course – plenty of chuntering about it in the government, I expect. You'll have to watch your back, but so do we all. Do you think the African church will accept a woman leader? I know it would upset the Queen if there were any further rifts in the worldwide Anglican . . . what is it you call it now?'

'Alliance.'

'Ah yes, a bit like the Commonwealth. A much better approach. Not so imperialist. I suppose it might be a little touch and go whether they accept your leadership, but your more traditional views on . . . relationships should assuage them. As a humanist, I really have little understanding of these matters. I would have liked an archbishop who supported gay marriage and encouraged her priests to work towards this ideal. But your appointment reflects a tiny step towards egalitarianism in the gender issue, so I suppose I shall have to be satisfied with that. And if you can establish some kind of Anglican unity here as well as abroad, it would keep the Queen happy and that would be a bonus.'

'I shall certainly do my best to win round my African colleagues, Prime Minister,' she said when there was finally a pause to fill, 'but their reluctance is theological as well as cultural, so we shall have to see.'

'Given the diplomatic skills I hear about, I am sure that if anyone can talk them round, you can. I suspect they fear liberalising views even more than they do a figurehead in a skirt.'

'You may well be right, but our African brothers and sisters are not the major problem I need to address.'

The Prime Minister looked startled.

'First, the church needs urgent modernisation if we're going to survive financially. We are not a heritage preservation society. We cannot go on maintaining the nation's historic buildings if they are not fit for purpose. We need to invest instead in a host of exciting projects that are paying dividends in helping the poor and bringing people to faith, even if they don't immediately put bums on the Sunday pews – or coppers in the collection.'

He nodded distractedly. Vicky felt slightly irritated.

'Prime Minister, these projects should be of interest to the government, since many of them plug the gaps in the welfare state, and support disaffected young people.'

She had his attention.

'So we need to bypass all the current legal wrangling over permission to sell, because the alternative is leaving them to become a local eyesore.'

'That will almost certainly invoke the ire of some of the Members' constituents, and the government doesn't have a budget to preserve them on its own. I'll have to talk to my ministers.'

'Of course.'

'You said, "first". Was there some other issue you intend to address?'

'Yes. I intend to fight for the restoration of freedom of speech.'

The Prime Minister sat up and stared at her, as if he were seeing her for the first time.

'We now have thousands of refugees in our country who have fled from oppressive regimes in their own. Many of them are black Christians who expect the human rights they have been denied, only to discover they cannot so much as work as a cleaner for their local council because they can't say they don't support gay marriage.'

'Homophobia must be eradicated from any free society.'

'It must indeed. But homophobia, according to the dictionary, is the irrational hatred, intolerance and fear of a group of people. That has nothing whatsoever to do with healthy disagreement on ethical and moral issues.'

'You are aware that I'm gay?' he interrupted.

'Of course I am, Prime Minister.'

'Would you marry me?'

Her argument had been cleverly ignored, she realised.

'That's hypothetical, because it's currently illegal for an Anglican priest to do so.'

'But if I asked you for a blessing?'

'I couldn't, because as you already know, I hold the traditional view of marriage, that it's between two people of different gender. But I would be delighted if you and your partner would come to dinner.'

He ignored her again.

'Gay marriage is about commitment. Society is stronger when we make vows to each other and support each other. I thought you'd be in favour of that.'

'I'm even more in favour of a society that allows for healthy debate and dissension, not one where the few ensure that anyone who disagrees with their views is silenced by the state. The loss of work is always the first step in persecution. When I first knew I wanted to be a priest the option was not open to women. I'm used to fighting for what I believe in. Which other national group provides seventy per cent of voluntary work, thanks you for the privilege and then pays for it? Without Christian goodwill you would face a national disaster.'

'Is that a threat?'

She was shocked by the aggressive nature of his tone.

'No, of course not. It's a fact,' she said amicably. 'Food banks, street pastors, alcohol rehabilitation units, many housing associations and credit unions, the national budgeting and parenting courses were all initiated by Christians, and in some areas half the welfare state provision is now owned by churches. I'm simply saying, take freedom away from Christian entrepreneurs with their charity, voluntary work, and reforms and you risk killing off the goose that lays the golden egg.'

The Prime Minister stretched an arm over the back of the settee, and took stock of her. His gaze made her feel a little uncomfortable.

'I can't work you out. You're an astounding mixture of the radical and the reactionary. We'll face the fall-out from your reforming zeal as it comes, but let me suggest to you that your stance on morality may well be seen as keeping the brakes on, rather than moving the church forward.'

'It will be seen by many as bigotry and intolerance, of that I have no doubt. It is a fearfully difficult thing to be out of kilter with cultural mores. So much easier to cave in for the sake of a peaceful life. But how far can we water down the essentials of Judeo-Christian morality, enshrined in biblical teaching, and still call what's left Christianity? If we don't bend we break, but by the same token, if we bend too far we fall over. Government legislation that is detrimental to the greater good of the people or that challenges their conscience must always be opposed.'

He bristled slightly.

'You don't plan to comment publicly on government policy, I hope?'

'It depends on the policy. I can't make any promises, Prime Minister. Surely the Archbishop's leadership role gives him, or her, the right to speak out if they believe it's in the best interests of the country, or voices the feelings of a voiceless minority.'

He put his head in his hands and groaned.

'That's not what I need just at this moment.'

Vicky tried to stop her lips from twitching in amusement. He was young, so young, and manifestly beleaguered on all sides, with little hope of surviving the next general election. He could have been her son, and the thought induced slightly disturbing feelings, maternal and protective.

'Generally speaking,' she continued, looking at him out of the corner of her eye, 'when it comes to issues of poverty and fairness, we bat for the same side.'

A wave of relief passed over his face, and he smiled.

For the next twenty minutes their conversation ranged across urban poverty and social unrest, overcrowded cities with inadequate resources in education, healthcare, housing and transport, and finally to another of her major concerns, the plight of Christians in countries where their human rights were being abused.

'You will take care what you say about China, won't you? They have us in their pockets. Bought up virtually our entire telecommunications industry. Planned it for years, I suspect. Always ahead of us with the technology – just biding their time. If we annoy them we could be scuppered.'

'I will be circumspect,' she promised.

By the time the Prime Minister showed her to the door, she felt they had established a working, if not warm relationship. How long it would last, whether because of her doings or his demise, only time would tell.

1988

In 1987 Synod had voted to allow women to become deacons – a splitting of hairs that meant they could become fully-fledged curates; burying, marrying, doing everything a first-year male curate did. But whereas the men were made priests after a year and allowed to preside at Communion, the women were not.

Meanwhile, armed with her first-class theology degree, Vicky had decided to teach RE and settled on a job in inner-city Newcastle. Gaining life experience in the big wide world before pursuing her career in the church seemed a sensible option. If she could hold the attention of children who could see no point in the subject, there was at least half a chance she might be able to capture the imagination of some bored and blasé Anglican congregation. That, she thought, must surely be a doddle after two years of coping with two and a half dozen wild and wilful teenagers at a time.

On the issue of women's ministry her vicar for those two years, Robin Martin, had, to all intents and purposes, sat on the fence. He was a rumpled, tired-looking man, with an immense Adam's apple that travelled distractingly up and down his throat like a miniature yo-yo. It was at least a diversion during his excruciating preaching.

'Lukewarm' was the only possible way to describe his response to her request to be ordained. Offering a candidate for ministry would earn him brownie points with the diocese. Just his luck that the one contender was a woman.

'So, Vicky. Tell me, why do you want to be ordained?' he asked, forcing his face into a smile.

'I've had a sense of calling since I was quite young.'

'Well, that is impressive. Of course, God lays his call on all our lives, and there are many possible directions that he may call us in. The teaching of children, your current career I believe, is a wonderful thing, don't you think?'

Vicky was rendered speechless, but he continued, 'This is a difficult time, of course. There is still much ambivalence in the church regarding the role of women.'

'We have a woman prime minister. No door can stay closed forever.'

'Ah, but can we use that argument, Vicky? After all, the church is not bound to reflect British social change. Two thousand years of church tradition is based on male leadership. Whether you base it on the premise that since our Lord was male, along with all twelve of his disciples, or the key New Testament passages of Scripture, that's the teaching of the church.'

'But many women followed Jesus. Weren't they disciples too? Last at the cross and first at the resurrection? Surely male and female were created equal? The differences are the result of human disobedience and the fall from grace.'

'Equal in value, not function. In terms of redemption, we are equal. We still have different gifts, abilities.'

'How? Why should that be?' she asked, almost mesmerised by the joggling cannonball in his neck.

The smile was becoming very tight around the edges.

'Vicky, let me spell this out for you,' he replied curtly. 'At a selection conference they will care not a fig what you think of the ordination of women: it's not yours to decide. They will ask why you want to be a curate. They will test your calling to that and that alone. It's not for you to argue the big picture.'

'Right. I see. But you will support my application?'

Without warning, he got up and showed her to the door.

'Since your mind is made up,' he said, turning the doorknob brusquely and ushering her out. 'I just hope, when and if you are ever ordained, you'll never have to mend a boiler as often as I have.'

She stood, bemused, in the corridor for several seconds. Not the greatest start to anyone's career. But she was on her way, nonetheless.

The next hurdle on the long assault course to ordination was the Diocesan Director of Ordinands, who advised the local bishop on the suitability or otherwise of applicants. He was a dishevelled-looking man.

In the half a dozen times or so she met him – it seemed mainly to delay the process because of her youth – his washed-out jumpers, unravelling at the sleeves, bore a variety of splodges she had identified as tomato ketchup, gravy – or was it chocolate sauce? – and mushy peas. If he had made it through, there must surely be some hope for her?

His vicarage was chaotic. An obstacle course of toys was strewn from front door to study. There were piles of papers on every available surface, and those that related to her constantly eluded him. When the phone rang, he would call out with a certain amount of exasperation, 'Can't you get that, dear?' and back would come a muffled response from some remote room in the house, 'I would if I could find the phone.' Or, on one occasion, 'I have a baby attached to my nipple. What's your problem?'

He would remove a doll or teddy or rabbit strategically placed in the only armchair and motion her to sit, while he perched on a broken swivel chair that regularly discharged a large amount of grubby-looking stuffing onto the carpet. Studying him, as he rifled through the pages of notes that eventually appeared from under the mounds on his desk, she couldn't help but wonder if he only had a haircut when his wife came across her pinking shears. As he explained the increasing, though still limited opportunities for female deacons, and the continuing battle for women's full inclusion in the system, it was tempting to imagine what a good haircut would do for his image. Still, it was hard not to like a man who interrupted his work to take a child on his knee, or at least to feel sympathy for one whose eyes were permanently bloodshot through lack of sleep.

Over the course of their many interviews she finally managed to convince him that her lack of life experience was not necessarily a deterrent to becoming a useful church leader. Finally, her name went forward for a 'selection conference', the three-day emotional assault course that constituted the interviewing process for candidates to the ordained ministry.

'Let's run through it, Vicky.'

'A rehearsal?'

'Focus,' he said sharply. 'Or do you not want to be accepted?'

He adjusted his voice: 'Miss Burnham, what makes you think you're called to full-time church ministry?'

'I knew from when I was very young that I wanted to serve in the church.'

'No, no, no, for pity's sake, don't say that. They'll think you're one of those women who wants to usurp the vicar's role by getting in through the back door. They won't touch you with a barge pole.'

'Shall I say I have a burning sensation in my guts every time I'm in church?'

Running a hand ferociously through his hair that left it sticking up like an old and grizzled toothbrush, he raised his eyes to the ceiling in near-despair.

'Vicky, I know this is tiresome, but bear with me.'

'I know, I know. Sorry. They'll put it down to indigestion. I'll simply say that I enjoy caring for people, listening to their problems and sharing my faith with them. Is that bland enough? Will that do it?'

'Good, good. That's it. Focus on the pastoral. You have no idea where the selectors stand on the issue of women's ministry and emphasising the caring role is spot on as the acceptable face of a woman's calling.'

'So no mention of preaching or leading services?'

'Let's say I wouldn't go overboard, though you could mention that you've taught in Sunday School. Up until recently a deaconess's role was supportive, enabling the vicar to get on with the more visible part of ministry. Things will change now, of course – but slowly! This is the Church of England, after all.'

'A tortoise?'

'Turbo-charged.'

'Since when?'

'Exactly.'

He smiled and ushered her out, grabbing up a child on the way to prevent it playing with the water in the dog's bowl.

'Best of luck,' he said, pumping Vicky's hand up and down with his free arm.

'Because I'll need it?' she asked wryly.

A harassed-looking wife appeared from nowhere, appropriated the child, and smiled at her apologetically. She heard the words, 'I've told you not to disrupt Daddy's work,' as the door closed behind her.

Vicky wasn't sure that the name 'selection conference' was the happiest choice. It smacked of survival of the fittest, a kind of ecclesiastical eugenics. It reminded her of school netball lessons where the team leaders chose the best players, and the rest felt like humiliated rejects. What if she were not selected? Looking around at the other sixteen candidates, three women and twelve men, it seemed not only possible, but probable. She was the youngest by far and the only woman not wearing a skirt. The one earring in sight was sported by a man. Good on him, she thought. He was the muscular sort with shaved head, a prominent gold filling, and poor skin. She offered him a smile, which he evidently took to be a smirk. The hostility in his response was palpable. Damn, she said to herself. What on earth am I doing here?

There were six examiners in all, five male and one female, chaired by Dennis Quilch, head teacher at a Church of England Comprehensive. He was a short, bald man with a face as round and polished as an apple. Prone to sweating, he kept mopping his brow with a large, checked handkerchief that he extracted with difficulty from his trouser pocket.

'We hope you will relax and enjoy your time here,' he said, welcoming the candidates. His fellow examiners nodded like a set of Russian dolls. He appeared to be unable to refrain from jiggling his feet and the squeaking of his brown lace-ups on the highly-polished wooden floor twanged already taut nerves. If he was aware of the tension, he was oblivious to his part in it.

Relax, Vicky thought – when you were being watched from morning till night? Some hope. Anyone who believed the examiners suspended their scrutiny between interviews must be sadly deluded. She didn't get much sleep. Nor did her fellow candidates, judging by their tousled, bleary-eyed look the following morning. The thought of having to deliver a presentation managed to put even the men off the breakfast fry-up.

Their presentations, accompanied by much quivering of hands and clearing of throats, were hardly earth-shattering, designed to please rather than inspire. Vicky had opted for, 'A Child-friendly Church', to showcase her knowledge of a radical new report called *Children in the Way*, that claimed the Church of England was jeopardising its future by making children feel unwelcome.

The title alone, on her first overhead, seemed to flick the off switch in the minds of the male candidates. Earring man yawned loudly. Undaunted, she made an impassioned appeal for services that were creative and imaginative enough not to bore the pants off the average child.

'The report highlights our very real rejection of children. For most of us they have indeed been in the way, not on the journey with us, and that means we lose them as soon as they're old enough to decide they don't want us or our God.'

Quotes on the overhead projector from the mums of her schoolchildren described the shushing and tutting to which they had been subjected when their children were small – those few who had tried going to church at all, that is.

'Attendance is plummeting,' she concluded, 'yet the Gospels tell us Jesus welcomed children. What does that say about us? A little bit of disruption is a tiny price to pay for the insights children bring us. Drive them away and we not only lose their parents, we lose our next generation of leaders.'

'Questions?' announced Dennis Quilch.

'So do we allow them to run riot?' demanded a young man with impeccable Home Counties pronunciation. He looked so young, barely out of university, judging by the school tie and overly large jacket. So why had she been made to wait for two long years, Vicky wondered?

'Whatever happened to dignity and solemnity?' he asked. 'Sunday School is the best place for children.'

Ah. Perhaps that was why. To give her more experience of the real world.

'That's exactly the point,' she fired back. 'Many churches no longer have the personnel to run Sunday Schools. Even if they have, it can't be right to force families to split up for a good chunk of their precious weekend time together, and many children are unhappy being separated from their parents. There's nothing wrong with Sunday School per se, but every child needs to experience adult church from time to time if they're ever going to cross the great divide, and when they do, it should be age-appropriate.'

'Proper discipline is what they need,' countered the public-school youth. 'Surely adults are entitled to quiet reflection and contemplation? Children should learn to sit still and shut up.'

'Well then, why don't you?' she snapped, the words out of her mouth before she had time to remember where she was. There was a stunned silence.

'I'm sorry,' she mumbled, 'I do feel very passionately about this.'

He was looking at the floor, red-faced and turned inward.

'No action songs, please,' shouted earring man, trying to get the argument going again.

'And no Tonka trucks and teddy bears at the Communion rail,' agreed a gruff, ruddy-faced man with a large, handle-bar moustache. 'Let's have order and decency in our Eucharists.'

There was a loud murmur of agreement.

Vicky was sorely tempted to tell them to stuff their dignity and decency where the sun didn't shine, but instead, with as much control as she could muster, said, 'I fear that you will have your silence one day – when there's no one left in the church to disrupt it.'

She sat down to the accompaniment of mutters and titters, and was teetering on the brink of collecting her things together and going home when the chairman said, 'Thank you, Miss Burnham. Very interesting. As someone responsible for young adults who take very little interest in faith matters, this is an issue that has been exercising my mind for some time. I thought the report was thought-provoking and I congratulate you on bringing it to our attention.'

She heaved a sigh of relief. There was some hope for the Church of England. But as she looked around the room, she became aware of a number of sullen faces and a new chill in the atmosphere. Resentment, amongst would-be vicars? Surely not.

The individual interviews, too, were not straightforward, the questions often dense and difficult, testing out her orthodoxy, spirituality, character and academic suitability. What did she believe? What did she read? She guessed that in response to the latter question highlights such as Germaine Greer, Betty Friedan, and her other favourite feminist writers were not what Dennis Quilch was looking for.

'I've been very struck by a book called *The Wounded Healer* by Henri Nouwen.'

'What struck you particularly?'

'He says,' and she quoted from memory, '*We must never disown our vulnerability. Lose sight of our own weakness, let power go to our heads and we're past helping anyone in their journey.*'

'A vital lesson for a priest, Miss Burnham,' agreed Dennis Quilch.

'Thank you, Donald,' she whispered under her breath.

Finally, just when she thought she might have cracked it, Selector Number Three called her for interview. He was some sort of advisor to the Bishop of Durham; quiet, unamused, always sitting slightly apart in his clerical collar and the traditional black shirt and trousers. His eyes skewered her, like a butterfly to a page.

'Are you always so bossy, Miss Burnham?'

Are you always so rude?

'Bossy? I don't understand what you mean.'

'You don't think you were a little forceful yesterday?'

Would you call a man pushy?

'If you mean I'm passionate about making the church more welcoming, then maybe pushy is what it needs.'

'What needs changing in you?'

'I'm twenty-three. Many things. But not my passion to see the church become more relevant to ordinary people.'

'Indeed, you're not only young, Miss Burnham, you seem to be in rather a hurry.'

'I've had a sense that this is what I should be doing since I was a child. So why delay?'

Damn, she'd just flushed the DDO's wisdom down the toilet.

'I think that's for us to decide.'

She nodded, silenced for once.

'You don't enjoy teaching? Isn't that enough of a vocation?'

'It's hard work, and I love the children. It's a wonderful privilege. But the church is what I want to do.'

Blow it, she'd done it again. He'd pushed her into it, the sneak.

'If you marry, will your husband enjoy being a clergy spouse, baking cakes and running the church fete?'

'If I were a clergy spouse, I wouldn't be baking cakes,' she replied curtly. 'No good at it. I'd have my own career.'

The grilling continued – 'What do you do with your leisure time?' 'How do you pray?' 'How would you deal with a case of domestic violence?' 'How would you feel if you knew women's ordination was still twenty years away?' 'How do you handle doubt?' 'What will you do if you have children?' A volley of questions with the occasional politically incorrect nasty thrown in. Only the church could get away with it.

By the end of the last evening her brain felt as responsive as a plate of scrambled egg. To cap it all, her period started – eight days early. No shops for miles. No machine in sight. She went to the warden's office and asked to speak to a female member of staff, who fetched her a couple of towels the size of hammocks. Women, apparently, were not regular visitors to this diocesan conference centre. She didn't push her luck and ask for paracetamol, but feeling far too miserable and sore to socialise, headed for bed to curl up with a hot water bottle.

Meanwhile earring man, alias Kelvin Craddock, had identified a local hostelry and taken all the male candidates with him. They returned at around 2.30 a.m., somewhat the worse for wear. Vicky was awoken by the sound of their sniggers as they groped their way up the stairs on hands and knees, then roared with laughter as they crashed back down to the bottom and started all over again. For fifteen minutes or so, she lay wide-eyed, willing someone, anyone, to open a bedroom door and shut them up. But no one did, so she eventually threw on a dressing gown and marched out to battle.

'Well, if it isn't the little Mother Superior,' jeered Kelvin, falling, face down, at her feet. 'Reverend Know-All,' he muttered, and promptly spewed up all over her new slippers.

'If you get accepted, this isn't a church I want to be a part of,' Vicky snapped as she gingerly removed the offending articles, and, head held high, padded back to her room barefoot, where she dropped them into a sinkful of water. Outside, the sniggers slowly died away. The pungent odour of beer-gone-sour made her want to retch. She shed a couple of tears, more from disgust than aggravation. But only a couple. She told herself the Kelvins of this world weren't worth more than that.

She had no idea who cleared up the rest of the mess, but it was gone in the morning, and no one said a word, the staff more long-suffering than they ought to have been. Rattling her way home on the train, she lay an exhausted head against the back of the seat and prayed she'd never have to cross the path of the likes of Kelvin again.

'It was bizarre,' she said to Bev that night on the phone.

She, Bev and Mandy had kept in touch throughout her university years, catching up by phone or on their annual week-long holiday together.

'Sounds worse than my vivas.'

'I'm trying to work out what they actually discovered about any of us. How could they tell what kind of ministers we would make? Yet the future of sixteen individuals, their families, and potentially, a large number of parishes in which they could serve, hinge on the decisions being made now behind those closed doors.'

'Hang on in there, kid. That's what I keep telling myself when lack of sleep makes me forget who I am, let alone why I want to be a doctor. We'll get there in the end – wherever that is.'

'That's the trouble. It's one thing to follow your dreams. It's another to cope with a bizarre institution like the Church of England. Do I really want to be a vicar? Maybe I'm not cut out for it.'

'If you're not, then I'm not cut out to be a doctor. At least it's not brain surgery. You can't kill anyone.'

'I nearly did.'

And Vicky recounted the Kelvin saga.

'If he's an example of vicar material,' Bev said, 'God help the Church of England.'

The irony was, Vicky thought as she put down the phone, despite her storms of doubt, to be turned down now would feel like the ultimate insult.

The Bishop's letter arrived ten days later, meting out her destiny in one short, bloodless sentence. She had been recommended for training. So it would be goodbye to her flat and the independence it had brought her, to teaching and the pupils she had come to love. For what? Three years without a salary, followed by a grossly reduced income and no roots, or home of her own. Was it Saint Teresa of Avila who said that it is the answered, not the unanswered prayers people should worry about?

What gross ingratitude, she said to herself, as she sank to her knees, finally allowing excitement to burst through the fear and uncertainty. Thank you, Father, for opening the door for me. I don't doubt that there'll be times when I'll wish I had never held this letter in my hand.

But you, in your wisdom, have chosen to keep the future hidden, leaving us with virgin territory to explore, and only your promise to be the guide we need through its troughs and its crests. So whatever the future holds, bring it on.

But what on earth am I going to say to the parents?

JANUARY 2020

For a week, until the Queen had been officially informed and the public announcement of her appointment could be made, Vicky lived in limbo, unable to share her knowledge with anyone else. In the end, she felt she had to speak to someone, and opted for Kelvin. Her chaplain would understand that he wasn't allowed to tell his wife, or even whisper it to a fly on the wall.

'So I have my patron taken away and am vowed to silence as well? Thanks,' he said, when she told him. She found the pained look on his face hard to bear, reached out and pulled him into a hug. He made no attempt to resist.

'I'll miss you terribly, Kelvin. I don't know what I'll do without you. You have been more than a chaplain. A real friend.'

'We'd better not let anyone find us in a clinch like this,' he said, pushing her away slightly, and forcing his face into a smile, 'or it'll all be over before it's even begun.'

'I hate the thought of there not being any spontaneity in my life any more, of having to weigh every word and action before I open my mouth or move a finger.'

'Not easy, but if anyone can cope with it and still be herself, you can. There couldn't have been a better choice – even though it'll break every heart in the Larchester Diocese. Mine included.'

Having someone who understood the agonising self-doubt and sense of inadequacy that overwhelmed her at times was an immense relief. Kelvin steadied her, encouraged her to clarify her vision for the role and write it down: to unify the UK church split apart by the defections over women bishops on the one hand and homosexuality on the other, to divest it of some of its more hierarchical structures, to encourage mission and financial stability through a radical divesting of its unviable buildings and an investing in innovative church planting, to stimulate Christian entrepreneurialism in the care of the poor, to campaign for persecuted Christians abroad living under Sharia law, and to give the majority African church more of a voice in the Anglican Alliance.

'It's a huge undertaking, Kelvin.'

'You need an ideal as a starting point. It will develop with the job.'

And then he talked her through the press conference, the pitfalls, the opportunities to say what needed to be said on this first occasion to speak in public as Archbishop. He even chose her clothes.

'That retro thirties suit, the slate-grey one with the long pencil skirt and the jacket with the nipped-in waist. Very nice. Very feminine. Chic but not severe. With your height and figure you can carry it off. And let's have some colour for a change – the china-blue shirt if you don't want to be too episcopal, more flattering than black, which can be hard on a fair complexion like yours.'

'It's not a day to be showy.'

'But no fake humility either. You're colourful, not a fading violet. You're a woman. Be what you are.'

'Okay, Kelvin. I take the point.'

It was at the end of that week of waiting that London fell victim to a new, frightening form of attack that brought the city to a standstill. In the middle of the busy morning rush hour, the underground's entire system went into meltdown. No signals, no lights, no communication, no power anywhere. Hundreds of trains halted where they were. Around one hundred and fifty thousand people were incarcerated in stifling, airless tunnels without water or sanitation. The evacuation was a lengthy, hazardous process and couldn't be attempted until the authorities were satisfied that the computer system had been manually bypassed. Were it to re-start without warning, thousands could be killed on the electrified rails, or by rogue oncoming trains. It was unsafe to send out rescue teams.

Unfortunately, unravelling the various control systems couldn't be done quickly and as time ticked on and a mass of humanity, totally unaware of the dangers, crept down several miles of track by phone-light after manually overriding doors or breaking windows, the authorities opted to kill the power to large swathes of London. The disruption was not well received. The mayor demanded a review of all emergency procedures.

Meanwhile, small children, very pregnant women, diabetics, people suffering from agoraphobia or who were disabled were among the masses shut in the dark without explanation, hour after endless hour, some in the deepest, longest tunnels for more than a day. Many people had to be hospitalised. Many more were severely traumatised. They said later that it was almost like being buried alive. Seven people died, three of heart failure, three of heat exhaustion, and one of hypoglycaemia. It was three days before trains began running again and a further two weeks before they could restore full service. The damage to the economy was colossal.

The cyber-terrorism that governments had feared for so many years had become a terrifying reality. The implications were chilling. If an enemy nation or an international radical group had managed to hack into a highly protected computer network and cause such disruption, what might they not be capable of? Power, water, fuel, communications were potentially subject to attack just like the transport infrastructure. Medical, manufacturing, educational, financial and government services, all dependent on computer systems for their day-to-day operations, were all vulnerable to sabotage, with immense risk to human life. Overnight, the world had become much less safe.

The rumour-mill turned with one bold theory after another: China, India, Iran, North Korea – all might benefit in different ways from collapse at the heart of one of the world's most important cities. However, the intelligence services quickly identified a recently converted and radicalised London Transport system administrator with links to known Islamist extremists. The attack had been master-minded from the inside – by a British man.

Even as the last victims were being rescued, anti-terrorist police rounded up the perpetrators. A haul of seized material revealed that it had been a carefully planned attack, and uncovered a video claiming full responsibility. The country breathed again. Nonetheless, government ministers could not sleep easily in their beds with the threat of a repeat episode hanging over them. Drastic measures were called for.

The moment the news had broken, Vicky rang the PM's office to offer her help. Gerard Lancaster rang her back immediately and reminded her to keep a low profile.

'Stuff that,' she said to Kelvin. 'As long as I'm Bishop of Larchester and families in my diocese are anxious for their loved ones stuck in those hell holes, I'll offer whatever moral and practical support I can.'

She put on jeans and an anorak, added her dog collar to establish her credentials, and as she set off, called out to Kelvin to contact the Bishop of London to ask his permission to trespass on his patch.

Kelvin shook his head in amused despair.

'Oh, and ask the vicar of St Botolph's if I can use his car park.'

She visited several of the many churches near tube stations where volunteers had gathered to provide warmth, shelter, food and hot drinks to the first victims to emerge, and the many family members waiting for news. She moved among the people, sat with them a while, held them, trying to offer what comfort and reassurance she could. Or simply washed and dried dozens of cups and plates. I'm well trained for this, she said to herself, smiling, recollecting her time with the tureens during the miners' strike.

She took orange juice to two small children whose father had been trapped in a tunnel for over twelve hours. They sat on her knee while she read them *The Lion, the Witch and the Wardrobe*.

'Can't we just watch the film on your e-phone?' they asked.

'You could,' she said, 'but since you've seen it already, this will be much more fun.'

And, she thought, keep them entertained a great deal longer.

The press, alerted to the presence of a bishop, descended on her and asked what message she had for those caught up in the crisis. She spoke about the strength of the human spirit, the need to hold on, to wait, pray and trust. And when it was all over, refusing to live with fear, and instead, building communities of hope out of the togetherness there had been in the streets.

Not a single journalist made any connection with the vacancy at Canterbury. She was, after all, a woman.

FIVE

> *It is only the desire, the passion, the thirst for God which turns suffering into conscious pain and turns the consciousness of pain into a protest against suffering.*
>
> JÜRGEN MOLTMANN

FEBRUARY 2020

The fourteenth-century guard room at Lambeth Palace, where the Archbishop once kept his personal army, had become his principal audience room once it was no longer deemed appropriate for a churchman to go to war. It was the ideal place for a press conference, though with its arch-braced ceiling, parquet floor and waist-high wood panelling, it put Vicky in mind of a glorified church hall.

She and Tom walked in hand in hand, to a barrage of whirring, clicking and flashing. She saw Tom's facial muscles contract.

'Sorry to inflict this upon you,' she whispered, out of the side of her mouth, maintaining a taut smile for the cameras. 'Stop clenching your jaw. Bad for the teeth.'

'I can't see anything but spots and zigzags,' he muttered. 'Couldn't leave you to face an ordeal like this on your own.'

'I do appreciate it,' she said, linking her arm through his. 'Your absence would have set off a maelstrom of false assumptions.'

'I just hope it does my image some good. Reflected glory for the hospital.'

The press conference was chaired by the Secretary General of General Synod, a man with a great deal of power in the Church of England. Dominic Naylor was large and imposing, fierce at times, with several joggling jowls and a nose as pitted as an old courgette. He was not, she knew, in favour of women bishops, and the occasion must have been something of a trial for him, though no one would have guessed. He was the consummate professional and a perfect gentleman.

'Take a few minutes to say what you have to say,' he whispered, as they faced the dense rows of journalists and the technology that would zoom her words and thoughts, along with every minute facial movement and mannerism, across the globe in seconds, 'then answer questions – as many as you wish.'

As she walked to the microphone, her stomach turned over. She took a moment to let it settle, surveying the throng, holding their gaze, acknowledging with a smile the journalists and photographers she recognised. She closed her eyes and prayed silently for a few seconds, then her voice broke through the profound hush. 'I think I can say that I'm as surprised as you all probably are. Who would ever have dreamed a mere six years ago, when women were given the chance to be bishops, that I would be standing here today? It is an honour I would never have dared to expect or presume, and more daunting than I could have possibly imagined, coming, as it does, at such a difficult and worrying time in our national life.

'But let me share a quote with you from the prophet Isaiah, who reminds us that though the mountains may shake and the hills be shattered, however frightening the crises we face, God will never abandon the world he has created and loves so much. No act of terrorism or sabotage, no evil whatsoever, can deflect his eternal plan for the universe, to renew and restore it one day to all its original glory. In that we can be absolutely certain.

'With such hope, this is an exciting time to take on the responsibility of leadership for the church. Traditional Anglicanism in this country may have declined. However, the erosion of formalised religion in the past thirty years has left us leaner but fitter – with a raft of exciting new kinds of churches, meeting in homes, pubs and community centres, on Saturday afternoons or mid-week evenings, much more convenient for young families. There are still the familiar Sunday congregations, of course – large, small, traditional, informal, black, white and multi-cultural. Many of them are engaging with their local neighbourhood, providing food banks, debt counselling, credit unions, local co-operatives, drug and drink rehabilitation, and parenting courses, as they engage in the vital task of sharing God's good news. They are responsible for over seventy per cent of the volunteering that takes place throughout this nation. What's more, it saves the government millions of pounds.'

There was a swiftly stifled titter of – what, disbelief? – and she used the time to take a sip of water.

'Let me give you an example from my diocese. Charley is a single mum of two boys, the youngest aggressive, bullied and being bullied at school, the eldest with no qualifications, out of work, drinking heavily, sleeping rough more often than not and in increasing trouble with the police. Charley is at her wit's end. Her job is at risk. She went to one of our charities that helps families in crisis. They got her onto a course that showed her how to cope and provided emotional support. The younger boy was diagnosed with ADHD, is now being given the help he needs and no longer needs to see the doctor. The older boy has been found a bedsit through the charity's supported accommodation project, and now has a job in a restaurant. He loves it and has stopped offending. His social worker has been reassigned. Cost all of that in terms of social value and you have an idea of how much of your tax, and everyone else's too, the church is saving.'

She was gratified with a short rumble of amusement.

'I am sad to be saying goodbye to the people of the diocese of Larchester who have embodied for me that calibre of care, but I am also immensely proud to be part of a church that seeks, as best it can, to live out the teachings of its master.

'The dynamic vibrancy that animates the sacred heritage entrusted to me today is largely due to the immense wisdom, integrity, holiness, dignity, and moral courage of so many of my predecessors. It is an honour to follow men of such calibre and godliness and I will endeavour to be worthy of the visionary and self-sacrificial manner in which they fulfilled their calling.

'I am so glad to have lived at a time when there are such opportunities for women. Had I been born a mere ten years earlier, I wouldn't be standing here as I am today. So I owe a wealth of gratitude to all the women and men who dreamed of it and fought for it, and with many tears and through substantial opposition, blazed a trail to this place and this moment.

'Finally, I want to express my thanks to my husband, Tom, for all his love and support, even taking time out of his own demanding job to be here today. The cost of his wife's calling has been more than many spouses would be prepared to accept. He will, I promise him, have the first call on my diary.'

There was a slight, further titter, but most of the journalists were already jostling to get in the questions they'd prepared or had been instructed to ask by their editors.

'Nathan Johnson, the *Telegraph*. There will, inevitably, be many who are dismayed by the appointment of a woman to the church's top job, particularly those in the African church. How will you handle those who can't accept your leadership?'

As the initial fracas died down to a background rumble, Vicky said, 'I understand and respect the genuine theological difficulties some may have with my appointment. But having very differing views and remaining united in Christ regardless is one of the strengths of the Church of England. I will do all in my power to accommodate the dilemmas faced by my colleagues. I don't see the role in terms of authority or hierarchy, so when it comes to my brothers and sisters in the African church, I can honestly say that my role is simply to serve their leaders to the best of my ability. Knowing them as I do, I trust that's something they will be able to accept.'

'Will a woman do the job differently from a man?' a female journalist shot from the floor, before the chairman could intervene.

'Combine sermon preparation with the hoovering, you mean?'

There was a short burst of amusement.

'You know, I'm not sure men and women are all that different. Some say we're better team players, and in Larchester I have worked closely with a small, very effective team, but then, so have my predecessors at Canterbury. I think perhaps women have certain freedoms that a man might not. You saw last week how easy it was for me to take a child on my knee. Much harder for a man.'

A pugnacious young man in the front row leapt to his feet, overpowering Vicky with an acrid smell of armpit odour.

'Jabez Corbett, the *Mail on Sunday*. Are you advocating a paedophile's licence, Bishop? Bearing in mind that priests in your church, and even bishops, have been prosecuted for the abuse of children?'

'We must do everything in our power to protect children. But we must also encourage fathering. Almost fifty per cent of children now grow up without any male presence in their lives, and suffer because of it. Parenting is not merely the domain of women. And I do believe that men in caring, professional roles, like primary school teachers or nurses, or even Sunday School teachers, must be released from the fear of contact with a child, as long as that contact is in an appropriate context.'

'Ben Daniels, ITV News. In the light of the recent cyber-attack, Archbishop, and the public's increased fears for its safety – to which I presume you were referring – what is your response to the secularists in the government who are calling for stringent measures against all forms of religious indoctrination?'

'There's a difference between a gentle, non-pressurised teaching or sharing of a religious faith that enables the hearer to lead a richer, fuller, more altruistic life, and the kind of radicalisation that leads to the killing or maiming of others. The former lies at the bedrock of our society. The latter seeks to be its destruction. These differentials are overlooked by the secularists and it's a matter I hope to discuss with the Prime Minister, so that we can come to some agreement over how to ensure the security of our country without encroaching on basic civil liberties.'

'Will your husband give up his work to support you?'

'Will having a woman at the helm make the church more attractive to the masses?'

'No, to both questions.'

'Helen Davis, freelance. When you trained, you couldn't have become a vicar, let alone a bishop. Why would you want to go into such a job?'

Vicky nodded. 'You're right. A deacon or curate was all women could be, second in command, at most an NCO to the manly officer. The battles women had won in society were only just beginning in the Church of England. But I had a sense of calling to be a fully-fledged vicar from when I was very young, and I always believed that the gates must yield to us one day. And I suppose I've always loved a challenge.'

1989

Vicky's heart sank at her first sight of St Christopher's. Colloquially known as 'the vicar factory', this particular college was a draughty, grey, stone mansion perched on the edge of the Peak District, just before it gave way to the sprawling, smoky mass of Sheffield below. Built at the turn of the last century by a steel works owner whose requirements revolved more around station and standing than common sense, it must have been nightmarishly cold even then, while any attempt at heating was now utterly defeated by dozens of cracks and crevices and leaking windows.

It had been transformed into an Anglican theological college in the early 1960s, courtesy of much chipboard and vinyl. Lecture rooms, dining room, common room, toilets, bathrooms and bedrooms had been hacked out or hammered on until barely a hint of its former grandeur remained. Health and Safety had contributed its fire escapes and fireproof doors (now painted with a lurid, pale-green gloss) in the early eighties. The carpets and curtains looked like job-lot leftovers from B&Q.

She had chosen St Christopher's out of a motley collection of theological colleges because it was evangelical without being narrow-minded, essential for someone who didn't want to find herself an anomaly at one end or the other of the Anglican spectrum – in a monkish catholic or macho conservative institution where the words 'woman leader' were held to be an oxymoron. At the end of the day, it was a privileged chance to do further academic research, this time a PhD in church and mission, though her mother made it absolutely clear there would be no financial or other support forthcoming for a daughter intent on being a perpetual student.

She quickly learnt the basics of survival, applying for grants to subsidise the meagre diocesan allowance from a mass of minor trusts with names like the Matilda Mountpleasant Ordination Candidates' Fund, set up by kind benefactors who had no idea how thinly their philanthropy would one day be stretched – £50 here, £25 there, a little piece of the cake for everyone. How a family could cope was beyond her power to imagine.

She realised her time at St Christopher's was never going to be easy, not at a time when the men were only just beginning to get used to the idea of women sharing their kingdom. But at the same time, acquiring the tools of the trade also proved more enriching than she had imagined. It was vital to face up to the why of natural disaster and personal tragedy, to think through the heart-rending moral decisions humans had to make – abortion, divorce, whistle-blowing, euthanasia – before they were let loose in the world, so that they could be more effective pastors. At St Christopher's none of the issues were shirked.

'How do we provide an explanation for people that's sensitive to their situation, yet true to the dictates of biblical Christian tradition?' she asked in an ethics seminar.

'We have no answers. Isn't that what mystery's all about?' shouted out Max, one of the male students.

'Oh, so when we're faced with parents who have just discovered that their new baby is severely special needs and they ask us why, we simply say, "It's a mystery. That's God for you. Totally arbitrary."'

'We listen, that's all we can do,' he spelt out slowly, as if he were speaking to a child.

There were nods from the men around the room.

'I know there are no easy answers,' she said, 'but surely we're called on to offer a little more than that? It's called hope.'

As they groaned and shook their heads at her, she suddenly became aware of the men's feet beneath the desks, many of them in the silliest of socks. Christmas presents from a mother? Not a wife, surely? Their feet suddenly seemed enormous compared to her dainty little pair in square-toed courts. So easily trodden on by such large loafers. What on earth was she doing in this male-dominated world?

The ethics tutor yanked them all into the discussion. 'Of course we listen, Max. But fight shy of the moral maze here, and when you're out in ministry, it could defeat you altogether.'

She found it hard to adjust to such close communal living. The raucous laughter in the dining room at lunchtime that thwarted meaningful conversation; the yells of protesting toddlers dragged around by harassed-looking wives with cumbersome buggies, overladen with bags, bottle and spare nappies; the sour body smell hanging heavily in the college library in the evening, after the husbands, sleeves rolled up, had spent the day escaping the pressures of home life to write an essay. Small wonder that occasionally one of the wives would blaze into the common room on a Saturday afternoon, where the men were slumped in armchairs in a semi-hypnotic state in front of the football, dump the baby on his lap and leave with the car. She rather admired them for it. Better that than the few who gazed adoringly at their husbands and said, 'We have a joint ministry.' If that were true, then why weren't they being ordained as well, rather than living vicariously off their husband's calling? She said so, loudly, just before a lecture one day. When would she learn to rein it in?

'We always knew you were a closet feminist,' Max called out.

'And a little red,' agreed another of the male students.

'Not closet about either,' she shouted back. 'Proud of the fact.'

Despite the constant niggles at each other, discussion of the most profound matters of life and death drew the ordinands together in a way no other environment could do. Their lives were inseparably entwined, not only by learning to live with their basic disagreements, but by confronting the same doubts, anxieties and fears. For all of them, the future came at a price. The loss of job status and prospects, the sacrifice of a decent salary, never being able to put down real roots of your own, saying goodbye to weekends off, in fact to any normal existence, for goodness' sake. However learned and dedicated the staff, the institutional culture dictated that past careers, achievements and experience now counted for little. Whether twenty-three or fifty-three, they were the raw material to bend and build into the leaders that would be useful to the Church of England.

Of the nine women living in what was known somewhat indelicately as 'the singles' block', Vicky was the youngest; Marjorie Townend, at fifty-three, the eldest. She, more than any, had cause to find the reversion to student life hard to bear, but she turned out to have the most to teach Vicky about how to face it with equanimity and grace. Her motherly proportions, tousled grey curls and gnarled face, sculpted by long years as a missionary in a sunny climate but troubled culture, camouflaged the resilience and depth of character that had been proven on the anvil of life. In apartheid South Africa, though she was reluctant to speak of it, she had faced bullying, beatings and unimaginable brutality. Her fearless stand had led to arrest, torture and a year of solitary confinement, all of which she described in a quiet, matter-of-fact voice and without an ounce of self-pity. What did any of them know of self-sacrifice compared to her?

It was to her, therefore, that Vicky often turned when the squabbles, frustrations, and imponderables threatened to rob her of her purpose, when she needed a role model in quiet Christian dignity.

'They said I was a feminist. I don't think I am – not the bra-burning type, at least. Do you think I am?'

Marjorie motioned her to take a seat on the bed that but for a desk and chair, filled the tiny, peach-coloured room. She arranged a cushion at Vicky's back, pressed up against the wall, then turned the chair round and sat on it, facing her.

'You want an equal world for women? That isn't wrong – unless you become offensive or start to think women are morally superior. Which we certainly aren't.'

'I do resent the men expecting us to be so meek and inoffensive in seminars. Why can't we pose the difficult questions, argue with the best of them? I won't give in to these stereotypes.'

Marjorie studied her for a while, smiling, then said, 'It's your outspokenness that makes you a threat.'

Vicky sighed.

'I can't be anything other than me. I often feel like a Japanese maple in a forest of tall trees – an exotic specimen. They call me "vibrant", "ebullient", or just plain "argumentative".'

'Not far wrong,' Marjorie agreed. 'I love your lively mind. And that you don't let them dominate you.'

'Yes, but when they do seem like they are actually willing to talk to me, it's usually a preamble to a request for babysitting,' Vicky said ruefully. 'Just because I'm single and female.'

'And I love your sense of humour too,' Marjorie said, patting her on the knee. 'You have to remember that we're living in a time of immense social and cultural change for the men. They'll never truly see us as their equals until we're priested.'

'How do you come to terms with that, Marjorie? After all you've been through?'

Marjorie raised her skirt slowly, and Vicky saw a long jagged scar puckering the skin all along the older woman's thigh. She gasped at the extent of the damage, then looked up into Marjorie's face, waiting for an explanation.

'Whenever my home was ransacked, the police would tell me the blacks had done it. But I knew. The blacks didn't have dogs. The police did. One night I was awoken by a noise and caught them at it. They released one of the dogs, and it almost tore my leg off.'

She lowered her skirt.

'Vicky, whatever ministry we're in will tear us apart in some way and leave its scars. And that may be especially so for women, as we take the lower place and simply serve. But that's the essence of ministry, if we follow our Lord's example – service. Some of these men are young, so young. Be kind to them. Some lessons can only be learnt with time.'

In the singles' block everyone seemed to have their issues. It seemed hopeless to expect that they might be dealt with before they were all inflicted on innocent congregations. There was a constant queue at Vicky's door, as one or other of a small coterie she had fostered took their turn to sit on her bed as if it were a psychiatrist's chair. Had anyone told her she would spend her ordination training playing host, in her bedroom, to a steady stream of eligible, would-be vicars seeking her out to feed their spiritual rather than physical needs, she would have doubted their sanity.

There was Phil Booth, the constant joker, whose tomfoolery hid a terror of death and funerals; Simon Marshall, whose short-lived marriage hit the buffers when his ex-wife ran off with his best friend; and Garth, who was gay, and terrified of being found out by anyone in power.

'If you were God,' Simon said, the day he heard that his ex-wife had remarried, as he shed bitter tears into a grubby handkerchief retrieved from his jeans pocket, 'would you choose such a weak and feeble hotch-potch of servants to change the world?'

'I'd certainly choose someone who did their washing more frequently,' she said, passing him a box of tissues.

Garth, of course, wasn't eligible, but so drop-dead gorgeous that his being gay seemed an awful waste of a man.

'If I were straight, I'd marry you,' he once said to Vicky, on a good day.

'I'll take that as a compliment.'

On other days his inner nakedness and near-despair made him so vulnerable that she was terrified lest any inadvertent cheap joke on her part would inflict fresh wounds on such raw flesh.

In 1987 the Church of England Synod had issued a statement of policy, affirming *the biblical and traditional teaching that sexual intercourse is an act of total commitment which belongs properly within a permanent marriage relationship . . . homosexual genital acts fall short of this ideal.* Garth deeply resented it.

'It makes me feel a second-class citizen for being what I am.'

'It's not about being, Garth, but doing.'

He looked up at her in astonishment.

'How can you be so naive, Vicky? What teenage bloke doesn't do? That statement turns me into "a fallen-short".'

'But we're all fallen-shorts. Christianity is hope for the fallen-shorts.'

It didn't so much as raise a smile.

'Sorry, Garth. I didn't mean to be facile. I am sorry for how you've been made to feel, but it was never intended as a rejection. Simply stating a basic principle. I'm heterosexual, but for me, as a single woman, sex is out.'

'For now,' he retorted bitterly.

'For the foreseeable future,' she shouted after him, as he got up and slammed the door behind him.

The truth was, she would have liked a man in tow. What single woman wouldn't? Preferably before she left St Christopher's and the dog collar deterred all but the most hardy. Weighing up the pluses and minuses of so much potential husband material was unavoidable when there was so much of it around. Put forty or so unmarried people together in one place for months at a time and the sexual tension was almost bound to stoke up passions that drove a few to the point of spontaneous combustion.

'Being cooped up like battery hens – it's a penance for being single,' Jan said one Saturday night in the corridor kitchen, where they cooked their own meals at weekends to keep the cost of catering down.

A research post-graduate, Jan had been ordained in the Episcopal Church of the USA, and vicar of a parish in Boston for several years. Here was a woman who fulfilled all Vicky's aspirations of what it meant to be a woman in leadership in the church – competent, dedicated, visionary, sharp and funny, without sacrificing her femininity. The male students mooned after her as she skimmed down the corridor on her never-ending legs, her short, shiny bob swinging, but they were too frightened to pursue her. She was just a little too American and sophisticated for would-be English churchmen, unnerved by a woman who could deploy words like a machete.

'Living in this kind of proximity to one another, you want to lay more than eggs – no matter how much you thought you had this celibacy thing sorted before.'

Jan's frankness always made Vicky laugh.

'So which of these many fantastic men do you fancy?'

'This lot? None of them. And don't you go there either. You, my poppet, are destined for greater things.'

'Don't be daft.'

'Hey, where's your ambition? You English do yourselves down all the time. Especially the girls. My church has just appointed its first woman bishop. Don't limit your horizons.'

'And end up an old maid?'

'Like me?' She dug Vicky in the ribs. 'It isn't so bad. Better than being married to any of these guys.'

They both laughed again.

'See? There's more to life than marriage. You wait, kid. You're not like the rest. Don't throw your future away on some misogynist parish priest.'

At times Vicky really wondered if she, or any of her fellow students, should ever be let loose on the world. She said so to Donald Williams when she stopped in on her way back from a flying visit to the north-east to catch up on Melanie, who had married the giant engineer she had dated in her final year, and had just given birth to an enormous baby boy.

Vicky's former university tutor had agreed to see her for an hour or so twice a year for 'spiritual direction'. She needed someone to accompany her on her journey into the unknown, and knew no one else with such insight and ability to knock her back into shape. To her immense relief, he agreed.

'Vicky,' he said quietly, after she had described her first months at St Christopher's, her angst about some of her fellow students, and her own self-doubt, 'you told me you found Henri Nouwen's *The Wounded Healer* a seminal book?'

She nodded. 'But what if the wounds become septic and poison us?' she asked. 'How can we be healers?'

'There is always that risk,' he agreed. 'But the outcome is far more likely to be fatal if we leave them unacknowledged. The ordinand who does that – or at least, who doesn't admit to any wounds – is a danger to themselves and others. If he or she cannot empathise, if they delude themselves into thinking they are somehow above the weakness and falli-bility that afflicts all vulnerable human beings, they'll never become decent priests. They should come here and peddle theology instead.'

He paused and frowned. Then his face lit up.

'Ah yes, it reminds me of my GP. He always spoke about his patients as if they were slightly inferior beings. Until his wife contracted Multiple Sclerosis. A terrible tragedy. But it made him a far better doctor.'

'So confronting our issues at St Christopher's is an essential part of our preparation?'

'Absolutely. Working through them is painful, but a vital part of our spiritual growth. But you can never be sure your friends have actually succeeded.'

'I can only learn to live with my own woundedness?'

He raised his expressive, bushy eyebrows in sympathy and nodded.

'Exactly so. We support each other as best we can, but in the end, leave them in God's hands. Ultimately, each of us walks alone with him.'

One morning, in the early hours, Vicky was awoken by a quiet, but unmistakable tap-tapping on her bedroom door. She put on the bedside light, tried to focus and read the alarm clock. 3.15 a.m. For crying out loud!

'Hang on!' she shouted, reaching for a dressing gown.

She opened the door a slit and found Garth, collapsed on the floor in the foetal position, shivering uncontrollably. He seemed to be suffering from shock. She got him into her room, sat him on the bed, wrapped him in a rug, and rocked him, as if he were a child. It seemed the natural thing to do. It was some time before he calmed down enough to speak.

'Interrogated. Police. For six hours,' he stammered, his teeth chattering so hard he couldn't get the words out.

'Why? How?'

'Police raid.'

'Where?'

'Gay bar in Sheffield.'

Vicky's heart sank. She knew he had gone to meet a friend for a drink. Both, it transpired, had been taken down to the station for further questioning.

'How old was this "friend" of yours?'

'Seventeen.'

'Grief, Garth – sexual relations with a minor! Is that what they're suggesting?'

He began to cry, and she held him close. It struck her how strange it was that she could never be this intimate with a heterosexual friend.

'I love him, Vicky,' he whispered into her neck, making it uncomfortably damp with the mixture of his breath and his tears, 'and now his parents will never let me see him again.'

'Charges?'

He shook his head.

'Thank God for that.'

'Is that all you can say?'

'It's a start. You could do without a criminal record.'

'I can't be ordained,' he said miserably. 'I can't live without love. I've tried.'

'No one's asking you to live without love.'

'Without sex, then. It's the same thing to a bloke.'

'We single women manage it.'

'It's not the same. You can always hope that you'll marry one day.'

'Marjorie, at fifty-three? Jan at forty-four? And who's going to marry a curate anyway? Virgins on our deathbeds, probably. That's the cost of the calling. We've all known it from the start. But that doesn't stop us loving and being loved.'

He lay down on the bed. She got up and switched off the bedside light, then without thinking, bent down and kissed him gently on the cheek. The dam burst and he was shaken by huge wracking sobs that jerked him around like a fragile tree in a storm. She stroked his hair until the violence subsided and he slept, fully clothed, shaken by the occasional sob.

She spent the rest of the night at her desk, intermittently watching him and studying every verse in the Bible on sex that she could find. Wasn't there some way, any way, that her theology could encompass the fulfilment Garth so badly wanted?

'Sod it,' she said to Simon the next night, when he rolled up at her room for a debrief. 'I've studied everything the Bible has to say about sex, and I still can't get my head around this gay thing. I can't see that its expression is any different from the heterosexual variety – it's a clear taboo outside marriage.'

Simon sank down heavily on her bed. That mattress wasn't going to last out her stay at this rate.

'Am I missing something?' she said, waving her Bible under his nose. 'Some of this lot seem to think that marriage is not a pre-requisite for intercourse, but I can't reconcile that with this book. What do you reckon?'

He stretched out on the bed, folded his arms under his head, and studied the ceiling. She checked his feet. Carpet slippers. Hallelujah for that. No muddy marks.

'If there's no ultimate authority in sexual matters, we drift into hedonistic narcissism, and frankly, I find the idea of a society where everyone indulges all their selfish pleasures thoroughly terrifying.'

'I know, I know, so do I. But in Garth's case, for example, what if it's a gene?'

'Can't be. The lack of procreation would mean homosexuality would die out. Anyway, they haven't found it yet. The jury's still out. More likely it's something to do with nurture, not nature.'

Simon's laid-back approach to the happiness of others, namely Garth's, began to wind her up. He was divorced, after all. Another Christian ideal out of the window, just of a different kind.

'Nature, nurture, what does that change? It's still not a person's choice. So who are we to deny them sex? That's the problem with these ethical issues. We can say we're against abortion in principle, but if a couple who know beyond doubt that their baby *in utero* is severely disabled and condemned to a life of suffering come to tell us they have made the incredibly painful decision to terminate its life, what choice do we have but to support them?'

'Of course we stand by them, but that doesn't mean sacrificing our ideals. It's a fallen world – messy at times.'

Her thoughts were coming so fast and hard she didn't notice his voice trailing off.

'But how do we walk with integrity? How do we follow our beliefs, our conscience, yet fulfil the overriding command to love?'

There was silence from the bed. Simon had nodded off.

Issues in Human Sexuality, a revised statement on sexual relations by the House of Bishops, was published several weeks later. The sexual act, it said, was limited to 'faithful, monogamous and heterosexual couples committed to one another for life'. Homosexual clergy were expected to be celibate, in keeping with their ordination vows.

'It seems a bit of a fudge,' she said to Simon, as they pored over its pages with the help of a glass of wine. St Christopher's had eroded her commitment to teetotalism. 'No such standards for the laity,' she added. 'They can please themselves.'

'They would anyway. But problems for the future, no doubt,' he agreed.

'And no hope for Garth,' she said, at the very moment Garth barged into the room, suitcases stacked outside the door, to say goodbye.

FEBRUARY 2020

'It has been suggested that you'll take a more relaxed approach to the job?' the freelance reporter Helen Davis continued.

'I'm not sure what that is,' Vicky said, 'but if you mean I'd like to see a church that not only does gravity and dignity, but that can laugh at itself too, then you're right.'

'For example, you're known for referring to cathedral processions,' Helen said, checking her notes, 'as, "a march of grim-faced penguins".'

Helen had certainly done her research.

'I did,' she agreed. 'We can take ourselves far too seriously. Religion without humour is intolerable – the domain of fanatics. There's more than enough of that around the world without the church adding to their number.'

'Quentin Curtis, the *Star*. The Lesbian and Gay Christian Movement accuses you of being homophobic, Bishop. Why shouldn't the clergy perform gay marriage now it's a legal institution?'

The chairman was about to interrupt, but she asked if she might respond. He nodded, reluctantly.

'If this issue was purely about homophobia, there would be no reason to refuse gay people a church marriage. But it goes much deeper. It's about conscience. No one should or, in fact, can be forced to do anything that their conscience forbids. Freedom of conscience, belief and speech is enshrined in the constitution of every democratic society. I have no time for churches who exclude anyone for homophobic reasons. We must open wide our arms to gay people, love and welcome them. As most churches now do.'

'But you'll maintain the church's anti-gay marriage stance?'

'The church is not against gay marriage. We are *for* the historic interpretation of an institution that precedes state and church, that in purely secular terms, evolved to ensure the creation, protection and preservation of the next generation. Gay marriage brings no legal rights that civil partnership hasn't already bestowed. And in fact, the demand for it has been surprisingly small.'

'So why does the church still not recognise clergy living in civil partnerships?'

'We do. Nonetheless, the priest's ordination vows commit him or her to a holy and celibate life. Each bishop must weigh that up when they appoint a minister. I, personally, have never tried to police what my clergy do in the bedroom and I don't expect them to make an issue of it either. But I do expect them to live by the promises they made. I have always taken a hard line on heterosexual priests who transgress their ordination vows and cast off their spouse simply because they may have fallen in love with the curate's wife.'

There was a sudden hullabaloo, the whole horde of journalists seemingly on their feet, waving, shouting, demanding to be heard.

Out of the corner of her eye, Vicky saw Church House's Head of Communications give a knowing nod to the chairman, who brought the press conference to a rapid close and escorted her out.

SIX

*God is not only a divine person who we can address in prayer,
but also a wide living space ... We human beings are giving
each other space for living when we meet each other in love
and friendship.*

JÜRGEN MOLTMANN

FEBRUARY 2020

The press response the following morning was mixed. Mike Barnes had laid the cuttings out on the table next to Vicky's desk. Her stomach churned at the sight of them.

'Grief, Mike, if I read these every morning it's a passport to irritable bowel syndrome.'

'Try to view them with a certain dispassion. Remember, not many people read the newspapers any more.'

'They read the London freebies all right.'

'But most people rely on TV or the internet for their news. And that was largely sympathetic. Reported what you said fairly verbatim. Found you refreshingly radical. Or something similar.'

Vicky snorted.

'So folk won't see the crazy mix of make-believe that's written here? I doubt it. Urban myths only need one initiator. Word of mouth does the rest. Ah well, an exercise in ego deflation is good for the soul.'

Mike picked up one or two and handed them to her. They smelt of stale tobacco, transferred from his ancient tweedy jacket with its leather-patched elbows.

'They're not too bad, really.'

Vicky wasn't keen on that 'really' and read them only reluctantly. 'Forget the usual breed of clerical leader – stuffy, worthy, with the faint smell of musty academia. This one is dignified, chic, with a smile that could charm a raging bull – and may have to, given the opposition her appointment is bound to attract.'

'Disarming, affable and attractive,' wrote Helen Davis. 'But don't be deceived. This woman hasn't got where she is without treading on toes in those steel-tipped stilettos of hers, and that isn't about to change. An inveterate moderniser, and openly dubious about the place of formal religion in current society, she will, inevitably, upset the traditionalists. Left of centre in matters political, her greatest accolade is for churches that supplement the welfare state by feeding the fives of thousands. But can she walk on water?

'After her famous March of the 4,000 from Wooten Grange to Downing Street to demand low-cost housing, she claimed that since her 1930s predecessor, MP Ellen Wilkerson, though eventually a member of the cabinet, was called "a bit of a nuisance", she would choose that as her epitaph. But it may not bode well for the first woman in this historic office if she meddles in matters that don't concern her, and doesn't deal with those that do, such as her stalwart refusal to support gay marriage. There are interesting times ahead.'

'The overall consensus seems to be that I'm "a breath of fresh air",' Vicky said to Tom that night as they prepared for bed, about the only time they had to catch up with each other. 'Not difficult, when you're the first Archbishop to wear a skirt.'

'You are a breath of fresh air, my darling,' he said, taking the opportunity of her ruminations to nip in front of her at the basin to brush his teeth.

'There is a rider, of course. Apparently my "unintelligent and incomprehensible homophobia might be almost quaint, if it weren't so downright bigoted". That came from Carson Rivers, the new chair of the Church's Gay Rights Association. He claims that my appointment was the church resorting to its usual fudge on the issue. He's such a hypocrite, that man. He doesn't say, of course, that he's even more disappointed by my lack of a male member. Strange how quiet he's gone on his opposition to the ordination of women since he took on the leadership of CGRA. So which is the greater – his misogyny or my homophobia?'

His mouth too full of toothpaste to reply, Tom raised his head, and nodded at her in the mirror.

'Dammit, Tom,' she grumbled, 'how do you always manage to sneak in before me?'

He spat into the basin.

'Can we have a two-sink job in the Lambeth flat?' he asked.

'You're joking! It's a down-size all round there, I'm afraid.'

Mike was waiting for her in the office when she went down the following morning. He shuffled from one foot to the other, several newspapers tucked under his arm. Fighting a rising sense of alarm, she beckoned to him to follow her into the study.

'Well?' she asked, closing the door behind them.

'No, no, Vicky, nothing too awful,' he said reassuringly, 'in fact, probably quite good, but the Church House press office wants to know why we never told them about this.'

He laid out several of the tabloids on her desk, the front pages covered in photos of her much younger self at the poll tax demonstration of 1990. Her small, rather bewildered face was ringed and arrowed.

'Supports your rather radical image,' Mike said, enthusiastically.

'But where in heaven's name did they get it?'

'You mean you don't know?'

She shook her head slowly.

'I had no idea anyone took any photographs. It was so many years ago, when I was at theological college.'

'And you've never seen this photo before?'

'Never. How did the press get hold of it?'

He stood next to her, studying the mass of tiny faces, enlarged and blurred.

'Looks like something taken by a surveillance camera.'

'Where would a photo like that have ended up?'

'In a file, I imagine.'

'Whose file, for crying out loud?'

He looked at her, raising his eyebrows meaningfully.

'Oh, this is ridiculous. Why, in heaven's name?'

'You don't imagine they didn't run a careful check on you?'

'But who would have discovered it was there and have access to the files?'

'Someone in high places. Someone who doesn't like you that much?'

She tried to dismiss the suggestion as fatuous. Why would anyone be that interested in an archbishop these days?

'Look, Vicky, the poll tax was very unpopular. Whoever found this photo hasn't done you any harm. Might even earn you brownie points.'

But Mike's reassurances floated past her. She was too busy reviewing her past, worrying about what other seemingly innocent activities might be taken as indiscretions – for an archbishop.

1990

Work placements for a would-be vicar could be stretching, and should be formative. In later years, Vicky would always describe hers as her wake-up call. She found herself in a Sheffield parish near the top of the national index of social deprivation. She had never seen poverty to match it since. Built in the late 1950s, the council housing estate had previously been an area of run-down, back-to-back tenement housing, known as 'Little Chicago' because of the level of gangster-like racketeering. Then whole streets were moved, neighbours kept next to each other, into 'streets in the sky', some as many as thirteen stories high, built into a vast concrete frame, filled in with yellow-orange- and red-brick curtain walling. From a distance the flats could have been mini cages, their inhabitants cooped up like battery hens.

The architectural style came to be known as brutalism. And brutal it was. The flats were riddled with damp. Noise levels were intolerable, burglary endemic, violent crime on the increase, security minimal. How could a child grow up in that kind of environment and emerge unscathed?

Her training vicar invited Vicky to accompany him to an assembly at the church primary school, the only safe place in the children's little lives. They performed a dance in honour of their visitors – the story of Noah. Each child jumped and pranced like the animal they had chosen to represent, and Vicky was entranced.

'Could they do it again?' she asked the head.

The head shook her head apologetically.

'Afraid not,' she said, ushering the children back to their classrooms. 'They're so under-nourished it's taken every ounce of their energy to perform it once. Don't even get milk to give them any more.'

'Malnourished children, in this country, in this day and age!' Vicky fumed at Simon, her pet socialist, when she got back to the college. 'Wouldn't you like to get hold of Thatcher and drag her up here to see the effect of her policies? What can we do about it?'

'I'll tell you what we're going to do about it. We're going to stop moaning about democracy turning into dictatorship and march for what we believe in. There's going to be a huge anti-poll tax demonstration in London on March the 31st. Come with me, Vicky.'

She looked at him askance. She had never marched for anything in her life. Protest was not exactly her parents' style. Nor that of the ladies of Harrogate College. Though she hadn't been above wielding a blow with her schoolbag when outrage required it. The memory of it made her smile.

'Come on, Vick,' Simon urged, seeing her weaken.

He was right, she thought. A charge levied on individuals rather than property would be pernicious in areas like the Sheffield estate, where larger than average families were squeezed into poorer than average accommodation. Why should they be faced with a local tax bill much higher than her well-heeled parents, living alone in a grand house?

On a sunny, spring day, armed with a packed lunch, they took a coach to London and joined around 200,000 protestors in Kennington Park. The fine weather and instant camaraderie made it seem like a grand day out, and Vicky half expected to see an ice cream van or two. Simon bounded around with pent-up energy. If he had had a tail he would have wagged it.

They set off for Trafalgar Square in an orderly fashion, at a fair pace, but came to a standstill inexplicably in Whitehall, where they waited and waited. The convivial atmosphere gradually leaked away, displaced by a growing tension and ever-increasing disquiet. Vicky could see nothing, but Simon, who was well over six foot, said there appeared to be a huge police presence blocking both the top and bottom of the street. They were stuck, unable to move forwards or backwards, jammed into a space far too small for so many people, feeling half-smothered as bodies pressed ever tighter against them. As the minutes ticked slowly by, patience wore thin. The fetid dampness of other people's perspiration invaded Vicky's clothes, her hands, her hair. Their rancid breath filled the space in front of her face and it was a fight to keep the mounting nausea and panic under control.

Feeling increasingly faint, she clung to Simon's arm for dear life as the pushing and shoving began. Like rag dolls, they were shaken backwards and forwards as the crowd surged first towards the rearward and then to the forward exits, both blocked by ranks of police. Scuffles broke out here and there. Police truncheons thudded into yielding flesh with a series of sickening thwacks, and then they saw that the line obstructing their advance had broken, and they stampeded like a herd of marauding cattle into Trafalgar Square.

Then, from nowhere, mounted police in riot gear surrounded them. She had seen them on TV, but had never imagined how menacing, how terrifying it could be to find yourself face to face with a barrage of faceless men on horses, waiting for the command to charge, to wonder whether you were about to breathe your last, thanks to a government that your country's democratic rights had put into power. The words, 'I'm a good, law-abiding citizen. It's my right to protest. I don't deserve this,' revolved round and round her head. But no one would hear. No one cared.

Vicky tripped over a stray foot and skidded across the road on her knees. She picked herself up and saw two jagged holes in her tights, just beginning to ooze blood, got a tissue out of her bag, spat into it and dabbed at the grazes.

'Okay?' Simon puffed, catching up with her.

She nodded, faintly.

'Can we go home now?'

'I think that may be a good idea.'

He grabbed her elbow and steered her across the square in the direction of the coach waiting for them south of the river, but before they could get out mounted police charged from a side street into the square, their horses snorting and whinnying loudly. Behind them, with the ear-splitting scream of sirens, four police riot vans moved in at speed, irrespective of who was in their way. And then every iota of restraint was lost. Armed with metal poles from dismantled scaffolding, the crowd launched into a full-scale attack.

Simon caught hold of her hand. 'So sorry, petal,' he gasped, dragging Vicky after him. But when they finally reached an exit, it was barred. They were caught in a trap, rained on from above by stones, bits of brick and metal. It was instinctive to want to look up, and she felt a sudden sharp pain as a missile glanced across her cheek. Thank God it wasn't her eye. She started to shake uncontrollably.

'What are we going to do?' she yelled at Simon, just as a truncheon missed its intended victim and landed heavily on his free arm. He yelped, but still held her firmly in his grasp as they circled the square, panting like hunted animals, looking for any way out. Smoke was billowing out of the South African High Commission. It filled her throat and nostrils and she could hardly breathe.

'Oh God, do something,' she shouted at the ever-blackening sky, 'and I promise I'll never protest again.'

'Pray on, babe,' Simon shouted, when suddenly, as if by magic, a dark tunnel opened up in front of them, and there, at the end of it, was daylight. And then they were out, free, taking in huge gulps of glorious fresh air, whooping with relief. But they didn't stop running until they collapsed against the side of the coach.

'Broken?' she asked Simon, gently touching his arm, after they had slumped into their seats, exhausted, filthy and battle scarred. He moved it gingerly.

'No, just badly bruised. You've blood on your cheek.'

She got out a mirror and examined the wound. Only a scrape. No stitches needed, thankfully.

'Never again,' she groaned.

'Shame. I thought you'd make a professional,' Simon said, grinning.

She couldn't help but laugh when she noticed his teeth and eye sockets shiny white in his smut-covered face, like a miner after a long shift down the pit.

At Easter she went back to Trafalgar Square to try and locate the little snicket, as they referred to small alleyways in Sheffield. In vain. All the same: no putting God to the test, she said to herself, no more marches for me. Then the poll tax was dropped. And there was something immensely empowering about the knowledge that individuals really could change the course of history, if they were prepared to switch off the telly and get up out of their armchairs. Even if it meant ending up with one or two scars in the process.

'A safer cause is what you need, honey,' Jan had said, eyeing the narrow scab that ran along just under her eye, 'one closer to home. You British girls, you can only be deacons in the church, huh? You believe you can vicar as well as any man? Well, my lovely, that small step ain't going to happen on its own. Here's the news: the battle is on. So how come you're not a member of the Movement for the Ordination of Women?'

Vicky had intended showing her solidarity with her sister campaigners after Lambeth 1988, the ten-yearly conference of worldwide Anglican bishops, when a silent MOW vigil had been harangued by a group of male clergy shouting, 'Keep the whores out of the temple.' But she had prevaricated, afraid of being associated with what was sometimes perceived as a group of subversive, strident harpies, risking their futures by chaining themselves to a church Communion rail, or throwing themselves beneath the feet of a cathedral procession. That now seemed a pathetic excuse. 'Little Chicago' and the poll tax debacle had toughened her resolve.

Looking round the little group that stood with candles at a silent vigil in Sheffield Cathedral in June 1990, while the men were priested and the women were not, the MOW members seemed about as aggressive as pet rabbits. Theological arguments notwithstanding, the animosity to which they were subjected didn't make any rational sense. Every demonstration always ended with one of the members crying in a corner, broken by the vitriol and abuse they received. But Vicky had made up her mind that she would never again let herself be cowed by tyranny or abuse.

FEBRUARY 2020

Despite the fears that the photo had generated, looking back on those days, Vicky's pride at the way she'd kept that promise to herself was reignited. And look at where it had got her. Right on cue, Nick called to offer his congratulations. At last. Relief flooded through her.

'Nick, thank heavens. Where have you been? I've been trying to get hold of you.'

'Not peevish, surely, Vicky? It doesn't suit an archbishop.'

She realised she sounded like a neglected wife and laughed.

'Of course not. It's just . . . I do rely on your sound judgement and common sense.'

'So sorry, business abroad. And now here I am – to congratulate you on your splendid appointment. Very well deserved.'

There was something about the way he said it. Not exactly half-hearted. Just not quite fulsome enough for Nick.

'You are pleased?'

Even as the words left her mouth, she was annoyed with herself that his approval mattered, that she had depended on the good opinion of this man for so many years. But he had taken her under his wing when no one else had, nurtured and encouraged her, smoothed out obstacles in her path at a time when few women could rely on the offices of such a high-profile figure. A man whose politics were as far removed from hers as Mars from Venus. That was what was so extraordinary about their alliance.

They had met at General Synod, when she was a raw, newly elected member and vicar of a tetchy, obstreperous congregation – and badly in need of a crash course in Machiavellianism. And Nicholas Hamilton-Jones, Baron Westburton and business entrepreneur, was just the man to give it.

1990

For a beginner, Synod was bewildering. The Assembly Hall at Church House, Westminster is an impressive circular auditorium, panelled in polished oak all the way up to a wooden gallery that, much like a court-room, hosts a media enclave, visitors and observers. Above the gallery fifteen massive arched windows circles the room, rising steeply to a thirty-foot glass dome, surrounded by thirty-two gilded angels and, in gold letters, the aptly prophetic words, *'Holy is the true light and passing wonderful, lending radiance to them that endured in the heat of the conflict.'* Synod members sat on chairs in tiers like theatre-goers in the round.

On her first day, she sat down next to Simon Matthews, relieved to find someone who could show her the ropes.

He pecked her on the cheek and whispered, 'Been in any good riots lately?'

She threw him a withering look.

'Don't worry. You'll soon get the hang of this little kingdom. Once a debate gets underway, members leap to their feet to indicate a desire to speak in it, if they haven't sent in a form already; the chair decides who gets picked. If you're called, you state your name, diocese and number; and they light up on the panel over there. A little amber light will flash to say when you're running out of time.'

'Like the boating lake. 'Come in number 78, your time is up.'

'When the red light flashes you stop.'

'Or?'

'The chair will interrupt you. And if you still keep going, they'll turn your microphone off. And it will be a good while before you get called again.

'Sometimes the debates are good, sometimes deadly, like finances or legislation or people's pet subjects. We've spent the past three years nit-picking over the wording of liturgical prayers for the new prayer book.'

'The one we've got is perfectly decent.'

'Oh, don't you start . . .

The gathered throng was predominantly elderly and male, with sparse grey hair much in evidence, dressed in clerical black or pin-striped suits, blinking behind the reading spectacles perched on the end of their noses, wearing bland expressions of non-expectation.

'If I am any judge of people, there's as much communal ability at creative writing in this room as in a penguin colony.'

'Ah, but it's theological and doctrinal accuracy that counts,' he countered.

'So God won't play if we don't get the wording right?'

'It's about being sure the people in the congregation get the right messages.'

'Do you know,' she said, 'I always thought prayer was talking to God, not to one another.'

So the proceedings began. The camera-wielders in the gallery trained their long-range sights on the speakers. Some were interesting and erudite, others entertaining enough to merit an echoey haw-haw, one exuded a rather aggravating superciliousness, while others nervously clutched at their notes, rambled, mumbled or spoke in a monotone. A few played to the gallery. And all the while the bishops, men in double-breasted suits and purple shirts, sat in their serried ranks, arms folded, legs stretched out in front of them, in an effort of concentration that all but wrote their thoughts across their faces: 'How long, O Lord, how long?'

As if intuiting her boredom, Simon whispered, 'Of course, the most interesting stuff gets done over coffee in the corridors of power.' Sure enough, one year later, that was exactly where Vicky was approached by Lord Nick, just after she had delivered her maiden speech – a contribution to a debate on whether to allow children to take the bread and wine at Communion.

She had begun by describing how her daughter Alice, at two and a half, had once processed down the aisle of her church with the four stewards bearing the collection, and, as they stood in a row at the front, had offered up her much-loved, well-chewed toy rabbit. 'Who are we to say that a child can't grasp the full meaning of the Eucharist? Do we? How can we deny Communion to a child who has manifestly grasped the concept of sacrificial giving?

'Eleven years have passed since the *Children in the Way* report. And how much of it have we implemented in our churches? Virtually none. Children are no more welcome than they have ever been. Not only do we need to involve them in Communion, but our churches should have child-friendly liturgies with accessible illustrations, proper crèche facilities, toyboxes, art and clay-modelling tables, and paintwalls. Children are not the church of tomorrow, they are the church today, and its leaders one day, if we haven't driven them away first.'

She had slipped back into her seat to tumultuous applause. Simon turned to her and said out of the corner of his mouth, 'You deserve that. You're the only one who hasn't bored the pants off everyone so far today.'

But her balloon had been well and truly pricked by Arthur Jackson, the rather pompous little archdeacon from Saffron Walden, known for his fierce opposition to women priests, and for his Hitler-like moustache. He demolished every argument she had made in the name of silence, sanctity, order and reverence. It was like her selection conference all over again, with an added swipe at working mothers. 'The church is not a nursery. It seems sad to me that so many women are out at work during the week, and don't want the responsibility of their children at the weekend either.'

He too settled in his seat accompanied by vigorous applause, and Synod adjourned for lunch.

Feeling slightly sick, Vicky followed Simon to the tea room, a frenetic, rumbustious sort of place, where anything less than a raised voice couldn't make itself heard, and people used some kind of elementary sign language to indicate whether they wanted tea or coffee. While Simon waited in a long queue, she was alternately slapped on the back, studiously ignored, profusely thanked, or acknowledged with a curt nod that could have meant anything.

'Simon,' she mouthed at him, pointing at the door, 'I think I need some air. I'll see you later.'

'Well done, that was masterly.'

She had popped to the cloakroom for her coat – a bargain in carnation pink that amongst the rows of uniform grey appeared a lone voice of protest against the triumph of dreariness – and had almost reached the front door. The voice behind her was deep, distinguished and attractive-sounding. She turned, hoping she wouldn't be disappointed, and took in a striking-looking man of around fifty, with thick, waving, iron-grey hair, a firm jaw, and penetrating dark eyes. He held out a hand to her and she took it, the cold metal of a large ring pressing into her palm.

'Nick Hamilton-Jones. You're not upset by that pompous oaf of an archdeacon, are you?'

Vicky smiled and shook her head, aware that her hand was still being firmly held.

'You've no need to be. He has his little coterie here, but the rest of us take him with a pinch of salt. Whereas you have genuine passion. And the ability to sway opinion with it. That's what the church lacks. I'd like to talk further. Can we do lunch?'

Vicky expected her vague nod as she withdrew her hand to imply, 'Yes, sometime.'

'Tomorrow?' he asked.

And she found she had agreed.

'I think I've just been chatted up,' she whispered to Jenny James, back in the Assembly Hall. She and Jenny had sat together since Vicky's first Synod, when she had become aware of the person sitting on the other side from Simon, a nondescript sort of woman in her early forties, tradition-ally dressed, with a grey crop, a scrubbed complexion, and large, rimless glasses.

'How rude of me,' she had said. 'Sorry. Vicky Burnham-Woods.'

And Jenny, recovering from a yawn, had introduced herself with a smile that unmasked an attractive bow-shaped mouth, lively eyes and dimples.

'Did you know,' Jenny said, under her breath, 'that the Talmud says, "Ten measures of speech descended on the world. Women took nine of them, men one." The writer had manifestly never attended General Synod!'

In that instant Vicky knew that she had found a soul mate.

Jenny, a MOW stalwart, who had attended all the major protests and vigils from Carlisle to Chichester, was vicar of four rural parishes, single, and surprisingly, despite her rather dour taste in clothes, something of a *bon viveur*.

'Let's do The Golden Calf,' she had suggested that first lunchtime, when they had just met. 'It's a bit on the expensive side, but what the heck, it's your first Synod, so let's push the boat out.'

Jenny had taken her arm firmly and steered her out through the phalanx of male clergy, too engaged in their scintillating conversations to notice a woman trying to pass. Jenny whispered, 'Chivalry is manifestly dead in the C of E, now that women are no longer prepared simply to clean the brasses and make the tea.'

They had jollied their way down Dean's Yard, as skittish as two foals let loose from the stable.

'You know that Victoria Matthews has just been appointed Bishop of Edmonton in Canada?' Jenny said excitedly, like a sixth-former whose best friend has just been picked for the hockey team. 'They allowed women priests in twelve years ago. We've done six. We're on our way, girl, we're on our way.'

Westminster's favourite clerical eating house, The Golden Calf, called after the Bible's best-known guest of honour at an orgy of eating, drinking and cavorting, was always a busy hubbub of noise.

'Smile at everyone,' Jenny whispered conspiratorially as they were shown to a table for two. 'You may not know them, but it doesn't do any harm to be pleasant. And you never know when you might need an ally. With your looks, I would flutter the eyelashes too.'

'Jenny,' Vicky protested, but Jenny was deep in the menu.

'You see,' she said, once they had ordered, 'we're in the doldrums. Made priests in '92. Huge progress. Now – nothing. Settling down again to our British-style don't-rock-the-boat mentality. The trouble with women is that we don't put ourselves forward. Not like the men. We need to engage politically, get ourselves onto the organisations with influence, fill policy vacuums with our agenda, make ourselves high profile, get onto every diocesan committee, get articles in newspapers. That's the only way we'll become bishops.'

Vicky raised her eyebrows.

'Don't you want to be a bishop?' Jenny asked in surprise, slamming the menu shut. 'After today's performance my money would be on you for it. You have a very melodious voice, by the way, pleasant to listen to.' She thought for a moment. 'A bit like the tinkling of a glass harmonica. They say George Eliot, the writer, had a face like a double-decker bus but men fell in love with her when she spoke. You . . .'

Amused, Vicky dismissed the compliment.

'I think women should be bishops. But when it comes to me personally, my heart sinks at the prospect. How do the men do it? I'm permanently exhausted as it is.'

'They have wives, dear, to cook and clean and see to all their bodily needs. And they have secretaries for all the rest. Once or twice, it's been the other way round.'

Vicky laughed out loud.

'Oh you can laugh,' she remonstrated. 'I have four PCCs. Get your head round that. It's hard work and it's lonely. Think I couldn't be a bishop? Not that I'll ever get the chance.'

After a parfait of smoked salmon and asparagus, a fillet of chicken Provençale, a meringue basket filled with kiwis and pineapple, and two glasses of Chardonnay, Vicky felt in no fit state to sit through a debate on the wording of a response to the government's policy on armaments transfer.

'I shouldn't worry about it,' Jenny said as they ambled back. 'I doubt our deliberations will have any influence on the powers that be. Fifty years of synodical government, of nervous energy, adrenalin, enough paper to destroy a forest, and plenty of hot air to burn whatever wood might be left, and since when has the government taken a blind bit of notice of anything we ever decided?'

But if the business bored Jenny rigid, the gossip was a source of unending pleasure and enjoyment. She was an expert in the private lives and predilections of most of the men present. So all those months after their first lunch together, when Vicky leant towards her and whispered in her ear, Jenny asked with glee, 'OK, so who's chatted you up?'

Several heads turned in their direction.

'Shhhhh,' Vicky giggled, discreetly moving her eyes in Nick's direction.

'Lord Nicholas?'

Jenny's eyes opened wide in surprise.

'Are you sure?'

'That he's chatting me up? No, not really. Why? He's taking me out to lunch tomorrow.'

'Flirting's not normally his style. A bigwig in the Tory party, but not known for womanising. Though, admittedly, the two do seem to go together. Now if you'd said the Archdeacon of Pooley . . .'

'So what do I do?'

'Go, of course. Never say no to lunch. He's a very clever man, and a powerful one. With a patron like that you could go far.'

'There's no such thing as a free lunch,' Vicky whispered back doubtfully.

'By the way,' Jenny murmured, as the perennially-revived debate on minor nuances in the wording of the new prayer book rattled on, 'don't take any notice of Archdeacon Arthur. Not many do.'

'I'm not. Silly man. If he has his way there'll be no church for him to bishop in a few years' time.'

'I got the impression the two archbishops and many of the bishops agreed with you.'

'When people realise just how fast we're haemorrhaging children and young people, they'll change their tune.'

'I wouldn't bank on it. I sometimes think we have a death wish. Anyway, I hear the archdeacon's over-large wife runs the show. Nothing gets past her – in a manner of speaking.'

'So I've heard. That smirk of his while I was speaking almost threw me. I imagined him making love, climbing up a vast mound of pink flesh and balancing there like Noah's ark on Mount Ararat after the waters receded.'

'You are so naughty,' Jenny guffawed, turning it quickly into a cough in response to the hostile looks.

'It's a great leveller – sex. Where does pomposity go in the bedroom?'

'Well, I wouldn't know much about that, would I, being single?'

'But imagine, Jenny, isn't that why God hit upon such a daft way of propagating the human species? It reduces men to a heaving, helpless mass of hormones that's supposed to remind them of their basic humanity. If ever I feel in awe of a man, I imagine . . .'

'I think I'd rather not know,' Jenny said. 'I always prefer to focus on food. Shall we celebrate your triumph when this is over?'

Nick didn't stoop to The Golden Calf. He took her to Claridge's.

'Lord W—'

'Nick,' he interrupted.

'Nick, I'm not dressed for this.'

'Nonsense. You look wonderful in that pink coat, and every woman should do lunch in Claridge's at least once in her life.'

He not only chose the venue, but the table, even the food, and for some reason she didn't mind. In fact it was a relief not to have to make dozens of decisions – the lot of every vicar on an average day. And it was, she ruminated later, the perfect choice.

'Still basking in yesterday's glory?' Nick asked, as the waiter took their order, and removed himself discreetly to leave them in peace. 'Because you should be.'

'Strange, it was nerve-wracking, yet seductively stimulating at the same time.'

'Sharing your vision should be, for anyone with a real passion for their topic. It's the gift of a good leader to take your people with you.'

'I can't wait to have another go. There are so many important issues buzzing around in my head.'

He laughed as the waiter reappeared with asparagus mornay, and arranged the pristine, crisp table napkins on their laps. Vicky was relieved she hadn't gone ahead with an earlier instinct to do it for herself.

'I look forward to it.'

'On the basis of my performance, I have been invited to chair a working party on children and the Eucharist.'

'Good. Excellent.'

'Not the same kudos as chairing a committee on sexuality.'

'But with potentially more lasting significance. Choose your battles, Vicky. Don't fritter away vital energy on what is never going to change. Now, tell me more about you, and that no doubt lovely family of yours.'

And she obeyed, as she suspected most people did. But then Nick was a charming and sympathetic listener, not allowing any interruptions to distract those extraordinarily dark eyes for longer than a second or two. She found herself sharing her life story through the sole meunière, the exotic cheeseboard, coffee and house truffles. She told him of all her difficulties in the parish with Ken the retired copper and Stan the hen-pecked newsagent, her two rogue churchwardens who had never wanted a woman vicar in the first place. And Nick had seemed hugely entertained.

'Humour them, Vicky. Make them laugh. Flatter them. And then enlist their support in selling your strategy to your PCC. And if they won't, leave them behind and work with people who do share your vision. You'll have the majority on your side. Of that I have no doubt.'

He wiped his mouth on his napkin, folded it, then threw it onto the table, a signal for the waiter to arrive with a bill that his lordship simply signed.

'Thank you,' he said to her, nodding courteously, then, as he walked round to pull out her chair, 'I did enjoy that.'

'So did I,' she said. 'Thank you so much, not just for lunch, but also the invaluable tips on handling unruly church members.'

They took a taxi back to Church House, and she promised to keep in touch. Heading for the ladies' cloakroom to touch up her lipstick, she realised that apart from the fact that he had two adult children from his first marriage and a toddler from his second, she knew no more about him. He feared boring her, he had said, with a vague wave of the hand, when she had tried to engage him on his business and political interests.

A week later a card arrived inviting her and Tom to dine with Lord and Lady Westburton at their Knightsbridge home. It was a pleasant enough evening, once Vicky had got over the shock of meeting Nick's wife, who was as far removed from her mental image of her as it was possible to be. Maura was a great deal younger than Nick, with kohl-blackened eyes and in a skirt so short it was barely there. Vicky had expected someone who would at the very least match his intellect, but, much as she hated to admit it, he had chosen a partner who seemed little more than a bimbo, with minimal interest in conversation. Since Tom spent the whole evening ogling her, though, she obviously had some attractions that Vicky was ill-equipped to appreciate.

When she said so to Tom on the way home, he protested, 'And he's an old charmer, with eyes only for you.'

'It's not like that, Tom.'

'I believe you – just, which means many wouldn't. I can see the head-lines now. The Lord and the Lady Vicar.'

FEBRUARY 2020

She had felt uneasy, but Nick never gave her cause for concern. His atten-tiveness was flattering, of course, but it fed a father-shaped, mentoring hole in her life, rather than any sexual desire. What she was to him, she couldn't quite define. But he had always been there for her when she needed encouragement, support or a shoulder to cry on, lobbying on her behalf in difficult Synod debates where she was the lead speaker, advising on business management and the art of gentle manipulation throughout her time as vicar, archdeacon and ultimately, bishop. Occasionally she wondered whether he hadn't had a hand in her promotion, and that worried her. But then she dismissed the idea as ridiculous. How could he? And why would he?

'My dear,' Nick insisted now down the phone line, 'of course I'm delighted. You think I won't enjoy having a hotline to the Archbishop of Canterbury? I'm incredibly proud of you. You've met our young puppy of a Prime Minister, I take it?'

'We had a rather robust discussion. He worries me. He's so thoroughly secular that he has no comprehension of the importance of freedom of speech in moral and ethical matters, no awareness at all of the value of religion.'

'That's our Prime Minister, the epitome of the post-modern man – no awareness of history, tradition, monarchy, loyalty, self-sacrifice, and I could go on. And have you had the pleasure of meeting that nancy boyfriend of his?'

'Nick,' she said, shocked to the core.

'A beautiful boy, no doubt, but nothing between the ears.'

It was tempting to make a reference to pots and kettles, but instead she said, 'Do be careful. Thinking such thoughts can get you into trouble these days, let alone saying them out loud.'

She heard the smile in his voice.

'Let anyone who dares, take me on. My legal folk have never lost a case yet. But less of this doom-saying. When and how shall we celebrate your success?'

In the end, Vicky would have neither the time nor the will to celebrate. The following day, news broke that she knew would impact her time in office in a way little else could. But a case of the finest claret arrived at Bishop's House regardless.

SEVEN

All human rights, be they social, economic, religious, or political are interrelated. They must be taken as a whole. The churches should give them equal importance and seek the application of all of them.

JÜRGEN MOLTMANN

MARCH 2020

'Have you seen the news?'

Vicky looked up from her desk as Jenny's face filled her screen, looking unusually sombre. She gave a quick snort.

'You must be joking. Too busy dealing with mounds of correspondence – mainly well-wishers, but with the occasional abusive letter from the loony brigade thrown in, accusing me of emasculating every male in my orbit and suggesting I submit to the authority of my husband.'

For once, Jenny ignored her.

'For God's sake, take a look at what our idiotic government plans to do next, and see if anything can be done. Best of luck – or perhaps I should say, I shall be on my knees in prayer if you need me!'

Vicky reached for her e-reader and scanned, with increasing horror, the news of proposed government legislation to curb what it referred to as 'the rising tide of extremism driven by organised recruitment networks harnessing alienated young adults with the aim of starting a full-on cyberwar.' To counter this threat an 'Anti-Proselytising Bill' would be rushed through Parliament in a bid to protect Britain's essential services and institutions.

She read on, feeling almost winded, as the implications sank in. Any religious activity in a public place, except in a building designated for that purpose, would be prohibited without special licence from the local council – including school and workplace meetings, outdoor services, and the handing out or posting of leaflets door to door. Places of worship would be closely monitored for preaching or activity that could be classed as doctrinaire, pressurising or offensive, or as an incitement to criminal behaviour (including aggressive recruitment). No new places of worship could be opened without a special licence that would only be granted on the basis of their proving they were not a sect. No new buildings could be bought or built for religious purposes without permission of the government.

On the face of it, the government was acting to prevent the increasing Islamisation of disaffected young people, predominantly black. The truth was that whether by ignorance or design, the bill threatened the right of every Christian to follow what they believed was biblical truth and obey Jesus' command to make disciples. It could, she imagined, be stretched to include any introduction to Christianity – Christianity Explored, Simply Christianity, the Alpha course. It was a secularist charter, benefiting no one, least of all the British public, whose rights to freedom of speech and religion were being eroded by subterfuge.

Jenny was right. She would have to act, but what should she do?

Don't give in to impulse, she commanded herself, as she almost ran upstairs to the chapel. The moment she closed the door, she realised she was too agitated to sit. Instead, she paced around its confined space, haranguing God with her need for his urgent intervention. Then she did what she had always advised her parishioners never to do. She took out her Bible and let it fall open at random. Ezekiel. Not her favourite book. Too much judgement and warfare. Chapter 33. The watchman on the city wall:

> If he sees the sword coming upon the land and blows the trumpet and warns the people and they ignore him, their blood shall be on their own head, but if they listen it will save their lives. But if the watchman sees the sword coming and does not blow the trumpet and warn the people, I will hold the watchman responsible for the people's blood.

That'll do. Thank you God, she breathed. I'll be the best watchman I can.

Back in her study, she pressed her video intercom and Marissa appeared on the screen.

'Marissa, get me the PM, will you?'

'Of course, Bishop.'

Vicky noticed that Marissa had reverted to calling her 'Bishop' since the announcement. Her face disappeared, but her dismembered voice said excitedly to whoever was with her in the office, 'Guess what? I've got to call Downing Street. She's on the warpath.'

'Ah, Archbishop, or is it still Bishop officially?'

'Archbishop Elect, officially, but you can always call me Vicky.'

'Ah, ah yes,' stammered the Prime Minister's voice as her computer whistled and his face came into view. 'Anyway, what a pleasant surprise.'

Vicky was taken aback by the charm offensive. He must surely know how she would respond to his government's actions. Or was he simply naive?

'Is all well? The family? The preparations?'

It was tempting to tell him to cut the crap, but she forced herself to submit to the time-wasting, though necessary, niceties.

'Family and preparations are fine, thank you, Prime Minister. And you and your partner? All's well, I hope.'

'We're good, when we get the chance to see each other. The usual burdens of government.'

'And that's exactly why I'm calling, as I think you may have guessed.'

'Ah!'

'I've been looking at the proposed anti-proselytising laws, and I'm wondering whether you appreciate their implications?'

He smiled at her wanly, and held up a pair of pale, unblemished palms as if to say, 'I have no idea what you mean.' Pontius Pilate, she said to herself. If nothing else convinced her of his deviousness, this feigned innocence did.

'No open-air services, no act of worship at the cenotaph on Remembrance Sunday, no carolling at Christmas, no Salvation Army bands in the streets, no Good Friday marches. And no street pastors, who do so much to support the police in preventing post-pub-and-club rowdiness and crime on a weekend night.'

'Oh,' he said mildly, 'I think you'll find permission will be granted for most of those.'

'Provided all those hundreds of separate groups can be bothered to go through what will no doubt end up being a complex, labour-intensive permission procedure for every individual event. And there would be no guarantee that a particular council would be sympathetic to their request. And as for monitoring churches for pressurising, offensive preaching, who is to decide what is pressure and whether it's offensive? It is totally subjective. We are a nation of the offended. The nature of preaching is to offend from time to time. As Jesus did.'

'You must surely understand the main thrust of these proposals – to prevent at source, if we can, any further cyber-attacks?'

'I fully sympathise with your concerns, but with the greatest respect, I can't see how this legislation will achieve your purpose. It will only alienate and radicalise the youth of our country even further. Not to mention giving offence to the moderate Muslims whose support you need to win.'

'And you know this how?'

'I know from experience here in Larchester that the only way to protect young people is to offer them acceptance, opportunity and hope, to listen to them, not penalise them. The truth is that these new laws will end up being used primarily against Christians, since the police will fear being accused of racism if they're seen to discriminate against Muslims. It's a denial of the basic human right of freedom of speech and religion for all.'

'Neither Civitas nor Liberty have expressed any concerns.'

'Because they're deeply secular organisations, and unaware of the difficulties this will make for Christians in this country. I suspect the bill may also alienate large numbers of the black community, who make up some of the largest, and most significant churches in London.'

'Ah, playing a racist card, are you?'

'I'm saying that the Judeo-Christian tradition is the moral basis for our democratic and legal system. Without it, what will be the yardstick for our social attitudes and behaviours? You are throwing out the baby with the bathwater. And something will move in to take its place. Quite likely, in many places, a more fundamentalist form of Islam.'

'Don't preach at me, Bishop,' he snapped. 'If you want the honest truth, members of my cabinet are fast losing patience with the fact that the church is still so resistant to the government line on equality.'

'Ah, so this is about gay marriage, not Islamisation and cyber-warfare at all?'

'Let's just say there are different ways to skin a cat.'

Was that a smile? Vicky dug her nails deeply into her palms in an effort to control her temper. How often had she preached that in every situation, before they launched themselves in, Christians should ask themselves what Jesus would say or do, then pray for the grace to say or do it? That, she was sure, was the key to love and unity, possibly to changing the world. But put on the spot, preaching it and living it were two very different things.

She took a deep breath and said quietly, but as firmly as she could, 'Prime Minister, I have already said that you must beware of overplaying your hand. You can only deny people their basic freedoms for so long.'

'Archbishop, I really wouldn't advise meddling in government policy,' he said smoothly.

The battle lines were drawn, it seemed. Hardly the best way to start, and not, she knew, what either of them wished for the relationship. Then how to ease the tension?

'Tell me,' she thought to ask, 'what is it about Christianity that you hate so much?'

'If you had to sit through as many dull services as I do, when there are so many more useful things I could be doing . . .'

'I sit through far more than you, if I may say so. And I couldn't agree with you more.'

He leant forward into the screen and looked straight at her.

'You couldn't?'

'I didn't ask what you thought of church, though. I asked what you thought of Christianity.'

'Is there a difference?'

'An immense difference. The church is a very human expression of faith, subject therefore to all our shortcomings, and I do apologise that it hasn't inspired you as it should. Christianity is dynamic, life transforming, a great adventure – never knowing where God might take you or what you might be called on to do. Full of surprises. I wouldn't be here now if that weren't the case. I never wanted it.'

'I got where I wanted.'

'And then? If it all eludes you at the next election? I'd give anything to run away and be a vicar somewhere out of the public gaze, somewhere I could make a lasting contribution to a local community. I suspect that's far more important than the macro. Though,' she said, interrupting his attempt to argue, 'it's tempting to want to change the world too.'

'Then do it,' he said smiling, throwing her the gauntlet.

'I'll do my darnedest, I promise you.'

One thing was certain, she said to herself, as the last vestiges of the Prime Minister faded from her screen, she had to find a way to bring the disparate groups in the church back together, for the sake of the country, to preserve their freedom of religion for future generations.

Just before Jesus died, he had prayed that his followers might be one. Had that prayer been answered? She often wondered, but if Jesus had prayed it, that was encouragement enough to pursue the ideal. In truth, there was only one church: his. Race and class, doctrine and denomination paled into insignificance by comparison with the task at hand.

The press wasn't blind to the implications of the bill, either, however, and besieged Mike Barnes for interviews. He released a short statement to the effect that the Bishop was exceedingly disturbed at legislation that could be used to curb freedom of speech and religion, two basic rights in any truly democratic society – and duly received a slap over the wrists from the Church House press office. They and they alone would determine what the Archbishop Elect might or might not say to the press.

'Not much freedom of speech in the church either, then,' she said wryly, to reassure her sheepish-looking press officer. 'Don't take it to heart, Mike. I know what a great job you've done for me.'

* * *

Neither they nor Church House, however, had any control over Tom's relationship with the press. Vicky was horrified that he should be subject to scrutiny at all. But in the great battle for sales, one tabloid journalist went grubbing around the hospital. Scrape hard enough and there will always be dirt underneath.

The newspaper claimed that Tom had a reputation for being auto-cratic and unpleasant. He was unpopular with the management, high-handed with his colleagues, rude to patients. As she read it, Mike watched her face with concern.

'It's clever, isn't it?' she said. 'Malice discovers something in which there's just an element of truth, builds it into a gun and shoots him with it. Of course Tom can be high-handed at the hospital – he's a consultant, after all. Especially when some petty diktat from senior management shows no understanding of patient care. He can be abrupt with colleagues who don't pull their weight, or patients who ignore his medical advice. But no one can fault him in his dedication. Or his skills.'

She had accepted that her own private life would be dissected into bits of a jigsaw puzzle, its constituent parts broken down for inspection and critiqued until no one remembered the whole picture. Any public figure is a legitimate target for quack analysis. But what did Tom have to do with it?

'Can anything be done, Mike?'

'Let's see if we can't find some very "pleased for him and his missus", satisfied patient stories and set the record straight,' he said, 'and blow Church House.'

Tom didn't blame her, despite a number of his patients ringing the hospital and asking for their care to be transferred to another consultant. She doubted she would have been so magnanimous under similar circum-stances. But he was privately incensed. So two days later, when he opened the back door to go to work and a journalist virtually fell in, he picked him up by the lapels and manhandled him halfway down the drive, shout-ing into his face, 'This is a private residence – or are you illiterate as well as stupid?'

The bad news was that his photographer had hidden in the bushes, ready to pounce as Tom left the house. He managed to get a close-up of the future Archbishop's husband snarling like a tiger with its prey between its paws. The good news was that the journalist was a small man, in body as well as mind, and a photograph of him dangling like a dummy from Tom's powerful grip did little for his street cred.

Tom, in fact, became all but a national hero – but from Vicky's perspec-tive, it was all a little too close for comfort. What if the Sophie Carpenter case were dredged up again? It was done with, over, finished. It must not be resurrected.

Was she mad to have accepted the post? But then, she so nearly hadn't gone through with ordination either, and look what she would have missed. That was the thing about a calling. Whatever the risks, however great the fears, it must be followed. What would be, would be.

JULY 1992

Every diocese demanded of its prospective curates that they spend three days on retreat before ordination, and as she prepared for it Vicky felt wracked by uncertainty. She had, after all, only been married ten days. The week honeymooning in a cottage in Devon had seemed so fleeting before the move here to the curate's house on a large council estate.

Unpacked boxes filled every available space. But the carpets were down and the curtains up and it might almost have felt like home, but for the constant, floor-shaking boom of a next-door teenager's hi-fi.

'I think I might even welcome silence,' she said to Tom, as she wrestled a small suitcase, and the large plastic wardrobe bag containing cassock and surplice, down the narrow stairs into the open-plan living area. 'Grief, I didn't realise these things were so heavy.'

Tom leapt up but she had already reached the bottom, so, seeing his help was no longer needed, he flung himself back into an armchair and slung one leg over the arm. Picking up the dictionary he had just dug out of one of the packing cases, he read out, ' "Retreat. Asylum, refuge, sanctuary", or, wait, here's another definition: "turning in the opposite direction and running like hell". That's your response to marriage, is it?'

'Don't sulk, my love. The honeymoon may be over but I've left you three evening meals stacked up in the fridge. To make up for taking the car. But I have to say, the sooner you learn to cook the better.'

He got up, drew her into his arms and kissed her.

'Really want to go?' he asked, rubbing her bottom lip with his forefinger.

She didn't. She still wasn't used to the male, musky smell of him, and longed to stay here in his arms, comfortable and secure.

'That's exactly why a retreat is compulsory,' she laughed, pushing him away. 'It comes from the Old Testament commandment to priests to refrain from you-know-what before ministering in the Temple because it made them unclean.'

'Tommy-rot.'

'Not then it wasn't, when they had no running water, and couldn't wash.'

'Then was four thousand years ago. Will the Church of England ever modernise?'

She planted a chaste farewell kiss on his cheek to pre-empt any more debate on the subject, and leapt into the car.

The directions she had been given for St Joseph's monastery brought her to a large, Victorian, neo-Gothic mansion that had seen better times. Once in open countryside, it now teetered on the edge of a brand-new, expensive commuter development, an anachronistic mausoleum with peeling paintwork and mossy walls. The bottle-green front door creaked open just enough for her to sidle into a dank and gloomy hallway smelling of beeswax and boiled cauliflower. An expressionless monk in a badly frayed cassock led her up the stone stairs and down a long, dismal corridor, to a cell-like room with a tiny window and linoleum floor. The only decoration was a large, wooden crucifix over the bed. She dumped her suitcase and cassock on the bed and picked up a scrappy timetable from the bedside table. The typewriter had a leaping 'e'. Word processors hadn't made it here yet, then.

The window looked out on a pretty, well-tended garden twenty feet below that dipped away to a gate in a hedge, then out to undulating fields extending to the horizon – and freedom. How many sheets would it take to reach the ground, should the need for escape prove overwhelming? Stupid woman, she said, shaking herself. All she needed to do was make her apologies and walk out through the front door. There was no failure in deciding, even at this stage, that ordination wasn't for her. A mere ten days ago, as she held his arm to walk down the aisle, her father had whispered, 'Still time to change your mind.' Her mother, pushing past them to a front pew, snapped, 'Don't be ridiculous, Cyril. What would we say to the guests?'

What would Tom say if she gave up now? He had just taken a job in paediatrics at Basildon University Hospital. It didn't bear thinking about. But the truth was that Jan's disappearance back to the States had deeply unsettled her.

'Why so sudden? What's the rush?' Vicky had asked, as she watched Jan piling bedding, table lamps, crockery and cutlery – all the precious stuff of hers that had become so familiar over the past three years – into a trunk labelled 'Boston'. 'You haven't even finished your PhD.'

'It's just too tough here for a woman in ministry. Your good old English misogyny is taking far too long to die.'

All the way to the airport Jan had remained tight-lipped and tense, until the moment they had said their goodbyes.

'Don't think badly of me, will you, Vicky?' she begged, the tears welling up in her eyes, before she almost crushed her with the force of that one last embrace.

'Why would I think badly of you? Write to me,' Vicky called after her as she disappeared into the no-man's-land on the other side of airport security. 'Promise.'

But there had been no communication, and the pain of that silence had been immense. Jan had been sister, confidante, role model. If she, with all her experience, thought it impossible for a woman to be a minister in the UK, what hope was there for Vicky?

She studied the crucifix above the bed and found it uninspiring – a manufactured Christ figure with lugubrious eyes, looking up into a bleak expanse of whitewashed ceiling. But perhaps that sense of abandonment and aloneness was an inevitable part of the human landscape. For him. For her, newlywed as she was.

Why hadn't she talked to Tom about her anxieties? There was no chance just before the wedding. And then, he had been pushed into a new job and home, in an area where he was a fish out of water. What could she say? Men didn't seem to be plagued by feelings of professional inadequacy, at least, not to the same degree as women. Paranoia, she could hear him say, dismissively, as if it were a uniquely female complaint. Some words by the American suffragette, Elizabeth Cady Stanton, suddenly came to her. *'Whatever the theories may be of woman's dependence on man, in the supreme moments of her life he cannot bear her burdens.'* This was one of those moments.

She had barely had time to throw a few bits of underwear into a drawer and hang the cassock on the door, when the supper bell clanged downstairs – an invitation to seventies school-dinner-style fare: a piece of lettuce, three slices of cucumber, half a tomato, supermarket coleslaw, a baked potato and a thin piece of ham, served up alongside piles of sliced packet bread at trestle tables in a draughty refectory. They sat together, the eight almost-curates, wordlessly passing the salad cream or custard back and forth, nodding and smiling at each other, shaking a head and pointing emphatically when they got the salt instead of the water jug.

It was over in twenty minutes. Food without conversation has little substance. They scraped their plates, stacked them on a trolley, and were ushered into a room with faded, floral curtains and a threadbare carpet where the retreat conductor, an archdeacon from another diocese, exhorted them to make the most of this unique opportunity to reflect on the demands and commitment of their calling. 'Modern life is so cluttered with words that we think we can't live without them. So here we fast, not from food, but from our constant human babble – which can be frightening if we have never done it before, but is nonetheless essential. Before we touch the darkness in others, we must confront the hidden, darker side of ourselves and bring it into God's light.'

It rained solidly for three days, denying Vicky the peaceful seclusion of the little bench she had glimpsed on arrival nestling under a copper beech beneath her window, and effectively imprisoning her in her cell. She stared at the wall, or at the door, where the cassock and surplice hung like some headless cleric, rebuking her inability to take up the lifestyle they represented with grace and fervour.

By the last day she was sick to death of her self, hidden or otherwise. She felt she had turned it inside out, upside down, shaken it about and generally become very bored – as was typical of an extrovert who relied on others for insight and stimulation. There had been no 'Aha' moments, no illumination from heaven, not even after the statutory half-hour with the retreat conductor, who assured her that doubts were normal at this stage, healthy even – a sign that she wasn't merely seeking status.

'Thanks, pal,' she muttered at the crucifix. 'For three days, I've done nothing but regale you with my uncertainty and inadequacies. And what do I get in return? Nada. Silence.'

She had had only two verbal exchanges since she had arrived, one with a monk who pointed to the bowl of stewed prunes at breakfast and whispered, 'We call these our little missionaries. They go into all the dark places and do you good.' The other was with the bishop, who popped in to rally his troops, patted her on the bottom and said, 'I've known some very fine women in ministry. You go for it, my dear.'

She was beginning to feel desperate for some kind of meaningful human contact, and it was Tom's voice she needed to hear most. She crept out of the house and headed down the drive in search of a telephone booth. It was madness. Tom worked long shifts and she had no idea yet of his on or off calls. The chances of finding him in were remote.

The drive, enclosed on either side by overhanging trees, was in total darkness. She rooted in the bottom of her bag for the tiny torch she kept for emergencies, along with hair grips, nail clippers, elastoplasts, paracetamol and a small screwdriver, but all she could lay her hands on was an array of lipsticks and throat lozenges.

'Women's handbags,' she heard Tom mutter despairingly every time she stood at her front door, unable to dig out the key.

'Teachers,' she countered, 'are prepared for any eventuality. Unlike doctors, obviously.'

Now, as her hands grasped a small, tubular shape, she felt a surge of triumph.

Emerging onto the main road after almost three days in captivity, the relentless flash of headlights, the roar of engines and the smell of their fumes were an assault on her senses. Where was that phone box? She continued for what felt like a mile up the road, the thought of hearing Tom's voice drawing her on, and at last found the box. It stank inside of mildew, rusting metal and the kind of human detritus she didn't want to think about.

'Come on. Pick up, please,' she begged the stale-smelling mouthpiece, as the ringing tone continued. Reluctantly she hung up, tears stinging the backs of her eyes.

The thought of going back to that lonely, oppressive little room was more than she could bear. And then she vaguely remembered passing a newspaper kiosk on her way to the monastery. Or had it been an hallucination? Why would there be one out here? But if there were . . . Chocolate. The sudden rush of saliva galvanised her into a march and then, there it was, her salvation, illuminated against the night sky. Open. She almost wept with relief, and took the last yards at a run.

Despite the heavy thud of her shoes and the thump of her elbows as they landed on the counter the man behind it didn't as much as look up. His head remained face down on his folded arms. Just her luck, the one time she really needed human help, and the only human available was asleep. Tough. Her need was greater than his. She reached out and shook his arm. He started, raised his head and blinked in an effort to focus. His eyes were red-rimmed. With the palm of his hand he rubbed his face from his forehead down to his chin, sniffed and muttered, 'Where the hell did you spring from?'

'St Joseph's, the monastery up the hill.'

He nodded. 'That figures. Silent, is it? They all end up here. Fags, was it?'

Feeling a little bad about her self-obsession, she said, 'Look, I don't want to interfere, but you seem a bit . . . down. Is there anything I can do for you?'

'That's funny,' he replied, with a forced smile.

'What is?' Vicky asked, uncertainly.

'You. Asking if you can help me. It's supposed to be the other way round. I ask you what I can help you with – ciggies, a newspaper, a can, or maybe chewing gum? That's my job. But since you ask, and I don't know why I'm telling you this, it's been a bummer of a day.'

She waited, watching him, willing him to trust her enough to share the reason for his distress.

'Took a short break this afternoon and found the wife had gone. Says she can't stand any more of this life – unsociable hours, financial uncertainty, me and my bad temper. So here I am, left to run the business, and no one to go home to.'

'Anyone else involved?'

She wasn't normally this bold, but this situation wasn't normal.

He looked up at her sharply and she thought she'd blown it, that he was going to tell her to get lost, as he probably should. But instead he shook his head.

'Children?'

'Just the one – seventeen. Never gets out of bed, lazy oaf.'

'Was there a note?'

'What is this? Twenty questions? Okay, okay, yes. Said she'd had enough of sitting here day after day, of my never being there for her, of not being appreciated.'

Misery was etched into every line of his craggy face. Vicky knew she must tread carefully, aware that one wrong word would make him clam up like an oyster.

'You said she'd left you with the business to run. What is she to you, business or marriage partner?'

'What's the difference?'

'For a woman? Everything.'

He thought for a while, and Vicky grabbed the chance to take a quick peep at her watch. Fifteen minutes until lock-up at the monastery. The tiniest flicker of comprehension crossed the man's face.

'You mean . . . I didn't treat her like a woman needs to be treated?'

Vicky nodded encouragingly, resisting the urge to shuffle from foot to foot.

'You could be right. She never wanted this place. But after they made me redundant I – well, it was my dream, and anyway I didn't know what else to do with the money. The other night she said I wouldn't notice the difference if she wasn't there.'

He paused, studied his hands that had been resting on the counter.

'I told her to go. I'd cope without her.'

'So she took you at your word?'

He shook his head slowly.

'I didn't mean it.'

'You still love her?'

He took a large, grimy handkerchief out of his pocket, and wiped his face with it.

'Then find out where she is, and tell her.'

He looked doubtful.

'It's not that simple.'

No, it isn't, Vicky thought. But I've only got eleven minutes. Come on, God. Do something for this poor guy. Get through to him.

He looked up at her, and frowned.

'If I tell the missus I want her back . . . you think it would work?'

'I can't guarantee it. But telling someone you love them can't hurt. You will have to be prepared for a long haul. Reconciliation doesn't happen overnight. And it'll cost you. You'll have to make changes. But what matters to you most? And now I'm going to pray for you – if it's all right with you.'

He nodded, but to her consternation, instead of closing his eyes, stared straight at her with something akin to alarm.

'Name?' she asked, lowering her eyes so as not to embarrass him.

'Kev,' he whispered.

'Then Father, give Kev a miracle and help him get his missus back. Show him what to do, and when. Amen.'

And she knew, at that moment, with one of those strange certainties that defy logic and reason, that the prayer was answered. When she looked up at Kev he was studying her face with amazement. 'I've never experienced anything like that before. I feel such . . . so peaceful. Are you my guardian angel?'

'Do angels eat chocolate? Because this one likes fruit and nut. Two big bars.'

She insisted on paying, though he was loath to take the money. Then she stuffed the chocolate into her bag, and set off down the main road at a run. There was no time to find the torch. She managed to negotiate the drive, but missed one of the steps up to the old oak door, just as it opened without warning. Cursing loudly, she found herself sprawled at the feet of the guest master, just taking the large iron key out of his habit pocket.

'Dear, dear,' he said, helping her to her feet, just a hint of a smile curving the corners of his mouth. 'Blessing rather than damning these steps might be a better way of sparing future visitors your predicament.'

Having satisfied himself that she wasn't hurt, he gave her a curt goodnight and disappeared down the corridor, leaving her to rearrange her skirt and bemoan another pair of wrecked tights.

Back in her room, she threw herself on the bed, retrieved the chocolate from her bag and bit off a large chunk. Well, she said to herself, lying back and letting the velvety sweetness fill her mouth and slip reassuringly down her throat, I can see why some women think this is a pretty good alternative to sex. At least it's always readily available.

The crucifix above her head caught her attention.

'So?' she asked, sitting up and facing it. 'A sign? A timely intervention for Kev, or for me? Or for both of us?' Why had their paths crossed at that particular moment? If not a ministering angel, she had been a messenger of hope. The very thing she wanted to share with a world that was dying for the lack of it, like a giant beached whale without water.

As she brushed her teeth at a sink so small there was nowhere to put a bar of soap, she said to her reflection in the single, tiny mirror in the room, 'Coward. You cannot shirk this enormous challenge just because it feels too big, or allow yourself to be defeated by disappointment and self-doubt. So help you God.'

She awoke the following morning, ordination day, after her first decent night's sleep there, to an excitement she could only describe as joy, irrational, unexpected, uncalled for. 'I'm going to live on a sink estate,' she said out loud, 'and I want to, because it's where I'm meant to be, doing what I'm meant to do. How barmy is that?'

She decided to forgo the breakfast prunes, and instead spent an hour reading and praying, a discipline she determined to maintain throughout her ministry. God first, husband next, and then the church. Always that order.

Murphy's Law. The rain had cleared and the sun's rays warmed her back as she walked out to the car. She laid the cassock and surplice on the back seat. Like a shroud. Ah well, she said, may that be a reminder to me to die to my selfishness.

As she drove off on her way to the cathedral, she kept one eye on the pavement, looking out for the kiosk. There it was, shuttered and silent. A good omen? But there was little time to wonder about Kev before the cathedral towers materialised in the distance, the stonework creamy white in the sunlight.

EIGHT

*I didn't go to religion to make me happy. I always knew a bottle
of Port would do that. If you want a religion to make you feel
really comfortable, I certainly don't recommend Christianity.*

C. S. LEWIS

APRIL 2020

The months leading up to her enthronement at Canterbury Cathedral
were a head-spinning whirl of preparations and decisions – the hymns,
the anthems, the readings, the robes, the guest list, food for the select
dinner afterwards. It was like a wedding on a grand scale, enacted on a
huge public stage but with no groom to share her limelight.

A pot of anti-wrinkle cream for men had suddenly appeared on the
bathroom shelf.

'What's with the face cream, Tom?' Vicky asked, as she got into bed
next to him.

'Oh, that?'

'It looks more expensive than anything I use.'

Tom continued reading, but finally gave in to her persistence.

'What you think are laughter lines, she thinks are premature wrinkles,'
he quoted. 'I was taken in.'

She peered into his face.

'I don't think they're wrinkles. I think they are great lines. Each one
chiselled out by life's experiences. That's what makes men their most
attractive.'

'I don't want the world to see me as the wizened old boy in the background – like Denis Thatcher.'

She ran her hands down his chest.

'You? Wizened? That'll be the day. I'll be fighting off the admirers.'

They laughed. That didn't happen enough, Vicky thought to herself.

The ultimate responsibility for the enthronement service lay with the
Dean of Canterbury Cathedral. And the new Dean was none other than
her old *bête noire* from her archdeaconing days, 'two-chevrons-apart'
Julian Riley. The former Dean of Westbury was a thin-faced, rather

pompous cleric, who reminded her of the television vicars she watched as a child, with his over-large teeth in his rather prissy mouth. With no bishopric in sight he had accepted this role, Canterbury's importance making up for the theoretically sideways move. But she suspected he would rather be sitting where she was now. She couldn't imagine he'd taken kindly to her promotion. As an archdeacon she had crossed swords with him on several occasions.

Vicky had waited impatiently to be lined up in his Employment Sunday procession, for a service at which she was designated to preach. The pecking order had to be right. In Roman times processions were a display of power and status. Manifestly, little had changed in the church in two thousand years.

They were to appear in reverse order of seniority – choir members leading the way, representatives of the Chamber of Commerce and the city's major industries in the middle, the Dean and Bishop at the very back. The Dean, whose obsession for detail was legendary, insisted they allow exactly two paces between themselves and those they followed, and walk in a dignified, upright manner, with expressions befitting the solemnity of the occasion. It was only when he had finished moving his chess players into place that he turned and saw Vicky standing a little apart.

'Archdeacon,' he complained, as if she were a tiresome child, 'why didn't you attract my attention? I've just got it right.'

The truth was that it had been such fun watching him that she couldn't forgo a little mischief.

'Sorry to spoil your symmetry, Dean, but I don't mind where you put me.'

'Nonsense,' he snapped, grabbing her arm and thrusting her unceremoniously into line in front of him.

It was unfortunate to have him so close, because just as they moved from the aisle into the nave she heard a loud stage whisper behind her.

'Two chevrons apart, Archdeacon.'

What bloody chevrons? she wondered. This isn't a motorway. And then she looked down, and saw the series of inverted V-shaped markings chalked upon the flagstones. After that, she couldn't resist standing purposefully on each of them all the way to her pew in the front.

Her own feeling about her enthronement was limited to the desire that people should have an occasion to take their minds off the fears spread by the cyber-attack on the tube, and the joyless, grinding austerity that had pursued the country for the past ten years; that they should reflect instead on a higher, more glorious and certain reality. But how to make the service joyous, alive and contemporary while maintaining the solemnity, dignity and formality of the occasion? How to placate, if not please, traditional old Julian? After all, he would be her Dean in Canterbury, with unrivalled access to her. She would do well to have him on her side, if she could.

There seemed to be all kinds of reasons why her suggestions were respectively impractical, improper or impossible, or all three. 'The first Archbishop to break with tradition by introducing a small orchestra was lambasted for lowering the tone,' the Dean reminded her.

'But he did pave the way for more imaginative, cultural inclusions, Welsh poems, African dancers and even bongos.'

The Dean turned up his nose. But Vicky was determined that being English, middle-class and Caucasian shouldn't mean the sacrifice of merriment in the name of buttoned-up spiritual sophistication. She and Tom had enjoyed the Bar Mitzvah of Mandy's son, the way the thirteen-year-old sang a portion of the Jewish law to demonstrate his fitness for adult status, and was showered with sweets from every side of the synagogue. Should she supply the congregation with Harrogate toffees to throw? Culturally relevant perhaps, but better the event didn't end in concussion and tears. Or, given the rebirth of the people's love of ballroom, how about a quick cha cha down the aisle with the Dean? Or a congregational conga? Just let go of your zimmer, Ma'am, and hang on to me.

And then it came to her. The Edenbury Arts Project. Home-grown in the Larchester diocese by clergy wife Chantal Pitcher, robbed of her professional dancing career on the London stage by a drunken driver who careered into her car and smashed up both her legs. Determined to see some good emerge from such a meaningless tragedy, she read in the local Edenbury paper that over fifty per cent of children raised in care ended up in police custody or were trafficked for sexual purposes, and offered the local care home dance and theatre classes. They were so successful that social services began to refer children with emotional difficulties, and the project expanded to incorporate a rock orchestra. To her astonishment, Chantal found herself with a large team of demanding adolescents, some of whom turned out to be outstanding young dancers and musicians, receiving several awards for their performances.

Julian was more than a little dubious. He balked at the idea of a rock version of 'Be Thou My Vision', and at a dramatised reading of Scripture, not to mention dancing in the nave; but he finally gave in to Vicky's persistence on at least some points.

'Anything else, Bishop?' he asked wearily.

'Oh yes. Since the Canterbury Cathedral choir is all-male, I wondered whether, on this particular occasion, they could be joined by some of the girls from the Salisbury Cathedral choir?'

'You're trying to make a point?'

'Mmm,' she said, non-committally.

The Dean sat in silence, pushing his fingertips together. When he eventually looked up at her, his eyes had turned to ice.

'Will you allow me to advise you?'

Vicky nodded reluctantly.

'I'd be very careful with this, if I were you. Competition between cathedral choirs is extremely fierce. Jealousies run deep. The Canterbury choir is and will be your own, whatever you think of their policies, so this might not be the best time to make a feminist point. If you are intent on it, so be it, but I have to warn you, collateral damage would be inevitable and potentially irreparable.'

'Whatever I do, I'm going to upset someone.'

'True, but when you do decide to tread on toes, be sure it's worth the pain it inflicts.'

'Thank you, Julian. That's helpful. As a compromise, could we ask Salisbury to send us one female soloist, perhaps for a single item?'

He sighed and conceded with a slight nod of the head.

It made no difference: the headlines read 'Archbishop Kicks her Choir in the Teeth'. The choirmaster had taken offence at the idea of a female Salisbury import. Vicky was manifestly a bra-burning feminist gone mad on political correctness, and the people could expect to hear God referred to as 'she'. What was more, the inclusion of contemporary dance and music was tasteless and improper. The Director of the Royal School of Church Music was 'incandescent' that the high quality they set out to maintain was to be publicly undermined by such so-called art – performed by amateurs, half of them probably inspired only by a drug-induced euphoria.

Vicky was incandescent on behalf of the Edenbury Project and apologised profusely to Chantal.

'Don't worry, Vicky,' she said. 'None of these youngsters reads the papers. And if they do find out, it'll make them all the more determined to prove the blighters wrong.'

Chantal's face had barely vanished from the screen when Marissa popped up to tell her that a number of African archbishops had announced they wouldn't be attending the enthronement of a woman. She issued an immediate statement assuring the African archbishops of her biblical views on sexual mores. Then, since the stumbling block appeared to be the one New Testament verse that forbade a woman to have authority over a man, she contacted each one personally to say, 'I see my role as one amongst equals, a friend, as Phoebe, Priscilla, Euodia and Syntyche were to the Apostle Paul, women he referred to as his "co-workers" in his letter to the Romans.' And though it hurt her theology, she added, 'Within your jurisdiction, I would always be under your episcopal, and therefore male, authority.' She sighed. Needs must. And it was true in a way. She could never successfully impose any decision upon the Anglican Alliance.

To her utter amazement and joy, all but one or two relented. Round one to her in the fight for global unity. She couldn't believe it was all going to be that easy.

Meanwhile, like any woman, and yet not like any other woman, she had her outfit to consider. The clerical shirt, of course. The rochet, the white cotton garment with the frilly cuffs that acted as a long-sleeved petticoat. But then? It was traditional for an archbishop to have his cloak, hat and scarf, otherwise known as cope, mitre, and stole, specially designed for the occasion. In bed, she trawled through pages of embroidered designs.

'What do you think, Tom? Gold has been popular, the colour of glory, but it makes me look jaundiced.'

Submerged in a crossword, his reading glasses perched on the end of his nose, he gave an uninterested snort, then muttered that it was a pity he couldn't choose the colour of his surgical scrubs, since green made him look sicker than the patients.

'And as for the mitre, I loathe wearing hats. They make me look ridiculous and flatten my hair.'

'Wear a couple of rollers underneath?'

'Thanks Tom.'

But then, she reflected, unlike some clergy, she certainly hadn't gone into the church for the uniform. In fact, from the very first day she had worn it, she had intensely disliked the separation from the laity it created and the stereotype it fulfilled, that the clergy were out of touch and irrelevant.

'Me big white chief, you Indians.' No, it was all wrong. That was not what church community was about.

1992

Vicky glanced at herself in the vestry mirror and turned away quickly to make room for the queue of other ordinands behind her. The other seven, ready to take the vows that would launch them into ministry in the

Church of England, all seemed anxious to take a good look at themselves in the robes they had waited and trained so long to wear, twisting and turning in front of the glass. They adjusted the white surplice with its voluminous gathered sleeves to ensure it sat correctly on the shoulders over the black cassock, or smoothed down the pleats on the hooded cassock alb, tying and re-tying the corded belt. The choice of garment depended on the churchmanship of the candidate, the historic cassock with academic hood for those with a low-church preference, the monkish alb for the more high church.

Vicky had opted for cassock and surplice, as expensive as a ball gown, her savings swallowed up by an outfit that she was convinced made her look like a penguin.

'What am I supposed to be? A telegraph pole?' she had joked to the fitter at the ecclesiastical outfitters, to disguise her heart-sink at the unattractive vision facing her in the mirror. The cassock hung straight from the shoulders to the ground, sack-like except for a belt at the waist. A man, especially a tall man with broad chest and strong shoulders, would probably look impressive in it. But a woman? There were no darts to emphasise any curves. Clergywomen evidently didn't have breasts, or waists, or hips. Or even legs. She slipped the surplice over her head. Taller than most women, she carried it reasonably well, but still felt defeminised.

The fitter was on her knees altering the hem.

'You're the first to mention it, madam,' the fitter replied, removing the pins from between her teeth. 'Many other ladies see it as a badge of honour for which you have all fought jolly hard.'

'The dog collar gives me a double chin.'

'But wearing it brings you such respect, madam.'

The fitter at her feet remained focused on the task at hand. The sacred garments were manifestly no joking matter.

Despite the extra layers, Vicky shivered. The cathedral robing room seemed chilly. A motley group of clergymen who had come to support the prospective curates and were dressing for the procession had hung their anoraks and carry-alls on a row of pegs on the wall as if it were a school cloakroom. They haw-hawed loudly as they dressed, each in turn making their own discreet little prance in front of the full-length mirror before vanishing jovially into the crypt to wait for the signal to proceed.

'Wonderful to wear these at last, isn't it?' one of the male candidates said, touching her on the arm.

'Er, yes,' she replied.

'Have a look at my stole. What do you think of my embroidery?' he asked, holding up the large gold cross stitched across one end for her to see.

Predictable, she thought.

'It's lovely,' she said.

She was actually pleased with her own – a depiction of the story of God's people crossing the Red Sea from slavery in Egypt to freedom, worked in azure, emerald, scarlet and turquoise, across both ends of the stole. If it was going to hang around her neck on a Sunday it might as well be worth seeing. An interesting visual for any children in the congregation. But she hadn't the heart to show it to him. Today, faced with the enormity of the commitment she was making, scarves hardly seemed like a priority.

Out in the crypt she found herself, inevitably, lined up alongside the one other female ordinand – a short, rather portly woman in late middle age, with whom she had developed a nodding acquaintance over the last few, silent days. We could be Jack Spratt and his wife, she thought.

'Beryl,' said her fellow ordinand, extending a plump little hand, as the marching orders were given and they processed into the cathedral, choir to the front, supporting vicars, legal beagles, archdeacons, dean and bishop to the rear. She tried not to resent the fact that the six male ordinands in front of her would get to repeat this process the following year when they became fully-fledged priests, while all she and Beryl could expect was perpetual curacy.

Unless, of course, the General Synod of the Church of England voted to allow women to be vicars in the coming year. Ladbrokes weren't taking bets on that yet.

She caught sight of Tom's back at the end of a pew near the front, standing head and shoulders above everyone else. He turned to face her as she walked towards him, much as he had on their wedding day a couple of weeks earlier, only this time, as she came level with him, he winked lasciviously, temporarily driving out all the serenity she had been trying so hard to preserve. She threw him a swift, silent rebuke as she passed, and felt his grin follow her to the altar.

Tom, of course, had not been party to the struggle of the previous few days, had no idea how close-fought the battle had been that had almost led to her not being here, but instead back in his arms at home, a disappointed heap.

Over an hour later, as she turned to stand and face the encouraging smiles of the congregation, Vicky knew, with a composure and certainty that wouldn't have been possible a mere twenty-four hours ago, that she was ready to make her solemn vows – to be diligent in prayer, and reading

Holy Scripture, to strive to make the love of Christ known through her word and behaviour, to be a faithful servant of Christ and an example to his people, to accept the discipline of the church and to take whatever steps necessary to grow in faith, love, holiness and grace. No easy path – but the one she knew had been marked out for her, wherever it led.

The dazzling sunlight was disorienting as she emerged from the dim cathedral into the hullabaloo of hundreds of family members and friends all jostling to reach their own candidate, and have their photograph taken alongside the beaming new curate.

Tom elbowed his way through the crowds, took her arm and kissed her.

'Okay, babe?' he asked, lifting a damp, straggling curl off her forehead.

'I will be when I can get out of the gear. It's so hot in here. I'm in a sweat bath.'

'Sexy,' he said with a grimace, reaching out to rescue her father, who had just been bulldozed into the wrong family grouping.

'Hello Dad. No Mum, then?' she asked as she hugged him, trying not to give in to disappointment. 'I thought she might just change her mind.'

Her father held her gaze and shook his head.

'No, Vicky. You know what she's like. I'm so sorry.'

'It's not your fault, Dad.'

'Isn't it?'

She laid a hand on his arm.

'How is she?'

'Not good. Probably best that she didn't come,' he said with a tight smile, patting her hand.

Vicky's heart sank. Nothing made her feel as helpless as her father's despair. He turned away from her and stood, blankly surveying the noisy, colourful mêlée around him.

Tom was ushering Melanie and Melissa towards her.

'You came all this way?' she gasped.

'The north-east isn't exactly the back of beyond,' Melissa retaliated, acerbic as ever. 'Civilisation has arrived, remember? We do have trains.'

'We didn't know what to bring to a do like this,' Melanie said, thrusting a huge cellophane-wrapped bouquet of flowers into Vicky's arms. 'I had a right job getting it here, though. And then I couldn't see much of the service past it.'

The scent of lilies filled Vicky's nostrils and she held them at arm's length, for fear of yellow pollen trails down the pristine white surplice.

'They're beautiful, thank you.'

'We were hardly going to miss it, were we?' said Melissa, 'Not after all those late nights in our room, defending your right to be here today.'

'I don't know what to say,' Vicky said, reaching out to hug them both, but hampered by the flowers that risked being crushed in between. She handed them to Tom, who took them, reluctantly.

Behind them, she caught sight of Bev and Mandy pushing their way through the crowds. It was hard not to see Mandy. Every head turned as she passed in a dazzling white suit, with red patent stilettos and clutch bag that matched her cherry-silk blouse.

'You look stunning,' Vicky acknowledged, extricating herself from Melanie's clasp.

'Perhaps a little glitzy for a cathedral?' Mandy asked, head on one side.

'Have you ever been into one before?'

'Never,' she said, 'and never again, if I can help it! Only for you.'

Before Vicky could reply, Bev had elbowed Tom from her side, thrust her arm through Vicky's and posed, while Melissa juggled an old Kodak, cursed it, shook it and managed, eventually, to get it to click.

'We're your oldest friends, remember?' Bev whispered, smiling seraphically for the camera, her auburn hair glinting in the sunlight. 'We've been waiting for this moment since you were knee high to a grasshopper.'

'We didn't know each other when I was knee high to a grasshopper. We were eleven when we went to Harrogate Ladies.'

'Stop splitting hairs, Vicky the Vicar. You always said this was what you wanted.'

Vicky was about to protest when Bev turned suddenly and grasped both of Vicky's hands in hers.

'I want you to know,' she said, looking straight into Vicky's eyes, ignoring Tom, who was standing directly behind them, semi-masked by the flowers, 'that whatever happens I'll always be there for you.'

Tears unexpectedly burnt Vicky's eyes. She let Bev pull her close, and buried her head in her shoulder to hide the emotion that had caught her unawares.

'Mascara,' Bev commanded loudly, holding her at arm's length. 'Vicars don't do tears – not in public anyway.'

Years later, Vicky would return to that moment over and over again. The promise was engraved on her heart. It meant so much to her – everything that friendship entailed. But those words would do her more damage than any knife. And she would reflect on how kind it was of God to hide the future from mere mortals, too fragile to bear it.

'Time to go. Luncheon at the church hall for our guests,' Tom announced. 'Off with the clerical gear and on with the party.' He handed Vicky the flowers, and pointed towards the vestry door.

She went several yards, then turned back to find her father. Where was he? There, standing, alone, in the shade of the cathedral wall.

'Dad, you will come back with us, won't you?'

He looked uncertain.

'I'd like that. Mum will have to wait.'

She reached out a hand. He took it and smiled.

APRIL 2020

Still undecided on the Archbishop's enthronement cope, Vicky went into the City, to the secluded back-alley shop of a company of silk weavers and vestment makers. A dismal shop front displayed a mannequin vicar modelling the latest in cassock albs. Once inside, an unadorned cope was brought out for her to try. It was almost too heavy to hold and had to be manoeuvred over her shoulders by two of the staff. She loved the way the ivory satin shimmered like a wedding dress, swishing as she moved, and it fanned out behind her. It would be stunning once embroidered, dazzling with a myriad metallic threads that glittered in the cathedral lights.

'It will be beautiful, won't it?' she said, standing in front of a long mirror, surveying her reflection.

The manager and his acolytes gathered around her, almost giddy with the excitement of dressing the first female Archbishop, nodding in pleasure as they pulled and tugged at the train, ensuring it hung correctly. They stood back to allow her to enjoy the full effect.

'So lovely. But I can't wear it. I'm so, so sorry.'

She caught a glimpse of their stricken faces in the mirror, and said quickly, 'It's no reflection of your work. It's to do with my qualms about all this pomp and circumstance in an organisation that should be committed to simplicity and service.'

Tight-lipped, they lifted the cope off her back, and the manager mumbled something about being at her service should she change her mind, then nodded a curt, silent acknowledgement of her thanks and farewell as she left. She walked back to the tube feeling dreadful. Pleasing people made life so much easier. If only that were always possible.

'What on earth am I going to do?' she asked Marissa and Kelvin in the diocesan office the next morning. 'I just cannot bear the thought of wearing all that paraphernalia. The cost of it alone – and for one occasion.'

'Like a royal wedding dress,' Marissa sighed. 'Doesn't it go on show somewhere afterwards?'

'I certainly hope not. Not with my sweat stains under the arms.'

'We'll have them airbrushed out of the photos,' Kelvin grinned.

'And it's so heavy.'

'The Queen didn't balk at her coronation.'

'Thank you, Marissa. The Queen wasn't post-menopausal and subject to hot flushes. I'll be a grease spot by the end of the day.'

Marissa suddenly sat bolt upright, her mouth open, her eyes wide with excitement. 'I think I might have it, Bishop. Give me a few minutes, will you?'

Half an hour later she hammered on Vicky's study door and rushed in without waiting for a reply, waving her notepad. She put her glasses on, took them off and let them dangle on their chain between her breasts, then put them on again. Kelvin followed her in, smiling benignly.

'Tony's sister, Maddy, was a missionary nurse in India,' she said breathlessly, 'and she's still in touch with some of the village women she used to visit. They set up a weaving and clothing co-operative, and she is their outlet in the UK. They produce a dupion silk that isn't terribly expensive, and their embroidery is second to none. Maddy could send them a drawing of whatever design you want. The money would be a fantastic boost for the co-operative. Not to mention the publicity.'

Vicky looked from one to the other, standing in front of her desk like two schoolchildren waiting for a gold star from the head. She got up and put her arms around them both, fighting hard to hold back the tears that seemed to be so near the surface these days.

'Marissa, you truly are a genius. You will come and work with me, won't you? I don't know what I'd do without you.'

'Well,' said Marissa, removing her glasses again and glancing coyly at Kelvin, 'there is something I've been meaning to tell you – but not today.'

It was only later that Vicky realised she had no idea who Tony was.

The mass of correspondence, both electronic and hand-written, continued to pour in from well-wishers known and unknown. Marissa had had a thousand 'thank-you' cards printed, but that wasn't nearly enough. Bishop's House looked like a florist's. The occasional bottle of passable wine persuaded Tom to admit that there were some perks. There was also the odd poison-pen letter, however, and a death threat. Marissa had been horribly shaken by it. The police took it away for forensic examination, and they heard no more. But generally, Vicky was deeply moved to have such a show of support – including the one or two who said, 'Show the boys how to do it,' or words to that effect.

'I gather the Archbishop normally receives around 150 letters a day, so this is just the beginning, Bishop,' Marissa said, filing letters into trays marked 'urgent', 'respond in time', 'personal', 'worth reading', and 'ignore'.

'Are you sure you won't come and help me with them in London?' asked Vicky.

'I'd certainly have considered it a few months ago,' said Marissa, the colour rising to her cheeks, 'but not now.'

'Oh?'

Vicky beckoned and Marissa trotted after her into her study like a little lamb.

'Um – Tony,' Marissa announced, before they had even sat down. 'He's a widower with two grown-up children. We met at a Churches Together event. He's a Baptist, you see,' she added apologetically.

'Some of them are very nice.'

'Yes,' she said earnestly, then giggled when she realised Vicky was pulling her leg. 'I just never expected to find . . . love, not at my age. Forty-seven,' she said, as if it were a surprise. 'Have you time to meet him?'

This certainly wasn't the same prim, sour-faced woman Vicky had met almost five years previously, whose expression would have curdled cream even before it was introduced to the whisk.

'Marissa, this is a man I have to meet.'

And so the two of them came for tea, Marissa like a teenager bringing the first boyfriend home to mother. Vicky was gratified to see that he seemed as smitten with her as she was with him.

'We have something to ask you,' Marissa said, nudging him in the ribs.

'Ah yes,' he said, hastily swallowing a mouthful of chocolate fudge cake, and clearing his throat. 'Er, Bishop.'

'Vicky.'

'Oh, yes, Vicky. Before you get your . . . promotion, would you do us the honour of marrying us?'

Their wedding was a last, wonderful duty before she moved to London.

NINE

We do not do good because it is what a bourgeois gentleman does; we do good because that is how the story ends! The resurrection of Christ was the enactment of God setting the world as it should be, and in this specific case, God enacted vindication on a political dissident who cared for the poor. This is our model for identity.

JÜRGEN MOLTMANN

MAY 2020

Several weeks before their enthronement, the Archbishop Elect is required to fulfil the medieval tradition of paying 'homage' to his or her sovereign before the 'Confirmation of Election' in St Paul's Cathedral makes him, or her, legally Archbishop of Canterbury. The vassal kneels at the monarch's feet. The Queen takes their hands in hers, and receives their oath of allegiance, repeated line by line, after the Home Secretary. As advisor, pastor and close confidante to the royal family, the Archbishop is then invited for dinner and an overnight at Windsor Castle, so that closer, trusting relationships can be formed.

The hairdresser came the day before to deal with Vicky's greying roots. Vicky switched off all her devices so as to shut out the world, and breathed deeply. Two hours of doing nothing, of letting the dizzying apprehension and excitement sink down from her chest, of clearing the crowded, busy brain.

She examined her reflection in the mirror. In the unforgiving light, her hair slapped to her head, it wasn't a pretty sight. She noticed newish furrows around the mouth, pouches of darkened flesh beneath the eyes, a slackness of the jaw that hadn't been there when she last looked. How time wreaked havoc with the human face. Mother Teresa had said that in their twenties, people have the beauty they're blessed with. At seventy-five, their faces are what they put into them. And there was beauty in every crease and furrow of the nun's lived-in, craggy face. Oh to grow old with a serenity like that.

If no longer exactly pretty, her face was possibly more interesting now than it was when she was thirty. Still the startling blue eyes and distinctive bone structure that made some journalists liken her to Meryl Streep. The actress's height and sleek, streaked blonde mane too, which might explain the comparison. But was it enough to keep Tom from straying? When they were out together she saw his eyes drift over a pert little bottom, a bare midriff, a fulsome décolletage. Good-looking as he was, he couldn't help but flirt a little with most of the women he met. Now, confronted with the future Archbishop's husband, some of them positively simpered. At work there were patients, students, female registrars, nurses, secretaries, a whole raft of competitors for his attentions. Could she, through the endless demands and pressures of the job, keep him at her side and in her bed? It was a question that had never really bothered her – until just a few years ago.

2017

She let herself into Bishop's House, poured herself a large glass of wine, threw off her shoes, and sank onto the settee with a sigh. She had just presented her five-year strategy for growth for the Larchester Diocese to diocesan synod and was exhausted from the debate it had provoked, though happy with the outcome nonetheless. A free hand to introduce a radical programme of modernisation – churches with congregations of less than twenty to be amalgamated, buildings sold, grants for churches with clear strategies for reaching children and the under-thirties, pioneer ministers employed to plant new 'churches' in schools, homes, pubs, clubs. 'Painful, but necessary,' she had spelt out. 'For too long we have been caught between the fear of local intransigence and the logic of necessary rationalisation. Now we must act swiftly, lest there be no church at all to hand on to our children's children.'

She fished her e-phone out of her bag, switched it back on and saw that she had three messages on voicemail, one from Jenny wishing her well with the debate, one from Tom saying he'd be late home, the third from a number that she had never seen before. The voice was female, slightly hesitant, but the diction was precise and clear.

'You don't know me, Bishop, but I need to speak to you urgently and privately, if you wouldn't mind.'

No name. A crank? How had she managed to get her private number? Vicky decided she wouldn't respond, got up and went to the kitchen to prepare herself a meal. But something about the message itched away at her like a mosquito bite. Eventually, she put the knife down and went back to the phone.

'Thank you for calling me,' said the voice, with a hint of surprise in it. Although visuals were withheld from her screen, it was vaguely familiar, but she couldn't put her finger on when or where she had heard it before.

'Who are you?'

'I'm sorry, but it really isn't necessary for me to say. It's just – I feel we women should support one another. Especially when it's a woman in your position.'

There was a short pause, then the voice said, 'Ask your husband where he was and who he was with last Thursday night.'

'Please tell me who you are.'

The phone went dead. Vicky was tempted to call the police, report an abusive call and have the number traced. But the woman sounded neither vindictive nor mentally ill. The call was only abusive if what she was insinuating wasn't true. It couldn't be true. Could it? Where *was* Tom last Thursday night? She went to her study and thumbed quickly through the diary. She had been officiating at the institution of the new vicar of Malmford. But there was nothing in it for Tom.

She ate half-heartedly, willing herself not to go over every opportunity Tom had had to be unfaithful, replaying the message over and over again so that she could find hints to suggest the woman was just a malicious caller. In the end, she was forced to admit that given their manic, entirely separate lifestyles, if he wanted an affair, nothing could be easier. Could she tell by looking at his face? What had she missed?

She went back to her study and tried to focus on sermon preparation. A vain hope. When he walked in tonight would she see the familiar old Tom she had trusted all these years, or a complete stranger? Had she been a naive little fool? Or was this a wicked hoax? Whatever, there was no way she could live with a wedge of distrust cutting between them. And then she heard the door and his footsteps approaching down the corridor, and her stomach lurched. She took several slow, deep breaths to stop her racing heart, as she waited for him to come and find her.

'Still up, Darling?' he asked, walking over to her and massaging the back of her neck, as he so often did, with his strong, experienced doctor hands.

Taking off her glasses, Vicky rubbed the bridge of her nose, turned and reached out a hand to him. He took it and she got up and led him across the room to the settee, where she sat him down next to her. He studied her face, looking slightly puzzled.

'Tom,' she asked, drawing a long breath, 'where were you tonight?'

He raised his eyebrows.

'Emergency appendectomy.'

She said nothing for a while and he began to look disgruntled.

'What is this, Vicky?'

'I've had a disturbing call – an anonymous call – from someone who appears to be suggesting that you've been having an affair.'

His eyes widened for a moment, then narrowed in disbelief.

'An anonymous caller. And you believe them?'

'Not necessarily. I'm just reporting what she said. She told me to ask you where you were on Thursday evening.'

Tom's outraged indignation pumped relief through her veins. More than anything she wanted to believe it was genuine.

'Thursday night? I told you where I was, having dinner with Myra, the Medical Director, trying to convince the Trust Board that their plans to reduce expenditure in general surgery were unrealistic.'

She nodded uncertainly.

'Vicky, I have to have dinner with many women – but it is strictly professional.'

'And no one could have seen you anywhere else?'

'Vicky!' The outburst was so full of wounded innocence that she felt a heel for asking.

'I'm so sorry, Darling,' she said, resting a hand on his knee. 'I just needed to be sure.'

He removed the hand and dropped it back into her lap.

'God, you know how to hurt a man. After all these years, you trust me so little?'

He got up and headed for the door.

'Tom,' she called after him. But he left the study, slamming the door behind him.

Vicky barely slept and spent virtually the entire night listening to his even, heavy breathing. If he had a guilty conscience, there was no evidence of it. When she finally awoke from a disturbed, early morning dream, he had gone, and the space he had occupied was cold.

APRIL 2020

Tom looked on with unmistakable pride as she knelt to take the oath of allegiance. It was obvious that the ritual meant a great deal to the Queen, and that she was not unaware of its particular significance on this first occasion of having a woman at her feet. As she covered Vicky's hands with her own, the honour felt overwhelming, and tears temporarily blurred Vicky's vision. The Queen noticed, held her gaze for a little while, then smiled appreciatively. Nothing gets past her, Vicky thought, not even now. Petite and dainty still, she was unusually upright for a woman of her age, and her hearing was acute. Her complexion, though criss-crossed with lines, was still soft pink and white porcelain.

Later, at Windsor Castle, Vicky was made to feel very much at ease. The Queen was working on a particularly difficult two-thousand-piece jigsaw puzzle, one of her great pastimes, and invited Vicky's help. Over dinner, her eyes, interested and alert, rested calmly upon her guests, taking in every word they said, sparkling with mirth when she found them amusing. She was a good conversationalist and since Alice, her daughter had just announced she was expecting a baby, delighted in coaching the new grandparents in the pitfalls, but mainly pleasures, of being a grand-, and indeed great-grandmother.

'And will you continue with your hospital work?' she asked Tom, turning her full attention on him, in a way few bothered to do, 'Or will you be the Archbishop's consort?'

'I shall continue with my work, Ma'am. I've always loved it and found it very rewarding, a welcome change from the world of the church.'

'Which can be rather all-consuming, I should imagine?' she said, nodding with understanding. 'Philip would have understood perfectly. And besides, the country needs its doctors.'

That led on to a discussion about her fears for so many young people whose families' financial limitations left them without access to higher education, or who were unemployed and unemployable, because what education they had had didn't prepare them to do the work the country so badly needed.

'Extraordinary when we're so short of skilled labour – electricians, metal workers, welders, roofies,' chipped in Prince Charles, right on cue.

'And your apprenticeship schemes have proved very successful, Sir,' Vicky interjected.

'They have indeed,' said the Prince appreciatively. 'Of course, literacy is of prime importance, but there's something very lacking at the heart of our education system if it can't prepare young people for a life in work.'

'But the current government won't fund or formally acknowledge them, will they, Darling?' Camilla added. 'And it's all rather frustrating. Why isn't skilled work seen as creative? Where has all the craftsmanship gone that we once so prided ourselves on?'

Vicky noticed how thoughtful and considerate she was towards her mother-in-law.

'Are you ready to turn in yet?' she whispered to her as they left the table, when the Queen appeared to be wilting.

'I think I might be,' the Queen agreed. 'Just one thing we wanted to ask the future Archbishop . . . disestablishment? A few of my bishops seem rather keen on the idea, claim it may offer new freedoms, protection from the rather heavy-handed approach of government we've been seeing recently. What are your views?'

'It's late, Ma'am,' Camilla said, gently taking her arm. 'Could you discuss this with the Archbishop on another occasion?'

'Yes, of course we can.'

'It upsets her rather,' Camilla whispered to Vicky.

'Ma'am, I'd be delighted to discuss the issue with you, but let me say, to reassure you, that I will do my very best to ensure the continuing link between church, state and monarchy.'

The Queen nodded, satisfied.

'The youngsters will look after you, won't you, William?' she said, turning to her grandson.

'Catherine and I would be delighted, Bishop.'

The Queen took her hand, as if to say goodnight.

'I must admit, I wasn't altogether happy with the idea of a woman Archbishop. At my age, I must be allowed a certain anxiety about such a major change.'

Vicky wondered whether memories of a somewhat uneasy relationship with a former female Prime Minister had coloured her thinking.

'But having met you, I feel very much reassured.'

'When they were first confronted with a woman priest, Ma'am, many congregations found it took some getting used to. But then they found they rather liked it.'

'And so shall we.'

'And I shall serve you, Ma'am, in any way I can,' Vicky said, meaning it with all her heart. She had a momentary, unsettling flashback to the republican rhetoric she had espoused in her youth, before she had any concept of the cost of a lifetime of duty and service.

'I hope she lasts a while yet,' she said to Tom, on their way to the guest suite, after a fascinating tour of the royal art collection and castle, followed by coffee and handmade liqueur chocolates. 'I have the feeling she could be a wise and wonderful friend and counsellor.'

'Rather her than Prince Charles?'

'I'll say. The logistics of a multi-faith coronation doesn't bear thinking about.'

Back at their suite of rooms they discovered to their amusement not only that their suitcases had been unpacked, but that they had been given separate bedrooms. The rochet that Vicky had worn for the Homage ceremony and dropped on a chair was now neatly laid out on one of the beds, having evidently been taken for a nightie.

'Can't blame them,' Tom said. 'That says it all.'

Vicky stood at the adjoining door between their rooms, waving a hand up and down the open space.

'Just checking to see there's no invisible thread.'

'Even if there was, don't you think they would have been broken by dozens of royal wanderers these past few hundred years? At least you escape my snoring for a night.'

'Tom,' she called him over as she explored further in his bedroom, 'come here a minute. Just look.' She pointed into one of the drawers of a large, antique oak tallboy. There, neatly and individually rolled in white gauze, were two pairs of his clean underpants.

'Good job I brought the boxers, not the jocks. I only hope they had no holes in them,' he muttered in astonishment.

'You're not going to expect that kind of treatment from now on, are you?'

May the 1st, when it finally came, was cloudy and unseasonably cool. A blustery east wind charged through the cathedral precincts, swirled around its arches and porticos, playfully lifting skirts, ruffling hair, tossing hats in the air and depositing them on the other side of the lawn, ballooning clerical robes so that it seemed as if Canterbury Cathedral were hosting a gathering of roly-polies. May Day, commemorating Joseph the Worker, the industrious carpenter father of Jesus, patron saint of the dying, of marriages, fathers, families, house sales and finances. Not particularly appropriate. And Witches Day in Portugal. Vicky hoped no clever-clogs religious correspondent would try and get any mileage out of that.

Tom, along with Alice and Dirk, over from Boston, kissed her goodbye and left her standing in the lounge of the Old Palace. She wished she could have held on to them for a few moments longer. As the front door closed behind them, and she moved to one of the large Georgian windows to watch the to-ing and fro-ing outside the west front, it seemed to her that this was how it would be from now on. Standing apart. This aloneness. The real persona hidden behind curtains, overshadowed by the role and its expectations.

A virtual screen in front of the cathedral meant that visitors without tickets could still watch the ceremony, and a large crowd had gathered already. Like a colony of bees in search of pollen, it swarmed this way and that with every new VIP arrival – royal, political, a smattering of celebrities; occasionally, when yet another unknown African archbishop emerged from the car, they would sigh back towards their original position.

Adrenalin pumped through her, forcing her to focus on the immense privilege that God had bestowed upon her. So many gifted women had fought for this moment. Then why was it she, not they, standing here? They were much better equipped for the task.

It was all so unreal, as if she were waiting for her cue to go on stage in a play. From a television in the corner of the room, BBC commentary droned away quietly in the background, odd phrases penetrating her consciousness – 'a break with tradition', 'known for her rather wicked sense of humour', 'popular people's choice', 'threat of large-scale division'.

The religious correspondent came on the screen. Vicky wandered over to the television, intrigued to know how she would be described.

'She's certainly different from all that's gone before.'

'And not just for obvious reasons?'

Laughter.

'Yes, Joe. She's only been a bishop a short time, but she's made her mark, dragging one of the country's poorest dioceses out of virtual insolvency to make it a model of social engagement. It's made her something of a local icon. Of course, some bitterly resented her modernising approach, but others found her a breath of fresh air.'

'She is very outspoken.'

'She is indeed, a Yorkshirewoman through and through, not afraid to say it how she sees it. Though whether that will continue in a role that demands such high diplomacy remains to be seen.'

'So far as I am able, it will,' she whispered to the screen.

'And speaking of diplomacy, she pulled off quite a coup – persuading the African church leaders, deeply opposed to a female archbishop, to come today.'

'Yes, quite an extraordinary feat.'

'But, of course, they welcome her more traditional approach in sexual matters. Is that diplomacy too, or does she actually hold to those views?'

'Whether her private views match her public statements, no one can say for sure. She has resolutely refused to conduct a gay marriage, but has attended one or two, which hasn't pleased the conservative evangelicals.'

'On another note entirely, all details about the Archbishop's cope have been a closely kept secret, a bit like a royal wedding dress.'

'She's very opposed to gratuitous spending, so whatever she's chosen, it's unlikely to have cost the church an exorbitant sum.'

'And of course, people won't be rushing out to M&S to buy copies of the cope on Monday morning . . .'

Mutual agreement and more laughter.

'No, it's not quite the same as a wedding dress.'

'But they may want to copy the evening suit she'll wear for the celebration dinner tonight?'

'Yes, there is a story behind that. The Archbishop has stated that she won't be wearing a cassock for formal occasions and banquets, which has ruffled a few feathers. We know she's opted instead for an outfit in episcopal colours. But will she wear the dog collar, that's the question? The Scottish designer Christian Kane offered her an evening suit he had designed for the spring fashion show. But we shall all have to wait and see.'

'And she's refusing to take the full Archbishop's salary?'

'She is indeed, in the belief that there should be no hierarchy in the Church of England, that all clergy should have the same basic stipend – and that's around a quarter of her potential pay.'

'And she's asking her fellow bishops to do the same. How do they feel about that?'

'She has repeatedly called for this throughout her time on General Synod, so no surprise. She can't simply impose it without the say-so of the House of Bishops, Archbishops' Council and Synodical legislation – but it has caused a certain amount of discomfort, shall we say, amongst her colleagues. Ah, and here is the Archbishop of York.'

Vicky's viewing was interrupted by Oliver Adams, chaplain to the previous Archbishop and long past retirement, who shoved his way through the door with a look of grave disquiet on his normally calm and kindly face, a large amount of gauzy purple fabric lying across his outstretched arms.

'Bishop, what on earth is this?' he asked.

'My cope, Oliver,' replied Vicky.

'I had a horrible feeling you were going to say that. But what is it made of?'

'A very sheer silk. If you hold it up to the light you'll see how beautiful the embroidery is.'

'But it has no weight. It feels . . .'

'Cheap? Absolutely right.'

He raised his eyes to the ceiling and shook his head.

'I was going to say, like a net curtain.' He sighed. 'Come on then, let's get you kitted out, my dear,' as if she were a patient in hospital about to don a surgical gown for a painful procedure.

'No "my dear", Oliver. Not unless you'd say it to a man too.'

He patted her arm.

'Sorry, Archbishop, I just feel protective of you. I have three grown-up daughters. Arms up.'

He slipped the white rochet over her head, as if she were a three-year-old. 'Honestly! I've been dressing myself for fifty years,' she laughed.

The rochet went over a deep rose-coloured clerical shirt and a long, midnight blue skirt that hugged the hips and fanned out like a fish tail – the Garbo look of Christopher Kane's design made her feel like a mermaid. Later that night, when she removed the clerical gear, she would replace it with a matching sequined bolero over the clerical shirt and dog collar.

By the time she had put on the rochet and the cope, she felt like Michelin man, swaddled under so many layers, despite the cope's light construction. She'd never survive five minutes in this lot, let alone an entire service.

'Be a gentleman and turn your back a moment, Oliver, will you?'

He looked surprised, then obediently turned away.

She lifted the layers and wriggled out of the skirt, then, voicing an all-clear, handed it to him and asked him to keep it until she came back from the cathedral.

'The men normally leave their trousers on.'

'The men don't have hot flushes.'

There was a sudden loud cheer from the crowds.

'The Duke and Duchess of Cambridge,' Oliver said, sidling up to the window. 'She's just announced she's pregnant again. A bit of a surprise, I gather.'

'They keep you in the loop, do they?' Vicky grinned, touching up her lipstick in a large, rectangular gilt mirror Tom had hung above a monumental antique sideboard.

She placed the mitre on her head, then gave a vigorous shake to ensure it was secure and wouldn't sink down over her eyes at a crucial moment. She had asked the female Divisional Commander of Larchester Police what she did on a night out when she took off the helmet, but hadn't had the time to do her hair. 'Wear a wig,' she had said. Vicky wasn't sure whether she was joking, and certainly didn't warm to the idea of carrying her hair around with her in a bag.

'Ah, Mahdi Khan, the new leader of the opposition,' the chaplain said from his vantage point, 'a Muslim. That would be another first. If the Tories get back into power.'

'He seems an interesting man,' she said, walking over to the window, aware of the tug of the cope, and the way it made her feel like Batman, 'but I'm not sure a Tory government would be good for the country.'

'Can't be worse than what we have, can it?'

She watched the ecclesiastical world making its way into the cathedral – moderators, patriarchs, papal representatives, cardinals and bishops from all over the globe. As colourful as canaries, parakeets and cockatiels.

'Whoever said the male of the species didn't like dressing up?' she said.

As she turned back to him, Oliver noticed that she was trembling slightly. He took her hands in his.

'Fear nothing, Vicky. Take the opportunity by the throat. Only the Duchess of Cambridge grabs the public imagination more than you do. You inspire, motivate and encourage. People warm to you and trust you. That's why the press has been so fixated on the minutiae of your life. But just think what those gifts of yours might achieve in God's hands! For such a time as this.'

'As Mordecai said to Queen Esther.'

'And she saved her people from extinction.'

'A hard call.'

'But a holy one.'

'It's stupid, I know, but I feel as if the honour of my entire sex rests on my shoulders. And I have no role models, Oliver.'

'You don't need them. Just be you.'

He rested one hand gently on her shoulder and prayed for her quietly, that God would give her the courage and strength she needed, then looked into her eyes and said, smiling steadily, 'Ready?'

She walked slowly across from the palace to the cathedral, the tall mitre on her head making her feel like an African woman balancing a bucket of water, smiling and nodding at the watching crowd who lined her way, stooping to chat to one or two of the children. A curly-headed little girl handed her a posy of flowers. Vicky kissed her, wondered momentarily what to do with them, then tucked them through her morse.

Arriving at the great west door, followed by the TV cameras, she took her pastoral staff and struck the door three times, the traditional way of requesting entrance to her cathedral, convinced that the hammering on the door couldn't be as loud as the thudding of her heart in her ribcage. She longed to lift the hair off the back of her neck, already sticky with perspiration, but couldn't reach it without tossing the cope out of the way.

The doors swung slowly open to what might have been a Breugel painting, an anonymous mass of hats, noses, mouths and eyes focused upon her. She took a deep breath, forced her facial muscles into repose to still the slight twitch under her left eye, and took her place in the long procession through the congregation, past the great, the good and the quite possibly wicked, believers and atheists, known friends and unknown enemies, through the centre of the world itself, courtesy of TV cameras.

As she walked slowly down the aisle, the cope, diaphanous and delicate as butterfly wings, fluttered and fanned out behind her. Embroidered on the back in emerald and gold were the words, 'Whom shall I send? And who will go for us?' God's call to the prophet Isaiah. How his heart must have sunk at the prospect, as hers had done, for he knew the people wouldn't listen and would even despise him for his message. He knew what it was to sit in stunned silence, torn between terror and excitement before the words of obedience, 'Here am I. Send me,' wrenched themselves from his aching guts.

As surely as Israel was Isaiah's people, this funny mixed bag of Anglicans was hers. And she, like the prophet, had been called to challenge them to an authentic lifestyle with radical, counter-cultural values – the sound good sense of faith, the merit of integrity, the sanctity of marriage and family life, the essentiality of caring for the dispossessed and under-privileged, the hungry and the lonely – values trumpeted yet passed over by governments with short-term policies that put their own interests first, and showed no concern for future generations, or how God and history might one day judge their efforts.

She became aware of the gasps of the congregation as she passed. Directly in front of her, Dean Julian's cope was a magnificent, shimmering garment in ivory and scarlet, heavy enough to sit firmly on the flagstones as he moved. Why hadn't she told him what she intended? She had never thought about the contrast, never intended causing him any discomfort. She had simply wanted to make the point that she was a servant, not a lord Archbishop. Judging by the response of the congregation, she had succeeded; though she prayed, silently, that it wouldn't be at the expense of her relationship with the cathedral clergy.

Reaching the front of the nave at last, to be welcomed to her cathedral and enthroned as Bishop of the see of Canterbury, she stooped to kiss the priceless sixth-century Gospels that Pope Gregory is supposed to have given to Saint Augustine in Rome when he commissioned him to go and convert the British heathens. That kiss sealed her commitment to take up the charge given to St Augustine so many centuries ago. That the British were any the less heathen in the twenty-first century, she rather doubted.

The second enthronement took place at the seat of St Augustine, a huge ninth-century stone chair, towering above the altar, with a commanding view down the entire length of the cathedral nave. She climbed the red-carpeted stairs, turned and sat in a space large enough for at least two of her, a poignant reminder that just as she failed to fill this physical space, so must she inevitably fail to fill the role's impossibly large responsibilities and expectations. To speak words of understanding, spiritual enlightenment and sustenance to every soul in the country, Christian or not, to be relevant, pertinent and ever gracious – how could she do it? In the face of virtually limitless opportunities for human error and failure. 'Oh God,' she whispered to herself, as she looked out at a resplendent purple pool of bishops, and way beyond them, a mosaic of bobbing splurges of cherry red, peacock blue and canary yellow – the be-hatted dignitaries and friends that made up the congregation – 'Go before and behind me, picking up my messes and covering the path with the strewn flowers of your grace.'

Into her mind flashed a vision of the magnificent tapestry in Coventry Cathedral. God sits there on his throne, and man is a miniature standing between his feet, no taller than his big toe. That was where she belonged – not on a throne, but between his feet.

As she smiled down on the crowds, here for an occasion that few perhaps had dreamed of seeing in their lifetime, the sun slowly emerged from behind the clouds, gilding the pale sandstone of the pillars, filling the vast space with its golden radiance. The stained glass of the cathedral windows, so muted and bland till now, came alive with vibrant, shining colour, anointing the heads and shoulders of the congregation with its dazzling rays. An immense wave of silence made its way through the cathedral, enveloping every individual in its breath-taking thrall. For several moments all rustling, fidgeting, whispering and coughing were stilled, as the entire congregation seemed to be caught up in the warmth of a divine presence that filled the building, blessing the people and bathing them in light.

The superbly crafted liturgy, deeply moving as it was, could never have fabricated such a moment. The adults stood transfixed, choirboys wide-eyed with wonder. The Dean's hands shook. But Vicky felt more profoundly at peace than she had been at any time since the PM's secretary had appeared on her doorstep. Now, enthroned in St Augustine's chair, she was Primate of All England and President of the Anglican Alliance, leader of the world's 82 million Anglicans – her name added to the pages of history, the first woman to hold the title in two thousand years.

Fanfares blasted through the hush, the sound resonating around the magnificent vaulted ceiling, while the congregation broke into cheers and clapped, and then the Edenbury dancers in shiny black leapt like panthers from every part of the building, to an insistent beat of African drums, performing their own electric interpretation of 'Here I am, send me'.

As the rock band launched into an upbeat version of 'Be Thou My Vision', Vicky made her way across the cathedral. The last guitar chord died away and she climbed into the pulpit, hoisting up the skirts of her robes, lest she mount them rather than the steps and ignominiously strangle herself on her first public duty as Archbishop.

She watched and waited as the shuffling settled and the throat-clearing died away. Then she began. 'What is heaven like? When I was a raw young curate on a funeral visit, the widow, who had seen many twin tombstones carved with the words, "Reunited in Death", asked me whether I believed that she would be back with her late husband there. Call it clergy instinct, but I sensed that I should be careful how I answered. So I told her, gently, that the Bible isn't clear on this point, that Jesus said there would be no marriage in heaven. "Thank God for that," she exclaimed. "The so and so was so awful down here, I wouldn't want to have to put up with him all over again up there."'

Hearty laughter gave way to some serious-sounding coughing that echoed throughout the building.

'Sentimentalised, erroneous versions of heaven have done untold damage to the Christian concept of hope. The Apostle John, condemned to hard labour for his faith, manacled, raw and bleeding, was given an apocalyptic vision of the future, the ultimate arrival of the kingdom of God. In the book of Revelation, he describes the new heaven and earth, where God reigns with absolute benevolence, where there is no more injustice, poverty, disease and despair, no more pain or tears. Isn't that the Utopia we all long for?

'But the Bible speaks not so much of our going up to heaven, but of our task in bringing heaven down to earth. Every now and then we get a glimpse of what that means – when the poor are fed, the wronged receive justice, the broken-hearted are comforted, the sick are healed, neighbours who haven't spoken for years are reconciled, the spiritually blind see and the dead in heart and mind receive a spiritual organ transplant. We experience a tiny taste of the kingdom of God breaking into our world now, though its fullest sense is yet to come.

'The theologian Jürgen Moltmann claimed that the post-modern "me" culture, promising people the power and choices they don't actually have, is a deception. The truth is, we are strongly influenced by political and economic forces outside of our control. But we are not powerless. We can protect human dignity and freedom only when we come together in community and decide for ourselves the quality of life we want for our neighbourhood. Christian communities are bringing glimmers of the goodness of heaven to almost every part of the globe, impacting the cultures in which they live, no matter how costly that might be. I heard recently of one African village where a woman discovered that her husband was sexually abusing their daughter. Since the forces of law and order traditionally side with the man, if the woman had complained she and her daughter would have been ejected from their home and left without financial support. So a large group of local women went to the hut and surrounded it. They stood there for days in complete silence, until the man felt so intimidated that he packed up his things and left the village.

'We in the United Kingdom live in interesting times, when Christianity, once the foundation of our British democracy and legal system, has been marginalised. There is a fairly widespread assumption that no one with a brain can believe in God. "Born again" is a term of derision. Christians are no longer free to discuss their faith because it infringes other people's freedoms. It's not politically correct. It can get you the sack. It simply isn't cool.

'The prevailing attitude of government is secularist, meaning without religious faith, yet every government follows its own pseudo-religion, with a creed and values it creates for itself, revolving around financial expediency and the maintenance of power, resulting in legislation without altruism or compassion. And that means there will always be enmity between these man-made, godless systems and the values of the church. So, while respecting our political leaders, we must nonetheless stand up for what we believe, challenge where necessary, and live the faith we preach.'

There was an isolated, short burst of applause. Vicky looked round, sorely tempted to catch the eye of the PM and some of his cabinet members, but forced herself to focus back on her notes and continue.

'That is the church I believe in and will fight for, a church that stands united against oppression, powerlessness, injustice and the discrimination of poverty, that demonstrates the life-transforming power of Christian love, that defends the freedoms that form the basis of any civilised nation – freedom of speech, freedom of worship, freedom from want, freedom from fear and intimidation. A church that is not afraid to say that we have what society looks for, has lost and longs for – the resurrection hope, the certainty that our deepest dreams will one day come true, that the eternal kingdom of God is an imminent reality, that the restoration of the perfection we knew in the Garden of Eden is God's ultimate plan for all humanity. So may I, by God's grace, be part of a church that dedicates itself to giving our nation a taste now of the joys that are yet to come.'

Vicky was about to leave the pulpit when a blood-curdling shriek filled the silence. From nowhere, an elderly woman in unremarkable beige skirt and cardigan appeared in the nave and ran towards her. Stopping at the foot of the pulpit, she pointed up at Vicky and screamed out, 'The great whore of Babylon. Sitting on her throne. She will be cast down into the great lake.' A hubbub of noise broke out in the cathedral. But no one moved. Vicky was imprisoned in the pulpit and there was no sign of security.

There had been a significant police presence in the precincts for weeks. Every inch had been covered by sniffer dogs checking for bombs. Nonetheless, this respectably dressed woman with deceptively innocent iron-grey curls had managed to make her protest – standing just beneath Vicky, close enough for her to see the gobs of spittle gathered at the corners of the woman's mouth. 'Whore!' she yelled again, shaking a fist. 'Bringing pagan cavorting into the house of God.'

Instinctively, Vicky came halfway down the pulpit steps to speak to the woman. She reached into her morse, took out the rather wilted posy of flowers and held them out to the woman, who seemed so ordinary, so harmless but for the berserk fury that had taken her. They were unceremoniously smacked out of her hand, and, finally, as a shower of petals rained down on both, security officers moved in swiftly, each grabbing an arm, and lifted her bodily towards the nearest exit, her feet dangling behind her as if she were a carcass of meat at Smithfield Market. The Dean, quickly recovering his presence of mind, introduced the Peace.

As she was greeted by guests and the few old friends who managed to battle their way through the hordes, the chief security guard appeared at her left shoulder, sweating profusely. 'So sorry, Archbishop. Nothing to worry about. We've taken care of her.'

'Who was she?' she whispered.

'She had a bona fide ticket. Claims she represents some traditional Anglican group or other. More like mental illness, I should say.'

'How sad. You'll ensure she gets some proper help?'

The officer stared at Vicky for a few seconds, apparently lost for words, then nodded and disappeared swiftly back into the crowds.

She was determined not to let one very disturbed soul ruin the day's proceedings. But the atmosphere had been disturbed, churned up like the sea after a sudden squall. Over the shoulders of the steady stream of greeters she looked around for Tom, hoping he was on his way to her side, but there was no sign of him. Then she caught sight of him, still in his seat, shaking hands with those within reach.

'Where were you?' she whispered to him afterwards, as they mingled for a few moments with the well-wishing crowd outside. A large, ungainly man in a dirty mac bumbled up to her and said, 'Haven't gone to church for years. Too many boring old farts. But I like you.'

'Good for you,' Tom said, taking Vicky's arm and escorting her quickly away.

'That's exactly why I needed you nearby.'

'Sorry, Darling, didn't realise. Didn't want to muscle in on your action.'

'What exactly is my action?' she asked, but never got a reply, as she saw Mandy emerge from the cathedral in a dazzling emerald-green trouser suit and come looking for her. Vicky pushed her way towards the familiar face, excuse-me-ing, smiling and nodding as she went.

'I'm so glad you came,' she whispered, maintaining the fixed smile.

'You will keep on with this getting-promoted business. Determined to get a good Jewish girl into church any which way. This one *almost* beats a Bar Mitzvah. But not quite.'

It was starting to rain as they left for London. Noah, her new driver, was waiting for them at the door to drive them back to Lambeth Palace.

'Do I really need a driver all the time?' she had asked Dan Clements, her Chief of Staff. 'Surely, the new navigation systems mean my own car will be fine to take me where I need to go most of the time?'

Dan had sighed at her apparent naivety and said respectfully, 'Archbishop, a driver will give you precious time to read, prepare, even pray.' Another freedom gone.

As they arrived at the palace gates, before the porter had time to press the button and let them in, a lone, bedraggled-looking journalist, who must have been waiting in the rain for several hours, appeared at the window and banged so hard that Vicky's heart missed a beat. She could hear his question quite clearly, but Tom shouted, 'Drive on,' to Noah, before it was finished. Noah put his foot down and they roared into the palace grounds, the gates closing behind them.

The celebratory dinner that evening took place under the auspices of the Nikean Club, set up in 1925 to promote ecumenism and provide hospitality to church leaders visiting the Archbishop. There were a great number of toasts. Vicky had been warned only to take a sip every time her glass was filled, lest Tom be forced to carry her out. So many pitfalls, so many more ways of making a fool of herself than she ever imagined possible.

A Roman Catholic cardinal became increasingly jolly as the evening wore on, telling endless vicar, priest and rabbi jokes about a foot from her face. Having Mandy as a friend meant she'd heard them all before. At one point Tom hoisted him physically out of her space, but since no one else wanted him in theirs, he was back for more by the time Tom had returned from the Gents.

'Time to bring the party to a close?' Tom asked.

'And how,' she said, forcing her swollen feet reluctantly back into her shoes.

The reality of waking up the following morning, buried beneath an avalanche of new responsibilities and duties, hit her with the force of a sledgehammer, and she closed her eyes. She remembered that Archbishop Cosmo Lang, who'd had the unenviable job of presiding over the abdication of a monarch, had once said the workload was 'incredible, indefensible and inevitable'. 'Do only what you have to, what only you can do. Delegate the rest,' said another of her predecessors. Great advice, but how practical would it be in reality?

She threw off her shoes before she reached the bedroom door, quickly followed by the designer suit, the clerical shirt and the breath-restricting pantihose that had held in her poor, protesting stomach. Mind-blown by an entire day of archiepiscopal good behaviour, she had an overwhelming urge to throw off all restraint and run around the flat stark naked, shouting obscenities. But she was too tired. Instead, she put on a pair of pyjamas and went into the lounge to find Tom.

'Did you hear him?' she growled, throwing herself onto the settee. 'The nerve of the man.'

'What did he want?' Tom responded wearily, half his attention on his e-phone. 'Fifty-five emails and a whole load of texts,' he muttered.

'Mmmm?' Her mind was blank.

'The journalist?'

'Grief, my brain has given up and gone to bed. He asked me whether I'd like to respond to the criticism that my sermon was too politically motivated, totally out of order for an archbishop.'

'Who's been talking to him?'

'No one. Anyone. Take your pick. The Dean, probably.'

'You didn't take it seriously? Didn't respond?'

'Of course not. Tom, you were in the car.'

'Good girl.'

'Don't patronise me.'

He held up his hands defensively.

'Whoa. Only trying to support. Have mercy on the cack-handed attempts of a poor male.'

'Sorry – done in. Even extroverts can suffer from an over-exposure to people. Suffocation by social intercourse, rigor mortis from a surfeit of niceness. I had no idea there were so many hundreds of bishops and cardinals in the world, not to mention moderators and sundry other chief honchos of other denominations, and I shook hands with them all. My wrist aches. My facial muscles have had more of a workout than any human should have to bear. Though probably good for keeping wrinkles at bay.'

'Personally, I thought your sermon was rather good,' Tom said, pouring them both a glass of red wine.

'I have a fan!' she said, toasting him. 'God be praised for that.'

'Won't score you brownie points with the government. Home Secretary had a face like a smacked . . .'

'Good. You have closed the kitchen curtains, by the way, haven't you? Anyone can see straight in when the light's on. Happy day for a photographer with a long-angled lens.'

She didn't remember much more. She felt Tom enfold her in a blanket, and kiss her gently on the forehead, but after that, blessed unconsciousness.

PART TWO

2020–21

Encryptogram user z3qa | to user bx4sw

Tears before breakfast. As anticipated. The fun begins.

Much appreciated our little chat re Joan of Arc. Who needs burning at the stake when we have our beloved press? So much more civilised. Let them put her on a pedestal – for now.

Good to know you share my feelings. Sources tell me she's turning over stones. Can you verify? Could seriously scupper our plans. A watching and waiting game. Your eyes and ears invaluable.

Won't forget this. Friendship matters. We'll talk again soon.

TEN

God weeps with us so that we may one day laugh with him.
JÜRGEN MOLTMANN

JUNE 2020

Lambeth Palace, with its towers and turrets, more miniature castle than palace, has been the London residence of the Archbishops of Canterbury since the twelfth century, when they began to worry that their power and influence over the London court was severely hampered by being stuck out at Canterbury. Built on the south bank of the River Thames, it is one of the few buildings of medieval origin left in London, although a rebuild in 1840 swept away a jumble of older, impractical constructions in an attempt to create a grand single palace. This is the Archbishop's home, as well as the hub of his, or her, national and international ministry.

Vicky soon discovered some of the little oddities that remained, reflecting the foibles of the former occupants. It had once been adapted to suit a particularly shy Archbishop, enabling him to go from room to room without ever having to appear in the main corridor – an option not open to Vicky, as many of those hidden routes were now repurposed or blocked off. Just as well his tenure preceded these days of televisual communication, she said to herself.

Her favourite room was the state drawing room, sunny and surprisingly restful with its elegant floor-to-ceiling windows overlooking the gardens and park beyond. Two magnificent crystal chandeliers, a gift from Waterford Glass, lit up the exquisitely restored, moulded plasterwork ceiling. This was where she would entertain religious and political leaders. The smaller, pink drawing room, used for a variety of meetings, was somehow more formal, and she found the rose damask wallpaper rather oppressive after several hours of deep discussion. The walls began to fold in on her.

The capacious study provided a great deal more than room for thought. She tried to cosy it up with voluminous, plum-coloured settees and silk scatter cushions, a profusion of table lamps, family photos, and personal knick-knacks. A large parlour palm, thirsty and fast-growing if she remembered to water it, softened a corner. Looking round at her creative efforts, she decided that this was now very definitely a woman's study.

Up an ancient square tower with a stone staircase winding up inside it, its steps worn by hundreds of years of footfall, was the Archbishop's private, three-bedroom flat. It was added in the nineteenth century, and fell a long way short of being the London penthouse it might theoretically be described as. In fact, it was really just a few rooms at the end of a corridor, modernised with typical 1970s disregard for the fineness of the building, like a pair of bed socks on an otherwise glamorously dressed woman. Any member of the large staff team employed to support the Archbishop could call in at any time. Fortunately, only a few did.

Tom guffawed loudly the first time he caught sight of the staff list – all twenty-four of them. 'Good Lord, Vicky – a Secretary for Ecumenical Affairs, for Public Affairs, International Affairs, Anglican Relations, International Development, Inter-religious Relations and for the Anglican Alliance, not to mention the Press Officer, the Events and Tours Manager and the New Media Editor. All managed by a Chief of Staff, and the best of luck to him. So this is our jolly, new extended family.'

Standing in the middle of the flat, he flung open his arms in a gesture of welcome.

'Come and give your new mummy and daddy a kiss.'

'Ah,' she said to him, 'you seem to have forgotten the administrative staff – a building manager, steward, cook, gardeners, gatekeepers and cleaners.'

'It's bloody *Downton Abbey*.'

'Tom,' she remonstrated, amused and just a little alarmed by his sarcasm. Thus far he hadn't mentioned finding his own little *pied-à-terre* again, and she desperately hoped that life in this stately home wouldn't give him renewed impetus to do so.

She hadn't the heart to tell him that the list, though it seemed long on paper, was, in reality, woefully inadequate. William Temple, Archbishop through the Second World War, claimed he did 'the work of a prime minister with the resources of a Head Master'. The last review of the job had not only borne that out, but claimed the job was fast becoming unmanageable – and that was nearly twenty years before, when the communication revolution was in its infancy. Now, it was out of control.

It consisted, in effect, of six separate jobs, each one extremely demanding: Bishop of the Canterbury diocese, if she ever managed to get there;

pastoral authority for the dioceses of the south of England, helping their bishops sort out recalcitrant clergy; leadership of the Anglican Church in the UK, including chaplain to the monarch and voice on spiritual matters to the nation; presidency of the worldwide Alliance of Anglican Churches, with its 82 million members and hundreds of bishops, all expecting the Archbishop to intervene in their own disputes and difficulties; senior representative in inter-denominational matters; and finally, spokesperson in inter-faith affairs in a multi-cultural nation, spearheading the response of the global faith community to poverty issues and the development of education and trade. When all six jobs were done, she thought ruefully, there would certainly be little time left for shopping, cooking, or washing her smalls.

To function effectively she would need a first-rate team. There was no reason why her predecessor's appointees should take kindly to a new boss – or she to them. So for her first week in office she invested time in getting to know her staff. Intimate chats in her study and the occasional coffee in a quiet café around the corner, helped her discern who shared her vision, and which potential trouble-makers needed winning round.

She managed to persuade Oliver to postpone his retirement for a few months and stay on as her chaplain. His wise and kindly presence would be invaluable to her. To her surprise, when she sat at her desk, buried beneath mounds of paper and an unachievable timetable, she didn't feel patronised by a fatherly arm around her shoulders. On the contrary, it was a comfort amidst the newness of it all that someone appropriate, trustworthy and discreet saw and understood.

Dan Clements, the Chief of Staff, manifestly did not. Known, with what she felt was a sad lack of political correctness, as 'the old woman of Lambeth', he was unusually tall, and painfully thin, with oily receding hair and a reputation for being a pernickety rules-and-regulations man. He seemed to expect her to drop easily into the slots her predecessor had left behind. A control freak, she said to herself. Always a tough nut to crack, but she couldn't afford to fall out with him.

'I hear you're something of a perfectionist, Dan. I won't have time to deal with the detail. So I need someone like you around.'

He bowed, unctuously, like a head waiter. She suspected that it was because she was his first female boss and he wasn't sure how to handle her. Vicky motioned him to a settee, but he remained standing.

'Can I ask what your priorities will be, Archbishop?'

'I'm deeply concerned by some of the government's current policies, particularly regarding human rights, so I would like, if possible, to be in the House of Lords on a regular basis.'

Clements gave a half-stifled snort.

'And when do you plan to walk on water, Archbishop?'

'Ah, you see why I need you, Dan.'

'Juggling your many commitments, ensuring each is done well, is tremendously important. Too much time at Lambeth, and you'll be accused of neglecting your diocese. Too much time on foreign visits and you neglect your UK responsibilities. Too much time in the House of Lords and you will necessarily neglect the church.'

'So whatever I do, I cannot win?'

'Quite so, Archbishop. But then we're here to fulfil our responsibilities, not necessarily to please.'

'Thank you for reminding me. And while I do take your point about the House of Lords, it is nonetheless imperative that I am there in the next month or so, when the anti-proselytising measures are debated, as I plan to give the strongest possible lead. Ultimately, it won't prevent their becoming law, of course, but it will make the church's opposition high profile. And that will be just the beginning.'

'As you wish, Archbishop,' he said stony-faced, turned on his heels and marched out.

Two days later, she called him to her study again, this time insisting he sit on the settee she had pointed out to him. He lowered himself carefully, then sat rigid, leaving the cup of fresh coffee she had given him untouched on the table. Sitting opposite him on the other settee, she broached the subject of altering the long-established daily schedule. Her predecessor, she began, had been a deeply spiritual man with a rigorous prayer life, which she had admired enormously, but he had lived an almost bachelor lifestyle.

'Firstly, I was wondering if we could move morning prayer in the crypt from seven to eight? That might make life easier for the staff who attend.'

She saw from the steely expression in his eyes that this hadn't gone down well, but was determined to hold her ground. If she didn't, she would never have a life of her own.

'And then real coffee and croissants for everyone, to prepare us for the challenges of the day.'

'Archbishop,' he said, as if explaining the rules to a child, 'we have a way of doing things here, based on what we know works best. Your predecessor understood that. Pushing the day forward will mean you won't get everything done.'

Vicky resisted the urge to snap, 'My predecessor had no hair and didn't wear make-up.'

'Trust me, Dan,' she said instead, 'I'm a bit of a night owl, and happy for evening events to start a little later.'

'That,' he said, his lips pressed tightly together, 'will make us all late.'

'I'll try to avoid that if I can.'

He conceded, because he had no choice, but with little grace.

The staff team slotted quickly into the new daily routine. At 9.15, there were diary and planning meetings, and a chance to respond to some of the 200 letters that arrived daily. Vicky's personal secretary, Ann Holmes, vetted everything that didn't come from the Palace or Number 10, and was an expert at sniffing out letters which needed special attention. She was a homely-looking, yet rather withdrawn woman in her mid-fifties, who had served several archbishops, dutifully if not devotedly, and kept her private life to herself. Vicky appreciated her quiet dependability, but wished she wasn't so hard to get to know.

Despite the rigorous filtering, she endeavoured to send a personal reply to as many correspondents as she could. It bemused her that churchgoers sent endless advice, each of them with their own hotline to God and a handle on how to solve the world's problems. One letter suggested which perfume to wear if she wanted to have the maximum impact, and it wasn't from the manufacturer. She wondered if any of her predecessors had been recommended an aftershave. Not those with beards, that was for sure.

She always responded to children, spoke to them online if possible, and with her e-phone camera showed them their drawings displayed on her wall. These 'meetings' were as important as any other, she explained to Ann.

And there were endless meetings, from ten to lunch most days – a delegation from a charity or pressure group, an on-screen conference call, a face to face with a faith leader overseas, if their technology permitted, a traditional phone call if not. Vicky had never appreciated, but nor it seemed did anyone outside Lambeth Palace, how many archbishops relied on regular support and advice from 'the centre'. To her relief, they did call her – a woman whose authority they struggled to recognise. She made them a priority. Their people suffered for their faith in ways she would never know, their churches attacked and ransacked, worshippers maimed, killed or imprisoned, their homes burnt down, wives raped, children taken into slavery. Or they might live at the centre of a disaster zone, living with the consequences of famine, flood and earthquake. Their stories left her shaken and heartbroken, overwhelmed by their courage and dignity, and deeply ashamed of any moans she might have at her own lot in life. By comparison, how puny were the difficulties experienced by Christians in the UK, even now.

'When are you coming to visit, Archbishop? The cameras follow you and people will see what we suffer. It will make all the difference.'

So, they still wanted her, even if it was only for her global connections, her potential access to governments, the World Bank, the World Health Organisation, the United Nations and many more international agencies working in the field of peace, poverty and justice. And, of course, her profile in the world media. An awesome responsibility, yet she was tied in those early months by her many commitments in the UK; even if, by comparison, it seemed like tossing breadcrumbs to well-fed pigeons.

Mornings were also for press conferences. She had a very enthusiastic press officer, intent on using any opportunity, even Vicky's leisure time, as grist to the mill.

'Anything to declare, Archbishop?' Sarah Mulherne asked at their first meeting, crossing a sleek pair of legs and flicking back her thick russet-coloured locks, as she grabbed her device. A former editor of a woman's page in one of the major tabloids, she reminded Vicky of a fox, composed and swift on the attack. Not at all the shambling yet canny Mike Barnes she was used to in Larchester. This new-generation PR peddler, using all the cunning known to woman in her battle with the press, would take some getting used to.

'Anything in the closet I should know about, bearing in mind that anyone and everyone can stitch you up, and almost certainly will.'

'You know about the accusations of an improper relationship?'

'Yes. Did you?'

'What?'

'Have a bit of vice versa.'

'Certainly not. Do you think I would be sitting here today if there was any truth in it?'

Sarah held up her hands in self-defence.

'Whoa, sorry, Archbishop. Just need to know what I'm dealing with, if you're to survive.'

'I think the story has finally died a death. I certainly hope so.'

'Hm,' she said, non-committally. 'Anything else?'

'Tom . . .'

'The child that died? Yes, got that.'

'The inquest verdict was accidental death,' Vicky said, a little too quickly.

How she hated having to shield Tom. What must it be like to have a wife whose job constantly exposed him to possible public censure? For all that she had shelved the whole thing at the back of her mind, the truth was that every time it was brought out again, she felt anxious and vulnerable.

'OK. But you'd better talk me through it,' Sarah said. 'I'd rather be prepared. Tomorrow?'

Then, moving on, 'There's a new musical opening in London about the suffragettes. How would you feel about hosting a talk-back session over drinks after the first night, with the audience, actors and journalists?'

Before Vicky had a chance to reply, Sarah continued, 'You're a cardi-aerobics fan, right? Planning is underway for a huge charity cardi-aerobathon at the old Olympics arena next year for world aid. Great PR.'

'I'll need to train.'

'Is that a problem?'

Vicky paused, thought of the crammed diary, realised it would probably mean going for that early rise she had tried so hard to avoid, and groaned.

'No. It'll be good for me.'

'Anything else you can suggest?'

'Hobnob with the *Hello* set, whip off my cope and mitre and dance around some celebrity's swimming pool in a bikini? But that would probably be poor PR, given the mid-life muffin top I'd be showing off.'

Sarah gratified her with a quick smile.

'Maybe not, then,' she said, snapping shut her device.

'By the way,' she added as an afterthought, 'any chance of reflections on TV or radio, I always grab them. Live is good – you can't be edited.'

'How many?'

'Up to you. I can get you at least a couple a month. We can do them from the little studio here, as we have an ISDN line to the BBC.'

'Who writes them?'

She looked at Vicky in surprise.

'You, of course.'

'Of course.'

'Let me just warn you – always be on your guard. It's horrid thinking we've done well, then getting mashed. And it will happen. But we'll bash 'em back with our positive stuff and try and get some balance.'

'Don't sink,' Vicky whispered to herself, as the door closed. 'Let me live each moment with equanimity, alive to every encounter, every interaction, every tiny joy and pleasure, for this moment, this experience, is uniquely itself. It will never come again. Nor will it leave me exactly as I am now. Let that thought transform the most mundane occurrences into unique opportunities, so that I welcome every face that appears at the door or pops up on the screen, however unscheduled, as if it were Christ himself.' She inhaled deeply and felt herself unwind.

At 12.30, when the staff officially stopped for lunch, Vicky ate sandwiches on the hoof, on the way to yet another engagement.

'Anything except fish,' she had said to Ann. 'Makes the breath faintly fishy for the rest of the afternoon.'

Ann nodded and made a note.

'And nothing with mayo in it. Impossible to maintain your dignity eating a gloopy sandwich with more of it smeared across your mouth and hands than between the limp pieces of bread. And get me tooth-picks, will you? No one will take the Archbishop seriously if she has lettuce stuck between her teeth.'

At 2.00 there was often a visit to a school, a church, a business, a project, or a hospice. Or she might host a reception, a seminar, a government minister, an overseas dignitary. She was warned that in the summer the palace would play host to large numbers of visitors, and that her fund-raising garden parties could raise a great deal of money for the charities of her choice. And play havoc with the hydrangeas she had asked the gardeners to plant.

At 4.30, whenever possible, she joined the staff for tea around the conference table in the library, where they reviewed the day and fought over the biscuit tin. It was a vital opportunity to build a sense of loyalty and co-operation in her team, to let them air their grouses and settle their minor disputes. At 5 p.m., as their voices receded, doors closed and silence settled on the corridors, her inner self seemed to unwind and settle too. This hour or so was sacrosanct, essential for reading minutes and briefing papers, for the preparation of talks and radio pieces, for in-depth Bible study and sermon preparation, or simply jotting down random thoughts that might be useful one day.

There had been so many occasions in these first weeks when she had been expected to spout relevantly, rousingly and wittily at the drop of a hat. And on virtually any topic – atheism, heresy, global poverty, high finance, business, civil law, ethics, morality, science, education, and, thanks to her gender, fashion and flower arranging. More formal speaking opportunities such as sermons and speeches for cathedrals and theological colleges, university colleges and the Lord Mayor's Banquet, which she might once have mulled over for a week and written up in half a day, now likewise fought for a bite out of this daily hiatus before Tom arrived home.

She had never allowed anyone to write her speeches and sermons before, but the sheer wealth of things she was required to do, and the competition with millions of other voices to be the best she could be, demanded collaboration. So after whatever consultation, briefings, reading, studying and meditation she could squeeze in, she wove her material together then tested it out on whoever she could find at the time.

'Is this hobnobbing below stairs really necessary?' Dan Clements asked her. 'The domestic staff have work to do.'

'That's the audience I need to keep in mind, Dan. If they find me comprehensible, relevant and challenging, there's a chance I might have a message for the general populace. If not, back to the drawing board. Constructive criticism is healthy. It's a chance to learn and grow. And they seem to be the only ones I can persuade to give it to me.'

He nodded impassively and left her to it.

Assuming Tom arrived home from work at a reasonable time, they sat down with a G and T to chat and then eat the food they now had a cook prepare for them. On a good day they might have an hour or so, though the time rarely passed without a tap at the door, and she would rush to get there with Tom's voice behind her muttering, 'What now?' On a bad day he would be so late that dinner was left in the microwave while she dashed off to the evening's round of receptions, anniversaries, inductions, Eucharists and dinner parties. She was rarely in bed before 1 a.m. Then up again at 6 a.m. to snatch time for a quick run, then prayer and Bible study, before getting ready to face the daily demands.

And the daily demands were endless, the urgent constantly robbing the important. The administrative staff did their best to prevent unwelcome encroachments into the cage they created for her, weeding out the non-essential and unsuitable, but some things inevitably slipped through the bars. Every day started with a carefully planned agenda. Unfortunately, this did not account for everyone else's agenda, much of which involved her input, and she ended up being bounced from one thing to another. She quickly realised that unless she was very careful there would never be time to do what she knew she had to do, namely to unravel the divisions in the church and re-knit them with a strengthened resolve to stand together against political discrimination, bullying, or injustice.

What struck her about the true greats – Jesus, Gandhi, Mandela, Mother Teresa – was that they seemed so unhurried. They stopped to give attention where and to whom it was necessary, refusing to allow persistent demands to distract them from their essential purpose. Their energy was never diluted, but kept concentrated, and applied with purpose where it really mattered.

It was vital she try to follow their example, however inadequately. She knew only too well how easily an exhausted mind could go on strike. She understood breakdown. Been there, done that, got the T-shirt, she said to herself: a lifetime ago, when I was an inexperienced young curate and knew no better. That was post-natal depression, argued a voice in her head, the hormones in free-fall. Huge life changes, stress, pressure, isolation – not just overwork. It could never happen now. Could it?

1992

Within a few months of starting her curacy Vicky was responsible for the parish magazine, the weekly newsletter, the Sunday School, the youth club, assemblies in the church primary school, the over-sixties circle and the mother-and-toddler group. That was apart from regular preaching, funerals, weddings, leading services and an ever-expanding visiting list that took in the local hospital. All without a car, because Tom needed it to get to and from work; and despite a total absence of workable public transport. The church alone was nearly a mile from home. After several weeks of thrice-daily hikes she bought herself a little moped and on days when the heavens opened, put up with looking as bedraggled as a cat that had fallen into the village pond.

She had settled into a large parish in north-east London, since Tom had no desire to follow her back to the frozen north. In her final year at St Christopher's she had rifled daily through the files holding ads for curates submitted by hopeful vicars using college as a kind of cheap matchmaking agency – but she couldn't see any that seemed the right match.

'Don't be so fussy,' said the college principal. 'Beggars can't be choosers. However open they say they are to women's ministry, the truth is few clergy really want a woman, since she can't stand in for them at Communion.'

'Especially a woman on the verge of matrimony who they think will immediately start popping out babies,' she finished for him.

There were several interviews, but whatever chemistry it required to bond a vicar with his curate did not materialise. No one else, it seemed, was prepared to live in a tiny box of a curate's house on a council estate in Killingdon, and Roger Davidson, the vicar, was desperate.

He was a clean-shaven, energetic little man with thinning white hair and rimless spectacles, whose uniform of ill-fitting moss-green trousers, Fair Isle tank top and scratchy-looking, marsh-coloured tweed jacket manifestly hadn't changed much since he was a boy in the fifties. When he showed her around the parish, in a flat working man's cap, she noticed that however out of touch he might appear, everyone knew who he was and greeted him with a friendly, 'Hello, vicar.'

'Typical social problems associated with deprivation,' he pointed out to her, as they walked past endless rows of back-to-back terraced housing, interrupted by the odd corner shop. He nodded at shopkeepers standing smoking in their doorways, and acknowledged the occasional shopper, weighed down by despondency as much as their heavy bags. 'Low house values, high levels of crime and fear of crime, unemployment, low skills and educational attainment, minimal public facilities, high levels of alcohol and drug dependency and teenage pregnancy, early mortality. Sure you'd want to come?'

Vicky looked around at the cheerless, treeless street-scene and determined not to let it depress her.

'There's such a sense of abandonment. A little bit of love could go a long way,' she said.

Her comment was greeted by a surprised glance of appreciation.

'You'll do,' was all he said.

The church's services appeared to reflect his own preference for the safe and reliable.

'Middle-of-the-road, no evangelical gusto or Anglo-catholic pomp here, thank you,' he said.

Vicky was disappointed. She disliked the balanced, rather bland traditionalism of an organisation toeing a line that wouldn't upset anyone, but wouldn't challenge them either. He watched her expression and said, 'Not what you would have chosen, eh? More the happy-clappy type?'

In fact, her own taste was actually fairly eclectic. She enjoyed the hushed reverence of the Anglo-catholicism of her childhood, but she wasn't going to let Roger patronise her for a style of worship she had come to appreciate because it allowed for more freedom of emotion and expression.

'No one refers to football crowds as happy-clappy,' she remarked quietly, forcing a smile. It didn't do to challenge one's boss before he had even taken her on. 'And the contemporary style has more appeal to children and young people.'

'Ah,' he said, 'then let me show you St Margaret's.'

The daughter church was a gloomy-looking pre-fab on a small, weed-infested patch of council estate, covered in broken glass, empty curry cartons and dog mess. A sad, hand-written notice announced that St Margaret's was open for morning prayer once a month at 10 a.m. Vicky peered through the cracked window panes. There were no pews, just a large, dismal space with chairs stacked up against the wall.

'Once you learn the ropes, you can have full responsibility for this place, and do with it more or less as you please,' Roger said curtly. 'I've enough to contend with without catering for the half-dozen or so that come down here – most of them because they're disgruntled with the other church.'

Her heart leapt. This was exactly the sort of potential she was looking for, but there would be Tom to convince. How could she drag him to a place like this, so far removed from his well-heeled family's home in Hove?

'Do you want to break off our engagement?' she asked when she brought him down to see Killingdon, and they stood surveying the curate's house, Tom with a look of disbelief on his face. 'I wouldn't blame you if you did. I'm asking such a lot of you. And this is my calling, not yours.'

He reached for her hand, his eyes never moving from the house, and she feared the worst.

'Just give me a bit of time,' he said. 'It's a lot to take in.'

By the time they arrived back at the vicarage, he seemed his old self, advising Roger in how to deal with his hernia, and explaining to Gill, his wife, the new procedures for varicose veins.

'I know I'm old-fashioned,' Roger confided as they were about to leave, 'but I do find it difficult paying someone to do what Gill has done for free for all these years.'

'Would you feel like that if I were your curate?' Tom asked.

'Well, no,' Roger admitted, 'but it wouldn't be the same.'

'Ah, but it would, wouldn't it?' Tom pushed, switching on his disarming, doctorly charm.

'You're right. I'll get used to it,' Roger beamed, patting Tom on the arm as he closed the door behind them. Manifestly, having his own medical consultant on hand more than compensated for being forced into taking on a female curate.

Roger turned out to be a hard taskmaster. His job, he insisted, was to teach her the ropes, and that meant two things. The first involved a course in traditional English vicaring. She must learn the liturgies off by heart, singing them with the correct intonation, syllabic stress and phraseology.

'Let your nasal passages thrum to lend your voice sonority,' he ordered, as he stood in front of her in an empty church, while she attempted to sing for him.

In vain did she try to suggest that the PA system rendered the careful use of the nose obsolete. Nor would he concede that chanting psalms had little relevance, if most people didn't know how to go about it.

'A congregation can't sing them without a strong choir to lead them,' she asserted.

'What's wrong with our choir, Vicky?' Roger asked in surprise.

She hadn't the heart to say that three warblers, a cat and two old crows hardly constituted a choir.

'Ah,' he said, wagging a finger at her, 'I know your sort. You'd sacrifice our faithful old regulars for the sake of the young who never come anyway. But haven't they suffered enough change without their church imposing it on them too?'

He may have had a point, but Vicky wondered whether there wasn't room for compromise, to at least hold onto the one or two children they had. She threw in the occasional modern translation for the Bible reading, the odd visual aid, overheads, and interactive sermons. The older members of the congregation didn't appear to object, but Roger told her not to waste too much time on 'that sort of thing', because 'folk didn't really appreciate it'.

He wasn't being deliberately unkind, but in forty years of ministry, he and Gill had never travelled further than a borrowed cottage in Ambleside, and seemed unaware that the world, let alone the church, was moving on. Then again, he was the boss, and who was she to challenge his preferred style of worship?

'I quite like the caterwauling,' Tom said, as he lay sprawled on the settee, listening to her practising. 'It takes me back to the Catholic masses of my youth. Except that they were in Latin and we didn't understand a word.'

'That's exactly it,' she snapped. 'It takes me back to my childhood too. Services were in English, but we didn't understand them any better.'

'What's wrong with a tribute to the 1960s?'

'You enjoy playing devil's advocate, don't you?' she said, hands on hips. She never knew whether Tom was teasing or baiting her. 'For the church, the 1960s were already a tribute to the 1860s. Nostalgia has its limits. The church is forever looking in its rear-view mirror, instead of through the front windscreen at the way ahead.'

'Hoity-toity, Mrs Moderniser. You're beginning to sound like Margaret Thatcher.'

She picked up a cushion and threw it at him.

'Anyway, the chanting could come in useful one of these days.'

'Like when?'

'When you become a bishop,' he grinned, 'and have to adapt to every tradition.'

The thought amused them both enormously.

The second part of Roger's unique induction style seemed to involve divesting himself of as much of his own workload as he could: it now seemed as if the empathy Vicky had so admired at interview was subsumed by his exhaustion. As he handed everything off to her, he seemed like a drowning man who had seen help on the horizon. In her second week she observed as he took two funerals. In the third week there were three, and she was expected to do them all, before she had had a real chance to familiarise herself with the service. The same with weddings. When she expressed her anxiety, he said, 'I thought marrying folk was the concession you women got when the C of E allowed you to become deacons. Get on with it.'

Funerals were one thing. The deceased couldn't complain if the service wasn't up to scratch, and the bereaved were too caught up in their grief to notice any minor omissions on the part of the minister. But for a wedding couple it was a forever moment, recorded for posterity, to be remembered for as long as the relationship lasted. She made a huge effort to ensure she did a decent job, and over time she became increasingly more tired, physically and emotionally, than she had ever imagined possible.

Gill said to her, 'You know, I didn't like the idea at first of Roger working so closely with an attractive young woman. But life is so much easier these days.'

Vicky forced her gaping mouth into what she hoped passed for a condescending smile.

Tom, meanwhile, had his own struggles, and was working long, unsociable hours. His boss, a specialist consultant surgeon, was brilliant at what he did, when he was there to do it. When he wasn't, he expected his registrar to cover for him – while he attended to private patients or played a round of golf.

Yet despite the frustrations and frenetic pace of life, Vicky loved the work more than she ever dared to imagine. To be received into the heart of a new family and community without having to earn the right to be drawn into their aspirations and disappointments, their joys and their grief, was a sacred privilege.

Her greatest satisfaction – and steepest learning curve – was the youth drop-in she started at St Margaret's. It began with a dozen or so kids who met for a social, snooker and some disjointed discussion about religion every Wednesday evening. The little group of largely unparented urchins was a microcosm of the estate culture. How to communicate concepts like unconditional love when these youngsters had never known it? Certainly not by throwing them out the moment they set fire to a waste-paper basket, smoked in the toilets, stole from her purse or called her a f****** cow, goading her with their offensive, destructive behaviour to reject them, because that was what they had come to expect of adults.

Yet tough love had to establish boundaries. So she gathered the regulars together, and they drew up The Saint Maggie Club Rules. No booze, drugs, fighting, bad language or abuse. Instead, respect, courtesy, a commitment to one another and their environment. Laminated copies were pinned to every door, including the loo, where they had most chance of being read. After a two-week trial period, every member was expected to sign the contract. And gradually St Maggie's became the safe, even cool, place to be on a Wednesday evening, and the numbers steadily grew.

Vicky recognised that she was doing everything a man could do and more – except preside at Communion. It riled her. Wasn't she a priest when she sat with the relatives of the deceased she was burying, sharing in their grief? Or when she prepared a couple for marriage and joyfully pronounced them man and wife? Or when a heartbroken young woman summoned up every ounce of courage to tell her that her stepfather had robbed her of her virginity?

General Synod finally recognised the possibility of her calling in November 1992. The wheels would turn painfully slowly, of course. The legislation would take at least a year to pass through Parliament, and then each diocese would have to arrange its own priesting ceremony. But just before her turn, as she began to feel she had the measure of the job, her world turned on its axis. She was pregnant.

Tom was thrilled.

'Okay, so we didn't quite get the timing right,' he said, standing behind her with his arms around her waist, staring over her shoulder at the positive pregnancy test. 'But since we have been overruled, we must take it as perfect timing.'

She loved it when Tom's faith challenged her own. There was no way she wanted to undermine it, but an 'Easy for you to say' slipped out all the same. 'Your career doesn't have to go on hold. And you don't have to explain it to Roger.'

'Darling,' he said, turning her round to face him and looking at her with such reproach, 'I'll do my best to ensure your career is disrupted to the minimum.'

Then he laid his hand on her belly and added, 'And as for Roger, I'll beat him to a pulp if he upsets you, or this little one.'

As anticipated, Roger was hardly thrilled.

'Maternity leave, no one to do your work, and we'll still have to give you accommodation, I suppose?'

It was only what she expected, yet the acrimony of his response still left her winded.

'Roger, I'll work right up to the birth, take the shortest maternity leave I can, then come back and work as hard as ever.'

'And who will look after the baby then?' he asked, pointing accusingly at her stomach.

'Don't worry. We'll sort out childcare. People do these days.'

'Sorry, sorry, sorry,' he muttered, raking his hands through the remaining strands of his hair. 'When I heard I could have a curate it was such a relief. At last Gill and I could have a life.' He rubbed his eyes and sighed at length. 'Ach, she'll love having a baby around. So,' he said, shaking himself, and opening the diary, 'I'll do all the funerals and weddings from now on.'

It took Vicky a while to make the quantum leap.

'Why?'

'We can't have you,' he waved his hands around the stomach area, 'you know . . .'

'Showing a bulge?'

'Bursting into tears all over the place.'

'Why would I do that?'

'I seem to remember Gill was very emotional when she was pregnant.'

'I'm certainly not planning to be.'

'No, no, no, quite,' he said, vigorously shaking his head.

There was a short silence. The conversation had become too difficult, but he couldn't seem to find a way out of his embarrassment. Vicky came to his aid.

'I'll do all that I have ever done right up to my time. You may even be rushing me to the maternity department in the middle of the mid-week Eucharist.'

Gratified, she noticed she had managed to raise a slight smile at last.

'I am . . . pleased for you,' he said, as he escorted her to the vicarage front door, patting her on the shoulder. 'Children are a blessing. We wouldn't be without our two. And their offspring.'

The pregnancy was uneventful and she continued to work as hard as she had promised Roger she would. The locals, who had stared at a woman in a dog collar, gawped at one with an ever-expanding girth, as if these symbols of sanctity and sexuality were a contradiction in terms. Young people catcalled, shouting out lewd comments in the street. Children with special needs came up to her in shops and fondled her belly. The baby was public property. Particularly for church members, who wouldn't so much as allow her to wash up a cup.

The older ladies, led by Emily Turner, a rosy-cheeked great-grand-mother with a tightly permed cap of white curls and a will of iron, were thrilled at the idea of a clerical baby in their midst. Emily was already drawing up a childcare rota and fighting with her cronies over who would have first access to the baby. They regaled Vicky with old wives' tales about how to tell the gender or to induce labour when her time came. And they terrified her with their childbirth horror stories. Tom, who knew only too well what could go wrong, was furious. He commandeered the moped for his nine-mile trip to work and back, so that she could keep the car. He would arrive home soaked to the skin and shivering, reassuring her that it was worth the effort – for 'our son'.

It was a long and difficult labour. Tom never left her side, although, drowsy with gas and air, she vaguely recalled begging him to go home and get some sleep. At one point she thought she heard him shouting, 'Do something, now!' and had a vague impression of running feet, of being hoisted through the air, and transported on a moving bed. She thought she might have screamed. But that was the last thing she remembered for some time.

Tom was cradling her right hand in his when she eventually regained consciousness.

'Thank God,' he whispered, lifting it to his lips, as she tried to focus. 'How are you doing?'

Her left arm appeared to be out of order, attached to a complex pulley system of bags and bottles.

Slowly it came to her.

'The baby?'

'We have a beautiful little girl,' he said.

She was bewildered and turned her head to look for a crib.

'Then where is she?' she panicked.

'She's fine,' he whispered, stroking her hair, 'we'll bring her to you soon, but you nearly didn't make it. A haemorrhage. You lost a very great deal of blood.'

'A caesarean?' she asked. 'I feel as if I've been run over by a double-decker bus.'

It was the following day, as she held Alice in her arms, that Tom told her gently that she had not only had a caesarean section, but a hysterectomy.

'It was the only way to stop you bleeding to death. That was the first priority.'

'No more children? Oh Tom, I'm so, so sorry,' she whispered, stunned by the shock of it.

And then the tears came thick and fast, almost choking her, tightening the stomach muscles that pulled on tender, wounded flesh, until she didn't know whether it was the physical or emotional pain that made her cry out.

'Don't ever, ever blame yourself,' he said, getting up onto the bed, so that he could put his arms around her. 'I still have you, we have each other, and this beautiful babe.'

He rested his head on hers and, enfolded in each other, they wept together, their tears falling on the baby who slept innocently and peacefully between them.

When Alice was three months old Vicky decided to go back to work part time. Tom thought it too soon, both physically and emotionally. Alice was a colicky baby and didn't sleep well.

'I knew this would happen,' Vicky said wearily, changing Alice's nappy for what felt like the hundredth time that day.

'What?' Tom's head jerked back in a gesture of injured innocence.

'It's all right for you. You go out to work every day, while I'm stuck here, working on a conveyor belt in a factory, food in the slot, processed and out again in fifteen minutes. Anyway, I promised Roger I wouldn't leave him to manage all the Holy Week and Easter services on his own.'

Tom shrugged. 'Have it your own way.'

'So much for being in this together,' she muttered under her breath.

But Vicky discovered quickly that 'part time' doesn't exist in parish work, where a lifetime of pastoral work would be no more than a droplet in the vast ocean of human need. And the logistics, let alone the emotional impact of juggling long working hours with a new baby, were harder than she ever imagined. She certainly hadn't bargained for the guilt.

'Emily,' she asked one evening, arriving home at seven, an hour later than planned, as Emily was about to give Alice her bedtime bottle, 'am I a bad mother working like this?'

Emily cooed at Alice, lying on her lap. The baby gazed adoringly back, gurgling merrily. Vicky felt an additional pang. Alice seemed more settled with Emily than with her.

''Course not, Darling,' Emily said, without looking up. 'You've God's work to do. And we all love this little one, don't we?'

Alice gratified her with a beatific smile.

'If I wasn't a minister, would it be different?'

There was a pause.

'I don't think so. My daughter-in-law went out to work to pay the mortgage. They didn't want to rent no more, and who can blame them?'

Vicky didn't feel reassured as she lifted Alice out of Emily's capable hands, so that she could take over with the bottle. But Alice began to grizzle.

'I love her like one of my own, don't I?' Emily said, reaching out to take her back and calming her with a gentle rocking motion and a rhythmical pat on the back.

'Thanks, Emily,' Vicky whispered, as Emily finally handed her back her sleepy daughter. Tears sprang to her eyes. 'I don't know what I'd do without you.'

'There, there,' Emily said, patting Vicky's back this time, before she headed for the door.

Vicky was torn. This would be her only child, and she didn't want to miss any of the key developmental stages in her life. But on the days when she was a full-time mum, she felt more fretful than the baby, balking at the limitations motherhood imposed. She tried to explain it to Tom as they ate together.

'I seem to find the separation harder than Alice.'

'Vicky, she adores you.'

'I want to be with her more than anything in the world. I hate leaving her. But when I'm with her, I want to be somewhere else. Does that mean I'm not a natural mother? Maybe it's as well we can't have any more.'

Tom reached out for her hand and said, 'Vicky, stop beating yourself up. You're a good mother to Alice.'

'But I keep thinking, "When she's older . . . we'll be free again." And it's stupid, because I'm missing the moment, and when she does grow up,

I know I'll miss the gorgeous smell of her little baby's scalp, and the feel of her tiny head nestling into my neck, and those wonderful, trusting smiles. Especially as I'll only ever have them this once.'

They were interrupted by screaming from upstairs. Another unfinished conversation.

Looking back at those months after Alice's birth, Vicky realised that Tom saw what she couldn't: like King Canute holding back the tide, she was trying to keep the pain at bay by immersing herself in parish work. But the blow of her loss of fertility was bound to overwhelm her in the end.

It was the funeral of a cot-death baby that finally punctured her defences. The parents were young, pole-axed with shock and grief, bewildered as to why a loving God should take their beautiful boy. And she had no answers, nothing that would ease their devastation and make it more bearable.

The funeral went as well as could be expected. She was doing what she thought was a decent, professional job, when the young mum ran out of her pew, demanding to hold the tiny coffin. Vicky nodded at the undertaker and he placed it gently in the mother's arms. Vicky led her to the altar step, sat down with her and continued the service from there while the mother lovingly cradled and rocked her baby. At the end, when she invited both parents to carry their little one out to the graveyard, she only just managed to hold her own emotions in check.

That evening Tom was called out to an emergency at the hospital. She put Alice to bed, holding on to her for longer than usual, laying her down with a new fear clawing away her peace of mind. The last thing she wanted to do was to leave Alice with a babysitter, but it was a parish council meeting and she had little choice.

Discussions revolved around the cost of repairs to the steeple, how much was left to spend on new hymn books, and methods of pigeon prevention, because wedding couples were complaining that it was nothing short of a disgrace to have the bride's train trailing through bird muck as she walked up to the church door. Vicky couldn't bear it another moment and made her excuses, weathering Roger's manifest disapproval.

She said goodnight to the babysitter, and as the front door closed, ran into the sitting room and gave in to the tidal wave of pain that knocked her to the floor and left her face down, her body wracked by enormous, breath-stopping sobs, as she wept for the baby she had just buried and grieved for the children she would never have.

The GP diagnosed post-natal depression and prescribed anti-depressants, but they only blurred the edges of life. They didn't solve the problem. She couldn't go on putting on a brave face, pretending to the world that nothing was wrong. If she lost Alice too, which was her constant fear, she knew she wouldn't, couldn't believe any longer. She might go through the motions, as she was doing now. But a minister's life is indivisibly intertwined with their work. You could fool a lot of people for most of the time, but not all of them all of the time.

At funeral visits she found herself parroting answers she wasn't sure she believed. Services were same-ish, the words of the liturgy a jumble on the page, sermon preparation a difficult chore. She hadn't had time for personal devotions for months. How could she, when church and child swallowed up every available second?

'Vicky,' Tom said in desperation, when he arrived home late one night and found her in Alice's room, sitting on the floor sobbing because Alice had been screaming for the past hour. 'Have a few days' break. Go up to Durham and see that magician of a tutor of yours. Catch up with some of the girls. I'll look after Alice. We'll be fine, won't we, babe?'

He had lifted her out of the cot, and she was nuzzling into his neck, quiet at last.

Packing her case felt like defeat, but she was too tired to argue. Tom promised to square it with Roger, and next morning she drove north. The A1 was a nightmare. Lorries jammed up the dual carriageway, determined to overtake each other but unable to get up enough speed, causing an endless tailback in the fast lane. She banged the steering wheel with her fists and yelled in frustration until she was hoarse. This was not a good decision at all.

By the time she had made a short detour into Barnard's Castle for a quiet sandwich and found her favourite café shut, she was in no mood to bare her soul to Donald. She had warned him she had been diagnosed with depression and demonstrated it spectacularly by bursting into tears the moment she sank into the familiar armchair. He, of course, was his usual gracious self, and all the more so after taking a look at the misery etched all over her face. He got up unhurriedly and reached for the box of tissues he kept on a shelf above his desk – for just these purposes, she surmised.

'Lovely to see you, Vicky, after all this time,' he said calmly in that familiar, reassuring Scottish lilt of his. She couldn't help but snort into the tissue.

'Like this?' she asked, blowing her nose unceremoniously.

'I'm just glad you felt you could come. So, tell me what's going on.'

Where to start? She simply let it all come out in an unco-ordinated stream.

'I had to bury a child, a cot death. I'm sick of funerals – three a week, of juggling childcare with the job, of being Roger's dogsbody. I can't have any more babies, and I don't think Tom loves me any more.'

'Right,' Donald said slowly, narrowing his eyes. 'Let's tackle those issues one at a time. Three funerals a week? And what else are you doing?'

'School assemblies, youth club, preaching, weddings, visits . . .'

'Whoa there,' Donald interrupted, which was very unlike him.

But once she had started, she couldn't stop.

'I know this job is an enormous privilege. To be alongside people during their best and worst of times, to have them confide their innermost secrets and share their hopes and fears, but it wears me out. They don't seem to see the real me – just this image of the bouncy, happy curate. I'm so afraid of losing touch with who I am. I have no one to expose my vulnerability to, yet I feel as if I'm carrying the pain and hurt of the world, and I don't know what to do with it and I can't take any more.'

Donald sat quietly, letting her weep, and then, as the tears subsided, said abruptly, 'How many more plates do you think you can juggle, and when will you face the fact that you're not Superwoman? Depressed? I don't doubt it, when you've no time to come to terms with your own pain. When did you last get a decent night's sleep?'

She dabbed at her eyes.

'Can't remember. I have a baby who wakes up several times in the night.'

'You're exhausted, woman. Sleep deprivation is a form of torture, you know.'

He waited to see if she had heard him and she nodded uncertainly.

'Ach, be a bit kinder to yourself. Is it any wonder the funeral of a wee child got to you when you're deep in your own grief? Grief cannot be short-changed. Numbness, anger, and depression are all part of the process. You have to go through them before there can be any resolution. And no one seems to be making allowances for you. Not your irresponsible vicar. Not Tom. Not even you.'

'Tom tried, but I didn't listen. Stupid or what?'

'No, not stupid.' He shook his head sadly. 'But I just wish someone would pastor the pastors once in a while.'

He sat reflectively, chin resting on his folded hands, then drew breath and said, 'So much change and disappointment to contend with all at once. And how is Tom in all this?'

'He seems to work longer and longer hours. I sometimes think he's keeping away from me. The sex is pretty lousy. If we ever get time for it.'

'And why do you think that might be?'

'Fatigue?'

'And?'

She realised he knew what she had been thinking, and started crying again.

'Because it seems pointless. A waste of sperm.'

'And is it? For two people who love each other as much as you and Tom? Have you told him what you feel?'

She shook her head.

'Talk to him, Vicky. Don't shut him out.'

'Has he been talking to you?' she asked. How could this man read her marriage so well?

'Oh, for goodness' sake, woman. No, I'm just a humble man. But you see, we men can't bear to see our women broken. We want to fix it for them, and when we can't, if they won't let us we feel helpless and . . .'

'Run in the opposite direction?'

'That's the risk.'

She finally managed a smile.

'Ach, Vicky,' he said, 'your smile is like the sun shining through the rain. Might there be room for the tiniest little rainbow of hope?'

'I have felt so hope-less,' she said. 'The desecration of my body has left me with such a sense of emptiness. I felt I had nothing left to give.'

'And that's entirely normal for anyone who has sustained a form of amputation. Instead of giving yourself time for the wound to heal, it was torn open all over again by that dear baby's funeral. But let's see if we can look at this differently.'

She looked up at him with bewilderment.

'Taking funerals forces you to confront your own mortality sooner than the rest of humanity. You are also grieving the loss of your fertility and womanhood. In other words, you're experiencing a very early and precipitate mid-life crisis. Combine that with becoming a mum, which is a major life change, and the child who reminds you continually of what you cannot have again, and is it any wonder that your emotions have gone on strike?

'Of course you can only go through the motions of ministry at the moment. But let the liturgy carry you. Hang on to the words of the funeral service you have to say,' and he grinned at her broadly, 'what is it, three times a week? Key statements of faith, wonderful promises regarding our eternal and everlasting destiny. Say them as a discipline. State them because they're true. It's at times like this, when we feel numb, that the liturgy sustains us. If the words of the prayer book float over your head, say them nonetheless, because they're touching parts of you too tired to respond just now. But one day, I promise you, they will.'

For a while they sat in a companionable silence, broken only by the spring birdsong outside the open window she hadn't consciously noticed until now, as blackbirds, sparrows, starlings and blue tits merrily went about the business of building new nests.

'I have been so unaware of nature, living on our estate,' Vicky said wistfully.

Donald nodded sympathetically.

'Okay, so here's a spiritual prescription for you. Work part time without guilt – even if it means getting tougher with that vicar of yours. Make time for Tom, bathe yourself in liturgical prayer, and rest whenever you can. And one more thing.'

He took a pristine piece of paper out of his desk.

'A quote to leave with you. I wrote it out for you, knowing you'd come for it one of these days.'

He handed it to her and she read, *For us, pain is a problem. For Him, it's a possibility.*

She looked at him quizzically.

'Who said it? I'm not sure where it originated, but my sister, Molly, clung to it. She developed multiple sclerosis in her twenties and died of it just a couple of months ago. She used to say, "It's not what happens to you, but what you do with it that counts." And she brought so much joy to so many.'

As she got up to go, Donald took her into his arms for the first time and gave her a fatherly bear hug.

'And have you a photo of this gorgeous baby?'

She delved into her handbag, retrieved a photo of Alice, and held it up for him to see.

'Ah yes,' he said, as he studied it, 'a wee beauty. And so like her mother.'

She turned at the door to thank him again, but he dismissed her with a wave, as if she were still one of his students.

'Just one thing,' she persisted. 'You remember when I was a naive theology student, you talked to me about being a wounded healer?'

He nodded, smiling.

'I guess I'm learning about the first part of that, at least.'

He studied her for a moment. 'In pain lies the gain, Vicky. No cross without cost.'

*   *   *

She spent the night with Melanie and her ever-expanding brood. With three children under the age of five, Melanie was a fair representation of a contented Mother Earth. Fortunately, her large, placid husband seemed to enjoy getting hold of as much flesh as a man could handle. He bathed the children, a rumbustious, wet and noisy business, then left 'the girls' to jabber and went out for a night with the lads.

'I don't know how you do it,' Vicky said to her, when number two child, her godchild, had been put to bed for the third time, and Melanie threw herself onto a sofa that sagged beneath her bulk.

'Easy, pet,' she yawned, reaching for the glass of wine she had poured for herself, 'when you don't plan to do anything else.'

'But you got a first in social sciences. Don't you ever feel it's wasted?'

'Raising this lot? You must be joking. Naw, I'm happy enough. And you? How's motherhood mixing with vicaring?'

'It's curdled,' Vicky admitted ruefully.

It was nearly two in the morning when they finally went up to bed. She heard Melanie get up with the children at four and felt a pang of guilt. Then turned over and went back to sleep.

'Come for a break any time,' Melanie said, with one child in her arms and another dangling from her waist, as Vicky left for Leeds the next morning. They both looked doubtfully at the children and laughed uproariously. 'Well, for the chat, then. And bring Alice with you. I'll not notice another.'

'Happy enough.' All the way to Leeds, Melanie's words from the previous night echoed in Vicky's head. Happiness wasn't part of the Christian parcel, was it? But according to St Paul, contentment was, though even he had to learn it the hard way, in beatings and imprisonment. What was her trial compared to his? Oh to discover that quality of being 'happy enough' that Melanie had, a sense of contentment with one's lot that enabled one to find rest for body, mind and spirit.

The three days with Mandy, now an accountant living in an upwardly mobile part of Leeds, were a whirlwind of restaurants, pubs, cinema and shopping. Mandy had taken annual leave and they slept until midday then stayed out until midnight. That was what the smart, fashionable new Leeds was all about, Mandy explained, as she marched Vicky into Harvey Nichols for a makeover.

'All right for you,' Vicky said ruefully, as they headed for the tea room. 'But on what I earn . . .'

'My treat,' Mandy insisted. 'My investment in the girl who's going to be one of the first women vicars, and is currently in danger of becoming as dowdy as the rest of them.'

'Mandy!' she said reproachfully, and couldn't help feeling a little put out.

'Okay, so when did you last look at yourself in the mirror? When did you last have your hair done? There's no virtue in letting yourself go. It's no advert for your cause.'

She had to recognise that Mandy might well be Yorkshire Jewish, up-front and in your face, but her ruthless honesty was always in her friends' best interests.

Bev, who had just got her partnership in a GP surgery in Otley, joined them for dinner on the last night. As they were savouring the last mouthfuls of their tiramisu, she said, out of the blue, 'Vicky, where do you stand on the homosexual issue?'

Vicky's heart sank. The last thing she wanted at that moment was theological controversy.

'Why do you ask?'

'No particular reason. Just that the papers seem to be accusing the C of E of homophobia,' Bev said.

'I guess I need to give it more thought,' Vicky said, wondering for the first time in months what Garth was doing, and why she hadn't bothered finding out. It was a cop-out response and Bev was too sharp not to know it, but she let it go, nonetheless leaving Vicky with the uncomfortable feeling that there was more to the question than met the eye.

There was no one at home when she got back. A note on the kitchen table from Tom said that he had taken Alice to his parents' house in Hove for a couple of days and would be back that evening.

Disappointed, Vicky went up to Alice's bedroom and sat in the dark, inhaling the baby smells that lingered in the room. She reached into the cot for Tracy the rag doll, and played with the little button nose that Alice loved to suck. For no reason she could fathom, she was suddenly overwhelmed with a sense of gratitude for all that life had bought her – a husband, a child, a job she loved. She sat for quite a while, barely aware of the passage of time, simply enjoying the profound stillness in the room, every fibre of her being expanding with a contentedness she hadn't known for some time.

Tom found her there when he got back, their sleeping baby parcelled up in a fleece bag in his arms. Vicky got up and went over to him to take a peek at their little daughter, then looking up at Tom, and seeing the questioning expression on his face, told him with her smile all he needed to know about her state of mind. He reached across the bundle in his arms and kissed her softly on the lips. Then he laid Alice in her cot, and they stood for some time, their arms wrapped around each other, watching Alice fall more and more deeply into the land of baby dreams. Then she took Tom by the hand and led him to their bedroom.

A week later, Vicky found herself making an unexpected journey to Surrey, where Marjorie had been serving her curacy. Simon had rung her to tell her that Marjorie was dying. She hadn't been well for some time, but in her usual no-nonsense way, she had refused to let anyone make a fuss.

She was in the local hospice, so weak she couldn't sit up, with the sallow, greyish pallor Vicky had come to recognise in the final stages of cancer. But the inner radiance that had always been her great draw couldn't be dimmed by disease or drugs. Nor was her sense of humour.

'A waste of money training me,' she said with a wry smile, as Vicky pulled up a chair and sat down at her side.

'Not from my perspective,' she said, laying her hand gently on Marjorie's arm. It felt crinkly, like crepe paper. 'You were like a mother to so many of us.'

Marjorie laughed dismissively, then reached for a glass of water. Vicky held it to her lips while she sipped.

'Have you heard from Jan?' she asked weakly, wheezing like a pair of old bellows.

Vicky put the glass back onto the bedside table. 'Not a word in all these months,' she said.

'It was all about a man. Often is.'

Vicky tried to keep her expression neutral, but Marjorie, as ever, saw past it.

'Don't judge her too harshly, Vicky,' she rasped. 'We can never know all the circumstances. That's why judging's not for us to do.'

'Why has she never contacted me?'

Marjorie took in several gulps of air.

'Perhaps because she feared your reaction.'

Vicky let it go.

'And Garth? Have you news of him?'

Marjorie turned her head and studied Vicky for a while, a look of intense sadness ruffling the calmness of her face for the first time.

'You don't know?'

Vicky felt as if an icy hand was passing up and down her spine. She shook her head.

'Garth killed himself. A few months ago. Went into his garage, got into the car. Put on a worship song. Turned on the engine. He couldn't reconcile . . .'

'Oh no, no, no, no,' Vicky moaned. She laid her head, face down, on the bedding that covered Marjorie's prostrate form. Slowly, Marjorie raised her one free hand and began to stroke Vicky's hair with it.

'Don't, Vicky, don't,' she murmured. 'Nothing you or I or any of us could do about it. His choice.'

'But you at least cared,' Vicky whispered. 'Unlike me – always so busy, so caught up in my own world.' Or had she ducked what she couldn't face? That she had no answers? Either way, she was culpable. She pushed it away. Too self-indulgent for now. This visit was not about her.

She lifted her head, pushed her hair off her face.

Marjorie watched her carefully. 'Always creates such guilt – suicide. Mourn Garth. Reflect. Should make us more compassionate, not crush us.'

She leant over the bed, reached for the oxygen, inhaled deeply and lay back down.

'And how are you, Marjorie? How does it feel, this last stage of the journey?'

'Hmmm, not afraid to talk about death? You'll be a good minister. Always knew you would be. I'm sick of visitors talking in corners in hushed whispers – even my training vicar. Just can't cope. Comes to the bed with a hail-fellow-well-met heartiness that drives me to distraction. Such a waste of time when there's so much to say. The Apostle Paul was so right when he said that if Christians can't face death with equanimity, we're the most miserable of beings. Especially ministers. Base our whole lives on false comfort. Sacrificed all for nothing. In the wrong job.'

The effort of such a passionate piece of communication had cost her, and she lay back on the pillows exhausted.

'I thought I was in the wrong job recently,' said Vicky. 'But I'm battling my way through.'

Marjorie turned her head to look at Vicky and reached for her hand. Hers was icy cold, yet her grip was surprisingly strong. She whispered haltingly, 'That's what I love about you, Vicky – your honesty. Never let . . . pressures to be . . . perfect priest suppress it. You're vivacious, clever . . . outspoken. You care and it shows.'

She gasped for breath, and Vicky squeezed her hand to stop her from continuing, but she took no notice. 'Charisma needs authority. That'll come . . . with experience. Then, you'll be exceptional. I shall watch from my vantage point in heaven . . . and smile, because I told you so.'

Vicky stroked Marjorie's arm, blinked back the tears and couldn't stop herself saying, 'I sometimes think I don't care enough. You at least kept in touch with Jan and Garth. I haven't.'

Marjorie looked into her eyes, and said as forcefully as she could, 'Each to his own gifting, Vicky. You have so much else to contend with, young family and all.'

She lay for a while, gazing into the distance with a beatific smile.

'I've worn you out,' Vicky said, but Marjorie shook her head slowly.

'What does it matter? I'm not going anywhere. Except into the arms of my Father.'

'I had better go all the same. To relieve the child minder.'

Marjorie released Vicky's hand and patted it, her eyes half closed.

'It's a beautiful road you travel on.'

Vicky thought she was referring to the spiritual journey and made some suitably pious-sounding noises of agreement. But Marjorie opened her eyes and, to Vicky's surprise, they twinkled with mirth. 'No, you twit – I meant the country road on the way back to the motorway. Never take . . . self too seriously, Vicky. Secret of survival for a minister.'

It pained Vicky enormously that Marjorie never lived to fulfil her dream of becoming a fully-fledged vicar. The first women were priested on 12 March 1994. Vicky's turn came the following April, and she decided to hold a belated, combined celebration with the awarding of her PhD, which she had delayed because of her wedding and finally managed to complete just before Alice was born. Her father wasn't well enough to attend, but Simon, Mandy, Bev, Melissa and Melanie, the usual suspects, all promised to turn out once more to toast the Revd Doctor Burnham-Woods.

With impeccable timing, a letter arrived from Boston the previous day. Vicky knew immediately who it was from and put it on the mantelpiece to open later, then couldn't leave it there, but tore the envelope apart and read it.

Dear Vicky

Over two years of complete silence. What must you think of me? The truth is I didn't know what to say, although that's a paltry excuse for the pain I must have caused you. All I can say is that I found it impossible to expose my betrayal of the trust you had in me. I feared you might be so disillusioned that it would jeopardise your own career, and I couldn't have borne that. Ruining one ministry was waste enough. And you have so much to give. But now I wonder whether the cover-up wasn't more for my sake. Your impression of me, our friendship, mattered too much.

So let me explain, if I can. I met Bud many years ago when I was training for church ministry at Archbishop Temple's College in Chicago. He and his wife had come over from New England for a year so that he could do foundational research for a doctorate in exchange for some teaching. They had one child already and his wife became pregnant again.

How can I ever explain the magnetism that drew this man and his student irresistibly together? It was frightening in its intensity. We knew it was wrong, but the head wouldn't get the message to the heart, however hard we tried.

Eventually, they went back to New England and I took up a parish in Boston, believing I could sublimate the passion I had for him in my work. Ministry certainly provided some compensations, if not consolation.

I wish I could tell you that we managed to keep our love pure and untainted. But it would be a lie. We went on meeting from time to time – pre-arranged liaisons, mainly at conferences, and each time, we vowed it was the last. In the end, the only solution was to flee. Which is how I ended up at St Christopher's. I planned to stay in the UK if I could.

But in the end, when Bud whistled, I came. I don't feel good about what we've done to his wife or their children. In fact, not a day passes when I don't feel deeply ashamed of it all – and I'll have to live with that for the rest of my life.

Bud has taken a teaching job at the Boston Theological Institute, and I work in the library part time. Otherwise I potter and tinker around the house we've rented, and I'm happy enough. A regular little home-maker. You'd never believe it. After all the rude things I said about those clergy spouses that wanted to share their husbands' ministries, rather than get ordained themselves, God bless 'em.

I'm sorry it's taken so long to tell you. Marjorie told me you were asking after me. If you can ever find it in your heart to forgive me, I'd love for you and Tom to come out here and visit with us.

Your ever-loving
Jan

Vicky dissected every word, convinced that if only she looked intently enough there would be some clue as to how this woman she thought she knew so well had thrown ethics, morality and calling to the wind to become a suburban little housewife. No, not even that. A married man's mistress. She read the words until they blurred, glistened and flowed into each other through the tears she was determined to hold in check. Such hypocrisy and deception. How could the woman crawl out of the woodwork after all these years, expecting to pick up the threads of their relationship as if the years of silence had never happened? She was livid at the inept timing that threatened to pinch the cherry off her cake.

She had been peeling and slicing carrots at the sink, and when Tom arrived home, she pointed with the end of the knife at the letter lying on the table.

'Jan didn't deliberately set out to offend you,' he said cheerily, scanning it. 'These things happen. Welcome to the real world.'

'Offend?' she shouted back. 'She betrayed me.'

He looked mystified.

'You men just don't get it, do you – the depth of sisterhood we developed. We shared our lives for two whole years. She was inspirational. She had guts. She was the one who always went on about being single-minded, not to let anything get in the way of our calling – even if it meant celibacy.'

'She was preaching to herself, Vicky. People do that when their morals are compromised. It doesn't mean she didn't mean it. It means she was human.'

'And that excuses it? You think I'd excuse you if you had a bit on the side?'

'Nope,' he said grinning, 'not the way you keep waving that knife at me.'

He took a bottle of wine out of the cupboard, and rooted in the drawer for a corkscrew. 'I think I'm in need of this,' he announced, as he settled himself at the kitchen table with a glass, then, looking at Vicky out of the corner of his eye, said, 'I wouldn't say no to a trip to Boston.'

'On your own, then,' she snapped.

'Oh, it's like that, is it?'

'Tom – don't you see? If being a Christian means anything these days, it means being counter-cultural, saying no to cheating, lying and deception, standing up for decency, faithfulness, and doing what's right.'

'It all sounds, well, a bit *Brief Encounter*-ish to me. Awfully nice in principle – but belonging to a bygone age.'

So they spent the evening before her long-awaited ordination arguing. All because of Jan.

Roger's ordination gift to her was full responsibility for St Maggie's. With the help of one or two members of the local Narcotics Anonymous she painted it from top to bottom, then pinned a poster to the board outside announcing a weekly, family-friendly service on Saturday afternoons. Mornings were out, as none of the locals were out of pyjamas before midday. A dozen or so children began to turn up regularly, some with a parent in tow, for an event that involved dramatised stories, artwork and a karaoke-style sing-along, complete with action songs. Vicky had a sudden picture of Kelvin, the earring man at her selection conference, and wished he could see her now.

Many of the children were listless and unresponsive.

'I suspect they've had nothing to eat before they came out,' Tom deduced, in medical mode.

'So we provide food.'

Vicky rang the ever-amenable Emily, who said she'd gather her army of grandmas to provide it. 'But where's the money coming from, Vicky?'

'Good point, Emily. I'll see if Roger will cough up.'

'You want a budget for what?' he shouted at their next catch-up. 'Have you any idea of the state of the church finances? I haven't enough money for the new service books we need. And God help us when the roof holds out no longer.'

But he capitulated in the end, until she managed to get a charitable grant.

Within a year the numbers had grown to thirty children and Vicky contacted the *Church Times* to suggest a feature. Simon Marshall saw it and rang to ask whether his younger brother, Andy, could join them for his gap year. He happened to be a brilliant musician. His attractions drew in several female students from a local college, who formed a special bond with Alice, and took charge of her when Tom wasn't around, enabling Vicky to increase her teenage drop-ins to two evenings a week. The CAB moved into the premises, along with the local councillors' surgery, and an NHS health promotion clinic. Quite by accident, they had become a community centre.

A rather pompous health and safety officer arrived one morning, claiming he had been informed that the kitchen was not up to standard. He clucked and tutted, fussed over cooker and cupboards, tried the doors, tapped the beams, made copious notes, and sent a report that concluded the building was unsafe and must be shut down forthwith.

Vicky was livid, not just at such petty-minded bureaucracy, but that someone had put him up to it in the first place. She suspected a neighbouring vicar who resented seeing children cross the boundary from his parish to hers. But anger would change nothing, so she contacted the local newspaper, which quoted her in full: 'We show children unconditional love and acceptance, and back it with moral values and spiritual truth, so that they can rediscover a sense of self-worth and find lasting hope for the future. If that doesn't offer children the best chance of health and safety, I don't know what does.'

The tabloids picked up the story and ran with it. The local MP brought the situation to the attention of the House. The Archbishop of Canterbury sent a letter of encouragement. Kind benefactors sent more than enough money to rebuild the kitchen and the toilets. Combined with a council grant, there was enough funding left over for a part-time centre manager.

'You're a star, a celebrity,' Andy announced with glee, as they surveyed their revived premises, 'a national treasure.'

'National treasures end up in museums,' she said, digging him in the ribs.

But that small taste of campaigning alerted Vicky to a power she didn't know she possessed. When she spoke in public, she saw the way people hung on to her every word, how she could shape them like clay on a wheel, moulding them to get the response she wanted. It was invigorating, but it made her feel unsettled, wanting more.

The silly things that had always annoyed her about Roger suddenly became intolerable – the way he dunked his biscuit in his tea at meetings, leaving a mushy mess of crumbs in the bottom of the cup that she, invariably, was expected to wash up. The way he nit-picked at her sermons, criticising her grammar, as if a failure in the English language was tantamount to heresy. ' "It gave Tom and me", Vicky, not "Tom and I". You are the indirect object. How many times . . ?' Most of all, the way he attributed so little value to what was going on at St Maggie's.

Vicky was now seeing Donald twice a year for spiritual direction, and she said to him, anxiously, 'The success of St Margaret's, the adulation of the media, and the response of the public are almost like a drug. I feel slightly high on it all. And now I seem to think I know better than Roger how to run a church. It just doesn't feel right somehow.'

'Ah, Vicky,' he said, 'brownie points for self-awareness. Roger has been faithful in his ministry in the only way he knows how. Your assessment of him may simply be a pandering to vanity and pride in self-righteous disguise. Both are poison to the soul. They're also destructive of decent working relations, and this is often a sign that the time has come for you to move on.'

' "Roger, this church just ain't big enough for the two of us," you mean?'

'If you don't,' he continued, ignoring her facetiousness, 'the criticisms will turn into disloyalty, and that would lead to division in the church you say you love. Divorce hurts many more people than the perpetrators. That's how it starts – small resentments that get blown up out of proportion. And that would be sad for everyone concerned.'

'It's not admitting defeat?'

'It's preservation.'

'I don't want to hand my centre on to someone else.'

'Since when has ministry been about what we want? And since when is it your centre? And as for that wee gift of yours of manipulating an audience, you'll treat it with respect, won't you? It's an awesome responsibility, abusive if you use it for your own ends.'

She left, chastened, and began to think about finding her own parish.

2020

Whenever she could, Vicky popped into the chapel to join the daily rituals of the order of nuns who lived in Lambeth Palace, maintaining an atmosphere of constant prayer. The ordered calm was always restorative and helped remind her of the essential lessons learnt throughout her almost thirty years of ministry. Only now, looking back, did she fully understand the significance of those early years in Killingdon, a journey that involved such a steep learning curve and that took her so much further than she had ever gone before in her ability to identify with the hurting and broken.

First among all the lessons she learnt was that if she truly wanted to serve she must not measure successful leadership by society's standards, but constantly return to the model of flawed and wounded vulnerability that Donald had helped her to understand.

ELEVEN

In expectation of the resurrection of the dead, the person who hopes, casts away the soul's protective cloak in which the wounded heart has wrapped itself, so as not to let anything more come near it. We throw ourselves into this life . . . by virtue of the hope that God will find us in death, and will raise us and gather us.

JÜRGEN MOLTMANN

OCTOBER 2020

Vicky's maiden speech in the Lords was a strenuous, impassioned attempt to sway not only the House, but also the wider public, to win them over to the value of the church and the Christian faith in British culture. She shared tales of the life-transforming power of Christianity in Killingdon, where disenfranchised young people had become not only useful citizens, but local councillors, teachers and school governors, bettering the quality of their own communities. She described how, years later, in Wooten Grange in the Diocese of Larchester, where the dispossessed were stripped of home and hope, boiling resentment that fomented civil unrest was assuaged only by the intervention of the church, providing whatever food and shelter it could.

'If this bill becomes law, the church will be severely hampered in its mission. So many life-enhancing projects will become dependent on the whim of local authorities, which, with an erroneous sense of political correctness, however well intentioned, may well refuse them because they still have little or no appreciation of the social benefits that faith communities bring.'

The Lords brayed and hear-heared, and nodded in their serried ranks like rows of toy drummers. Lord Kilmarton, whom she recognised from General Synod, kissed her hand, an anachronism in this day and age, holding it far too long. He never mentioned the bill. Instead he said, 'Lovely to see you finally made it to the House.' A strange, almost backhanded compliment and a veiled reference to the fact that she had never made it there as bishop, for want of a vacancy.

The bill was defeated and sent back to the Commons twice, but the support of her fellow Lords was not necessarily a PR advantage, easily caricatured as they were as the elderly bulwark of reactionary traditionalism. The press acknowledged her fervour, but little else. One leading opinion-former averred, 'It's impossible not to want to follow Boudicca into battle and storm the barricades – a pleasant change from the usual dull vagueness of the church, but all the pep and pizzazz in the world cannot hide the paucity of her argument. A truly Christian minority would be prepared to sacrifice their so-called precious rights for the safety and security of us all.'

Despite these lengthy delays in the House of Lords, the anti-proselytising measures passed, inevitably, into law, with a fairly minor modification ensuring that local authority decisions were made at council meetings, not on the whim of an individual.

Nick Hamilton-Jones took her out for dinner that evening.

'Don't give in to disappointment, Vicky. You were impressive. You succeeded in getting the bill defeated twice. You made your mark,' he said, pouring her a large glass of Chablis.

She waved a hand at him, but he went on filling her glass.

'Medicine, my dear. You need it.'

If there was one thing she was determined she would never do, it was to allow alcohol to become her crutch. When she had started to drink an occasional glass, she discovered how easily she could become dependent on the way it muted and mellowed her feelings, and she knew too well the damage that could do. But Nick didn't appear to hear her.

'Where will it all end, Nick? I see nothing but disaster ahead.' She grasped his arm and moved his hand away decisively. 'I need to think straight, to respond wisely, and I need a clear head for that.'

But she sipped her wine nonetheless, its calming effect, the subdued lighting, the quiet opulence of Le Gavroche, and Nick's soothing good sense acting to take the edge off the anxiety she felt.

'Such an underhand and ineffective way of dealing with the issue,' Nick continued, one eye on the menu. 'What we need are more resources to protect our cyberspace – not an outsized shovel to crack a tiny nut.'

'And the Tories would rescind it, would they, Nick?'

'No idea,' he said, without looking up, the slightest upward twist playing at the corner of his lips, 'but I would certainly encourage them to do so. Meanwhile, since there is no sign of their immediate rise to power, what now, my Boudicca?'

Vicky laughed despite herself. He put the menu down and took off his half-moon spectacles.

'For me, the *filet de boeuf*, for you perhaps the sea bass?'

'I must try to rally the troops, unite our forces, and fight on. Threaten civil disobedience ultimately, if we have to.'

'The government won't believe you. They know Christians are far too nice to withdraw their voluntary labour and make people suffer.'

'There are ways and means of protesting without causing undue misery to the innocent, so the government may yet be in for a surprise. What would you advise?'

'Keep your gunpowder dry for the time being. Work behind the scenes. Placate. Aggravate. Negotiate.'

'Without the press behind us?'

'Woo them, Vicky. The press is like a pack of dogs. Feed them rich pickings – the stories that show the charisma of the new Archbishop – and you'll have them eating out of your hand. I'll drop a word here and there. See if we can't find you a pet journalist or two.'

Placate – the first step. Unite the church. But how? The national outcry following the failure to admit women to the episcopacy seven years previously, had led to an accelerated vote in Synod, not allowing adequate time, claimed its opponents, for legislation that would safeguard their consciences – Anglo-catholic on one side, conservative evangelical on the other. So they went off in a huff, the conservative evangelicals by far the larger group, the more determined Anglo-catholics having already defected to Rome in 1992, when women were priested. The conservative evangelicals had simply spent the entire twenty years insisting on their right to refuse a woman vicar. Submitting to the authority of a female bishop was another kettle of fish altogether.

The divisions in the C of E were, in fact, highly complex. Some Anglo-catholics opposed to women bishops were gay, and some evangelicals who were against ordaining practising gay priests were for women bishops. It all defied simple definition, but the simplest version was that in one corner stood the modernisers, embracing a secular, contemporary agenda of diversity and non-discrimination, in the other the conservatives, appealing to the authority of the Bible and the traditions of the church. And since the huge, vibrant African church stood in the latter corner, that camp was by far the most powerful internationally, if not at home. The African church now dominated the International Anglican Alliance, and their bishops offered episcopal oversight to any UK churches that couldn't accept the oversight of a woman bishop. These were the churches she needed on board, if her campaign was going to have any real impact.

The problem was that there was no one group of dissident conservative evangelicals for Vicky to approach. Typically for such configurations, various pressure groups had grown, splintered and faded in turn, with the current front-runner the most hardline of them all: React.

React's head honcho was Malcolm Davies, the bane of her life when she was Archdeacon of Westhampton. Their relationship had never been a success, from their very first encounter some fourteen years ago at her 'meet-the-new-archdeacon' bun fight. She had been keen to organise something, only too aware that not all the clergy were pleased with the appointment of a woman to the post. She had anticipated the odd moan, even some gnashing of teeth, but not the kind of group dynamics that would have stymied a social psychologist. A number of the men simply studied their mobile phones, while a few others whispered to each other and laughed out loud, refusing to join in the main body of conversation. They were like a difficult class of Year Nines, or the youth group at St Margaret's. But these characters were nearer fifty than fifteen.

She looked surreptitiously around for the source of the disaffection, and to her horror, hiding slightly behind his neighbour, beheld none other than Kelvin Craddock. She thought at first that she must be hallucinating. There was no way he could have been accepted for ministry after his disastrous behaviour at their selection conference, surely – let alone turn up in her diocese? But no, it was the same thick-necked, shaven-headed Kelvin with the earring and even now one or two red eruptions on his face. He inadvertently caught her eye, and the surge of hostility threatened her equilibrium. Don't think of bedroom slippers, she said to herself.

Addressing the room at large, she said, 'I know an archdeacon in a skirt is unwelcome for some of you, but if you have an issue with it, I'd rather we discussed it as adults.'

'What's to discuss?'

Vicky took note of a hostile-looking vicar in his early forties, sitting slightly apart from the rest, flexing his jaw muscles. He was all sharp edges, from his closely cropped dark hair and black-rimmed spectacles, to the shoulder-blades and elbows that poked through his crisply ironed shirt. He probably had a submissive little wife at home to press it for him. Stop it, she commanded herself.

'Malcolm Davies,' he said curtly. 'My church is the largest in the diocese,' he announced, 'and I attribute it to the fact that we obey Scripture and don't countenance women in leadership.'

There was a groan or two, some embarrassed titters, but he held her gaze with an insolence she would never have countenanced from a child in her classroom. And yet, when she thought about it rationally, she could almost sympathise with the Malcolm Davieses – intelligent, able men whose chances of career advancement were minimal, passed over by women who, from his jaundiced perspective, would never have his authority or expertise. It was going to take every interpersonal skill she could muster to disarm men like that and turn them, if not into allies, at least into colleagues.

Careful not to avert her eyes, she said, 'Most of you in this room could do this job as well, if not better than I could. But you knew when you went into the ministry that few of you would get the so-called status positions. But the Christian faith is about service, not status. You, in parish work, are at the coal face. And my job is to do my best to ensure your well-being and facilitate your work. When it's tough, I'll support you however I can.'

Malcolm's derisive little snort dissipated the first appreciative silence. He swung backwards and forwards on his chair with studied nonchalance. Round one to me, Vicky had said to herself. Until the Bishop informed her that Malcolm had emailed him to say that she would never be welcome in his church.

'Nothing I could say or do would make him change his mind, he says.'

'In industry he'd be on a disciplinary.'

'But this is the Church of England, Vicky. I have to respect everyone's theological foibles.'

Round two to Malcolm, then.

Her next encounter was some years later, when there was trouble in the parish – a raft of complaints from locals about his high-handed manner, clamping their cars if they were parked on church ground, refusing to do christenings if they didn't attend church regularly, his propensity for telling the bereaved at funerals that their loved one was rotting in hell. It made great copy for the local, and occasionally for the national, newspapers – the archetypal vicar-you-love-to-hate, accompanied by a stock photo of him with his mouth soured by distaste, as if he had permanent acid reflux. It drove the diocesan press officer to distraction.

'Let me find you some arsenic,' he had said, when she told him where she was bound.

'Prayer might be more proper?' she countered, and then they both raised their eyes to heaven, shook their heads and laughed.

'Hello, Archdeacon, come to tell me off, have we?' he asked, when he had seen her standing on his doorstep.

'No, Malcolm, it's a waste of breath. But the Bishop would like to know whether there's any truth in the letter he's just received that you've closed the cemetery to dog walkers.'

'Of course I have. There's nothing my enemies like better than cover-ing the path in canine excrement, in the hope I might stand in it.'

'Shit,' she said, despite herself, swallowing an overwhelming urge to grin.

'As you say, Archdeacon.'

'Malcolm, here's a quote for you to chew on. "Beware of no man more than of yourself; we carry our worst enemies within us."'

'Which atheistic philosopher are you spouting at me now, Archdeacon?'

'Charles Spurgeon, actually, Malcolm.'

Bingo, she thought as she left the angular figure with a puzzled expres-sion, standing on his doorstep. The words of the great evangelical preacher might just stand a chance of getting through. If they didn't, there was no more she could do. If Malcolm ended up with a broken nose, he had no one but himself to blame.

And now here he was, some ten years later, sitting opposite her in her study, squirming slightly in her armchair. Greying around the hairline, more furrowed in the forehead and around the nose, otherwise as uncom-fortable in his body as he had always been. He had categorically refused her invitation for a chat when she had first spoken to him, even declining a face-to-face on screen, until she resorted to flattery, mingled with a hint of soul-sickening female helplessness. Resistance to the current, grave situation, she claimed, could only be effective with his support. She couldn't spearhead it without him. Only he had the necessary influence with some of his 'brother' conservative groups. They would listen to him. And so, finally, he had agreed to come and see her at Lambeth Palace, in the corridors of church power.

'Malcolm,' she said, leaning towards him, her hands clasped together on her lap, 'you and I both know that the current legislation is intolerable. Evangelism is at the heart of what we both believe. But how can our folk fulfil their calling without breaking the law? We must have a united front if we're going to stand up to such bullying. And you're the one I need on board to achieve that.'

He looked past her out of the window, seemed miles away, pulled, she suspected, this way and that by responsibilities to his following and the sense of his own power. She held her breath. And then he said, after a short eternity, 'I do understand, Vicky, but under the circumstances . . . I'll have to talk to my members.'

'And you would approach some of the other conservative groups?' she asked, as submissively as she could manage, endeavouring not to let her face betray her distaste. 'Perhaps you could all come here together to discuss the situation?'

He turned one of his most ingratiating smiles upon her.

'Not so fast. But I'll see what I can do.'

'Meanwhile, I shall continue my crusade in the press. Speak out when I can. Defend the right of all people to speak publicly of their faith.'

To her amazement, he shook her hand as he left, not heartily, not exactly warmly, but with measured consideration nonetheless. Was there a new, grudging respect in his eyes? Or was she imagining what she so badly needed?

Shortly before her first Christmas in office, one of the more sexist tabloids lobbed in a typically unhelpful distraction from the issues that really mattered, announcing to the world that the Archbishop wore a lacy black basque. They even displayed a photograph of it, taken from the Marks and Spencer's Special Collection website. 'This gorgeous basque has a diamond mesh and floral lace design and comes with rear hook fastening and detachable suspender straps.' The Archbishop had, apparently, left the straps on.

Setting aside her concern for the respect she might have sacrificed from the conservatives who tended to park their humour outside the church door, her instinct was to be amused. Her Chief of Staff felt otherwise.

'It's pathetic, Dan. Who cares about this sort of trivia?'

'It's demeaning, Archbishop, reduces you to the level of a . . .'

'A tart?'

He reddened, but there wasn't the slightest abatement in the fury on his face.

'Manifestly one of our staff was responsible for the leak. It's a sackable offence and I won't rest until I find out who it is.'

'Oh, Dan, so the nation knows I'm a normal woman. There's very little real damage done. Best ignore it. It'll soon be forgotten.'

'What example does it give to the rest of the staff? What information might they not sell in the future?'

He went on sleuthing until the trail led him to a young Filipino cleaner, a single mother called Dalisay. He dismissed her on the spot, but instead of complying with his orders and leaving the building, she doubled back to the Archbishop's study and threw herself at Vicky's feet, weeping and begging for mercy. She claimed she had been chatting with a friend over a drink at the pub. They must have been overheard. It was foolish, indiscreet, wrong. But she had received no payment, and she had the rent to pay, children to support. Vicky took her by the elbows and lifted her up, sat her on the settee with a box of tissues, and, with a sinking heart, promised to speak for her.

'It sets a very bad precedent, Archbishop,' Dan said, making no attempt to keep the irritation from his voice. 'It undermines my authority here.'

'I know, I know. You're right. It goes against all the rules, Dan, but just this once. She won't find any other work without a decent reference. She is deeply penitent. She will never do it again. We can use this to remind the staff of the dangers of idle gossip. And still show ourselves to practise the mercy that we preach.'

'You may preach mercy, Archbishop, but I run your home. If I'm not allowed to do so in a professional manner, my position becomes untenable.'

'I'm very sorry to hear that, Dan.'

They had reached a stalemate.

'I have no alternative but to offer you my resignation. With immediate effect.'

Vicky nodded and her lack of protest seemed to rile him further.

'But I warn you, you won't hear the last of this. There are many ways of handling difficult . . . issues. As the last Archbishop discovered to his cost.'

Stunned, she asked, 'You're not threatening me by any chance, are you?'

He merely smiled, turned on his heels and walked out.

The blaze of media publicity that followed his departure was far more damaging than the basque episode. He told the press that he couldn't tolerate the new Archbishop's 'abrasive, headstrong and wilful style'. Vicky was even more upset by his claim that she had never been the Appointments Commission's first choice, merely the result of another Church of England fudge when the male preferences had fallen by the way.

Was it true? Was she a last resort? Or was this only the man's thwarted ego speaking? Could Gerard Lancaster have misrepresented the Crown Nominations Commission so blatantly? She finally raised him on her computer late that evening, demanding to know the truth, and after some prevarication, he admitted that the first two choices had fallen by the wayside.

'Gerard,' she groaned, 'can't you see what this has done, how you've undermined me at just the time I need to inspire confidence in my leadership?'

The PM's secretary protested.

'I did not lie, Archbishop. The vote was unanimous, except for one abstention. And the PM's office is about to send out a news release that will say so – without mentioning the abstention, of course.'

'If you'd been honest with me in the first place, it mightn't have been necessary. The Crown Nominations Commission doesn't have much of a reputation for discretion, though heaven knows why they find it so hard. I only hope you haven't set Anglican unity back by years.'

A thought occurred to her.

'If I asked you which of them had spoken to Dan Clements and why, where would you place your bet?'

'I really have no idea, Archbishop. I'm not a betting man. You must look to your own house for that.'

She snapped him off her screen, and sat for some time at her desk, her head in her hands. Who was on the Commission? Even if she knew who had broken ranks, how could she ever prove it? Church politics! She loathed them. In that moment she longed, like the Psalmist, to have the wings of a dove and fly away from it all. She looked up and checked the clock. Time for compline with the nuns – the only source of genuine calm currently available in her world.

Giving Dalisay her job back won Vicky the love and loyalty of her domestic staff. Would that the media was as amenable, she said to herself. Nick rang to tell her not to take the recent skirmishes too seriously, that for an astute operator there was plenty of time to regain lost ground, and he promised to look into it. But it seemed to Vicky that her former Chief of Staff's vicious attack had unleashed a tempest of bad press. Sarah also urged her to wait for it to subside, but meanwhile, there seemed no end to the genius of journalists in finding half-healed scars that simply needed a pick or two to re-open and bleed. Every part of her past, private and public, was turned over, picked at and elaborated upon.

'I think you should see this one, Archbishop,' Sarah said to her the day before Christmas Eve, retrieving one newspaper out of the bunch. She laid it on Vicky's desk, turned over the front page and pointed. There, taken presumably from a local archive, under the headline, 'Archbishop's Blighted Childhood', was a grainy reproduction of a black-and-white photograph of her mother, standing proudly behind some of her young pupils, who sat, musical instruments on their laps, ready for the annual school concert. Vicky's stomach lurched. She swallowed and forced herself to look. Her mother was smiling for the camera, eyes half shut, possibly because of the sun. She never drank on the job. Of that Vicky felt sure. But the journalist had found a former teacher prepared to swear that Audrey Burnham had made regular appearances at school functions in a state of inebriation, that her staff had been relieved when she was pensioned off, and that none of them had mourned her lonely death from cirrhosis of the liver.

Vicky stroked the picture with a fingertip, too full of emotion to trust herself to speak for a while.

'I am so, so sorry, Mum,' she whispered to her.

'Are you okay, Archbishop?'

Her sharp intake of breath was half sob.

'Not really, Sarah. If this below-the-belt stuff is the best our journalists can come up with, news reporting is in a more parlous state than I thought.'

'This is cheap,' Sarah agreed.

'Thank God most of the people who knew her are gone. Why roll in the muck like this?'

'Because that's what the swine do,' Oliver said, as he came into the room, and laid a gentle hand on her shoulder.

'Am I completely naive? I didn't realise that public scrutiny could be so downright cruel.'

Oliver removed the paper from her hand and replaced it with a mug of hot coffee.

'Your relationship with her can't have been easy,' he said, scanning the article.

'It wasn't, but she didn't deserve this. We made our peace at the end, and that's how I want to remember her.'

Oliver patted her shoulder, turned, and motioned to Sarah to follow him out of the study.

1996

Vicky's father died in the October of 1996, without warning, shortly after she became vicar of Potbury, amidst the West London sprawl. She had seen very little of her parents since taking on the new job. In those early days her congregation provided her with quite enough disapproval without facing her mother's. But she suspected it had upset her father, not least because he loved his little granddaughter. It niggled at her conscience. Why hadn't she been able to weather the difficulties with her mother, at least for his sake? But Harrogate was hardly round the corner, and there was so little free time, with Tom doing on-calls and she working weekends. Synchronising a day off was a miracle. Or were these merely excuses for the detachment she had built so carefully, so that she wouldn't have to face the wreck her mother had become, and the helpless heartbreak it caused her father? She sometimes wondered whether she hadn't opted for dealing with the problems of the world because she couldn't handle her own. And now that her father was dead, she bitterly regretted not having scaled his defences to tell him that she understood, and that she loved him.

'You've come,' Audrey had said in surprise, when they turned up for her father's funeral and she opened the door to them.

'Of course, Mother. We told you we were coming. Why would we not?'

Audrey nodded dumbly, and then her reserve broke. Vicky reached out and held her as she wept, then led her into the kitchen and made a cup of tea, while Tom took Alice and a bag of toys into the sitting room.

'To find him like that in bed,' she said, wiping her eyes. 'I thought he was asleep. The shock. I'll never get over it.'

Vicky held her hand and they sat with their tea, remembering Cyril, his thoughtfulness and kindness, his love of Alice, but after that there wasn't a great deal more to say. So they discussed the funeral arrangements. She was aware of the usual vague whiff of alcohol around her mother, but Audrey seemed fairly lucid as she outlined the terms of his will. He had left everything to Vicky.

'I don't know why he did that,' Audrey said vaguely.

'So that you'll always have a roof over your head, Mum. And enough to live on.'

She eyed Vicky, aware, possibly for the first time, that it would be a waste of time to deny her demons.

And then they sat in uncomfortable silence, neither daring to broach the subject that had driven the final wedge between them, until Audrey said, 'You remember that boy you used to know at university?'

'Which boy, Mother?'

'The posh one. What was his name?'

'Ralph Cooper, or Mark? Mark Bradley-Hind.'

'That's the one. Did you see that he's just become an MP in that by-election in Gloucestershire?'

Vicky shook her head.

'I don't get much time to read the papers.'

'I kept you the cutting.'

Vicky was not terribly interested, but Audrey got up and trotted over to the kitchen drawer where she kept all the bric-a-brac that didn't have a dedicated place, and drew out a tatty piece of newspaper. Vicky took it from her and scanned it briefly. The same old Mark, smooth and suave now that his weaker features had been mellowed by maturity, a very Tory gentleman being congratulated by Prime Minister John Major.

'They gave him a safe seat,' she said, more to herself than her mother. 'Typical. And goodness, does he smirk.'

She handed the cutting back to her mother.

'The sleaze party,' her mother commented, studying the photo, and pointing at Mark. 'Says there he left his first wife for his secretary. Your father and I stuck together through thick and thin because that's what you did in our day. Back to Basics? They make our Prime Minister look a fool with their antics. Do you think it affects their work?'

'I think it must,' Vicky said. 'If a man cheats in private, he'll cheat in every other part of his life.'

'Tom had better watch it then. He won't get any mercy from you.'

Audrey managed to stay sober for the actual funeral, but by the time they left her in the evening, she was very much the worse for wear. She tried to lift Alice to kiss her goodbye, staggered backwards, and let her fall. She was mortified and made an effort to wipe Alice's tears with the faithful cologne-soaked handkerchief, but Alice wouldn't let her near.

'She doesn't look well,' Vicky said to Tom, as they waved goodbye from the safety of the car, looking back at the frail, doddery little figure standing at the gate.

'You wouldn't be well either, if you drank a bottle of whisky a day.'

'She's not eating properly. Her hair is thin and she's looks pasty. How on earth is she going to cope without Dad?'

Tom shook his head in sympathy.

'Not a lot we can do, Darling. We can't have her with us unless she stops drinking. We've Alice to think about.'

Vicky turned around to check Alice, who was dozing off, her thumb in her mouth, her other hand clutching Tracy the rag doll, who was entangled in wisps of her fair hair. She had been more shocked than hurt, thankfully.

Life in the next weeks and months was consumed with work. In those early days of female vicars, there was a temptation to show how grateful they were for being given the chance to prove themselves, which, in very basic terms, meant more bottoms on pews, and that, in its turn, meant hard work. Alice needed time and attention too, but even she had to fight for it. So apart from an occasional phone call, Vicky had precious little opportunity to think about her mother, who, as she was to discover a few months later, more or less drank herself into oblivion.

'A blast from the past, Vicky.'

'Paula. How are you? And how long has it been?'

'I was trying to work it out. Around twelve years.'

'And are you still in Harrogate?'

'We are indeed – and that's why I'm calling, because I didn't know if anyone else had been in touch with you. Your mother was taken into hospital last night. One of the neighbours rang me, but she didn't know how to contact you. I found you in *Crockford's*. The good old clerical directory has its uses.'

Vicky felt as if her heart had stopped.

'I haven't managed to get up there for a while. Any idea how she is?'

'Not good. You're welcome to a bed with us, if you need it.'

When she reached the hospital's admissions desk, an officious receptionist was loath to let her in. 'See that?' he said, pointing to the sign with visiting hours.

'See this?' she said, taking her dog collar out of her handbag and inserting it into her shirt collar. It did the trick.

Audrey had been an emergency admission, vomiting blood. 'It's advanced cirrhosis of the liver, as I expect you've guessed. Not much we can do except keep her comfortable,' said the Ward Sister apologetically, escorting Vicky into a pleasant, sunny side-ward, painted buttercup yellow, with floral orange and green counterpanes on the four beds – a pattern that did little for the emaciated, jaundiced complexion of the figure in bed four. Her stomach was so bloated she looked nine months pregnant.

'She'll need constant care from now on,' the nurse continued.

'And how long's that?' Vicky asked, lowering her voice.

She shrugged sympathetically.

'Days? Weeks?'

They walked up to the bed.

'Your daughter's here to see you, Mrs Burnham,' the Sister said cheerily, in that abrupt change of tone nurses reserve for the patient. 'Come all this way. Isn't that nice?'

Vicky covered her mother's hand and said, 'Hi, Mum.'

Audrey opened her eyes and stared at Vicky, struggling to focus.

'I'll send the social worker,' the Sister whispered. She smiled benignly round at the other three patients in this little outpost of her kingdom and swept out of the room.

Though Audrey seemed hardly aware of her presence, Vicky talked to her quietly for around an hour, stroking her hair, telling her about the weather, about Alice, anything that might interest her, before the social worker bustled in with a pile of files in her arms. She was an older woman with strong features, a brisk manner, stout legs and a permanent look of disapproval. The badge that swung on the lanyard around her neck named her as Vanessa Curtis.

'You'll be taking her home with you, I imagine,' she stated curtly.

'Could we have this conversation somewhere else?' Vicky asked her in a hushed voice. She nodded and Vicky followed her to a small office further down the corridor.

'No,' she said firmly, as they both sat down. 'If my mother lives, I can't take her back with me. I have a responsible job and a small child. I'm not there during the day. And she's a liability.'

Vanessa Curtis studied her for a moment, opened the relevant file and put on the reading glasses that were attached to another cord around her neck.

'Hmmm,' she said, studying the notes carefully. 'Drinking a long time, then?'

Vicky nodded.

'Since you were young?'

'She used to tell me her "dizzy spells" were because of the ear problems she had as a child.'

The social worker looked up at her over her glasses, and her face softened a little.

'Tough for a child.'

Vicky had never spoken to anyone before, apart from Tom, about her mother's drinking. And yet it was as if she had waited all her life to hear those four short words. Healing, comforting words for the frightened, lonely child that longed for some recognition of the bewilderment and helplessness she had endured on an almost daily basis. Vicky nodded, unable to speak for the lump that blocked her throat.

'Well, we can't interfere with your career then, can we? Not when you've had such a fight to get it.'

Vanessa Curtis smiled knowingly.

'Your mother's condition may not improve sufficiently for discharge, of course. But if it does, we might be able to find some kind of residential care for her. Does she have a house you can sell to pay for her care, perhaps?'

Vicky nodded sadly. 'My father thought of that. It's mine to sell.'

Audrey came round two days later, while Vicky was sitting at her bedside reading.

'Vicky?'

It was a tiny croak. Her face was mottled and crumpled like a sunken lemon soufflé against the whiteness of the sheets. Two tiny rivulets of tears made their way slowly from her eyes down the crevasses of her face and disappeared behind her ears. Vicky took her hand.

'I feel so rotten.'

Her eyes closed and she appeared to be sleeping. Vicky got up and closed the curtains around the bed. As she sat back down, Audrey's eyes flicked open again without warning, and she looked at her daughter in alarm, as if she had just seen her for the first time. She snatched her hand away.

'You didn't want to see me again. And I don't blame you. I've let you down so badly.'

The tears flowed again and Vicky took a tissue from the box on the bedside table and mopped them gently.

'I'm sorry too, Mum. I should have come sooner. I just . . . seem to spend my time caring for everyone else. But that's no excuse.'

It was true, nonetheless. Her job used up so much of her emotional energy, she had little left over for those who should have mattered, and now she bitterly regretted it.

Audrey reached out a hand and grasped Vicky's arm. Vicky felt the uncut fingernails digging into her flesh. With every ounce of strength she possessed, Audrey raised her head slightly and spluttered, 'Whatever I've said in the past about . . . you know . . . women being priests, I want you to know I'm proud of you.'

She collapsed back onto the pillows and Vicky stared at the pinched, lemony little face of a once proud and clever woman, now so shrivelled and lost in the hospital bed. How she wished she could scoop her mother up and travel back in time together to re-make their relationship into something more like what it might have been.

'I know,' she said, 'I know.'

Audrey was now squeezing her hand so tightly that the stone of her engagement ring bit uncomfortably into her little finger. She tried to release the grip a little, but Audrey held on and begged, 'Don't leave me, don't leave me.'

'No, no, I'm not going anywhere.'

'Can you ever forgive me? Not just for that, but for . . . for this. Me, what I've become.'

'Why, Mum, why? If you could just tell me why.'

Audrey turned away from her, wheezing slightly. She focused on a small, round hole in the curtains.

'You don't plan it. It just creeps up on you. It kept the ghosts at bay.'

'What ghosts?'

What had she missed? What hadn't she known?

'You had Dad, me, a lovely home, the job you'd always wanted, respect in the community.'

'Your father . . . a kind man, but I couldn't love him like I loved Billy.'

'Billy, Mother – who was Billy?'

'Billy,' Audrey murmured, smiling for the first time since Vicky had arrived, but with a wistfulness that wrenched at her guts. 'Killed. Explosion on an oil rig. I was pregnant. Not married. So I found Cyril. What you did in those days. Baby boy, stillborn at twenty-six weeks. Nothing left of Billy. Always loved him. Cyril knew. Always knew.'

Why, why, why, Vicky yelled inside, had she never known? Damn her mother's destructive self-sufficiency, her dignity and her utter privacy. Some secrets were so deep you could drown in them – unless you reached out to someone for a rope.

Audrey was panting now with the effort of speaking. Vicky poured her a glass of water from the jug on the bedside table, lifted her and held it up to her mouth so that she could take a sip. Her bones jutted out from her flesh, and felt as brittle as twigs as Vicky laid her back down.

'When you came, I . . . resented that you weren't Billy's child. All my fault. Lousy wife. Bad mother.'

She was crying openly now, whimpering as she gasped for air, each tiny sob wracking her desiccated body. She patted Vicky's hand repeatedly and the fluttering of her fingers felt like the tap-tap-tapping of a dying bird on the window of her heart, desperate for warmth and peace. In all those months that Vicky had stayed away, her mother had never once demanded she go and see her, or complained that she hadn't. Stupidly, she had seen it as rejection, thought it was because of her ordination. How could this woman priest have been so blind to the need that was inside her own house? Why had she allowed her mother to push her away and not understood that it was a facade to hide her sense of guilt and failure? It was to protect her that she had never let Vicky get close, for fear she might see that she couldn't love her enough. And she did it out of misguided love. That was the terrible irony. Then, when the facade threatened to crumble, she surrounded herself with an impenetrable wall of booze instead, anaesthetising herself against a broken life.

'I know you only wanted the best for me, Mum. I understand. I forgive you,' Vicky whispered in her ear, 'if you can forgive me for not being there for you when you needed me?'

Audrey nodded, turned her head to look at her daughter, and smiled. Vicky leant over and kissed her on her cheek, the first time in memory that she had ever kissed her mother. As Audrey's eyes closed in sleep, Vicky stayed as close to her as she could, whispering in her ear the familiar words of the old service of evening prayer: 'Lord, now lettest thou thy servant depart in peace according to thy word; for mine eyes have seen thy salvation which thou hast prepared before the face of all people; to be a light to lighten the Gentiles and to be the glory of thy people Israel.'

The hospital rang her at Pete and Paula's at 7 a.m. Audrey had died during the night.

Paula drove her there for one last farewell. Looking at her mother's face, she saw that death had indeed ironed out the pain, the sorrow, and the despair; but it had also smoothed away her essential character, her essence. All that remained was an empty husk. Her mother had gone. But she felt certain, nonetheless, that in the going, Audrey had found peace at last.

Clearing out her childhood home was almost unbearable. In the loft were box-loads of old photographs, all of her, drawings she had done when she could barely hold a pencil, toys that were chewed and dog-eared, Noddy books and school reports, old textbooks crammed with years of school essays. On the mantelpiece in the sitting room stood a framed photograph of her ordination as deacon, her father at her side, Audrey conspicuously missing. It hadn't been there when she came for her father's funeral, of that she was sure.

Like a wasp in a honey trap, her mother had suffocated slowly in an age, environment and culture that had never been kind to her. The fulfilment of all her upwardly mobile aspirations had never afforded her the sense of self-worth and satisfaction she sought, because it couldn't. It couldn't reach her unresolved grief through the layers of perceived failure she had heaped on top of it. The more she struggled to survive, clinging by her fingernails to the image she had created of the perfect family, the more exhausted she became, until she was just too weary to hold on, and let alcohol carry her away.

2020

Vicky wasn't sure how long she had sat at her desk looking at the press cutting with its faded photograph. How could some ignorant editor take what was precious to her and trample all over it like that – such a private, personal glimpse of redemption, ground into the dirt? Nothing was as disheartening as such inhuman disregard, or as demoralising as the personal experience of it. Yet no government had ever truly grasped the nettle of controlling the worst excesses of the press. Too concerned for the impact on their own short-term reputation.

As she examined the piece of newspaper in her hand, it occurred to her to wonder what kind of a mother she herself had been. She was far, far closer to Alice than her mother had ever been to her, but they were of a different generation, where friendship between a child and a parent was more the norm. Had she nonetheless sacrificed her daughter for her career?

TWELVE

With every righteous action, we prepare the way for the New Earth on which righteousness will dwell. And bringing justice to those who suffer violence means to bring the light of God's future to them.

JÜRGEN MOLTMANN

FEBRUARY 2021

Canterbury quickly became Vicky's place of escape from the madness of the capital. Whenever she left the Old Palace there to go back to London, she felt like a convicted criminal being driven off to Wormwood Scrubs. She intended to be in Canterbury every other weekend, even if it raised the pressure bar higher the rest of the time.

The fact was, life in the goldfish bowl was getting to Tom. Financial pressure to generate more income for its upkeep had led to a substantial increase in guided tours of Lambeth Palace. Tom was forever falling over camera-toting tourists who either stared at him, trying to work out who he was, or clicked their cameras at him as if he were a Madame Tussauds' dummy. When he found a tourist on their private toilet, the cleaner having inadvertently left the flat door open, he lifted him out, mid-business, by the lapels. The poor man bowed his way backwards down the corridor, fastening his trousers. Tom began looking through the London property listings.

Vicky feared their drifting apart again, and a regular weekend in Canterbury, if they could get away on a Friday evening, gave them a little breathing space, and their own front door.

'We are still us?' she asked him, one spring evening, as they sat watching twilight gather around the cathedral, luminous in its floodlit glow against the darkening sky. The windows flashed with flames of fire cast by the last of the sun's dying rays. Rows of tiny lamps highlighted a path for the black silhouettes who scuttled home to family and tea, or to dress up for a Saturday night out. A shining fingernail clipping of a moon emerged from behind the tower, and the distant voices of tired shoppers gave way to the gleeful whooping of the city's night revellers.

'I hope so,' he said, reaching out an arm and putting it around her shoulders. 'Do you think I'd still be here with you if we weren't?'

She looked at him in alarm.

'I sometimes fear it's a close-run thing.'

He silenced her with a kiss.

On her fifty-fifth birthday he arrived in the bedroom with a tray – orange juice, coffee, toast and, wedged in the toast rack, a buff envelope. She opened it slowly, watching his face, which remained impassive, even when the membership card to an exclusive Canterbury health spa fell out onto the bed. She picked it up and studied it, struggling with a mass of conflicting emotions.

'Oh Tom, what a lovely thought, but . . .'

'It's valid from today,' he interrupted, handing her a parcel. In it was a soft, silver-grey track-suit.

'I never thought I'd marry track-suit woman, but needs must.'

'What if I'm recognised?'

'For crying out loud, in that? And if it doesn't bestow anonymity, a white towelling robe will. So,' he said, picking up the trousers and tossing them at her, 'put it on and let's go.'

'Submission to my husband?'

'If that's what it takes to make you see sense.'

It was one of the most relaxing mornings she could remember. No need to think, simply submit to the unravelling sensations of massage, sauna, steam room and jacuzzi. She swam, she lazed, she brunched, Tom resolutely coming between her and the newspapers. She was so relaxed that she let him escort her from the car back into the Old Palace, then pick her up and carry her to their room.

'Strike while the iron's hot,' she whispered into his ear.

'Nookie with a freshly massaged, hot Archbishop? Now there's an offer a man can't refuse.'

'Just don't give yourself a hernia, Superman.'

From then on she tried her best to keep Saturday mornings in Canterbury free for the spa. She had abandoned the running, too dog-tired to get out of bed in the morning, but now she started running midweek again – from Lambeth Palace along the Thames, in wind, rain, sleet, sunshine or snow, galvanised by the thought of all the sponsorship money she could raise for '28 Too Many', her charity of choice, committed to the eradication of female genital mutilation in the twenty-eight countries in Africa where it was still practised, inflicting immense emotional and physical pain on the women subjected to it. As an added bonus, running gave her a clarity of thought, a depth of concentration and an energy she felt she had lost. On Saturdays there was the gym, a swim, a massage and possibly further recreational activities when they got back, before she leapt onto the merry-go-round of local afternoon meetings and visits, leaving Tom in a heavy, happy sleep.

On Sundays, he'd either accompany Vicky to wherever she was preaching, or take himself off to the cathedral. He had always got on with Dean Julian better than she did and she appreciated the balm her good doctor seemed able to pour into the wound, giving her the chance to preach there more regularly. Ever since the enthronement, there had been a chill in the atmosphere, mainly from the music director and some of the canons, who hadn't forgiven her perceived slight. The churchwarden, Clive Marshall, whom she tended to think of as a little sweetie, and who happened to let slip that he had been on the Commission responsible for her appointment, did his best to win them round. But cathedral staff, it seemed, had an exemption from the seventy-times-seven imperative for Christian forgiveness.

She saw Clive at the door one Sunday evening after she had preached to a fairly substantial congregation. She always had to resist the urge to pump him for more information about his fellow Commission members. The only other name he had mentioned was his friend, Frank Hardiman, another cathedral stalwart.

'You knew Frank died ten days ago?'

She didn't, and was aggrieved that she hadn't been told.

'In his sleep, the night after a particularly upsetting cathedral chapter meeting, where he adamantly refused to accept the conversion of a broom cupboard into a further disabled toilet.'

'He died as he lived then, defending his corner?'

Clive smiled sadly.

'He never spoke ill of you though, not after we had appointed you. Defended you to the hilt, in fact. Difficult as he could be, he was a loyal and generous friend. I'll miss him.'

Vicky touched the top of Clive's arm. She had wondered whether Frank was the one who had spoken to the press. But now the truth was out: he had spoken up for her. So much for grubbing around in the dirt, for making facile assumptions based on face value with no real knowledge.

'Oh, I almost forgot,' Clive added, 'honestly – old age creeping on – there's a couple here who say they know you. He's a vicar just over the border in the next diocese. Americans, judging by the accent.'

'That's not just over the border, Clive,' she teased, allowing herself to be led across the cathedral, conscious that the sight of a small man hanging onto the cassock of a woman who towered over him, as if he were about to dance around a maypole, was probably causing some carefully stifled hilarity. And all the while she had an increasingly sinking feeling that she knew where this journey would end.

'Vicky, after all these years,' she said, arms outstretched, with the same wide smile. Her face was sun-crinkled and sprayed with brown freckles, but Jan's eyes were as animated as ever, and the bob still a silky chestnut. Vicky did a quick mental calculation. She must be well into her sixties, but didn't look anything like it.

'This is Bud, my husband,' she said, turning to a tall, powerfully built man with a square jawline and close-cropped grey hair. He pumped Vicky's hand until her arm ached.

'Were you ever a basketball player?' she asked him.

He laughed heartily.

'If the stereotype fits, Ma'am.'

'Archbishop,' Jan corrected him.

'Vicky, for crying out loud,' she said, dismissing the title with a wave of her hand.

'Coffees?' Clive asked. Vicky mouthed her thanks and off he popped, glad in all probability that his neck could be relieved of the pressure of looking up at three giants.

Vicky and Jan chatted for some time. Politely.

'I'd ask you back to the palace,' Vicky explained, 'but I'm dashing back to London.'

'Maybe next time?' Jan suggested. 'Bud's parish is only fifty minutes away.'

'And you? Did you ever go back into ministry?'

Jan bit her lip and gave a slight shrug.

'A little, here and there.' Then she shook herself and said, 'But you've achieved enough for the both of us. I always knew you had it in you. Didn't I say so?'

Vicky nodded, and decided on the spur of the moment that if the conversation was ever going to get beyond the superficial to the meaningful it must at least be honest. 'Yes, you did, but I wish you hadn't just abandoned me the way you did. You were one of my few models of women in ministry, and I missed you a great deal. Friends matter, and there have been too few of them in my life.'

'You didn't write back to me.'

'I didn't know what to say. I felt betrayed. After all we had shared together.'

She had never destroyed the letter, though. It was still there, somewhere at Lambeth, stuck between the pages of an old Bible on one of her many bookshelves.

There was nothing more Jan could say, so Vicky said a swift goodbye and retreated back to the vestry to remove her robes. Sitting in the passenger seat on the way back to London from Canterbury, she retrieved her e-phone from her handbag and barked out a number of letters for Ann to download and deal with in the morning. As she snapped her bag shut, she said to Tom, 'Strange. I must have approved Bud's licence to minister in the UK, but I have no recollection of it.'

'And would you have approved it had you known who it was?'

She hesitated.

'I don't know. But I just can't get over the way Jan has wasted her gifts. But that's sin, I suppose – wasted potential.'

'Jan made her choice. Do you have to be so judgemental, Archbishop? You can't be her conscience.'

'But she seemed so . . . wistful. I don't doubt she thinks Bud was worth the sacrifice, but it obviously hasn't been easy.'

Tom was quiet, his eyes glued to the busy motorway.

'I suspect they know that now,' he said after a while. 'So perhaps, since we're all sinners, it's time for you to bury your disapproval. Where's the redemption that you preach so often? Or is it just a general principle, not for personal use?'

Vicky felt cut to the quick, and was tempted to defend her corner. But she knew better than to try and pull the wool over Tom's eyes.

'OK, you're right – preacher's malaise. Do what I say, not what I do. So – what do I do?'

'It'll come to you,' he said, patting her on the knee.

Meanwhile, back at Lambeth, there were changes in her team. Oliver retired at last, and she asked Jenny James to become her chaplain. Jenny was reluctant to leave parish ministry at first, where at least, she said, she ran her own show, but decided Vicky probably needed her more, if only to save herself from a surfeit of sobriety and self-restraint.

There was also a new Chief of Staff to find. To Vicky's amazement, Ralph Cooper responded to the advert. 'Those few months of working with you in Larchester were amongst the happiest of my life,' he wrote, in a personal greeting attached to his application, sent by way of explanation. 'Besides, remember BLEO? Of course you do. I'm still on the case, you'll be glad to hear. It wasn't difficult getting some details for the British partner company, but finding out who or what really lies behind A.T. Developments – the "A" stands for Artemis, apparently, not sure about the "T" bit yet – is proving much harder. It would be easier to keep you in the loop if I were at Lambeth.'

Vicky emailed him back promptly, 'I enjoyed working with you too, and of course I still want to get behind the Wooten Grange business. Thanks for your help with this. Of course, as regards the staff post, the usual procedures have to be followed. But I'm delighted you've applied.'

The usual procedures, fortunately, ensured that with his past experience as a former government economist and diocesan secretary, Ralph was eminently qualified for the job and shone out as an outstanding candidate. He was duly appointed.

2006

As a fairly new archdeacon Vicky had used the opportunity to preach in Westhampton Cathedral on Employment Sunday, as an excuse for a fairly left-wing sort of sermon on the unacceptable face of capitalism. She had decried the fact that for the sake of shareholder profits, many employees were forced to work longer hours for less pay. It wasn't very different, she argued, from the benighted Victorian employers whose Protestant work ethic was enforced on their workers more than on themselves, with only an occasional, rather grudging day's holiday, despite the God-given Old Testament pattern of extended periods of festival and recreation. Capitalism was often blind to the potential for exploitation of the relatively powerless.

Standing in the line-up at the cathedral door afterwards, offering the statutory farewell handshake, she had been collared by 'Red Roy', a local MP and old union man with broken veins on a bulbous nose, and beads of sweat on his forehead. He pumped her hand so hard her shoulder was almost dislocated, loudly proclaiming what a gift she was to Westhampton. Looking past the effusive MP, hoping for an escape, she caught sight of someone she had never expected to see again.

'A blast from the past!' he said quietly, as she extricated herself from Red Roy's clinch and moved him on, aware that a certain aura of eau de body had now attached itself to the front of her surplice.

'You know Ralph Cooper, then?' Dean Julian asked with surprise before she could respond, moving in on them to hijack the conversation. He had shown no interest in any of her previous encounters. 'Ralph is new to us. An economist. A favoured advisor to the Conservative Party. He is helping us out with our fund-raising appeal. We are so fortunate.'

He bowed slightly, and Ralph smiled in acknowledgement.

'Vicky and I go back a long way,' Ralph said to the Dean, his eyes focused upon her.

'Almost twenty-five years,' she said, weighing him up.

The Dean, uncertain whether to feel impressed or excluded, muttered his excuses and turned his attention elsewhere.

Maturity had enhanced the good looks she remembered. But then, time was often kinder to good-looking men than to pretty women. The silver speckles that glinted in his thick dark hair and eyebrows, the creases from his nose to his wide, square-shaped mouth, lent dignity and sophistication to his features. Ralph's rugby-playing frame had turned into a broad-shouldered ruggedness. If anything, his waist was more defined. Whereas hers, she reflected thankfully, subjected to the skin-stretching ravages of pregnancy, was hidden beneath cassock and surplice.

'Lindy,' he called, and a leggy, exotic-looking woman with immaculate make-up and artfully contrived waves of dark hair cascading over her shoulders extricated herself from an animated conversation with the Dean and came to Ralph's side. 'Meet Vicky. We were friends at university in Durham. Vicky, this is my wife, Lindy.'

Lindy looked her up and down, wide-eyed, then turned back to Ralph and repeated incredulously, 'University friends? Apart from Mark, you've never spoken about any university friends.'

Ralph responded with a sheepish smile. Lindy stowed her clutch bag under her left arm, extended a ring-covered hand, and said, 'Then you must be an exceptional lady. She must come to dinner, mustn't she, Ralphie?'

Before Ralph had time to reply, Lindy's attention had been grabbed once more by the Dean, leaving Vicky with lipstick on her cheek and the scent of Chanel No 5 lingering in her nostrils.

'What on earth are you doing here, Ralph Cooper?' Vicky hissed, one eye on the rank and file queueing at his heels. 'You had no interest in faith of any kind, as I remember.'

'Long story. Lunch?' he whispered.

'When?' she asked urgently.

'My card,' he said, taking it from his pocket and passing it to her as inconspicuously as he could. Smiling at the man who was next in line, she deftly raised her surplice and stuffed it into a cassock pocket, just before her hand was once again scrunched into mincemeat.

They met the following week at Clos Maggiore, reputedly one of the best French restaurants in London, tucked away from prying eyes in a tiny Georgian town house in Covent Garden. They were seated in a cosy, oak-framed conservatory with a sky-filled glass ceiling, almost cobalt blue on this sunny spring day. Two miniature trees on either side of the room enfolded them in a lacy bower of blossom, filling the air with its heady scent. She looked around uncomfortably, hoping she wouldn't be seen having an intimate lunch date with such an attractive man. But without her dog collar the archdeacon was as anonymous as any other woman in London.

The wine list alone was ninety pages long. As Ralph studied it, she examined the unusual paintings on the wall.

'Is this your regular, then?' she asked him.

'Yes, largely,' he said, removing his reading glasses. 'Like it?'

'Mmm,' she said appreciatively, 'a bit of a change – for me.'

'You don't lunch much?'

It always surprised her how little outsiders understood her world.

'Oh, I lunch regularly – in church halls with peeling green gloss paintwork and defunct boilers, where the fare consists of sandwiches made out of curled cardboard, or cold quiches so soggy the pastry coagulates in your gullet and almost chokes you. Those are the decent lunches. Woe betide you if the Methodists are providing it.'

'No bar to drown your sorrows, I should imagine?'

They were still chuckling when the waiter arrived for their order, which included a wine that cost the same as her entire hospitality budget for the month.

'So, tell me,' she said, as the waiter melted away with a deferential inclination of his head, 'what were you doing at the cathedral? I'm intrigued.'

'Well,' he said, twiddling the stem of the wine glass between his thumb and index finger, 'it wasn't my idea. Lindy was modelling when we met. She never expressed any intention of having a family until an unexpected pregnancy turned into a miscarriage. From then on she was obsessional about having a baby. But it never happened.'

A shadow crossed his face.

'Three attempts at IVF almost destroyed her. We discussed adoption and surrogacy, but she couldn't go with either of those. In the end she suffered a serious bout of depression.'

'I'm so sorry, Ralph,' she said, touching his hand that now lay very still on the bleached white cloth. 'We have one child, Alice, the joy of our lives, and I found it very hard to be told there would be no more.'

The wine arrived. Ralph sniffed the tiny sample that had been poured into his glass, tasted it thoughtfully and gave the command for it to be served.

'Lindy was getting too old for modelling. But she had nothing else in her life. It was Mark, believe it or not, who suggested charity work.'

'His usual altruistic self?'

They both laughed.

'She met the Dean on some committee or other, and the rest, as they say, is history.'

'Not to me it isn't. Why start going in the first place?'

'She went to some charity anniversary celebration at the cathedral and came back saying she had felt the presence of God, that it was a comfort.'

'And you?'

'The music is wonderful. Where else can you be treated to a choir of that quality every week for free? And . . .'

'And it doesn't demand belief of you.'

'No, but I'm nearer than I used to be. Toe in the water, perhaps.'

'And the Dean values you, obviously.'

'I create money. It's about time I made it serve some useful purpose.'

'Good,' she said. 'So what is it you get up to? Government stuff?'

'That's a bit grandiose. I actually work in corporate financial services, but Mark calls me in now and then. He's a rising star in the party – shadow something or other to the treasury.'

'So I gather. Well, that was what he always wanted.'

'And you, as I heard on Sunday, are as radical as ever.'

'Oh I don't know. The older I get, the more jaded I become about politics. And the more certain that only Christianity holds out any hope. That's what I preach and if it seems left of centre, there's little I can do about that.'

'It was an excellent sermon, by the way. Even if I didn't agree with it all. It took me back twenty years. You always could pack a punch. Remember those debates in Durham?'

Vicky smiled in recollection.

'We really thought we knew what life was about, but we were so very, very young. Anyway, I cut my eye teeth, as they say. Strange, when we look back, how apparently insignificant experiences turn out to be formative.'

'I have followed your career fairly closely. So has Mark, of course.'

As they tackled the guinea fowl, she asked, 'And how is the golden boy?'

'You know Mark. More Tory than the Tories – still a huge fan of Thatcherism and the free market; which you, I take it, are not?'

She guffawed loudly.

'It didn't work out with Fiona.'

'I know. It was the title he fell for.'

'And he was on the rebound.'

'Loyal as ever, eh Ralph? I hope he knows what a good friend he has. But I doubt it. It always annoyed me that you were so in his shadow.'

Ralph gave a wry smile.

'Both parents are dead, by the way; his mother with bowel cancer, his father shortly after from a massive stroke. So Mark has inherited his share of the Bradley-Hind estate. Libby, his sister, runs her own riding school and stable there.'

They were finishing off with a mouth-watering chocolate fondant when it suddenly occurred to her to ask, 'Offshore accounts, Ralph – are they legal?'

'Yes, though you have to declare the interest you receive in the UK for tax purposes. Why?'

'No reason,' she said, shaking her head nonchalantly.

But she couldn't help coming back to it a moment later: 'But supposing you don't declare your interest?'

She noticed that Ralph looked uncomfortable.

'Okay, I understand,' she said, holding up her free hand. 'I was just asking you to explain.'

'Offshore accounts are protected by the bank secrecy principle.'

'So in practice it would be extremely difficult for the UK government to acquire information on or access to an offshore account?'

'Quite,' Ralph said, standing up abruptly and tossing his napkin onto the table.

He helped her into her jacket with consummate politeness, taking great care to smooth down the fabric so it sat just so.

'I've enjoyed this enormously,' he said. 'Can we do it again sometime?'

'Thank you,' she said. 'It's been really lovely to catch up.'

On the train home an alarm bell sounded in her head. Was there really any such thing as a free lunch? When he rang two weeks later to make another date she pleaded a full diary – which was true. The following week, though, she wasn't as quick with a good excuse, and he obviously wasn't pleased.

'Look, Ralph,' she said, 'I really enjoyed our lunch, but being seen alone with an attractive man isn't a good idea. Once for old times' sake, but not as a regular thing.'

'Can a man and woman never be friends without sex getting in the way?' he asked.

A throw-away remark, but one that told her her instincts had been sound.

'Something like that. The tabloids would love it.'

'Of course, Archdeacon. We must preserve your reputation at all costs.'

'It's not my reputation that matters here, Ralph. Tom and Alice are what matter.'

After that, their paths crossed occasionally at cathedral functions and each time he regaled her with evidence of Mark's outstanding political ability, that must surely put him in line for party leadership one day. Maybe it was Mark he should have married, not Lindy.

And then she lost touch, didn't see him again for several years, not until she became Bishop of Larchester. In response to concerns expressed in the House of Bishops about a UNICEF report that had highlighted the destructive impact of the UK's materialism and consumerism on the well-being of its children, the Archbishop of Canterbury had proposed that she be elected their 'children's champion'. It was a neat little act of buck-passing. Perhaps the title sat better with a woman, and her fellow bishops were glad to find something appropriate for her to do that might satisfy her crusading zeal. How little did they know her. She appropriated the role with gusto and made an immediate appointment with the government minister for children and families. Her declared aim was to find out why the recommendations in the Mothers' Union report on the sexualising of children and the need for more stringent controls on advertising, so warmly welcomed by the government, had not been acted upon.

As she was leaving Whitehall with the usual unconvincing assurances, she was almost mown down by a man advancing into the building like a ship in full sail, newspaper under his arm, talking loudly into his mobile phone, then repeating the conversation to a colleague several steps behind him. He made a distracted, rather lame apology as he dodged to avoid her, inadvertently kicking her shin in the process. And then they both stopped dead in their tracks and stood, looking at each other.

'Vicky?' he asked uncertainly, folding his phone and dropping it into the pocket of a cashmere overcoat.

She couldn't help but stare. The floppy piece of fair hair that used to fall into his eyes was now stretched across his pate in an attempt to cover increasing baldness. There was a slackening of the jaw. A few broken veins in the cheeks. But she would have known him anywhere.

'Mark Bradley-Hind, as I live and breathe,' she said, lifting her leg to rub her aching shin. 'Still with the kick of a mule.'

Ralph, standing several paces behind, finally emerged and kissed her. She was about to say, 'Well, well, if it isn't Batman and Robin,' but it would have been cruel and she held her tongue.

'You were the one with the kick, as I remember,' Mark said, with a sardonic smile, taking in the high-heeled, black patent shoes, the crisp suit, the dog-collared crimson shirt and large, silver pectoral cross, swinging against her chest. 'You've done well in your chosen profession.'

'So have you. Almost made it to where you always wanted.'

'You too.'

'I don't think so,' Vicky said. 'I couldn't have mentioned any aspirations to be a bishop, since women weren't even vicars at that stage.'

'Of course,' he acknowledged, with a condescending tilt of the head.

The conversation was becoming ridiculous, and they both smiled uncomfortably in acknowledgement of the fact.

'Great to see you,' he said.

'And you.'

'Must all have a drink one of these days, mustn't we, Ralph? For old times' sake.'

Ralph was about to make a courteous response, but before he had a chance to speak, Mark swatted him on the chest with his newspaper, and they both said a curt farewell.

The meeting, for reasons she couldn't quite put her finger on, left her feeling shaken. Later, trying to explain it to Tom, all she could say was, 'It had . . . a bad feel about it. What's the saying? As if someone was walking over my grave.'

'Well, you know what I think of those two cowboys,' Tom said dismissively, as men do about their lovers' previous male consorts.

'Do you know a Ralph Cooper?' Kelvin asked just a few months later, appearing at her study door.

She nodded.

'What does he want?'

'He wouldn't say. Want me to find out?'

'No, get Marissa to find a space in the diary – but make sure it's at a time when one or both of you are here at Bishop's House.'

Kelvin looked askance, waiting for enlightenment.

'I may need a bodyguard, Kelvin.'

'No problem, Bishop,' he grinned, demonstrating the muscle power in his right arm.

Ralph was shown in late one afternoon, and he couldn't have been more restrained. In fact, she quickly became aware, as she led him into the sitting room, that he was clearly in some distress. He slumped into the chair she offered him, refusing to remove his coat. It looked crumpled, as if he had slept in it. Unshaven, his eyes red-rimmed, he remained slouched at an angle, barely looking at her. He refused a cup of tea with a curt shake of the head.

'Thank you for seeing me, Vicky. Or should that be Bishop?'

'Vicky will do fine.'

'I wouldn't have come, except that I had nowhere else to turn.'

She wasn't sure she believed him, but had never known him to be a liar. People can change, said the caution in her head.

He fiddled with one of his coat buttons, then cleared his throat.

'You knew I was working with Mark?'

'I hadn't realised it was full time.'

'It became full time when he joined the shadow cabinet.'

There was a long pause, while Ralph rubbed the back of his neck.

'I hate being disloyal to a friend . . . former friend,' he corrected himself.

She sat very still, her gaze fastened on his face, while his never left his shoelaces. In all the time she had known him she had never seen him like this, and she found it extremely disconcerting. Under Mark's thumb, yes, but never without the essential self-confidence that came from education at a top public school – the relaxed certainty of being born to be in control. The clock in the hall just outside the door registered the passing seconds.

Ralph drew breath slowly and said, with some effort, 'I became aware of certain . . . anomalies in the handling of the office budget. Inconsistencies. As his financial chap, all I wanted was some kind of an explanation.'

'Questioning his integrity – that must have gone down well.'

'We had a massive row. He . . . sent me packing. There was never any proper contractual agreement – it was all on a consultancy basis. I had no recourse, and he knew it.'

'But your old lot will take you back?'

He looked up at her momentarily and shook his head slowly.

'No one will touch me. All Mark has to do is drop a word here and there. He's not a man to thwart. He has so many powerful allies. I'm finished, Vicky. I don't know what to do.'

He hung his head.

'Lindy?' she asked.

'Divorced a while back. Another man. I still felt bad about it, that I had let her down somehow. I gave her the house.'

He wiped his mouth with the back of his hand. She waited, watched him struggling for words. His eyes rested on hers, begging for understanding.

'Mark and I, we've been inseparable for over forty years, since our schooldays. Only you know how close we were. No one else would understand. They'd probably think we were gay.'

'I know only too well the bonds between you, Ralph. You're like brothers. I can't believe the breakdown in your relationship is permanent. Give him time.'

Ralph held up a hand to stop her.

'Then you don't really know him.'

Vicky suspected that was true, that she had never really known what he was capable of.

'And I don't know that I want reconciliation, that I could face living with the possibility of criminal charges one day.'

'Should you go public?'

'I haven't enough evidence.'

They lapsed into silence again, Vicky uncertain as to where to go from here. The man before her was broken. He appeared to be fighting to hold all the pieces together lest he fall apart completely. Despite the whispering of her better judgement, she reached forward and laid a hand over his.

'I've earned a small fortune over the years. But at the end of the day, I have nothing to show for it.'

'How will you manage?'

He shrugged.

'After the divorce, I bought a simple one-bedroom flat in North London. I imagine it would fetch a decent price. But I need something to *do*.'

He hesitated, embarrassed, turned away from her to stare out of the window, chewing his lower lip. Aha, she thought, now he's about to tell me the real reason he's here.

'I saw in the papers that the Church of England is in a financial mess – one diocese bankrupt, yours right on the brink. I . . . I could help.'

He looked at her again, hopefully.

'You don't know of anyone that might take me on for a while?'

'As a financial consultant? Or on a voluntary basis?'

'At a hugely reduced rate, at least,' he said quickly. 'I'd be worth every penny.'

A thought occurred to her. She dismissed it once, twice; but it wouldn't go away. And she found herself saying, 'Actually, I have a temporary vacancy for a diocesan secretary. Mine resigned suddenly due to ill health and it has left me in a bit of a pickle.'

Even as she said it, she suspected he knew already, had been tipped off somehow. 'The job involves responsibility for an annual turnover of over

£12 million, an investment portfolio currently valued at £13.5 million, and for maintaining diocesan assets with a net worth of £130 million. That should be chicken feed for someone like you. But it also involves the care and supervision of the diocesan administrative staff, visionary thinking and the management of change as we respond to new challenges. Think you could manage that – on a temporary basis – for a little while, until we get round to the formal recruitment process?'

Now it was actually on the cards, his uncertainties returned. 'Of course, I know almost nothing of the workings of the Church of England, except what I've picked up on the internet.'

'You can learn, can't you? You're absolutely right. We're in dire straits. What I need is someone who's a wizard with money. I can't offer you anything like the sort of pay I know you're used to – but your expertise would be invaluable.'

The beginnings of a smile played around Ralph's lips.

'There must be a God.'

'There is indeed,' she agreed, as she showed him out.

Tom arrived home as Ralph was leaving, and offered him a peremptory shake of the hand at Vicky's cursory introduction as they passed in the hallway. As the door closed behind him, she explained to Tom who Ralph was. 'What did he want?' he asked, throwing his jacket over a chair.

'Not sure. A job, I think. Seemed timely somehow. He's going to be acting diocesan secretary for a while. I need someone to sort out the financial mess I've been left with.'

Tom whistled.

'Oh Vicky. I hope you know what you're doing.'

It's an almighty gamble, she admitted to herself, but didn't say so out loud. Life without risk wasn't life at all.

Several weeks after Ralph had started to work for her, Vicky summoned him to her study.

'A job for you,' she said, motioning him to a seat, a slim, buff-coloured file in her hand. 'I presume you've heard about this vast abomination that's in the process of being built in Wooten Grange?'

'Who hasn't? Your campaign was fairly well covered in the press.'

'Initially, until they knew we had lost the battle we knew we were going to lose. Too many vested interests.'

'I remember seeing an impressive photo of you standing arms outstretched in front of one of the bulldozers.'

Vicky smiled wryly. 'A great image. Good copy. But now it's old news, forgotten – despite the fact that it's a small-scale humanitarian disaster.

Thus far only exclusive new homes that sell at extortionate prices. No sign of the low-rental social housing that was promised. And already, the new inhabitants are up in arms, maintaining they were never informed about having "low-grade dwellings" on their doorstep when they bought.

'Many of the former inhabitants were left homeless. Some were taken in by relatives, or accommodated in poor-quality local government provision. Either way, multiple occupancy and a dreadful environment for children. Even if social housing does get built, I doubt they'd be able to afford it, thanks to the cuts in their benefits.

'That said, the local churches have been fantastic, working together to provide food, shelter, money counselling, and detached youth work, starting an old-fashioned "friendly society" offering loans at minimum interest. Never let it be said that national welfare doesn't start with us. But there's a limit to how much we can do.'

Ralph, looking slightly at a loss, held out his hand to take the file she now handed carefully over to him.

'I share your frustration, but I'm not sure what you want me to do.'

'Sorry, yes, I get a bit carried away. This matter is very close to my heart. I just want to know who is behind it all. Kelvin did some research for me at county hall. It appears as if planning permission was a done deal. No council was going to turn down such a large investment. More to the point, it seemed like there was government pressure to make it happen. But after that he hit a brick wall. Nothing but prevarication and secrecy.'

Ralph opened the file and began to read.

'And you still have no idea who's behind A.T. Developments or the Brazilian Leisure and Entertainment Organisation, or who their other partners are?' he reflected, stroking his chin.

'No, none.'

'And you want me to find out?'

'Can you?' she asked uncertainly. 'I thought, with your financial background . . . ? It feels like there's something malicious behind this, not just your common-or-garden money-grabbing capitalism. Who is responsible, and how do they get away with it?'

'Vicky, you're asking a lot. These trails can be very hard to follow, and we may not like where they lead. They may even get us into . . . a certain amount of hot water.'

She nodded, frowning.

'I know. I've thought about that. But if you're up for it, I am. I don't feel I can stand by and watch such a grave injustice without at least trying to discover the truth. We owe the people of Wooten Grange that much.'

THIRTEEN

2020

And now Ralph was a member of her staff once again, this time at Lambeth Palace. The BLEO trail might have gone cold once again, but he had no intention of abandoning the hunt.

THIRTEEN

Yes, dearest Amy, God has lent you to me all these years. He only knows what a strength, comfort and joy you have been to me. In sorrow He made you my staff and solace, in loneliness my more than child companion, and in gladness my bright and merry-hearted sympathiser. So, darling, when He asks you now to go away from within my reach, can I say nay? No, no Amy, He is yours – you are His – to take you where He pleases and use you as He pleases. I can trust you to Him and I do . . . All day He has helped me, and my heart unfailingly says, 'Go ye.'

LETTER TO MISSIONARY AMY CARMICHAEL
FROM HER MOTHER, 1895

MARCH 2021

Having so little time for friends was always one of Vicky's greatest sorrows. Occasionally, on a whim, she would call up Mandy late at night. But Bev no longer figured in her life. Melanie, Melissa, Simon, and even Katya, her trusty churchwarden when she was vicar of St Chad's, were now predominantly Christmas card correspondents only. Her social networking presence was entirely impersonal, carefully managed by her staff.

Her only real soul mate was Alice, her beloved daughter – and she was on the wrong side of the Atlantic. At the end of 2019, not that long before the PM's secretary made his fateful visit to Bishop's House in Larchester, Alice had married Dirk Peterson, an American IT specialist she met on a temporary posting to Boston. They were wed in Larchester Cathedral. Katya's daughter, Ania, Alice's closest friend since childhood and as dark as Alice was fair, was her bridesmaid. Tom, naturally, gave her away and Vicky, struggling through with a lump in her throat, managed, somehow, to take the service. It was one of the most difficult, yet most joyous things she had ever had to do.

It had been wonderful to see Katya again after so many years. A Polish immigrant Vicky had met when she was vicar of Potbury in West London, Katya had been left penniless when her husband made off with all their savings and spent them on a one-way ticket to the USA. She took on a variety of menial, low-paid cleaning jobs to support herself and Ania. Home was one room in a tiny, multiple-occupancy terraced house, sharing a kitchen, bathroom and lavatory with three other, not especially clean, residents. The first time Vicky had invited her to the vicarage, Katya gawped at the size of the space in amazement and admiration, and Vicky saw the rather characterless modern box in a whole new light.

Katya, looking chic, a new urchin haircut emphasising her elfin features, was now an office manager for a large construction company. And there was a partner in tow, a swarthy, muscular man of few words and watchful eyes, whom she proudly introduced as Ethan Douglas, a detective sergeant at the Met.

In other ways, the wedding was a bitter-sweet affair, since Dirk was sweeping Alice back to the US almost as soon as the ceremony was over. Although Alice hadn't lived at home for some time, not having her within reach of a short car or train journey left Vicky feeling utterly bereft.

That night Bishop's House seemed cold and empty.

'Just the two of us,' Tom had said, as they arrived home in the early hours of the morning. Vicky followed him into the sitting room, kicked off her wedding shoes, slumped on the settee, and rubbed her aching bunions. Tom joined her, put an arm around her shoulder, and they sat for a while in almost total darkness, even the timer lights having switched themselves off at midnight. She felt too emotionally wrung out to go to bed, and unwilling to give in to the tears she knew would come the moment she laid her head on the pillow. Tom was unusually quiet, unusually still, suffering too, she guessed, from the loss of his little girl.

'We'll rattle around a bit,' he said.

'How often can we get to Boston?'

'As often as we can.'

'My job permitting, you mean?'

'You said it. We have the financial wherewithal.'

'I'll try, Tom. Really, I'll try. I can't bear the thought of not seeing her regularly. Technology is all very well, but it's just not the same.'

'Just the two of us, now,' he said eventually, taking her hand in his and squeezing it gently. 'As it was in the beginning . . . Always so moving, isn't it, to hear those vows again? To remember the promises we made to each other. Would you have had me, knowing what you know now?'

'Would you have had me, had you known what was coming? That's more to the point.'

'The two of you? You, and your alter ego, the Bishop?'

She hit him over the head with a cushion.

'Ouch. Is that a new form of episcopal blessing?'

'There is no real competition, Tom, you know that, don't you?' she said, serious now, putting the cushion down and stroking the side of his face in the darkness. 'You and Alice have always been first. And even though she's gone, we still have each other.'

He stroked her palm, and she was surprised to see tears glittering in his eyes.

1992

As Tom rolled back over on the bed, panting, Vicky gave in to an irresistible urge to laugh out loud. He heaved himself up on one elbow, and leant over her, frowning.

'Does everything amuse you, Vicky? Is nothing sacrosanct? This is our wedding night, for crying out loud.'

'Sorry, my darling,' she said penitently, cupping his face in her hands and drawing him down so that she could kiss him, tenderly, on the forehead, the nose, and then the mouth. 'I didn't mean to hurt your feelings, but it is funny, you have to admit. All the hype, the frustrating, agonising wait. For what? This heaving, pushing and faffing about.'

'If you say so, babe, but I've never slept with any woman who found losing her virginity such a laugh.'

He lay back, staring up at the ceiling.

Vicky didn't exactly welcome having the collective host of his ex-lovers barging in on the first night of their marriage. But that was her fault. It would have been better to tell him that she found the feel of his naked skin against hers, the smell of him, the taste of him, the converging of their flesh, an utterly intoxicating sensation, but she was afraid the words would turn the sacredness of it into a trashy novel.

Instead, she snuggled into his side and whispered, 'I wasn't casting any aspersions on your performance, Tom. I'm so very, very happy. Being one flesh with you is more wonderful than I could ever have imagined. But it's not exactly, well, graceful, is it? Young people are sold short by the media with its images of slick, skilful sex from the very first attempt. Without a sensitive, thoughtful lover it must be hellish – at least for some girls.'

Tom reached out and stroked her hair, then held it back from her face, so that he could look into her eyes. 'Just for once, could you pack your social conscience into a drawer at the very back of your mind, and focus all your attention on the situation at hand?'

She nodded, ruefully. If Tom was guilty of bringing his exes to the party, she had opened the door to an even greater multitude. The bedroom was getting crowded.

'You will always be the main focus of my attention,' she murmured, weaving her fingers through the strip of fluffy hair that ran the length of his chest to the soft mound of his belly.

'Don't make promises you can't keep,' he said, pressing a forefinger gently to her lips. 'I'm not naive. I've seen your single-mindedness when it comes to your calling. I hope I have the same dedication to mine. But let's be clear about this. Putting each other before the demands of our work is going to be hard graft.'

'I certainly intend to make plenty of time for *this*,' she breathed into his ear, her hand moving slowly down his body.

Later, as she lay awake, listening to the gentle but regular snuffling from the other side of the bed, trying to adjust to the idea of sharing such private space for the rest of her life, she marvelled again that she had ever agreed to a date with the man lying naked next to her, let alone married him. Was it the challenge to her reforming zeal? The compulsion to discover why anyone with a modicum of intelligence would behave as he had? Or simply the chance to escape the vicar hothouse for an evening and spend time with someone whose life did not revolve around the latest edicts from the General Synod of the Church of England?

'Vicky,' he had tried to assure her, as they sat down at a table in Il Trattoria, the menus barely in their hands, 'please believe me, it was a temporary aberration. I never normally attend those sort of medical parties, precisely because they're so renowned for serious, stupid drinking. But when your colleagues are forever berating you for taking life too seriously, when they intimate that you think you're above them, it's join 'em, or lose 'em – their goodwill, at least. I had no choice. Then realised as soon as I got there that it was a Catch 22.'

The speech was a good one, but perhaps a tad too polished. But the menu, in which he had shown no interest, was shaking in his hands. She had never had that effect on a man before and found it disarming.

'Just to test whether my presence was pure condescension, they coerced me into one of their drinking competitions, and I ended up rat-arsed. Exactly as they intended.'

His penitence was beginning to seem more genuine, but she wasn't prepared to let him off the hook. Not that easily.

'Ah, you were pressganged into it, then – the party and the drinking?'

He held out his open palms.

'No, I'm not trying to excuse my behaviour. But no doctor is an island. A medical team must work together. It's in the patient's best interests. I couldn't see how else to break down some of the barriers I seemed to have created just because I'm not quite as clubby as the rest of them.'

She gestured at the menu, and he began to peruse it in a half-hearted sort of way, giving her a chance to study his face when sober. She took in the firm curve of the jaw, the midnight shadow that emphasised the small cleft in his chin, the narrow channels that ran from a straight, strong nose to a wide, full mouth, and the early crinkles at the edge of those wonderful eyes that she hadn't been able to erase from her mind. This didn't look like a man who was easily led. Quite the opposite. After all, what was she doing here with him? Loath as she was to admit it, she had been rail-roaded by a beguiling individual with an elegant bedside manner, who knew what he wanted and how to get it. She gave a start, suddenly aware that she was staring.

'And did you achieve your objective?' she asked drily. 'You don't think your colleagues would have respected you more if you'd maintained a gentle but dignified refusal?'

He put the menu down, and said earnestly, 'Yes – that's why I feel so wretched, Vicky. All I did was make a complete fool of myself, and there is no one to blame but my own weak self. I can't think why you ever agreed to come out with me.'

'Nor can I,' she agreed, as the waiter arrived to take their order. Everything on the menu looked so tempting. She chose quickly, then secreted a copy in her handbag as a souvenir. Tom was too busy thinking of a suitable response to notice. Instead, he covered her hand with his and said, 'You were so . . . luminous. Your face, your beauty penetrated even my drunken state. I thought I'd been rescued by an angel. I just had to see you again.'

She had no intention of letting him think that either his eloquent expression of regret or his flattery would break down her determination not to be taken in. Though she had to admit that in her current theological habitat, rare was the man who displayed such honesty, humility and charm. Such *savoir faire* with a woman. It was that urbanity, more than anything, that caught her off guard. It was in such stark contrast to all those would-be vicars.

The wine menu arrived and she asked for water. Tom raised his eyebrows.

'I almost never drink,' she said. 'It's personal, not theological. I could get used to it, I think. But at the moment, the very smell of it turns my stomach.'

She looked away from him, not wanting him to see the sudden, unexpected emotion that filled her eyes with tears. Then felt his fingers lightly touch the back of her hand again, sending an electric jolt through her body.

'Then you were even more amazing the other night than I realised. So now I've seen you at your best, and you've seen me at my worst. Do you think there's any chance we could have a relationship where the reverse becomes true?'

Tom wooed her with a dedication and ardour that undermined all her best attempts to keep a cool head, and two months later, he asked her to marry him. She should have been delirious with joy. Instead, she was plagued by doubts about the wisdom of such a liaison, so she put him on hold and dashed up to Durham to consult with the one voice of reason she knew she could fully trust.

'Vicky, I can't tell you whether or not to marry Tom,' Donald said from the comfort of his favourite, well-worn armchair, with the benign smile he reserved for delivering disappointing counsel. She must have looked stricken, for he relented a little. 'Tell me more about him.'

'He's kind and considerate, open and thoughtful, fun to be with, a very committed doctor. Since boyhood all he has ever wanted to do is relieve pain and suffering. In fact, in many ways he's everything I ever hoped for.'

'But?'

'He calls himself a lapsed Catholic. He's been coming to church with me virtually every week. I don't think it's just to please me. Faith meant something when he was a boy, he says, and he's not against it. As he grew older, it just slipped away from him.'

'Mmmm, residual faith, liberated yet wistful, slowly re-awakening.'

'But is it . . . re-awakening? How can I tell? I'm training to become a soul doctor at large, delving into the deepest recesses of people's beliefs, checking up on their spiritual health. But I wouldn't feel able to submit Tom to that kind of prying.'

'I'm sure you can't,' Donald said, shaking his head vigorously. 'If you take a young and tender plant out of the soil every five minutes to check whether its roots have taken, you risk destroying it. It's not for us to barge into another human being's sacred place with God – not without their permission. And you're just too close to Tom.'

She must have looked dubious, but Donald pursued. 'Come on, Vicky, if some re-awakening were not taking place, he'd be trying to get out of the hothouse, not wilfully running towards it. Who would knowingly commit themselves to partnering someone with a calling so strong they're throwing themselves into an institution that still doesn't fully recognise their right to have it? It's asking for trouble.'

She couldn't help but smile. That was Tom all over. There was nothing he wouldn't do for a patient when vital treatment was delayed by bureaucracy, ineptitude or unconcern. The heartlessness of the system made him obstinate, determined, bullish. The church had no idea what was coming to it if this man became a clergy spouse.

'He certainly won't hold me back. He is that rare thing in a man – instinctively egalitarian.'

'Ah, some of us do exist,' Donald nodded appreciatively.

'It's his innate sense of fair play. He says what's good for the gander, must be good for the goose.'

They both chuckled at the idea.

'What worries me is that I can't make him see that it's going to take more than a hide like a rhinoceros to be married to someone who belongs body, soul and spirit to the Church of England.'

She noticed the new leather patches sewn onto the elbows of Donald's jacket. He sat now with them resting on the arms of his chair, pressing his fingertips together, staring into the distance, as he so often did when faced with one of Vicky's more impenetrable conundrums. Then he turned to her suddenly and said, 'What do you want of the man, Vicky? If that's how you see your calling – a total, all-consuming commitment to an institution – then stay celibate, for God's sake. And yes, before you ask, I'd say that to a man too. Marriage is a calling as well. For two to become one flesh is more than a romp between the sheets now and then. It requires the greatest altruism you'll ever have to give. Sometimes your calling will take priority, and sometimes his. You can't go into it planning to make a cuckold of the man from the start – forced into second place by your job. The test is, do you love him enough to put him first – always?'

She concentrated and let Tom's face fill her mind, then nodded slowly. 'I think so.'

'Thinking so isn't enough.'

'I love him so much,' she whispered, eventually, choking slightly on the words. 'I was so afraid it would compromise my vocation.'

'Oh, away with the hair shirt, woman! What is it they call it today – being "up yourself"? I expect it's very rude, but it makes the point. A vocation it must be, but a job is also what it is at the end of the day. Get it into perspective. Marriage is a wonderful estate – a lifetime of sharing your bad habits and dirty laundry. If you are called to it, the quality of sacrificial love you show your life partner will enhance the quality of selfless love you give to all people.'

2020

'The PM has asked if you'll see him. He says it's urgent,' Ann said, her head looming up on Vicky's screen like a dismembered ghost. 'He wants to speak to you face to face. At Number 10.'

She was appreciating this room more and more, Vicky thought to herself, as she looked at the new paintings hanging on the wall of the terracotta room.

'Archbishop,' said Liam Cavendish, bursting through the door and clasping her hand. 'Thank you for coming.' He motioned her to a seat, swept his hair out of his eyes, straightened his tie, and said without any further preamble, 'I am under considerable pressure from my colleagues in the cabinet to introduce fresh legislation that requires Anglican clergy to carry out their responsibilities in a state church to marry whoever requests it.'

For a moment Vicky anticipated feeling as if she had been stabbed with a sharp blade, but to her surprise the pain never materialised. In fact, she felt a deep sense of excitement, as if she was sitting in a boat that had just been freed from its moorings and was about to sail out to sea.

'In other words, Prime Minister,' she said with a strange, unearthly calm, 'you want to force the clergy to conduct gay marriages?'

'We feel there should be no exemptions in our anti-discrimination legislation. Your ministers should fulfil the obligations they took on at ordination to serve the whole community – and not just the heterosexual part of it. In exchange for which, the government might see a way of putting pressure on local councils to let you rid yourselves of your extravagant monuments.'

'Kind of you,' she said, taken aback by such an open attempt at bribery. 'But you do realise that this new legislation would bring you into conflict with canon law, which is equally binding, and states that marriage is between a man and a woman.'

He dismissed her with a wave of the hand.

'Parliament is supreme. We'll simply have canon law changed.'

Vicky couldn't help but smile. The naivety of the man. He manifestly had no idea of how complex that might be, of the battles he would face in Synod.

'So you will remove the so-called "quadruple lock" imposed by a previous government that forbade the Church of England from offering gay marriage?'

She smiled again, and he nodded, warily, slightly unnerved by her reaction.

'I think I would welcome that,' she said.

His head jolted backwards in surprise.

'I always thought it rather tiresome, not to say patronising, that a government thought it necessary to lock us up like an antique, bone china dinner service.'

'So, the church is now ready to support and perform gay marriage?' he asked, wide-eyed in amazement.

'Ah, no, I didn't say that, Prime Minister. On the contrary, I don't think we've changed our basic position at all. I'm simply saying we are quite capable of following our consciences without the protection of the state.'

'But if we remove the "quadruple lock", as it was called, the clergy will inevitably face a challenge in the European Court of Human Rights.'

'With respect, Prime Minister, that must be our battle, not yours.'

'And if their judgement makes performing gay marriage compulsory?' he asked.

'Compulsion is the resort of a totalitarian state,' she replied, evenly. 'There can be no democracy without a plurality of beliefs and views, and the freedom to maintain them.'

The Prime Minister made no effort to hide his annoyance.

'The law cannot change the heart,' she added. 'Tell me, what will you do with those who refuse to do their duty, as you put it? Sack them, as councils and other government organisations summarily dismiss any staff, from cleaners to teachers, prison officers to the police, who openly disagree with gay marriage? You see, we're not government employees, so I'm afraid that avenue is closed to you. Fines? We won't pay them. Imprison us? We'll clog up your already oversubscribed prison system. So how will you force us not to follow our consciences? Torture? Beheading? I wouldn't be the first Archbishop to be burnt at the stake.'

She smiled, but Liam Cavendish ignored her, crossed his right leg over his left, and started to tap his left foot on the ground, so that his right foot swung backwards and forwards.

'So, as I suspected,' he snapped, 'I can't rely on your support?'

'I'm afraid not. The church's position is that it's not for the state to re-define a historic institution, based on the fundamental complementarity of men and women, that is the foundation of a stable society.'

'And you'd face the consequences the law would impose?'

'Of course. We would have no choice. Out of interest, what do you intend to do with the imams, the rabbis, the Sikh and Hindu leaders who refuse to perform gay marriage?'

'That's the sticking point, of course.'

'Ah, so we can be anti-Christian, but God forbid we should look anti-Muslim?'

'I think we had better bring this conversation to a close,' he said, rising swiftly to his feet.

'I'm so sorry we seem to have locked antlers again, Prime Minister,' she said, following him to the door. He held it open for her, but she stood her ground on the threshold, and turning back to him, said, 'With the greatest of respect, I fail to understand why this particular matter should so exercise the government, when there are so many more pressing demands. The country is in a parlous financial state, the fissure between rich and poor becomes ever more marked, our transport network is at a virtual standstill, and healthcare is deeply challenged. I would be happy to work with you on any of these priorities. But freedom of conscience is non-negotiable, the right of every individual in this democracy of ours.'

He indicated that he was holding the door open for her. Still she paused, shaking her head.

'It seems as if we are further down the road to a totalitarian state than I had feared. Some of us simply will not accept it.'

'And what will you do about it?'

It was almost a sneer.

'There are many ways to make our feelings known.'

'I do hope the recent press hullabaloo hasn't upset you too much. Most unfortunate to be wrong-footed so soon in your new role.'

Vicky realised that the Queen was referring to the basque episode.

'Ma'am? Oh, that. Such nonsense. I took it with a pinch of salt.'

'One does wonder why people can't maintain any discretion these days.'

'I find it a futile exercise, Ma'am, to try and work out what the press hopes to gain from such disclosures. Apart from selling newspapers, of course. Though I'm not sure how the underwear of a middle-aged cleric would boost their sales, or indeed have any interest for the great British public.'

'Quite so,' she smiled.

'I was more upset by the revelations about my mother.'

'It is very hard when our parents, whom we love, are subjected to that kind of prurience.'

Vicky found the Queen a sympathetic listener. They met once a month, and for occasional weekends at Sandringham. At first she mistook the Queen's natural shyness for aloofness, as many apparently did. Once Vicky had grasped how private a person she was, it made the relentless schedule of royal visits all the more remarkable. Though the Queen never admitted it, they left her physically and emotionally drained.

How she managed the charming informality that never came at the cost of royal dignity or mystique, though, Vicky could never quite work out. It was a remarkable gift. But as the Queen got to know her new Archbishop, she warmed, and as they gained each other's confidence, they began to genuinely enjoy each other's company. Vicky suspected that being a woman was actually a bonus. The unique sisterhood that could spring up between two women was particularly precious for two who were so alone, set apart for special duties.

In what she now saw as her naive younger days, Vicky had been very taken with the idea of the disestablishment of the church from the state, resenting the fact that all measures passed by General Synod had to be sanctioned by Parliament. What business was it of several hundred MPs, most of whom had no insight into church affairs? But when it came to the current monarch, the loss of the church's figure-head would be a grave loss indeed. She took her role as Supreme Governor of the Church of England seriously, and was concerned that disestablishment, on the distant horizon at the start of her reign, now hovered ever closer with the reduction of bishops in the House from twenty-six to twelve. She expressed her anxiety to Vicky in no uncertain terms.

'The concept of our established Church is widely misunderstood, and that is such a pity. It has created an environment where people of other faiths and no faith can live freely, following their own belief systems. It helps to build a better society, and does so much for the common good. Yet few in our government appear to appreciate the fact. A further reduction in the number of Lords Spiritual, and I fear that a break between crown, church and state might be inevitable.'

'Apparently we bishops are out of touch with the people.'

'That strikes one as ridiculous, though we're not permitted to say so, of course. Surely, a bishop's presence in the Lords is an extension of his or her responsibility for the spiritual oversight of the people? They are an important independent voice. Of course they make no claims to direct representation. But who in the House of Lords does?'

So astute, Vicky thought. If only Her Majesty could make her views more public.

'And they do seek to be a voice for people of all faiths, not just Christians. We have raised our concerns with the Prime Minister, but . . .'

She and her Archbishop shared a knowing look.

'Ma'am,' Vicky said, treading carefully as she broached the subject, 'I fear there might be an even greater clamour for disestablishment if the government removes the current legal strictures they introduced some years ago that enable Anglican clergy to be absolved from their duty to marry whoever requests it.'

The Queen looked at her in alarm.

'Same-sex marriage? But surely the clergy must have the right to follow the teachings of the church as stated in canon law? Government statute cannot simply ignore it.'

'I was informed that Parliament is supreme. The new legislation would scrub out the exemption and conscience clauses, and so canon law would have to be changed.'

The Queen was visibly shaken.

'That would create such a row between church and state, which we have tried so hard to hold together.'

'And greater demand for disestablishment, of course, which would be perceived by many as a means of freeing the church from state intervention in our affairs.'

'In this democratic country of ours, no government could possibly overrule freedom of conscience in this way. Could it?'

The Queen recovered herself and remained silent, lost in thought. Vicky was acutely aware of the danger of stirring up dissension at the Palace, but felt she had no alternative. If she couldn't rely on the support of the Supreme Governor, her position was untenable. She said, 'I'm not sure how free this country is any more, Ma'am. Some people appear to be much freer than others. Secularists can't bear anyone having special privileges in the name of religion. To them, any belief simply seems like bigotry.'

The Queen remained silent, her mouth slightly pinched, her brow furrowed, but maintaining her composure.

'We're trying to take this all in, Archbishop,' she said, eventually. 'We are Supreme Governor of the Church, but we have not been consulted. What would be the impact of the new legislation? Resistance? Fines?'

Vicky shook her head.

'I can't say at the moment, Ma'am. Though I think we would have to refuse to pay any fines – on principle.'

'Imprisonment? These are our ministers. We would have something to say about that.'

The Queen paused for a moment, still struggling to absorb the implications of what she had just heard.

'Where will this all end? Is there nothing you can do?'

'I don't think so,' replied Vicky. 'The only power I have is in name.'

'Ah yes,' the Queen smiled, 'a little like us.'

And then she added pensively, 'Though there might still be something we can do.'

Vicky left the Palace feeling slightly cheered, for reasons she couldn't quite define, except that here was someone in her nineties who understood frustration and helplessness, yet continued to execute the duty she believed God had bestowed upon her at birth without acrimony or complaint. Her role, Vicky said to herself, has required life-long dedication and self-sacrifice, while I balk at the few years of mine.

Over their next few meetings the Queen invited Vicky to discuss her anxieties for the church, the potential impact of the anti-proselytising laws, the financial difficulties faced by the dioceses, the growing unrest in the country. She was an insightful and perceptive companion, asking her Archbishop whether she thought there was a chance that the country might ever return to the Judeo-Christian values that had once made Britain great. Vicky said she thought it might, describing the growth of spiritual hunger as people were bewildered by the drop in their living standards, the meaninglessness of political bluster and the naked aggression of a lost, young generation. It comforted the Queen to think so.

They also had a great deal of fun together – which she hadn't anticipated. They chuckled a great deal – often at the foibles of men, be it the Lords in Parliament or the bishops in Synod. The Queen thoroughly enjoyed Vicky's descriptions of the neighing and braying, snoring and wheezing, that turned the debates into a farmyard, especially after lunch.

'As some of us get older,' the Queen confided, 'we have to be very careful not to embarrass ourselves by dozing off at inconvenient moments.'

'Yes, Ma'am, but with respect, if some of them ate more healthily and desisted from the wine, it might be a lot easier.'

The Queen laughed.

She never mentioned same-sex marriage again specifically, but let Vicky know, nonetheless, by inference, that she wasn't averse to action, if her responsibilities to her clergy required it. What she intended, Vicky couldn't conceive. She was only glad that someone had a plan.

FOURTEEN

The truth of human freedom lies in the love that breaks down barriers.

JÜRGEN MOLTMANN

APRIL 2021

Vicky never came to terms with having Alice so far away, especially once Caleb, her baby grandson, was born. Once or twice a week she and her daughter would get hold of each other for a chat, usually at around 1 a.m. British time, early evening in the US.

'How goes it, Mum?'

'It goes.'

'Is that all?'

'One or two, er, political difficulties, shall we say? But aren't there always?'

'You sound knackered.'

'I am. This job is more of a killer than I could have ever imagined. My only chance to relax is at the health club in Canterbury. And that's not nearly as often as I'd hoped. I think your father finds it hard. He's talking about buying himself a studio flat.'

'Don't worry about Dad. I guess he just wants the equivalent of a garden shed – somewhere for a man to keep his bits and bobs. He needs some kind of non-church space.'

'You're probably right. I'm just feeling a little wistful for that old thing called a life. It's the ordinary things I miss, like shopping. I have just been told – diplomatically, of course – that it would not be wise to pop over to Oxford Street – at least, not without a paper bag over my head. Apart from the security risk, I might get harangued by the disenchanted, God forbid, or oddballs with a grudge against women. And then the following morning the press would tell the world what I bought. As if anyone is interested.'

'Oh but they are, Mum. Your famous basque ended up in our newspapers. You'll just have to come out here. Great shopping, I promise. And your grandson is dying to see you again.'

There had been one short trip to see the new baby – too little, too long ago.

'And how is my little man?'

'Just gone off for the night. Take a look at him.'

Alice moved over to a crib and crouched, so that Vicky could see the baby.

'Angelic, isn't he? At times like this you wouldn't believe the racket he can make when he's awake.'

Vicky had thought of explaining the 'political difficulties' to Alice, then thought better of it. She suddenly felt so tired of it all. What she needed was to be drawn into a world beyond her palaces – Alice and Caleb's world, where that calm and cosy, familial contentedness would free her from her archiepiscopal prison. Finally they said their goodbyes and Vicky went, daughter- and grandchild-sick, fretfully to bed.

From the moment she first held Alice in her arms, she had always known that no matter how demanding and restricting motherhood might be, no matter how much she longed for an uninterrupted day's work or a decent night's sleep, there would come a time when she would do anything to turn back the clock and have her child again, dependent, cuddlesome, and simply there.

1996

'Alice, are you ready for church?'

'Why do we have to go to silly church?'

'Because your mummy is the vicar,' Tom said, buttoning her into her coat.

'Church is boring.'

'I know, precious,' Vicky said. 'I'm bored too, so I'm going to change that as soon as I can. Meanwhile, Ania will be there. And you can play together.'

'With everyone going shhhhhhhhhh?'

Tom wiped the spray off his cheek and she giggled.

Vicky put up with the moans at the church door every Sunday and the barely disguised twittering behind her back. What she couldn't stand was the way Alice was subjected to scowls and tuts as she pushed her toy buggy up and down the centre aisle during, and even after services. The child was only four, and doing no harm whatsoever. Ironically, it meant Tom ended up spending most dry Sunday mornings supervising Alice and Ania on a muddy patch of grass outside the church. It would have been simpler and more fun to have taken them to the park.

'Do you know what?' Vicky exploded after one morning service, as the girls ran back into church to thaw out, Tom and Katya in tow. 'Someone has just complained about unruly children desecrating the church "garden". Apparently, it's as much God's dwelling place as the interior, and he doesn't want it spoiled.'

Tom's eyes widened in disbelief.

'What did you say to them?'

'I said, "If we are God's children like he says we are, his dwelling place would be a grand adventure playground."'

'Good for you,' Katya said. 'Don't let the buggers get you down.'

Despite herself, Vicky's fury dissolved into amusement.

'Where did you learn language like that?'

Katya shrugged her shoulders.

'It helps sometimes.'

The following week Vicky set out a trestle table at the back of the church, covered in paper, pencils, pastels, crayons and waterpaints, beads, buttons, straws, threads and pieces of fabric. And there the girls played happily, one blonde head, one brown, bent studiously over their creations, throughout the entire service.

Ken, churchwarden and former police sergeant, lumbered across to her the moment the service was over, as she stood shaking hands at the church door. He was apoplectic, his fists clenched against his hips. In an effort to prevent himself doing something he might regret? Vicky suspected so, and was determined not to be intimidated by it.

'How dare you desecrate God's house in this way, Vicar!' he spluttered.

She felt the spray of his spittle flecking her face, and raised a hand to wipe her cheek, then manoeuvred him forcefully out of the hearing range of the girls.

'These are children, Ken. Do you think God doesn't welcome them in his presence?'

'It's not them,' he blustered, waving a hand in the direction of the table, 'it's all this . . . paraphernalia.'

'Children drawing, Ken? Isn't that a reflection of God's creativity?'

'You didn't even ask your churchwardens. We have no faculty.'

'We don't need permission for an art table, Ken,' she said, affably.

'The Bishop will have something to say about this.'

How could Ken think the Bishop would censure her when it was he who had imposed her on the church? Ken had never recovered from that, essentially. He and his fellow churchwarden, Stan – a silent, bespectacled local newsagent with an army haircut – had already turned down five other candidates the Bishop had sent, and had been issued with an ultimatum. The Anglican bush telegraph had carried the news of her work at St Maggie's far and wide, and the Bishop seemed to think she would be a good catch for his diocese. So unless Ken and Stan had very good practical reasons for turning her down, they were left with a woman or permanent vacancy.

The only woman this congregation had seen conducting worship was the Vicar of Dibley. Unfortunately, Geraldine Grainger, though not the usual media buffoon, was a hard act to follow. The only similarity in their situation was that Vicky's Parochial Church Council was also a collection of irksome oddballs.

St Chad's, Potbury was a hideous 1960s monstrosity – all corners, flat surfaces and high brick walls, more like a prison than a church. It stood on the edge of an identikit 1950s estate in the great West London sprawl, housing the upwardly mobile in rows of *Monopoly*-style three-bed homes, as if in the race to keep up with the Joneses everyone had to have an identical start in order to satisfy the British sense of fair play.

Such was the inflated value of housing in the London area in the nineties that first-time buyers would have been lucky to afford a garage, and the locals here were now largely London commuters and small businessmen of the middle ranks. There was one little row of shops, half of them now non-retail offices, no community centre, a tiny scrap of park and no pub where people could congregate. Just this afterthought of a church – with a congregation of around eighty on a good Sunday.

The vicarage, joined to the church by a narrow covered way, damp and mildewed – like a rank umbilical cord – was rectangular and characterless. The residual class system of the sixties persuaded diocesan surveyors that from the outside vicarages should resemble a council or police house, so that locals could see that the occupants were not throwbacks to the Victorian era with ideas above their station. And so another eyesore was created.

Inside, it strictly followed the official Anglican rules on every detail of the build, from the size of the toilets to the number of light fittings, dictating that every vicar should have a house large enough to be functional, but small enough not to lead to any misapprehension of luxury. A generous study, but a dining room so bijou that they would be hardpressed to fit a table into it.

'Whatever happened to the concept of vicarage hospitality?' she asked the archdeacon on their guided tour. The kitchen – modernised, said Ken the churchwarden with a measure of pride, a mere fifteen years ago – was lit by a single strip light. The cupboard and drawer fronts in mottled mustard were falling apart, and the minimal tiling was made up of the white variety used predominantly in public conveniences. The vinyl on the floor, a square tile-effect in beige and gold, was stained, worn through in places and literally dog-eared around the edges. The smell of the animal had lingered.

Tom stared, poked, prodded and tutted, which made the poor archdeacon nervous. He was a rotund little man, who addressed his words to Tom most of the time, eyeing him apprehensively.

'Good-sized kitchen and meeting-rooms over at the church. No need to entertain here. Especially not when the clergy spouse is er . . . male,' he said, laughing at his own little joke, then clearing his throat when Tom crushed him with one of his most withering looks.

'Don't worry,' Tom whispered, 'when the big bucks start coming through, we'll do something with this place.'

Tom had secured his first consultancy in general surgery at the Royal Free Hospital in London.

'It's not ours to do anything with.'

'I don't care. I can't live with that turquoise bathroom suite. You and Alice deserve a bath where the enamel isn't brown from a succession of clergy family ablutions, and I shall have a proper shower.'

There was little anyone could do with the church. The large empty worship space was unadorned, badly lit and impossible to heat. The congregation mumbled its way through the hymns, while the organist, an elderly lady who wore a felt hat and a large tweed coat that seriously hampered her movements, struggled to keep up, often a couple of beats behind.

In those early weeks Vicky put as much preparation into preaching as she could – to share her vision, to stir and challenge an apathetic congregation, to allay their fears that a woman wasn't up to the job. One bumbling woman was all it took to undermine her entire gender. More to the point, it was a theft of time not to deliver something of worth to a captive audience.

But no matter how hard she tried to be relevant, challenging, and inspirational, it never seemed to make a scrap of difference. The nearest she came to a token of acceptance in the whole of her first year was a comment from Stan's wife, a lady so large she looked as if she might have eaten her churchwarden husband for breakfast. An inch from Vicky's face, overpowering her with a heady mixture of Givenchy and sour gastric juices, she had said, 'May I say, dear, how attractive you are – for a woman priest.'

Vicky took a step back and, to her surprise, found herself saying, 'Some male vicars aren't bad either.'

Mrs Stan gave her a very strange look as she frogmarched her husband out of the church door. But Vicky was heartily tired of being called a 'woman priest', rather than plain 'vicar'.

Ken the copper certainly set out to make her life difficult. At Communion, to make an obvious point, he would march past her to any male permitted to administer the bread and wine. He argued interminably at PCC, opposing every suggestion she made on principle.

Vicky decided a pastoral visit was due, to see if they could reach some understanding, and if not, to secure his resignation. His wife, a faded little woman in a beige twin set, with fuzzy, over-permed mouse-brown hair, brought in a tray of tea and biscuits.

'Stop fussing, Flo,' he ordered, as she pointed out the extra hot water in a plastic thermos flask. She backed towards the door with a forced smile. The man, Vicky could see, was a bully at home too.

'Tell me, Ken,' she asked him, keeping her eyes firmly focused on his, 'why stay on as churchwarden when having a woman vicar manifestly upsets you so much?'

He blustered for a moment. He was not accustomed to forthrightness from a female. He took a gulp of his tea and cleared his throat.

'To take a stand. To show local people that I fundamentally disapprove.'

'In that case, why not transfer to a church with a male vicar?'

'St Chad's is my church and it has been since we came to live here, over thirty years ago. You think you can just come in here and turn over all our sacred traditions? Over my dead body.'

He leant towards her and eyeballed her with a glare that in its day must have cowed many a criminal. But she held his gaze.

'I have no intention of abandoning ship as you steer it towards disaster,' he said. 'It needs a safe pair of hands at the helm.'

He eyed Vicky's hands, clasped around a flowery china teacup, and added, 'I've seen out three vicars already, and I'll be here long after you've passed on to new pastures.'

It was futile to argue with the man. Short of turning over her art table, there was little he could do, so she bypassed him, enlisting the support of newcomers to the congregation, gradually introducing better crèche facilities, toyboxes, Plasticine and paintwalls, a monthly family-friendly service, and child-friendly liturgies with accessible illustrations. Week by week the numbers of children grew. It helped that the organist retired, making way for a decent pianist and the occasional guitar. But her determination to liven up St Chad's and make it more relevant to its community began to take its toll on her own family life.

At her initial interview, the archdeacon had gone out of his way to say that she mustn't take advantage of the flexibility of the job. Proper childcare arrangements must be made. Would he have said such a thing to a man?

'The parish deserves professionalism,' she assured him curtly.

Tom's work meant that they could now afford a decent nursery for Alice, but Vicky knew she was leaving her there far too many hours. She was reading to her one night when Alice said, 'Lily's mummy is just like that mummy in the book.'

'How's that, sweetheart?' Vicky asked her. 'Aren't I?'

'No, silly,' she said. 'You don't make cakes and things. You're the vicar.'

Either the book was maintaining old-fashioned stereotypes, or Alice was telling her something.

Tom often worked late, and then he had a long commute home. When he arrived, he usually found a babysitter in residence. When Vicky arrived home late after yet another meeting, they often ended up arguing when what they really needed was to unwind and catch up.

'What am I to you?' he shouted one night. His chilli con carne had emerged from the microwave in a glutinous, congealed mess, and she hadn't rolled home until midnight.

'Which is my time in your busy diary?'

'You're just as bad, never around for an evening meal because something unforeseen has happened during surgery, or a patient has had a relapse, or the Medical Director has called an urgent meeting.'

'You knew life would be like that when you married a doctor.'

'Oh – and you didn't when you married a vicar? Or is it still that old cookie – that ultimately the woman has to be there for her man?'

'You don't have to work while Alice is small. I earn enough to keep us both.'

Vicky felt as if she had been slapped.

'Work? Is that what this is about? You knew how important my vocation was to me when I married you.'

'Vocation? Oh, please don't make me argue with God. I don't stand a chance.'

And with that, he swept up his pillows and stomped off to the spare room.

Vicky spent a miserable couple of hours pacing the floor in fury, justifying herself to him in his absence. How could he expect her to care for Alice, shop, cook, and fulfil all the expectations that went with her job?

At 2 a.m. she crept down the corridor and hesitantly opened the spare bedroom door a crack. His eyes were closed, and she was about to make an unhappy return to their bed when she heard him call out softly, 'Vicky?'

'You were having me on – pretending to be asleep.'

He laughed out loud, and she threw herself on top of him, beating his chest with her fists.

'Don't let's quarrel, Tom. We have to accommodate each other's lives. That's what we agreed. Marriage is about mutual self-sacrifice.'

'Easy in the abstract, harder in reality. Surgery can be life and death. I can't simply abandon a patient.'

'I know. It's always the pressure of everyone else's agendas and crises. But so is my work. I'll do my best to be at home more. If I can.'

Tom didn't respond immediately, and she waited.

'It's just . . . I feel left out of your world. Church members have to have their lengthy one-to-ones with you. I'm the spare part, the one that stops them getting their pound of the vicar's flesh. As if they were the real partner, and I'm just the demanding lover.'

He sounded peevish, but had a point.

'You,' she said, kissing him hard on the mouth, 'can be a demanding lover any time you want.'

'I can, can I, when all I get are your fag ends? Your worn-out leftover moments at the end of the day.'

She cuffed him across the head with a pillow.

'Not enough sex, then?'

He grinned. 'Something like that. And by the way, your cooking's lousy at the moment too.'

'Who's in charge of the diary, Vicky? Reshuffle your schedule,' Donald commanded, when she went up to Durham for her regular appointment. 'You'll not survive if you don't.'

They met in his home, now that he had retired from academic life. His tiny study was mannish and musty-smelling, with wall-to-wall shelving crammed with ancient and new theological books all mixed in together. 'Can you not take an hour or so off late afternoons for your wee girl? You need a break too, woman. Who else works three sessions a day? Can your man manage one early evening a week, to coincide with yours?'

So she began to carve out an Alice-shaped break between 4 and 7 p.m. most days. Any attempt to disrupt it, except for a real emergency, be it from the Bishop himself, was met with the same response: 'Sorry, prior engagement.' It wasn't a lie. Alice was a priority. Vicky knew her daughter mustn't grow up resenting the church because it took her mummy away from her.

Tom arranged to come home early on Fridays, her day off. Alice went off with Ania and Katya for a couple of hours so that they could have some 'quality time' together. Invariably the phone would ring. 'I know it's your day off vicar, but . . .' She had learnt by then that most crises, bar death, can be left for twenty-four hours, by which time they have often resolved themselves. To respond quickly would really be about her own need to be needed. Instead, it was better to allow people the space to discover their own inner resources.

The doorbell was harder to ignore, what with the lights on inside and the car parked outside. 'One of these days I'm going to answer wearing a very revealing negligee,' she said to Tom, removing her clothes for a second time. 'And I'll ask, "Is your need as great as Tom's right at this moment?"'

One Sunday evening, Ken collapsed in the middle of the service. Tom, who might have saved him, was babysitting, and by the time someone had run to the vicarage to get him, Ken had died of a massive heart attack.

'An answer to your prayers, Vic?' Katya asked, tongue-in-cheek, as they sat on a park bench some days later, watching the girls chasing each other up and down the slide.

'He said I'd change the church over his dead body. And now I'm burying him.'

They both fought to repress the smile that threatened their faces, then gave up and giggled like teenagers.

'Stop it,' Vicky said. 'This is awful. I'd much rather he'd changed than died. He would have been remembered so differently. Anyway, Flo already has a new dress for the funeral. She told me so. I think she might blossom.'

'So, who will be your new churchwarden?'

'You,' Vicky said, almost without thinking. But she realised with surprise that she had thought about it. It had occurred to her that Katya's swift grasp of English must reflect a far greater degree of intelligence than her cleaning role required.

To her surprise, Katya said, 'I hoped you might ask.'

'You'll make a good churchwarden, overseeing all the practical issues in the church.'

'Good on my CV.'

Vicky looked at her quizzically, and she said abruptly, 'I can't be a cleaner for the rest of my life, Vicky. My parents were teachers.'

Vicky touched her arm. 'You go for it, Katya.'

When Alice started school, Vicky found it hard to let her golden-haired little baby go. She looked so grown up in her uniform, her curls tied up in a wonky ponytail, wispy tendrils escaping in every direction, her lunch-box packed with the sandwiches she had insisted on making herself – little dots of peanut butter spread across her face from one ear to the other. Katya collected her in the morning, and Vicky picked up both their girls in the afternoon, because Katya had managed to find herself an office job.

With Alice out for most of the day, she managed to write her first book, *Hope in Practice*, a Moltmann-esque exploration of the ways in which the St Maggie's experience might prove a useful model for practical demonstration of the kingdom of God. The *Church Times* hailed it as radical, intelligent and forward-thinking, and it established her reputation as a minor expert on community-based mission.

In 2000 the Venerable Alison Clark, the church's first female archdeacon, tabled a private member's motion in Synod, designed to force a real debate on the topic of women bishops. It requested that further theological study be done on the role of bishops, to pave the way for discussions within the next two years on women's admission to the episcopacy. Within an hour it attracted over a hundred signatures, enough to ensure it a public airing.

As she rose to her feet to introduce the motion, a tiny woman with a presence that nonetheless filled the chamber, the Venerable Alison said, 'When I am old I shall not be wearing purple.' It was some time before the clapping and cheering died down enough to let her continue. The motion was passed, a working party established. And that was the start of the slow, painful, almost-endless process to make women bishops.

'Congratulations, Alison,' Vicky enthused as she edged her way out of Synod and found herself standing next to the archdeacon.

'Nothing not to pass – bland,' Alison said in her matter-of-fact way. 'I'll never see it, of course. Retire in a couple of years. Makes you demob happy. That's why I did it – don't care whose toes I tread on. Not that I ever have. But it may clear the way for girls like you.'

'Can't see myself in the corridors of power,' Vicky admitted, a little sheepishly. 'Too much the rebel.'

Alison raised her eyebrows questioningly before turning to push her way through a phalanx of back-slapping well-wishers. As Vicky watched her go, Alison turned momentarily and called to her, 'Never rule yourself out of anything.'

The reunion was Bev's suggestion. She called out of the blue to ask if the three friends could meet. The last time Vicky had seen her was at Mandy's wedding fifteen months earlier, at which point she had been polite, but rather distant. Vicky hoped that she had recovered from whatever was affecting her mood that day. But something told her that she might not have done.

They opted for a Garfunkels off Oxford Circus – not very imaginative or chic, but cheerful and private if you managed to get a more secluded table, which they did, because Bev had rung and reserved it.

Mandy was there when Vicky arrived, looking as chic and dainty as ever in a business-like silver-grey suit, with a skirt that only just covered her dignity as she sat with one leg crossed over the other. Her dark hair tumbled in loose curls onto her shoulders. She looked more than well. She was positively glowing.

'Marriage suits you,' Vicky said approvingly, as the pair kissed then hugged in greeting.

She acknowledged the compliment with a coy nod, and added, 'That and being a director in Marcus Freeman. Who'd have thought that fish and chips and pizzas could be so much fun?'

When she took the fancy of one of the Freeman sons, Mandy had married into a global food-service empire.

'Please tell me this place isn't one of yours?'

She grinned.

'Grief, no. At least – not yet.'

'So how are you coping with the cut and thrust of big business?'

'Like a duck to water. After all our pontificating on women's equality, you should see me flash my eyelashes when I want to clinch a deal. But who wouldn't – when the result is the house and the pool and all that?'

'Then what the heck are we doing here, slumming it with a vicar-style celebration?'

'Search me. Bev's choice. God knows what's coming. But tell me about you while we have the chance,' she said, examining Vicky's face carefully.

'Fine,' Vicky said.

She raised an eyebrow, perceptive to the last.

'Okay, so those stress lines on your forehead are—'

'Juggling a job with motherhood.'

'Tough?'

'Has been.'

'And I thought it was all garden parties and cream teas. Have I been watching too much *Vicar of Dibley*?'

'Substitute funerals and cold quiche suppers and you'd be a bit nearer the truth.'

'Christians don't do slap-up catering like the Jews, then?'

'I wish. It's all soggy pastry, slimy potato salads and Iceland sponge cakes.'

She pretended to heave.

'Such suffering for your calling. I'll think of you next time I'm being wined and dined at The Connaught.'

'Thanks. The trouble is, the Vicar of Dibley always comes out on top. I don't.'

'Poor Vicky,' she said ruefully. 'But tell me about Alice? How's my gorgeous little goddaughter? Where are the photos?'

Vicky barely had time to whip them out of her bag when Bev appeared, in a pin-striped trouser suit and brogues. The thick, long auburn locks, once the envy of all, were gone, replaced by a boyish crop that seemed too severe for someone with such bold features. Her nose had never seemed so long to Vicky before.

Bev kissed them both peremptorily, as if they had seen each other the previous week, sat down heavily and picked up a menu.

'Have you ordered? No? Too busy catching up,' she said, catching sight of the photograph on Mandy's placemat. Mandy looked at her watch. 'Fifteen months conflated into seven minutes and thirty seconds. We've barely started!'

Bev was too distracted to catch the mood and called the waitress over. She ordered a burger and fries, and a trip to the salad bar. Mandy said the salad bar would be fine for her; her standard lunch as a figure-conscious businesswoman, Vicky imagined, as she ordered some pasta.

'So,' Bev said, when the trip to the salad bar had been accomplished and they were about to tuck in. 'No point beating about the bush. I've invited you both to tell you that I have found the love of my life. I wanted my oldest friends to be the first to know.'

'Fantastic, Bev,' Mandy enthused.

'Wonderful,' Vicky chimed in, a little too loudly, conscious that they were both making an effort. Wasn't it a little over the top to summon them to hear the good news in person like this? Why hadn't she just told them over the phone?

'So who's the lucky man?' Mandy asked, scooping up a forkful of tomato salad. 'Do tell.'

Without a moment's hesitation, Bev said, 'She's called Sandra.'

'Sandra?' Mandy and Vicky both said in unison.

Mandy's fork had halted in mid-air, several inches from her mouth. Her eyes, when they caught Vicky's, were as round as two slices of cucumber.

'Yes. Sandra.'

'So?' Mandy asked, with a slight shake of the head. The fork managed to find its way into her mouth.

'So what?'

'Who is she? And where did you meet her?'

'In a gay bar. She's a graphic designer.'

'And are you happy?'

'For crying out loud, Mandy, don't patronise me. I've just told you she's the love of my life. Why wouldn't I be happy?'

She got up from the table abruptly and threw her serviette onto her chair. 'Let's get a refill from the salad bar.'

Mandy had just enough time to flash Vicky another fleeting look, one that said, 'You could knock me down with a feather,' before she and Bev trooped off to reload their plates with grated carrot and pickled beetroot.

The atmosphere remained forced as they sat back down at the table. Bev said, almost wilfully, like a child demanding pudding before she's finished the main course, 'I want Sandra to meet my closest friends.'

'We'd love to, wouldn't we, Vicky?' Mandy said, in a placatory tone.

'Would you, Vicky?' Bev asked, turning to her.

Vicky nodded, playing with her pasta. 'Of course I would.'

'I want you to be happy for me.'

'Why do you need our approval, Bev?' Vicky asked carefully. She was fast losing her appetite, the food apparently congealing on her plate before her eyes to create a glutinous, unappetising mess. Why hadn't she chosen the salad? 'I've never asked your approval for the things I do.'

'This is different. My parents have refused to meet her.'

'So would mine,' Mandy interjected. 'You can't blame them for that.'

'Why not? I'm their daughter, for God's sake.'

'Try to see it from their perspective,' Vicky suggested. 'Give them time.'

'Best parsonical manner, eh, Vicky?' Bev said bitterly. 'Their perspective? Homophobia, that's their perspective.'

Vicky tried to placate her. 'They're probably trying to come to terms with it all, mourning the fact they'll never see your children.'

'Who says we won't have children?' Bev said, skewering Vicky with her look. 'Or does that shock your Christian morals?'

Vicky shook her head. She was not shocked, simply trying to acclimatise to this new reality, and work out how to accommodate her beliefs alongside the needs of someone she dearly loved. She had openly supported the new legislation that enabled gay couples to adopt, on the grounds that a loving home was always better for a child than social care. But, somehow, the deliberate withholding of a parent of the opposite gender seemed like self-indulgence. She formed her words with immense care.

'Maybe . . . I wouldn't say it's the ideal.'

A picture of Garth, alone in his car, his only comfort the words of the songs on his CD, formed in her mind. She reached out a hand and laid it over Bev's.

'Whatever you do, it will not change our friendship, because I do love you, Bev, and I want you to be happy.'

'It won't change our friendship, won't it?' Bev snapped, snatching her hand back. 'Do you know what? You can f*** off with your holy ideals, Vicky,' and with that she picked up her bag and marched out.

They sat in stunned silence. Mandy called the waitress over and ordered a bottle of wine.

'I need this,' she said, pouring them both a glassful. 'Don't let's beat ourselves up. She was spoiling for a fight.'

'With me,' Vicky said ruefully.

'With you,' Mandy agreed. 'But don't all our actions affect our friendships? I mean, if I went off with another man, wouldn't it impact our relationship?'

'Oh, I don't know Mandy, I don't know,' Vicky said, her head in her hands, massaging her scalp with her fingertips.

'I can't change four thousand years of Judeo-Christian morality just for me. But I'd never turn my back on either of you. You mean too much to me. Of course I want to meet Sandra. That's what's so galling.'

'But Bev wants more than that. She wants approval, not just acceptance.'

'I know, I know. How I hate being thrust into the "heartless bigot" box for having ideals. It would be so much easier not to bother, it really would.'

Mandy insisted on paying the bill, hugged Vicky close as they said goodbye, and, patting her on the back as if she were a gripey baby, said, 'Don't fret. She'll come round.'

*   *   *

Nine months passed before Bev demanded the chance to bring Sandra to the vicarage.

'Of course,' Vicky replied. 'What kept you so long?'

Sandra was a gentle, soft-spoken younger woman in an elegant dress and tiny pearl earrings. Vicky liked her immediately, though wondered whether she wasn't a little conservative for Bev, whom she obviously adored.

'And how have your church members taken to having a woman vicar?' she asked, evidently trying to make polite conversation. The artlessness that Vicky found rather childlike and charming appeared to wind Bev up.

'Oh for goodness' sake, Sandra,' she snapped, helping herself to a chocolate from a box Vicky had left open on the coffee table, 'after five years, what do you think?'

'Yes, of course,' she acquiesced. 'Well, that's good, isn't it?'

Bev sighed loudly.

'Our good news,' Sandra said uncertainly, trying to placate her partner whom she watched nervously out of the corner of her eye, 'is that Bev's parents seem to have accepted us as a couple at last.'

Bev smiled weakly and shrugged. Sandra looked embarrassed, so Vicky said she was pleased for them and moved the conversation on.

'I do have some news of my own,' she said. 'I've been appointed Diocesan Director for Women. It involves meeting women who want to go into the ministry, and sussing out those who should and who shouldn't, before forwarding them for formal selection.'

'And the bishop has made her a canon,' Tom slipped in. 'One of the first women to hold the title. More balls than most.'

Sandra looked bewildered.

'Honestly, Sandra,' Bev barked at her. 'Don't make me spell it out.'

Vicky was bemused by Bev. What was she playing at?

The conversation around the meal table was stilted and difficult. Alice watched her godmother warily, her thumb in her mouth, something she rarely did when food was in front of her. And they all heaved a sigh of relief when Bev announced shortly after the meal, to Sandra's evident surprise, that they had another engagement and would have to leave.

They didn't hear from Bev for a number of years, despite the repeated messages Vicky left on her answer machine. They never saw Sandra again.

✠

2020

Alice! If she tried hard, Vicky could almost think her way back to relive those ten years at St Chad's and recapture the child she had loved so much then, making sandwiches for her school packed lunch when she could barely hold a knife, sitting cross-legged on the school hall floor, looking up at her mother with proud and rapt attention as she took an assembly, sitting at the kitchen table drawing intently, head on one hand, as Vicky dealt on the phone with yet another long, involved parish crisis; snuggling up to Edward, Tom's father, and holding his hand as he wept after Tom's mother, Mary, finally had to be hospitalised with dementia.

Was that just Alice's nature, Vicky wondered, or did the daughters of vicar mothers have a heightened opportunity to develop life skills such as patience, poise and compassion? After Mary died, when Edward was struggling for something to live for, it was Alice who found it for him, introducing her fluffy, white-haired grandfather, with the craggy face and twinkly eyes, to all her friends. They fought to sit on his knee at church on Sundays. Alice had to fend them off. But when the ice cream van tinkled its way into the street, she would run out and round up whoever she could find, because Grandpa was rattling the spare change in his pocket, and that meant there was enough in there to buy ice creams for half the neighbourhood.

Where did those ten years go? Why must time slip through our fingers in this way? Almost before she knew it, she was Archdeacon of Westhampton and Alice, now a teenager, was wrenched away from her familiar friends and facing a new life. And still, she never complained. The passage of a beloved child into adulthood would always be a kind of bereavement, however wonderful the man or woman they became.

FIFTEEN

There is nothing more difficult to take in hand, more perilous to conduct, or more uncertain in its success, than to take the lead in the introduction of a new order of things.

NICCOLO MACHIAVELLI

MAY 2021

Stories of harassment of religious groups had started coming in – albeit in a small way. Two new churches, meeting in local schools, were informed by the council that they should find alternative premises. A landlord refused to go on renting a room to the church group that used his pub, lest he be prosecuted. Muslims in the Larchester diocese, known personally to Vicky and who could not be further from the extremist end, were refused a licence for a new centre.

She did all she could to ensure that every grievance inflicted on a religious group became high profile, following the initial news with a press release from the Archbishop's office denouncing the idea that such lamentable fall-out from the legislation could have any association with the potential of a cyber-attack: 'This is nothing less than an attack on the freedoms of innocent, law-abiding citizens, and is totally unacceptable in a democratic society.' The Home Secretary responded on cue with a depressing repetition of the party line: 'The Archbishop has scant regard for the safety of our citizens if she can't see the effectiveness of the government's actions,' citing the closure of a Muslim college in Birmingham that had been a cover for an extremist madrasa.

It was imperative that she have the entire UK church on board. She spent more lunches than were good for her waistline harnessing the support of the Roman Catholics, Methodists, Baptists, URCs, and the newer non-denominational church groupings that had been growing in significance since the turn of the century – the list was endless. She had also finally enlisted the Muslim Council in her cause. But not a word from Malcolm Davies. She suspected his stalling was all part of a power game.

Eventually, late one afternoon, Ann announced, 'I have Malcolm

Davies.' It was the middle of Vicky's time for preparation and quiet, normally sacrosanct. She groaned.

'Put him through.'

As his unsmiling features materialised in front of her, her stomach gave a lurch of anticipation.

'Good evening, Malcolm. How are you?'

There was no response to her greeting, simply a perfunctory, 'I've consulted with my members, and with the leaders of most of our "fellow travellers", shall we say, and we feel that in this instance, it would be helpful if we stood together.'

In other words, a yes. They would unite behind her. She allowed herself a well-hidden sigh of relief – no, more than relief – a sigh of joy. Until he added, 'There is a problem, however.'

'I'm listening.'

'You are aware that the Dean of Canterbury has invited the presiding bishop of TEC to preach in your cathedral, and that she is being mooted as a speaker at Synod?'

Vicky's heart sank. Julian had put her on the spot. Informing her that Bishop Myrna Elliotson, head of the Episcopal Church in the USA, was visiting relatives in Kent, he suggested with what she suspected was a brilliant piece of malice aforethought that it would only be common courtesy to invite her to participate at the cathedral. Vicky could hardly say no, despite the International Anglican Alliance's long-standing disagreement with TEC over its recognition of priests and bishops in same-sex partnerships, and its ousting of clergy who refused to accept them.

Nor had it stopped there. Once word got out that Bishop Myrna was being invited to Canterbury, there had been increasing murmurs from interested factions in Synod that she should be allowed to address them as well. Vicky had stalled, fearing the impact on her tentative relationship with the African bishops.

TEC's relationship with the African church had broken down completely. For over twenty years there had been extensive posturing from liberal American bishops and conservative African bishops alike, the former claiming that the African bishops were intellectually and theologically inferior, the latter accusing the Americans of being simply unbiblical. It was a mess.

At the most recent Lambeth Conference in 2018, the African church had grown to such proportions that it was the most powerful lobby in the Anglican Church. Archbishop Gabriel Ajomo of Nigeria openly accused the more liberal Western bishops of glorified humanism. 'If you are so superior, tell me, why are you in such decline? When you again have the authority of millions of believers behind you as we now do, then maybe we will listen to you. Meanwhile, in the great race to save the nations, we run with the baton we received from Britain in the days when it was truly great, before it lost the fire in its belly. We will take the true message of salvation onward to the furthest corners of the globe.'

Watching the African bishops dancing around the Communion table on the last night of the conference, Vicky had had to admit that she felt more at one with their joyous expression of faith than she did with the more restrained, intellect-driven approach of the predominantly white, English-speaking parts of the world.

Chairing the conference, her predecessor as Archbishop had looked like a rag doll shaken from side to side in a tug of war between two small children, his pleas for tolerance, understanding, and unity falling on deaf ears. And then, in a master stroke, he pulled a rabbit out of his mitre. Since it was manifestly obvious that much of the Anglican Communion was in shreds, he had set out a form of managed schism. The new International Anglican Alliance would consist of a loose association of archdioceses, each a law unto itself with its own arch-bishops and bishops representing its theological and moral preferences. But like any group of international distributors for a global brand, they would come together to share their vision, not their differences, every ten years – and still pay lip service to a benign leadership from Canterbury. Rather like the Commonwealth. Under the new rules, TEC must allow their clergy and churches freedom of conscience, and cease to confiscate the buildings and land of traditionalist priests. It would be a case of live and let live, in an uneasy community under one large umbrella, if not real unity.

Whether the warring factions would ever let go of their treasured convictions and find true common ground was a matter for conjecture. But from her standpoint, Vicky had certainly felt that any attempt to preserve the 500-year old tradition of Anglicanism was worth a try. How Malcolm's conditions would fit with that, she could hardly begin to conceive.

'Yes, Malcolm, I am aware that Bishop Myrna is to be our guest.'

'Then let me make it clear that it would be anathema to have her speak at Synod. And that her appearance at your cathedral will set back our joint cause significantly.'

'Malcolm, I understand exactly how you feel about Bishop Myrna.'

A red rag to a bull, she thought to herself.

'But it's not "my" cathedral,' she continued. 'The Archbishop of Canterbury is not the Pope, as you know. I have surprisingly little authority over these decisions, but I shall see what can be done. Leave it with me.'

'Of course, Archbishop. But you know our position.'

She groaned inwardly as he faded from view. What next? Grovel to Julian? Try to bully the standing committee of Synod? Malcolm's negotiating position did have some attraction for her, in that it would enable her to maintain her integrity with the African bishops. One thing was for sure: there would be fall-out from this whatever she did, heaven help her.

The power structures in the Church of England often seemed as complex as the configurations on a map of Britain's rail networks. Or, indeed, the UK's government structure, on which in large part it seemed to have been modelled. Lambeth Palace was its Downing Street, while Church House, with its own civil servants, was its Whitehall. And the Archbishop's staff and the bureaucrats were often in competition, deeply suspicious of one another and wary of being outdone, or out-manoeuvred, by one other. The relationship was a little like a marriage gone bad, where the pair keep declaring a truce in the hope it may eventually work out, mainly because they can't afford a final separation. Being caught in the middle was not an enviable place to be.

The Church Commissioners were the civil servants in chief, responsible for clergy payroll and pensions, the ministry of bishops and cathedrals, and the vital management of the church's assets that they both entailed. Sir Douglas Lovelock, the self-made layman who headed the Church Commissioners in 1992 when their unwise wheeling and dealing in the property market virtually wiped them out, once said, 'The great problem of the Church of England is that no one, I repeat no one, is in charge. There are a number of power centres – Lambeth, the Archbishop, Synod, the dioceses, the bishops in their splendour, the Church Commissioners and many other bodies. No one single person can say, "This is what we are going to do" and make it happen.'

Things had changed very little since then. Unfortunately for Vicky, the Commissioners were the ones who controlled the purse strings at Lambeth Palace, which cost around £1 million a year to run – so that gave them a certain power over her actions. They also conferred a budget of £80 million on the Archbishop's Council, a national advisory body for strategic thinking and planning set up to support the Archbishop in promoting spiritual and numerical growth. The twenty or so members were a mixture of lay and clerical, unpaid and chosen for their expertise, a commanding management layer of top dogs in industry, finance and government. The church needed its resources well looked after if it was to have any clout.

But since Vicky now got to chair the ethical investment committee that imposed restrictions on how the Church Commissioners invested the church's money, it was a case of swings and roundabouts. Companies involved in military products, pornography, alcoholic drinks, gambling, tobacco, human embryonic cloning, weekly collected home credit and other organisations not aligned with the church's values and teachings, were strictly disbarred. As she sat up late one evening, glancing through the list of investments, one particular company caught her eye – the 'Athena Corporation', an international agency dedicated to the redevelopment of areas of the greatest social need, with particular strength in South America. Athena was a Greek goddess. Where else had she come across Greek goddesses recently?

'Ralph?' she asked the next morning as she walked into his office, slapping the list down on his desk. 'Am I being paranoid?'

He looked up at her, bemused.

'Many would say the Archbishop has good cause to be.'

She gave him her long-suffering look.

'The Athena Corporation – ring any bells with you?' she asked, pointing out the name she had underlined.

He looked blank.

'A.T. Developments,' she pushed. 'Didn't you say the "A" stood for Artemis, the goddess of hunting? Now here's the goddess of wisdom and both have links with South America. What do you think?'

'God knows.'

'Well, obviously, but I have no idea who or what this corporation is. The Church of England only invests in bona fide companies, right?'

Ralph shrugged.

'OK, OK, just my fertile imagination. Forget it.'

Seeing Ralph installed in his new office, looking very much in charge of her household, and as handsome as ever, gave her a surprising, though not entirely unwelcome, frisson of pleasure. Steady on, Archbishop, she commanded herself, and changed the topic of conversation quickly.

'I'm having an urgent tête-à-tête with Dominic today to see if he can help me scupper this possible Synod visit by Bishop Myrna.'

'That's nice for you,' Ralph smiled, pursing his lips.

'Yes, I'm not looking forward to it. He seems to be very matey with

Lord Kilmarton. I've seen them whispering in the corridors once too often.'

Dominic Naylor, the Secretary General of Synod, had always made it clear that he hadn't been happy with the appointment of a woman Archbishop. He was never anything other than courteous, but Vicky felt his eyes shift away from her when she spoke to him sometimes, and his choice of friends made her a little uneasy.

'What do we know about Kilmarton? Apart from the fact that he's so maddeningly superior when he speaks in debates that he can't see past the end of his own nose.'

She felt that hand of his clasping hers, brittle and bony, criss-crossed with lumpy blue veins, and shuddered slightly.

'A major funder of the Tory party,' Ralph said. 'One of the country's wealthiest industrialists. And, unlike some, not particularly known for his philanthropy.'

'He certainly wasn't keen on women bishops.'

'Actually, he's not that keen on male bishops either. I've just been going through some of your predecessor's correspondence so we can archive it, and found a letter lambasting him for his "irresolute, lily-livered left-wing sympathies". That was over the Archbishop's attack on government plans to semi-privatise the NHS.'

'Not sparing with his adjectives, is he?'

'Don't make an enemy of the man if you can avoid it.'

'Too late for that, Ralph, I suspect. Anyway, I may ask Dominic what he knows about the Athena Corporation.'

'Do take care, Vicky.'

'With Dominic? Why?'

'I don't know. Just a feeling.'

General Synod was the place where she felt most impotent, a figure-head with little executive power, a somewhat ineffectual guide rather than a director. She once said to Dominic, 'I'm not sure what Synod achieves. Every decision is watered down until it's drowned in indecision. I don't want to be remembered as the Rt Revd Ms Compromise.'

'Then you won't achieve anything at all,' he had said curtly.

It was all so perverse. Surely this central body of the church should be leading the way in radical, cutting-edge, truly Christian innovation? Vicky had certainly tried to lead it that way once or twice in the past.

2003

As a mere vicar, she had introduced a motion she felt sure would scupper any chances of promotion she might ever have and hit the House of Bishops where it really hurt – in the pay packet.

If, as the Church Commissioners claimed, the stipend was a living allowance, not a salary, it seemed incongruous that bishops, archdeacons and deans should earn, in some cases, up to one hundred per cent more than the rest of the clergy. The word 'stipend' was described in the dictionary as, 'Distinct from a salary . . . a payment for a role which cannot be measured in terms of a task.'

Too right the task can't be measured, she said to herself, so how could the senior clergy weigh up their worth against their juniors in this illogical way? Someone had to be brave enough to bite the bullet.

'Typical,' Jenny said, when Vicky told her what she proposed. 'In with both feet. You think the bishops will vote for a large pay cut? You're crazy. All you'll do is alienate them, and find it hard to get a move when you want one.'

'I agree that they should have generous expenses – help with heating those vast palaces, reliable transport and a worthwhile hospitality allowance.'

'Oh, wonderful. Have us all round to tea more often, Bishop, because it will be worth your while. It's the poor wife who'll get lumbered.'

'I know, I know. But it would be a much fairer system.'

'Think of your job prospects.'

'Everyone always does. That's why they never rock the boat.'

'Suit yourself. But don't say I didn't warn you if you end up persona non grata.'

Vicky felt disgruntled. Her career was her concern, no one else's. And she had no intention of bowing down to the god of ambition. She would do what she had always done: what she knew she had to do.

She laid her private member's motion on the table in the anteroom, then withdrew to a corner to watch from afar, like a mother in the playground on her child's first day at school. A certain dean, whose name she couldn't remember, wandered over to her and made an attempt to engage her in scintillating conversation, but she couldn't stop her eyes from wandering to the table, and he gave up in the end. Within an hour she had a longer list of signatories than any of the other motions laid out on the table beside hers. For many of the clergy, this was, it seemed, a very real matter of concern.

On the morning of the debate, she spent an inordinate time in front of the mirror. 'Vanity, vanity,' she said to herself, re-working her hair for the tenth time. Feeling the part is half the battle, she argued back at her reflection, before rehearsing her script one last time. No notes, she had decided, or everyone would see the tremor in her hands.

As she moved towards the microphone 500 expectant people, representing some of the most intelligent theological minds in the country, not to mention all the people who would hold her future in the palm of their hands, turned to look at her. Never had she felt so entirely alone. In the gallery the journalists leant forward, notepads at the ready. One lone camera was trained upon her. Lord have mercy, let it only go out on Sky, she prayed. Let me not be important enough for the BBC.

She caught sight of Simon, intently waiting and watching; Jenny, anxious and tense; and Nick, smiling encouragingly. Thank God for friendly faces. Other than that, all she could see as she surveyed the scene was a purple mass of bishops in one block, a black-suited, dog-collared cluster in another, and a variety of shapes, sizes and colours in between. An Alice-in-Wonderland voice in her head said, dismissively, 'You're just a pack of cards, all of you.' It settled the nerves – a little.

She began with a quote from Abraham Lincoln. ' "I can make more generals, but horses cost money." In the Church of England,' she said, 'the generals cost the money, but the horses, funded from the pews, come cheap.'

The enthusiastic applause helped her warm to her subject. 'The differentials in clergy stipends create an ecclesiastical hierarchy. And a hierarchical system is not biblical. It does not reflect the teachings of Jesus, who washed his disciples' feet and told them not to lord it over one another. This is not the fault of our bishops, who do serve us, often lovingly and sacrificially, but I believe that nonetheless, we need a more radical approach to tackle this unhelpful indicator of status in the church. To begin the process, I humbly suggest, first and foremost, that all differentials in the pay and pensions of the clergy, whatever their role, should be removed. A stipend is a stipend – a payment that enables each of us to do the work we have been called to do, and whether that is as a curate or as an archbishop, the difference is in kind, not quality.'

She detected an icy draught or two from the purple phalanx, but pushed on all the same.

'I am aware that this is a tricky subject. The very nature of a bishop's role requires more expenses, and that should be reflected with generosity. I would also like to suggest that "senior" offices, as they are called, should be held for a limited period, at the end of which the dean, archdeacon or bishop would return to doing the work of a parish priest, rather like the Franciscan monks and nuns whose vow of humility limits their time as a "superior" and requires them to return to the lowliest ranks. We cannot, however, expect such a radical approach to be palatable if it involves a huge cut in the stipend upon doing so.'

The motion generated a great deal of debate. It was defeated, as she knew it would be, but by a smaller majority than she had anticipated.

'And at least the matter has been raised,' she whispered to Jenny, as she turned to respond to a pat on the shoulder and found her own diocesan bishop standing beside her. She took a deep breath.

'Well done, Vicky,' he said, to her immense surprise. 'An excellent and necessary debate – brave, well presented and persuasive. Don't be disheartened. There are many who do agree with you. It's just a little too radical, too soon. And a little too painful, as you so rightly say,' he said wryly, patting his pocket.

2020

Throughout all her subsequent performances in Synod, it was always Nick she wanted to impress. His advice before and after was essential to her, like wind to a windmill. If he thought she had done well, she knew she had, and it was praise indeed. If he felt there was need for greater clarity, more concentrated argument, he would tell her so.

'A good speaker can convince their audience of almost anything,' he said to her. 'You have that ability. It just needs a little fine tuning – a pause here, a punch there.'

She trusted his judgement implicitly and would endeavour to incorporate his suggestions the next time she spoke. On the whole, he was right.

'Nick, do you have any idea who is behind something called the Athena Corporation?' she asked him, a couple of days after she had spoken to Ralph. There was no one else to ask. Dominic had told her, tartly, that the ethics committee was not his department and that meddling in their affairs was not something he intended to start.

'Who?' Nick asked her.

'The name appears on the list of Church Commissioners' investments. It's a rather large amount of money. I wanted to find out more about it.'

'Is that wise? Doesn't the ethics committee decide policy, not individual investments? It could be construed as meddling.'

'You're probably right. It intrigues me all the same.'

'Any particular reason?'

'Well . . .' she said, and then realised how foolish her explanation would sound. 'Let's just call it female intuition.'

'Do nothing in haste,' Nick advised. 'Let me do the digging, see if I can find out what this is all about.'

'I would really appreciate it.'

She also told him of Malcolm's demands. 'It annoys me to have the tail wagging the dog.'

'Important not to let those kinds of emotions rob you of a clear head. Ask yourself whether his demands are so unreasonable. The Episcopal Church has hardly played by the rules – they've shown scant regard for the Alliance. Bishop Myrna will no doubt make a lot of mileage out of it. The Dean will use it to score a point or two. But keeping the African bishops onside might be more useful to you. They're by far the larger group.'

'It's not about numbers, though, is it, Nick?'

'No, not entirely. But when it comes to political action against these confounded proselytising laws, you need all the support you can get.'

Her first port of call in making a decision over TEC was the House of Bishops. Synod members always suspected, with some resentment, that this was where the major decisions were made. But Vicky had discovered during her time as bishop that the bishops could barely agree on what to order for lunch, let alone on how to run the church.

They were, after all, a rather mixed bag. Balding or hirsute, genial or aloof, larger than life or as silent as a university library, they constituted one of the last-surviving male enclaves – a churchy gentleman's club. Individually, most of the members were delightful. En masse, the haw-hawing and back-slapping could be demoralising, but it papered over the cracks of some serious differences of opinion. Bishops were chosen for their character, determination, vision, leadership and management skills, so how could forty-four strong-willed males ever yield a point? Certainly not to a woman.

Her first meeting in the chair had not gone well. She opened it by reading the letter the mystic Evelyn Underhill had written to Archbishop Cosmo Lang in around 1930. Her demand for a renewal of the spiritual life of its ministers at a time when the church was divided and in a parlous state still seemed incredibly apposite almost a hundred years later:

We look to the clergy to help and direct our spiritual growth. We are seldom satisfied because, with a few noble exceptions, they are so lacking in spiritual realism, so ignorant of the laws and experiences of the life of prayer . . . In public worship they often fail to evoke the spirit of adoration because they do not possess it themselves. Hence the dreary character of many church services and the increasing alienation of the laity . . . God is the interesting thing about religion, and people are hungry for God. But only a priest whose life is soaked in prayer, sacrifice, and love can, by his own spirit of adoring worship, help us to apprehend Him.

'You're trying to tell us our clergy aren't up to the job, are you, Archbishop?' asked the Bishop of Carbury, barely letting her finish. Holding her gaze, Toby Macdonald, whom she always thought of as the ginger man, folded his arms, stretched out his legs as far as they would go, and crossed one over the other.

'I certainly ensure mine use the proper liturgies and rituals,' chipped in Greg Davidson, the Bishop of Normington, a dapper man with a neatly clipped black beard on the first of his two chins, and the largest pectoral cross Vicky had ever seen filling the expanse of his cassock front.

In the normal run of affairs, the two men, one evangelical, the other Anglo-catholic, would never, by any stretch of the imagination, be comrades in arms, but they had become bedfellows in the face of a common enemy: a female Archbishop. It was tempting to say, 'Now, now, boys,' but the Archbishop of York caught her eye and rose quickly to her defence.

'Come on, gentlemen – you get the point. Archbishop Ramsey credited Evelyn Underhill with saving the Church of England single-handed in the inter-war years. Of course her wisdom speaks to us today. Why not call the clergy to a life of greater prayer and holiness? How else are we going to deepen the spiritual life of the nation?'

With his ability to bounce back good-naturedly in the face of every difficulty and criticism, the youngest-ever Archbishop of York reminded Vicky of Tigger in *Winnie the Pooh*. He had the smooth complexion, appealing grin and boyish good looks that last way beyond the usual ravages of middle age. His high spirits and exuberance lifted the atmosphere the moment he rose to his feet, no matter how fraught the issue. In her first months, Vicky would often have cause to wonder how she would do without him. His advice could be a little irregular, mind you. The solo girl chorister that caused her all the problems at Canterbury Cathedral had been his suggestion, but it was her fault for pursuing it, and she put it down to his lack of experience, for at other times he had an almost uncanny knack of reading a situation, and his support was unwavering. She sometimes called him simply for the banter. She could just imagine what he would have to say later *vis-à-vis* these two rogue bishops. Who now conceded the point, albeit in a reluctant, fairly offhand manner.

Having met them as a bishop, Vicky had expected the pair to be difficult, despite the fact that neither had expressed any hardened theological objections to a woman leader. Their real problem lay in having her as their senior. Goodness knows how either would have fared in any sphere of life other than the C of E, the misogynist's last shelter from the real world.

If ever pearls were fed to swine, Evelyn Underhill's were on that first day. Money, or the lack of it, always hijacked the agenda, not the quality of the spiritual life of the clergy. How, if churches wouldn't pay the full tax, or quota, levied upon them by the diocese, would the diocese survive? How would it find the means to pay the fines incurred by clergy perceived to have transgressed the anti-proselytising laws? The most anxious were the least willing to accept the radical but necessary step of closing dying churches and selling off unnecessary buildings. The very suggestion heralded a concerted neighing and whinnying.

Vicky found herself stifling a yawn. When she could bear the endless tangents no longer, she rose to her feet and said, 'You all know my views by now. Year on year we impose higher taxes on our parishes. The ineffective don't pay it, the more successful churches are crippled by it. No other organisation can inflict a five per cent rise on its customers without consultation or come-back.'

'What alternative would you suggest, Archbishop?' asked the Bishop of Normington, sourly.

'Cut diocesan jobs and administration, as I did in Larchester.'

'Even if we cut administrative posts, falling numbers mean less money, Archbishop, or is arithmetic not your strong point?' asked the Bishop of Carbury.

There were a couple of sniggers.

She ignored the sarcasm and said, with a broad smile, 'Then let's ensure that numbers start going up. Take the burden off the growing churches and cut their share. It will give your churches an incentive to mission.'

She ignored the gasps.

'Find out how many churches with congregations of thirty or less use them and heat them only once a week and struggle to keep them in good repair. Sad though it is, they really aren't viable. I have received certain assurances from the government that they might be prepared to pressurise local councils into making it easier for us to sell them. The resources can be invested in new church plants.'

'Despite the anti-proselytising laws?' asked the Bishop of Carbury, surveying her through his pale lashes.

'Despite them,' Vicky insisted.

In due course they broke for lunch. There was a small amount of chuntering and disgruntled muttering, though several of the bishops thanked her for being so outspoken and told her how encouraged they were by her fearlessness in the face of the new legislation, and her vision for the renewed, more vibrant church of the future.

In the afternoon session, a possible change in legislation to impose the conducting of gay marriages engendered a mixed response. Some said it would change very little. Many of their clergy had been performing some kind of rite anyway, with or without episcopal support. Others said the majority of their clergy would refuse to do them and were willing to face the consequences. His feet twitching relentlessly, and with an expression of utter boredom on his face, the Bishop of Carbury said, 'Personally, I think the solution is simple. We disestablish to avoid any legal obligation to marry. We're certainly not gaining anything at the moment by being a state church.'

Vicky felt aggravated, unreasonably, since she knew disestablishment made sense. 'I think, Toby, that that will have to wait for the next monarch.'

He raised his eyebrows.

'The Queen has strong feelings about this matter, but I'm not able to say any more at the moment. Simply that for the time being we must remain united and pull together if we want to defeat the denial of religious freedom in our country.'

Vicky was gratified by fairly universal nodding.

'These are indeed difficult times,' said the Bishop of Marchington, 'and there are some signs of a greater unity, a rallying around the Archbishop in her campaign, after several years of deleterious schism, so let's do all we can to encourage it.'

'On that note,' Vicky said, 'let me explain recent developments. React has been in conversation with the other groups of conservatives, and they are prepared to stand with us against government bullying – on condition that Bishop Myrna Elliotson's invitations to Canterbury Cathedral and possibly Synod are withdrawn. I'd appreciate your views.'

'Oh, for heaven's sake, yes, let's banish the woman. She's insufferable,' said the Bishop of Carbury, holding up his hands as if it were unnecessary to ask the obvious. And then he appeared to recover his manners. 'Genuinely, I think it's the best thing to do, Vicky. If you could persuade the conservative churches to start paying their quotas again as well, it would be well worth it. They tend to be the wealthiest churches in any diocese.'

'TEC's numbers are now tiny,' added the Bishop of Normington. 'The potential of offending them matters much less than the risk of losing the support of the African church.'

'It would show our brother bishops there that you have . . . are prepared to take a tough line on morality,' he said, recognising, it appeared, the need to sound more irenic. 'And we do need them onside. They'll be running the Alliance soon, the way things are going in this country.'

The response appeared to be strongly in favour of turning against Bishop Myrna and TEC, but it was hard for Vicky to discern the bishops' real motives, hidden as they were behind the politics.

That was her main problem every time she met with her bishops – the fact that bubbling away beneath the surface was a fair amount of disenchantment with her personally – and not just the initial appointment. Few bishops welcomed her radical suggestions for rationalisation, amalgamating tiny congregations and closing defunct buildings. They might recognise the need, but had little stomach for the local battles it would entail. Some resented her call on the church hierarchy to forgo the huge differentials in stipend and her refusal to accept an archbishop's salary. 'All very well when the main wage earner is a medical consultant,' they huffed and puffed, as was reported now and again in one of the newspapers. Others disapproved of her 'nepotistic' appointments such as Ralph Cooper.

She had decided to tackle that head on, however. Mentioning Ralph's work on a recent report, she took the opportunity to say, as she closed the meeting, that she hoped it was obvious her appointment of him was vindicated; and to touch on the fact that despite malicious rumours to the contrary, he had undergone the due interview process and emerged as the best candidate. The church was lucky to have harnessed such talent. She felt sure she heard a 'Yes, Mummy' from somewhere, but it was impossible to be certain.

'I felt like knocking their heads together,' she said to the Archbishop of York when he popped up on her screen later that evening to see how she was. 'They behave like naughty schoolboys and I have to resist the overwhelming urge to slap them down as fiercely as I know how, otherwise I'll just be pushed into a fall-back position of maternal disapproval. I bite my tongue. I am rational, sensible, open to debate, reason and logic, blow it, in the hope that we might achieve some strategic, visionary objectives.'

'And you do it so well,' he enthused. 'I'm tempted to say ignore them and they'll go away.'

'I know that on home ground, most of them are good men, godly and prayerful. They care passionately about their communities. They give a hundred per cent of themselves and more. But together, they're a living nightmare.'

'You're just one CEO, with forty-three managing directors. Cut yourself some slack. It was never going to be easy. And you have called on them to give up their salaries. Stab a man through the wallet and it might as well be his heart.'

'That was never going to go down well,' she said ruefully.

'You certainly know how to pick a fight,' he chuckled. 'But wasn't it Churchill who said that the secret of success is going from failure to failure without losing your enthusiasm?'

'Something like that. And that was during the Second World War.'

'Sounds about right.'

'And the TEC saga? What are your feelings?'

There was a short pause.

'Difficult. The majority seemed in favour of sacrificing friend Myrna to the wolves. But it won't win you any favours in certain places – least of all the press.'

'That's nothing new at the moment. And it will win us the support of React.'

'Well – best of luck.'

In the end, given the clear lead from the bishops, React had to be her choice. The Dean was incandescent, and there was fury, too, in North America. Bishop Myrna raised the spectre of TEC's leaving the International Alliance. Dominic Naylor expressed his concern that Synod had not been fully consulted. The press declared her actions high-handed, nay, incomprehensible. A sign of inexperience, of a fundamental misunderstanding of modern culture's trajectory, to kowtow to the traditionalists in such a way.

Vicky was beginning to fear that in her desire to tackle the big issues boldly she was making too many enemies, both within and outside the church. She had willingly sacrificed support abroad to harness the support of the conservatives for her campaign at home. She hoped it would not prove a pyrrhic victory.

SIXTEEN

> Totally without hope one cannot live. To live without hope is to cease to live. Hell is hopelessness. It is no accident that above the entrance to Dante's hell is the inscription: 'Leave behind all hope, you who enter here.
>
> JÜRGEN MOLTMANN

JUNE 2021

The purge began in earnest. The first religious proselytisers to be arrested were four Jehovah's Witnesses, for going door to door with the *Watchtower*. They put us to shame, Vicky thought when the news flashed up on her alerts. Then Christians began to be harassed for a host of supposed violations of the act. A hospital chaplain was sacked for suggesting to a patient that Christianity might offer the comfort and hope he was looking for. A schoolteacher was dismissed for admitting in the classroom, when asked, that she believed Jesus was the only way to God. A Salvation Army band was refused a licence to play on a beachfront bandstand for fundraising purposes. A young mum was given an official warning for inviting her neighbour to the local church's toddler club. An IT specialist was arrested and fined for inviting a colleague to his teenager's baptism. When he refused to pay the fine, he was imprisoned for seven days. Several churches were threatened with action for naively continuing to distribute their parish magazine around their villages. When Vicky read one of them, she struggled not to laugh. It was as seditious as a bottle of milk, sadly.

Many churches continued to offer the Alpha course and other equivalent introductions to the Christian faith, but could advertise by word of mouth only, meeting at secret venues in people's homes, running the risk of betrayal and prosecution. The laws had turned anyone with a grouse against religion into an unofficial secret police force as tenacious as the Stasi, always on the lookout for the slightest contravention to the act so that they could it report to the police, who more often than not felt impelled to take action.

Local councils felt they had no alternative but to withdraw their funding of church-based welfare initiatives. Charities that could show they were not faith-related were offered funding instead, but there were nowhere near enough of them, and they simply couldn't mobilise volunteers at the level required. So the councils tried to reinstate their own short-term crisis provision of food, furniture, clothing and shelter, but since thousands of council staff had been made redundant over the years, there were too few of them with the capacity or experience to co-ordinate such a major undertaking. It was exactly as Vicky had warned it would be. Some of the most vulnerable – people with a disability, who had been made redundant, who were fleeing domestic abuse, whose benefits had been delayed, or whose cash had been stolen – were left hungry, homeless or both, unable to access the basic human necessities. Inevitably, some had no alternative but to sleep rough and beg. Given the numbers affected, there was little the police could do. A night in a police cell was a luxury.

And then, in response, the church began to rally. Paid staff at food and furniture banks announced they would work without pay, like the other volunteers. They would depend entirely on the goodwill and donations of members.

'Okay, so the councils have removed our funding, but it's not all bad,' Kelvin said, when he spoke to Vicky one evening from Larchester. 'It shows we're not in their pockets. Food, shelter, furnishings, counselling – we provide it all voluntarily, for love, not because the government funds it. No compromising our message. Harder to tell a genuine case from a scrounger without the voucher scheme running, but what the heck if we can prevent a kiddie from going to bed hungry?'

'Only now we run the risk of criminal charges?'

'Well, yes. What other organisation would pour so much time and energy into such a cause, fund it themselves, and then say to the government, "Thank you for the privilege, would you like to send us to prison for it?" Suckers for Jesus, that's what we're called to be, and that's what we are.'

'Kelvin,' Vicky said, quickly swallowing the lump that had formed in her throat, 'I am more proud of these folk than I know how to say. And say it I will, at every opportunity.'

Vicky's press conferences became an almost daily occurrence.

'What's your response to the prison proselytising case, Archbishop?'

Two prison officers had been caught praying together in an empty cell during their lunch break. They were summarily dismissed. A number of prisoners then 'confessed' to having been 'forced' into chapel by the pair against their will. Both men were arrested and awaiting their court hearing.

'Such is the topsy-turvydom of our current situation that, presumably, if the prisoner officers had been caught *in flagrante delicto*, they would have got away with a caution,' Vicky blazed. 'This country's dire shortage of prison staff makes the whole business a total nonsense. The flimsy evidence on which it's based threatens to make it a huge miscarriage of justice.' On the BBC's *Question Time* she added, 'I do wonder whether the government thinks the police have nothing better to do than to seek out such soft targets. But then it requires much less effort to bang up some poor law-abiding Christian than to build the evidence that would nail a genuine criminal. And what a waste of the taxpayer's money, at a time of such economic stringency!'

'The police have no choice but to administer the law, Archbishop,' said the evening's government stooge.

'These laws are turning our country into a police state as repressive as the former Soviet Union. Many church activities have had to go underground. Voluntary care is restricted because the volunteers are threatened with incarceration. How can the government justify such lunacy? This misguided law threatens the freedoms of everyone in this country, of religious faith and none, and turns neighbours, colleagues and business contacts into informers. We don't know who to trust. Working relationships are undermined, neighbourliness is threatened, friendship is betrayed. We used to censure a child for being a tell-tale. Now adults are positively encouraged to snitch on each other by the government.'

Sustained applause followed. Vicky took a sip of water, the simplest way of averting her face from the cameras, lest she come across as smug. As the terror of cyber-war receded with time, the tide of public opinion appeared to be marginally on the turn. But it was too soon for any hint of complacency.

Whenever possible, until the 'infringements' became too numerous, Vicky endeavoured to visit as many of the church projects as she could, to listen, encourage, raise support, and strengthen their determination. To be a small but ever-present thorn in the side of the establishment. One in particular, always close to her heart since its early days when she was a teacher in Newcastle, became her special cause. The Verity Trust was born when a gang-motivated stabbing in a school playground on the other side of the city had galvanised the desperate head teacher into inviting Tony Patterson, a twenty-year-old church-based youth worker, to help him deal with difficult behavioural issues. Other schools, including Vicky's – at her instigation – had followed suit.

The Verity Trust had expanded over the years until it had teams of committed volunteers, rock bands, actors and mobile bus-based youth centres that went into over 200 schools, prisons, and some of the most deprived neighbourhoods in the north-east, teaching drug awareness, anger management, sex and relationships, overcoming prejudice, and self-respect. Then a zealous county council suddenly instructed their schools to blackball the trust, refused to give its buses parking space, and gave them notice on the building they had lent them as an 'Enterprise Centre', a business and training hub for unemployed young people.

'It's total madness, Vicky,' Tony said to her, as he gave her a guided tour of the centre, and showed her the café, hairdressers, cycle recycling and car maintenance businesses they ran. 'We may be faith-based, but we're not faith-biased. We work with young people of every faith and none. Maybe some of our volunteers have become a little more up-front about their beliefs recently, but they're young too. And you know what young people are like. Tell them they can't do something . . .'

'The church's greatest growth spurts are often in times of repression and restriction,' she said, shaking her head in disbelief as she looked around. 'But try telling the government that. Tony, this place is amazing. So needed.'

'The biggest disaster would be the closure of our pioneering work on addictions – alcohol and drugs, and especially porn No one owns up to it. An epidemic. It leaves young people unable to live productive lives. They can't study or work, and they can't make relationships because they expect any partner to look and behave like a porn star. When it comes to addictions, only an alternative, Christian lifestyle frees them – but I'm not supposed to say so. It's not politically correct.'

'Could get you arrested.'

She thought for a moment.

'If we rang round the church leaders, got you a network of decent church facilities to use as clubs, drop-ins and for training, would it help?'

'Much harder to work without the schools' support, expecting young-sters to come to us, rather than us going out to them.'

Then, as he reflected on it, he brightened slightly and she noticed how it smoothed out some of the lines on his face – lines which hadn't been there when she had last seen him, at her enthronement in Canterbury Cathedral.

'Local teachers are not best pleased. They'd put the word around for us. And then, the youngsters have their own very effective bush telegraph.'

'We're not giving in to this brow-beating, Tony.'

'We have no intention of giving in or giving up.'

'And you will continue the youth arts festival you run with the Edenbury Project every year?'

He nodded emphatically.

'And the Urban Heroes award ceremony?'

'If we can find anyone who'll let us have a venue.'

'Oh, I think you should go national with it.'

He raised his eyebrows.

'Any suggestions?'

'Canterbury Cathedral? Westminster Abbey?'

The words were out almost before she had registered them herself. In fact, she had almost said 'Buckingham Palace', but decided at the last moment to stay on her own turf. It would be difficult enough to convince two reluctant deans. Though the positive publicity in hosting such large national youth events might just convince them. She suspected the same thought had crossed his mind, as a wide grin spread from one of his ears to the other.

'A great idea, Archbishop, if we can pull it off.'

'We must,' she said simply.

He nodded, sobered by the thought.

'I refuse to believe this is a lost generation,' he said. 'We cannot allow ourselves to let crazy legislation rob them of their potential.'

Her anger at the treatment of the Verity Trust galvanised Vicky into tackling the Prime Minister again.

'The government has created a crisis of epic proportions, Prime Minister. But for the church, which continues to provide crisis welfare – at great cost and risk to many of our members – the situation would be far worse. This legislation is barbaric, a return to Elizabethan times,' she said, as he appeared on her phone screen, his lips pulled into a tight line that indicated very clearly just how he expected the conversation to go.

'No plans to burn anyone at the stake,' he retorted.

'Haven't you? It might feel a bit like that to those who've lost their jobs, their livelihood, their reputations, and in some cases, their freedom. Not only that, but you risk sacrificing some of the country's most effective welfare, youth and social programmes. I thought you admired Tony Patterson? You've contacted him often enough for advice. Given him an OBE, for goodness' sake.'

'Everyone is free to share their faith,' he sighed, spelling it out, word for word, as if to a recalcitrant child, 'privately, as long as they don't give offence. The government is not responsible for the decisions of local government.'

That old cop-out, Vicky said to herself.

'As I've said before, Prime Minister, offence is an entirely subjective emotion, that's inevitably become a weapon to beat anyone who speaks of their faith, even church ministers. How do they share it "privately" at a funeral, for example? How do they know they won't give offence and be reported for it? How can any true Christian, following the call of Jesus to make disciples of all nations, put law before obedience?'

'I thought it was Christian to obey the law?'

She thought she detected the hint of a smirk. This Prime Minister was like an ignorant puppy, snapping at her heels, unaware of either the dignity or responsibility that should go with the role – and of the power of the people if pushed too far.

'Christians cannot obey laws that contravene their beliefs.'

Why couldn't he grasp that? He mumbled a closing dismissal as he faded from her screen, retreating, she suspected, from an argument he knew he couldn't win, and thought he didn't need to, protected by the trappings of government from personal responsibility for anything.

Battle-weary, she went on from Newcastle into the wilds of Northumberland for a couple of days, needing to be alone. In a little cottage she had borrowed overlooking the sea, she could think, achieve spiritual, mental and physical equilibrium again. It was a coastline she knew well and loved deeply. Beneath the sitting-room window, beyond the cliffs, lay a rich aqua carpet of sea, sparkling like myriad sequins whenever the sun deigned to emerge from behind the clouds. When it vanished once more, and the sea turned ashy, blending into a leaden, lowering sky, she was left looking at a desolate, stony-grey canvas. Pictures of her life, or so it seemed – moments of intense clarity of vision that illuminated the path ahead, and other times when lucidity disappeared, the horizon was distant and she needed simply to plod on through the mist and the murk.

She walked for miles, her worries unravelled by the forward propulsion of her limbs, the wind whipping her hair across her face, the scent of gorse in her nostrils and the taste of the sea spray on her lips. She sat on the cliffs, watching the skylarks wheel and dive, listening to the lap-lapping of the waves on the shore, as great gusts of wind hurled themselves at her, stopped dead, regathered their strength and blasted her again, like a carpet beater knocking out of her all the accumulated anxiety, stress and frustration of the past year. She opened wide her arms to it, oblivious to the departure of the sun, until she became so spine-tinglingly cold that it felt as if her bones had been moulded into a sculpture. Still she could not move from this hallowed place of rest and renewal, of re-invigoration for the next stage of the journey. Not until the roar of an engine, the creak of a car door and a blast of Radio One assaulted her senses and recalled her to the wider world of humankind.

She went back to the cottage and rattled off an open letter to the 20,000 or so clergy for whom she had some pastoral responsibility. She told them how proud of their courage and determination she was, how moved she was by the commitment of those who continued to engage with the needs of their local communities, despite the risk. They and their congregations had her full support in sharing, preaching and living the Gospel whenever, wherever and however necessary. 'True Christianity will always be in conflict with secular, contemporary values – unless it is a watered-down version of the faith. We follow a crucified Christ. "If you suffer as a Christian, do not be ashamed, but praise God that you bear that name" (1 Peter 4:16).'

She flashed it to Sarah in London, asking her to send it, along with an article in defence of her actions, to the media, starting wherever she felt was most appropriate. Sarah offered an exclusive to the *Guardian*, who had shown respect for the Archbishop's social justice concerns, despite their innate suspicion of faith; but to their fury, the *Telegraph* released the story first.

'How on earth did the *Telegraph* get hold of it?' Vicky asked Sarah, two days later, as they studied the front page together. 'Archbishop Throws Down the Gauntlet.' The headline and report made her sound like a tub-thumping radical going out on her own, rather than a general inspiring the troops; not nearly as sympathetic as an exclusive in the *Guardian* would have been.

'Honestly, Archbishop, I have no idea,' Sarah said, shaking her head and holding out her palms in a gesture of total helplessness. 'Needless to say, the *Guardian* is now seriously questioning our integrity. There was obviously a leak . . .'

'A leak? How, Sarah? I was in Northumberland. I only sent the letter to you.'

'Archbishop, are you saying . . . ?' Sarah asked defensively.

'No, no, not at all. It's just so . . . utterly baffling.'

'When I find the culprit . . .'

'When you find them, give me half a chance to get my hands on them!'

Despite their being wrong-footed, the publicity was exactly the rallying cry Vicky had hoped it would be. By the end of the week, she had the declared support of virtually every dissenting group that had broken away from the Anglican Church over the appointment of women bishops, both Anglo-catholic and evangelical. There was a significant surge in church attendance as the public decided to see for themselves what all the fuss was about. But there was no moment of triumph for Vicky. She had engaged with the powers of darkness, and vengeance was swift. One of the tabloids claimed that Tom was tired of sharing his bold and publicly embarrassing wife with the entire world, and had decided to buy his own flat.

Tom denied that he had ever revealed his plans to anyone else, and dismissed the allegations that she used her feminine wiles to disarm her opponents as the sexual fantasies of a few frustrated clerics.

'But do I bat my eyelashes, wiggle my hips, wear my skirts too short, too tight?' she asked Ralph.

An unflattering photograph taken mid-blink was supposed to demonstrate her seductive charms. Studying it, she wondered how anyone could believe that this middle-aged woman with the dog collar and droopy eyelids could seduce anyone, let alone a dry-stick clergymen.

'I'm asking as a friend. I need a man's honest opinion, and Tom refuses to take the whole thing seriously. Do I flirt?'

'No, not exactly,' Ralph said, studying the photograph over her shoulder. She turned to him.

'What does "exactly" mean?'

Ralph looked decidedly uncomfortable.

'You are a very feminine woman, Vicky. You're not afraid of your sexuality. You hug, you touch people, you even hold them when they share their pain with you. No male Archbishop has been able to do that. It's great. So don't let the jerks behind this put you off your stride.'

'Who do you think it is? The Cray twins in the House of Bishops?'

'Is that what you reckon?'

'I don't know. I'm trying to think who even knows what perfume I wear – other than Tom, of course.'

'Ah yes, "the dizzying aura of Paloma Picasso". They might have recognised it.'

'Come on, would you have known? Would any man? Tom only knows because he buys it for me.'

'Well, whoever it is either has it in for you or fancies you,' he said, with a wink.

'Ralph, this is no joking matter. A male Archbishop would never have this to contend with. It's sick.'

Ralph looked at her with concern.

'Just dismiss this sort of tosh, Vicky.'

'It's humiliating. It undermines me. Distracts from the vital challenge we face.'

She sat for a while, rubbing her forehead in a vain attempt to assuage her total bewilderment.

'I sometimes have the feeling someone's listening at keyholes, intercepting conversations and messages, even rifling through my things. How did the *Telegraph* know about the email I sent to Sarah from Northumberland? Who told the press that Tom couldn't cope with the pressure and was looking for a flat?'

'Had he mentioned it at work?'

Vicky thought for a moment and nodded with relief.

'You're right. He probably did. Some mischief-making little colleague will have tittle-tattled. Stupid of me. Over-reacting. Next I'll imagine the lights are flickering.'

'No, your instinct is usually fairly sound. I suggest we get police advice – just in case.'

'Come on. I may not be a national treasure, but I'm hardly a national threat either. The police won't be interested. And why would anyone want to know my business?'

A thought occurred to her that made her want to laugh out loud.

'You know something, Ralph, if anyone did think of tapping my emails, they'd be comatose after five minutes, poor things. If they're not about the deadly minutiae of church legislation, I'm sympathising with Alice about teething and nappy rash.'

'Still,' Ralph said, without a smile, 'better check it out.'

The detective inspector's expression couldn't have said more clearly that she was being paranoid. It was written all over his florid, pock-marked face as Ann brought him into Vicky's study. His tired-looking beige mac was flecked with tiny spots. Ash holes, Dr Watson, Vicky said to herself.

'Detective Inspector Wright,' Ann said, as he held out a fleshy hand to her.

'And Detective Sergeant Douglas,' he said, introducing his side-kick.

Vicky recognised the detective sergeant at once.

'Hello, Ethan,' she said, reaching out a hand to the neat, rangy, dark-haired man in a leather jacket, who moved restlessly from foot to foot as if he were warming up for a chase. The jacket creaked as he moved. 'How's Katya?'

Ethan nodded, acknowledging her smile of recognition, but kept a polite, professional and physical distance, standing slightly behind his inspector who turned to give him a quizzical look.

When the look was ignored, the inspector brushed past Vicky in a waft of perspiration and cigarette, and took a perfunctory look round, Ethan and Ralph close on his heels.

'Well, my lady . . .'

'Archbishop will do fine, thanks, Inspector.'

'Well, your . . . Archbishop, you don't need me to tell you that phone tapping and bugging are strictly controlled in this country, and only licensed in a court of law if serious criminal or subversive activity is suspected. Now Ma'am, er Archbishop, what criminal or subversive activity might you be involved in? A spot of terrorism, perhaps?'

He chortled at his own joke. From behind his boss's back, Ethan caught her eye, and raised his eyebrows apologetically, the first sign he'd given that he had any opinion of his own.

The inspector took one last glance around the room, then lumbered his way to the door, turned and said, 'Let us know if you have any more concrete evidence for your suspicions, won't you, my – er, Archbishop? Not much we can do otherwise.'

Before Ethan could follow him out, she tapped him on the shoulder and said quickly, 'Is Katya okay?'

He turned and nodded. She held out her phone and buzzed her number to his.

'Transfer this to hers, will you? Tell her to get in touch. I miss my friends.'

Ralph escorted the men to the main entrance.

'Is there any chance at all the Archbishop might be under some kind of surveillance?' he asked Ethan, when the inspector had taken himself off to the 'little boys' room' down the corridor.

Hands in his pockets, Ethan shrugged.

'It's not likely. Someone telling tales is more likely.'

'You didn't check for bugs.'

Ethan shook his head and smiled.

'Not much point unless there's more to go on. They're as small as fleas these days, anyway. You can put them anywhere, but the nearer the subject the better. Keep tabs though, if you're worried.'

'She's convinced something's going on,' Ralph said.

'You?'

Ralph shrugged.

'Not sure. But she's not given to flights of fancy. And some things don't add up. The press is always one step ahead of her.'

Ethan said, 'The easiest way to monitor her activities would be to have a mole.'

'Someone here, at the Palace?'

Ethan nodded, searching Ralph's face. Ralph stroked his chin.

'Not sure who'd be able to get close enough for long enough.'

'Who would want rid of her anyway?' Ethan asked, eyes narrowed, his hands still firmly in his pockets.

Ralph snorted.

'How many names do you want? Can we meet up somewhere?' he asked, noting the inspector lumbering his way back down the corridor, zipping up his trousers. 'I could do with talking to you about something else, if you don't mind.'

He saw the detectives out and sauntered back down the corridor.

'The inspector was right to dismiss me as an obsessive, post-menopausal neurotic,' Vicky snorted, as Ralph appeared back at her study door.

'He never suggested any such thing,' said Ralph.

She felt herself flushing. 'He didn't have to. I may be making a few waves but it was ludicrous to suggest that someone would think me a danger to national security, or a serious enough threat to anyone else to go to those kinds of lengths. Let's just drop it, Ralph, shall we?'

The Synod of July 2021 was always going to be difficult, more or less dedicated, as it was bound to be, to discussion of the church's official policy on gay marriage – with those who willingly performed blessings on the union of gay couples accusing those who couldn't of homophobia, and being accused themselves of apostasy, of having left biblical Christianity behind.

Somehow the Archbishop was expected to steer a steady course through what were pretty fundamental disagreements in terms of theological and cultural approach, holding the two factions together in the quintessentially Anglican spirit of generosity, tolerance and grace. And Vicky was determined to do it without resorting to the usual synodical law of fudge and flimflam that Dominic Naylor seemed to favour. But she would have to do it under his watchful, apparently disapproving eye.

In 1987, one of her predecessors, Robert Runcie, had said of Synod, 'In this earthly tabernacle of Christ's kingdom there are many mansions, and all of them are made of glass.' It was never more true than in a debate like this. They were doomed if they voted to marry gay couples, and doomed if they didn't, by a press and population that oscillated wildly between demanding the church to be all-inclusive or in favour of traditional morality.

Vicky opened the Synod without mentioning the issue, hoping to inspire members with a broader vision. 'The biggest challenge we face is not secularism or the rapid growth of other faiths. It's the apathy of the church: we too often come across as insipid, uninspiring, and unimaginative. We think we are strapped for lack of cash, but we are actually strapped for our lack of innovation and commitment. We think we are silenced by government legislation, but in fact we're silenced by our own fears and inadequacies. God has all the resources we need to enable us to bring love, healing, and transformation to our communities. We must challenge the marginalisation of the elderly, the demonising of the young, the prejudice towards the stranger and the bigotry shown to gay men and women. We carry the presence of the transfigured Christ wherever we are.'

The tension grew palpably as they dispensed with the mundane, necessary business and neared the key debate. Opening it, Vicky said, 'The greatest, the first freedom is freedom of conscience, of speech, and of belief. It exists to protect the believer, not the belief. The church must defend that basic human right for all, without dismissing our detractors as "Christophobic". Disagreement in a diverse society is necessary and healthy.

'In this hall are people of integrity on both sides of this argument. How we conduct our discussions here is as important as their outcome. We must be free to disagree with courtesy and grace, caring deeply for one another and for those who will have to live with our decision. The language of hate, be it accusations of homophobia against those who uphold the traditional view of marriage, or of making a pact with modern culture against those who don't, is at best subjective, at worst disingenuous. Let there be no attempt to demonise those who don't hold our views.

'Let me say that my own views have not changed. The biblical and social recognition of committed heterosexual bonding has been a constant for thousands of years, existing long before either church or state as part of an evolutionary process ensuring the survival of the human race.

'It provides for the creation, protection and preservation of future generations in a social continuity and stability that we re-negotiate at our peril.

'Civil partnerships are important, for the protection of the legal rights of those in partnerships other than marriage. But in the eyes of the church, marriage is a sacrament, holy and differentiated from any other kind of relationship. The state cannot therefore re-define it according to contemporary culture, and in doing so risks undermining its foundational benefits for a healthy society. We, the church, now have a double duty, therefore, to uphold its value, as we are indebted not only to nature, but also to biblical revelation.

'Let me end by saying that when it comes to official church policy, we, as the UK members of the Anglican Alliance, should not ignore the feelings of our African, Asian and South American brothers and sisters, who are deeply troubled that we are having this debate at all in a country they once looked to for moral probity.'

In the event, after some heated discussion, the motion to adhere to the church's traditional view of marriage was upheld by a fairly substantial majority. If anything, attitudes had moved back in that direction over the past few years, a number of waverers swayed perhaps against the government in the face of recent persecution. A good number of Synod members were clearly upset by the outcome, but Vicky was much relieved to have a decision that strengthened her authority in the International Alliance.

She walked out of Church House to a mixture of jeers and cheers, applause and catcalls. A foul-smelling tomato missed her left shoulder by a fraction of an inch, spraying her jacket with pips as it hit the wall behind her. A few landed in her hair. She pulled them out, and sprinkled them nonchalantly on the ground, standing with a resolute calm and smiling as the cameras flashed and clicked. The press would not get the 'disgusted' captions they were hoping for.

The attack, when it came, was far more personal and vitriolic. One of the tabloids claimed that Tom had more interest in decent wines than he had in the Christian faith, that he and Vicky squabbled about his drinking, and more hurtfully, that Alice had moved to America because she just couldn't get far enough away from her mother.

'Where do these stories come from?' Vicky asked Sarah. 'Marvellous tales of mystery and imagination – if they weren't so soul-destroying.'

'The price we pay for a free press,' Sarah said, raising her eyes heavenward.

'Oh, I believe in a free press – the freedom to print what is accurate and true, rather than the whimsy, myths and lies that enable a newspaper or magazine to steal a march on their competitors.'

'Journalists just do what they're told these days. Or get sacked. That's the reality,' Sarah said, utterly matter-of-fact. 'I happen to think they quite like you. You don't bore them. You give them good copy. But even a media darling has to take a bashing or two. You were doing too well. Time to bring you down a peg or two. To remind everyone the Archbishop is human.'

'Lest the country succumb to a religious ideology, God forbid?'

'You said it,' she agreed, re-examining the cutting.

'The booze story sounds like it might have come from someone who remembers you both at some party or other . . . ?'

Vicky thought hard. 'Possibly when I was a vicar. There were occasional deanery do's. But clergy parties were so boring for Tom. He enjoyed a drink or two. But he was certainly never drunk. Who would say so?'

'Any clergyman piqued by your rise, or simply gossiping with his colleagues.'

'As the clergy do.'

'Do they ever. And the tasty morsel is passed around, until eventually, hey presto, it's gospel truth, and the press prints it.'

2004

The vicar's final 'treat' before Christmas was always the deanery party. Vicky had already braved the toddler club party, the playgroup party, the Sunday School party, the Mother's Union party and Alice's nursery school nativity. The thought of another mince pie made her nauseous. 'Bah, humbug,' she said to herself that afternoon, as, with a kitchen knife, she dug lumps of ground-in lard out of the church carpet, the remains of cheap pastry trodden underfoot. 'Show me the minister who loves Christmas.'

She resented giving up a precious free evening at such a busy time to spend it with around two dozen clergy and spouses, many of them elderly men who had retired long before women became vicars, but she didn't want to be antisocial, or ungrateful for the area dean's hospitality.

Tom had entertained his colleagues on the tale of last year's little bash. The previous area dean and his wife, though pleasant enough, had been somewhat . . . buttoned up. Not the partying type. Having so many people invade their home was manifestly something of a trial.

At around ten he and Vicky had found themselves alone with a couple whose company they particularly enjoyed, perched on the carpet in front of a real fire in the dean's study, their glasses full and a spare bottle of plonk lined up on the hearth. They were totally absorbed in putting the church to rights when the door opened a crack, and their host, in pyjamas and dressing gown, popped his head round it and said, 'Remember to switch off the lights when you go, won't you?'

'A rather low capacity for fun – the clergy,' Tom had said. In contrast with his medico parties, the deanery do was like afternoon tea at Buckingham Palace. Vicky only managed to drag him along by bribing him with the promise that she would be at his side to support him at the next liquor-sodden, raucous doctors' do.

Vicky was running late, and Tom wasn't home yet. She wasn't pleased to have to get out of the shower and squelch across the bathroom floor to the bedroom phone, wearing nothing but a towel. She just prayed the babysitter wouldn't arrive at that particular moment.

'You dripped on me, Mummy,' Alice complained, as Vicky stepped over her and the enchanted Lego castle she was building outside the open bathroom door.

'It's Marilyn, Mrs Woods. Mr Woods asked me to tell you he has been unavoidably detained. Sorry about that. He said to tell you he should be home about 8.30.'

The pseudo-sophisticated voice was always slightly grating. She wasn't sorry at all. Vicky suspected that Tom's secretary had a bit of a crush on him, from the reverential way in which she said 'Mr Woods', as if he were God himself. She seemed to milk any opportunity to annoy the wife with her superior knowledge of his movements.

'Thank you, Marilyn,' Vicky replied, more graciously than she felt. It wasn't the secretary's fault he was late – even if she did sound supercilious.

'Sorry,' Vicky apologised to the new area dean, as he flung open his front door, waving a bottle in one hand.

'A problem bowel,' Tom added, with his usual charm.

'Good to see you,' beamed the new dean, removing the cigarette from his mouth so that she could kiss him on the way in. The contrast with his predecessor couldn't have been more marked.

'Kind of you, Geoff, to feed and water this large mob,' Tom said, sounding more hopeful than he had been in the car.

'No, no, no, not hard work at all. One of the beauties of being divorced. The parish ladies take pity on me and do all the cooking. And since they can't run their business without us, the undertakers, bless 'em, have coughed up for the booze.'

Tom disappeared from her side the moment he had hung up his coat, as he caught sight of the claret on the kitchen table. Vicky was left to fend for herself amidst a charm of magpies – half a dozen large-bellied, dog-collared, retired vicars, swinging on their heels as they reminisced about the glory days of parish ministry, telling the same anecdotes they told every year.

'Remind me, whose wife are you?' asked a tall, distinguished-looking, white-haired man, stooping and turning his ear towards her mouth to catch her reply.

'I'm not a wife,' she shouted into the orifice, 'I'm the vicar of St Chad's.'

He looked nonplussed, then regained his composure, and said, 'Ah, yes, yes, yes, of course. The younger generation. I was a cathedral dean, you know. Still preach occasionally – at eighty-one. Come and meet the wife.'

Invariably, since the genders tended to segregate, she found herself manoeuvred into the wives' corner. When she had had her fill of it, and the food, she wandered over to find Tom in the middle of a group of her fellow clergymen, laughing heartily. He put an arm around her shoulders to draw her into the conversation, but the mood changed almost at once, and discussion dried up and became stilted. She caught Tom's eye and moved hers towards the door. He looked at his watch, raised his eyebrows in mock surprise, and after she had expressed her appreciation to Geoff, followed her obediently out to the car.

'Not a bad night,' he said, tossing the keys into her lap. 'Good food. Wine not bad.'

'Mmmm,' she replied. 'Who was it who told me at our first date that he wasn't the clubby type?'

'So?'

'I'm glad you enjoyed yourself. I just get fed up with socialising with vicars' wives. They're not my colleagues. What do I have to do to be accepted into the boys' club?'

'Give it time, Vic,' he said soothingly. 'They have to get used to the idea.'

'How's that going to happen when at chapter Communions they don't let me serve them the bread or the chalice, let alone say the magic words? It's as if I don't exist.'

2021

So which of the clergy present on that occasion, if it was that night, might have tittle-tattled about Tom's drinking? Who would want to damage his reputation so much, or hers by extension? Tom, who was forcing himself to remain immune to such malice, told her she was over-reacting, that it was all a load of tabloid trash. But only a robot could fail to react at the personal nature of the jibes, no matter how determined she might be not to let it get to her.

'From what you say,' she said to Sarah, 'it seems young men and women set off with the best of intentions to be serious, objective reporters, and are bullied into writing the sort of rubbish that can't possibly fill them with any sense of pride. Shall we do a press release on that? Want some quotes?'

Sarah groaned.

'Archbishop,' she pleaded, 'don't try to fight on every front. Let's try some "soft" PR for a change, give the public an insight into the real woman behind the role. Lord Westburton rang me to suggest we talk to Helen Davis. She's a freelance who does some hard-nosed pieces, but also writes more restrained, domestic stuff for the women's pages and mags. I've spoken to her and she says she'd like to do a personal portrait, countering some of the fantasies we've had to contend with recently. Wants to portray you as a dynamic but accessible role model for ambitious young women today.'

Vicky was dubious, but welcomed Helen all the same, warmed to her open, freckled face and short, girl-next-door, brown curls, showed her around the palace, and shared the joys and privileges of living in a grand historic institution. They went up to the flat for coffee and cake, and as Vicky waited for the kettle to boil, engaged in the relational small talk that women do, chatting about family, fashion, running, gardening and baking.

It was a relief, for once, not to be drawn or challenged on some of the profound and thorny issues facing the church, to chit-chat instead with a bright, intelligent, interested and disarming young woman. Helen asked her what it was like to be an icon, where she shopped, how she coped with the pressures on her marriage, what were her favourite leisure pursuits, and ended by asking her whether she was upset by the announcement that, for financial reasons, the Mother's Union was being forced to sell Mary Sumner House, its London base for over a hundred years. Vicky said that she was immensely saddened, that the Mother's Union had done and did strategic work in encouraging and supporting family life in the UK, not to mention their vital and dynamic role in Africa particularly, where they helped to bind women into a force to be reckoned with.

Helen's article, when it appeared, in one of Vicky's least favourite tabloids, had become an editorial opinion piece, not the lifestyle article Sarah had pitched. It talked about exactly what they had wanted – and took it in exactly the wrong way. It claimed the Archbishop was a paragon of domestication, and no more, a woman who would have liked nothing better than to bake cakes, open bazaars and chair the Mother's Union. There was, she wrote, no evidence whatsoever of the razor-sharp intelligence, political cunning and shrewd manoeuvring necessary for anyone leading a threatened species like the church:

> I looked in vain for the dynamic, trail-blazing amazon I had been led to expect. Far from carrying all before her like a river in full flow, she's

more of a water feature for the back garden, spouting neat little homilies about the importance of the family and the home.

Let's not kid ourselves that this was the best man for the job. Her appointment was a knee-jerk reaction by a beleaguered Church of England, which, when their first choices fell by the way, decided to make an unconventional gesture that grabbed the headlines and proved they were capable of surprise. She obviously has her gifts, but they're more mumsy than Machiavelli, more pastoral than pragmatic. In fact, she is a born Archbishop's wife. It's time the C of E went out and found a real leader, and left the Archbishop to her flower arranging.

The feature was peppered with quotes from anonymous clerics who expressed their disappointment with Vicky's first year of office, deploring the tokenism that had inflicted female leadership on a church that wasn't yet ready for it.

'Not what we were hoping for, was it?' Vicky said furiously to Sarah. 'And all from a woman. Where on earth did you find her? Who has she been speaking to? How could you be so naive, Sarah? We have been well and truly stitched up.'

'Vicky, I am so sorry. The vicious cow owes us big time.'

Sarah marched backwards and forwards across Vicky's study, her mouth set in a tight red gash. 'An outrageous, pound-shop, liquorice-allsorts bag of cheap put-downs.'

'Nice description,' Vicky said. 'So what are you going to do about it?'

'I'll get the Archbishop of York to rise to your defence.'

'An able, gifted woman,' he said later that day in response to a planted question at a school visit in Newcastle. 'The Archbishop has a fine mind, is deeply caring, a collaborative, astute and visionary leader, who has pulled off an extraordinary feat in uniting the church at a crucial time.'

'Not exactly earth-shattering,' Vicky said when she saw it. 'A bit . . . clichéd, but it'll have to do.'

The following day, the Archbishop of York's tribute was met with a stinging attack on Vicky's ineptness and indecisiveness by one of the religious correspondents on a different paper.

'On what basis?' she asked Sarah in total bewilderment. 'Now it feels less like a mean editor creating a story, and more like a conspiracy. Who's feeding this attack and why?'

Sarah shook her head.

'Someone who resents a woman leader, or doesn't like your campaign against the government, or fears your popularity with the people. Take your pick,' she said. 'There are so many possibilities out there. But I have my suspicions.'

'Try me.'

'What about our beloved Dean of Canterbury?'

Vicky was deeply shocked.

'What makes you think it's him?'

'My sources tell me that "inept" is an adjective they've heard him use for you. But hey, I could be way off the mark. But if I find it is him, I'll nail him.'

She picked up a letter opener off Vicky's desk, and stabbed it, forcefully, through the newspaper article, skewering the photograph of the writer.

'Bless your enemies, Sarah,' Vicky said, smiling.

'You bless them for me, Archbishop. I'm clean out of blessings at the moment.'

'So, so sorry about all of this, my dearest girl,' said a short text from Nick. 'I thought Helen was kosher. Always served me well in the past. Mea culpa. I owe you dinner.'

A bouquet of two dozen white roses arrived at the palace. The scent of them filled Vicky's study.

The press negativity also brought a welcome text from Katya.

'I was too scared to call you, Vicky. You are the Archbishop, after all. And so grand. But when I read all that crap they said about you, I just had to get in touch. Maybe you need an old friend? It must hurt a lot.'

So one Saturday, when Tom had a works do that prevented them from going to Canterbury, Katya came to spend the evening with her. She was dressed in black from head to toe, apart from a vivid, red glass bead necklace and matching earrings, and looked stunning, as if she were twenty years younger. Vicky had ordered in a meal for two from her favourite French restaurant. They ate, catching up on Ania's and Alice's news.

'So, you're a grandma,' Katya said. 'So how does that feel?'

'Wonderful and sad. Both at once. I never thought I'd feel, so . . . utterly besotted. The genes seem to have a way of recognising each other. But it's sad not seeing him grow up, that he only knows me at a distance.'

'And you can't get away because of the job?'

Katya ate thoughtfully.

'Ania says she doesn't want children. She says she can't bring them into such a terrible world. All those things you say in the papers about hope, I cut them out and show them to her.'

'And does it make a difference?'

She shook her head sadly.

'Ach, the next generation. So disillusioned. So turned in on themselves.'

'And Ethan? How is that working?'

Katya laughed.

'Oh, Vicky, you forget. We've been together many years now.'

'I'm sorry. I am out of touch. Not married yet?'

'Ah, my old vicar speaks. No, not yet. Ethan doesn't like the commitment of it. But I am working on it, I promise you.'

She fiddled with her wine glass, drained it, then swallowed hard.

'There is something I wanted to tell you. I probably shouldn't, but I worry for you.'

Vicky refilled their glasses.

'Thanks. Ethan came to see you a while back? He told me what happened. That boss of his is a bit of a . . . plodder. Or is that "plonker"?'

She pointed at her head.

'Ethan . . . didn't think you were . . . what's the word?'

'Paranoid?'

'He's been poking around. He thinks, I don't know why, that maybe you do have some enemies in unexpected places.'

Vicky opened wide her eyes and stared at Katya.

'Please, please,' Katya said, waving a hand in reassurance, 'don't be alarmed. He's looking out for you. He's on your side. Just take care, that's all I wanted to say.'

After Katya had left, Vicky felt too agitated to clear the dishes. She got out her Bible, tried to read to quieten her mind, but ended up pacing the floor instead. The possibility of concerted scheming and plotting against her, of someone deliberately planning mischief and mayhem, made her heart race. But surely, she said to herself, this was what you signed up for at the start – to be misunderstood, slandered and maligned? Minor adversities compared with the sufferings of persecuted Christians in Asia or Africa. Though, the murder of one's character was a kind of death.

Yet if she allowed fear to make her back away from the risk of challenging government, society and church, she would become yet another silenced voice, another passive member of an ailing society. So, she said to herself resolutely, do what you have to do, and take the taunts, the spitting, the hammering in of the nails like a man, Victoria Burnham-Woods.

'I am what I am and what I am needs no excuses.'

She was singing it in the bath when Tom came home.

'Changing genders then?' he asked, bemused.

'Hmmm?'

'*La Cage Aux Folles*, Darling. The Broadway musical about trans-sexuals.'

He came over to the bath, kissed her on the forehead, and looking her up and down appreciatively, added, 'That, of course, could be one way of satisfying those disenchanted with a woman – but a bit drastic, all the same.'

SEVENTEEN

The knowledge of the cross brings a conflict of interest between God who has become man and man who wishes to become God.

JÜRGEN MOLTMANN

OCTOBER 2021

There were so many visits, in the UK and abroad, that the myriad sights, sounds, conversations and events she'd experienced blurred into each other, and Vicky couldn't remember which visit was which. But her first trip to China, in the autumn of 2021, was one of the most memorable. Though its economy was not as buoyant as it had once been, its growth rate still hovered at around seven per cent, making the UK look like a very poor relation. It also had one of the largest, most vibrant churches in the world. The government claimed there were 25 million Christians in the country, 18 million Protestants and 6 million Catholics. An independent figure put it at a conservative 70 million – more Chinese at church on a Sunday than in the whole of Europe.

With the permission of the State Department of Religious Affairs, Vicky went as a guest of the Self-Patriotic China Ecumenical Churches, to deepen the relationship between their religious communities and the Church of England. From a government perspective, the official, state-sanctioned churches, whose primary allegiance was to the Communist Party, were the church in China – other churches did not exist. Fourteen years earlier, a predecessor at Canterbury had offered them theological training for their ministers, but there had been little take-up. Vicky wanted to know why, but she also wanted to highlight the plight of the 'less official', house or underground churches, still experiencing a measure of state harassment.

The whistle-stop tour of Shanghai, Nanjing, Xi'an and Beijing, crammed with university lectures, visits to church-based initiatives, and meetings with religious leaders, academics, local officials, and business executives, left little time for tourism. Still, it was a fascinating introduction to the dynamic, rich and colourful culture of China.

Vicky's hosts were genial and meticulously polite and the last thing she wanted was to offend them, but even as she congratulated the government on its support for some impressive church-backed welfare projects in child and rural healthcare, she asked after the lawyers, writers and religious leaders whom she knew had disappeared, victims of arrest, imprisonment and the confiscation of their property.

She had warned the Foreign Office that she would employ a carrot-and-stick approach and was made aware that ministers would not be pleased at her meddling in international affairs, risking some delicate, highly lucrative business deals. But she simply could not close her mind to the hundreds incarcerated in stinking, rat-infested, urine-soaked cells. If China was now a senior partner in the fellowship of nations, the suppression of religious freedom could not be overlooked. What price a human life?

She galvanised herself to capitalise on every ounce of diplomacy and female charm she possessed, and smiled, beguiled, cajoled and captivated her way to some concrete assurances from the Chinese government that a long-negotiated, massive investment in the UK's nuclear programme, dear to the heart of the government, would not only go ahead, but as a token of goodwill, would be announced publicly at a press conference on her last day. The Chinese kept their word, and summoning her most gracious smile, she thanked them for this new partnership between 'our countries, and our churches'. Britain would receive theology students and send university lecturers to China. And China, in this new spirit of co-operation, would release from prison certain church pastors, whom she proceeded to name, aware that the cameras were still trained upon her. With a curt nod or two, and some rather tight smiles, the government officials conceded. She heaved a sigh of relief. She had gambled on Chinese pride, and won.

Back in her hotel bedroom, she received the grudging, 'sailing close to the wind as ever, Vicky' congratulations of the Prime Minister.

'Not that close, Prime Minister,' she said to his pinched, tiny face on her e-phone. 'No enterprise is more likely to succeed than one concealed from the enemy until it is ripe for execution.'

There was a studied silence.

'Machiavelli, not Burnham-Woods,' she added.

The press hailed the visit as a triumph. Flashing through the copy the following morning before breakfast, catching words like 'masterful', 'ingenious' and even one appearance of 'stateswoman', she thought again about Helen Davis's ludicrous, disparaging article. Not Machiavellian enough, eh, Ms Davis? More fool you. How does any woman survive in the Church of England as archdeacon, let alone a bishop without taking lessons from the statesman who said, 'Before all else, be armed'? It had almost been her motto in Westhampton.

2006

The archdeaconry of Westhampton. Not the easiest post she had held in her life, but a church picnic in contrast with what was to come. Yet it was her private rather than professional life that would prove the most challenging – because of the impact of the Sophie Carpenter case on her relationship with Tom.

By the end of her time at St Chad's, she had gathered that one or two bishops were on the look-out for a woman capable of filling the most senior post they had to offer, but she never, for one moment, expected to be considered. At his request, she set off to see Bishop Richard Brooke on a foul November morning, torrential rain making the lines on the M25 almost invisible and slowing traffic to a crawl. Spray created a blinding shield across the windscreen whichever lane she was in, and an ominous rattle in the rear announced a long-suffering and unhappy exhaust appealing for attention. By the time she arrived at Bishop's House she felt utterly frazzled. Her suit was rumpled, her head thumped and an inner voice convinced her that the job would be so consumed with buildings and their fabric, there was no reason why she should want it. 'You,' she commanded the exhaust, as she grabbed her briefcase from the back seat and slammed the car door shut, 'stay where you are till we get back home.'

She had tried to recall the Bishop from her times in Synod and had a vague impression of a rather distant, dour individual with a magnificent mane of silver hair and a fine aquiline nose – a rather intimidating headmaster type. Not a man she would have earmarked as a boss, but she could hardly afford to be picky.

As he showed her into a comfortable, chintzy sitting room, decorated in a soothing duck-egg blue, the Bishop appeared more genial than she remembered.

'Coffee? Tea?'

He disappeared out of another door at the far end of the room, and within minutes of his return and a question or two about her journey, the door opened slowly and a faded, middle-aged woman in twin set and tweed skirt emerged with cups, a large cafetière and a plateful of digestive biscuits. Without so much as a glance in her direction, which Vicky ascribed to a long habit of discretion rather than deliberate rudeness, she placed the tray between them, folded her hands and said, 'Anything else, Bishop?'

'No thank you, Margaret.'

Then she disappeared through the far door as swiftly and silently as she had arrived.

'Margaret, my secretary, a wonder of efficiency,' he exclaimed appreciatively to the well-ordered tray she had left behind her. 'Now then, where were we?'

Vicky didn't feel the vagaries of her exhaust were worth returning to, so smiled sweetly and said nothing. He ran a large, heavy hand through the copious, silver hair, his episcopal gold ring glimmering in the light from the standard lamp.

'Ah yes, let me tell you how I see the archdeacon's job. I expect you've heard that it's all gutters and downspouts?' he asked, with a hint of a smile, pressing the plunger into the cafetière with such force that a large spurt of coffee flooded the tray.

'And eradicating bats from the belfry?' Vicky added, watching his vain attempts to mop up the slick with a few paper serviettes. She resisted the temptation to come to the rescue of a helpless male.

'A terrible caricature,' he said, as she took the proffered, damp cup and saucer from his hand. Wedgwood? Certainly not Ikea like hers.

'It's a wonderful office – the eyes and ears of the bishop. Essential,' he said, leaning his forceful frame towards her.

When he seemed satisfied that she had taken the point, he picked up his coffee, sat back, and crossed one leg over the other.

'I can't know the minutiae, whether one church is failing to pay its way or its vicar is having a nervous breakdown, which vicarage needs a new bathroom. I don't always know when we have an outstandingly good incumbent who deserves a pat on the back, or when one of them is up to no good and requires a shot across the bows. I'll have you for that . . . if you accept, of course,' he said, taking an abrupt swallow of his coffee. His eyes never left her. 'You will of course be one of the most senior women in the Church of England.'

She had wondered when the bait would be laid.

'Yes,' she said, 'I realise. There are still very few female archdeacons.'

'Exactly. Which is one reason I've asked you. That and your undoubted gifts,' he added quickly.

Ah, let's not forget my gifts, she thought, otherwise she might be tempted to think the offer was mere tokenism.

'I am honoured to be asked.'

He gave a gracious nod of acknowledgement.

'I would be, even if I were a mere man,' she added, and to her relief he broke into a hearty laugh. A humour-otomy would be catastrophic in a bishop who was going to be her boss.

'My only hesitation,' she said, as his laughter died away, 'is that we know each other so little. I only hope I wouldn't disappoint your expectations.'

'I have no doubt on that score,' he said. 'I took plenty of soundings and wouldn't have asked if I had any reservations.'

There was a rather grand coal-effect gas fire glowing in the grate and he sat and stared vacantly at the false flames for a while. Then he looked up suddenly and said, 'I'll never forget that time at Synod when you demanded that the church hierarchy should give up our larger pay packets. You were so convincing that you almost got away with it.'

'Almost?'

He chuckled to himself.

'Better luck next time. Only now, Archdeacon – it will cost you! I thought then, I'd rather have that woman with me than against me.'

The archdeacon's house was grander than any they had lived in thus far – a modern, detached house, bought, rather than purpose-built, on an estate full of aspiring career couples, who, judging by the frenetic comings and goings of 4x4-fuls of children, were lucky if they ever managed a couple of hours *en famille*. So like us, Vicky said to herself. Except that her new motor for the extra travelling that the job entailed was a rather more environmentally friendly, little pink Honda Jazz. Not what she had planned to buy, but irresistible. She had fallen in love with it the moment she saw it.

Tom claimed to be delighted with her promotion. A longer commute was a small price to pay. He then proceeded to find fault with every aspect of the move, from the date for her induction to the colour of the new curtains and carpets, as if they were her choice alone. He was particularly vociferous on the choice of a new school for Alice. They had agreed to send her to the local C of E comprehensive, but when she didn't settle in her first few days, he developed an aggravating, 'told-you-so' tone to his voice.

'Give her a chance, Tom,' Vicky begged. There were still packing cases everywhere, and she was wandering around the house looking for a final resting place for the shoe polish, resenting the fact that had she done the unpacking single-handed, it would have been done by now. 'We knew it would take a while.'

'She's lost without Ania,' he said, watching Vicky rummage through endless amounts of tartan wrapping paper. 'They grew up together. It's unfair on her.'

'Shoe polish?'

He looked at her quizzically.

'Where shall we keep it?'

'How should I know?'

'Gee, thanks for your help. Moving is stressful for all of us, Tom. I can't tell you how much I miss Katya.'

The thought seemed to rile him.

'Yes, but Alice didn't ask to be moved, did she?'

'I know, I know. But what do you want me to do?' she asked, temporarily interrupting the unpacking to talk to him. 'You agreed I should take the post. So did she. We said it was a big honour, and that she could have her own mobile phone to stay in touch with Ania. They phone and text all the time.'

Tom kicked one of the packing cases.

'We may have to send her to a private school.'

'I don't like the idea, but if you think it best. It's early days yet.'

He shrugged, put his hands in his pockets, and stalked off.

One of the most dispiriting things she had to contend with in those early days of senior ministry was that around half the parishes in the diocese imposed some restriction on what she could and couldn't do. The evangelicals wouldn't let her preach, the Anglo-catholics wouldn't let her officiate at the Eucharist.

'Caught between the devil and the deep blue sea,' she called to Tom one evening after a particularly dispiriting church visit, as he was brushing his teeth in their en suite bathroom, an unexpected luxury. She was sitting in bed with the Synod papers for the following week – the perfect bedtime read. Jenny said they should be marketed for insomniacs.

Tom came into the bedroom wiping his mouth on a towel. 'I'd like to see a patient refuse a female surgeon on the grounds she might be premenstrual and gung-ho with the knife.'

The picture made her smile.

'Not quite the same thing. But I'm blowed if I'm going to lose sleep over what I can't do when there's so much I can.'

'That's my girl,' he said, as he climbed into bed, patting her on the knee. 'No defeat.'

It was the most physical contact they had had since the move.

'By the way, Vic,' he said, reaching for his book and glasses, 'what do Alice and I do now? Where do we go to church while you're doing whatever it is you'll have to do?'

'Try your local? Find somewhere Alice enjoys?'

'Fair enough.'

'It won't be quite the same. Not being the vicar's other half.'

'Thank the Lord for that. I was getting a little tired of playing Prince Philip.'

Vicky was taken aback. Tom may never have been an active committee man, like some clergy husbands, but he had always been at her side on Sundays, and she thought he had coped quite well with it.

'Was that really how you felt?'

He shrugged, put on his glasses, and buried himself in his book, precluding any further conversation, leaving Vicky to the church's higher education strategy and a disturbed night.

The next morning, as she drove to St Wilfred's, in one of the far-flung parts of the diocese, to support a vicar seeking permission to move its brass-eagle lectern, the conversation came back to her, and she acknowledged with a leaden sensation in the pit of her stomach that there was a lot that Tom didn't tell her. Sophie Carpenter for one, a no-go area for conversation that was all it took to make the rest seem superficial. With a real sense of disquiet, she realised that like protecting a sore on the body for fear of causing it further damage, they subconsciously avoided what couldn't be said, and she wondered how much of what they still had to say to each other was of any real significance at all.

The pressure on Tom to get waiting times down had become intolerable, requiring longer and longer hours. More and more he was an absent partner, even when he was present – withdrawn, distant, uninterested in her work. Having lost her church family at St Chad's, struggling to find her feet in a strange new world, she needed him more than ever, and felt isolated, a lone swimmer in a hostile sea. Sometimes it seemed as if being in a marriage was a lonelier place than being out of it. She blinked back the tears. There had to be better places to cry than at the driving wheel of a car.

Meetings of the St Wilfred's kind were tiresome. In the end, whatever the Bishop said, she was indeed besieged by problem drains, gutters and boilers located in creaking, barn-like churches, damp, peeling church halls, and neglected vicarages. Either that or keeping the peace when congregations decided to 're-order' – the official name for a major modernising of the interior. Any works, alterations or additions to parish churches, even just moving those Victorian brass-eagle lecterns, required

ecclesiastical planning permission, known as a 'faculty'. It began with a
visit from the DAC, the Diocesan Advisory Committee. If a modification
got past them, there were manoeuvres with the local Civic Society, the
Victorian Society and National Heritage. The process was a nightmare,
with Vicky deploying every tactic known to woman to achieve the church's
object, not to mention holding the vicar's hand for moral support. She
had little expertise in historical, financial and legal matters – but she
learnt fast.

Life was essentially one long meeting. Diocesan policy and strategy,
developed by the Bishop and his staff team, would need delivering to and
through a raft of committees, many of them chaired predominantly by
the archdeacon. This was where gender differences seemed their most
stark. Some of the women asked so many questions that it was difficult
to complete any business. The men interpreted that as evidence of the
inferiority of female reasoning powers, while they remained doggedly
focused, never asked for information, and held forth, at length, whatever
the subject. Vicky became adept at looking interested and engaged, even
while mentally writing a shopping list or planning the evening meal. To
save her sanity, she pinned a wonderful Garrison Keillor quote to the wall
of her office in Church House: 'God writes a lot of comedy. It's just that
he has so many bad actors.'

The only opportunity to say anything of any real significance was at
the annual archdeacon's visitation, where she swore in the newly
elected churchwardens. Once a year she had some 400 clergy and other
church leaders in her power. She was determined not to bore them early
into the pub, but to leave them with something memorable and
worthwhile.

'The church,' she said, at her first visitation, 'should be the face, hands
and voice of Jesus. That's the awesome responsibility you take on today.
It requires the loving acceptance of all comers, putting them at their ease,
making them feel totally at home in your building. That means running
the heating, providing a decent cup of coffee, and any biscuits other than
soggy Rich Teas. It means ensuring the loos are lockable, clean and in
good working order. Some have given up on church for want of a piece of
toilet paper.'

The titter was gratifying. She had them eating from her hands.

'One of our greatest strengths is that we're the only place in society left
where people of every age, every background, and every level of intellect,
can mix freely. If we want to offer the world a community with a radically
alternative lifestyle based on self-sacrifice and generous spirit, let's
demonstrate it in the small things, as well as the great.'

The area of responsibility she most enjoyed was the pastoral care of the clergy. She didn't want the diocese to be a distant, faceless employer, unaware of the pressures and struggles of employees who gave pastoral care to others, but received little enough of it themselves. She had been there, knew only too well from experience what a thankless job it could be.

'Well?' the Bishop would ask on Monday mornings, over the top of his half-moon spectacles. 'What's going on out in the jungle, Vicky? Any naughtiness amongst the boys? I suppose that should be "and girls" these days, but sadly, I'm only too aware which of the genders has the greatest tendency to play away from home.'

He said it in such a lugubrious tone that it took Vicky all her effort to keep a straight face.

'How should I know, Bishop? Strangely enough, when any of them do plan some nookie on the side, they don't usually give me prior warning.'

When the clergy did stray, the collateral damage was like the fall-out from a grenade – for the family, the church, the wider community, and the nationwide church, if the press got hold of the story. Of all the professions, though, the clergy had the highest reported level of sexual misconduct.

'What makes them succumb to the extraordinary madness of an affair, costing them career, house, reputation and family?' she asked the Bishop. 'Stress, loneliness, depression? Or perhaps they feel they've been proper and good and passed over for so long that they subconsciously look for a way to throw off all restraint and remake their image? Whatever, we do so little to prevent it.'

'Suggestions?'

'Confront it. It's an issue that's rarely tackled during training. Let's bring in psychologists, offer seminars on the professional conduct of the clergy, let them talk about the issues that put them at risk.'

'Try it,' the Bishop sighed. 'But getting them to attend will take the persuasive powers of a car salesman.'

Being the Bishop's trouble-shooter regularly required the negotiating skills of Solomon. Whenever a church council wrote to him to moan about their vicar, which they did with frightening regularity, Vicky was sent to mediate. What PCCs most often wanted was dismissal. They didn't seem to comprehend that, just as in the secular workplace, sacking was not an option, except for a criminal offence or gross indecency. And a minister's misdemeanours, even if real, were usually far less exciting than that. Convincing a PCC of the fact, though, appeared well-nigh impossible. 'Stop spouting and just ditch the blighter, Archdeacon. He's a waste of space,' said one voluble churchwarden.

'Mind you, some vicars do have it coming,' she confessed to Simon one evening. She had come home early, knowing Tom had a half-day off, but there was no sign of him. Disappointed, she had rung Simon instead. 'I'm permanently amazed at how inept the clergy can be – useless at even basic volunteer management. On the other hand, some get lumbered with a dominant, unsympathetic squirearchy who think all they have to do is snap their fingers (and maybe cough up some money) to make the vicar dance to their tune. If they don't get what they're paying for, they want him or her out.'

'Bullying. Sadly, there's plenty of that. Discerning where the fault-line lies must be difficult,' he commiserated.

'It is. Even harder to know what to do about it.'

'Rather you than me, oh Venerable Machiavelli, that's all I can say.'

'One aggrieved church claimed their vicar wasn't pulling his weight, got fed up when they couldn't get their own way through official channels and hung posters all over their village displaying his photograph with the caption, "Have you seen this man?" '

Simon burst out laughing.

'You have to hand it to them. He must have been a real lazy blighter.'

'Yes, but what a poor image of the church to present to the village,' she said ruefully. 'I sometimes really feel the need of a traffic hold-up on the way home just to let the steam out of my ears.'

She put down the phone, and looked at the clock. Still no sign of Tom. She spent the evening emailing out details of her professional conduct seminar to her fellow archdeacons in other dioceses. Word about its success had travelled. Novelty meant it hadn't been nearly as difficult to work up the numbers as the Bishop had feared. Harder to gauge whether it was a success, she thought wryly. Only time and good behaviour would tell.

She was in bed when Tom arrived home.

'I came home early,' she said as his silhouette appeared in the bedroom door.

'Hmmm?' he asked, apparently in the process of sending a text.

'So that we could spend some time together.'

He still didn't appear to hear her.

'Where were you?'

'What?' he asked distractedly.

'It doesn't matter.'

*   *   *

As he opened the door of his rambling, untidy Victorian villa, Donald took in her new, shoulder-length haircut, the tailored suit, the heels, and the pink Honda parked outside. He seemed amused.

'Ah,' he said knowingly, 'the Venerable Vicky.'

As he motioned her to follow him into his study, he said, 'You were never as tall as me before, were you, or am I shrinking as well as going gaga?'

It was the first time she had seen him since becoming archdeacon, and she was struck at once by how doddery he seemed. His feet didn't appear to do what he wanted them to do, and his clothes hung on his large, bony frame as if they were suspended from a hanger.

'I think it's the heels,' she said, slipping them off as she sank into the familiar armchair opposite his.

'Aye, well, that and a touch of Parkinson's on my part.'

'Oh Donald, I'm sorry,' she said, but he waved a hand dismissively.

'At eighty, what can I expect?'

'Eighty?'

She was suddenly horrified at the way time was slipping past them both.

'And I haven't seen you for over a year. It's shameful.'

'You've been busy,' he smiled. 'Besides, this relationship is supposed to respond to your needs, not mine.'

As he let himself down into the armchair, she tried to remember what busyness could possibly be worth staying away from this wise and godly mentor, for whom time was now at a premium. The skin around his jawline sagged in loose folds, but his voice was still strong and resonant, and his eyes, as they focused on her, though a little rheumy, were as alert as ever. Patches of white stubble, missed by the shaver, glinted in the sunlight from the gracious floor-to-ceiling window of his study.

'So, how are things?'

She told him that it had taken longer than she had expected to adjust to the new role. 'There's no community to welcome you and take you to their bosom. No work pattern, not that clergy ever have much of one, but now, with no services to plan and lead, no funerals or school assemblies to do, no role in the community . . .'

'Easy to fall into bad habits?'

She heaved a sigh.

'No routine to ensure a personal discipline of prayer and reflection?'

'I try.'

'Guard it with your life – most of all now, when there is no pattern to your day. In these later years I've had to become more, not less disciplined about it. A fixed devotional time helps us become sponges absorbing a few wee drops from the eternal springs. We can't understand God. He's too vast for that. But we can soak him up into our lives. Thirsty plants benefit more from a slow drip-drip than occasional soakings.'

He stretched out his legs comfortably, folded his hands as if in prayer, then rested his mouth on them.

'A dogsbody job, archdeaconing, I've always thought,' he said a moment later.

Dear Donald, as perceptive as ever.

'That just about sums it up.'

'Stranded in a no-man's-land between the bishop and his dependants. A lonely place.'

A lump constricted her throat. He knew where she was at just by looking at her, as he always did, no matter how hard she tried to hide it, to be brave, to be strong, to hold herself together.

'Vicky, you need your support networks more than ever. How is your family?'

'Alice had a bumpy start with the move, but she seems to have settled at last. She's growing up fast. She's clever and good. And I'm so proud of her.'

'And the great doctor?'

Vicky was painfully aware of her momentary hesitation.

'Okay,' she said lightly, in a way that invited no further discussion.

'I see,' Donald said slowly, then changed the subject swiftly.

'Of course,' he said, 'your experience of parish ministry prepared you for your role.'

She looked at him, puzzled.

'The older I get, the more cruel and unkind our society seems to be. All this "You are the weakest link, goodbye" nonsense. So uncharitable. We are all weakest links – vulnerable, inadequate, human. Our greatest fear is that we will be found out. Of all people, the clergy should know that weakness in God's hands is strength, not failure. But they have no one to say, "Well fought, soldier." Never forget what that feels like. Be there for them – in their self-doubt, disappointments and failures.'

'That is one enormous commission,' she admitted, 'and what I so want to do, but how not to let it get subsumed by endless meetings, downspouts, spires and pigeon droppings is beyond me.'

'Oh, you'll get there, Vicky,' he said reassuringly. 'Of that I have no doubt. Let me, as ever, quote you some Moltmann.' He fished a book out from beside his chair, opened it at a marker and read: *The knowledge of the cross brings a conflict of interest between God who has become man and man who wishes to become God.'* Never be seduced, by power, status or hierarchy, into thinking you are superior. Simply be you. It's all you have to give.'

They sat in companionable silence for a while. She knew it was a clever tool the wily old bird tended to use when he knew that there was more she needed to tell him. And she fell for it every time.

'Donald,' she said slowly, unsure of how to articulate what she needed so badly to explore, 'did you ever have a subject about which you fundamentally disagreed with your wife – something that became a no-go area?'

He was pensive for a while, staring at the ceiling, and said, 'No, I can't think that there ever was.' Then he turned to face her. 'That must be very hard?'

'I can't go into details – medical matters. But it has left me with a major moral dilemma.'

Concern was writ large on Donald's face.

'Tom refuses to discuss it. And I don't know how to bridge the gap.'

Tears sprang to her eyes. She let them fall, then rooted in her handbag and finally managed to retrieve a tatty piece of tissue. Donald watched her carefully throughout, then got up and handed her the familiar box of tissues.

'Obviously I can't tell you what to do,' he said, as he sat heavily back down. 'Tom's confidences are between you and him, and that's one place I dare not tread. But it seems to me that apart from prayer and patience there is little to be done, except to go on loving your husband. He has an inalienable right to be sustained and consoled by you in all matters, and it sounds as if he needs it more than he has ever done. Give him the gift of your time and trust, Vicky. And leave his conscience to God.'

Later, as he escorted her to the door, he said, 'Vicky, you have been entrusted with two other human lives. Always make Tom and Alice your priority.'

She leant over and kissed him on the cheek. 'Thank you,' she said, 'for always being there.'

'As long as I have breath in this ancient body, and this aged mind of mine continues to function, I will be,' he said, patting her reassuringly on the arm. 'You know that.'

2010

In 2010, after twenty-three years of Labour government, the Conservatives came to power again and Mark Bradley-Hind was appointed as a minister with a brief for higher education. Intrigued, Vicky watched him being interviewed on his views on proposed legislation that would more than triple university fees.

'The proposals are part of a progressive package that will put higher education on a stronger footing for the future.'

The standard party line – slick, inane and meaningless. It would leave students with around £40,000 of debt. But what did Mark know about debt?

It was strange to see him on the TV like that after so many years. The fresh-faced, bright-eyed, boyish look had been superseded by that world-weary, sardonic expression so often assumed by politicians, sick of listening to what they dismiss as the uninformed rants of unintelligent voters. But then, Mark had always had an unerring belief in his own superior judgement. His eyes, she noticed, once as soft and brown as a cow's, were now almost black. As she watched him, a frosty shiver shot up her spine, leaving her feeling slightly chilled, though she couldn't, for the life of her, say why that was.

Meanwhile, the church, like the rest of the country, was beginning to succumb to the gloom of the ever-deepening financial crisis, which had left a multi-million-pound hole in the pensions scheme. The Pensions Board proposed raising the retirement age from sixty-five to sixty-eight, and to increase from forty to forty-three years the length of service required before a full clergy pension could be claimed. At the General Synod debate Vicky spoke out vigorously against the proposals. Forty-three years of service meant very few clergy would ever qualify for a full pension, especially since so many were asked to work 'in the world' before training for ordination.

'The clergy have been caught up in one of the greatest social upheavals of all time, when Sunday trading, mistrust of institutions, post-modern individualism and a breakdown in traditional morality have driven a rail-road through church communities, demolishing some completely. Many have had to take on several parishes and we all work harder than ever. The meagre stipend clergy are paid leaves no surplus to invest in a home of their own, or in a private pension. Having served us well, should we then condemn them to a grinding poverty in old age? This is not just irre-sponsible. It is downright wicked.'

Her speech was greeted with whoops and cheers, until a member of the Pensions Board argued that such was the number and longevity of the clergy in retirement, that there was a grave danger funding would run out altogether and no pensions would be paid at all.

Vicky rose to her feet again, infuriated by such overt manipulation.

'I am so sorry, Mr Smethwyck, that we take so long to die. But given the increasing stress of the job, I suspect that this current inconvenience to the Pensions Board may be about to decline, as the rate of coronary heart disease amongst the clergy rises to the levels that you require to balance the books.'

She didn't win, of course. Though why Synod capitulated with barely a firecracker, let alone a decent volley of cannon, she would never understand, except that a paralysing terror of losing even the meagre pension they might currently expect had spread its tentacles into the minds of the clergy members. She suspected that the Church of England could have found a way of being more generous to its former troopers, had it the will and the heart.

This and a host of other topical issues, such as the defeat of legislation to allow women to become bishops, thrust the archdeacon into the media limelight. She was regularly caught on camera, interviewed as she left Synod, pursued for comment, and invited onto current affairs programmes. She was even offered a photo-shoot wearing designer gear, which she decided not to accept, tempting though it was, lest it compromise her authority.

Jenny claimed she had overheard a cameraman refer to her as 'hot totty for a churchwoman'.

'The media always has its darlings,' Vicky said, dismissively, 'the favoured one or two spokespeople who get into the researchers' address books and are rolled out every time a comment is needed, because they don't actively drive the viewers to slitting their throats with boredom. But it's a five-minute wonder.'

There was, as she clearly foresaw, a temporary fall from grace for her media career in 2013 when she openly opposed the government's intention to introduce same-sex marriage, praising a one-million-strong demonstration in France, where the French government was proceeding with similar plans. 'Why are we British so passive about what matters to us, compared to the French, who truly value family life and get out there to say it?' she was quoted as saying. 'Why haven't we done the same here?' The press, annoyed at having Britain negatively compared to a manifestly half-baked country like France, accused her of homophobia, at least until it became known that the French demonstration had been organised by a quirky comedian and a gay atheist.

The financial crisis began to cause serious difficulties for the Westhampton diocese.

'How many clergy can we lose, and how quickly?' asked the Bishop at the weekly staff meeting.

The assistant bishop nodded his accord and checked a list he had obviously prepared in the event of such a question. It was news to Vicky.

'But Richard,' she interjected, 'can we think through the implications first? It would force remaining clergy to take on one, two or even three more churches, each with its own Sunday services, PCC, decrepit buildings, falling numbers, and financial problems. It will drive some of them to their knees and save us little money in the long run.'

'Yes, but are there any viable alternatives, Vicky?' the Bishop asked wearily, removing his glasses and rubbing his eyes.

'Forgive me, but this approach smacks of knee-jerk reaction, rather than strategic planning. All is far from doom and gloom outside our creaking structures. There's as much interest in spirituality as ever, and new kinds of churches are proving appealing. They meet in pubs or homes outside of the institutional setup.'

Bishop Richard gave her one of his most dismissive, withering looks.

'And your point?'

'When Marks and Spencer had a hard time a couple of years ago, they closed some unprofitable branches, but invested in new ventures. Close the buildings, but keep the clergy. It would be more cost effective.'

The Bishop sighed at length.

'And you're prepared to take on the local council, the Civic and Victorian Societies every time we try to close a church, are you?'

He had a point. She knew only too well how many years of legal wrangling could be required. Preserving Victorian history was all very well, but most of the members of the preservation societies never darkened the church's door, yet still expected the worshippers to foot the astronomical bills for the upkeep and heating of an unusable, monstrous Victorian monument, even in areas of high unemployment.

'Let the buildings fall down round our ears, Bishop.'

'And have the council take us to court?'

'We can't pay – whatever the courts decide.'

'Thank you, Vicky, we'll bear it in mind,' he said, looking at her down his long, aquiline nose, and the rest of the staff team returned to the discussion of reducing and retrenching.

'But the Archbishop of Canterbury's special grant, ring-fenced for new mission projects, where has it gone?' she muttered.

'Paying off debts,' whispered a fellow archdeacon.

It was outrageous. She made to speak once more, but as she opened her mouth the Bishop cut her off with a warning look, and she closed it again immediately, like a goldfish.

Damn, damn, damn, she muttered under her breath, on her way out to the car, you're going to have to do better than that if you want to modernise the C of E, Victoria. Bishop Richard was probably tired. More likely it was yet another example of pragmatism as he faced up to the deepening crisis. Move the clergy like pawns on a chessboard into the few vacant livings, lumped together to save money. Managed decline. At his stage in the game, with retirement beckoning, he hadn't the will to handle revolts against church closures. People were much easier to dispense with than buildings, it was as simple as that. Eight years without a single creative suggestion for expansion. Without accepting one from her. Despite saying to her, a mere two months previously, 'Why do you think I appointed you? Simply to win a round in the gender game? I did it because I recognised that I'm easily cynical and dispirited and that I need your fire and vision to remind me why I'm here, and to keep me focused.'

She tossed her briefcase into the boot, aware that her superficial frustration was at risk of turning into an increasing boredom. Find your fire, Richard. She was ready for a change. But the episcopal doors had only just been flung open to women, and she didn't see herself as a candidate, not after her controversial performances in Synod. So where did an archdeacon go from here? Should she head back to a parish somewhere, or sit tight and wait for an invitation that might never come?

PART THREE

2022–24

Encryptogram user z3qa | to user bx4sw

That damn woman – the neo-socialist claptrap she passes off as Christian conscience!

Blasted W.G. business. She must keep stirring things up. All for a bunch of low-lifes. Our friend anxious about it. Time to put a stop. She's parried the minor thrusts, deflected the darts. But it can't last.

That man of hers sniffing around. We'll handle him – but final grenade has to come from your people. Government cannot be seen to encroach on Anglican affairs. Deficiencies in leadership in church and state not so far apart. How many support you?

Remember. If we fail we all go down together. Relying on you. Will show appropriate gratitude when the time comes. Would a family holiday be appreciated?

EIGHTEEN

We think sometimes that poverty is only being hungry, naked and homeless. The poverty of being unwanted, unloved and uncared for is the greatest poverty. We must start in our own homes to remedy this kind of poverty.

MOTHER TERESA

JANUARY 2022

'Doris is 88. Let me tell you about how she spent Christmas Day. She spent it alone, in front of the television, in a freezing house she was afraid to heat because of the cost. Her only visitor was a carer who popped in for half an hour at midday to heat her a cup of soup. And what is particularly cruel is that Doris has three grown-up children, all with comfortable homes, who couldn't agree which of them should be burdened with their mother. And Doris is only one of around a million of our elderly who are abandoned simply because they are frail and their needs are time-consuming.'

Vicky used her New Year sermon of 2022 in Canterbury Cathedral to bemoan the death of family and community, and the increasing heart-lessness of a society rejecting traditional Judeo-Christian values. 'This shocking inhumanity seems to be a peculiarly middle-class British phenomenon. The less well-heeled are far more likely to orient their lives around their parents' home and wouldn't dream of neglecting a mum or a gran. The French and Italians value grandparents, aunts, uncles, cousins and eat together regularly on Sundays. In China, despite the rapid cultural change, age is revered for its wisdom, and it would be unthinkable not to have the eldest member of the family at the head of the table. In the so-called "developing" countries that we so often dismiss, elderly parents usually live with their grown-up children once they are too old to fend for themselves, demonstrating a humanity alien to trend-driven, immoral Britain in our comparative wealth and comfort, and with a gulf between young and old that we are simply not addressing. Whatever happened to "Love your neighbour as yourself", let alone "Honour your father and mother"? For myself, I certainly did not spend enough time with my own mother in the later years of her life. She wasn't easy, and I was busy. The usual excuses. So I understand the pressures, but I also bitterly regret it.

'Let us make it our resolve to live counter-culturally in a hard, unloving society, obeying the biblical injunctions to offer hospitality, to share our bread with the hungry, to welcome strangers and comfort the lonely – whether they're members of our own family or our neighbours, particularly the elderly. Secularism is morally and socially bankrupt. It cannot engender compassion, altruism or generosity, as it cannot change the human heart. It leaves a vacuum which Christianity can and must fill, for we value human life. We want the punitive, anti-proselytising laws that threaten the sharing of our faith and its values revoked – of course we do. But meanwhile, let's demonstrate that we hold the one and only key to a whole, healthy and caring community.'

The press had reported her words almost verbatim, impressed that she had eaten her Christmas dinner in a care home and spent part of Boxing Day in a homeless shelter, while Tom had been on duty at the hospital.

On 3 January, she was surprised to see Will Goodacre, the Bishop of Marchington, appear on her screen, a man whose gentle, dignified bearing belied a steely determination not to be messed with. In both Synod and in the House of Bishops she valued his sound judgement and support. But Will was not fond of modern technology and usually resorted to more traditional methods of phoning.

'Good morning, Archbishop. Well, I trust? A rather unusual Christmas, I gather. Joyous, nonetheless, I hope?'

She could do little more than nod before he continued, 'Forgive my contacting you so soon after the holiday, when you no doubt have many other things you'd rather be tackling, but I would value your advice. It concerns the rather . . . appalling situation that faced you in Larchester. It appears Marchington may have its own Wooten Grange.'

Vicky tutted and, supporting her chin between her thumb and first finger, leant further into the screen. The Bishop stretched across his desk, picked up a scrap of newspaper and put on his reading glasses.

'This came in just before the holiday:

> L.H. Properties is pleased to announce that the planning application for a major development on the Marchway estate was approved yesterday. The scheme represents a multi-billion-pound investment with 7,500 elite new homes, as well as 11.4 million square feet of offices, hotel and leisure space, a multiplex cinema, a shopping mall and casino.'

He paused a moment, removed his spectacles.

'I imagine you're aware that the Marchway is one of the most deprived areas in the diocese, with several thousand families facing severe challenges – and not a word about what happens to them in this grand scheme. These ideas have been talked about for a bit, but what we've got is on a huge scale. It will change the epicentre of the whole city.'

'All too familiar. Is there any mention of who's going to finance the scheme?'

'Yes, an India-based company, apparently.'

The Bishop put his spectacles back on and examined the press cutting.

'"Delhi Land and Leisure Construction", it says here. My secretary had a copy of the plan emailed over to us from the Council – nothing specific about social housing, despite the obligatory mention in the preamble.'

'No, not if they want to sell executive homes. It is a legal obligation, of course, but my suspicion is that there may be a very long wait.'

'What do you recommend we do?'

'Alert the press to your concerns. Protest in the strongest possible terms. I'll get my former press officer to send you our news releases. It's obviously not the same company, so maybe they'll deliver in the end. But be prepared and watch out for the bulldozers moving in.'

He looked at her sharply. 'I'm not sure what you mean.'

'If it goes off like Wooten Grange – and of course it may not – but if it does, the church needs to start planning right now. Childcare, food, accommodation, warm clothing, budgeting advice, whatever you can provide – it will be needed, I promise you. Have you got someone who can co-ordinate a response on that scale?'

He thought for a moment, then smiled.

'Yes, I think so. Eddie Macdonald. Local businessman and entrepreneur.'

'Send me his details and I'll put him in touch with the planning group in Larchester.'

'And those laws?'

'Oh, stuff the law, Bishop. At least, in situations like this.'

'Vicky, thank you,' he said, looking fully into her face for the first time. 'I must confess, I feel rather helpless.'

'One thing we're not, Will, is helpless. Or forsaken. May God give you wisdom.'

Wisdom was exactly what she would need for herself when, before the end of the week, the Church Commissioners imposed savage cuts on the Lambeth Palace household in their annual budget. They would be forced to reduce their spending by around a quarter, and that was bound to mean redundancies. Vicky hated the idea of disrupting the fragile efficiency of her staff team, all of them already under pressure to work harder and for longer hours than they should be asked to.

They knew roughly what was in the wind, but on the evening when the actual figures finally came through, Ralph had already left for home. Vicky was about to forward them, so that he could start work at once, then realised she had a meeting that evening just around the corner from his flat. It would be easier to go through them with him. Noah had been promised a night off, so she drove herself.

She feared that her driver must be one of the first to go. The new auto-drive navigation systems that enabled cars to take themselves to any destination, at least when they were talked to nicely, made his role unnecessary. Her heart sank at the prospect. Noah was an unobtrusive, often reassuring presence. And Dan had been right about one thing: she did appreciate the luxury of being able to work in the back while he drove, even though the rumours that the new car computers were by no means fool-proof and drivers were discovering themselves on the London Eye or in the Thames, were definitely apocryphal.

'I'll pop in quickly on my way home,' she said to Ralph. And that was all she had planned to do. Fifteen minutes, no more.

But as she rang the bell to the flat and the familiar voice on the intercom said, 'Come on up,' she felt a sudden, unanticipated surge of excitement at escaping from the Palace and her public persona, the responsibilities and restrictions. The last thing she wanted was to go back to that lonely flat in the vast Old Palace, empty as usual, with Tom out who knew where. And once inside Ralph's cosy, lamp-lit home, with Schubert playing in the background, and a bottle of her favourite claret open on the coffee table, the urge to throw off her shoes and ensconce herself in a corner of his comfortable, feather-stuffed settee was stronger than any voice of caution. She told herself that the staffing issue was urgent, that it was imperative she tell him about the Marchway estate development and set him off in search of the owners of Delhi Land and Leisure Construction. In reality, her most urgent need was for a taste of normality. The chance to do what every other middle-aged woman in the country could do – unwind, chat, relax and laugh a little.

It was after 2 a.m. when she looked at her watch and, with a start, got up to go.

'I'll call for a taxi,' Ralph said, clicking the screen in his hallway. 'And I'll bring your car to the Palace tomorrow.'

He accompanied her to the outside door. It was bitingly cold, and they stood on the doorstep with hands in pockets, stamping their feet, their breath two frosty streams of vapour intermingling in the chilly night air. The street was deserted and silent, its inhabitants burrowed in their beds behind closed curtains, the only light streaming out through the glass doors of the block of flats. They were alone. So how, for crying out loud, was that one, innocent, goodnight peck when the taxi arrived captured on camera to accompany the headline, 'Archbishop's Naughty Night of Nookie'?

'We'll vehemently deny any suggestion of a sexual encounter,' Sarah assured her.

'We most certainly will – since there wasn't one. The headline is libellous. Tell them we'll sue for defamation of character.'

'Would you?'

'Yes, absolutely. Except that we cannot defend the fact that I was at Ralph's flat until the early hours.'

Stupid, stupid, stupid, Vicky said to herself, biting her bottom lip as she studied the photo, and saw in close-up her lips pursed and pressed against Ralph's cheek. And then a thought occurred to her.

'Who took that photograph? Ask the newspaper where they got it, how they know my movements. Remind them of the phone-tapping business of a few years ago. Tell them, and any other paper that wants a comment, that we're making it a police matter.'

Sarah turned abruptly on her heels and left the study with renewed vigour in her step.

Vicky rested her head on her hands and rubbed her scalp with her fingertips. She was so heartily sick of it all – the constant negotiations with the media, the threats, the self-protection that forced her into the role of the bad-tempered termagant. Would she always have to be on the defensive, watching her front, her back, hedging her bets, restricting her every move, never knowing who was watching and waiting in the shadows, ready to stab her in the back? Or worse, which of her supposed friends would be looking out for ways to shaft her? As Bev had done. A betrayal that had almost paralysed her, the disbelief and pain were so great. How could anyone lie so deliberately and consummately? And then she thought of Kelvin. He had suffered a similar fate – and survived.

2016

Bishop Richard had called her at 8 a.m. – on her day off. Tom had groaned and turned over, while she had wrestled her way out of the bedclothes and fumbled, eyes resolutely shut with sleep, for the phone on the bedside table.

'Good morning, Vicky.'

'Good morning, Richard.'

She tried to keep the early morning crackedness out of her voice.

'Sorry to disturb your day off, but we have a rather tricky situation. Kelvin Craddock, vicar of St Martha's, on the Wellesdon estate?'

'Mmmmm.' Vicky groaned inside. 'I know exactly who you mean.'

'A seventeen-year-old, pregnant girl in his parish claims Kelvin's the father of her child. Conduct unbecoming. I've suspended him, and can't see him, of course, lest it prejudice our investigation. But he'll need support. Can you get over there?'

'I can't think he'll be pleased to see me, but I'm on my way.'

Well, well, well. Kelvin Craddock. Donald's voice resonated in her head just as she had heard it that night, so many months ago now, when she had called him in crisis and begged him to tell her what she must do to rediscover her peace. 'Serve your clergy, Vicky, including those you don't even like. The discipline of it, however numb you may feel at first, will eventually be your healing.'

She felt like Superwoman as she leapt out of bed, slipped on jeans and jumper, picked up the dog collar, then threw it back in the drawer. Too officious. She brushed her teeth, popped in her lenses, and put on a slick of mascara, then she pulled her hair up into a slide, grabbed her briefcase and crept downstairs. No sign of the car keys. Nothing for it – she had to wake Tom after all.

'Car keys?' she asked urgently, standing over his sleeping form.

'Where you left them,' he croaked irritably.

'No they're not,' she said, her voice rising in annoyance.

He sat up reluctantly, rubbing his eyes, and mumbled, 'Right-hand drawer of your dressing table.'

'I never put them in there.'

But there they certainly were. Tom made a strangulated 'told you so' sound.

'If you didn't put them there, how did you know where they were?' she snapped at him.

But he had lain down again and made no reply.

She hadn't seen much of Kelvin since the difficult "Meet the Archdeacon" session she had organised at the beginning of her time in the job, where he had been the source of much of her difficulty. He had gone out of his way to avoid her then, but she had managed to confront him as he tried to slip past on his way out.

'Hello Kelvin, long time no see. How are you these days?' she had asked, attempting to offer some kind of olive branch to the man.

'Not so bad,' he grunted, pushing past her, towards the door.

'Come on, Kelvin,' she had called after him, 'we're grown-ups. Let's be friends. Or if we can't manage that, we need to have a working relationship, at least.'

He had turned back, shrugged, and said, 'As you wish, Archdeacon.'

'Don't let Kelvin get to you.'

Standing next to her was a tall, pleasant-faced man with fair hair flicking up on his collar. He was casually dressed in well-fitting blue jeans, shirt sleeves rolled up to the elbows, jacquard sweater draped round his shoulders. So few clergy had that kind of effortless, unself-conscious style. So few had any style at all. He gave her a genial smile and held out his hand.

'Tim Hutchings. Likes to pretend he's a hard case, our Kelvin. Soft as curd cheese underneath. Know his story?'

She shook her head.

'Street-wise, a bit of a fighter, until the chaplain at Borstal took him under his wing and helped him turn his life around. Now vicar of Wellesdon, and that's as rough as they come. Not many would take it on. So we forgive God's little vessel his jagged edges.'

'Don't judge a book by its cover?'

Tim inclined his head.

'Thanks, I'll remember that.'

'Let me know if you have any problems with him.'

'You'll sort him out for me? You think I need a minder?'

He looked at her out of the corner of his eye, then grinned broadly.

'Oh, I expect you can take care of yourself.'

'But I'd like to get through to him.'

'Ah, feminine determination. Can't resist a challenge,' Tim teased, but in a winsome way, so that she couldn't help but laugh.

'But would it get you anywhere?'

'Probably not,' she agreed. 'But that won't stop me trying.'

Despite her good intentions, however, she and Kelvin had spent years stalking around each other in a sort of stand-off, like two cats vying for the same patch.

She was at St Martha's in twenty-five minutes, thankful that few other fools were out and about at this time on a drizzly Saturday morning. The vicarage stood in splendid isolation on a large, treeless, mud-and-grass island covered in litter, broken glass and dog mess, overlooked by high-rise blocks on three of its sides. It was an ugly, red-brick monstrosity, surrounded by a heavily graffitied ten-foot wall, topped with decorative spikes of glass set in concrete. The lurid blue front door matched the drainpipes. The word 'pervert' had already been sprayed in red, next to the gate.

The door was opened, slowly, suspiciously, by Glenda, Kelvin's wife. In the dismal early morning light, her eyes were two dark hollows sunken into a pale, pinched little face. A small woman anyway, she appeared to have shrivelled into defeat. She pulled her cardigan tightly around her front, and with a nod, beckoned Vicky to follow her into a gloomy, musty-smelling hallway. 'Archdeacon, Kelvin,' she announced, unceremoniously, pushing open the door into their sitting room, making way for Vicky and closing it behind her, leaving her in the lion's cage.

Kelvin was slouched in an armchair, his eyes red-rimmed, a heavy grey stubble speckling his head and chin. She sat down in the armchair opposite him until he finally looked up at her, a bleak expression on his face.

'Come to gloat?' he asked, averting his eyes.

'What do you think? No, Kelvin. I've come to see if there's anything I can do.'

He snorted.

'Nothing you or anyone can do. An ex-con is always an ex-con, no matter how long ago or how much good you've tried to do since. You'll never believe me, whatever I say, so just bugger off out of it . . . Archdeacon.'

Vicky knew that the couple had had an outstanding ministry in one of the most deprived, soul-destroying estates in the country. Behind the belligerent, abrasive exterior, the man cared passionately and deeply for the local people, feeding dozens of hungry kids every Sunday, housing people when they were homeless, refusing any improvements or creature comforts here in the vicarage, when it already looked so grand compared to the rest of the neighbourhood; and perhaps knowing anything new would only get trashed anyway. She was filled with a sudden determination that if Kelvin was innocent and it lay within her power, she wasn't going to let him, or the church, be robbed of such dedication.

'There's nothing I can do if you don't tell me exactly what's going on. So try me.'

He sighed, but for the first time a degree of animation surfaced in his voice.

'She came round to drop in the PCC minutes. Her mother's the PCC secretary. Made up to the nines. Seventeen going on twenty-seven. She asked for a glass of water. I never let any kids in on their own, but what could I do? I stood her in the hallway, closed the inner door, and went to the kitchen to get her a drink. When I turned round, she was there. She'd followed me in. She made a kind of clumsy attempt to come on to me, poor kid. But I shoved her off and told her to find someone her own age. She yelled and screamed a bit, threw the water at me, bless her, but eventually took herself off.'

Vicky was struck by Kelvin's apparent compassion for the girl. His lack of hostility was not only commendable, it convinced her, possibly against her better judgement, of his innocence.

'And where does she claim the encounter happened?'

'She says I took her up to the bedroom.'

'Show me.'

Kelvin raised his eyebrows in surprise. He got up with apparent reluctance and led Vicky upstairs.

'Don't be shocked, Archdeacon,' he said on the way up.

'Vicky,' she corrected him, wondering what was to come.

It was a stale-smelling, cheerless room, painted in a lurid emerald green that ate up any light from the low window. But filling one wall was a painting – a large, almost Salvador Dali collection of cubes in pink, blue and beige. Glenda, unmistakeably. Naked.

'She was quite a looker,' Kelvin said, following her gaze.

'She certainly was,' Vicky agreed, doubting that any man could have sex with another woman with his wife's body so flagrantly on display. Unless . . . she wasn't a total innocent when it came to men's fetishes, but somehow, it seemed unlikely.

'Did you paint it?'

He nodded.

'It's good. Very good.'

'How many months till this baby's born?' she asked on the way back down to the front door.

'Four. A DNA test will soon show that I'm not the dad. But will that be enough to convince anyone I didn't have sex with her?'

An idea began to form in Vicky's mind.

'Maybe not,' she said, as she left him standing on the doorstep. 'But there could be a way to convince them. Don't despair, Kelvin.'

He shrugged, went back into the house, and closed the door without looking round.

It was Vicky's responsibility to explain to the small congregation in Kelvin's church the following Sunday why their vicar was 'on leave'. With every fibre of her being she had to fight the urge to say, 'Don't judge.' Instead, watching a multiple of reactions settle on the faces – shock, confusion, disgust, or plain sorrow – she simply promised a full investigation and urged them to wait until all the facts were known.

She said a similar thing to the press, aware that it was a fatuous waste of time. Kelvin was going to be assumed guilty until proven otherwise. But she was determined that was exactly what she was going to do.

Gathering evidence against colleagues for a clergy tribunal was not a favourite part of her job. So much was at stake, and she had seen several excellent priests fall foul of temptation and find themselves out in the cold. It was imperative she see the girl and take a statement. And so she ended up with the diocesan solicitor at her side, sitting on a large, shiny, dog-eaten settee, facing the heavily pregnant young woman and her larger-than-life mother.

'Donna, where did this assault take place?' she asked.

'In the bedroom, of course,' said the mother without hesitation.

'Describe the room to me, Donna, will you?' Vicky asked.

'It had four walls, a window and a bed in it, for crying out loud,' the mother responded.

'Donna?'

The girl simply nodded, without looking up.

'Was there anything on those walls?'

The mother opened her mouth, then shut it quickly, silenced for once. The girl shook her head.

'Donna, you were never in that room, were you?'

'It must have taken place elsewhere, then,' barked the mother. 'Tell her, Donna.'

The girl began to cry silently. After a while Vicky said gently, 'Would you like to withdraw your accusation, Donna?'

The girl nodded again.

When the baby was born a DNA test proved conclusively that Kelvin was not the father and the investigation could finally be dropped.

Meanwhile, Kelvin had lost his confidence, his reputation, privacy, mental and emotional well-being and five months of his life and ministry. Though he appeared to bear the girl no ill will.

'Terrified of what that battle-axe of a mother would say, poor kid. So she made up the story, never thinking the mother would see it as a potential gold mine.'

As Vicky said goodbye to him and they stood face to face in the vicarage on the day that his name was cleared at last, she gave in to a sudden instinct to reach out and put her arms around him. He stiffened at first, then relaxed into her embrace, his face pressed into her shoulder to hide the tears.

'You know,' he said, pulling back from her and rubbing his face vigorously, 'I always thought you were a bit up yourself. And that pink car of yours just confirmed it. But now you'd better get out there before some bright spark lets your tyres down, or decides to nick it altogether.'

'Couldn't resist it,' she said, ruefully. 'Shall I change my image?'

'No. Stay just the way you are. Thank you, Vicky,' he added quietly.

'You still owe me a pair of slippers, by the way,' she flung back at him as she headed to her car.

A few months later Vicky was asked to be Bishop of Larchester, and she asked Kelvin to join her there. He needed a new start, and she needed a man of compassion and integrity to be her chaplain.

2022

On those mornings when she was tempted to stay in bed and pull the sheets over her head, it was only the memory of that victory, with its ultimate triumph of truth, and the restoration of an apparently irretrievable relationship, that had the power to strengthen Vicky's determination not to give in to bullying, brow-beating or her own self-pity and paranoia.

When they met a few days after the 'Naughty Nookie' headline had appeared, the Queen patted her hand: the first real physical contact between them.

'Ah,' she reflected, 'your recent experiences remind me of my *annus horribilis* some thirty years ago. Such mess and mayhem in the family. Much of it compounded by the press.'

'I know there were family problems, but I don't think people remember it now,' Vicky said, in an attempt to reassure Her Majesty, 'and I suppose that's true of most difficulties. "This too will pass."'

'They do indeed. But one wonders how the photographers so cleverly manage to present a perfectly ordinary expression as a grimace in order to support the notion that one is displeased. Ah well, we survive. And so will you, Archbishop. We have always admired your inner strength.'

The tears came to Vicky's eyes. She couldn't prevent it. She blinked them away, embarrassed.

'About that matter we spoke of a while back,' the Queen said, tactfully changing the subject. 'The Prime Minister has at last briefed us fully on the matter, alerting us, as he so kindly put it, to any possible fall-out. Since we are Defender of the Faith, one might say it was a little late, I feel. How many of our clergy might be affected? What might it cost the church in fines?'

'We're not sure of the implications at the moment, but if there are fines, I imagine the church would have to foot the bill, which in the end, these days, can only mean the people in the pews. But my soundings tell me many clergy would rather go to prison than sacrifice freedom of conscience, not merely on their own behalf, but in order to establish the vital principle of free speech in this great democracy of ours.'

'Quite so. And very laudable. But how likely is it that calls for disestablishment would follow?'

'I think it highly likely, Ma'am.'

The Queen sat back and took a deep breath. She remained deep in thought for a while, then shook herself and said, 'Really, Archbishop, we don't think this can be tolerated – an attack on an ancient institution of which we are the Supreme Governor. Are we to have no say, when our ministers are robbed of their right to conscientious objection and are then threatened with the power of the state?'

The enormity of the implications left Vicky stunned and temporarily speechless. One could hardly say to the monarch, 'Do you realise what you're saying?'

'Ma'am,' she tried hesitantly, after a while, 'are you suggesting triggering a constitutional crisis?'

'Archbishop, we know what we are suggesting.'

No room for argument, Vicky said to herself, feeling as if she had been slapped on the wrist.

'Remind me,' said the Queen, 'who was it who said, "The only thing necessary for the triumph of evil is for good men to do nothing."'

'It's attributed to the philosopher Edmund Burke, Ma'am, but there is little evidence that he actually said it. It became more widely known when Dietrich Bonhoeffer used it in his brave stand against the Nazis.'

'Of course, of course,' she said with a knowing smile, 'exactly so.'

For a moment Vicky thought she detected something close to a twinkle in the Queen's eye.

'We cannot, of course, compare ourselves with such great men, but at my age, one rather rejoices at the chance to make a few waves.'

'Ma'am?'

'Archbishop, I am ninety-six. How much longer can I reign?'

'By God's grace, a while longer . . .'

She silenced Vicky with a wave.

'No need for indulgence, Archbishop. We are prepared for whatever will be. But one wonders whether perhaps it isn't some kind of test, or perhaps a special grace, to be given such an opportunity at this late stage.'

She rose, with extraordinary briskness, from her chair.

'We will wait to assess the response of our people, of course, but we must also be seen to support our Archbishop, must we not?'

Vicky felt her heart sink. The last thing she needed was to be seen as the influence behind the throne. As if reading her thoughts, the Queen added, almost playfully, 'But have no fear. We shall be sure to let it be known that this is our decision and ours alone.'

This time there was a definite gleam in her eye.

'We have no intention of sharing this . . . historic moment.'

She lost her balance slightly as she reached for the stick hooked over her chair. Vicky went to her rescue, and took hold of her arm. Her hand was shaken off determinedly. But as she stood close to this diminutive, frail yet dignified woman, she couldn't stop herself from giving her a quick, peremptory hug, before the Queen pulled back abruptly, her face showing a mixture of surprise and perhaps the slightest glow of pleasure.

'So sorry, Ma'am,' she said, 'but you see, you are so greatly loved that it gets harder by the moment for your people not to show it.'

Vicky returned to Lambeth feeling deeply concerned. Had she advised her monarch wisely and well? Surely she had barely had the chance? The Queen's personal well-being mattered to her enormously, and she couldn't decide what impact a constitutional crisis might have on her monarch's popularity, and consequently her happiness. But the Queen appeared deeply contented with whatever her lot might be henceforth. And who was Vicky to discourage her from doing what she manifestly saw as her duty – a last, memorable, moral obligation?

Ralph, for his part, was concerned only for Vicky's reputation. He had the 'Naughty Nookie' press cutting on his desk.

'I don't think your press officer does enough to protect you,' he said, as they examined it together, their heads too close for comfort. She stood back from him, painfully aware now of the need to put a certain distance between them both.

'The blame game, Ralph?' she asked him. 'Not you too. What could she have done? We shouldn't have been so stupid. And anyway, the truth will protect me – however long we have to wait for it to come out.'

'You can be so naive, Archbishop. Who cares about the truth these days?'

'So cynical?'

'So honest.'

'Never lose confidence in the truth, Ralph.'

She studied the photograph again.

'But how did anyone know I was at your flat? I didn't see anyone in the street that night. Did you?'

He shook his head.

'There isn't a time I haven't thought about it in the last couple of days. There is CCTV outside, of course.'

'But who would take the trouble to watch it?'

He swivelled round on his desk chair to face her, fiddling with his pen. 'There might be a reason. Let me explain where I've got to with my investigations into Wooten Grange and its new counterpart up north. Yes – I have made one or two discoveries about our new friends, Delhi Land and Leisure Constructions. Company law is hugely complex, as you're probably aware. I've been chasing up old contacts from my days in the city – some, shall we say, a little broader in their application of moral criteria than others. Word gets around amongst the fraternity.'

'And?' Vicky pushed him.

'I didn't want you to worry. But I'm beginning to wonder whether there isn't some connection with . . . this,' he said, waving at the photograph on his desk.

Vicky felt slightly queasy and pulled up a chair opposite him.

'BLEO is a South American company, as it purports to be. And DLLC is a bona fide Indian firm. But behind them both lies the same silent partner – or perhaps partners. British, I think; and with the know-how needed to negotiate all the legal wrangling entailed in such a vast project, and the ability to manipulate all the powers that be in their favour.'

'This is beginning to sound like a political thriller.'

'Don't mock. When it comes to business crime, fact has always been more ingenious than fiction.'

'So who is, or are, these silent manipulators?'

'Every time I get anywhere near finding who or what might have some connection with A.T. Developments, or this new parent company, L.H. Properties, otherwise known as Lakshmi Holdings, the trail goes cold and he, she, whatever, disappears into the ether without footprint, finger-mark or any trace.'

Vicky started.

'Lakshmi? You did say Lakshmi?'

Ralph's eyes widened as the import of the name slowly dawned upon him.

'Another goddess?'

Vicky nodded.

'My contacts have no knowledge of the Athena Corporation either, for that matter.'

'Sometimes, I . . .' she began.

He shook his head in disbelief.

'Paranoia maybe, over-reaction probably, but I sometimes feel as if my computer has been tampered with, or that I'm being watched.'

Vicky felt a sudden chill in the room, and shivered.

'Be careful, Ralph, won't you?'

'I'm sorry. I told you I didn't want to alarm you. But I'll find out who these sods are – if it's the last thing I do.'

Meanwhile, the government announced its intention to rescind the 'quadruple lock' legislation that forbade Church of England clergy from performing same-sex marriages, and, indeed, to introduce new measures that would enforce the performing of the same as a duty on every religious faith and denomination. As the Bill then made its tortuous way through the Commons and the Lords, both government and country were deeply divided between those who saw the change as a threat to the basic human right to freedom of thought and expression, and those who proclaimed delight at the church being brought to heel at last. The media dithered between the two, as it sought to gauge the public mood, largely conceding that the clergy could not be forced to act against their moral conscience, but attributing that 'conscience' to institutional homophobia.

In the House of Lords Vicky said that the church was certainly anxious, but by no means cowed, at the threat to its liberty. 'Article 19 of the Universal Declaration of Human Rights, which is legally binding on member states, guarantees "everyone the right to freedom of opinion and expression; this right includes freedom to hold opinions without interference . . ." If the European Court of Human Rights, at some point in the future, decides against ministers of religion on this matter, which I imagine will be extremely unlikely, since gay marriage is no more than a cherry on a cake, bestowing no new rights that gay men and women do not already have in civil partnerships, it will not change our determination to follow our conscience in this matter. For this legislation is the thin end of a dangerous wedge that threatens our very democracy.'

The bill had the narrowest of majorities in the Commons, the government's whip eroded by a vociferous back-bench revolt. And for the first time in history a bill was unanimously defeated in the Lords, who, acting in their capacity as protectors of the constitution, rejected it as a threat to the key principle of human rights, and went so far as to send a delegation to the Commons to say so. A furious Home Secretary announced that the government would invoke the Parliament Act to override the Lords and push it through regardless. Pundits began to talk about the nation teetering on the brink of a constitutional crisis.

NINETEEN

In every no of God there is a hidden yes. In every end there is a beginning. If you are seeking it, it will find you.

JÜRGEN MOLTMANN

MARCH 2022

Cook's night off. The BBC 7 news hummed in the background as Vicky prepared the evening meal in the kitchen, waiting for Tom to come home. Her notes for the lecture she was to give the following morning on 'Faith, Human Rights and Dignity' for the International Ecumenical Development Agency lay on the counter next to the chopping board, so that she could have a quick run-through. Tom swore that one of these days he'd find a fingertip in his casserole.

Subconsciously, she noticed that the timbre of the voices had changed, had become more urgent, excited. She raised her eyes to the screen, and saw the familiar face of the royal correspondent, standing outside Buckingham Palace. She grabbed the remote and turned up the volume. It passed through her mind that the remote would now stink of onions, but blow it, this was more important. It appeared that the Queen had taken the opportunity of a joint appearance with the Prime Minister at an event in the City of London to celebrate the unique qualities of the British constitution and her commitment to the charge to uphold the freedom of her people in their personal and religious lives, even 'as I have shared privately with the Prime Minister' in the face of a secularising government that might threaten to ride roughshod over issues of personal conscience. It was being read as a clear signal that she had previously summoned the Prime Minister to Buckingham Palace and advised him that as Head of State she would be unable to support legislation that the Lords deemed a contravention of the British constitution.

The correspondent explained that as the monarch, with a history stretching back centuries, the Queen represented the British nation in a way transitory politicians never could. However, no monarch in the past few hundred years had ever intervened, in their constitutional role as supreme arbiter, in matters of government to the extent of refusing the Royal Assent. So in indicating so clearly that she would do this, and in making it public, Her Majesty had made an unprecedented commitment, confident as she was in the resistance of most of the electorate to a move for which they hadn't been given the chance to vote.

'You did it, Ma'am,' Vicky whispered to herself, as news analysis suggested that the government would have to wait for the Queen's death and the succession of a new king before any further legislation on the matter could be brought. She felt a little like one of her predecessors, Archbishop Cosmo Lang, rumoured to have schemed to ensure that Edward VIII abdicated in favour of his brother, George IV, because George was a man who shared his moral values. But she had not schemed. The Queen had needed no persuading.

'Looks as if the clergy are not going to be imprisoned after all, at least not for another few years,' she said to Tom as he walked through the door.

'Good,' he said, coming up behind her and sliding his hands around her waist.

'I didn't fancy having to bring your favourite Pinot Grigio to Wandsworth.'

Vicky's video glasses bleeped on the kitchen table and Tom reluctantly released her. The Archbishop of York.

'Well done, girl,' he enthused. 'We seem to have cracked it.'

'I wouldn't put it quite like that. Perhaps a little overt persecution wouldn't have been such a bad thing. Given us the chance to explain to the people what we believe and why our faith matters to us so much.'

He sighed.

'You're made of tougher stuff than I am. Give me the quiet life. But all power to the old Queen's elbow.'

'She has taken an enormous risk.'

'Did you know?'

Vicky remained quiet, motioned with a hand, as inconspicuously as she could, to alert Tom to the need to stir the casserole.

'You did. And said nothing?'

The Archbishop sounded a little peevish.

'I couldn't. You know that. Besides, I wasn't altogether sure. Do you . . .?'

She paused, unsure how to phrase the question.

'You don't think people will imagine I put her under pressure, do you? I really don't want that. Because it isn't true.'

Tom, stirring vigorously, pointed at his watch, and then at his open mouth. She had an engagement to go to.

'You are made of fairly persuasive stuff. But no, I think the nation knows by now that behind her gracious demeanour, our monarch is also one determined lady.'

Vicky felt a sense of relief, the tension in the pit of her stomach diminishing.

'Thanks,' she said to the Archbishop. 'Must go. Have to give a welcome talk to the new students at the Holy Trinity Brompton Christian University. Haven't eaten yet.'

Plenty of noisy, strident republicans and secularists held forth on the news and – to some degree – in the streets, but the mood of the nation was clear: they might not fully understand the issues, but they rallied around their beloved, elderly monarch. The government withdrew the bill, and, unable to recover from such serious damage to their authority, soon lost a vote of no confidence in the House. A general election was called.

Vicky contacted Liam to say her farewells.

'To gloat?' he asked her. He had refused to appear on screen.

'I cannot gloat, Liam, not with the press I've had myself,' she said, 'though I do feel that a blow has been struck for human dignity and freedom.'

'Blow you and your freedom. I have no doubt the next census will show that religion is still on the decline in this country. It is time that public policy caught up and stopped privileging religious groups. They are increasingly irrelevant to British life and any government will accept that fact.'

'Even if the census does show a decline in religious belief, it would be very unwise not to recognise the contribution to national life of those who do still believe.'

'We'll see,' he said.

'We certainly shall.'

A general election gave Vicky just the breathing space she needed. An archbishop has a moral obligation not to make any political statements during an election campaign. It would have been grossly irresponsible to sway the voters, whether or not she had swayed the Queen.

But now was a good time to plan the protest against the anti-prose-lytising laws. What she needed was someone with first-rate organisational and pastoral skills to draw in key religious leaders from across the nation, someone with the wisdom of Solomon, the patience of Job, the prophetic power of Isaiah, and the crusading zeal of the Apostle Paul. Kelvin. His years as her chaplain in Larchester had done much to equip him for the task.

Kelvin, who had never fitted in in Larchester since the change of helmsman, accepted the post with alacrity, and soon they were drawing up plans to make the greatest possible impact.

'A festival, not a protest rally, that's what we need, Kelvin. A carnival – like the gay pride march, only better. But with the colour, the noise, the floats, and the banners, the best bands and dancers, and street performers. Like the great Old Testament pilgrim festivals in Jerusalem, when the Israelites marched up to the Temple. And everyone will see it, and hopefully, be tempted to join us. If we want people to take a day's holiday from work we'd better make it worth their while.'

'Wait – that's it!' said Kelvin. 'We'll ask for a strike from voluntary work – as long as real emergencies are covered and no one is without food or care for twenty-four hours. Let's bring the welfare state to a standstill, so that whichever government is in power will realise how beholden they are to our goodwill.'

'We don't do welfare to be seen, Kelvin.'

'No, of course not, but let it be a thank-you to all those thousands of volunteers, a chance to celebrate their achievements. Everyone needs appreciation.'

'And other faiths?'

'We will bend over backwards to welcome them, of course.'

It soon turned into a massive operation – one she was relieved to leave entirely in Kelvin's hands.

She should have known it was all going too well. A tabloid, hungry for a story that wasn't about electioneering, chose that moment to run with the lie she had worked so hard to repudiate several years ago as a bishop. And they ran it as fact, on page one, with an old photograph of Bev, head down, her hand half masking her face, the victim: a very picture of misery. And Vicky, next to it, in full archiepiscopal finery, looking every inch the proud churchwoman taking the moral high ground. She sat studying the article for some time, as if it might contain a clue as to how this could have happened, too devastated to get up from her desk. These character slurs were difficult enough for her to take, let alone Tom. So belittling for a man to watch his mate violated and scorned, and be unable to protect her.

She called Sarah back into her office.

'This is outrageous,' she fumed, slamming the paper on her desk. 'We had a retraction and an apology several years ago. So where has this nonsense come from? Has Bev Aldridge gone back to them? Would that allow them to print this monstrous rubbish?'

'They're probably piqued at being beaten to the last good story,' she muttered.

Vicky frowned and shook her head.

'Naughty Nookie,' Sarah explained. 'and revenge for your stance on gay marriage.'

'Tell me why my sex life is of such interest to the general public.'

'Because you're Archbishop?' Sarah hit back. 'That's like being the Virgin Mary.' Vicky had never seen her so harassed. 'I'll find out what's going on, Archbishop,' she said, taking a deep breath and blowing it out loudly, as she reached for her e-phone.

'Whatever happens, I'll always be there for you,' Vicky repeated to herself, when Sarah had left the room. She threw herself onto one of the settees. She could see Bev so clearly as she'd been on the day of her ordination – bright, bold, cheekily brash, manhandling Tom and the large bouquet out of her way so that she could be close to Vicky, holding the crook of her arm. What had happened to that Bev, the woman she'd known so well and loved? What had Vicky not seen?

2015

She had heard nothing from Bev for years, though she and Mandy still spoke from time to time, and had lunched in London once or twice. Then, towards the end of her time as archdeacon, there was a surprise message on her answer machine – Bev demanding they meet as soon as possible. Vicky should have been glad to hear from her, but instead her heart sank. She called Mandy to find out whether she had any inkling of what it was all about. She hadn't.

'I'd always hoped she'd bring Sandra back to see us,' Vicky said, 'but she never did.'

'I think the relationship wasn't all Bev wanted us to believe it was. She was embarrassed,' Mandy said. 'They were still together, last I heard, but that was a couple of years ago, and I think it was more limping along by then.'

'And how's juggling a full-time job with two children?' Vicky asked her.

'You don't need me to tell you. But they're fine. Growing fast. When are you and Tom coming to see us?'

'I'd love to, but weekend work makes it a tad difficult.'

'A bummer where friendship is concerned.'

Vicky promised she would do her best, knowing, even as she said it, that it was unlikely. How would they ever find a date that worked for all their diaries?

'Let me know how you get on with Bev, won't you?'

She met Bev at the London Review Cake Shop, on the basis that, since the conversation was likely to be trying, she might as well enjoy the cake.

'How's Sandra?' she asked, as they walked through a passage in the bookshop's history section to its jewel of a teashop beyond, and found a table in a secluded corner.

Bev frowned. She was dressed in an open-necked shirt, and jeans that emphasised her boyish hips. The crop had grown into a short, shiny auburn bob that was much softer on the face.

'You look great, by the way,' Vicky said. 'Very un-doctorish.'

'What's that supposed to mean?'

Vicky was taken aback at how aggressive she sounded. Or perhaps it was simply defensive.

'Women GPs, like women vicars, are hardly renowned for their chic,' Vicky said.

Bev gave a small snort, and announced, 'It's all off with Sandra.'

'Why? I really liked her.'

'It wasn't working,' she snapped. 'And anyway, because of Celia. I wanted you to know in case there's any fall-out – which could affect you.'

Vicky began to wonder whether the venue was a good idea after all. The sight of mouth-watering, homemade cakes, normally so desirable, was beginning to make her feel slightly queasy.

'Who's Celia? And what fall-out?' she asked uneasily, as the tea, a large chocolate brownie and a luscious piece of carrot cake were brought to their table. 'Why should it affect me?'

'Celia, my practice nurse. She was married to a clergyman. It's caused a bit of a furore in the local press. It – well, it might lead back to you.'

The tightening in the pit of Vicky's stomach intensified.

'What's it got to do with me?'

'I'd like to tell the papers we have the support of an archdeacon.'

'We?' Vicky put down her cake fork, eyeing the chocolate brownie, which sat on her plate, suddenly inedible.

'Celia and I. She's my new partner now, you see.'

Over the past few years, as curate, vicar and archdeacon, Vicky had been subjected to deception, manipulation and verbal abuse, but nothing compared to this. She found herself trying to muster every technique she could remember to keep her anger in check. Inhaling deeply, she said, 'Why on earth would you bring me into it, Bev? Why mention me at all?'

'Because of . . .'

Bev played with the cake on her plate.

'The way that church of hers treated her, their homophobic attitude – it makes me so mad. I think we deserve some support, the help of a friend in high places.'

Vicky was speechless for a while. She had a strong urge to slap Bev, but treating her as the child she appeared to be would only provoke a child-like tantrum. So she marshalled every ounce of reasoned calm she possessed and said, in the most measured way she could manage, 'One, I'm not, as you call it, in "high places". I do a dogsbody, practical job. Two, your sexual orientation does not make adultery acceptable. And three, you have no right to presume on how I would feel or what I could say to the press in your favour.'

Bev stared back at her sullenly.

'Principles before people, eh Vicky? Self-righteous as ever, that's what I expected, really. Maybe that's why I dropped you in it.'

It was Vicky's turn to feel as if she had been slapped. All she wanted was to be true to her ideals. Was that so unacceptable?

'There is nothing wrong with principles, Bev,' she fought back. 'Everyone needs them. I'd never turn away from you, or Celia either, or deny you both a welcome in my home. But you're asking me to publicly condone adultery. And I can't do that. What about Sandra? What about Celia's husband? How must they feel?'

Bev went on fiddling with the cake on her plate, mashing it into tiny crumbs, before collecting them together, pressing them onto the back of her fork and shoving them into her mouth.

'Our friendship means nothing to you, does it?'

'Oh Bev, how can you say so? This job costs me friends all the time, and I can't afford to lose a single one. You and I go back a long way, and I've always loved you.'

'Why can't you be happy for me, then? I've two stepsons now.'

'How old?' Vicky asked, trying to smile, but her heart sank at the thought of the turmoil inflicted on two innocent children.

'Seven and five. And we plan to have at least one of our own.'

This was so much to absorb in one afternoon that she began to feel she had mental and spiritual, as well as actual, indigestion. Even so, she couldn't stop herself asking, 'Is all this best for the children? Taking them from their father?'

'What would they miss? I've never needed one,' Bev said sourly.

Her words brought Vicky up with a start.

'But your father, your brothers? You always seemed such a close family.'

'Close is about right. My brothers – well, the older two anyway, sexually abused me – for five years,' she said flatly.

Vicky's eyes opened wide. She stared at her friend.

'Oh Bev, I'm so, so sorry. I had no idea. All these years and you never said. Did you ever tell anyone?'

'My mother. Told me my imagination was as filthy as a French public toilet and my mouth like a furnace in hell. Said if I ever repeated anything like that again, she'd beat the living daylights out of me. All that ever mattered to her was her lads.'

'But you never told us.'

'No one talked about it in those days. Like you never told us your mother was a drunk. Though we all knew.'

Vicky was shaken, but she banished the distraction, forced herself to focus on Bev.

'Yes, she was. But there were reasons. There always are. We were too young to understand. No one could have rescued me, any more than we could have helped you, had we known. But I made my peace with her at the end. Have you spoken to your mother about it since? Had any . . . support?'

'Counselling? No,' she said, scrunching up her serviette and throwing it on the table. 'Counselling's for the patients. I handle my own stuff my own way.'

Vicky opened her mouth to protest, then thought better of it as she saw Bev reach for her bag. She sincerely hoped Bev's patients received more compassion than she did. But since it seemed like Vicky was the preferred choice of punch-ball, they probably did.

At least Bev paid the bill this time, tight-lipped, brusque, thrusting the change into her purse without making eye contact with the woman running the teashop.

'Was everything okay, ladies?'

Vicky nodded and mouthed a grateful thank-you, thinking that everything was certainly not okay. She grieved for the appalling abuse Bev had suffered and for the pain it so obviously still caused her, for the friendship they had once had, and for the victims caught in the crossfire of her new relationship. And now there was the added worry of a possible call from the press.

'Would you marry Celia and me?' Bev asked wryly on the way out. 'No, of course not. Silly me,' she said, slinging her bag over her shoulder as she stalked off.

An invitation to Bev and Celia's 'wedding' arrived a few months later – a civil partnership, with a supplementary blessing borrowed from a Californian church to be hosted by some rogue vicar. Bev had obviously informed the press that Vicky planned to attend, because her phone rang incessantly. Amidst all the confusing international political stories and interminably dreary bank crises, the tabloids were delighted to be presented with the story of a vicar's wife, seduced by her lesbian doctor boss, who was a close friend of that well-known cleric and media commentator, the Archdeacon of Westhampton. Any endorsement would rekindle the church's own homosexuality debate and embarrass Vicky's superiors. But no endorsement was forthcoming. The archdeacon simply told the diocesan press officer to say it was a private matter. Without a statement from her, the newsworthiness of the scandal shrank exponentially. And Vicky sincerely hoped it would go away for good.

She and Tom did attend the ceremony, however. In her earlier days as archdeacon she had had her own, very private, little tussle with temptation, one she would rather forget. But having stared into the abyss, and been dragged back from the brink by divine mercy, she hardly felt in any position to judge. The guilt of it still stalked her like a lion its prey. Tom didn't know, must never know how nearly she had betrayed his trust.

The photographers were out in force, looking out for her. Dog-collarless, she held the brim of her hat protectively over her face, and clung to Tom's hand. Apart from the pleasure of catching up with Mandy, it was a rather held-in, cheerless affair, Celia's family and friends having mostly refused to attend, in support of her abandoned husband. Those who did, looked out of place and ill at ease, remaining on the fringe of the group. Vicky's heart went out to Celia's two bewildered-looking little boys.

She heard no more until she was a bishop. But the call, when it came, was inevitable, and she was prepared.

'Why won't you marry us and bless our union, when Celia makes me so happy?' Bev pleaded. 'We've been together a while now.'

'You know, Bev, that I'm not officially allowed to, even if I wanted to.'

'But you could break ranks, for a friend. Be a little radical for a change. As the first woman bishop, you're supposed to be a trailblazer.'

'The implications are too enormous to consider. I'm glad Celia makes you happy, Bev, but I'm a Christian, not an existentialist. Happiness isn't the barometer of what's right.'

'I can't believe you could be so unloving.'

'Bev, you know that's not the issue. I do love you – but let me remind you that Celia was married to someone else when you started your relationship. She loved him, then. That matters. Her children matter.'

At which point, the phone went dead.

Vicky sat for some time afterwards, twisting and turning the thing in her mind, testing her conscience. Could she ever budge, for Bev? The unambiguity of the Bible on the sacrament of monogamous, male–female marriage was inescapable. Jesus did not condemn the woman committing adultery. But he did tell her to stop. Obedience was no easy option. As if she didn't know it. And she had done her best to live out what she believed, even if it had taken every ounce of determination she possessed.

In the end, she feared in her heart that as much as, or more than Vicky's approval, what Bev wanted was to be seen to have won her personal battle against Vicky's traditional views and the church she saw as coming between their friendship. That victory might come through forcing Vicky to bend to her desires, or by exposing her to ridicule; it wasn't entirely clear if she truly cared which. As the first female bishop, every charity across the country wanted the acknowledgement that Vicky's support would give them. Being used for other people's purposes seemed to come with the job.

Two or three weeks later, Mike Barnes, her press officer, came into her study looking grave.

'I've had a call, Bishop, from a journalist who wanted to know whether you knew a Dr Bev Aldridge in 1983?'

'Yes, we were at school together. Close friends. Still are. In some ways.'

Vicky felt the usual knot of apprehension forming in the pit of her stomach when Bev's name was mentioned, but nothing further seemed to come of the enquiry, so she heaved a sigh of relief and put it out of her mind.

The next day there was a meeting with the local Christian gay and lesbian group in the diary. Nothing untoward happened, and Vicky was able to engage in what seemed to be quite a positive question-and-answer session at the end.

The day after that Mike stood in front of her desk with a small press cutting in his hand, looking slightly sheepish. It was a tiny diary piece from one of the tabloids. She took it from his hand and read, 'It's not surprising the Bishop understands the difficulties faced by gay men and women when she herself engaged in a rather intimate relationship with a female friend in her teenage years.'

It felt as if a lead weight had been dropped from a great height onto her head.

'Is this saying what I think it is?'

'That your relationship with Bev was rather more than friendship? I'm afraid so. I've had calls from various newspapers, as you'd expect, but this one is now demanding a full interview. After all, what wouldn't it give to be the one to knock the church's episcopal golden girl off her pedestal?'

Vicky was so flabbergasted she could hardly speak.

'But it's complete and absolute nonsense.'

'The journalist claims he has a sworn allegation in writing.'

'That doesn't mean it happened.'

'My advice would be to deny the allegations off the record in the strongest possible terms, then sit tight and ignore the whole thing. That way, it's more likely to stay a diary piece.'

'No. If I ignore this, they'll still go public on Bev's say-so. Even if they don't, it will always be there, at the back of their minds, poisoning everything I do, because they'll all be assuming that my integrity is a sham. I can't leave stuff like this in their cupboard – a little nugget to be launched like a grenade just when they feel the moment is right. Ask to see the allegation, will you, Mike? Let's see what she's saying.'

That evening, as she and Tom finished their meal, she said, carefully, 'The papers seem to be suggesting I had some sort of homosexual encounter as a teenager.'

His propensity to fly off the handle seemed to have increased with her promotion.

'That little bitch! I'd like to screw her head off. The hospitality she's had in our home. I always thought she had mental health problems – easy to cover up if you're a doctor. Tell the press you'll sue if they go to print.'

'The Church of England never sues. It hasn't the money, and they know it.'

'But we can.'

'What with? It would cost us thousands.'

'Our house savings.'

'Oh, Tom,' she said, reaching out for his hand across the table. But he withdrew it.

'I'm not having half the hospital staff, not to mention my patients, sneering at me behind my back because they think I'm married to a dyke. It's difficult enough as it is with your face in the local paper most evenings.'

Mike and Kelvin walked into her office with a copy of the allegation the following morning. Bev had claimed that on 1 October 1983, staying in the home of a friend, they had engaged in a mutually consensual act of a sexual nature.

Vicky Skyped the diocesan registrar, and allowed the men to listen in to their conversation.

'I have no remit, Bishop, to advise you legally on issues pertaining to your social life. But since I don't want you go to court and risk diocesan assets, I'll be a sounding board and point you in the right direction.'

'I appreciate that. I'm prepared to fund any legal action myself.'

'In that case, take a look at the date in the allegation. Where were you that night?'

'How can I remember something that's supposed to have happened over thirty years ago?'

'You must. Your whole defence stands on it. It's your word against hers. She is a doctor, and you are a bishop. Doctors are trustworthy, whereas bishops, given their record on paedophile priests . . . do I need to say more?'

She sat there for some time after Kelvin and Mike had gone back to their desks, wracking her brain for any glimmer of a memory that might be hiding there. She went up to the attic where they kept boxes of old photographs waiting to be filed and went through them all. There were several of her with Bev and Mandy, looking so, so young, but none were dated on the back.

She went back to her study and Skyped Mandy, praying that she would be in. Miraculously, she was working from home that day. Vicky quickly dispensed with the niceties and explained the reason for the call.

'God, Vicky, how could she do this to you?'

'It was supposed to have happened at your house.'

'But that's ridiculous. By then my mother didn't approve of either of you – because of all that business with the DJ, if you remember.'

'But didn't we once stay overnight – when they were away?'

'Yes,' she said uncertainly, 'but I think that was earlier, before the parents put me in purdah. Leave it with me.'

Vicky spent a miserable hour pacing the floor, willing her memory to co-operate, praying for inspiration, and then, suddenly, almost from nowhere, it materialised. 1983. She had been assuming it was right in the midst of their time in the sixth form together, but no: 1983 was the year she went away to university. Slowly, she dragged pictures out of the archive onto the imaginary screen in her brain – the preparation, the shopping for clothes, ordering textbooks, packing the trunk, saying goodbye.

And then the phone rang.

Mandy was breathless with excitement.

'It was the year we all went off to uni.'

'I know, I know, I've just worked that out too.'

'October the 1st was a Saturday. But Vicky, you went up to Durham on the Friday. I remember because you were in agonies working out how to persuade your dad to let you go early, without making it too obvious you couldn't wait to get away. And here's the thing – I thought of you arriving in Durham while my mother was lighting her Sabbath candles, because I said a special prayer for you. That could only have been a Friday night.'

'Thank God, thank God, thank God,' Vicky breathed. 'But we did stay with you one night, I do remember that.'

'Yes, but it was a great deal earlier, as I said, and we all shared my big double bed, and chatted most of the night. I was there the whole time.'

'Except when you went to the loo, or fell asleep.'

'And what could you have done with me around?'

'Mandy, you'd swear to this if it was needed?'

'Of course, Vicky. I cannot let her get away with a downright lie, despite all the years of friendship there are between us.'

Vicky hung up and slid to the floor, where she sat, hunched up, for some time, weeping in sheer relief.

The following morning Tom's solicitor was instructed to send a letter to the newspaper, rebutting the allegation. It stated that on 1 October 1983 the Bishop had already arrived at Durham University to begin her undergraduate studies, a fact that could be proven in court if necessary, and that she therefore demanded a printed retraction and full legal costs. If they wished to continue the case in court, she would be happy to see them there.

The tabloid did not respond for a while, presumably weighing up the will and wherewithal of the Bishop to fight a full legal battle, balancing potential costs against newspaper sales. But finally, after several nail-biting weeks, a small retraction and apology appeared.

She showed it to Tom as he left for work.

'Finished with,' he said, blowing her a kiss.

'I hope you're right.'

Time after time she went over to the computer, on the verge of trying to reach Bev. It was madness. It could only cause more hurt and pain. But she had to know why. Finally, she picked up her courage and video-called her.

The first time she was cut off. The second time Bev appeared on the screen, sullen and hostile.

'How could you do this?' Vicky asked quietly, her anger caged by a massive act of will. 'Lie about me, so viciously – and to the papers?'

'How could you and your church do this to me?' Bev shouted back. 'Continually deny who I am and the happiness that should go with it? Besides, it wasn't a complete lie. You did love me. You said so.'

Vicky was silenced by disbelief. She hardly knew this strange child-woman any more.

'Don't try to deny it.'

'I didn't mean love in the romantic or sexual sense. We never had a sexual relationship.'

'It was close. Whenever I kissed you, it was reciprocated.'

'Oh Bev, it wasn't like that, though. I have no recollection of anything faintly resembling love in the sense that you mean it.'

'That day at Mandy's house . . .'

Vicky was beginning to feel very disturbed. She was speaking to a fantasist. She had had one or two on the phone before. Those, though, had been unknown to her. This was a friend. 'Which day, Bev? The day I was already at university, you mean?'

'You've blotted it out. Typical.'

'I haven't blotted out anything. It never happened.'

'If you must know, I did what I did because you are in a position now to change the church's attitude to us. But you won't. You'll just maintain the status quo and pretend that's okay. Well, it's not.'

'Bev, I am so sorry, but I can't talk to you any more. I think you may be unwell.'

As she cut Bev off her screen, the sound of her ranting rang in her ears, and she felt deeply worried for Celia and her children. But there was little she could do for them.

2022

Setting aside her memories of that difficult time, Vicky got up from the settee and went back to her desk. Fortunately she had no public appearances that day, so there was no opportunity for the press to bounce her into any comments. But the phone rang incessantly as the tabloids hung out in hopes of a bigger and better revelation. Ann was dizzy with exhaustion and Sarah the colour of sago. So many questions. Did the Archbishop accept the job knowing this was in her past? Was this at the heart of her homophobia? What did her husband make of it? She suddenly remembered to call Tom, to warn him he might find himself the subject of a great deal of unwanted media interest.

'Yes, yes, they've been on to us already, Mrs Woods,' said the latest all-knowing secretary. 'But don't worry, I know how to protect him.'

The cheek of the woman. Implying that she didn't.

'Thank you. Just refer them to my press officer.'

Vicky prayed silently and fervently through every meeting, every encounter. It was impossible to concentrate on anything else. Her very integrity, not just her career, was on the line. 'I'll always be there for you.' The words, continually ringing in her ears, seemed to mock the hope that anyone's dignity might be retrieved from the mess. Bev, Bev, Bev, she cried, in the odd moments she had to herself, what happened to you?

Sarah looked a great deal more buoyant when she bounced into Vicky's study at around 6.30 p.m.

'Well, they've given me a run for their money,' she said, breathlessly, 'but I think I might just about have cracked it.'

Vicky offered her a stiff smile. She was glad to see her press officer flushed with success, but suspected that besmirched reputations were not that easily restored.

'Stories of this nature are apparently kept on record,' Sarah explained.

'But it was proved to be erroneous,' Vicky flashed. 'How dare they hold onto what they knew were pernicious lies?'

'I know, I know,' Sarah apologised, holding up a hand to calm her down. 'But that's how it works. They're filed and sealed with a glued label. Some inexperienced young journalist set out to find a coup that outdid the Naughty Nookie story. The editor says the journalist found the file, and whether the label had come unstuck, or he simply didn't see it, he thought his career was made. He'll be making the tea for the next year.'

'But the story is out there, Sarah, on the front page. And mud sticks. What did you say to them?'

'Demanded a full retraction on the front page. Threatened them, and any other paper that prints the story, with legal action.'

'And?'

'They tried to bluff their way out – at first. Said the church has no money, ha ha. I reminded them that if they checked their records, we had been prepared to go to court the first time round and would be again. And that the Press Standards Association would take a dim view of a newspaper using information that had already been shown to be libellous. The loss of a sticky label was hardly the greatest defence. So – they caved. I not only have our front-page retraction, I have also negotiated us a little financial demonstration of their goodwill, one that might just solve your staffing problems, for the next year at least.'

Vicky shook her head in disbelief. So, she could keep Noah on to drive her, at least for another year or two.

'You are a wonder, Sarah, and I am immensely grateful, but it still worries me that many people will be convinced there's no smoke without fire.'

'Look at it this way. Perhaps it's not such a bad thing that these two slurs on your reputation have come at almost the same time.'

'Since when is slander not a bad thing?'

'Well,' she said carefully, 'they do rather cancel each other out. Is this "nookie" you're having with women or men?'

'Both? They'll say I'm bisexual next.'

They both managed to laugh. But Vicky could see her point. One sexually explicit story was destructive. Two, especially with a retraction, began to look like cheap gossip. Overkill might just work in her favour. She could only pray that it would.

But as for the explanation that some young journalist had just happened to find the story on a forgotten file . . . she scrunched up the cutting and threw it in the bin.

TWENTY

Christian hope does not promise successful days to the rich and the strong, but resurrection and life to those who must exist in the shadows of death. Success is no name of God. Righteousness is.

JÜRGEN MOLTMANN

MAY 2022

Shortly before the general election a second set of findings from the 2021 ten-yearly census – on ethnicity and religion – was published. Vicky hardly dared to look at the précis that Ralph handed her, convinced that Liam would be right, that the country had become increasingly irreligious, that it would present the new government with a secularist charter. Watching her face, Ralph said, 'Go on, Vicky, take a look.' She scanned quickly. Muslims up from 4.8 per cent to 6.2 per cent. People of no religion down from 25 per cent ten years ago, to 16 per cent. 'Interesting,' she murmured. Those who called themselves Christians up from 59 per cent, to 70 per cent.

'This isn't possible,' she gasped, checking the figures several times.

'Back up by 11 per cent, almost to where it was in 2001? It certainly seems to be.'

'I told Liam secularism would leave a vacuum,' she agreed, 'but I never thought we could fill it.'

'Why not?' asked Kelvin, who had followed Ralph into her study. 'Force Christians underground, secret meetings and meals in homes – a bit of cloak and dagger works wonders for the faith. And then there's the team spirit engendered, people pulling together in providing community social welfare programmes. Attractive, that – to feel part of something useful. Say thank you to the government from me, next time you see them.'

'Churches all over the country have been reporting slow but steady growth,' Ralph added.

'Not all.'

'Enough. And then there are all the African and Eastern European churches.'

She managed a broad smile.

'And just when I need extra muscle the most.'

A thought occurred to her.

'When these laws are finally repealed – as they will be – we'll need a strategy for growth. We haven't enough clergy. Lay leaders are wonderful, but they're either retired, or have a job to do. And they can't administer Communion.'

Kelvin groaned.

'So what might you be plotting now, milady?'

The Conservatives were elected to power by the narrowest of margins, which meant that the UK had its first Muslim Prime Minister, Muhammed 'Mahdi' Khan.

'Mark Bradley-Hind, Secretary of State for Health?' Tom exploded, as they watched the announcement of the new cabinet on TV the following day. 'What the hell does he know or care about people's health?'

Vicky's heart sank too at the news of Mark's appointment. What might he not be capable of, now that he was in the cabinet? But she kept the thought to herself. It already felt as if Tom held her personally responsible for the most ill-conceived of Mark's political comments. Having him at Health was the worst possible scenario for Tom's blood pressure and her peace of mind.

Their dedicated daily hour for each other often descended into a wordless slouch in front of the box. If work allowed for it at all. Occasionally Tom would make some snide remark about ringing her secretary for an appointment.

'I can't do less, and I can't create more time,' she snapped at him, exasperated by her helplessness to change the situation. And they would relapse into exhausted silence.

Vicky invited Mahdi to meet with her at Lambeth Palace as soon as their diaries would allow. He was a soft-spoken, kindly-looking man, with gleaming white teeth and bright, enthusiastic eyes, older than his photographs portrayed, his dark hair just showing the slightest bit of grey at the temples. She wondered whether his publicity people had resorted to a little Photoshopping to support his campaign.

'Mahdi,' she said, bowing respectfully, 'how lovely to see you again. And now in your new role – no longer the opposition.'

He bowed back, beaming at her.

'Archbishop Vicky. Always such a pleasure.'

They had what the media might refer to as 'a full and frank discussion'. Politics aside, they had always got on well, but in their official capacity, neither was prepared to give the other much ground. Mahdi knew that for Vicky the church was no longer 'the Conservative Party at Prayer', at least not with any real accuracy. And she, for her part, was aware that behind the gentle charm of the man lay a shrewd and forceful individual, who would never have got to where he now was without the ruthlessness and determination of a dictator. Not a man to cross until she had to, she had decided.

'Vicky – I want to be very clear that this government is firmly committed to a neo-liberal ideology,' he stated at the beginning of their meeting, presumably to ensure she knew where he stood from the start.

She raised her eyebrows, struck by the bullish approach, and he elaborated, presuming she hadn't understood.

'A market philosophy is the most effective way of determining the world's political and economic priorities. Private enterprise, liberalised trade and an open market promote globalisation, and will ensure that we remain a key player.'

She noticed the dark circles under his eyes. Already.

'Let me tell you now, Prime Minister,' she said, as gently as she knew how, fearing he might balk at a warning from a woman, especially one in a dog collar, 'my fear is that your free market means the fat cats grow fatter at the expense of the dispossessed, and if that proves to be the case you will find me a fearsome enemy. I cannot stand back and see social injustice knowingly perpetuated by our own government, at home or abroad.'

'We are a democratically elected government.'

She noticed his voice had risen now, and that he had started to wring his hands. His discomfort worried her. Figuratively pushing the man up against a wall wasn't the best start. Even so, she felt it best to set out her stall from the beginning.

'Of course. But you have such a tiny majority in the Commons that it doesn't give you a mandate to walk over the masses who didn't vote for you.'

'Do you really think you should be meddling in politics? It's not your job. My people don't like it.'

She couldn't work out whether 'my people' were the Tories or Muslims, and decided to appeal to both.

'Prime Minister, a great mystical writer called Evelyn Underhill claimed that the spiritual life must govern our behaviour in all our personal, social and national obligations. Our faith must influence the movements we support, the papers we read, who we vote for, our attitudes to social and international justice. It's simply not true to say that spirituality and politics have nothing to do with each other. It is my job to speak for the people, whether they're Anglican Anglicans or not, since we are still a state church.'

'At the moment,' he interrupted.

'At the moment,' she nodded. 'I have been critical of a Labour government, as you know only too well, when its policies trample on basic human rights. When opposition is weak, someone has to speak out – especially when poverty abounds in what is, comparatively, such a wealthy society. Surely, because of our respective faiths, we can agree on that?'

'Muslims, like Christians, are committed to helping the poor, as it says in the Koran.'

Common ground at last. She heaved a sigh of relief.

'Having had a run of prime ministers who thought their beliefs were only a private matter, I'm delighted to hear you will stand by the values of your faith – the values we share.'

He nodded courteously and smiled again at last. His was a disarming smile, suffusing his whole face with warmth and what appeared to be genuine respect. He took both her hands in his, which she found a little disconcerting. She had been led to believe that out of respect for a woman's modesty and in case she was menstruating, most Muslim men wouldn't touch a woman. Either he wasn't so strict a Muslim, or he recognised that she was past both modesty and menstruation.

'Dear Archbishop, I really do hope we can work together, and even be friends.'

'Wonderful. I would love for us to talk about the anti-proselytising laws, when the time is right.'

'Ah, that.' His expression lost some of its geniality. 'I can make no promises.'

'Then I shall have to continue my fight to have them repealed. Surely, as a practising Muslim, you must be concerned with their potential impact?'

'We have to start from where we are. Anyone who wants to lead his party makes compromises.'

'Don't you agree that these laws run the risk of restricting essential expressions of faith for Christians and Muslims alike?'

'With respect, Archbishop, most Muslims don't want to make a fuss. We get on with our faith quietly.'

She was tempted to say that that was exactly the problem. That the Christian faith demanded that its followers fight for the truth and defend the poor of every faith and nation, while Muslim acts of charity tended to be for their own, not for those they saw as 'the infidel'. In addition, of course, many Muslims worldwide did indeed see it as their duty to proselytise.

'Not all. Perhaps what we need is for ordinary Muslims to make more of their faith, to resist the extremists on the one hand, and on the other to say that they won't be hidebound by legislation that curbs their chance to make converts?'

'You preach at me, Archbishop?'

'Forgive me, I do. I have a tendency to get carried away.'

He laughed.

'I know you, and your reputation, well enough, I think. As you know, I like some of your ideas, especially on care for the family and the elderly, and I look forward to a happy, constructive relationship.'

She reassured him before he left that she hoped for that too, but in fact, she was seriously worried about the reality of such a commitment, when the basic assumption of his party was that the poor were somehow responsible for their lot. She knew he believed that if his own family had arrived in the UK penniless and had pulled themselves up by their own bootlaces, the rest of humanity should be able to do the same. Unemployment and poverty were humiliating for a man like Mahdi. He would never see the provision and receipt of welfare as evidence of a rightful, common humanity.

As the months went by, she began to see that she was right to be worried. The new government, with UKIP yapping at its heels about undeserving immigrants, and a cabinet largely dominated by a privileged mentality, stuck on the stereotype of people in poverty spending their money on booze and fags, used the ongoing crisis to argue the case for a cashless benefit system. Recipients would receive only stamps for food, basic clothing and a tiny amount of fuel, ignoring all other, basic needs. Vicky heard of one woman who asked for baby food and was given tins of custard as that was all her stamps allowed.

There was no room for flexibility. No money could be given for a deposit on rent, not even for a miserable, little room – at just a time when rented accommodation had become unaffordable for anyone on a low wage, let alone the genuinely unemployed. The homeless were trapped in their home-lessness. Seventy years of the welfare state had unravelled almost overnight.

Housing associations, many of them church based, which for years had taken the strain of providing social housing, were stretched to the limit. Homeless shelters were subject to regular police raids. Any children found with their parents would be taken into care, shelters deemed an inadequate and unsuitable environment for a child. Though Vicky couldn't help but feel, cynically perhaps, that the real reason was because it lowered the UK's rating in the very public European child poverty index'.

Incensed by the daily evidence of contempt for people who, often through no fault of their own, found themselves in dire straits, Vicky delved as deeply as she could into any reserves of funding she could find. She contacted charitable trusts, major donors and philanthropists, and begged for additional support.

Eddie Macdonald, the Bishop of Marchington told her, had successfully galvanised an army of volunteers to care for the dispossessed of the Marchway estate, and had set up the first pharmacy bank, providing nappies, baby milk, shampoo, shower gel, sticking plasters, toilet paper and even sanitary protection, the necessities not covered by benefit stamps.

'You must come and see it for yourself,' the Bishop said, sounding fairly upbeat. 'I have the feeling you'd find it inspirational.'

'I would love to come, Will. As soon as I can. It's just . . . a little busy at the moment.'

Meanwhile, however, the badgering of Christians under the guise of legitimate concern for the rule of law continued almost on a daily basis. Vicky took the opportunity on a number of occasions to express the fear that the UK was becoming a police state.

Despite – or perhaps because of – the regular news releases that winged their way from Lambeth, the stories were not always picked up by reporters. Did the lady protest too much? Well, they haven't heard anything yet, Vicky said to herself. Though she feared nonetheless that the one-track story of her constant conflict with the government might well be running the risk of overkill.

'Do I rant?' she asked Tom.

'No,' he replied, one ear tuned in to the cricket scores. 'You're at your best when roused. Political fury fires your oratorical gift.'

It was reassuring, but too pat. She wasn't convinced.

'All I know is that the future welfare of our country cannot simply be left to the politicians.'

She made herself a cup of coffee, took it to the sitting room, and switched on the recording of an interview she had done for BBC News to promote the anti-proselytising protest and festival, suddenly anxious to see how she came across.

'While your predecessors chose to exercise discretion in their criticisms, you are more . . . outspoken,' said the interviewer.

Shifting uncomfortably on the sofa as she watched, she took a sip or two of her coffee, then held it close for warmth, to soothe away some of her angst.

'My predecessors all critiqued the government when they thought it necessary.'

'One MP said that you took whatever weapon was to hand and plunged it into their guts. "Police state"? You don't mince your words.'

'I think women often are more ruthless with words.'

'Why is that?'

'Perhaps because we haven't the physical fighting strength of a man, we resort to verbal prowess. Fundamentally, I cannot stand by and watch unrestrained free-market capitalism divest so many of their dignity.'

'How do you respond to the criticism that church and politics should be kept apart?'

'The right-wing press complained for years that the C of E was too wishy-washy to raise its voice in support of traditional Christian values. But when we do raise our voices, they shout us down as soon as we depart from their script. The prophet Isaiah said that true religion was to loose the chains of injustice, to set the oppressed free, to share our food with the hungry, to provide the poor wanderer with shelter, and to clothe the naked. If that's not political, what is? Jesus moved the goalposts even closer together. "Lord, when did we see you hungry and feed you, or thirsty and give you something to drink? When did we see you a stranger and invite you in, or needing clothes and clothe you? When did we see you sick or in prison and go to visit you?" "Truly I tell you, whatever you did for one of the least of these brothers and sisters of mine, you did for me."'

'But surely that can be done on a personal level, without necessitating an attack on the government?'

'Of course – it must be. And many churches are – and at great cost and risk. But morality isn't just a private matter. It's all very well for a government to pursue prosperity, but if, in so doing, it creates an underclass rather than increasing the welfare of all, what point is there in economic blessing? One of my predecessors said that political systems without an ideology were like a compass without a magnetic north, leaving the pointer wavering all over the place. Events have proved him right.'

'So you are the magnetic north?'

'That sounds pompous. No. But I want people to see that you need a direction. I suppose I try to model that, at least. Someone has to, if our politicians won't.'

Goodness, she thought, how schoolmarmy she seemed. How preachy. The interviewer must have thought so too, as he changed tack.

'And you manage to remain friends with the PM?'

'The Prime Minister is a very decent man, with a great deal of integrity. But self-made men have little sympathy with those they see as the left-behinds.'

'He is a Muslim, though. He has strong religious principles, supports the right of Christians to express their faith in the workplace.'

'Being allowed to wear a cross is a very minor concession. I'll believe it when the anti-proselytising laws are repealed.'

'You think it feasible?'

'They must be. I won't give up until they are.'

'You're not a stranger to organised protest, of course.'

'I think I'd call it passive resistance rather than protest. No, I'm not.'

'Not that it was altogether successful?'

'You're thinking of Wooten Grange? Not on the face of it. But who knows for the future? We must follow our consciences and do what we have to do.'

Switching off, Vicky told herself she couldn't have spoken otherwise – but it didn't make for a peaceful life.

Another of the hardship-inducing steps the government took early on in office was to unveil plans for an insurance-based healthcare system – the first step, it seemed, towards unravelling the NHS. Vicky knew that however little she wanted to see him, the time would come when she must confront the new Secretary of State for Health. Adequate healthcare, surely, was essential in any civilised society. And besides, she wanted to share her deep concerns about the apparent heartlessness of some health-care staff, reflected in tales of unspeakable indignities and cruelty inflicted on the elderly. She knew a little about that first-hand.

2016

The letter inviting her to become the first woman bishop was lying open on the kitchen table when the phone rang. Ernest, Tom's father, had been rushed into hospital with severe chest pains. Now in his late eighties, he lived independently, drove at frightening speed, and flirted with a raft of merry widows he had met at the local 'University of the Third Age'.

Vicky arranged for Alice to spend the night with friends, cleared her diary and was ready to go, but couldn't make contact with Tom. A medical secretary, not the indomitable Marilyn for once, had no idea where he was and manifestly couldn't care less.

'I'll let him know you want him when I catch him, Mrs Woods.'

'You could tell him his father's desperately ill in hospital and that I shall have to go without him. He can come on when he can.'

There was silence on the other end of the line, just long enough to register the need for a little sympathy. 'Sorry, Mrs Woods. Of course. I haven't seen him all day, but I'll try and get a message to him.'

'Marilyn not in today?'

'She rang in sick, Mrs Woods.'

Ernest was on a geriatric ward, dozens of tubes attached to his right arm, a machine monitoring his heartbeat beeping reassuringly. Usually so dapper and conscious of his appearance, now he looked dishevelled and confused, his pyjama jacket cross-buttoned, his eyes gummy, his thick white hair tangled and knotted. He was conscious and as she took his free hand, turned one of his wonderful smiles on her. It almost broke her heart.

'When did you last eat?' she asked.

He removed his hand and waved it dismissively.

'Can't manage it. Not like this.'

Vicky marched up to the nurses' station, where several nurses had their heads in the *Daily Mail*, cooing over the latest photos of the royal children. As she stood there, one or two looked up lethargically.

'Mr Woods has had no food since he arrived.'

'He didn't want any.'

'That's because he's too weak to feed himself. He has his dignity.'

'Next meal's at 5 p.m., love.'

'That's two hours away! I'd appreciate it if you could fetch me something.'

It wasn't long before Vicky was threatening to go to the CEO's office with a formal complaint.

A little while later, she pulled the curtains around Ernest's bed and spoon-fed a plateful of slimy scrambled egg into his mouth.

'Feel such a fool,' he gasped.

'You've had a major coronary. You're lucky to be alive. But we'll get you mended.'

'Tom?' he asked.

'Coming – as soon as he can,' she lied.

It was ten in the evening when Tom finally appeared at the bedside. Ernest's face lit up at the sight of him.

'How are you doing, old boy?' Tom asked.

'Less of the old, thank you,' he wheezed, and dozed off contentedly.

'Where were you?' Vicky snapped as they left the ward.

'With patients.'

'No one seemed to know where you were.'

'What is this? The Inquisition?'

She relented, and took hold of his hand. Unnecessary aggravation, when his father was so ill, was the last thing he needed.

'Sorry. I've booked us into a Travelodge. Not far away.'

Alone in their room, it was obvious from Tom's behaviour that he was in no mood for conversation. This was not the moment to discuss the letter she'd left lying on the kitchen table.

When they arrived back at the hospital the following morning Ernest was in the operating theatre, having his leg set. He had fallen out of bed.

'One of your nurses left the side of the bed down, Sister,' Tom said quietly, repeatedly clenching and releasing his jaw.

Word of his professional standing had evidently been passed around, as the respect only given to senior doctors emanated from every nurse in his orbit. The Sister was deferential, though guarded.

'I can't say, Mr Woods,' she replied, her eyes firmly on the floor. 'It was the night team. There will be an investigation, of course.'

As they sat there, staff scuttled past them like frightened rabbits, but in a quiet moment the patient in the bed opposite motioned Vicky over.

'He kept asking for a bedpan, but they said they were too busy, he'd have to wait.'

'How long for?'

'Couldn't say for sure. Well over an hour, though. That's why he tried to get out of bed.'

Sadly, Ernest never made it back to his bed. The shock triggered a further coronary and he died on a trolley, in a public corridor, alone.

'We'll sue,' Vicky said, her hand resting on Tom's, as they sat in the Sister's office after they had received the news, two tepid cups of weak tea sitting on the table in front of them.

'I'm a consultant, Vicky. Hardly good practice.'

'Then how does anyone ever effect change in this God-forsaken system?'

'Not by suing. The NHS is no better, no worse than the institution you work for. The bigger and more anonymous it is, the greater the danger that its staff feel disenfranchised, unsupported, unimportant. They treat the patient as they are treated themselves.'

'And that excuses their offhand, unhelpful manner?'

'Of course it doesn't. Many of them go into nursing with high ideals, but they're soon buried beneath a mound of bureaucracy and pressure.'

'How can you be so . . . forgiving?'

'Because I know the system.'

'Oh, Tom, to them he was just an anonymous old man. To me he was a dear friend. To you, a lovely dad. This was no way for him to go.'

Tom stared straight ahead, his eyes filled with tears, then he shook himself and said, 'I won't let this rest. I'll have a word with the Chief Executive. Scare him with the threat of trouble in high places.'

'Well, maybe, but it still stinks. Your average man-on-the-street doesn't have that kind of come-back.'

'Hm,' he said, standing up and holding out his hand to her. 'Come on, Vicky. No more crusading, not today.'

She didn't tell Tom about the letter waiting at home on the kitchen table that night either. They ate half-heartedly in a second-rate restaurant and went early to bed, where they sobbed in turn in each other's arms, until their immediate grief was spent. Then they simply held each other until they finally dozed off. It was a long time since they had done that.

2022

She had taken some time with her appearance, knowing he would be at the reception, deciding on a suit that she knew was figure-hugging and flattering. She was glad she had, and not a little gratified to see that time, stress and lifestyle had continued to wreak havoc on the once fabled good looks of the new Secretary of State for Health. What remained of his hair was clipped close to his skull like stalks of corn. His complexion was pasty. Wrinkles in the flesh below the ears lent a dissolute slackness to the jaw, and those extraordinary dark eyes were hidden behind an unflattering pair of heavy, horn-rimmed spectacles. His face had become unfamiliar and that realisation steadied her. She noted that his waistline had thickened considerably too.

'Not taking your own public health advice seriously then, Minister?' she asked, with a slight twitch of the lips, her eyes resting upon his paunch when, unable to avoid her any longer, he finally came over to greet her and planted a cold wet kiss on her cheek.

'No time in this job, Archbishop, as you can imagine,' he replied, summoning a waiter, and gesturing at the canapés on the plate held out in front of them. She declined, but he reached out and took one.

'Make it a salad rather than the three-course meal at lunchtime, perhaps?' she said, making small talk. But he seemed determined to bow neither to informality nor humour.

'Preachy as ever, Archbishop?'

'No. Just thinking about your well-being. You know, if the fast-food industry didn't keep getting planning permission for outlets in areas of high urban deprivation, there might be an increased chance that the people wouldn't spend money they don't have on food that doesn't do them any good? Think of the savings to the NHS!'

He looked away from her around the room, as if her conversation bored him.

'You always know better, don't you, Vicky? Forgive me – Archbishop. People who are determined to eat junk food won't get free healthcare. And that will save us money. They'll have to learn to make right choices.'

'Lucky them. And what about you?'

She bit her tongue. She had told herself she wouldn't allow their conversation to be reduced to childish squabbling.

'I can afford treatment when I need it,' he said, curtly, swapping his empty glass for a full one, as a trayful passed them both. She shook her head at the waiter and said a brief thanks.

'My point exactly. One rule for the rich, another for the poor. Whatever happened to free healthcare for all at the point of use? The NHS motto has been the bedrock of our society for almost eighty years.'

'High time we modernised, then. I know you understand that concept,' he said, turning back to her and smiling affably.

'Absolutely. But never at the cost of the frail and vulnerable. And that's exactly who will suffer if you introduce medical insurance.'

He dismissed her with a wave of his free hand. 'I don't see why I should discuss health policy with you, Archbishop, and especially not here and now.'

She stared at him, too affronted to speak. His eyes rested on hers like an alligator weighing up its prey. She noticed that the whites were laced with red veins. He said, coldly, 'Instead of harping on about government failures, you should take a look at your own. Dissent amongst your bishops, bad blood in Synod.'

What did he know about her bishops? It sounded like he knew things that didn't concern him. And if so, how?

'But then,' he added, 'you always did like to get your own way.'

'I'm not sure I follow you. In what, for example?'

He hesitated for a moment, took a gulp of his wine, wondering, perhaps, whether he was about to go too far.

'In, for example, the appointment of Ralph Cooper to your staff.'

'Ah, Ralph. Too honest for his own good – and that's exactly what I need him for. Nothing to do with what I am sure you could only see as disloyalty in your nearest and dearest. Three ex-wives must make you apoplectic.'

Damn, damn, damn. Why did she have to descend to vindictiveness? Why could she not maintain some dignity?

'With the rumours about your own marriage, I am not sure you have the right to lecture others!'

Her stomach lurched.

'Yet you maintain your objections to gay marriage, and bang on about human rights for your beloved vicars. How fortunate for you that our dear Queen sides with you.'

She decided to change the conversation, to strike for another cause near to her heart before he made an excuse to drift away.

'Speaking of human rights, that brings us to another issue I wanted to raise with you.'

He flinched.

'If a doctor prays with a patient or discusses their spiritual needs, they're reported within moments and can be dismissed without a hearing. But not a single nurse has reported a doctor for performing female circumcision, though we know that it happens to thousands of British girls – yes, not just abroad but in this country. As far as the charities involved in helping such girls can establish, perhaps a fifth of all such "operations" are performed by healthcare providers. And though it is against the law, there still hasn't been a single prosecution. I know you have been sent dossiers that document a number of cases, and had plenty of evidence to justify a closer look at the practices of certain doctors, so can I ask you to do that?'

He shifted slightly on his heels, but remained impassive, smiling at passers-by, who greeted him with a nod.

'Mark, these small black girls are voiceless. The only people who actually get to exercise their supposedly universal human rights in this country are those who can shout sufficiently loudly – the educated and well-heeled, those who know how to marshal their arguments and lobby.'

Feeling the opportunity slipping away, she went on, 'These girls need someone to stand up for them. Their lives are blighted.'

He didn't reply, but simply knocked back the remainder of his champagne. She paused, then said softly, 'Mark, can't we try to lay aside the past and let go of the acrimony it causes?'

The look of long-suffering on his face made her feel as if she were a recalcitrant child promising to be good. 'Thank you, Archbishop,' he said loudly, but before he had a chance to move pointedly away, she added, 'I do beg you to reconsider the moral implications of leaving large numbers of people without proper healthcare. It is not appropriate in this country of ours that has led the world in this.'

As she made her way out of Whitehall she felt slightly sick. It had been pure vanity to believe she could take on that man and either win him over or score any meaningful points. Knowing him as she once had, how could she have been so naive as to think that their past history didn't matter? He had always been the least forgiving person she had ever met. Ralph was right. Dent his pride and he would almost certainly come back all the more resistant to any further incursion, inflicting his own damage in retaliation if he could. She would have to let the Archbishop of York take over on matters of health.

'We hold the trump card,' Sarah reminded her, slyly, when she arrived back at Lambeth, indignant and disgruntled, and recounted the essence of her encounter, leaving out the personal details. Sarah furiously began to tap the small screen on her lap, reading as she went.

'Heading: Archbishop Challenges Health Secretary to Support the Vulnerable. The Archbishop of Canterbury has made a personal appeal to Mark Bradley-Hind to address two health issues that she believes are vital for any civilised society to confront: the need for a comprehensive healthcare system that is accessible to all, and for a clear stand against female genital mutilation.'

She stopped and looked up at Vicky.

'The Times has campaigned against female circumcision for years. They'll be delighted with your support. We'll give them a head start, then send the press release to the other papers. Should get us some good cover.'

Vicky wasn't sure. Mark would see it as acting purely out of pique. On the other hand, she had given him every opportunity to make some kind of conciliatory gesture and had received none. Why not gain such important matters maximum publicity?

Sarah was right. The story made a huge splash. No one was left in any doubt where a civilised society ought to stand on this. Mark was cornered into making some inane response about the inappropriateness of mixing religion and health. But had her judgement been sound? She was certain that he wouldn't take it lying down. What had she unleashed?

TWENTY-ONE

With every righteous action, we prepare the way for the New Earth on which righteousness will dwell. And bringing justice to those who suffer violence means to bring the light of God's future to them.

JÜRGEN MOLTMANN

APRIL 2023

In April 2023 the government came to her. The Wooten Grange problem had escalated. 'Cashless welfare' and the restrictions it placed on securing rented accommodation had led to the farcical situation of one or two councils offering the homeless vouchers for tents instead. Now around 2,000 people, dispossessed of their homes and unable to afford any alternative, had set up the UK's first 'tent city' on the site of a disused gasworks around half a mile away from the shining new mecca of luxury homes, shops and leisure facilities. Drinking water was collected in buckets from a single standpipe. Chemical toilets, showers and a soup kitchen were provided by the local churches. It looked like a refugee camp in war-torn Africa.

Residents of the smart new Wooten Grange development complained bitterly about the eyesore on their doorstep, and threatened to take the law into their own hands if the council didn't get rid of it, and sharpish. They didn't care where the people went, they just couldn't live there. But the council suffered from the usual decision-making paralysis, and the encampment grew almost daily, as hundreds of homeless arrived from all over the country, keen to express their support. They were joined by a number of political activists, and the rumour-mill said many were armed with a variety of weaponry, conventional and definitely otherwise, that could cause havoc if used in anger.

Local churches did their best to keep the lid on any violence, but at the same time as expressing their gratitude, the council also accused them of contravening the anti-proselytising laws by buying people's conversion with food and water. When it did finally decide to act, therefore, it was to close down the food bank. The churches, however, had had a tip-off.

Overnight, they moved the whole operation and multiple truckloads of canned and packeted food to alternative premises. Tensions continued to escalate as the council's prevarication allowed battle lines to be drawn. By the time the bulldozers appeared, accompanied by a phalanx of police in full riot gear, it seemed violence was inevitable.

Vicky offered her help to the government as soon as the problems hit the news, but was told by the Home Office in no uncertain terms that this was a matter for the police and that a dim view would be taken of any interference. On day three of the stand-off, a couple of security guards apparently snuck off for a cigarette round the back of a kitchen tent and somehow managed to cause a camping-gas explosion that destroyed half of the tented communal area and left them and two protestors with serious burns and several more with minor injuries. It heralded the outbreak of war. At which point the PM rang and asked Vicky if she would head up negotiations.

'Prime Minister, I am sure you know what my answer has to be – I would not be doing my duty in the face of this appalling situation in an area I know and love so well if I declined. But if I am to stand any chance of success, I will need some negotiating tools. Primarily, these people need assurances that reasonable, affordable, alternative accommodation will be provided. What can I give them? I know that a large number of the new flats are empty – too pricey to sell or rent.'

'But Vicky, there will be such opposition from the home owners if we put these troublemakers right in the midst of them.'

'With respect, Mahdi, it's better than their having their fancy new houses trashed. And anyway, the vast majority of these people once had and loved their homes in Wooten Grange, and are still awaiting the social housing that was promised. They are only "troublemakers", as you call them, since being summarily thrown out of those homes. And that's shameful in a relatively wealthy country like ours.'

'Maybe we could put them up in church halls, or disused factories – spread them around the country?'

Vicky thought at first that the Prime Minister must be joking. Then she remembered that he wasn't given to jokes.

'No, Prime Minister,' she said, as forcefully as she could. 'That might dissipate the current pressure, but it will *solve* nothing. Everyone has the right to shelter and privacy, and they have done nothing to deserve forcible dispersion away from their friends and families – an old trick used by invading empires to reduce unrest in conquered territories. They need real homes, as close as possible to the ones they were forced out of. If they don't live quietly and peaceably, there are laws that will ensure their ejection. But I know these people, and I promise you they will be impeccable neighbours.'

After two days of more or less pitched battles, with some horrific footage of wounded tent people being aired around the world, the Prime Minister called again. Meanwhile, she had prepared her plan of campaign. Every church minister and imam, every youth and community leader in the Larchester area, along with two well-known local premier league and England football players, a smattering of other sports personalities and one or two local TV celebrities, were invited to join her at Wooten Grange on Friday 21 April.

She spent the Thursday working to persuade the police to agree to her strategy. Of course, there were risks. She knew how dangerous such confrontations between police and protest groups could be. She remembered the London poll tax riot only too well; had a scar, albeit tiny, to show for it. But the police had demonstrated that they had no viable, safe alternative, so there was no choice for them but to rely on her instincts and inside knowledge, and let her make an appeal directly to the Wooten Grangers.

'There's no such thing as life without risk,' she said to the Chief Constable, and he conceded, with the proviso that an armed response team would be at the ready.

'Then I beg you,' she conceded, 'don't get involved unless I signal for help.'

At dawn the following morning, a quarter of a mile or so from the tent city, Vicky and her team of forty met to pray together for protection and a positive outcome. They sang, 'Light of the World, You Stepped Down into Darkness', just as a golden ball of a sun forced its way up through pink-tipped clouds, and appeared to hang, suspended in the sky above them.

'How wonderful,' said one of the ministers, gazing up at it. 'A sign?'

'Maybe,' Vicky nodded. 'A reminder, certainly. "The sun of righteousness risen with healing in its wings." Healing is what we need.'

'I tell you what, though,' he murmured, 'at this point I know how it felt to be in the charge of the Light Brigade.'

'Not as bad as facing Barcelona,' grinned Paul 'Jacko' Jackson, one of the footballers.

And they went off, laughing, to breakfast and a final briefing meeting with the police.

By midday a large, belligerent mob of demonstrators had congregated at the tent city side of the large brownfield site. Vicky led her team slowly forwards towards them, coming to a standstill halfway between the police and the rioters. Her mouth was dry. She could feel her heart pounding in her ribcage as the angry, baying mass stood stock-still, watching them, waiting for their next move. At some covert signal, they set off at a measured pace, heading straight for Vicky, a variety of weapons grasped tightly in their fists.

'Sit!' she commanded, as the furious rabble came ever closer. And the entire team dropped onto the filthy, litter-strewn ground, many of the ministers on their knees, others with their heads bent down over their folded legs. And still the hordes kept coming, closing in on them. And then, a mere twelve yards or so away, the raucous din gradually died away to befuddled murmurs and mutterings, as the advance came to a sudden, dishevelled halt, close enough for Vicky to catch the whiff of body odour on the breeze. She had counted on their being disarmed by surprise, but knew too that all it would take was the tiniest, unguarded gesture on her team's part to be seen as provocation. They froze stock-still. She held her breath.

The stand-off seemed to have lasted for an age, but was no more than a couple of minutes, when a local lad broke through the mob from the back, shouting, 'It's Jacko. Ho Jacko, can I have your autograph?'

The England striker called back, 'Of course you can. Come over here then, mate.'

The lad swaggered slowly over to his hero, while the others waited nervously, watching for a trap. Jacko offered him a seat on the ground next to him, and he took it, grinning at his mates, calling out to them. Once they had established that there was no police trap, they weren't going to be outdone and followed him across. They sat and bantered with the two footballers, giggling and nudging one another like schoolgirls who had just met their favourite pop idol. Soon a steady stream of demonstrators was wandering across, joining them on the ground, and they began singing football songs and hymns alike, ignoring the occasional rallying cries of the serious activists, who for their part gently melted away, disheartened and defeated.

The food vans rolled in, as Vicky had arranged, with plentiful supplies of free pies and buns, fish and chips, soup, fruit and ice cream. Someone had found a football and starry-eyed youngsters dribbled it around with two England players. Women sat chatting to their favourite soap stars. An impromptu band formed from nowhere. It was carnival time. Vicky was kissed and hugged like a long-lost relative.

'Hey darlin', what's it like living in that grand castle, then?'

'I'll let you into a secret. I only have a tiny bit of it.'

'You don't say.'

The negotiations that followed over the next days and weeks were tortuous, and several times events took a turn for the worse once more. But eventually, affordable homes were found for the locals who had been genuinely dispossessed. And along the way the government was forced to back down on some of its more ruthless cuts to benefits.

'Well done, cleverly executed, Archbishop,' Ralph congratulated her. 'Even the press had to hand it to you.'

'Not so clever at all. Elementary, my dear Cooper. Just trying to put myself in the shoes of people living with despair. It's the simplest things that cheer them, that touch their hearts. A favourite footballer. A visit from a celebrity. And it's not all singing and dancing, believe me. The press is already chasing after tales of "low-lifes" who refuse to work and are now living in undeserved luxury accommodation.'

'The Secretary of State for Health must be delirious with joy.'

'Well, maybe not. He certainly hasn't sent me roses.'

'Whoever *is* behind that development must be incandescent, having "riff-raff" living on their prestigious housing estate, their rent paid for by the government.'

They both chuckled.

'Here's something for you, Ralph,' she said, serious once more. 'I did a bit of asking around while I was there to see if there was any gossip that might offer us a clue as to who was behind the mess. One of the local councillors told me she had wondered, initially, whether some of her fellow councillors hadn't been bribed.'

Ralph's eyes narrowed, but the gleam in them was unmistakable.

'What makes her think so?'

'An unprecedented rash of home improvements, holidays abroad, new cars . . . She's promised to send us a list of suspects. But she has no idea who was pulling their strings.'

'Hard evidence is what we need. It'd be a start.'

The date planned for Vicky's own national protest event was rapidly approaching.

'What if it's a dead duck?' she asked Kelvin.

He looked at her in astonishment.

'Oh ye of little faith! The plans are going really well.'

'But what if no one turns up? I don't think I can cope with an "I-told-you-so" from the government. We'd be finished.'

'No, we wouldn't. We'd fight them in the European Court of Human Rights.'

'Expensive, unpleasant, risky.'

'The government is banking on that. So let's put them under a little pressure first. The people won't let you down.'

'I only hope you're right. Because I'm off to brief the PM about it, and he isn't a happy bunny.'

She had only just arrived back from a robust interview with an aggravated, uncomfortable Mahdi, when Tom walked in just as she was settling into her favourite corner of the settee. Her greeting died on her lips the moment she took stock of his grim expression, and the ashen pallor of his face.

'Tom, what's wrong?'

'Are you going anywhere?' he barked, barely looking at her.

'When?'

'Now. Tonight.'

She stared at him for some time. No matter how difficult their relationship had been at times, he had never spoken to her like this.

'From the tone of your voice I take it this isn't a spontaneous offer of a romantic night out?'

He didn't respond.

'I have a meeting with the William Cadbury Trust to plan their 100th anniversary service.'

'Cancel it.'

She was about to protest, then thought better of it.

Fortunately, Ann was still at her desk, working late. The Archbishop never cancelled meetings, not even for a cold or the flu. Vicky expected a raised eyebrow at the very least, but the secretary's face remained completely impassive.

'Of course, Archbishop.'

She walked slowly back up to the flat, her hands folded across her stomach in an attempt to still the churning in her guts and the instinctive feeling that whatever might pass between them tonight, she and Tom's lives would never be the same again. He was slouched in the large armchair, legs stretched out in front of him, staring vacantly into space. In his right hand was a large whisky, which he rotated abstractedly, so that the ice cubes swirled round and round in the tumbler.

He started as she came into the room, looked up at her momentarily, then averted his eyes. She sat down on the settee opposite him, folded her hands in her lap like a dutiful wife and waited, willing him to say something that would relieve the thudding in her chest.

'Vicky,' he said eventually, clearing his throat, 'there's no easy way to tell you this, so I'll just say it. Tomorrow morning one of the tabloids will reveal that a few years ago I had an affair.'

It took her a moment to take it in. Then her guts went into free-fall.

'But it isn't true Tom, is it? If it's libel . . .'

He waved a dismissive hand and said nothing more, fixing his gaze on the ice in the glass. The clinking annoyed her. She needed to focus, to let the words she had heard sink in, to make some sense of them. She had misheard, misunderstood. He would never betray her. Never make her look a fool. It couldn't be true.

But as she examined that familiar face, searching for the man she thought she knew, an inner voice assured her that it was true. She realised she had always known. From the moment she had received that anonymous call. Where had he been on all those late nights? Why had he removed himself from her, not just physically, but emotionally? The bed was cold, even when he was in it, and she was left feeling vulnerable and alone. She just hadn't been able to admit it to herself, didn't want to believe it. So she believed his protestations instead. It was the easy option.

'When? Who?' she whispered, swallowing the sob that was constricting her throat, forcing back the tears. She would not suspend her dignity as she had her reason.

'How do the papers know?'

'She told them. It was when you were Archdeacon of Westhampton, and finished just around the time you were made a bishop. It was Marilyn, my former secretary. You remember her?'

The smell of Marilyn's cheap perfume filled her nostrils, as if the woman was actually in the room. How could he sleep with – that? And then come home to his wife? How had she not known, not smelt that awful woman on his skin? She was filled with a total, terrible contempt for him.

'Marilyn! How could I forget her – the patronising bitch? No wonder she looked down her nose at me. As shallow as a puddle. Is that the best you could do, Tom, really? It doesn't flatter either of us.'

He continued to stare into his glass, took a mouthful of its contents, then lapsed into silence.

'Tom,' she barked at him, determined to goad him into some response, 'before I took this job on they checked me out for anything the media might exploit. How could you hide this from me? You swore it wasn't true.'

He sighed deeply, and looked up at her for the first time.

'What do you expect me to say? You think I'm proud of myself? I wanted to spare you pain. How could I know she'd sell her salacious little story?'

'It must have been obvious to you what sort of a woman she was.'

Tom ran his free hand through his hair, as he did when he was under pressure. On this occasion it aggravated Vicky immensely. She had thought she was the only one close enough to him to know all his little mannerisms. The sudden awareness that she might not be chilled her to the marrow, formed splinters of ice on her tongue.

'The tarty blonde secretary, Tom. It's such a cliché. You couldn't even be bothered to look beyond your office. Or are you going to tell me it was the male menopause? A crisis in your manhood? That you want to trade me in for a younger model?'

'It wasn't about age.'

'What was it about then? God knows I've had my chances, but I've never been unfaithful to you.'

'I don't know how to explain it, Vicky,' Tom said, furiously rubbing his forehead. 'Marilyn was just there when you weren't. Can't you understand what it was like, night after night of coming home to an empty house? I needed the company. More than the sex.'

'Company? You were scraping the barrel on that one. And it was all my fault, was it?'

He shook his head and held up the palm of his hand to her.

'No, I'm not blaming you. I'm trying to explain. You're right, Marilyn was hardly a catch, throwing herself at me the way she did. I insisted we be discreet, given the importance of your career.'

'Well, thank you, I suppose.'

Tom took a sip of his Scotch, then studied the ice cubes again as they spun and tinkled against the glass.

'Have you any idea how difficult your career has been for me? Do you think I enjoy being the spare part that no one knows what to do with? They make polite, superficial, boring conversation, because in reality, they'd much rather be talking to you. That's the thing about being married to such a . . . charismatic woman. People are attracted to you like moths. Not just because of what, but because of who you are. Everyone wants a share of the brilliance. And there's none left for me.'

He paused for a moment, gulped a large amount of the peaty liquid from his tumbler, and continued.

'I can never say in public what I actually think and feel, even about the NHS, because there might be media breathing down my neck. You're never at my side at social events or at dinner parties with colleagues, because you're always somewhere else. Even patients I've never seen before, lying half-dressed on the examination couch, ask me about you. I'm almost surprised they don't ask me to get them your autograph.'

With every ounce of her being Vicky longed to reject his excuses, to make clear that the blame for his appalling behaviour remained firmly and solely at his door, but she couldn't. The truth of it stung her, and tears hovered just behind her eyes once more.

'Why didn't you tell me?' she asked, quietly.

'And what would you have done if I had? Given up the job? That would have been the only solution. And what sort of a heel, what sort of a pathetic male would stand in the way of his wife's illustrious career?'

'It would have been better that than this, Tom,' she whispered, the tears spilling over, despite herself.

They sat for a long while in silence, as the darkness gathered around them. Vicky hadn't imagined such desolation possible. She didn't have the energy or will to move. She hadn't the heart to switch on a lamp, didn't want to see his face, or let him see hers, ravaged by his revelation.

Eventually Tom shook himself, put down the empty glass, leant forward and reached out for her hand. She folded one over the other and kept them firmly in her lap. Tom nodded and withdrew.

'I don't deserve your forgiveness. But I don't want to lose you, Vicky. I only realised it when I feared I might lose you to cancer. I was utterly devastated. The Marilyn thing was all over by then anyway. It was sheer stupidity. Never going to last. It's you I love, always have and always will.'

Vicky felt solid, unmoving, a statue made out of heavy-duty glass.

'Vicky, please. We've had so many good times together since. We'll weather this too. I'll tell the press it was short and swift, that I was a first-class prat.'

He came over to the settee, sat down next to her and reached out an arm. She jumped up as swiftly as if she had been burnt.

'Don't touch me. Don't come near me. And don't even think about sharing my bed.'

'I wasn't. I've rented a little pad of my own in Chelsea.'

'When were you going to tell me about that?'

He shrugged apologetically.

'So, you were prepared for this?'

'No – I got the flat some time ago. You knew I was looking. But Marilyn just called me today to say that she had gone to the press.'

'Why now, after all this time?'

'I really have no idea. She said she was sorry, but that she had no choice.'

'Sorry? Sorry?' Vicky yelled. 'What help is that? Of course she has a choice.'

Tom got up slowly and went into the hall to collect his jacket. Then he came back into the room and stood looking at her, in the hope, she suspected, that she might have something more accommodating to say.

'I'm going to ring Sarah now to discuss what we say to the press in the morning. You'll need to be there – and you'll say what you said you'll say?'

'If that's what you want,' he nodded.

'For now.'

'I'll bed down in the guest accommodation tonight, then, and head off in the morning after the press briefing. I'll need to collect a few things later,' he said, then left the room without turning around again.

For hours after he had gone, she paced the floor, alternately screaming in fury and weeping, replaying in her head every harsh word, every missed opportunity for rapprochement during those difficult years of her marriage. Should she have foreseen this? Could she have prevented it? What more could she have done? Had her pursuit of professional satisfaction blinded her to Tom's needs? Of course, she wasn't innocent herself. Had she taken such comfort from her own little dalliance as to resist putting in the necessary effort from her side – efforts that might have averted this crisis?

2012

On a chilly November day Vicky drove out to fulfil one of her least favourite chores as an archdeacon – a meeting with local vicar Tim Hutchings and a representative from the National Heritage Trust. Tim was desperately trying to convince the Trust that converting the unused back half of his Grade II listed church into a community centre with coffee bar, playgroup and meeting-room facilities was a caring, public-spirited venture that would ensure the future of the building. That something big was required was obvious to Vicky as soon as she saw the vast, greystone edifice, marooned on a desert island between two dual carriageways, inaccessible but for pedestrian bridges.

She had met Tim at several meetings since their first encounter and was impressed by this thoughtful, soft-spoken giant of a man, with eyes the cornflower blue of the sweaters he wore. He walked her and the Trust representative around the church. It was dark and dank, freezing cold, with brown patches of damp spreading like the huge, splayed fingers of a dismembered hand across the walls.

'A sorry state,' Tim said, his breath condensing in the glacial air. 'Would you want to spend an hour in here? We worship in the church hall – much easier to heat.'

'Well, there you are,' Vicky said to the man from the National Heritage Trust. 'If you can't provide the funding to modernise this building, the diocese will either have to sell it or let it fall down around our ears. Because we certainly don't need it, and neither does Tim.'

As he took his leave, lamenting the demise of the country's historic worship sites and the inability of the congregants to rescue them, she turned to Tim and said, 'Come on, my fingers are numb. Let's go to the vicarage, and get the kettle on.'

'I've got an even better idea,' he said. 'Let's lunch. There's a decent Italian down the road. You deserve it – after the way you handled him.'

'Hmm, I wish I could say he'll cough up the money, but I have my doubts. Serving the community is just not on the agenda.'

After they ordered he touched her gently on the arm and asked, 'That Malcolm chap isn't giving you any grief, is he? I hope not. You're highly rated amongst the clergy for the way you fight our corner.'

'I don't take the Malcolms of this world to heart. Strange, though, he comes from a tradition that eschews the idea of taking Bible verses out of context, but bases his theology of the role of women on one verse – "a woman shouldn't teach or have authority over a man" – which was meant for a particular context. I'm not sure we're much good at identifying which things are really meant to be absolute for all time, and which are merely personal and cultural preferences.'

'His wife does run round after him,' Tim agreed. 'And no, he doesn't lift a finger to help in the home.'

'Not like you nice "new men"?' she asked archly, thinking of Tom, who was committed to sharing the housework in theory, but rarely even got round to emptying the dustbins or changing the toilet roll.

'Of course,' he said. 'We are the new breed. So darn nice.'

As they tackled their pizzas, Tim said thoughtfully, 'Yes, I do sometimes think that many of our theological preferences are simply based on personality.'

'That's an interesting concept – go on,' she said, vigorously cutting at a slice that promptly shot off the plate and landed in her lap. Amused, he waited for her to retrieve it.

'There's tomato puree on your shirt,' he said quietly, pointing to her right cuff.

She examined the damage. It was a white shirt, too.

Tim leant over, fished a wet wipe out of his briefcase, then gently rubbed the livid patch until it was a pale pink.

'Told you I was a new man,' he grinned, then, seeing she was the same colour as the patch had been, continued quickly, 'I mean, if we like order, structure, no loose ends, and take ourselves seriously, we're most likely to be conservative. If we're more extrovert, fun-loving and rule-averse, we'll probably be charismatic, while the introverts, wedded to silence and contemplation, tend to lean towards Anglo-catholicism.'

'You could be right,' she murmured, then added, on the spur of the moment, 'Come for a meal, you and Jo.'

He looked surprised and pleased.

'We'd love to. When?'

They got out their diaries and decided on a week from the following Friday, providing their respective spouses were free.

Tom was, but hardly willing. 'Another Friday night spent entertaining. Great.'

Since when had her genial, extrovert husband become so antisocial?

'Tim and Jo aren't hard work. You'll like them.'

'They'll talk shop.'

'I'll stop them, I promise.'

There was no sign of Tom when their guests arrived. Vicky, who prided herself on her multi-tasking, nonetheless found it impossible to successfully welcome guests, put them at ease, organise pre-dinner drinks and cook a meal all at the same time. Fortunately, Alice was there to set the table, watch over the pots, knock up a fantastic pavlova, organise the welcome drinks and even play her part engaging the guests in interesting conversation. Her daughter was a marvel, but Vicky feared she was beginning to be put upon. She relied on her not just for her practical skills, but for companionship too. But Alice was a teenager and entitled to her own life. Vicky made a mental note to encourage her daughter to go out more.

'Tom,' she hissed, as he walked in nonchalantly, putting his briefcase on the kitchen table a fraction of an inch from the raspberry pavlova and picking up the post. 'We have guests, remember?'

'Nothing I could do. Damned departmental meeting to discuss cuts to the budget. Three-line whip from the business manager. As excuses go, dinner party didn't cut any ice.'

'Fine. But go and say hello – now!' she commanded, picking up the briefcase and thrusting it at him. 'And put that in the study.'

He opened his mouth to protest, thought better of it and marched out, pulling the kitchen door shut behind him.

She found him a few moments later chatting to their guests, the embodiment of charm. Only she could hear the slight edge to his voice.

The first course was barely served when Jo, a vivacious primary school teacher with shiny, cropped brown hair, and the picture of apple-cheeked vitality, launched into a tirade about the reductions in the Church of England pensions.

'They pay you little enough,' she said to Tim, 'and now they condemn you to old-age penury, but for the luckless wives who have to work like dogs to subsidise the church.'

'But won't pension changes affect teachers too?' Vicky asked, desperately steering the conversation off the church.

Jo shook her head. 'Not the same.'

'And it must affect the doctors,' Vicky added, looking meaningfully at Tom.

Tim quickly picked up on her lead and said, 'Yes, Tom, how goes it in the great world of the NHS?'

'Oh,' he said blithely, 'people come to me ill, and I make them better. That's the job.'

Vicky had never known him sound quite so superior, and it made her toes curl. She hoped their guests wouldn't notice, but Jo was far too astute for that.

'But that's not true, is it? You're not God. People die. You can't always prevent it.'

'If they're elderly, or have spent a lifetime abusing their bodies with booze, fags and bad food, their chances are slimmer. But these days, we're fairly confident. We know how to make do and mend.'

'That makes you sound like a plumber.'

Tom said disparagingly, 'Well, it's just a little more complex than plumbing.'

'And then there's the importance of personal interaction, of course,' she added.

'Ah, the caring doctor,' he said, in what Vicky imagined was his most patronising bedside manner. 'I don't think it's all that important. People need the surgeon to solve the problem, not mollycoddle them. We leave that to the nurses.'

Vicky could not begin to imagine what was eating at her husband. The silence that followed was so deep it was subterranean. But somehow she and Tim struggled on making polite conversation until it was late enough for their guests to use the babysitter as an excuse to make their exit.

Tom vanished as they stood at the door. Jo apologised for upsetting him.

'No, no,' Vicky reassured her. 'He's just had a bit of a bad day. Things aren't easy at the moment. Big pressures in health. Just as in education.'

They pecked each other goodbye, while Tim gently patted her arm in silent sympathy. It was exactly what she needed and she smiled a grateful thanks.

Tom had his back to her at the sink when she joined him in the kitchen to clear away the evening's debris. She suspected it was deliberate, so that he couldn't see her face. They scraped the dishes, fed the dishwasher, and washed and dried the pots in a heavy silence.

As she was reorganising the fridge to accommodate the leftover bowls, she felt his hands from behind slip gently around her waist.

'Sorry, Vic, sorry, sorry, sorry.'

She stood up, unmoved and resentful, still as a statue, aware of the warmth of his breath on the back of her neck.

'I don't know what got into me. I sometimes feel I live and breathe the Church of England these days. I suppose I resent it.'

She turned to face him and reluctantly let him hold her. He rocked her slightly, as though comforting a child, and her anger began to dissipate.

'Tom,' she whispered into his shoulder, 'what is happening to us?'

He shrugged, let his arms drop and turned away.

'No,' she begged, 'please don't make it worse by pretending there isn't a deeper problem. It's not just the job, is it?'

He leant back against the counter and faced her, arms folded, looking down at the floor. After what felt like an interminable silence, he drew a long breath, looked up at her and said, 'No – you're right, it isn't just the job. What I really cannot bear is you demanding the moral high ground.'

It was that again, always that. It always would be. The Sophie Carpenter case.

'Tom, I'm only trying to follow my conscience.'

'Doctors have to make appallingly difficult judgements all the time – and whatever I may have said to your friends tonight, we do it based on what we genuinely believe is best for the patient and their loved ones. To minimise their pain. Do you think I feel good about having a child die on the operating table?'

'No, my darling, of course not,' she said carefully, desperately trying to weigh Tom's feelings against the need for honesty and truth. 'I know how much it distressed you. I suppose I just wonder whether you didn't then act to make life easier for yourself and the hospital, rather than the family concerned.'

Tom ran his hands through his hair, then held them out to her in desperation. 'That's exactly it. You judge me from your perspective, never trying to see things from mine. I can't live in a relationship where I'm made to feel inferior, defective in this way.'

'Oh, Tom – that was never my intention.'

She realised as she said it that; far from supporting her husband, she had left him feeling diminished, and he had, inevitably, been forced to remove himself, psychologically at least, from the source of pain.

'And you've been holding that in all this time?' she said to him. 'No wonder I couldn't seem to reach you.'

She went to put her hands on his shoulders, but he intercepted them and held them in his. Looking straight into her eyes, he asked, 'Can you live with me just as I am, Archdeacon, not assessing my faults and weaknesses and holding me to account for them, as if I'm one of your charges?'

'Don't do that, Tom,' she said. His grip was hurting her wrists.

'What?'

'Call me Archdeacon – even in jest.'

'Okay,' he said, releasing her a little, but never wavering in his gaze, 'just answer my question.'

The tears sprung to her eyes, and she could only manage a nod. He took her into his arms and murmured, 'Vicky, I should never have burdened you with my moral dilemma. It wasn't fair. And now I can never undo it. So we have to find a way of living with it.'

She pulled away from him and crossed the kitchen in search of the tissue box.

'You know,' he said, as she blew her nose loudly, 'one way would be for me to have my wife back.'

'I thought you welcomed my promotion,' she said nasally.

'I did – until it took you over.'

'I need to do it well, Tom.'

'Oh, you do that all right. It's obvious that our steady stream of guests all adore you. But add good and justifiable ambition to the lure of popularity and I'm afraid it could easily curdle the mixture.'

'My first responsibility is to be a good wife and mother. You know that's what I want – even if work responsibilities push it aside sometimes.'

'Bulldoze it aside, more like,' he said ruefully. 'Come here.'

He reached out for her again, and she let him enfold her in his arms and kiss her gently on the forehead. 'I do worry about you. When do you take time to potter, garden, shop, bake, listen to music, do the things that normal people do?'

'Shouldn't that question be rephrased: when do *we* do those things?'

'You're right,' he said. 'Tell you what, let's designate next weekend a weekend just for us, when we can do all those things. And if Alice is out, it could even be a dirty weekend. Now that would make a very pleasant change.'

But Jenny James was coming to stay the following weekend. Vicky had forgotten and didn't feel she could put her off. Jenny had holiday to use up and, being single, didn't know what to do with it. With so few friends locally, Vicky had been looking forward to her company. If only it hadn't been that weekend.

Tom took himself off to visit his father. 'Been promising ourselves a round or two of golf for some time,' he said tightly, as she kissed him goodbye, the palms of her hands resting against his chest.

'Our weekend's on hold, not cancelled,' she promised, as seductively as she knew how. But he pulled away from her and got into the car with a derisive little snort.

The following week, out and about on various visits, she remembered that she had recently been involved in appointing a thoroughly nice, bright-eyed and bushy-tailed young couple to a well-heeled but difficult parish in the north of the diocese. Lambs to the slaughter, she feared, and decided to do an impromptu call to see how they were coping. She stopped at an off-licence on the way to pick up a bottle of wine for them, and rang to let Tom know she would be late home.

'Marilyn?'

'Yes, Mrs Woods?'

It was the voice the secretary reserved for tiresome and nuisance callers. At least, Vicky hoped it wasn't only for her.

'Is Mr Woods around?'

'No, Mrs Woods,' Marilyn said with a weary sigh.

'Could you tell him I'll be a little late tonight?'

'I'll tell him Mrs W., only, we know what he's like, don't we? Never remembers anything unless I'm there to remind him. And I'm just about to go off home.'

She could have knocked the woman's condescending little head off.

The young couple were not at home, however, and before she knew it, Vicky found herself heading for Tim Hutchings' vicarage, which just happened to be a mere couple of miles away. As he opened the door his face broke into an enormous smile.

'Is it convenient? I was passing and just thought I'd pop in and see if there were any developments with National Heritage.'

'Funny you should ask,' he said, ushering her in. 'We heard today that we've got our grant – on condition that we preserve a substantial "worship space" at the cost of the "coffee space", which they have reduced to an area that might just be big enough for twelve people, as long as they're slim and sit on each other's knees.'

'Cosy,' she said, following him into the kitchen.

'Infuriating. We'll get round it – moveable chairs, serve refreshments at tables in the worship space.'

'Well, let's celebrate with this, then,' she said, handing him the wine.

'Thank you,' he said, hunting for a bottle opener. 'It's great to see you. Jo has a parents' evening and the boys are at football practice.'

They sat at the small kitchen table, chatting companionably, sipping their wine. After walking on eggshells with Tom, being with Tim seemed effortless. Vicky was always surprised at how easy it was to be with him, how reassuring to find someone with whom she could share her thoughts and feelings, without worrying that they would become a source of gossip throughout the diocese. How liberating just to laugh.

She heard a click of the front door and looked up at the clock. Goodness, they had been sitting there for well over an hour.

'Hi?' Jo called out.

'In the kitchen,' Tim shouted back.

'Vicky,' Jo said with genuine pleasure, 'how lovely to see you.'

'I'm just off,' she said, standing up quickly.

'Must you?'

'Afraid so. Alice will be wondering where I am.'

'And I must collect the boys,' Tim said, escorting her to the door.

'I'm so glad you came,' he said warmly as she left, gently touching the top of her arm once more. 'We should chat more often.'

The house was empty. Alice had gone to the cinema with friends. Tom must have got the message and never came back at all that evening, his dinner left sitting in the microwave. If it weren't for Alice, she might just as well be living on her own, Vicky reflected ruefully, as she ate from a tray on her lap.

She found herself thinking about the two pigeons she had watched that morning through the window, perching on a branch. They had had the entire tree to themselves, but chose to sit virtually on top of each other, their heads and bodies wrapped up in one another. That was what she missed, she thought wistfully, skin against skin, the feel and smell of it, the warmth and comfort of contact and closeness. The painful reality was that they might as well be sleeping apart. They rarely made love these days, and when they did, it was peremptory and unsatisfactory, from her perspective anyway, with little sense of any one-flesh intimacy. We go through the motions of a relationship, she thought. We are polite. 'Sherry, dear?' How she loathed that reduced term of affection – 'Dear'. Darling-gone-dead. She was suddenly overwhelmed with sorrow, a mourning for the loss of love and its joyous companions, romance and passion. She got up hastily and switched on the television before she could become too maudlin.

Midsomer Murders made satisfying viewing. The nasty got their comeuppance, the wicked were unmasked, and decency triumphed in the end. And at least she wasn't Archdeacon of Midsomer. Any clergy who made more than the briefest appearance to take a wedding or a funeral were lucky to survive a Sunday service. If they did, they were pretty much guaranteed to be the murderer.

'Flavour of the month, that's all. I won't last,' she said to Tim Hutchings a few months later, as they lunched in some country pub in the middle of nowhere, well outside of the diocesan boundary. They were lunching pretty regularly, but had agreed that being seen together might send out the wrong message.

'But you're always popping up on my TV screen these days,' Tim said. 'Do you enjoy it?'

She flushed with pleasure.

'For now. But I won't let myself be taken in by it,' she assured him, waving a spoonful of crème brûlée as she spoke. 'Fair-weather friends. Adore you one moment. Bite you on the bum the next. And it certainly doesn't give you kudos in the church.'

'Jealous lot that we are,' Tim agreed.

'*Midsomer Murders* is not far wrong. Westhampton all over.'

They giggled at the thought of it.

In the car on the way home, she reflected on how seductive the lure of the media could be. It was pure presumption to think you had been chosen for a unique opportunity to speak to the millions on God's behalf. As if he needed it. More likely, she needed something to fill the cavern that Alice's departure to Leeds University had carved out of her middle. Career woman that she was, she had always assumed that 'empty nest' syndrome would pass her by. But saying goodbye to Alice, even for a term, had been a surprisingly heart-rending bereavement. She would come in late from some boring meeting and rush upstairs as she always had, expecting to see the strip of light under Alice's bedroom door that would tell her Alice was awake and reading, whereupon she would tap, put her head around the door and leap into bed next to her daughter, so that they could laugh at the foibles of the diocese's various eccentrics. But now there was only ever darkness under the door. No one to laugh with. Chatting on Skype was not the same. The image was always so distorted. The sound always vanished at the most crucial moment. Perhaps, if she were painfully honest, her newfound lesser-celebrity status simply stroked her vanity, and went some way to assuaging the emptiness that the lack of a child, of a community, and increasingly, of a husband had engendered inside her.

'A reporter at the Beeb has just called me a breath of fresh air,' she said to Tim when they met for coffee at his vicarage several weeks later. She always found herself saying things to Tim she would never dream of saying to anyone else. He made his interest in her so obvious that it made her dizzy, almost adolescent. It crossed her mind that his attraction for her was the same as the media's. It filled that darned emotional void, at least until she needed the next fix. But she dismissed the idea. She couldn't give him up. Her first waking thought in the morning was how she could engineer seeing him. Her last thought in the day was whether she could see him, or at least speak to him, tomorrow. All those pomp-ous conversations with the Bishop about how the clergy might be saved from sexual folly by openness, honesty and seminars on the subject now seemed naive and ill-considered. Who could she be honest or open with? Jenny? She had no intention of telling her about Tim. Jenny would tell her to grow up and get over her adolescent crush. Besides, there was nothing to tell. Like a junkie, she denied her compulsion so that she could indulge it, freely.

'You are indeed a breath of fresh air, Vicky,' Tim said, gazing at her with those gentle blue eyes of his. He reached out a hand and laid it over hers. Left it there. It was the first time their flesh had touched. A slight movement of his fingers sent an electric shock pulsing up her arm. She had never known how erotic a hand could be. But fighting its way through the intense pleasure that begged for more and drew her towards him like a magnet to iron, came an unexpected, momentary sense of panic. What was she doing here? There was no one else in the house. They were alone together. Except – there were the boys' football boots piled up in the corner. And Jo's anorak hanging from a hook. Her knitting in a basket by the fire. There was no room for Vicky here. But if she waited another minute or so, she would force her way into their world and smash it apart. Of that she had no doubt.

She leapt to her feet.

'Time to go,' she said, dragging her hand back and gathering her things. She was aware of a momentary anxiety ruffling the surface of

Tim's normally composed features, but he got up, smiling, and escorted her to the car.

She came home to find Tom sitting in the kitchen with a glass of wine and the newspaper, engrossed in the story of the *News of the World*'s phone-tapping exploits.

'You're home early,' she said, leaning over him from behind and pecking him on the cheek. He barely registered her presence.

'How did they think they'd get away with it?'

'They probably will,' she replied, going to find herself a glass.

'Have you seen the list of victims? Not just celebrities.'

'Well, they'd be sorry if they tapped my phone – all gutters and boilers. Any journalist listening in would get rigor mortis through boredom.'

And then it struck her, a sudden realisation that hit her so hard it almost winded her. The frequent, flirtatious conversations with Tim. Their easy intimacy. The personal nature of their conversations. Nothing improper had ever been suggested, but anyone with an ounce of prurience could have created a nice little pot-boiler intrigue for the masses, and disaster for those they loved. Their protestations of innocence would have counted for nothing. Adultery was so much more than leaping into bed.

She would never know whether it was simply some strange irony, or God hammering home his point in his own distinctive way – but that evening, she and Tom watched the television together, for the first time in months, a dramatised version of the life of the comic actress, Hattie Jacques. She vaguely remembered the enormous, larger-than-life lady with the dimply smile and alluring face from the *Carry On* films she had seen as a child. Her cinema persona was funny and jolly. In reality, a pointless affair culminating in a miserable, two-year marriage put paid to her happy home life forever.

When the programme was over and Tom got up to switch off the TV, Vicky said, 'It must be a kind of madness. Why would anyone throw everything away for something so obviously doomed from the start?'

Tom grunted and headed for bed, leaving her to ruminate on the words that had just fallen from her mouth. Wasn't it exactly that, a madness – the girlish excitement that anticipated any meeting with Tim, the adrenalin rush when she finally saw him, the zing in the marrow and the somersault of the stomach, when he looked at her, said her name, and especially today, when he touched her hand?

Here she was, a menopausal woman, lamenting the ageing process and the slow but certain loss of her looks, the de-sexualising that her job entailed, the loneliness of being unsupported by her husband, and ultimately, not being able to even articulate any of it to the man who should have been there for her. A tiny voice in her head told her she was entitled to happiness. She deserved Tim. But Jo and the boys had done nothing to deserve the unhappiness her selfishness would cause them. This addiction of hers was as noxious as heroin, and just as hard to fight. But fight it she must, for his family and for hers, for the reputation of the church she served, for all her colleagues, and for all out there, for whom the assumption of her integrity was unacknowledged, though its betrayal would be another nail in the coffin for their perception of the church.

She sat on, long after Tom had gone to bed, until she came to the conclusion that cold turkey was the only certain way to treat addiction. But at the thought of never having Tim to herself again she started to sob, great wracking spasms that convulsed her whole body and were all the more violent because they had to be internalised and silent for fear of disturbing Tom. 'I just wanted someone to want me,' she moaned, embracing her body with both arms lest it burst open with the misery that was fighting its way out, and rocking herself backwards and forwards.

She tried desperately to sublimate her pain with mental images of Alice, now a poised, beautiful and self-possessed young woman; of Tim's two innocent, mischievous, rosy-cheeked boys that looked so like Jo. She knew she could never willingly inflict such terrible hurt on them all. But how to live without seeing Tim, without that meeting of mind and spirit, that all-consuming attention that made her feel valued for herself? How could something that felt so life-enhancing be so wrong? And yet it was. It countermanded everything she believed in, everything she had based her life on.

Then she did something she had never done before at this hour. She called Donald. Sheer madness to disturb anyone, let alone a poorly old man, at this time of night. But it seemed to her that a sensible madness was required to conquer the senseless madness that threatened to drive her headlong into disaster.

The phone rang for some time before it was answered. His wife whispered a shaky hello.

'Who's that?' she asked suspiciously.

'Oh Gwen, I'm so sorry to disturb you at this time of night. I know it's late, but Donald isn't still up by any chance, is he?'

'An emergency?' she asked.

'Something like that.'

'He went to bed a wee while ago, but hold on, let me just see if he's asleep or reading.'

'Please don't wake him if he's asleep.'

She was gone for what seemed an age, hobbling, Vicky imagined, as fast as her elderly frame would carry her, but when she came back, panting slightly, she said encouragingly, 'You're in luck, Vicky. Deep in some fascinating new book or other. I'll take the phone through to him. He'll be with you in just a moment.'

'Vicky, my dear?'

There was no weakness in his voice, no resentment, only undisguised pleasure, as if he had been waiting for her call all evening. She felt embraced in his musty-smelling, old tweed jacket.

'Oh Donald, I'm so sorry to get you out of bed, but I've got myself into a bit of a mess.'

She described her relationship with Tim, and the reality check that now left her feeling so utterly desperate.

'Oh dear, oh dear, this is exactly what I feared the last time I saw you. That emotional separation from Tom was going to leave a gap that you would be tempted to fill elsewhere. An adultery of the heart and mind, if not the body.'

Though she knew it already, it was still a shock to have Donald's verbal confirmation.

'I know, I know. And I know what I have to do, but never thought it would hurt so much. I need you to help me.'

'Vicky, it will hurt. There can be no competing, detrimental emotional interests in the life of someone who has given themselves to God. A clean cut is the only option. I have no pill, no anaesthesia to offer you.'

'But I feel so desolate. How do I live with the pain of it?'

'You know how, Vicky. But since you've called me, you obviously need to hear it. Duty, responsibility, love, to God first and then to your fellow human beings. Give yourself to Tom, even if he can't give himself to you at this moment. It's what you vowed when you married him. Find clergy other than Tim to support and serve, including those you don't even like. The discipline of it, however numb you may feel at first, will eventually be your healing. Lay down what you want and think you need. Take up your cross. We lose ourselves only to find more of God. He is waiting to carry you through this. He will be enough for you.'

'Thank you,' she whispered.

'Vicky,' Donald said firmly, struggling for breath. She became painfully aware of the energy the conversation was costing him. 'I have every confidence in you, that you will not allow evil intent to distract you from your life's vows and calling, and you will survive, purer, truer, stronger, I promise you. By God's grace we fall only to rise higher.'

It was the prescription she had anticipated and needed. A good slug of kick-up-the-backside medicine. A reminder of the commitment she had made to God, to one man and to the church. This was the bedrock of her sanity, of her very existence.

She and Tom had made a child and a life together. She could never walk away from so many shared memories, anniversaries, little intimacies and peculiar foibles. Or betray his belief in her and the sacrifices he had made that had enabled her to come thus far. When she imagined the future stretched out in front of her, there was only one man at her side, and that was Tom. Sometimes silent and surly, generally steady, strong and dependable. 'The only man for me,' she murmured, as she slipped between the sheets next to his inert, sleeping form in the bed, so close, yet so far apart. She lay awake for at least another hour, praying silently that the emotions she had once felt for him would kick in again. And that he hadn't gone away from her forever.

She awoke from a disturbed, disrupted sleep with swollen eyes and a heavy heart, glad that Tom had already left for work. 'A clean cut,' she repeated to herself, as she reached for her Bible. It fell open at the story of the woman caught in the act of adultery. She couldn't help but laugh out loud. Who could ever doubt God's sense of humour? 'Go and sin no more,' Jesus said. She got up, gave herself as fully as she could to the commitments in her diary, made a conscious effort to drive Tim from her mind.

He rang a day later to suggest a meeting at his vicarage.

'So sorry, Tim,' she said, as coolly as she could. 'I can't make it.'

She had a strong sense that had she gone, her defences would not have prevented her from crossing the boundary, and she breathed a short prayer of thanksgiving that it had been nipped in the bud just in time.

'When can I see you then?'

It didn't seem possible to discuss the nature of the relationship, to admit that they had already gone further than they should, to make an issue out of what had merely been the usual pastoral visits.

'Not for the foreseeable future,' she said gently, swallowing away the ache in her gullet. 'A very full diary.'

'Of course,' he said politely. 'I get the message.'

She put the phone down, blinked back the tears and quickly moved on to the next matter on her agenda.

'Tom,' she said, over dinner that night, reaching for his hand, 'let's have that weekend we've talked about. Let's go away – somewhere chic and expensive. Let's push the boat out.'

He didn't jump at it. In fact, there was little reaction at all. She felt gutted. Then reminded herself it was probably a protection against having his hopes dashed more often than he deserved.

'Okay,' he said later as they cleared away the debris of their meal, 'if that's what you'd like. Where do you want to go?'

'I've always wanted a trip on the Orient Express.'

He whistled.

'A woman of simple tastes,' he said, picking up her hand and kissing it.

That trip on the Orient Express to Venice, shortly before she became Bishop of Larchester, was a small taste of heaven. Those moments of revived love were imprinted in graphic detail on her memory. Yet she now knew that either side of that trip, he had been seeing Marilyn. The hurt of that knowledge was almost unbearable.

She sat for hours after he had gone, her whole body shuddering, as if the blow had been physical. She tried to remember what had first attracted her to this man, this total stranger with a life she knew nothing about. This man whose body was more familiar to her than her own. That tiny white scar on the inside of his left thigh, where he had fallen as a child trying to climb a wooden fence and almost done himself a far more serious injury. The mole on his right shoulder. The pattern of his chest hair. All the little details that made him hers alone, he had shared with another.

Was it so naive to expect monogamy in this day and age? Society, with its usual double standards, would certainly expect it of the Archbishop's marriage, if not of their own. And archaic as it might seem to people out there, she genuinely believed that one flesh meant exactly that, that his body was hers and hers was his, inextricably joined from their first union. Yet he had taken what belonged to her, and given it away, like a bottle of cheap plonk.

What had she loved about him? Did she still love him? Would she ever want him back as a husband again? And if she didn't, could she continue as Archbishop? Would she want to, anyway? In her mind's eye she saw them, cabinet ministers and bishops alike, revelling in her humiliation. That left her with the bitterest taste of all. Tom, oh Tom, how could you do this to me? How could he do it to himself? She couldn't see the hospital trust being thrilled with this little piece of publicity.

She shook herself. Her mind was running on too far ahead. For now, she simply had to survive the physical and mental punishment of the next few days. Then she would decide whether there was anything to be retrieved from the dishevelled mess of their relationship.

The dam finally burst, and she wept until she fell asleep, fully clothed, on the settee.

She awoke feeling cold, stiff and empty and couldn't remember why. Then reality dawned and she started crying all over again. Come on, Victoria, she commanded. If she didn't take charge of herself, no one else would. Self-pity does no one any good. Least of all you. So get on with it, woman.

She splashed cold water on her face, took some time with her hair, painted on a happy face and went to fill Sarah in. This was going to test her press officer's PR skills to the limit.

TWENTY-TWO

Since resurrection brings the dead into eternal life and means the annihilation of death, it breaks the power of history and is itself the end of history.

JÜRGEN MOLTMANN

MAY 2023

Vicky wanted her press statement to be as honest as possible, lest it negate or trivialise the heartache of thousands of women who found themselves landed with wandering men. She simply said that she was deeply saddened, that the demands of both their jobs would put pressure on even the most loving of relationships, and that she hoped theirs was strong enough to withstand such a painful breach of trust. She considered using words like forgiveness and redemption, but they sounded prissy and pompous. Besides, it would be dishonest to claim to have come so far so soon. Forgiveness was the last thing on her mind. The media would have dismissed it as trite spiritual flimflam – and they would have been right.

At the end of the statement a short quote from Tom said that he profoundly regretted an affair that had ended some years ago, that their marriage had been a strong and loving partnership, and that he was confident it would survive what had been a foolish and temporary aberration on his part. It was more optimistic than Vicky felt, but Sarah seemed to think it would help them avoid being buried under a slag pile of intrusive requests and insinuations without requiring any concrete commitment to reconciliation from the Archbishop.

The tabloid that had bought the story ran it, inevitably, on page one in full colour, with the headline, 'Adultery of Archbishop's Husband'. The photograph showed a glossy Marilyn in a sleek, scarlet satin sheath, standing behind Tom, who was seated in front of her, wine glass in hand. She was draped all over him, her hands folded on the front of his dress shirt, while his head, thrown back in laughter, was cushioned by her ample bosom. They were in a row with three other posing, smiling couples. A departmental bash at the hospital by the look of it – one of the many Vicky hadn't been able to make. So much for discretion, Vicky thought as she studied it. But if that was the only visual evidence for their grand passion, it was a poor job.

The press coverage that followed couldn't have been more hostile – the antagonistic response of a media longing to expose an idol's feet of clay, and beaten to the scoop by a low-grade tabloid. Several newspapers concluded that if indeed it had been over for several years, she must have known about the affair, and hidden her knowledge of it so as not to skew her chances of Canterbury. 'The Archbishop claims she was ignorant of the affair. Was she really too busy to see the lipstick on the collar or smell the scent on the lapels? It seems very unlikely. How can Vicky Burnham-Woods preach on the sanctity of marriage, when her own has manifestly been anything other than faithful?' It didn't help Vicky's cause that one of Marilyn Morton's fellow secretaries admitted having rung the Archbishop with a tip-off some years ago.

The tabloids showed no mercy to either party. True, Tom was never at her side, had little interest in religious matters, was known for his offhand attitude with junior staff and was rarely seen without a glass in his hand, but give the man a break. His wife was an aggressive, man-eating career woman who appeared to prefer the company of her Chief of Staff. Unsurprisingly, the peck-on-the-cheek 'Naughty Nookie' photographs were resurrected from the archives. Likewise a number of veiled references to alleged 'improper adolescent activity' that may have led to 'issues' in the relationship. In other words, despite her outspoken support for traditional marriage, the hypocrite was evidently a predatory bisexual. By inference, Vicky was too busy flirting with everyone else in sight to bother with her husband.

There appeared to be no shortage of people willing to anonymously aver that they never showed each other any affection, lived very separate lives, even that they didn't share a bedroom.

'Once or twice, when he had a heavy cold, I moved out because of the snoring,' she fumed. 'Really Ralph, can't you stop your staff from selling porkies to the press?'

'Not when they're offered such mouth-watering sums. And certainly not if they're put up to it. But if I discover anyone at it, they're out.'

'Sorry,' she said, sitting at her desk, her head in her hands. 'This is just too awful.'

Ralph reached across to touch her arm.

'Don't,' she commanded. 'There's no privacy anywhere. And it could make matters a thousand times worse.'

'I have the Archbishop of York. Will you speak to him?' Ann's dismembered voice intoned from Vicky's computer. His fragmented image materialised on the screen in front of her.

'I can't imagine what you're going through. You must be gutted. I'd kill Amélie if she did that to me.'

'Thank you for your support.'

She reminded herself that he was a man, a youngish man who had never known real hardship, a comprehensive kid who'd got a first from Cambridge, and had a brilliant sporting, as well as academic career. Blessed with good looks, a beautiful wife, and four delightful teenage children, he also had the perfect family. Even if he didn't have the greatest pastoral sensitivity.

'Change the locks at Lambeth and throw his things into the garden.'

It was supposed to make her laugh, but she couldn't even manage a smile.

'The press would love that.'

'I'll do my best to keep the dragon bishops at bay, but you know what they're like. It doesn't help that you're a woman.'

'Not one of the boys?'

'Quite. Stay strong. Let me know if there's anything I can do.'

'Take on some of my engagements, perhaps? I need a bit of space.'

He squirmed like a worm newly dug from the soil.

'Er, well. I do have a very full diary myself. But if I can, I will. Of course.'

One or two of the bishops were much less supportive. The Bishop of Carbury was quoted as saying, 'It's not good for an institution that's supposed to model Christian values if there are domestic difficulties at the top.' Well done, Toby, she muttered when she saw it. Always so helpful. 'Unless she can get her act together she may have to stand down.'

The Bishop of Normington, pictured with his large pectoral cross protruding from beneath his black beard as if it were about to puncture a hole in his throat, was his usual pompous self. 'It's hard for all of us to maintain the standards we preach, but unacceptable if we are not seen to live by them. I suspect that divorce is out of the question, but they may arrange some kind of amicable separation that enables them to soldier on and make the best of a bad relationship.'

How could he presume to pontificate on their marriage?

Suppositions and hypotheses, fables, fantasies and fairy tales rattled on for days. The constant drip-drip effect wore down Vicky's emotional defences. To find your man has opted for another woman was the worst rejection imaginable. It suggested failure – as a lover and companion. The media assaulted her femininity when it was at its most vulnerable. They would never challenge the masculinity of a male bishop, describe his figure, his legs, his mannerisms, his sex appeal or the lack of it, so why was she fair game just because she was a woman? The only consolation was that in recent photographs Marilyn looked gratifyingly over-ripe and blowsy.

By day nine or ten, Vicky felt dizzy and disoriented. Ann had been wonderful, cancelling as many diary events as she could, passing some onto the Archbishop of York, or other amenable bishops. But she couldn't avoid everyone; and it was more important in any case for the world to see her smiling face and believe she was unfazed by the fuss.

In just a couple of weeks it would be their festival/protest event. How might that be affected? Kelvin was convinced the show of support would be greater than ever. She wasn't sure. And there had been no word from Tom.

Nick came to her rescue, bought her flowers and perfume, cosseted her, took her out for dinner and reassured her that she was intelligent, gifted and beautiful, and that Tom needed his head examining. Why hadn't she married a man like Nick?

'Oh, Nick,' she said to him, after she had struggled her way through a plateful of Sole meunière, 'you are just what I need to bolster my flagging ego.'

It wasn't enough. Jenny James found her in the corridor outside her study, bewildered and shivering, teeth chattering uncontrollably. Jenny escorted her back to the chaplain's study and tucked her up in an armchair with a rug, a jug of coffee and an almond croissant.

'Eat,' she commanded.

Vicky fingered the croissant, put it to her mouth, but her stomach turned over at the smell of it.

'I can't.'

'You need the sugar, Vicky.'

'This is how my chaplain pastors me – with carbs and calories.'

'Once I've fed your belly, I might be able to feed your soul. Not before.'

She watched her take a few nibbles.

'Look, you managed to work through worse than this.'

'What can be worse than this?'

'Cancer, for one.'

Vicky managed a weak smile.

'You can weather this storm too. Come on, Vicky, give the man some slack.'

'Not you too,' she groaned.

Jenny ignored her.

'He could have had virtually any woman in his orbit and he went for that little tart. He took it, yes, but only because it was handed to him on a plate. What does that tell you?'

She shook her head, mystified.

'It was testosterone talking, that's what. Idiocy, but not incomprehensible or unforgivable. Don't let her ruin your life. She's got her money and her fifteen minutes of glory. Don't give her any more than that. Come on, Vick, fight back. Don't hand it to the boy bishops. If you take leave they'll say you can't cope with the job. Prove them wrong.'

'I have the consecration of Emily Porter in the cathedral tomorrow,' Vicky stated flatly.

'Another woman diocesan bishop. Moral support at episcopal gatherings.'

'I know, but I'm hardly in the best state for an encouraging, pastoral interview this evening.'

'How many of her guests are you entertaining?'

'A dozen at least,' Vicky sighed, extracting herself from the blanket. 'A houseful of them. Not really in the mood for Happy Families, but I can't let her down.'

'That's my girl. The resources you need to do the job are there, inside you. The Holy Spirit, that is, in case you've forgotten. And that's what you need for the rally next week too. That power of yours to inspire an audience Vicky, to ignite their passion to go out and change the world is awesome to watch. Only now, with your natural gift totally depleted, you'll really have to depend on God to get you through.'

'I don't want to say stuff that I don't live out myself.'

'Don't get maudlin on me. Which of us clergy live out our pontifications all the time, however hard we try? It isn't hypocrisy, because we do our best to live up to what we preach, insofar as we are able. Don't beat yourself up. Self-pity isn't attractive, Archbishop.'

'Thank you, chaplain. I had that coming.'

'My only aim is to put fire in your belly and steel in your spirit.'

'You usually succeed.'

'Me, or the Master? I'm going to pray for you now, that he'll lift you out of this slough of despond, and renew your hope, your peace, your passion.'

The following morning Vicky could hardly get out of bed. She staggered over to the mirror and groaned. What a sight. Her face was bloated, her eyes bulbous and swollen. She looked like a puffer fish. Not the best morning for a houseful of special guests and a cooked breakfast to go with it.

In all those years as archdeacon she had gone through the motions of being married. Now she had to go through the motions of being Archbishop, for the sake of a new woman bishop, who shouldn't, on this long-awaited day, have to pay the price for her misery.

'Come on, God, answer Jenny's prayers, even if you don't seem to be hearing mine,' she muttered as she got back into bed for a few blessed moments and opened her Bible. She had been struggling through the book of the prophet Jeremiah for some weeks. All judgement and retribution. She tried to focus, to concentrate. Words on the page blurred before her eyes. They were just words. Then one verse leapt out at her from the page as if illuminated: *'For I know the plans I have for you, declares the Lord, plans to prosper you and not to harm you, plans to give you a future and a hope.'* Positive plans. A future. Hope. Let it be enough to cling to, to feed on, to carry her through the day.

Bishops are consummate performers. They have a responsibility to rein in personal feelings so tightly that burning the toast at breakfast, a difficult phone call with wilful offspring, even the worst of bad hair days is not allowed to interfere with their professionalism. Like any actor, she said to herself as she carefully applied concealer to the bags under her eyes, we must be in complete control of the performance. Not that it should be a show, but simply that when their bishop shows up, the punters have a right to expect the best. It comes with the job. We are chosen because we can be relied on not to be tetchy, touchy or temperamental, but always dignified, courteous, encouraging and inspirational. Which is what I shall be, she said to her reflection, as she outlined her lips in a bright shade of pink.

Vicky's faith had always underpinned everything she did. She had promised herself at ordination that she would never recite familiar liturgy without meaning the words she said. But on this day, she had no choice but to go into autopilot. And somehow, she managed to deliver more than mechanistic ritual and a lifeless sermon, to smile and chat attentively to the hordes, to swallow a dry and heavy piece of Victoria sandwich, and wash it down with an enormous quantity of tepid, metallic-tasting tea.

She scolded herself in the back of the car as Noah drove her home. Be gentle with yourself. You can't pretend spiritual fervour. God knew the intention of your heart. You were determined to give Emily a good launch, and you did. She was grateful, bless her.

'OK, Archbishop?' Noah asked with concern.

He must have seen her lips moving, and wondered whether the crisis had addled her mind.

'Fine. Just thanking God for helping me survive today.'

Suddenly, she felt angry, so angry, that Tom had robbed her of her integrity. The selfish bastard. She hoped he had moved his things out by the time she got back. And yet, in the deepest recesses of her heart, she wanted him to be there, waiting for her, looking at her with the love he had had for her in the early days of their marriage. But clocks don't go backwards. He had protested his innocence so vehemently that she had believed him, which made those weekends in Canterbury, the few days on the Orient Express, even the tower of strength he had been through her illness, all the more a lie. How could she ever trust him again now?

She started crying again. Fool, she chided herself through gritted teeth. Don't let Noah see you like this. Stop this now. Be a man.

The day of the anti-proselytising rally was finally upon her. The previous night sleep had evaded her. It hadn't helped that Tom had rung to say he would come to collect his things the following evening. She had a fearful headache and took two paracetamol, but still tossed and turned. Recent events churned around her head, and she began to wonder – if it really took two to mess up a marriage, then she needed to assess seriously what part she had played, other than the superficial issue of working every hour God gave? What was it Donald had said to her just after the death of the child that had driven the wedge between them? She had written his words down in her journal.

She got up, fetched the relevant volume from her bureau, and took it back to bed with her. 'Your husband has an inalienable right to be sustained and consoled by you in all matters. Give him your time and your trust.' Had she given him either of the most precious gifts that were hers, and only hers, to give? Or had she, in fact, withheld them, as a form of punishment for his contamination of her conscience? She had questioned the integrity of his professionalism and perhaps, from that point on, had given him merely the dregs of her day. With a profound sadness, she switched off the light and allowed sleep to overcome her at last.

The following morning, she couldn't think of anything she wanted to do less than to stand before crowds, urging them to stand firm, be strong, follow their consciences and live with the consequences. And then she reminded herself that Kelvin had been negotiating with the authorities for months for the privilege of holding such a large event in Central London. Lacking any awareness of irony, they had threatened him with the enforcement of the anti-proselytisation laws – until she had intervened and asked them whether they had the resources to arrest as many as a million people. She owed it to all who came to make it a day to remember. The sun shone, which was a blessing in itself, as, for the first time in the history of voluntary service, Christians across the country withdrew their voluntary help for a day. Kelvin was jubilant when Vicky arrived at the centre of command, one white van among many stationed in Hyde Park, behind the stage erected for the speakers. He was listening to the media reports and watching the cameras. Hundreds of coaches were bringing people from towns and cities across England, Wales and Scotland. Crowds arrived at the train stations, on the tube, and they just kept on coming. Some had been travelling all night and sat around with makeshift breakfast picnics.

'How many do you reckon?' he called out to one of the technicians.

'Difficult to say, but at least a million.'

'And still an hour to go.'

The National Council for Voluntary Service claimed that 75 per cent of social enterprise and support work had been forced to close down for the day. A BBC reporter suggested that it left vulnerable people suffering undue hardship.

'No, no, no,' insisted a feisty meals-on-wheels volunteer from Nether Wallop. 'We couldn't leave our elderly friends to go hungry. We plated up salad meals and left them in their fridges yesterday, with homemade cakes, chocolate and orange juice to boot.'

London was gridlocked. All police leave in the capital had been cancelled and additional support drafted in, but they were forced simply to stand by and look on as organised chaos ensued, in the most peaceful way possible. At the appointed time for the official march to begin there were so many people in the streets that there was no way they could go anywhere. But no amount of waiting appeared to dampen their high spirits. Kelvin had recruited the most popular performers. Stationed on floats and platforms along the route, the noise echoed off the buildings and through the streets. Everyone seemed to be singing. Children sat on their parents' shoulders waving flags and banners. Wheelchairs were decorated with ribbons, balloons and streamers.

'You have to see this, Vicky,' Kelvin shouted, grabbing her arm and pulling her back towards the TV screens. Scanning the crowds congregated all over London, apparently uncaring now about getting anywhere, just enjoying the day, Vicky felt herself unwind, just slightly. Nuns held the hands of toddlers. Purple-shirted bishops rubbed shoulders with chatty, tattooed teenagers. Mothers' Union members walked arm in arm with ex-convicts from the Christian Prisoners' Association, the Association of Blind Catholics were led along by presenters from God TV, and members of the Legion of Mary communities danced to black

Pentecostal bands. Representatives of the Church of Scotland appeared to be sharing samosas and shortbread with the Muslim Doctors' and Dentists' Association. Quakers marched alongside uniformed members of the Federation of Military Christian Fellowships. Sikhs joined in the singing and chatted happily to members of React.

This was passive resistance at its best. In Hyde Park, where Kelvin had organised the largest tea party in history, volunteers had brought along thousands of cakes, and there was feasting and dancing. Salvation Army bands, black gospel choirs, and Christian rock bands took their turn at entertaining the crowds. It was carnival time. A grand day out.

Without thinking, Vicky threw her arms around Kelvin's neck.

'You're a genius!' she said.

'Hey,' he said, extricating himself. 'You're in enough trouble as it is. But I think you should see this as a huge vote of confidence in your leadership, whatever the media, and some of your fellow bishops, have to say.'

Vicky walked onto the platform to a volley of cheers and whistles, and a loud and lengthy ovation. A mass of blurred faces stretched as far as the eye could see, and beyond. The crowds settled slowly into an expectant hush. It was overwhelming, and paralysed her for a moment. She prayed audibly that she would speak truth, not tosh, which raised a few laughs, then took a moment to smile at her audience, and said, 'When you were a child, what did you dream you'd be?'

There were a few shouts within range, and she repeated them. 'A train driver, a zookeeper, a fireman, a footballer, a singer, a ballet dancer, an astronaut? So why isn't Hyde Park filled today with astronauts, footballers and film stars?'

There were some further laughs, some pointing at the celebrities who stood behind her on the platform.

'Ah, well, yes, we do have a few of them around, and I'm so grateful to them for their support.

'I must have been a boring child. I only ever dreamed of being a vicar. But that wasn't a possibility when I dreamed my big dream. Not for many years. If you had ever told me I would stand here in my current capacity I don't think I would have believed you. Dreams are vital to us. The great American prophet of racial equality, Martin Luther King, believed that one day his nation would rise up and live out the true meaning of its creed – justice, equality and acceptance for all people.

'His dream has been built upon to ensure freedom of belief and practice throughout the Western world. Let me read you Article 18 of the Universal Declaration of Human Rights: "Everyone has the right to freedom of thought, conscience and religion; this right includes freedom to change his religion or belief, and freedom, either alone or in community with others and in public or private, to manifest his religion or belief in teaching, practice, worship and observance." These freedoms are protected unconditionally. No government has the legal or moral right to deny them to its people. My dream is not, as some will say, to take us back to a dark past when religion was forced on anyone and everyone, but rather that we will live out the true meaning of this promise, in the face of a secularist creed that has become a religion – or perhaps I should say an "anti-religion" – of its own, a creed that would deny us the ability to share the biggest and best truth of human existence – indeed, the only truth that can make men and women truly free, and that has always been at the heart of our nation, with its rich history and cultural life.'

The volley of cheering and clapping lasted for some time.

'The alternative is that our country will be reduced to little better than a police state, like Stalinist Russia or Maoist China. We already live in a society where colleague betrays colleague, and neighbour betrays neighbour, and we no longer know who to trust. Every British citizen stands at risk of prosecution for expressing views that fail to meet with government approval.

'We stand here today, not just for religious liberty, but for freedom of speech, freedom of conscience, freedom of debate and discussion, freedom to share our stories and our faith, without the fear of losing our jobs and finding ourselves imprisoned just for being who we are. We stand not just for those who have religious faith, but for the common good, for every man and woman in this once great democracy of ours.'

Another prolonged, enthusiastic response. The exuberant acclaim of the audience, the bright, encouraging faces that she could see at the front, drove all other thoughts away, focused her mind completely and roused her to give this moment everything she had.

'Western society teeters on the brink of financial and moral collapse. At this critical time in our history we must hold on at all costs to the right to share the only real message of hope our nation has, which for me is best enshrined in the words of Job, perhaps the most ancient book of poetry upon this earth: "I know that my Redeemer lives, that in the end he will stand upon the earth, that after this skin has been destroyed, in my flesh, I will see God."

Hyde Park erupted. She had to fight to continue.

'We demand the repeal of the pernicious laws against sharing our faith publicly. We demand the freedom to let God's good news of restoration and redemption ring out across our country, in every block of flats and office building, in every shopping mall and football ground, on every hill-side and from the mountain tops. That is my dream today.'

She finished to what seemed like interminable applause. Eventually she was able to interrupt it sufficiently to point at the heavens and proclaim, 'His is the kingdom, the power and the glory.' The crowd broke out spontaneously into the Lord's Prayer. She led them, overwhelmed by the power of the moment as over a million people joined in, and the sound of it boomed around Hyde Park and echoed in the heavens above. As it ended, the black opera singer Gina Carroll came to the microphone and sang a slow, electrifying version of 'Amazing Grace'. She was followed by a Welsh male voice choir in 'Guide Me, O Thou Great Jehovah'. The London Community Gospel Choir took over, followed by various bands who played on until, concerned about contravening noise restrictions, the master of ceremonies finally brought the singing to an end and the people went wearily, but cheerfully, home to bed.

It was late when Vicky finally arrived back at Lambeth Palace, thoroughly exhausted, but happy for the first time in weeks. She had just poured herself a glass of wine, slipped off her shoes and put her feet up on the sofa when she heard the familiar click of the key turning in the lock and remembered. Damn, it was Tom coming to get his things. She heard his footfall approaching, down the corridor towards the door. The handle turned and he walked in, then stood looking at her for a while.

'You're here,' he said.

'Where else would I be? The Palace goes with the job, remember?'

'Vicky, please,' he begged, carefully sitting down next to her on the sofa, 'I've missed you so much. Can't we talk? Really talk?'

'Tom,' she moaned, 'it was the protest today. I'm exhausted. It's late.'

'Sorry. First chance I've had to get away from work.'

The words she had read last night came back to her – they were obviously still revolving around her head: 'An inalienable right to be sustained and consoled by you.' She pulled herself up from a slouch to a more upright sitting position.

'Okay,' she said, 'okay. But I need to know about the affair. Tell me exactly what happened. All of it. The truth.'

'There's so little to tell,' he muttered, looking away from her distractedly.

She folded her arms and steeled herself.

'Try me.'

'She threw herself at me – but you know that already and it's no excuse,' he said quickly, before she had time to interrupt. 'I suppose I was flattered.'

'Lots of women throw themselves at the handsome consultant. Why was this one different?'

'I've wondered that myself, so many times. Chemistry? Timing? That somewhere deep inside me I wanted to punish you for your . . . abandonment? It's like a lover, you know, the church. It pushes its way between us. It steals your emotional energy. Leaves nothing over for me.'

'No tangents. Where did you . . . ?'

'Cheap hotels. Her flat. Once in the office, after everyone had gone home.'

'Risky. She liked that, then?'

He ignored the jibe.

'I never really loved her. Before long I didn't even like her. It annoyed me, to be treated like a trophy she had won at the fair. It was the kudos of having seduced a consultant she wanted, not me, not really.'

'And you, what did you want?'

He sat for a while reflecting, then said, 'Adulation, adoration, company, intimacy, touch. For God's sake, Vicky, just a little normality, a moment's peace from the breakneck progress of our joint careers.'

Vicky felt desperate. Their marriage could never offer him that.

'So all down to me, then?'

'No, no, no, I'm not blaming you. I'm trying to explain. And doing a lousy job of it because at the end of the day, I have no idea why I did it. Except that she was available, and that it was risky, exciting, to throw off the restraints that your job imposed on me.'

He became agitated, lowered his head and ran his hands repeatedly through his hair.

'Vicky, I did a terrible thing to you, to us. I have hurt and humiliated you.'

Into her head flashed a picture of him on their first date, excusing his drunken behaviour. She remembered again with a heart-rending clarity how that ability of his to take responsibility for his own actions, the vulnerability portrayed all over his face, had broken through her defences back then, and reduced the walls she'd constructed against him to dust and rubble.

'When did it go so wrong?' she asked him, resisting the urge to reach out and stroke his hair. 'Presumably it all started when I was archdeacon?'

He nodded.

'I always intended to talk to you, get it out in the open, but then . . .'

'Then what?'

'You became a bishop.'

'Ah yes,' she said, 'I was afraid then of what that would do to our relationship. But I didn't know that the damage was already done. Maybe if
we'd had that time away together when we originally planned it . . .'

2016

Those in the know may have expected the appointment of a woman
bishop to happen quickly. Once the legislation came into force, a public
demonstration was needed. But why did it have to be her?

She read up about the Diocese of Larchester. The northernmost part
of the Greater London sprawl reflected the merciless and deepening social
separation of the country at large – small rural communities where
wealthy commuters had appropriated every decent brick and barn and
dwelt in bucolic comfort, to large, privately owned near-slum areas where
those least able to exercise choice were condemned to a place least chosen.
On the council estates a high-density mixed-race population lived in
shabby housing with a diet rich in all the wrong kinds of food, fighting
off diseases that shouldn't exist in the twenty-first century, like scabies
and rickets, and where too many households were ravaged by poor mental
health. In some places unemployment was running at nearly forty per
cent. The area was like a giant matchbox with frustration, disillusionment and despair rubbing up against privilege and middle-class
complacency. One tiny spark could set it alight.

In short, it was exactly the challenge Vicky needed: it would be an
immense privilege to lead the church in Larchester, to identify with the
pain of the dispossessed, to challenge the unfeeling institutions that
starved them of resources, little caring that they might be storing up
disaster, to try to encourage regeneration and kindle some kind of hope.
But could she do it? She had seen in Westhampton the way the strategic
nature of the role died a slow death in the face of the daily grind of civic
functions and church services. She felt confident her motives were good,
but might she be lying to herself; what if she truly only wanted the job for
the kudos?

And then there was Tom, who would be cast more publicly in the role
of consort. He had his own work, of course, and few would expect a man
to roll in the tea trolley – but he would have a lot to come to terms with.

She did what she always did in a crisis. She took herself up north to see
Donald. He really wasn't up to seeing anyone, but made a special excep-
tion for her. 'Ah, Vicky,' he said haltingly, rearranging the blanket around
his legs with trembling hands. 'A new chapter.'

'I don't know,' she exclaimed. 'My life is already too complicated, too compromised. Who am I, an almost-adulterer, to be a bishop?'

'Who are any of us?' Donald said mildly. 'The great spiritual writer, Richard Rohr, describes the grace we're given in failure as "falling upward". If you are open to your crisis, God can use it to propel you into a spiritual growth you could not have imagined before. It may well be a blessing in disguise. Now you know your weakness. It's your strength you have to worry about. That will tempt you to self-reliance. Vanity, even.'

'The excessive belief in one's own abilities or attractiveness to others,' she said to him. 'I looked it up once.'

'Indeed. One of the seven deadly sins. Related to the word "vainglory", originally meaning futility. The sin of being self-, not God-focused. When that happens, we wander away from our home near his heart and squander our true potential. Life becomes rather futile.'

'Everyone tells me I charm to get my own way. Half the time I can't see it – but then I realise it's exactly what I do, and it makes me far too cocky, too convinced of my own rectitude. I know I must eradicate this unholy awareness of my strengths if I'm to be the woman God intended me to be. As I get older there are fewer and fewer years left in which to redeem the potential I've wasted so far.'

'Ah, little Vicky, always so hard on yourself. God knows this image-obsessed world of ours is unwittingly seductive. He also knows your desire for a pure and holy devotion. And promises to meet the desires that are deeper than we know.'

'But would being a bishop bring me nearer to God, or lead me deeper into a dangerous self-reliance?'

'How can I tell you that? But going into it with eyes wide open is a good start. Stay focused, not on your gifts, but on the giver. Channel them continually into service, even – perhaps especially – service you balk at, that seems menial, beneath you, so that pride will be swallowed in true humility.'

'And Tom? What do I do about Tom?'

'If you believe, after some waiting and listening, that this is right, you must trust the same God who is speaking to you, to speak to him. While you, of course, will do your best to minimise the difficulties he fears.'

Donald lay back in his chair and closed his eyes. The effort had exhausted him and she got up to go. He took her hand as she was about to leave.

'Vicky,' he said, opening his eyes briefly and looking straight at her, 'what do you really fear?'

She blurted out, surprising herself as she did so, 'Being pilloried by the press, despised, hated, when I stand up for the values I believe in. You see how vain I am?'

'Moltmann said that suffering was inevitable if we live by the truths we believe. If we succumb to the cultural views and mores of our society, we are no longer living out our Christian calling. No longer disciples. Radical, sacrificial living. The cross, Vicky, it all boils down to that.'

She bit her lip and nodded.

'But after that, the certainty of resurrection,' he added with a beatific smile.

He squeezed the hand she held out to him.

'Ach, you'll be fine, lass. And I'm more proud of you than I know how to say.'

Before she dared to broach the subject to Tom, it was Alice, now in London on the Lloyds Bank Graduate training scheme, that she consulted. They met for a treat one afternoon in the imposing Orangery tearoom at Kensington Palace and sat companionably together in the rather grand surroundings of what had once been Queen Anne's entertaining pavilion.

'You can't turn this down, Mum, you know that,' Alice said earnestly, tucking a strand of long fair hair behind her ear. Vicky constantly marvelled at how she had managed to produce such a shrewd and sensible daughter. At sixteen Alice had been as grounded as any thirty-year-old. These days Vicky often wondered who was mothering whom.

'Did you ever resent it?' she hazarded. 'I mean, my being out so much when you were little? My being owned by the church?'

Alice thought for a while.

'I'd have liked to have seen you a little more, but any child with parents holding down two such demanding jobs would say that. But no, I don't resent it. That's where I got my independent streak.'

She smiled reflectively, and Vicky studied her face, with its wide, upturned mouth, straight white teeth, and her father's coruscating blue eyes. If she had achieved nothing else in life, this lovely young woman was enough.

'The other girls at school would moan about what was in their lunch boxes, so I used to say to them, "Do what I do. Make your own."'

'You make me feel a failure.'

'No, no, no,' she said, reaching out for Vicky's hand. 'I was proud of you, doing a job that made the world a better place. Breaking new ground for women like me, as you always used to tell me. And as for being a clergy kid, it means you learn to mix with anyone and everyone. I had dozens of surrogate parents, aunts, uncles, brothers and sisters.'

'I can't tell you how relieved I am. You always fear as a parent that you're scarring your child for life.'

Vicky poured them both a fresh cup of tea.

'What does a bishop do, exactly?' Alice asked. 'I know they ponce about in purple, but there must be more to it than that.'

'Where to start? Pastoral care of everyone in their diocese and especially of the clergy, of course, maintaining relationships with the civic authorities, contributing to the development of plans for local communities, encouraging local church and non-church initiatives, resolving conflicts, supporting international development, participation in national bodies like the House of Bishops and General Synod, chairing a committee or two, leading voluntary organisations.'

Alice nodded encouragingly. 'Mum,' she said, as Vicky stopped to draw breath, 'the job was made for you. You'll be brilliant at it.'

'But with the financial crisis going on so long and still biting so hard, it will take ruthless and unpopular measures to hack off the dead wood and support new growth.'

'You can do it if anyone can.'

'And your father? Do you think he'll be able to live with it?'

'You haven't told him?'

'The letter came just before Grandpa died.'

She nodded, thoughtfully, then exclaimed, 'Well, he'll be a bit stony about it at first – he hates your not being there for him – but he'll come round, I promise.'

It was Alice's confidence in her abilities that gave Vicky the courage to show Tom the invitation at last. He actually smiled, and she wondered whether Alice hadn't softened him up a little. She could wrap her father around her little finger.

'Well,' he said, 'it's great to have some good news at a time like this. Ernest would have dined out on it for years. "My daughter-in-law, the Bishop."'

She accepted the job, but with a rider. No pay rise. She would simply be paid the standard clergy stipend, plus a contribution towards heating the rather uncomfortably grandiose residence. It was one of the larger episcopal palaces, yet had survived the most recent cull on the grounds that the rooms were small enough and the ceilings low enough to make the heating bills manageable. But it was still big enough to house three families comfortably, and with only Vicky and Tom living there, it felt a little extravagant.

'I'm thinking of asking the Church Commissioners if we can't convert part of the Palace into two flats, each with its own separate entrance,' she said to Tom, as she sat in a window seat in the sitting room, watching the squirrels tearing up and down the extensive, landscaped garden. 'The rent would offset the running costs.'

Tom, sherry glass in hand, looking every bit the lord of the manor, strolled across the room to her and, looking out over his well-clipped lawn, said, 'Come on, Vick, if we were buying our own place like normal people we could afford a house like this.'

She turned and gave him a look.

'Well,' he said, grinning, 'maybe not quite as big as this.'

On reflection, she thought Tom better-looking in maturity than he ever had been. He wore his dark hair, now tipped with grey, swept back from his face, emphasising the high forehead and chiselled jawline, and lending greater depth to those remarkable eyes of his. No wonder his female patients fell in love with him. She really needed to keep a closer eye on him.

'Doesn't it strike you as funny,' she said, accepting the sherry that he had poured for her, 'that we have an entire Bishop's Palace with ten bedrooms to choose from, yet we sleep in the same one, in the same space? Presumably bishops and their wives once had their own separate suites of rooms, while the domestic staff had separate living quarters altogether.'

'It doesn't strike me as funny at all,' he said, standing behind her, as they watched twilight slowly descend upon the grounds, enfolding them in an ever-darkening stillness. 'It means we still have a marriage. I'm one of only two men in the country who gets to sleep with a bishop.'

He gently massaged her shoulder with his spare hand.

'I do love you, you know.'

It was the first time he had said so since their move, and she had needed to hear it.

She still hankered after the easy meeting of minds she had known with Tim, but when they rose up she tried to push those memories away, to concentrate instead on rebuilding her communion with Tom.

She thought back to their four-night trip to Venice on the Orient Express, just a few months previously. The expense had been gargantuan, but what price a relationship, she had asked herself, and at such a crucial time?

Alone in a small, enclosed space, the distance between them seemed as deep and wide as the Channel. Despite the breath-taking scenery, the gourmet food, and the cosy opulence of their private cabin, she couldn't seem to reach him.

But once they reached Venice, the alchemy of the place worked its magic. Tom relaxed, became more present, more attentive, more alive. In a gondola on a twisting canal, they sat as close to each other as the two pigeons on the branch she had watched with such envy, and somehow, he metamorphosed at last into the dashing young beau she remembered, grasping her hand to point out a sudden, spectacular view or a stunning architectural feature.

On the way home, encompassed by the dazzling, snowy magnificence of the Italian Dolomites and Swiss Alps, she knew again the intimacy of intermingled breath, flesh and heart as they lay entwined, rocked by the steady motion of the train in their cosy cabin bed.

Yes, she thought: the way is hard, but it will be worth it.

2023

'Was Venice a dream, a lie, a mockery?' she asked him now.

He shook his head.

'Venice was the most real thing in our relationship for years, my darling. I vowed then to end it with Marilyn the moment I got home. And I did. I never slept with her again after that.'

He was still sitting on the sofa next to her, but she could barely make out his features in the dark. She was afraid to reach out and put on the lamp, lest it disrupt the moment.

'You have hurt me more than you will ever know,' she said softly, as a clutch of gloating ecclesiastical faces paraded their way through her mind like characters from a Trollope novel.

'We were closer after that, though, weren't we? Until you became Archbishop, and then I didn't seem to be able to do anything to stop us drifting apart again.'

'I can't duck the blame for that,' she admitted sadly.

'What I'm asking you is whether you can you find it in your heart to forgive this fool of a man who has brought you such grief, yet loves you more than life itself. Life can be pretty intolerable with you at times, but it is even more intolerable without you.'

He started to weep. But not like any woman she had ever seen. His anguish seemed to heave its way out from a desolate place where he had stored it, choking him in the process, in the most terrible body-wrenching groans. Had she contributed to this? The solid lump of ice in her guts began to thaw. Should she tell him about Tim? But what was there to tell? That she'd had an infantile infatuation, borne of his neglect? It sounded like tit for tat, and would do very little except to absolve her own conscience. But she needed to remember that Tom wasn't the only one with repenting to do.

'Tom, I can't bear to see you like this,' she said. Her instinct was to wrap her arms around his neck, press her cheek into his and comfort him. But still she held back, and simply touched his arm. He clamped his hand over hers. The sobs subsided slowly and he rubbed his eyes with his free hand.

'Could you ever see yourself taking me back?' he asked, still too over-wrought even to look at her.

She didn't know what to say. Her pragmatic mind buzzed, but she couldn't let it rule the roost. Remaining married could simply be the means of maintaining a wounded, resolute dignity that enabled her to carry on with the job. She could see herself saying to the press, 'We are working at our relationship', while the reality was that it was a conven-ience, as the Bishop of Normington had suggested it would be. Sticking a plaster over the wound without ever dealing with the infection. She couldn't live like that. Whatever she did had to be wholehearted.

But then his arms encircled her and all resistance melted. She had missed that familiar, musky male scent of him, a mixture of body oils, aftershave, freshly laundered shirt, and a vague hint of antiseptic. Despite herself, she still wanted the gentle touch of those long surgeon's fingers.

'We can't ever go back, Tom,' she whispered, 'but I'm prepared to see if we can find a way forward.'

'To stay together?' he asked, pulling away from her.

'Together,' she conceded. 'We'll need help. I'm in such a fog, I can't find my way through it.'

'Counselling?'

'Could you put your male pride on hold?'

'If that's what you want.'

'I think so, yes. Something external to us, to make sure we stay the course and get things fixed as properly as we can.'

He leant towards her to kiss her on the lips, but she turned her head and switched on the lamp.

'Leave your things here. Just take what you need right now. And I'll see you soon.'

TWENTY-THREE

If love stops, we make a fixed image of each other. We judge and pin each other down. That is death. But love liberates us from these images and keeps the future open for the other person. We have hope for each other, so we wait for one another. That is life.

JÜRGEN MOLTMANN

JUNE 2023

Sister Agnes, one of the gentle nuns downstairs, who had replaced Donald as her spiritual director, recommended a discreet marriage guidance counsellor attached to their retreat house in Kent.

Meg was not at all what Vicky imagined. She was bird-like and wrinkled, with tight white curls and twinkling, penetrating eyes that wouldn't allow for any prevarication. The disarming, dimpled little smile concealed a shrewdness that made them both say the things they never intended to say, but that needed to be said.

And the dirty laundry all tumbled out of the basket. To be picked over, sniffed at, and examined for stains. For Tom's part, the lack of her presence, the lack of her support, the lack of any life other than the church, and the lack of sex.

'When we're apart, when I'm away, I want it – I want you,' she tried to explain to him, 'but when we're together, it barely ever enters my head.'

'Because you're so busy you haven't time to think about it.'

She acknowledged it, reluctantly.

'But primarily because of the menopause. Do you think I like seeing my libido limp away because it's extraneous to requirements these days, but that's how it feels.'

'Why didn't you say?'

'I didn't want to admit to ageing, I suppose. I don't think I realised how much it was affecting me. Or us. And there seemed so many more important things to do.'

'And that's the nub of it.'

'No, it isn't Tom. I need affection. I need to be courted, to be wooed, but you never as much as tried. Whether any remaining spark of passion can be reignited now, when all that was sacred between us has been defamed, I can't tell. I'm worried that Marilyn will forever be insinuating her busty body between us.'

'And Ralph?'

'Ralph? I have never slept with Ralph. How could you possibly . . .?'

'You spend more time with him than you spend with me.'

'We work together. That's it. Nothing more.'

Meg observed them both for some time, then smiled benignly from one to the other, as if this was the moment she had been waiting for. Then she said to Vicky, 'What you are trying to ascertain is whether you can continue to be successfully married to a person you no longer trust. The answer, quite simply, is you can't. In a very real sense, your marriage ended when Tom began his affair, and the marriage vows you took were broken. Marriage is a contract between two people, and when one person violates the terms, the contract is null and void. That may sound harsh, but what you're doing, at last, is facing up to the reality of your situation. The question is, not can the broken marriage continue, but can a new marriage emerge? Can acts of betrayal or a loss of integrity be forgiven? Can trust be rebuilt? I believe that redemption is always possible – but it depends on your willingness to co-operate – with each other, and with the redeemer of all things.'

She turned to Tom.

'A new relationship will probably have to include some form of restitution by the person who broke the original agreement.'

Tom looked at Vicky and nodded slowly.

'Think about what that might be,' Meg instructed him as they left.

He was quiet at the wheel of the car on the way back to Lambeth. Though he had moved back in, he was sleeping in a different room.

'I like what she said about falling in and out of love many times in a marriage,' he said. 'Falling in love with the same person over and over again must surely be the healthiest way to live.'

'And the cheapest.'

He turned to her and grinned.

'Ever the pragmatist.'

'Better for the children,' she said.

'It's what you've always preached, Archbishop,' he said. 'Have you told Alice?'

'Of course. Couldn't let her see it in the papers first.'

'What does she say?'

'That we must forgive seventy times seven, as it says in the good book.'

'And what did you say?'

'That I never thought it would be put to the test like this. Strange, isn't it, when your children start telling you how to live?'

'Awe-inspiring. It makes me feel we got something right.'

'You will give me time?'

He nodded. She said to him after a while, 'Tom, I've been thinking. This breach of contract wasn't your fault alone. I need to make restitution too. I could go back to parish work. Like a previous Archbishop of York.'

'And announce to the world that a woman can't do the job? I'd never forgive myself.'

Several days later, as she and Ralph were at her desk in the study at Lambeth, discussing the job description for a new secretary of public affairs, Tom marched in looking more buoyant than she had seen him look for months. He was never normally home in the middle of the day and they both stared at him surprise.

'I've resigned,' he announced, throwing up his hands in what Vicky could only describe as glee.

'You've what?' she gasped. 'Why, Tom?'

She wondered for a moment whether she hadn't given him the idea of making such a sacrificial gesture and was horrified at the thought of it. He loved his work.

'I was called into the CEO's office when I arrived at the hospital this morning, and told that I had been suspended, pending a full investigation into my conduct. I asked on what grounds, and they came up with some lame, half-baked excuse about events in my private life making me a risk to patients. I asked if anyone had made a formal complaint, and they couldn't tell me.'

'Of course they couldn't,' Ralph said with a snort. 'Not when the pressure comes from the very top.'

Vicky started as the extent of her ignorance and naivety finally began to dawn.

'No, Ralph. It can't have been.'

She studied his face for some reassurance, but he gave her none.

'He wouldn't stoop to this? Would he? I can't believe it – even of him.'

Tom moved to her side and put an arm around her shoulder.

'He couldn't have put Marilyn up to it?' she asked helplessly.

'I'm fairly sure he did. When you're a senior government minister,' Ralph said, with feigned cheerfulness, 'you can do almost anything you like.'

'But why? How can a man be so embittered?'

'Many years ago I did warn you what he was like. But still you've antagonised him, Vicky. Made him look inept. He's already had the humiliation of watching your star rise, while he was pipped to the top post by a jumped-up little . . .'

'Muslim?' Tom said, unabashed as ever, in the face of the rules of political correctness.

Ralph nodded.

'What's more, you thwart the government continually. Wooten Grange was their Achilles heel. You provoked a showdown – and won. Mahdi invited you in, but I can't imagine his ministers were happy about the outcome, or the way you unpicked their policy on benefits.'

'So, he strikes.'

Ralph rubbed his chin.

'I have a feeling that it isn't over yet. I think there's more to this than wounded pride or political hubris, but I can't quite put my finger on what.'

'But to make Tom pay for it! How could he do that?' Vicky asked, clasping the hand that still rested on her shoulder. She looked up at her husband. 'I'm so, so sorry, Tom.'

He kissed her gently on her forehead and said, 'I'm not. It might turn out to be the best thing that could have happened. What is it I've heard you preach so often about all things coming together for good?'

She smiled at him lamely and he leant forward and whispered in her ear, 'My restitution,' then stood up and, shaking his head, said, 'But my word, what did you do to our Secretary of State for Health, to have this effect on the man?'

Mark! What had she once seen in him? She couldn't remember. The only image in her mind now was of the rather dissolute-looking, older version she had seen a mere few weeks ago. It was hard to believe now that he could have once been an object of such overwhelming passion and utter despondency.

1983

She told him she intended being ordained that first time he bought her a drink at the 24 Club. Mark had laughed and she thought that was the last she would hear from him. But to her amazement and utter dismay, he sent her an invitation to be his partner at the prestigious Durham Union Society Michaelmas ball. She would never fully understand why she accepted, wondering later whether there wasn't some truth in the claim that physical chemistry is based on a subconscious search for the best breeding partner. Or perhaps it was simply the vanity of being asked out by the most desirable man in her orbit. There was certainly no rational sense in pursuing a relationship with the President of the Durham University Conservative Association. Nonetheless, it turned out to be a magical evening of gourmet food, champagne and first-class bands, set against the enchanting backdrop of Auckland Castle, home to the Bishop of Durham.

'What must it be like to live in a place like this?' she asked Mark, as they wandered, hand in hand, through the gracious, stately rooms, he in dinner jacket and vivid red bow tie and cummerbund, she in a black evening gown with a velvet bodice and full taffeta skirt.

'You haven't seen my folks' little pile yet,' he said, smiling.

'Is it like this?' she asked, panic-stricken.

'No, not quite. But nice.'

The following morning, as she sat cradling a magnificent bouquet of lilies and agapanthus, she asked herself over and over again what on earth a *petit bourgeois* grammar-school girl with socialist leanings, feminist tendencies and dreams of disrupting one of the country's most established institutions, was doing with a wealthy, public-school educated Tory boy. And one with plans to restore the male honour of the party by becoming a more right-wing Prime Minister than Mrs Thatcher herself, to boot. She had held her tongue, reluctant to provoke a row on their first date and ruin such a lovely night, trusting that morning would restore her common sense. Instead, her malady had worsened. She had never felt like this before, her insides in turmoil at the mere thought of that one other human being, leaving her dizzy and disoriented, victim to wild and wonderful sensations that were frighteningly tantalising, unbelievably pleasurable and totally irrational. That kind of romantic love, if that's what it was, wasn't predictable or reasonable. But it was too late already to nip it in the bud. The man had conjured with her mind. She was addicted. As so many girls before her, she suspected ruefully.

For reasons she could not understand, he pursued her, and they became what Melanie called 'an item', hardly ever out of each other's company. Prince Charming was attentive, thoughtful and a great deal wealthier than most students. He phoned when they were apart, took her to lovely little out-of-the-way restaurants, sat gazing into her eyes, hanging on her every word. He couldn't possibly find her so tantalising, she said to herself, yet he said he'd never felt like this about any other girl, letting her know in the process that there had been more than just a few.

'You're only twenty-something,' she said to him bluntly, 'too young to know what you really feel.'

Yet in her heart she hoped he did.

'Funny little Vicky, always the realist,' he countered, brushing her lips with his until she couldn't think straight. Her sexual feelings were at a high pitch and he knew it, knew how to apply pressure without making it too obvious, knew how to bend girls to his will. And she was only just in control enough to recognise that if she gave him what he wanted, she would forfeit the self-respect inherent in a belief system where virginity, once given away, couldn't be retrieved.

They argued about it endlessly, though they argued, in a jocular sort of way, about most things, from the government of the country to the films they saw. It always ended with his taking her on his knee, explaining in reasoned tones why she was wrong and he was right. It took her a while to realise why this made her so uncomfortable – she felt as if she were a ventriloquist's dummy, being groomed to parrot his world-view. It riled her and she tried to resist because it wasn't an argument amongst equals, but the warmth of his body liquefied the fiercest opposition, and before she knew it they were a living testimony to the triumph of passion over politics.

In retrospect, she wondered whether her resistance to his sexual advances was all that kept Mark at her side. He was intrigued by the first girl to hold out against his determination to take her virginity. Then she convinced herself that this quintessentially desirable man simply wanted an ordinary little northern girl for who she was, not as a rare, exotic feather in his cap. Only when she spent a few days of the Christmas vacation in his baronial home and saw him in his natural habitat did she allow herself to question whether their romance really was the stuff of fairy tales.

The parental 'pile' was a mock-Tudor mansion complete with battlements, high towers, half-timbered upper facades, and mullioned stone windows, a stately home fit for a lord of the manor. But Mark's father was strictly new money, a bigwig in one of the major banks, who addressed everyone in his orbit as if they were staff, and expected the appropriate, dutiful response.

'Theology?' he growled, on her first night in his home, his resonant tuba of a voice raised just enough to be heard down the entire length of the oak table that filled a baronial-sized dining room. It had been polished to a mirror finish and the exquisitely cut wine glasses that sat in burgundy pools of candlelight threw distorted shadows onto the walls.

Vicky started. She had been trying to work out which cutlery to use for the melon. She looked across at Mark, who raised his eyebrows in warning, then turned to his father. The man was unprepossessing in many ways, with an ill-defined chin, and sparse, tawny-coloured hair stretched across a freckled pate. Although he was of medium height and build, he gave the impression of being a great deal bigger than he was, simply by putting his weight, quietly and forcefully, behind whatever he said. Vicky couldn't imagine him in anything other than the jacket and silk tie he was wearing for what Mark had called 'an informal, quiet family dinner'.

He studied her over the top of his half-moon glasses, waiting for her response. The hint of disparagement in his tone annoyed her, but she bit her tongue and simply nodded a smiling response. But he wouldn't leave it alone.

'Who studies God these days? Where will that get you?'

He tugged a large black grape off a bunch poised decorously on top of a pyramid of fruit in the centre of the table and popped it into his mouth.

'Leave her alone, Daddy. She can study whatever she wants,' piped up Libby, Mark's younger, horse-mad sister, who was pursuing a life of equestrianism on the basis that while there was a son at university, a daughter could please herself. They were alike, she and Mark, but the boyish features that were attractive on him did her no favours. Nor did dragging her hair back from her face into a tight and heavy ponytail at the top of her head, so that, from behind, she resembled the animals that took up so much of her time.

She was silenced with a look from her father, and didn't raise her head from her plate for the rest of the meal.

'So, tell me,' asked the lord of the manor languidly, skewering her with his look as he had just skewered a piece of melon to his fork, 'what do you plan to do with a degree in theology? Teach, presumably?'

It was her turn to be silenced, with a pleading look from Mark. Virginia, his mother, didn't miss it. She didn't appear to miss anything that concerned her beloved son, as she sat in silence, watching him fondly. Vicky understood now where Mark's whiff of entitlement came from. It went with being the only son of these parents.

Virginia and Mark's father seemed an odd match. She was a tall, rather stately woman, taller than he was, with a razor-sharp nose and a short, iron-grey haircut that she carried off by having excellent cheekbones and startling, almond-shaped, grey eyes. She was wearing a high-collared white shirt with a cameo at the neck, and a longish tweed skirt. Too traditional, Vicky suspected, to have any sympathy with the girlfriend's feminist aspirations. But Mark adored her, and he was evidently the centre of her universe. From the way Virginia looked at her, Vicky deduced that she was not what Mrs Bradley-Hind had had in mind for her son.

'Yes, I suppose so,' she said offhandedly, twisting the stem of her wine glass with her hand. Mark nodded enthusiastically, and his father, with a slight sigh, wiped his mouth with his white linen napkin and took a slow, appreciative mouthful of wine.

'Thank you,' Mark whispered to her later, taking her into his arms in the oppressively dark oak-panelled hallway.

She tried to pull herself free, but his grasp was too tight for her.

'For what?' she hissed. 'For helping you save face?'

He nodded sheepishly.

'I don't know how they would have responded if you'd said you wanted to be a vicar.'

'They were manifestly not impressed with the idea of teaching either.'

'No, but it's less loaded. Can't upset the old pair, can we?'

She was tempted to say, 'But it's all right for them to upset me?' but held her peace, aware that open disagreement would earn her no brownie points.

'Walk? Talk? Scrabble?' he asked.

'No, I'm a bit weary. I think I'll just head for bed.'

Reluctantly, he let her go.

'Condemned to port with the old man,' he sighed, as she left him at the bottom of the staircase.

When she reached her en suite bedroom – all mock beams, chintz and lavender potpourri – and sank down on the bed with a sigh of relief, she realised she had left her glasses in the sitting room. Damn. She was as blind as a bat without them, so there'd be no cosying up with a book if she didn't go back down. Waiting for silence to descend on the house, she got ready for bed, then, wrapped in her fleece dressing gown, crept downstairs, holding her breath, willing the joists not to creak, praying that there was no one was in the sitting room.

The study door was slightly open as she tiptoed past. A coil of choking cigar smoke wafted out into the hall and she had to stifle the urge to cough. She became aware of voices, Mark's and his parents', raised in what appeared to be a disagreement over money.

'I hope you know what you're doing,' she heard Mark's mother say.

'For crying out loud, Virginia, if I don't know how to keep it in the family, who does?'

'This offshore account is legal? That's all I'm asking.'

'Would I do anything that wasn't?' he said, as if he were soothing a child whose toy needed mending. 'Godfrey has been a family friend for years. He's entirely reliable, as you know only too well.'

'Godfrey's getting on.'

'Nicholas is taking over his affairs. He's a very sharp young man. Making some interesting investments. I have every confidence in him. Nothing to worry about, Virginia, I promise you.'

'You must trust Dad,' Mark chimed in curtly. 'Let's face it, Mother, what do you know about money?' And then he added in a more conciliatory voice, 'You go on up to bed and I'll come and tuck you in.'

Vicky shot into the sitting room, retrieved her glasses as quickly as she could and sped back up to her room.

Virginia caught her alone in the hall the following morning. She was wearing a lavender cape and on her way out to a WI meeting. A matching felt bowler with a small feather in its band sat jauntily on her head. Hearing Vicky come down the stairs, she turned on the threshold and filleted her with her eyes for a few seconds.

'You do know Mark is far too young to know his own mind, don't you, Vicky?'

She must have looked as startled as a rabbit caught in the car headlights, and grasped the bannister for support.

'He's far too clever and responsible to consider a serious relationship at this stage of his life, with a no doubt illustrious London career ahead of him.'

Vicky nodded dumbly.

'Durham is a very tiny lake when he has the whole sea to fish from, and virtually limitless opportunities to make a decent catch.'

And with that she swept out.

Vicky was furious with herself for being so tongue-tied. A pushover. The quick and clever responses that would have enabled her to hold her ground always seemed to arrive two minutes too late. On reflection, though, it was probably just as well. Virginia would then have dismissed her as insolent, as well as socially inept.

Those few days in Mark's home were incredibly difficult. Vicky felt completely out of her depth, and out of sorts too. The moment they were out of hearing range they didn't merely argue, they rowed, about everything from what to do and where to go, to the existence of God and the relevance of religious faith – both equally far-fetched in his estimation, and completely overrated as subjects of intelligent conversation. They rowed about the effectiveness of Thatcher's free-market policies, and most of all, they rowed about her not fulfilling his parents' aspirations as a suitable partner for their son.

On her last night, some time after she had switched off the light, Mark let himself into her bedroom, clad only in a pair of boxers, and slipped into the large double bed. He had tried his luck throughout the stay with dogged and annoying regularity, and she was running out of excuses to hold him off. From her perspective his mother's behaviour was the perfect anti-aphrodisiac. She was still incensed.

'Ah, so that's why you won't let me have my wicked way with you,' he whispered into her hair, his hands writhing around her body like the tentacles of a giant octopus. She disentangled herself, shoved him off with brute force and sat up abruptly.

'My mother has come between us,' he groaned.

The picture wasn't a happy one, but it made Vicky smile. At least there was something to thank her for. Mark emerged slowly from underneath the sheets, and sat with his arms folded and his mouth turned down at the corners.

'It's not just your mother,' she argued. 'I'll tell you again what I always tell you, that for me, sex isn't just a pastime to be indulged in as and when we feel like it. It's a gift given to enhance one life-long relationship.'

'That God of yours is such a bore.'

'And don't try and manipulate me,' she snapped at him, moving to the far side of the bed. 'In any case, it's not boring to refuse someone whose parents have made it abundantly clear that I'm not what they have in mind for their son. That's self-preservation.'

To her horror he leapt out of bed, ran round to her side of it, and went down on one bended knee.

'Marry me, then. This summer. If that's what it takes to prove I love you and don't give a fig what my parents say.'

She leant down to take a closer look at him, trying to decide if this was just one of his usual ploys to get his own way. He looked so comical wearing only his boxers, naked-chested with his arms stretched out wide, that she was sorely tempted to throw herself into them. But even then, she couldn't distinguish the genuine from ruse, so what hope was there for their future?

'Mark, get real,' she begged him. 'You'll be starting a career in the city, and I have two more years of my degree to do.'

'What's a degree? I'll earn enough to keep us both.'

'And it's only theology, after all. Is that what you're trying to say?'

He ignored the sarcasm, just as he always avoided what he found unpalatable.

'I love you too much to let you go. And you love me?'

'You know I do. Will you get up from the floor, for goodness' sake? We'll talk about it in the morning. Let's sleep on it.'

'Together?'

She threw a pillow at him and pointed at the door.

Back in Harrogate, she went straight to the vicarage to find Paula. Paula took one look at her face and said, 'Pete, take the kids to the park.'

'I don't know what to do,' Vicky said, fiddling with a loose thread on the arm of the chair, while she tried to unravel a mass of disconnected thoughts and feelings. 'I love him so much – but we don't agree about anything. He doesn't understand me, he doesn't understand my faith. He wouldn't let me tell his parents about the vicaring, and they hate me anyway.'

'Hmmm, so tell what isn't so good about the relationship?'

Vicky managed a short smile, then let out a long sigh.

'You're right, it doesn't have anything going for it. But I can't let him go.'

'If you don't, Vicky, he'll go on making you deeply unhappy. The warning signs are there. Or why would you have come round to ask me what I think?'

In her bedroom that night she got down on her knees, and for some time she argued with the insistent voice in her head that told her that Mark had to go. When all the arguments ran out, leaving her feeling spent and anguished, she finally gave in to what she knew to be the voice of reason, and wept, heartbroken, for what seemed like hours. Then slowly, a reality beyond her powers of rational comprehension broke into her emptiness, suffusing her with an almost ethereal quality of calm such as she had never experienced before. It was a strange physical sensation, a kind of gentle embrace that soothed away the pain and filled her with the certainty that life could go on without him, might even be a great deal better without all the bickering. She eventually fell into bed, exhausted, as light began to penetrate the thin cotton curtains.

She awoke at ten, still feeling extraordinarily peaceful, threw open the curtains to the same old street, but in a world that shone with endless, new possibilities. This feeling can't last, she said to herself. But it did, for several days – right up until Mark met her at Durham Station.

'You positively glow,' he said, as he swung her and her heavy case down from the train.

'We'll talk about it later,' she said, as he held out an arm for her, and she took it out of habit. He turned and looked into her face.

'So it's not seeing me, then?'

She dug him in the ribs.

'Vain to the last. You know, there always will be someone else in my life, someone altogether bigger than you.'

'Ah, the invisible third party.'

Their relationship struggled on for longer than Vicky intended. Somehow, she couldn't find the right time or words for what she knew she must do. They argued bitterly about the miners' strike, Mark applauding Mrs Thatcher for destroying such a powerful union, Vicky convinced Thatcher was destroying the miners' livelihood and communities. But their personal disagreements were even deeper than their political ones. Mark accepted that she wasn't prepared to throw away her degree to marry him, but still expected her to encourage his aspirations, while showing little interest in hers. He said Thatcher was wonderful, inspirational and sexy – to older men, of course. But if she wasn't exactly a freak, she was certainly a rarity, one of those little tricks of history in fallow times, when men are wanting and a woman with the heart of a lion and the constitution of an ox emerges to plug the gap – Boudicca, Cleopatra, Elizabeth I, Catherine the Great. But this, he stressed, was not the norm. Men were made for power. And now, a new generation of male shooting stars were set to make their shining debut in the political galaxy. He, of course, was one of them.

She bided her time while he took his finals – with a maddening minimum of exertion and a great deal of bravado – but with them out of the way she knew she had to broach the subject. He had booked a post-examination celebration at an expensive restaurant on the river. She planned to wait until after the meal to explain that there was no way he would be free to change the world tied to a vicar-wife. But before she had a chance to say anything, he produced a ring. Appalled, she was taken completely off guard and rushed out to the Ladies.

By the time she emerged he had paid the bill and they walked along the tow path in heavy, angry silence, despite the balmy summer air. She tried to explain the reasons for her decision, but he couldn't, or wouldn't, listen. That she should hold fast to her intention of pursuing a career that wasn't even open to her was beyond his ability to grasp. It always had been, she realised. Any career other than supporting his was out of the question.

'But this is a calling, Mark. I can't just walk away from it.'

He found it hilarious that she could even consider condemning him to a lifetime of clergy accommodation that wasn't Auckland Castle.

'You really mean you would expect me to live in some 1960s, jerry-built council house, like our local padre in Suffolk?' he asked, snorting at the thought of it. 'God, what a pitiful existence.'

The silence descended again as she waited for him to realise that she was in deadly earnest, that nothing he had to offer was going to make her change her mind.

'So that's it then? You don't want my ring? You don't want me? All this time I've waited for you, done without sex to please you, to show you what a patient man I am, and you never really wanted me.'

'Mark, I did. God knows I do,' she said, reaching out for his arm, but he flicked her off as if she were a fly landing on his sleeve, turned around and stormed off in the opposite direction down the towpath.

'I've always loved you,' she shouted after him.

He turned, and with a look that was as near to loathing as any she had ever seen, that shook her to her very core, said quietly, 'Don't. Just don't.'

And with that, he walked out of her life.

Or so she thought.

The last days of term were almost unbearable. She alternated between blaming herself for not releasing him sooner, and doubting the wisdom of her decision, and longing to ring him up to apologise and tell him she couldn't live without him. She might well have made a complete fool of herself, trying to hurl herself into his arms despite knowing he would never take her back now, were it not for the blessed Mels, her two friends with the combined sensitivity of a block of granite. Perhaps that was why she needed them as friends.

'We always knew it wouldn't work, Mel and me,' said big Melanie, handing Vicky a mug of thin, grey student coffee, as she sat in their room, licking her wounds and looking for diversion.

She raised her eyebrows.

'I mean, let's be honest – you weren't his type.'

'Not gorgeous enough?'

Melanie giggled. Vicky knew she was right.

'No, no, no, I didn't mean that. You were just chalk and cheese. And then all that recent stuff – well, we knew, didn't we?'

Melissa nodded, pursing her lips in disapproval.

'What recent stuff?'

Melanie looked at her, disconcerted, blushed and pushed a few escaping strands of hair behind her ear.

'What recent stuff, Melanie?'

'Oh. I assumed you knew. I'd never have said otherwise.'

'Then tell me now. Please. It will help.'

'Word on the block was that he was shagging Fiona whatshername, you know, the earl's daughter, his vice-president at the Tory Association.'

'Since when?'

Melanie shrugged.

'Maybe a few weeks?'

'The little toad,' Melissa added.

Vicky felt as if an IRA petrol bomb had gone off in her guts, that her whole body had exploded into the air and fallen to the floor, shattered into a thousand pieces.

'Why didn't you say anything?' she heard herself ask, from a very long way away.

'Wasn't that why you called it off?' Melissa asked.

She noticed Melanie catch Melissa's eye, and both went silent.

'No, I didn't know,' Vicky managed to whisper, smiling inanely, 'but I'm so glad you told me.' She got up in a daze, heard herself say, 'I'd better get on with that essay,' and staggered back to her room, wondering how she was ever going to put herself back together.

Mark never appeared at the 24 Club again, a self-banishment inflicted by wounded pride, she suspected, though Ralph popped in one evening as she sat there alone. He went straight over to her, sat down heavily at the table without as much as a greeting and began to swing backwards and forwards on his chair.

'Drink?' she asked him.

He shook his head and she waited, watching him. The swinging came to a sudden halt and he pierced her with a look of such intensity that she felt uncomfortable.

'Vicky, take care,' he said without preamble. 'Don't underestimate Mark. He's passionate in love, but poisonous in hate. This is a man who always gets what he wants. No one has ever denied him anything. He's not to be crossed.'

'You're not threatening me, are you, Ralph?'

He shook his head vehemently, looking slightly shocked.

'Just warning you, because I'm fond of you, in case you're not aware of it, you idiot.'

'I love Mark, but I had no choice but to call it off. There were too many differences. It could never have worked between us.'

'Then beware,' Ralph said.

She was tempted to laugh at this rather crass attempt at playing the prophet of doom, but he was so deadly earnest, his heavy brows knotted in anxiety, that she kept her face straight. But she was bewildered.

'Why? What on earth can he do to me? People break up all the time. He'll just have to learn to deal with it, like any other sensible bloke.'

'But Mark isn't a "sensible bloke". He's the proverbial elephant that never forgets. Not a perceived slight, at any rate. Just keep out of his way, I beg you.'

'That shouldn't be difficult, now that he's on his way to some illustrious career in the city. And anyway,' she said as an afterthought, trying her best to disguise any sense of pique, 'I gather he has someone else, in fact, has had for some time.'

Ralph studied her face, then shook his head in disbelief.

'You thought he'd survive all this time without sex, Vicky? What planet are you on?'

She was flabbergasted at such a blatant betrayal of her private affairs.

'If he couldn't be faithful to me now, he never would be. And that's not good enough,' she muttered through her teeth.

'If you mean Fiona, I don't think she means very much to him,' he said as he got up to go. He paused for a moment with his hands on the back of the chair, and his face softened. 'Actually,' he said, delivering his parting shot with a wistful smile, 'you picked the wrong man, Vicky.'

Three months later, Melissa sheepishly handed her a small cutting from *The Times*:

Friday October 5ᵗʰ, 1984

> Lord Charles and Lady Diana Atherton of Ashbury are delighted to announce the betrothal of their daughter, Fiona, to Mark Bradley-Hind, son of Virginia and Max Bradley-Hind, Chief Executive of the Leeds and Wetherby Bank and Chairman of Bradley Holdings.

'At least his mummy will be pleased,' Vicky said.

2023

'Stuff Mark Bradley-Hind. This is Britain. We have rights,' Vicky said, returning to her desk to access Tom's home computer and check out the terms of his employment contract. 'We'll fight the Trust. We'll go to tribunal. They have nothing on you.'

'But it wouldn't be difficult to engineer,' Ralph warned her. 'Not for the Secretary of State for Health. He's already scoured the hospital for gossip, and found what he wanted. He managed to induce or threaten one woman to put the knife in. What else might he unearth?'

Vicky knew at once, and felt sick at the thought. Tom saw it, and put his arm reassuringly around her shoulder again.

'Don't worry, Vick. Like I said, I resigned. I'm not going to fight. No point. No more of this horrendous publicity.'

'I just feel so . . . helpless.'

'I know. But we won't let him win. I've a more than decent pension. And I feel freer than I've felt in a long time. So when do we go to Africa? The Archbishop will need a man at her side. Even if it's only to fight off the bugs.'

TWENTY-FOUR

*Without new certainty in Christian faith and action, . . . there is
no political relevance in the struggle for the liberation of the
oppressed and for justice in the world.*

JÜRGEN MOLTMANN

AUGUST 2023

Ralph's e-phone vibrated in his jacket pocket as he was wandering down
the corridor at Lambeth. He saw Ethan appear on his screen.

'Hi, Ethan. I'm good, thanks. You? Any news? Wait, I'll find somewhere private. The whole world can hear us here.'

He went into his study and shut the door firmly.

'I'm in my study. What? Oh, right, okay, I'm heading out again.'

Ralph left his room and wandered back down the corridor and into the
garden.

'Go on. The goddess companies, yes. What have you got on them?
Who? You're sure? Couldn't be a mistake? The Fraud Squad? Umm, I
suppose so. You tell me how you want to handle it.'

He shook his head.

'No, no, she's in Africa anyway. She doesn't need to know at the
moment. I won't tell her until she gets back.'

The screen faded and he sat staring at the wall of shrubs for some time.

'Oh God, oh God,' he said out loud, 'this is really going to hurt.'

'You're not just coming to make official restitution?' Vicky asked Tom, as
they prepared for a heavy two-month schedule of visits overseas.

'Not in the least. I've always wanted to travel.'

He came up behind her and nuzzled her neck. 'The company is an
additional perk.'

He turned her to face him but she pushed him away gently and
continued packing. While her senses craved the familiar touch, taste
and smell, her mind wasn't yet ready to release her body to him.
'Retirement' appeared to have had an almost instant rejuvenating effect
upon him. He was like a young buck and she wondered how long she

could go on playing the coy doe without repressing the spring in his step.

The official trip had come just at the right time, with the press still chuntering on about their marriage, scrabbling for the tiniest hint of a sham reconciliation, and shamelessly fabricating it when there wasn't enough evidence to support a new scoop. Vicky had issued a press statement claiming that Tom's early retirement would enable them to have more time together to 'rediscover the romance they had once shared'. Sarah thought it a bit tacky, and so did she, truth to tell. But she suspected it might appeal to the less cynical, more susceptible majority of the public, particularly its TV-soap-loving women. And besides, it was true. Mind you, it didn't dampen the media gunpowder completely.

'Archbishop, is it true that your husband resents your job and still wants a divorce?'

'My husband is accompanying me on a number of important visits overseas. What does that tell you?'

As she put her wardrobe together and laid her clothes in the case, she reflected that it was a sad and sorry irony that she no longer felt any of her youthful wanderlust. Now that the opportunity had finally come, and exciting as it was, part of her would have much preferred to stay put and sit by the fire with a good book. How unappreciative, how unfair that such a privilege should be given to such a home-loving woman. Yet how could she not go when it meant so much to the African church? She had been moved already by the stories she heard and the appeals she received almost daily, by what she knew of the overwhelming generosity of the people, their resilience, their enthusiasm, their unalloyed joy, even through near starvation or in fear for their lives.

Bud Schuler had been her Secretary for International Affairs for just a few weeks. Her heart had sunk when she saw his application, but the interviewing committee, including Ralph, was unanimous that he was the best candidate. She could have told them what she knew, to scupper his chances, but forced herself to hold back. Tom was right. Where was her sense of forgiveness? In the end, she was glad she had not said anything. He and Jan had been an indispensable support to her just when she was feeling at her most bereft. Phone calls from Mandy, an occasional visit from Katya, were all very well, but how she valued having people close at hand. And she suspected that her pain had brought home to Bud and Jan once more the devastation and heartache they had inflicted – so that there was an element of expiation in their solicitude. Not that they ever said so, of course.

Bud had arranged a tight, but fascinating schedule. It began with a gruelling whirlwind tour of the major European institutions in Strasbourg,

Brussels, Geneva and Vienna. She lunched with the President of the European Commission and the President of the European Parliament, attended a number of embassy dinners in her honour, and spoke several times on issues such as the importance of a united church response to the unemployment and poverty caused by the crash of the euro, cultural and religious diversity in the new Europe, the urgency of responsible steward-ship of the environment, and the need to maintain ethical and moral standards in the interests of health and well-being.

The hotel bedrooms they stayed in, so bland and same-ish, with flocked wallpaper and heavy drapes in shades of aubergine and beige, were disorienting. After four stops, she couldn't remember which was which or even where she was. There was never a mirror in the strategic place for hair dryer and styling tongs. And only rarely full-length mirrors, essential before performing religious duties to ascertain that a stray edge of the full episcopal regalia wasn't caught up in her knickers.

She crashed into bed at night so full of the day's events that she couldn't sleep. Unlike Tom, who was unconscious the moment his head hit the pillow, she was a martyr to insomnia. She tossed and turned, beat and pummelled the pillows into shape until Tom, roused at last by her restlessness, could stand it no longer and turfed her out. She frequently spent more of the night reading a book or writing a sermon than lying down. A chance to pray, advised more ascetic, spiritual friends, and she did try. But eventually, it was easier to resort to the little pills her doctor had given her. How she would adjust to sleeping with-out them once she got home, she had no idea. It would be ironic to have spent her life persuading young people to avoid drugs, only to develop a dependency on them herself.

Then, on to Africa, now the largest and leading voice of the International Anglican Alliance. The aim of the visit was to offer support and encouragement, build bridges, to secure relationships threatened by her gender. 'I am here as your friend, under the authority of your own archbishop.' If that was what it took, she was prepared to say it. And it opened most of the doors. Having her man at her side helped.

The snow-capped peaks of Kenya, the lush greenery and misty moun-tains of Uganda, Nigeria with its sudden waterfalls cascading off sheer rock faces into the black gorges below: Africa took their breath away. There was little time for tourism per se, but once away from the towns, off the beaten track, they got a glimpse of the real continent. Leaving behind the wide streets lined with shops, the bustling crowds wearing a surprising mixture of smart and colourful traditional dress, they headed out to rural villages in a four-wheel drive that bumped and bounced them over potholed roads and bone-shaking corrugated dirt tracks, leaving them coated from head to toe in a layer of fine dust.

'I can taste it on my lips,' Tom complained, but she could tell by the grin from ear to ear that for him this was a grand *Boy's Own* adventure and he was loving every minute of it.

And then they would emerge without warning from that grey and dusty haze into scenes of the most heart-stopping natural beauty. Massive lakes and wide, snaking rivers, royal blue and diamond-spangled beneath the glare of an African sun. Dense, scented tropical rainforests filled with startlingly coloured vegetation would enfold them in their heavy foliage, until, beguiled and diverted, they would suddenly come upon a small, bedraggled-looking settlement and be brought down to earth with a bump. Here, listless adults tried in vain to care for children in ragged clothing with grotesquely protruding ribcages and distended little bellies, who lay lethargically in the sun while predatory insects fed on their every infected orifice. They were so helpless, their condition so appalling that it broke Vicky's heart. All it took was one failed harvest to turn grinding poverty into a disaster.

Bud had arranged a special programme for Tom. When he wasn't being the Archbishop's consort he was a hero of *Mission Impossible*, rushing around hospitals and clinics and remote health outposts, talking to patients, listening to the medical staff, tapping out notes on the equipment and drugs they needed so that he could send the details to his hospital contacts and the Secretary of State for International Affairs. Whether the minister would be pleased was another matter.

Several times, on official church visits together, Tom was treated as the chief guest, while Vicky was relegated to being his lady. But what did it matter?

She loved the way the local tribespeople moved to the rhythm of a band, and found it impossible not to get up and join the dancing. Even Tom managed a jiggle and a sway. The British church, with its stiff upper lip, still had a great deal to learn about more dynamic expressions of faith – and could well start with the cultural traditions of its African brothers and sisters.

UK journalists were not so sure, unwittingly stuck, it appeared, in the old colonial conditioning and the patronising attitudes that went with it. 'Archbishop's Antics Make Us Sweat', said the tabloid press the following morning. The English expected more decorum from their Archbishop. Did they expect her just to sit and watch, like the Queen? She rushed a quote off to Sarah: 'Bad enough that we expect African visitors to submit to our culture when they come to our churches, but far worse if we stand on our dignity when we visit theirs.'

Wherever they went people were appreciative of their visit, thrilled to see them. They were showered with gifts the givers could barely afford, Vicky ending up with a profusion of beaded necklaces. They had to explain on many occasions that they couldn't take anything more home with them on the plane. The 'giftmeister' on the team had the job of taking charge of all the presents, cataloguing them so that they could send a proper thank-you later, and getting them safely back to the UK without having to pay enormous duties to the tax authorities.

The world was supposed to be small, but after spending days on planes, boats, trains, and many, many hours on trucks or in cars and 4x4s, in extreme weather conditions, with a myriad of strange smells and tastes and sights, wonky beds, poor sanitation and the intermittent need to spend a great deal of time on the loo, it seemed immense and boundless.

And then there were the back-to-back meetings, the endless preaching, politicking and diplomacy, the carefully prepared and the completely off-the-cuff speeches, all requiring intense concentration to focus on what needed to be said, to remember who was who and who had said what. Why hadn't she the physical stamina of her predecessors who had coped so well with such a punishing schedule and the lack of creature comforts? Being on the go from morning until night left her feet and cheek muscles aching, her hands numb, and her brain addled; in short, totally exhausted. She was also aware of a niggling pain in her lower back – a chill from the beds and the potholes, the heat and the sweat no doubt.

But the acclamation of the crowds, delighted to see their Archbishop, whom they saw as a celebrity, carried her along on a wave of endlessly renewed energy and determination. Africa supplied her need for encouragement and affirmation. Africa helped her remember why she was Archbishop, and to be sure that she wanted to continue for a while yet. Unbelievably, Africa, with its creaky beds and scratchy mattresses, its debilitating humidity and merciless insects, somehow helped to restore her marriage in the fullest sense. It was impossible not to succumb to the indescribable romance that assaulted the mind and senses in that extraordinary continent.

But there was also the dark, frightening side of Africa, areas like Southern Sudan and several smaller, lesser-known states that had been increasingly subjected to Islamising forces and the oppression of Sharia law, where the romance of Africa had given way to the rule of terror. Despite the reluctance of the UK government, which couldn't guarantee their safety in Al Qaeda-dominated territories, Vicky insisted on adding them to her itinerary, so that she could bring the constant harassment of many small cells of Christians to the world's attention. Slavery, rape, starvation, beatings, imprisonment were common experiences. Many had been beheaded on trumped-up charges of blasphemy.

They found the atmosphere oppressive. Adolescents wielding Kalashnikovs strutted around, always on the look-out for anyone with forbidden cameras, radios, or CDs. To comply with Islamist rules, Vicky took off all her jewellery, covered her head, her arms and her ankles, and felt a disorienting loss of individuality and identity.

Meeting with local women, she was heartsick to discover that they were denied both education and a living, imprisoned in their own homes, and sometimes reduced to starvation with their children. Amputees whose hands and feet had been severed for minor crimes begged on street corners. These countries had slipped back into the dark ages.

Vicky and Tom were welcomed under sufferance, as a show of tolerance for the benefit of the Western press. Tom was loud in his criticism, thankfully mostly in private. One day, however, out alone, having managed to evade official supervision and their security guards, he tripped over what he thought was a bundle of rags lying across their path; until it moved, and a man sat up and waved him away with a grizzled stump where his hand had once been. Tom bent down and took the stump in his hand. 'How?' he mouthed at the man, holding out his own hand. The man's eyes wandered slowly over to a group of Islamist soldiers, barely out of school, laughing and joking but with one eye on them all the same. Tom placed the stump carefully back in the man's lap, rose to his feet with a curse and marched towards them.

Vicky had discovered he was missing and gone out after him, half-running round the corner just in time to recognise that purposeful walk she knew only too well. She called after him in a panic, but he didn't appear to hear.

Two of the soldiers, seeing him coming, swung their rifles around and waved them at him, simultaneously warning him off and tempting him forward.

'Tom!' she screamed again, running towards him and grabbing his sleeve.

He shook her off and stood, eyeballing the young men for some time while Vicky's heart raced, until two of her official escorts caught up with them and manifestly shouted out a command to the young men to lower their weapons. Tom turned, grabbed her hand, and pulled her away.

'Don't ever do that again,' she muttered.

'I just can't bear it,' he snapped back at her. 'It's so inhuman.'

'There are better ways to fight it.'

'If you're talking about diplomacy, you must be kidding – it hasn't got a chance.'

It was a struggle to respect the Muslim faith when its fundamentalist form led to such infringement of basic human rights, and it was vital for the British church to show fellow Christians, suffering under Sharia regimes, that they had not been forgotten. The moment Vicky got back to the UK, she made an appointment to see the PM. He listened with his usual courtesy, but as she spoke of the need for action, his eyes drifted away and his mouth settled into lassitude.

'Mahdi,' she pleaded, desperately trying to rouse him, 'the situation for Christians in Nigeria, Somalia, the Sudan and Egypt has been difficult for years and is now becoming intolerable. They are subject to the worst kind of indignities. They have no representation in government, no entitlement to education for their children, and no protection in law.'

'What do you want me to do about it, Vicky?' he asked wearily.

He made her feel like a tiresome child.

'I challenged the governments to allow Christian organisations to build schools and hospitals. They were very amenable in our meetings, but the moment I left the country the crackdown continued as before. If they won't do so themselves, I need you to persuade their governments to give our aid organisations the right to provide healthcare and education wherever it's needed, whatever the faith of the people.'

He flinched. He seemed an extraordinarily passive man to be a prime minister.

'Mahdi, if Muslims were treated here as Christians are treated there, there would be an absolute outcry.'

He conceded the point, but sighed heavily.

'We cannot interfere in the sovereign affairs of other countries, Vicky.'

'I don't want to interfere with any delicate negotiations, but make no mistake about it, if our brothers and sisters are oppressed and murdered, the church will protest.'

He bowed politely.

'That is your right.'

'In this country, yes, it certainly is.'

'By the way,' he said as she got up to go, feeling decidedly disgruntled, 'the government is proposing certain revisions to the anti-proselytising laws.'

Her heart sank. Surely the legislation couldn't get any tighter?

'What "revisions"?'

'To . . . remove them,' he squeezed out.

She firmly resisted the twitching smile of triumph that longed to play around the corners of her mouth. To betray her glee would be undignified. And his scowl encouraged no more than a courteous nod.

'That's . . . wonderful, thank you.'

'Good. I did think you might be . . . grateful. Might be prepared to back off from protesting for the time being? Maybe encourage some more partying?'

In the event the impact of the act was reduced so as to forbid only proselytising done with a view to stirring up acts of violence. Vicky was in the gallery of the House of Commons to hear the results of the vote confirmed, so overwhelmed with joy and relief that once back at Lambeth, she simply couldn't settle, not even to write the tribute to the thousands whose support had made it possible, which she knew she must send to the press. Instead, she went outside and stood by the Thames for a while, gazing at the glittering, star-filled sky, watching the reflections of the lights of the Parliament building dancing on the river, as she breathed in the balmy night air. Thank God, thank you God, she whispered. Bizarre the way the secularists seemed to have mirrored so closely the Sharia-style restrictions she'd witnessed recently; but no more. The church was free to carry on its mission unhindered.

There was little time to enjoy her triumph, though. In July 2023, war broke out over the disestablishment of the church. A large, all-party body of MPs had introduced a Commons early-day motion demanding that the Church of England be deprived of its special relationship with state and monarch, claiming that in a multi-faith society, represented by a Muslim Prime Minister, it was an anomaly to have an established church that reflected such a small minority. The move was engineered, she had no doubt, by the Prime Minister himself, hiding behind a display of innocent ignorance for fear of jeopardising his relations with the Queen. Many of the clergy, however, supported the idea, believing it would afford them much greater freedom to be self-governing. Others felt it would be a sad end to a 400-year history that was part of Britain's heritage and emphasised the importance of religion in national life.

She rang the Archbishop of York to plan a united front.

He said, 'I think many of the bishops are keen to see it go through. The anti-evangelism laws, despite our successful campaign to have them repealed, have severely dented their confidence in the government. They resent it having any power over us.'

'I have every sympathy with them.'

'So they feel it's time to put an end to this nonsense of them having to approve any changes to church policy we decide upon.'

'Care to hazard a guess at how many feel like that?'

'Half? Maybe more.'

'And what are your feelings?'

'Mixed. I think it's a bit of an anachronism. We are no longer truly a state church, as we no longer represent England at prayer. Cutting ourselves loose would give us more autonomy, break down the divisions between the denominations.'

'Yes, that's true. But it's not the whole story. We shouldn't underestimate the Queen as an asset – and it would upset her terribly.'

'I'll support you in whatever you decide. You know that.'

Chairing a tetchy House of Bishops was difficult. Carbury, unsurprisingly, was first to his feet in support of disestablishment.

'We now have a lot of Muslim and Hindu MPs. Why should they have a vote on matters that concern the church alone? Nor do I see why the arch-traditionalists in Parliament, who rarely darken the church's door, should have the right to get to their feet and bleat on issues they know nothing about. It's time for the church to come of age, cut loose, stand on its own millions of feet and concentrate on mission.'

'But, Toby,' Vicky replied, 'isn't maintaining a Christian presence in every community a vital part of that mission? An established church belongs to the nation, and not just to the people who attend it. Therefore everyone has a view on what the Church of England does and should do, and the right to express it, even if they never go to a single service. That's a nightmare for us a lot of the time, but it is also an amazing opportunity to reach people and I would hate to kill off those expectations.'

'And when it comes to renovating the bell tower on that lovely old building, how often do those same people who never attend but think they have the right to tell the church what to do, ever play their part? No, they expect the regular congregants to cough up and repair it on their behalf. Even if the regular congregants are heartily sick of being stuck in an ancient monument that threatens them with frostbite every week and would far rather move into the local pub.'

He had a point.

The Archbishop of York rose to Vicky's defence.

'Toby, many of us agree with you. But we also agree with the Archbishop that we cannot cease to see our role as serving the entire nation and become merely congregational in our attitudes, closed and self-contained.'

'There is no reason why we should,' the Bishop of Carbury argued back, 'but we deceive ourselves if we say we serve the nation. Most of the nation doesn't want our service and it's patronising to suggest that they do.'

They were at an impasse when they broke for coffee. Vicky had just picked up a cup and was about to go and find the Archbishop of York to thank him for his support, when she was intercepted by the Bishop of Carbury.

'A word, Archbishop?'

'So formal, Toby?' she muttered, escorting him out into the corridor. He looked around to ensure they weren't being overheard.

'Shall I have them check the lights for bugs?' she asked.

He was not amused.

'You're not going to win on this, you know, Vicky. There's a great head of steam behind me.'

'Hot air, Toby? Not the most flattering way to describe your supporters. Besides, the Queen will not be handing out brownie points for this.'

His head was so close to hers that she could smell the coffee on his breath.

'She won't live forever.'

'Then let her have her last years in peace.'

'It all depends.'

'On what?'

'Some of us feel . . . compromised, shall we say, by the most recent appointment to your staff. An American priest who left his wife and children to run off with his student. Long live adultery. Surely we're not condoning the moral values of TEC, are we? What next – a married gay priest? It really won't do.'

'You want me to sacrifice Bud for the Queen? Nice one, Toby, but I'm not sure she needs my help. The unpicking of church and state would require a mountainous legislative process, at least a dozen acts, not to mention the unravelling of current constitutional relations with Scotland, Wales and Northern Ireland and the fifteen Commonwealth countries of which the Queen is also Head of State.'

'Well, Vicky – if you're confident. But I think you should have thought more carefully about the implications of surrounding yourself with your cronies. None of us benefits if the press accuses you of nepotism, do we? Doesn't look good for any of us.'

And with a sardonic smile and a nod, he scuttled off.

Vicky was determined not to give in, but when he got wind of it Bud offered up his resignation against all her protestations. She asked one of the northern bishops to find him a parish, but Bud turned her down.

'Banished from court and exiled to the frozen north – a very ancient British tradition. Usually the prerogative of royalty, though,' he said wryly. 'I think it's better that we go back to the States, where we can't be used as a stick to beat you with.'

'I'm so, so sorry. I hate having to ask this of you.'

'Don't worry, Vicky. There's always a choice in these situations. We can feel we've been screwed by men and resent them for it. Or, we can receive it from God, and thank him for moving us where we need to be. Personally, I feel happier with the latter. I'll serve wherever I'm sent. And Jan and I are so thankful for the months we've had with you.'

'So am I, Bud. So am I. I'll miss you both terribly.'

She sat at her desk long after Bud had gone, unable to focus on anything, feeling not just bereft, but as if she had been smeared with manure. Was this job going to cost her everything that mattered to her most, even her very integrity? All those vows she had made to herself to be open and honest, not to chop and change her words and actions to fit the demands of political manoeuvring. 'And look where it's got me,' she yelled, hurling a paperweight at the far wall. Its progress was halted by the coat stand before it reached its target, fortunately. 'Can't even aim straight,' she muttered.

'Nothing can make a person more disillusioned with God than his people,' she said to Jenny the next day.

'Tell me something new. Is it this Bud business?'

She nodded, barely looking at her chaplain.

'I need absolution. Sometimes I wonder whether I go on believing simply out of habit. Few other jobs have faith as a prerequisite. It's too easy to go through the motions of talking about God without stopping to think whether I really believe what I'm saying, or I'm just saying it because it's what I am paid to say.'

'If that really was the case, you wouldn't continue.'

'Wouldn't I?' she asked, looking up at Jenny with surprise. 'How can you be so sure?'

'Because I know you.'

After watching Vicky's face for a while she added reflectively, 'Sounds to me like you've put your feelings on hold, rather than your faith. Faith does sometimes require a going through the motions. Until the day that you can really feel again.'

'I believe in the sun even when it isn't shining? I should have learnt that by now.'

Vicky shook herself. 'So, upwards and onwards?' she asked.

'Something like that. I think it's time to lay the politicking aside for a while. Think micro not macro, people not policies. Do what you were called to do, Vicky. You love meeting young people. I'll fix up some school visits.'

'Ever practical.'

'Someone has to be, before the real woman inside you is swallowed up by the glittering image she presents to the world.'

Jenny was right. The challenge of meeting bright, probing young people looking for answers was exactly what she needed, to remind her of the why and what she believed. Does God exist? Hasn't science disproved him? Why doesn't the church like sex? (That question accompanied by embarrassed, or occasionally by raucous laughter, of course.) What happens when we die? And the inevitable question: Do you spend your life in church? Questions that exercised her faith muscles and forced them back into shape.

The total ignorance of this new generation of all things biblical made her laugh and despair in turn. In one assembly she asked why it was daft for the good shepherd to abandon ninety-nine well-behaved sheep to go in search of the rogue one.

'Because they'd have been nicked,' piped up one little lad.

'Why aren't you wearing your nightie thingy?' one of the girls asked, her eyes focused on Vicky's peep-toe patent sandals with their bows and three-inch heels. They made honeycomb out of school parquet floors, but she never could resist gorgeous shoes.

'Love the flash,' said another, pointing at her episcopal cross. 'Where do you get one of those?'

She took it off, gave it to the girl, and let her wear it for the duration of the session. At the end, the girl handed it back with such reverence that when Vicky put it back on, still warm, it had far greater significance for her.

In one school, a young black man sat on the edge of the group, swinging on the back legs of his chair, his eyes firmly on the floor. When one of the girls bravely described how her mother had died of breast cancer, and asked Vicky why a loving God would allow such suffering, he finally raised his head, challenging her with a look.

She struggled to answer as honestly as she could. There was no dissembling with young people. They smelt insincerity at a hundred yards. Some words of Moltmann, her unseen guide and mentor throughout so many years of ministry, unexpectedly came to mind. Faith and hope together, he wrote, were *not only a consolation in suffering, but also the protest of the divine promise against suffering*.

'Suffering,' she said, 'was never God's intention when he made men and women. He hates it. Jesus died to defeat death once and for all, so that one day there will be no more separation, grief and tears. No more suffering.'

'You believe that stuff, do yer?' the young man jeered, with naked hostility.

The teacher ignored him and invited some of the other children to put their questions to the Archbishop.

'You believe in heaven, do yer then?' he persisted, the chair making a loud crash as it landed back on its four legs.

'Mikey!' the teacher warned.

'No, no,' Vicky said to her, 'let him speak.'

'Yes, I believe in heaven, Mikey,' she said. 'One day this world will be transformed, filled with God's presence, and there will be only love. All hatred and pain will be forgotten forever.'

There was a momentary pause, and in it, she saw his eyes fill with tears. He quickly regained control, and sniffed loudly.

'And how do you know that for sure?'

'Only because Jesus promises eternal life to those who follow him. And I don't believe he was a liar.'

'Jesus.' He thought about the word for a while. 'He was a good man, right? And look what they did to him. The good die young. The evil gets away with it.'

'He wasn't just a good man, Mikey. He was either God or a con artist. They're your two alternatives. Personally, I believe that he is God.'

For several seconds the ticking of the clock was the only sound in the room.

'Miss,' hazarded one of the girls, her hand in the air.

'Archbishop,' the teacher corrected her.

'Miss Archbishop, Mikey's older brother was murdered. Stabbed by one of the Black Bullets gang.'

'And no one's been done for it,' added the girl next to her.

Vicky made a point of going over to Mikey before she left the classroom. She reached out a hand to him but he stiffened, so she simply touched him on the arm.

'I hope they catch the guy who did that to your brother,' she said.

He nodded without looking at her.

'We will if the police don't,' he muttered.

'Mikey,' she begged, 'don't throw away your life too. God says he's the one who will judge. There will be justice one day, I promise, for everyone.'

She had clicked her way down the school steps and was standing at her car with the head, chatting about the national syllabus, and how a one-size-fits-all curriculum could never work for the range of children in a school like this, when she heard a softly spoken voice behind her say, 'Miss . . . Archbishop . . . Ma'am.'

They turned and Mikey was standing there, his jeans so low slung she wasn't sure how he managed to keep them on. He shuffled in his shoes, his hands thrust deep in his pockets.

'Thanks,' was all he said, looking up at her briefly.

She nodded and he sauntered back up the steps into school.

'Was it my imagination or was that halfway to a smile?' she asked the head.

'I think it may well have been. Thank you from me too,' said the head, grasping her hand and holding onto it as tightly as if she were drowning.

'The Verity Trust,' Vicky said to her. 'Get them into the school. They're highly experienced at working in a gang culture. They'll achieve wonders with young people like yours, and no laws to stop them now. And if it's okay with you, I'll get my PA to ask them to make direct contact with Mikey.'

Vicky sat in the back of the car feeling more satisfied than she had in many months. She had been so aware of doing something useful and worthwhile as a parish priest at St Margaret's and St Chad's, but it was so long ago that she had forgotten how it felt. Promotion wasn't everything, that was for sure.

In a fit of righteous indignation she scribbled off an article which found a home in the *Times Educational Supplement*:

Monday September 25th 2023

Everywhere I go I meet hungry, angry, hurting children, disillusioned with a state that doesn't seem able to promise them any outcome for their education. In poorer areas forward-thinking schools provide breakfast in the morning, then are taken to task for not feeding minds. Everywhere, children are pressured to achieve and discarded when they don't.

Schools are full of committed teachers dedicated to the cause of enabling children to grow up to be better citizens, committed parents, more caring human beings. In these challenging times, they long to rise to the challenge of meeting emotional and developmental needs, not just the 'Three R's' basics. That's education at its best. But they are thwarted at every turn, because that simply isn't on the government's agenda. A raft of recent edicts shows that academic results remain the only indicator that matters, and the straitjacket of formal testing is still the chosen method to gauge such results.

All the children I meet ask penetrating questions about life and death, despair and hope. To which they receive no answers, for RE has

been watered down and relegated to virtual non-existence. These
young people know almost nothing of world religions, including
Christianity, which played such an essential part in our legal and moral
history.

The Secretary of State for Education wasn't pleased, and invited her to
visit him. He braced himself as she came into the room. She began to
wonder whether Whitehall had installed a special Archbishop advance
warning bell that rang as she arrived.

'If you're not happy with our policies, Archbishop, I'd rather you came
to me before you go public. You are still a state church, remember?'

'Actually, I answer only to God and the Queen, not the Prime Minister,
and I cannot sit back and watch the educational system that inspired so
much of the world's schooling become a narrow, blinkered pursuit only
of hard results. There are dozens of youngsters in our schools up and
down the country who are not academically bright. Many will not go
on to further education. Some will never work. But should we simply
abandon them? What we need is a system that can adapt to every child,
and help them contribute to society in whatever way will be most
beneficial.'

'The children you're referring to are virtually unteachable.'

'With respect, this is one area a boarding school education such as
yours might not equip you to rule on. Every child has potential.'

He flinched.

'If we're going to survive in the global financial rat race this country
needs business men and women. That is our goal. And that's where we
invest. Simple as that.'

'So – what? No art, music, film, theatre, literature, religion – just
remove them all from the syllabus? As for the idea of giving financial and
educational incentives to the well-heeled to produce more children, isn't
that social engineering at its worst?'

He gave a slow smile of acknowledgement.

'Necessary in a top-heavy population pyramid – too many old people
taking up too much of the nation's resources, not enough younger workers to keep the economy growing. We need more children, and good
workers too, to pay for the care we'll need. Call that social engineering if
you like.'

'Manipulating people into doing what you want from them is always
suspect.'

'Forgive me, Archbishop, but I don't see what this has to do with the
church. As I understand it, your department hasn't had much success at

enhancing the lives of young people so far, so I advise you to get on with improving your own record and leave education to us.'

'Maybe you don't have the full picture, Minister,' she said, smiling, as she handed him an invitation to the National Young Heroes Award ceremony in Westminster Abbey, and the Youth Arts Festival in the Albert Hall the following evening. Booking the Royal Albert Hall at a hugely reduced price, thanks largely to the efforts of Kelvin, now permanently on her staff as a roving innovator and initiator, had been quite a coup. 'I think you have a rather limited view of the church's impact on young people. True, we have been through a disastrous period of being out of touch and losing a generation, or even two. But we are making up for lost ground, with some extraordinary achievements in the past ten years. I'd love you to be my guest and to see for yourself how the church is bringing hope to a new generation.'

Young people from all over the country arrived in the centre of London in their coachloads, brought by the Verity Trust, the Edenbury Arts Project, and hundreds of other youth projects for two days of celebration, beginning with a ceremony to honour acts of real dedication, care and commitment to the local community, and ending the following evening with a grand showcase of outstanding artistic talent. To her amazement, the Secretary of State cancelled a prior engagement to attend the first event, and stayed on afterwards to congratulate the chosen heroes individually.

In between the two events Vicky had organised a daytime symposium for her young guests, with as many bishops as were free to attend, so that the latter could hear for themselves what young people wanted from the church. She opened it by speaking on the reality of hope.

'The pundits say that the younger generation is given over to something called hedonism – which means that the only thing that matters is pleasure right now, what you want when you want it. You know only too well that this doesn't work. It doesn't bring real lasting happiness or fulfilment. Christians, though, are not into immediate gratification. We look to the future, to the day when God will sort out this beautiful world of his and make all things new. And that won't make us so focused on heaven that we forget to be happy today, which is what everyone tells us. Instead, that hope for the future *is* our happiness today. It's what keeps me going when I get bogged down in the mess of politics and the media. You know what it means to discover hope for the future, a hope that inspires us to believe we can help make a better world today in preparation for the perfect world that is to come. And we church leaders are here to listen to your ideas on how we can do that together.'

Looking around at the array of eager faces in the main auditorium of Church House, Vicky's stomach gave a lurch as she caught sight of a young man she recognised in the front row. Mikey. As their eyes met he gave her a broad smile.

'I know it's a logistic nightmare finding accommodation for all these young people, and I know it's expensive,' she said to Kelvin later. 'But it's worth it. The only way for the church to stay in touch with the generation that could be our leaders one day. We need to make it an annual event.'

Hearing the young people share their hopes and dreams, their vision for their friends and communities, Vicky had been deeply moved and impressed. They seemed aware, not only of the difficulties faced by their peers, but of the increasing numbers of older people living alone and needing loving support, a garden tidying, a bit of shopping fetched in, some company. She realised with excitement that their eyes were being opened to a potential army of surrogate grannies and granddads, people who needed life transformation just as much as their own mates, and with money from the Church and Community Fund she invited Tony Patterson to co-ordinate a national youth social justice network, so that resources and ideas could be shared. She also managed to make several seed-funding grants available to some of the most innovative projects suggested, little guessing that even this would soon come back to haunt her.

TWENTY-FIVE

Christians talk of justice but what they really mean is 'just-us'. If you look at the history of the constructive influence of faith in public life, it always thrives when it fights for interests of humanity and the common good.

OS GUINNESS

It began to be abundantly clear that the figures in the census were no flash in the pan. The church was indeed growing.

'We're demonstrating our relevance at last,' said the Bishop of Marchington at the House of Bishops.

'I put it down to those laws,' said the Bishop of Normington cynically. 'Tell young people they can't do something and it's a sure sign they'll think it's worth doing. Perhaps we shouldn't have fought them after all.'

Vicky was momentarily tempted to slap him. Fortunately for him her arm wasn't long enough.

'But it's now we're reaping the real benefits,' Will Goodacre continued, 'as we harness all the new interest. But we must ensure that people have vibrant communities to which they can belong, or we risk losing them again.'

'Come and see what's happening in Marchington,' he said to Vicky afterwards. So she went. Eddie Macdonald took her first to the Marchway estate and showed her around the united church's pharmacy, food and furniture banks, the advice and job centres, the childcare and family support clubs, the credit union and debt counselling service, the new housing association aiming to provide shelter and ultimately social housing for anyone left homeless. The breadth of it all took Vicky's breath away.

'The council is now outsourcing virtually all social care to us again, the bits they've still got money for, that is,' Eddie said with evident pride. 'We can respond so much more quickly than anyone else to local need.' Then he shook his head and added, 'But I sometimes wonder if there isn't a danger we lose our cutting edge.'

'You mean, too much emphasis on the body and not enough on the spirit?'

He nodded.

'It's an inevitable tension,' Vicky said. 'We care because we're called to, but it doesn't necessarily bring life transformation.'

'I think we were at our most effective when we did it all for love, without council funding. We didn't risk losing our spiritual focus. I wonder whether some kind of national welfare delivery programme might be possible – so that we can share key issues, provide ourselves with a central resource.'

'It would certainly save churches having to re-invent the wheel. I'll send Kelvin Craddock to help. He seems to have a special gift for bringing disparate groups of people together.'

'I have a name if you want it.'

She looked at him in some surprise.

'The Well. Welfare and well-being – God's inexhaustible supply.'

'I like it.'

'And,' he added, as the Bishop arrived to join them both for lunch, 'we need to include a new service – community troubleshooting and peace-making, a group of trained and skilled individuals who will mediate between the national government, or local government, and the people whenever it becomes necessary.'

'An interesting idea,' she admitted.

'Yours,' he said, looking a little awkward for the first time in their conversation. 'Your handling of the Wooten Grange crisis was inspirational.'

'And how are you finding the growth spurt, Will?' Vicky asked the Bishop, as they shared a sandwich in a new high-street teashop that doubled as a church in the evening and at weekends.

'Wonderful. All we've ever hoped and prayed for.'

'But?'

She had noticed a certain hesitation before he spoke.

'I'm totally exhausted. I haven't enough clergy to handle it. We've trained dozens of new lay ministers to run places like this, but I still have so many darned civic duties that I haven't time to deal with all the extra pastoral responsibilities it brings.'

'Hiya, Bish.'

He was greeted by two young women wearing the most outlandish outfits Vicky had ever seen, skirts barely visible beneath their baggy, off-the-shoulder jumpers. She felt herself about to tut, and stopped abruptly, horrified at the self-revelation of the older woman she seemed to have become. The Bishop, meanwhile, had wiped the mayonnaise off the corner of his mouth, jumped to his feet, and was warmly kissed and petted, before he was permitted to return to his sandwich.

'I love the way these new church people don't bow and scrape to me,' he said, replacing the serviette on his lap. 'Where were we?'

'You're exhausted.'

'Ah yes, but I really wanted to raise the issue that congregations like this one here can rarely have Communion – it only happens when they can commandeer a local vicar, but of course most of them are too busy serving their own churches to oblige. And understandably, the churches resent having to have an unknown come and do it.'

'So you let the lay minister . . . ?' she prompted, encouragingly.

'As long as they don't use the official liturgy, of course.'

'Of course, Bishop,' she smiled reassuringly.

Lord preserve us, she said to herself, despairing at how complicated the church had made Jesus' simple act of togetherness and remembrance.

'I sympathise,' she said. 'Let me think about it.'

'Vicky, why does my heart sink when I hear from you these days?' asked the Archbishop of York. 'I think to myself, what now? Who are we going to upset this time?'

'I'm so sorry. But we really must do some radical thinking about church structures if we're going to sustain this period of growth.'

'You're thinking . . . ?'

'Experienced ministers selected to provide episcopal pastoral support to lay church leaders. Some kind of priest-bishop role. Let's see if we can get something through the House of Bishops.'

'Give the old codgers apoplexy?'

'Archbishop,' Vicky said in mock rebuke, 'you can be so rude. You'll be an old codger yourself soon enough.'

'Comes on by the minute in this job.'

'It is only a first step, of course.'

'What is?'

'Priest-bishops.'

'Ah, that. For a moment I thought you were referring to my encroaching codgerliness.'

She laughed.

'No, I'm wondering how we make Communion accessible to all these new churches – all very well helping lay leaders do a better job, but not very Anglican if people can only take Communion once in a blue moon.'

'Any suggestions?'

'Yes, as it happens. I suspect most of the Celtic communities – Northumbria, Iona, Holy Island – have liturgies for a simple service of bread and wine.'

He groaned.

'Ah, now you really risk putting the cat amongst the pigeons – undermining the role of the clergy.'

There was a pause.

'Okay, okay – let's float it,' he said. 'But I hope you are good at swimming, Archbishop.'

As they were about to walk into the House of Bishops he turned to her and said, 'You look great, by the way.'

'Thanks,' she said, genuinely touched.

'Give 'em that big smile of yours. Switch on the legendary sparkle. You're going to need it.'

'Since when do I switch it off, Yorkie?' she asked, poking him playfully in the ribs.

They paused for a moment outside the door. She pulled down her suit jacket, lifted her head and shoulders, took a deep breath and went in.

She laid out her ideas, both for an informal priest-bishop role within local church networks, and for lay leadership of a simple service of bread and wine. The former was greeted with little antagonism, but the latter occasioned a heated, acrimonious debate.

'A severe shortage of clergy,' she had said to the bishops, introducing the subject, 'forces us to face deep challenges in enabling people to receive Communion regularly, but I believe this may prove a serendipitous situation, a God-given opportunity, that forces us to revert to the model of the early Celtic church of a weekly meal of bread and wine in the home, itself based on the early church practice that went before it. We cannot go on denying people Communion simply because we haven't enough clergy to go round, or continue to run what clergy we do have ragged, dashing from one service to the next, when they need to be doing mission on their own doorsteps.'

Greg Davidson, the Bishop of Normington, leapt to his feet with a look of outrage on his face almost before she had finished speaking.

'This is highly irregular, Archbishop. Lay leadership of Communion is what you're talking about – and doing it by the back door doesn't make it any better. I won't be part of a church where the clergy have no distinct sacred role or duty, and our most precious sacrament is left to any old Tom, Dick or Harry to deliver, who probably has no concept of the seriousness of what they're doing.'

'Which of us can claim they truly grasp the full import of these precious symbols?' Vicky asked him.

His large pectoral cross swung wildly across his paunch as he pawed the floor in agitation.

'The laity certainly doesn't. You open the door to sectarianism.'

'On the contrary, Greg, if we do nothing these new congregations will either go independent or align themselves with another denomination that can provide for their needs. Finding imaginative ways to keep them in the church is the only answer.'

Vicky suppressed the smile that played around the corner of her mouth at the sight of the panic on the bishop's face. She thought she might have won her point, but the mutinous look of fury with which he settled back in his chair told her otherwise. Some clergy seemed to have this need to maintain a mystique that enabled them to feel superior to their congregations, as doctors were once tempted to do with their patients. How could she ever penetrate it? Small wonder Jesus' toughest criticisms were reserved for religious leaders.

'Greg, I am not taking away the priestly role from the clergy. I am simply suggesting that we examine a number of Celtic liturgies for Agape meals of bread and wine, and give permission to use them as and when appropriate.'

'So, should we take it that you will try and force this through Synod?' called out the Bishop of Carbury, supporting his colleague, as ever. Despite herself, Vicky raised her voice in sheer exasperation.

'I know some of you feel – and are willing to say all too publicly – that I do not listen. I have never stopped listening, but we must act, and on difficult issues it may be that there will never be consensus among us. Certainly change will never be bloodless.'

The Bishop of Normington got up and left the room. The Bishop of Carbury followed. She turned to the Archbishop of York, who simply raised his eyebrows and shrugged. But by the time the rest of the gathering went their separate ways late that afternoon, the battle was all but won.

The following day Sarah stormed into Vicky's study looking like thunder. They had survived so much together, Vicky couldn't imagine what had thrown her so badly now. Surely not the theological machinations of the House of Bishops, though the press always enjoyed a little conflict in the ranks?

'Archbishop,' she said, 'did you know a priest in the Larchester Diocese by the name of Kirk Black? Died a couple of months ago.'

Vicky froze.

'I did, unfortunately. He was accused of sexually assaulting a child. But all charges were dropped. We couldn't touch him. It must be around eight years ago.'

'Nine, to be precise. The boy is now a twenty-one-year-old man.'

'Don't tell me,' she said, with a heavy sigh. 'He's gone public.'

Sarah nodded, making no attempt to hide her annoyance.

'Now how did I guess?'

'Not only that, he's claiming you were culpable by giving the aforesaid Mr Black a licence to carry on.'

Vicky gritted her teeth with sheer exasperation.

'I knew it. I knew this would happen.'

Sarah gave her a stony look.

'It wasn't a case of allowing Kirk Black to carry on. I had no choice. The boy's parents wouldn't bring charges. They said testifying would traumatise him. I suspended Black and we carried out a full investigation. There was no doubt in my mind that the allegations were true. There were too many stories of his "special relationships" with the choirboys. But Kirk was a barrister before his ordination, and he employed a lawyer buddy, one of those sharp-shooting types, who warned us in no uncertain terms that we would be sued for mouth-watering sums if his client was unfairly dismissed.'

She noticed that Sarah hadn't erased the critical expression from her face.

'Look,' Vicky said in desperation, 'bishops' legal costs had gone through the roof. The new disciplinary measures gave clergy so many rights that we couldn't sack them for anything other than gross indecency that was witnessed by half the world. And I still paid £300 an hour to be told I had no choice but to reinstate him.'

She remembered then that she had rung Nick too, that he had backed up the legal advice that forced her to send a paedophile back to his parish.

'I hated reinstating him, but we drew up a strict code of conduct with the churchwardens. I warned him that he would be carefully supervised, that if he was ever seen anywhere near a child I would withdraw his licence immediately, legal proceedings or no, and that he would never get another parish. I also kept a complete record of my actions on file, because I knew it didn't bode well.'

'I suspect the press won't find it difficult to prove he had further contact with children,' Sarah said disparagingly.

'Look,' Vicky snapped at her, banging her clenched fists on the desk, 'I know this is a tough one but we need to fight it with every weapon we've got. I loathed what Kirk Black did. What kind of a monster would it make me if I had simply covered it up to protect the church? I kept records to show that I did all that could be done. You can get them. Release them to the media. Paste them on every blog page. Use every network and outlet we possess.'

A thought occurred to her.

'Then get your camera and record my full defence so that we can put it on YouTube and people can hear it from my own mouth.'

As Sarah rushed out to do battle with the media, Vicky called after her, 'Sarah, I have done the scapegoat thing and I am heartily sick of it. Not this time. I followed procedures by the book. I want the world to know how our hands are tied, and to judge my actions for itself. Oh, and get Jenny to find out if the young man will speak to me.'

'Is that wise?'

'Wise or not, there are things we simply have to do.'

The young man, Jack, refused to see her in person, but agreed to a video link conversation.

'Why now, Jack?'

He looked uncomfortable, evasive.

'I know what happened must have blighted your life, and I am so deeply sorry for it.'

'I didn't want to get you into any trouble,' he stammered.

'I understand. You know Kirk Black died of cancer a few months ago? Is there anything I can do or explain that would make this more bearable for you?'

He shook his head sadly, and shortly after brought the call to an end.

The story appeared to rattle on in the press for a while, but fizzled out when no more victims came forward. The media dogs must have found some fresher food, Vicky said to herself.

It was a tense and sombre General Synod that November. The difficult mood in the House of Bishops was always going to make itself felt. And her robust self-defence in the paedophile priest furore had manifestly not satisfied everyone, though this was neither the place nor the time to defend her actions. The church, she believed, needed to turn its attention to far more pressing matters, such as the establishment of 'The Well' in fighting the poverty that was becoming an indigenous part of national life. She spoke about the dangers of becoming inured to the commonplace.

'The images of pain and suffering all around us and on our TV screens can fill us with compassion fatigue, but if we don't feel, we have lost our humanity. The media tries to tell us we live in a post-Christian age, but God help us if that is the case, because all the best in our society came from our Judeo-Christian heritage – the abolition of slavery, the establishment of schools, hospitals, poor relief, prison reform. Shaftesbury, Wilberforce, Nightingale, Barnardo, Elizabeth Fry, Josephine Butler never found human tragedy wearisome, or lost their reforming zeal. They understood that transformational activity in the world was a visible sign of the immanence of the kingdom of God. Together, we today must pick up the baton they hold out to us and run with it, and encourage even greater Christian entrepreneurialism now that we have fought off the pernicious laws intended to hold us back.'

There were one or two nods, an odd murmur of assent, but generally, little eye contact, little response. No mutinous looks or hostile gestures, just a thick and heavy grey blankness. The proceedings lumbered along for three days with no let-up: discussions were leaden, reactions deadened, as if everyone were six foot under water. Some important resolutions were made, and progress was definite, albeit slow. A motion was passed to involve other denominations in the forming of 'The Well'. Agreement was reached to make the two-day youth festival an annual event. Nonetheless, Vicky went back to Lambeth trying to shake off the growing anxiety that somewhere, above the surface, there existed an alternative universe from which she was completely excluded. Was this suffocating blanket of fog over everything merely her imagination? And if it wasn't, what could she do about it? She tried to shelve her anxieties, intending to take soundings in the New Year.

December meant speeches and sermons for World AIDS Day, a conference on Anglican Engagement with World Religions, a debate in the House of Lords on religious education in schools (what was left of it), an Advent Carol Service in Westminster Abbey, and the Christmas Day service in Canterbury Cathedral. There were Christmas and New Year messages to write for BBC TV, Radio 4 and Radio 2, and personal greetings to be sent to every archbishop throughout the Anglican Alliance.

Then there was the demonstration she had promised the Prime Minister she would organise in support of Christians in Muslim countries. The media dismissed it as a fatuous waste of time for all concerned, and had to rustle up journalists quickly when almost 200,000 people turned up in coaches, minibuses and even on bicycles, from as far away as Cornwall, Northumberland, even Scotland, congregating in the evening twilight in Parliament Square and its surrounding streets. Christians were learning how to make their presence felt and their views known – at last. Kelvin had arranged for several separate processions to march by torchlight to the embassies and high commissions of all the relevant countries. A policing nightmare, except for the fact that the crowds stood in silent, near-immobile vigil for the entire night.

New high-level security had to be installed at Lambeth Palace following terrorist threats from Islamist groups. Vicky felt as if she were being watched by eerie red and green eyes that blinked at her in the dark. The last remaining vestiges of personal freedom appeared to have gone.

She said so to the Home Secretary, who had not been best pleased to be landed with the responsibility for her welfare.

'Yes, but to all intents and purposes you are now protected from harm,' he replied. 'And that's the main thing.'

But she didn't feel secure. It now seemed to her that human beings were never inviolate as long as their reputations were exposed to attack. And she appeared to be particularly vulnerable to this pernicious kind of harm. The press was still grubbing around, looking for chinks in her marriage, skeletons in her cellars, flaws in her sermons, dissatisfaction from the bishops and Synod, any evidence of dysfunctionality in her private or professional life. 'Don't be afraid of those who kill the body but cannot kill the soul.' She repeated it like a mantra, every time she picked up the daily newspapers. 'You can crush every part of me except my soul – which will never die.'

But if she could sideline her dismay at the press and shelve her anxieties about Synod, at least until after Christmas, she couldn't go on ignoring the persistent, niggling pain in her lower back. She finally took herself off to the doctor's. Within forty-eight hours she was lying in an MRI scanner. Within a week she was sitting in front of Stephen Gibbons, a sober-faced consultant and good friend of Tom's. She appreciated the way he didn't discuss her ailments while she was lying in a state of undress on the examination couch, vulnerable and prone, making no comment until she was fully clothed, so that he could address her face to face. Tom took hold of her hand.

'Well?' she said to the consultant. She had been here before.

2016

She had been a bishop for a few months and was working on the implementation plans for the long-term strategy that had recently been passed by the diocesan synod, when there was a tap on the door and Marissa's head appeared around it. 'You haven't forgotten your mammogram later this morning, Bishop, have you?'

'Bishop' and 'mammogram' – it seemed oxymoronic, two words that just didn't belong together. She had indeed forgotten this little encroachment into her time that no male bishop ever had to contend with. One of the joys of reaching fifty.

She had never been squeamish about exposing her upper torso, but still, as she drove to the screening unit, she found herself hoping that she wouldn't be recognised. She needn't have worried. Without the purple shirt and dog collar she was a woman like any other, and the radiographer was so focused on the relevant part of her anatomy that she barely looked at her face. The process – the breast almost unrecognisable, squeezed as flat as a chicken sandwich filling between two chilly glass plates, was uncomfortable, though worth it, no doubt, for the thousands of women whose cancers were caught at an early stage. And then she didn't think any more about it.

The day after receiving that anonymous phone call about Tom, and her heated altercation with him about it, she slipped surreptitiously down to her study first thing to pick up her post, hoping to avoid Marissa and Kelvin. She had had a dreadful night and didn't feel up to any chit-chat with her staff. There on her desk lay an unopened letter with the NHS logo across the top. Marissa must have left it for her. She opened it without really thinking, wondering whether she should try and make contact with Tom, apologise again for doubting him, but it seemed more sensible to wait until he decided to come home.

As she mused, various phrases in the letter suddenly came into sharp focus: 'anomalies in the mammogram', 'further investigation', 'please make an urgent appointment', and, 'usually nothing to worry about'. The shock of it caught her off guard and she had to sit down. Instinctively she reached up inside her clothes, feeling for some kind of lump. For a second there was a heart-lurching flash of hope that this was all a mistake. The scans had been jumbled. She had been sent the wrong letter. But the breast screening unit confirmed her identity and made her an appointment for the following week.

'Usually nothing to worry about,' the receptionist repeated brightly on the phone.

Were there ever dafter words, when a loaded gun with a 'C'-shaped bullet was pointing straight at your head?

She made herself a cup of tea, then went back up to the bedroom and sat, propped up against the pillows, embracing the comforting warmth of the mug in her hands as she tried to deal with the double whammy that life seemed to have landed in her lap.

'Not feeling too good this morning, Marissa,' she said on the interconnecting phone. 'Give me a while, can you?'

'Certainly, Bishop,' she said tartly. 'Not like you. You have no appointments until 11 a.m., but there are a wealth of messages and correspondence to deal with when you feel up to it.'

Blow the letters, blow the phone messages and the emails, Vicky said to herself. A life can suddenly seem so short, a meaningless, tiny drop in the vast ocean of time when confronted with its possible end. How ironic that she should be facing the possibility of breast cancer, of all things. The first woman in this man's job faced the loss of her essential femininity. Voluntary and necessary castration. As if her very femaleness was rising up to attack her, determined to prove her detractors right. No one with boobs could do the job – because they themselves would let her down.

If it was cancer, what then? What would she do? How would she face a possible mastectomy, chemotherapy, the loss of her hair? Could she continue without anyone knowing – especially if she suddenly started wearing a wig? She shook herself. Stop being so melodramatic. It might be nothing. But she did need to talk to Tom now.

He arrived home early, marched straight into her study, anxiety written large across his face. She got up and went to him, and he swept her into his arms. They stood for some time, her head buried in his shoulder, he gently stroking her back. It saddened her that it had taken the possibility of death and final separation for Tom to hold her close. There was no mention of the phone call. That had been swept into a dark corner somewhere, and she didn't feel like retrieving it at this stage. She pulled away from him, but he held onto her.

'One of the team might come in.'

'So?'

'I don't want anyone to know.'

'I'll get on to the breast guys, make sure they look after you. We'll get the best.'

'Tom,' she laughed, looking into his troubled face, 'we don't even know that there's anything really wrong as yet.'

The new appointment involved another mammogram, the results of which gradually wended their way down the corridor to a specialist breast doctor, while Vicky waited for an interminable thirty minutes, the hands of a large wall clock tick-tocking every one of them. She had sent Tom back to his department. He was too jittery to be of much support and she couldn't handle his anxiety as well as her own.

She was eventually shown into a bland consulting room, where she sat, as at a job interview, facing a kindly-looking man with large, bushy eyebrows. He introduced himself as Stephen Gibbons, a colleague of

Tom's, and the smiling, self-possessed woman at his side as Lesley, a specialist breast cancer nurse. He asked if he could examine her.

She stripped to the waist and lay down on the uncomfortable, paper-towel-covered leatherette couch, while he poked, prodded, ran tests and, finally, sat down heavily in his chair again.

She dressed and found herself facing him across the desk once more, Lesley at her side. A bad omen. She finished buttoning her jacket as he examined the mammogram, his face giving nothing away.

'I'm so sorry,' he said, in a voice that sounded as if she hadn't got the job, 'but you have cancer.'

She was aware that he and Nurse Lesley were watching her carefully for her reaction. She actually felt surprisingly calm. The previous week, though she hadn't thought about her for years, Marjorie had come to mind, reassuring her that death was not the worst thing that could happen to a Christian. Besides, she had already achieved more than she had ever dared to dream or expect. The practical implications were what bothered her.

'So what now?' she asked evenly.

Her poise appeared to throw them slightly.

'We won't know exactly until we do a biopsy and find out what kind of cancer you have. But for a start, a lumpectomy, then we'll decide on further treatment when we know what we're dealing with.'

'It feels strange', she said, 'to be at risk from an enemy I can neither feel nor see.'

Lesley handed her a card as she escorted her out. 'My contact details,' she said. 'Call me at any time if you have questions or need to talk.'

Now that was a role reversal, she thought, as she walked the endless corridor miles to Outpatients to find Tom. No one had considered that she might have a need to talk for some years. She still felt extraordinarily at peace, or was it a kind of benevolent numbness bestowed on the mind that would slowly wear off as it came to terms with reality?

She put her head around Tom's consulting-room door between patients. One look at the expression on her face told him all he needed to know. But then he had guessed all along. There was a large desk between them, leaving little other space in the room except for an examining couch, but they reached across it for each other's hands.

'No one must know, Tom.'

He looked at her in surprise.

'Imagine what the press would do with this? First woman bishop and she gets the big C before she's barely begun. Will she die in office? They'll pursue me for months, looking for any sign of my imminent demise.

They're intrusive enough without that. And then there would be the letters, cards and calls from people I've never met, let alone those I have, all requiring a response.'

Tom ran a hand through his hair, as he often did in extremis.

'Damn, damn, damn,' he said under his breath.

'And then at every service and meeting, I'd have to cope with the embarrassed and don't-know-what-to-says, the presumptuous who think they do and are entirely inappropriate, and the terrified for whom cancer is a death sentence. No, Tom, no one must know.'

'Not even Alice?'

'Possibly. Let me think about it.'

All the way home the only thought that exercised her mind was how to get through the treatment without anyone finding out. What excuses could she make? And then a possible solution occurred to her.

'Marissa, that letter from the NHS?' she said, as she arrived back at the diocesan office. It was lunchtime. Kelvin, being a man, had inevitably gone out to fill his grumbling stomach, so her secretary was alone.

'Come into my study a moment, can you? I want to talk to you about it.'

'It was from the breast screening unit,' Vicky said, as Marissa sat opposite her, perched uncomfortably on the end of an armchair.

'Oh no,' Marissa gasped, her defensive facade crumbling. 'Not cancer. Why you?'

Vicky nodded, marvelling at how typical everyone's responses were.

'Why not me? That's life. It's okay. I've no intention of dying – not quite yet, anyway. But I do need treatment, and you can imagine the furore in the press if they find out. Somehow we have to try to carry this off without anyone knowing. Can we do that, Marissa? Can you use your genius to manage the diary and cover for me?'

Marissa pulled herself up and sat very straight.

'Of course I can, Bishop.'

'Call me Vicky, from now on – when we're alone. I'll take as little time off as I can.'

'Take as much as you need, Bish . . . Vicky. Leave everything to me,' Marissa announced, suddenly reaching forward and patting her hand, which shook her a little. 'We'll pull this off together.'

Vicky was tempted to say, 'Jolly good,' but found herself instead saying an equally hackneyed, 'I knew I could rely on you.'

Marissa beamed a gratified smile, a first.

The surgery was swift and uneventful. She was back on her feet within forty-eight hours. Waiting for the results meant a further, no doubt interminable, ten-day wait. If patience was a Christian virtue, this experience would make a saint of her.

She threw herself into her work. With an ingenuity that took Vicky's breath away, Marissa had slotted every urgent meeting into this short period of opportunity, quietly aware of the further assault to Vicky's body that might be lying in wait when the ten-day sentence was up. As long as she stayed focused on the issues at hand, the nagging anxiety and the pull of the stitches didn't bother her unduly. Whenever a sudden shaft of apprehension threatened her tranquillity, she used the words from a familiar psalm, that she had so often used to comfort others, as a kind of mantra: 'Though I walk through the valley of the shadow of death, I shall fear no evil.'

The night before the test results she couldn't sleep and sat up late writing her Christmas letter for the diocesan magazine.

'In early October?' Tom demanded, shaking his head in disbelief. 'Won't you come to bed?'

'I can't just lie there tossing and turning.'

He nodded reluctantly and left her to it.

There's nothing like the assumption that everyone else is having a wonderful time to make you feel jaded, lonely and bypassed. As a child raised in a fairly dysfunctional family, Christmas never lived up to the fantasy I had spun in my imagination – happy families nestling cosily around an open fire, fairy lights twinkling on a sweet-scented fir tree, melt-in-the-mouth mince pies, carols sung in soft harmony around the piano. I knew nothing of the dramatic scenes that ensued in everyone else's homes when mother-in-law took over the kitchen, Granny left her hearing aid at home, Billy rode his new bike over the baby, and Daphne announced she'd become a vegetarian. It would have shocked me beyond measure had I known that my fantasy was a media-induced lie, and that many people lived in dread of this major event in the Christian calendar.

Last year, the BBC asked a group of teenagers how they would be celebrating Christmas. With their heads down the toilet, they said. What terrible, bogus celebration binge-drinking is, when having fun means total oblivion.

The church a has more authentic celebration to offer. The problem is that by the time the festival proper arrives, the extraneous trappings – the endless shopping and canned jollity, the nativities and carol services, the works dinners – have inoculated

*even the most faithful of us against the sheer gob-smacking
miracle of the incarnation. And exhausted clergy are simply
relieved the end is in sight.*

*But if Christians don't tap into the true wonder of the festival,
sharing it in our homes and churches and with our neighbours,
who else will? As more people than ever attend church at some
time during the season, searching for that something that will
give them a sense of significance, purpose and joy, what an
incomparable opportunity to offer a real experience of
Emmanuel, God-with-us.*

God with me, she whispered to herself all the way to the hospital, sitting
in the waiting area, the corridor, the consulting room. Tom was with her,
his hand in hers, as she was given the prognosis – a revolutionary new
drug, a further operation, radiotherapy; but, after that, every hope of
complete remission. Vicky nodded, unable to speak, blinded by the tears
of gratitude that welled up in her eyes. No chemotherapy. Thank God,
thank God. She might just manage to maintain her privacy and dignity.

The second bout of surgery was a little more radical and she spent a
night in hospital. She arrived home dizzy with exhaustion, the anaes-
thetic still circulating around her system. Marissa ordered her to bed. She
managed Vicky's absence then and throughout the intensive radiotherapy
treatment that followed, with such an imaginative variety of plausible
excuses that even Kelvin was satisfied.

When yet another mammogram finally gave Vicky the all-clear, she
managed to persuade her amazing secretary that a hug might be in order.

'Do you know,' Vicky said to her as they shared a glass of champagne
in her study, 'the new hospital computer reminds staff to wash their
hands, and tells them when it's time for each patient's medication? It even
flags up a warning when a patient hasn't emptied their bowels. With a
programme like that, we could run the diocese really well.'

For the first time she heard Marissa laugh.

Vicky suddenly had an overwhelming longing to see Donald again, and
called to ask if she could make an appointment.

'An appointment?' tutted Gwen, his wife. 'You're a friend, Vicky, and I
think maybe you should see him before it's too late. He would certainly
want to see you. But don't expect a great deal of him. It's an awful long
way for you to come.'

'I'll take the train, and however he is, a few minutes with him would be
worth a trip halfway across the world.'

She found him lying on a daybed in the room that was once his study, but now served as a sick room, a commode tucked away in the corner.

'Vicky,' he said, his face lighting up as she walked into the room. He stretched out a tremulous hand, which she took in hers, and made as if he wanted to sit up.

'Don't even try,' she warned him.

'No,' he said, lying back, 'it's got the better of me in the end – the accursed Parkinson's. But I gave it a run for its money, did I not?'

'You did that, Donald. Nearly ninety. Not a bad innings, considering.'

'Life is like water falling on the ground which cannot be gathered up again.'

'Who said that?'

'A bishop who doesn't know her Bible?' he chortled. 'And you? How are you?'

'A touch of cancer.'

His eyes, that had never missed anything, locked on hers, expressing anxiety and concern.

'No, no, no. You have so much living left in you.'

'It's been dealt with – surgery and radiotherapy. I'm relieved it's all over, but a bit shaken.'

'Not surprising. Fine-tunes the spirit. Makes us question our priorities.'

She was determined not to be drawn into her issues, not this time, and asked, 'And you, are you ready for the last great adventure?'

He chuckled. 'Are you coming over all pastoral with me? To be honest, I'm getting a bit tired of trembling uncontrollably and can't wait for the new body. And, of course, the eternal party, where I, even I, your dour Scottish mentor, will don the kilt and dance for all I'm worth. That'll be a sight for sore eyes.'

Fighting back the tears, Vicky lifted his trembling hand to her mouth and kissed it.

'No fear, Vicky,' he said softly. 'Remember that. No fear. Fear, if it finds a niche in our souls, blights our lives and drives out the love of God. But he who loved us from the start, when there was nothing in us worth loving, won't abandon us at the last.'

'Donald, I . . .'

She paused a moment, determined not to let her voice break.

'I want to say thank you. It seems so inadequate a word for all you've done for me. But will you do one last thing? The patriarchs of old, when they were dying, used to lay their hands on the heads of the next generation and bless them. You have been such a father to me. Would you do that for me?'

He nodded weakly, smiling at her with such tenderness that she could barely bring herself to look at him without the fear of breaking down completely.

As she knelt by his bed, he laid his large, once strong hands on her head, and whispered, 'The blessing of honesty and integrity, of courage and dignity, fearlessness and perseverance, of purpose and hope, joy and laughter, love and peace, of the indwelling of the Holy Spirit in all his fullness rest upon you for the remainder of your earthly days, however few or many, whatever God calls you to do.'

As he was praying the sun came out, anointing their heads and shoulders in the radiant warmth of its golden rays, streaming through the floor-to-ceiling window in the room. And then she realised that for those few wonderful moments, Donald's shaking had ceased.

'Vicky,' he said quietly, watching her as she got up and prepared to go, 'it has been such an honour to journey with you all these years. And if these things are at all possible, I will carve out a little window in heaven, so that I can sit and watch your progress. "Rage, rage against the dying of the light" – it isn't true, you know, for the Christian. The light gets brighter and brighter the closer we get to the end of the journey. Rejoice, rejoice in the brightening of the light. From one degree of glory to another – however tortuous the path, however many the setbacks, or your perceived weaknesses and failures. All to make us more like him, till the day when we see him, face to face, and dwell with him forever in never-ending light.'

She nodded, blinking away the tears again, leant down and kissed him one last time on the forehead.

'Until that morning, then?' he called after her as she reached the door.

'Until the morning, Donald. Rest well.'

He died peacefully at home four weeks later. She was unable to attend the funeral as she and Tom were having a fortnight's break in France, but she was so glad she had gone up when she did and that their farewells had already been said.

'Two weeks in France – now, Bishop?' Kelvin asked, bewildered.

She suddenly realised how unfair it had been to him not to take him into her confidences. He obviously realised something was seriously amiss, but had covered for her faithfully, holding his peace.

'I know, I've had a lot of time off,' she said, touching the top of his arm, which he now allowed her to do. 'Not been too well.'

'I thought so,' he said, looking slightly injured. 'Couldn't you trust me, Vicky?'

'Personal. Women's stuff. I didn't tell anyone. And that's why Tom and I need this little break.'

'Oh,' he said, comprehension wiping the confusion from his face.

Men, she thought to herself, could be so wonderfully credulous and easy to deal with, at times.

2023

As she buttoned herself up and looked questioningly from the consultant to Tom, Tom smiled back reassuringly and grasped her hand. Not a good sign. He was never normally demonstrative in public, and certainly not in front of a colleague. Stephen had her scan in front of them both on the desk.

'You don't need me to tell you that this isn't good news,' he said.

It went through her mind that it must be hard for a doctor to find the right facial expression at a moment like this. How to deliver devastating news? Maintain a certain gravity? Hold sympathetic eye contact? Smile sadly? He opted for the last.

'I had hoped you'd say I'd slipped a disc while doing the hoovering, or pulled a muscle while I was swimming. Though actually, I get little time for either.'

He shook his head.

'Neither, I'm afraid. The cancer is back – metastases in the spine this time.'

His disappointment was palpable, and she found herself switching to pastoral mode. How can I make this easier for him? Stupid, a voice said in her head. This is about you now, not him. Leave him to deal with his own feelings. You need to deal with yours. But she had no feelings. She felt completely numb. Tom likewise, she presumed, for he said nothing, simply clung to her hand.

'Strange,' the consultant said, 'I deliver this kind of news several times a week and never let it get to me. But in your case . . .'

'Why should I be any different?'

'Maybe because I don't normally have such a high-profile patient.'

'And a fat lot of difference it makes. Come on, tell me the prognosis.'

He paused. Kept his gaze steady.

'And maybe, because I applaud so much of what you've tried to do, and want you to have the chance to see the fruit of it.'

'So, you're telling me I won't.'

'Let's not go there just yet. Fortunately, the tumours are all on the outer part of the spinal cord, which means it's worth trying surgery, always the best option if we can avoid weakening the spine. And then intensive radiotherapy, of course. And drugs, lots of drugs, until you rattle. Let's see how you respond to treatment before I get out my crystal ball.'

TWENTY-SIX

We shall only become capable of new beginnings if we are prepared to let go of the things that torment us, and the things we lack.

JÜRGEN MOLTMANN

DECEMBER 2023

They drove the first part of the way home in silence. Tom stared straight ahead at the road, his brow furrowed, his mouth pinched. She knew that look so well. The pent-up anger that couldn't find its way out. Even when Alice had had the usual childhood ailments he had never believed that he or his could become the patient. It insulted the sense of inviolability bestowed by the stethoscope around his neck. So Vicky hadn't told him about the back pain, hoping too, she saw now, that if she didn't mention it, it might simply go away.

'Are you okay?' she asked eventually.

'Perfect,' he said, clenching his teeth.

She laid a hand on his thigh, looked up at his face, and saw the beginning of a tear forming at the corner of his eye.

'Feeling pretty desolate, actually.'

'Oh, my darling. I am so sorry.'

'I'm a doctor, for God's sake. Isn't that an irony? I feel so helpless.'

'And doctors' families never get ill or die? I never knew the career choice conferred automatic immortality. It's life, Darling. You don't have all the answers to the human condition. Sooner or later, we die.'

'And in your case, it should be later – a lot later. After the hell you've been through, couldn't God at least have given you that?'

'But Tom, I've lived the life I've had. To the full. Had opportunities others have never had. And I'm so grateful for that.'

'But what about us? We've barely had any time together – the time we might have had in retirement. That's what I resent so much.'

'Don't spend your time fighting what is,' she said, patting his thigh, 'or we'll waste the time we do have. I'd have loved to share a long retirement with you. But if it's not meant to be, we'll have to wait for eternity instead.'

'Blast eternity,' Tom yelled, revving his way furiously through a yellow traffic light.

'Tom, let's not look too far ahead. All we ever have is the present, this moment. Let's enjoy it while we can,' she begged.

He turned to her momentarily and there was a look of such despair on his face that all she could think to say was, 'I'm not dead yet. We will fight this. Together.'

And he gratified her with a nod.

At home, alone, with Tom safely sent out in search of Christmas presents, she threw herself onto her bed for her own internal wrestling match. How, on top of all the other pressures heaped upon her, could God have landed her with this? All the hackneyed old questions came tumbling out. Why me? Why now? Haven't I given you my best shot? Listening to herself, she thought, I sound just like the heroine of a TV drama. The reality was that this time there could be no dissembling or subterfuge, and the thought of having to face such a private trauma in the public glare was almost unbearable. What would Donald have said to advise and console her? She was almost pole-axed with her longing to hear his wise and loving voice.

After an hour or so of ranting at God, and still feeling utterly disconsolate, she snatched up her Bible off the bedside table and opened it. A piece of scrap paper fluttered out to the floor. She picked it up and read something she had written years ago. Moltmann, inevitably. *'Our resurrection hope helps us to say a full and entire yes to a life that leads to death.'*

She studied it for some time through a blur of tears. This was exactly what Donald would have said to her. His voice couldn't have been clearer if he had been in the room. This short little life of hers, at whatever age she died, was but the preparation for an eternity that was more wonderful than anything she could begin to imagine, and must therefore be lived as such to her final breath. And that thought enabled her to release a small, uncertain, 'Why not me? Why someone else? And why not now, when my life has been so full and I have had the chance to achieve all I was created for?'

She thought she had said her yes to mortality all those years ago, when she had cancer for the first time, but the truth was that the roundabout of life had caught her up again and swirled her round so fast that she had simply been too busy to reflect on it. And then, in recent months, the continual bombardment of press brutality had made her so unhappy that she hadn't stopped to realise how truly blessed she actually was.

How quickly bad news shifts one's perspectives, like Tom's new 3D camera that allowed him to refocus pictures after he had taken them, because it captured all the rays of light travelling through any scene. Her marriage had revived. She had a wonderful daughter, son-in-law and grandson, the technology to see them whenever she wanted to, and the means to visit from time to time. So many long-term friendships that had lasted the test of time. Not to mention the privilege of connecting with the minds and hearts of millions of ordinary men and women in this nation and beyond.

She had come close to letting the demands and difficulties of the job rob her of the beauty of life itself. Not so much its grand highlights, though she had enjoyed more than her fair share, but the simple, ordinary things she had taken for granted – the interactions with so many fascinating people on a daily basis, a thoughtful, encouraging word or touch, the banter of the staff, the merry laughter of children as they toured the corridors and gardens, the sunsets tinting the world pink through the windows of her study, the snow painting a magical winter scene she could watch, entranced, from her cosy, lamp-lit room, with Bach playing in the background. There was a desolation in the thought that she might not have this for very much longer, then a burst of unalloyed joy in the realisation that she would, forever, if she held tight to that resurrection hope. Whenever fear found an entrance, she whispered the words of Evening Prayer to herself: 'Support us Lord, all the day long of this wondrous life, until the shadows lengthen, and the evening comes, the busy world is hushed, the fever of life is over, and our work done; then Lord, in your mercy, give us safe lodging, a holy rest and peace at the last.'

Alice and family joined them in Canterbury for a bitter-sweet Christmas. She was pregnant again, and there were moments of tearfulness at the thought that this baby might never know his grandma.

'I'm so sorry, Mum,' she apologised, blowing her nose and taking several deep breaths, 'I should be strong for you.'

'Your hormones are all to pot – that's pregnancy for you. Just having you here with me is all I need. And let's not cross any bridges till we need to. The consultant hasn't issued me with a death sentence – yet! Though sooner or later, it's inevitable. For all of us.'

'Cheery thoughts for Christmas,' Tom murmured from behind his newspaper.

Vicky nodded in Tom's direction and Alice took her cue. She went over to her father and took his hand. He needed the comfort of her presence as much as Vicky did.

They had a family consultation on how public she should make her illness, given that she couldn't continue to work through it. Alice thought she should be honest about the reasons for taking leave. She was entitled to a little sympathy. But Vicky insisted that the actual nature of her condition should not be made public, not even to Ann or to the rest of her staff. It was enough coping with her family's anxiety, let alone having to deal with everyone else's.

On 2 January 2024, she made the announcement that she would be taking some time off due to ill health, and on 3 January a surgeon removed three smallish tumours from her spine.

The press was in no doubt that she was having a nervous breakdown. Hardly surprising, she said to herself, when they had been fed the line that she wasn't coping, but blow them for swallowing it so readily. She was still annoyed by the anonymous bishop who said, with crocodile tears, 'The Archbishop has been experiencing difficulties for some time. It was inevitable that the stress would take its toll, and she has our every sympathy. It is such an impossible job to do.'

Tom was incandescent.

'After the way you've worked day and night for the past four years! How dare any of them suggest you're not up to the job? They'll all look stupid when the truth comes out. Tell them, Vicky.'

She shook her head.

'Have the entire world watching me when I go back to work, waiting for my imminent demise? I can't.'

'You're probably right. The press won't admit their mistake, will they? They won't apologise. They'll just hope their readers will forget what they wrote.'

It pained her that this was so much harder for Tom than it was for her. Perhaps one of the most difficult things about having a woman in the post was the fact that her other half, full of testosterone-fired aggression, felt compelled to hit out in defence of his wounded mate. But Tom had always been denied that outlet for his pain. She took the newspapers away from him.

'Tom, let them say whatever they want. We won't let it touch us.'

She was barely out of hospital when a private member's motion was tabled for General Synod:

> This Synod expresses its appreciation for the work of the Archbishop
> of Canterbury in the creation of 'The Well' – enabling the church to
> address more effectively the worrying increase in poverty in our
> country.

'Some public appreciation at last,' Tom said, handing her the Secretary General's email.

'Yes,' she said reservedly.

Tom studied her face.

'You're not pleased?'

'It's just – I don't know. Maybe I'm just not good at accepting compliments.'

Two days later an amendment was added, proposed by the Bishop of Carbury, and seconded by Lord Kilmarton. This seemed reasonably innocuous on the surface, but the devil, as always, was in the detail:

And being also mindful of the all-too-evident pressures on the Archbishop of Canterbury, this Synod requests the House of Bishops:

1. to instigate an urgent review of the day-to-day responsibilities of the Archbishop, with a view to sharing some of them more widely in the House;

2. to establish a committee of the Synod to oversee and co-ordinate the engagement of the Archbishop of Canterbury with all the offices of state;

3. to work with the Archbishops' Council in establishing clear guidelines for the spending and accounting of all the discretionary funds available to the office of the Archbishop of Canterbury.

'This is horrendous,' she muttered as she read it, installed on the sitting-room settee, suddenly bathed in a lather of perspiration. She thrust away the rug that covered her, loosened her wrap for air and rang Dominic Naylor, careful to block all visuals, lest he see her state of undress.

Though apologetic, the Secretary General was as maddeningly laid back as ever.

'I know, Archbishop. This really is a rather grievous business.'

Was that all he could say? Might he even be behind it? Who was?

'It questions my professionalism, suggests I am incompetent and misspend what little budget is actually at my discretion, and removes any freedom I have to act in the future without the say-so of Synod and the House of Bishops. In short, it's a cynical attempt to disempower me completely.'

'Quite so, Archbishop. But entirely within the rules.'

'I cannot oppose it. But nor can I let it pass. It's nothing less than a vote of no confidence. Can you offer me any guidance on how to handle it?'

'This is a difficult one, and I wouldn't presume, Archbishop. But . . .'

She waited, and then he said more gently, 'I have no doubt you will be given the wisdom and the words.'

The press recognised the implications at once, citing her ill-thought-out and high-handed proposals regarding the modernisation of the church, allegations of doubtful morality – referring, she imagined, to the intimations about her purported relationships with either Bev or Ralph or both – her irresponsibility in allowing a paedophile to continue in ministry, her apparent inability to cope with the work, and misuse of the Church and Community Fund. It was an impressive list, considering she had been in office a mere four years.

The Bishop of Carbury publicly professed his sympathy, suggesting that the stress and pressure had been too much for her, that it accounted for many of her errors of judgement, and that additional support might just enable her to avoid a future breakdown. The allegations of misuse of Church and Community Fund money had come from Kilmarton, it seemed, on what basis she couldn't imagine. He claimed she had used the church's money for what he referred to, in deliberately inflammatory language, as her 'anti-Muslim vigils'. It was far from the truth, as the accounts would prove. However, it also emerged that Class B drugs were discovered during a police raid on one of the new youth projects she had recently funded. Unfortunate, she had to admit, but hardly an abuse on her part.

In fact, it was hard to take any of the no-confidence accusations seriously. But because of the close ties between church and state, which she had played her part in defending just a few months ago, there was every chance this move had the government's blessing. Why hadn't she seen this coming? She had been foolhardy in confronting ministers, criti-quing their policies, challenging their integrity – even if it had been in the name of the marginalised and dispossessed. And as for the church, with its power groups and cliques, its institutional torpor and resistance to her attempts to create a freer, more innovative culture? Every day the storm clouds had been a little thicker, a little blacker, but she had not considered the possibility that they would finally burst.

In the recesses of her mind she heard Donald's warning voice: 'Ah, Vicky, suffering is the inevitable cost. Rejoice that you've been chosen.' But she didn't want to be a martyr. She was shocked, angry and feeling down, at a time when she was post-operative and weak, and needed the chance to recuperate before the radiotherapy began. How could Carbury and Kilmarton believe that they had enough support for their plot to get rid of her? Who was behind them, lurking in the shadows? Had her own naivety been the cause of her downfall? Her helplessness drove her near to tears.

'You won't even be well enough to go and defend yourself,' Tom griped, clenching and unclenching his fists until his knuckles were white, as they sat together in the sitting room, he slouched in an armchair, surveying the morning papers on his tablet, she in her dressing gown, sipping her coffee. Quite the Darby and Joan, she said to herself. Like any normal old couple. She could get used to this. But his words infused a sudden strength into her aching backbone.

'You want a bet?' she said to him, consciously straightening herself up. 'I'll be there. Even if it kills me.'

She even managed to laugh, despite the pull on the stitches.

'And I can't think of a better way to go.'

'Not funny,' Tom snapped, running his hand through his hair in desperation.

At Vicky's request the wonderful Sister Agnes paid her a visit from downstairs. Vicky was resting on her bed, too weary to rise that afternoon. The mere sight of the sister's placid, almost line-free face, surrounded by the simple white band that kept her unruly grey hair in place, soothed her spirit.

'You've been having a hard time of it, Cariad,' she said in a soft Welsh voice.

She had told Sister Agnes the first time they met that she was to call her Vicky, not Archbishop. But Cariad – or darling – was the word she preferred. And so it remained.

'You know what's going on?'

'Of course I do. We're not completely cut off. Even I have an e-reader these days. How can we pray effectively unless we know what's going on? So tell me now, how is it you're lying on your bed?'

Vicky told her about the cancer, and Agnes knelt down beside her, took hold of her hand and began to stroke it gently. All the tears Vicky had held in check for Tom's sake burst through the dam she had erected and kept in place so firmly for the past week. The pain in her guts was so intense it far outweighed any pain in her back, and she wept like a child, for her betrayal by friends and colleagues, and for the life she might soon have to lay down.

Sister Agnes stayed silently by her side, except for the occasional, 'ssshh' of sympathy, like a mother quieting her baby. And when the flood slowly began to abate, she pulled a tissue out of one of the voluminous pockets in her habit, and handed it to Vicky.

'It's clean, Cariad.'

Vicky loved the mischief in those twinkly eyes of hers, and smiled despite herself.

'Now then, is there anything I can get you? A cup of tea maybe?'

Vicky shook her head, bemused by the practicality of the woman, so unlike Donald, who would never let himself be side-tracked by such minor niceties.

'In that case,' said Sister Agnes, 'let me give you three pictures that might help you face your current desolation. Just relax now and let the Holy Spirit do his work.'

Vicky closed her eyes and waited.

'First, I want you to imagine you're on a long mountain climb. It's a steep path and you're struggling. The mist comes down and you're enveloped in it, unable to see a foot in front of you. Now, the inexperienced townsman would hurry along and soon have to stop, dead beat and completely lost. An experienced mountaineer, on the other hand, knows that the only thing to do in the mist is to halt in his tracks and camp out under the small tent he's brought with him, quietly smoking his pipe. He moves on only when the mist has cleared away.

'For the second picture, I want you to imagine you're on board a ship, facing a turbulent storm. What will you need to do in that little cabin of yours? Put your most precious stuff away for safety, that's what, and just keep by you the essential, reliable, simple things you'll really need till the storm passes – a bottle of water, a good book.

'And lastly – now this'll make you smile – you're on a camel in the desert, overtaken by a sandstorm. All you can do is dismount from your camel, fall prostrate, face down, on the sand, covering your head with your cloak. Maybe you'll lie there three hours, maybe six, or a day, until the storm is past, but only when it's over can you continue your journey.'

After some minutes, Vicky opened her eyes and saw that Sister Agnes was watching her carefully, with those penetrating blue eyes of hers. Vicky smiled at her and nodded slowly.

'Do you see what I'm saying, Cariad? I think you do. When you face what Baron Friedrich von Hugel called "the flinty furlong", which is where you're at, the crucial lesson in the midst of the storm is – here, let me read to you what he says,' and she delved into the other pocket of her habit. She brought out a pocket Bible and withdrew a scrappy piece of paper covered in handwriting:

to form no conclusions, take no decisions, change nothing during such crises, and especially, at such times, not to force any

*religious idea or mood on oneself. To turn gently to other things,
to maintain a vague, general attitude of resignation, to be very
meek with oneself and others: the crisis goes by, thus, with great
fruit. What is a sense of God worth which would be at your
disposal, capable of being comfortably elicited when and where
you please? It is far, far more God who must hold us, than we
who must hold him. And we get trained in these darknesses into
that sense of our impotence without which the very presence of
God becomes a snare.*

'There you are. He puts it better than I ever could. So don't try to be
brave, or work out what you must do or say to get you through and out of
the storm. Don't even wonder where he is. Just be, my dear, and let him
carry you and care for you. Wait – and he will see to the rest. He's brought
you thus far. He won't let you down now.'

Sister Agnes laid her hand on Vicky's head. Her palm was smooth
and cool and smelt of lavender. She prayed for healing of the body, for
light on the path, for peace in the dark moments, for rest of mind and
spirit, and for ultimate vindication and the triumph of truth. Then she
kissed Vicky on the forehead and disappeared as calmly and quietly as
she had arrived.

And Vicky fell softly into a deep, deep sleep.

Ten days after her operation, before the radiotherapy began, she dressed
in her work clothes and went gingerly down to her study to clear some of
the admin that she guessed would be piling up.

Ann found her sitting at her desk.

'I can manage, Archbishop,' she said indignantly.

'I don't doubt it for one minute,' Vicky said apologetically. 'I just
thought, given the . . . situation, I'd better deal with anything urgent.'

Ann harrumphed, sorted through some papers and placed a small pile
in front of Vicky.

'That's in order of importance,' she said, and marched out of the door,
as Ralph came in, not hiding his surprise at her presence.

'Okay?' he asked.

She nodded, glancing at a card that Ann had left for her to see, signed
by a clergy wife whose marriage had been threatened by her husband's
breakdown. Vicky had spent some time trying to help her in her early
days as bishop, despite Marissa's insistence that she had more important
things to do. She gave the husband unlimited leave and the money for a
proper break.

*I shall always be grateful for the way your intervention saved this
little family, and gave us back our happiness. Our loving prayers
are with you through this difficult time . . .*

She was suddenly aware that Ralph was watching her, concern writ large
on his face. She stood up without support, motioned Ralph to an
armchair, walked over and sat down opposite him without flinching.

'Ralph,' she said, 'I'm so sorry not to have . . .'

He waved a hand to stop her.

'No need to explain,' he said. 'I respect your privacy. Just tell me, is it
stress?'

She smiled at him and shook her head.

'Jenny and I thought not, but I think she might be a little . . . hurt.'

'I'll speak to her,' Vicky reassured him. 'Minor surgery. I just needed
some time to recuperate.'

'And look what happened while you did. The dogs! Such a good example to the nation, this church of ours!'

'They're a minority, Ralph, always remember that,' she said, smiling.

'I spoke to Tom. He assured me that you were coping. But I do need to
talk to you urgently. Are up to it?'

She nodded.

'Then take a look at these. They're from our old friend, Mark Bradley-
Hind, to none other than the Archbishop of York, Ryan Talbot.'

He handed her a piece of paper, an inscrutable expression on his
face.

She took it, watching his face, but no clarification was forthcoming. It
was a printout from the Encryptogram secure messaging service, recording a series of incriminating messages clearly referencing her over the past
three and a half years. Mark was hostile, dismissive of her politics. No
surprise there, but why on earth was he writing to Ryan? With an increasingly heavy heart, she scanned down quickly through some fairly
unpleasant stuff, typical of Mark, she imagined. Would the man never let
go of his animosity?

' "Neo-Socialist claptrap? Good to hear you share my feelings?" What
does he mean? Why should Ryan share his feelings?'

Ralph said nothing, waiting for her to grasp the full import of what
she was reading. When it did finally sink in, she felt as if a machine gun
had just blown a hole through her middle, leaving her guts hanging
out. Ryan! Why? There had to be some mistake. She checked the name
of the recipient, once, twice, over and over again, unable to bring
herself to speak.

She was conscious of Ralph's eyes trying to read her reaction. The concern had returned to his face.

'Where did you get this?' she croaked at last, then cleared her throat, hoping it might clear her mind at the same time.

'Ethan – that detective sergeant of Katya's. He's been promoted, something he was a bit cagey about – seconded to the Fraud Squad. Anyway, seems to be working well for our purposes. They have a monitoring device on Mark's phone, cracked his Encryptogram account.'

'On Mark's phone?' she asked, feeling strangely dense and distant, wondering how much of her confusion was due to the strong painkillers.

'Why? How?'

'You can guess why, Vicky. You raised it with me all those years ago. It was the reason he and I parted company. Some of Mark's financial practices aren't what we might call entirely above board. The Fraud Squad have had him under surveillance for some time to find out who else was involved.'

'If this is police business, surely it's top secret? Why did Ethan give this tip-off to you?'

'We only have those addressed to the Archbishop of York. Ethan thought, given your current circumstances, you ought to know. He relies on your absolute confidentiality, of course, until the investigation is complete.'

'Of course,' Vicky said, still feeling slightly dazed. She rested her head on her hand.

'We don't have Ryan's replies. Can't be sure he's done anything criminal.'

Ralph studied her anxiously, then said gently, 'Vicky, think. Even if his actions are not strictly criminal, doesn't it seem to you as if there has been a well-organised, concerted attack on your character? The leaking of information, the personal nature of some of the allegations, the timing of them and the sheer vitriol behind them? I don't just mean Carbury and his cronies. Or even Kilmarton. I suspect they're stooges. Inflexible, aggravating and unpleasant – easy to manipulate though, for the right person. But to me, this has always looked . . . planned.'

Vicky thought hard, but her brain still refused to function fully.

'Mark?'

'Oh, we know that he has a lot to answer for, and no doubt persuaded the PM not to do anything to prevent this scurrilous vote in Synod. But there's more to it, somehow.'

A thought occurred to her.

'I always had the feeling that the press was one step ahead of me. Ryan always knew I wasn't the Nominations Commission's first choice. Who else could have revealed such secret information to Dan Clements?'

'Well, there was Dean Julian, I suppose.'

'He was on the commission too? Why on earth would he have voted for me?'

'A little pressure from the top, perhaps? Or maybe he's not quite as narrow-minded as we think.'

And then it dawned on her, and her stomach revolved.

'Ryan gave me the Paloma Picasso perfume one Christmas. You remember how it was specified in the press as evidence of my so-called flirtatiousness?'

She studied the messages again, reading some of them out loud, shaking her head in disbelief as she reached the end.

'So what you're telling me is that it's my most trusted colleague, and friend, who has orchestrated this blessed no-confidence vote.'

She lay back against the armchair, exhausted.

'Why? Why would he do this to me?'

Aware that she was hyperventilating, she made a conscious effort to take slow, deep breaths.

'What are you going to do with this?' she asked Ralph, pointing at the email printout on her lap, unwilling to touch it now, lest it besmirch her in some way.

'Show it to him. Terrify him into decent behaviour. It's dynamite. The Archbishop of York himself and possibly other senior church officials in cahoots with a government minister to bring down the Archbishop of Canterbury? Great story. So much for that Synod vote.'

'No, don't, Ralph. That's blackmail, more or less. And it would never clear the air, always leave room for doubts about my character.'

He opened his mouth to protest, but she interrupted.

'Let me talk to Ryan. This . . . betrayal,' she bit her lip and swallowed hard to clear the constriction in her throat, 'I need some time to take it in.'

She was desperate to escape to somewhere quiet, to be alone, to think, to cry – if the tears could get through the wall blocking her brain from her feelings. She got up and made for the door, trying hard not to limp.

Ralph watched her in astonishment, got up to assist her.

'Vicky?'

'No,' she barked, shrugging him off. 'Give me an hour, then come up to the flat. Bring Jenny.'

She paced the floor for as long as the pain would allow, sat until discomfort set in, then got up again and held onto the dresser, calling

Ryan every rude name she could think of. The Judas! What sort of low-life could stoop to this?

After around thirty minutes or so of sustained rage her anger abated enough to prevent her rushing into some vengeful reaction she would later regret. She could hardly criticise his hypocrisy if she didn't herself live out the law of love she preached. God give me strength, she muttered, but I can't forgive him. Grace was not that cheap. But in time, if forgiveness was an act of the will, not the heart, she would find a way to get a full explanation, and try to understand.

Unbidden, her mother's voice suddenly forced its way into her consciousness. 'Stop pacing the floor like an animal in a cage, Vicky, and get on with your homework.' Her mother was right. Baron von Hugel even more so. Let the storm pass, then pick yourself up, dust yourself down and get on with it.

She went to tidy up her face in the mirror, and was shocked at how wan and weary she looked. Inevitably, she supposed, given the ordeal she was facing. In the early days of their marriage, she and Tom had always managed to see the funny side of the foibles of patients and church members, and it had saved their sanity. Not much to laugh about in the current situation, she reflected, as she blushered a little cheerfulness onto her cheeks, then went and put on the kettle as she waited for Ralph and Jenny.

'This is insufferable!' Jenny exclaimed loudly before Vicky had barely had the chance to open the door. 'You have been well and truly stitched up. If anyone did that to me I would be angry enough to knife them. I can't believe such behaviour from anyone who calls themselves a Christian, let alone from someone with his responsibilities!'

'Knifing isn't exactly Christian either,' Vicky grinned, as Jenny took her, gingerly, into her arms.

'I'm not made of porcelain,' she said, extricating herself and showing them into the sitting room.

Vicky sat down slowly on the settee. The solicitude on both their faces as they watched her made her want to laugh out loud.

'The pair of you. You look as if you're waiting for a funeral.'

'Just tell us what's going on,' Jenny insisted.

'I have cancer,' she said, in as matter-of-fact a way as she could. 'Primary breast cancer when I was Bishop of Larchester, secondaries now in the spine.'

Ralph couldn't conceal his horror. Jenny managed to hide hers beneath a veneer of professionalism.

'Why didn't you tell us?' she asked.

'Because of what I see before me now. All I have to do is say the big C word for everyone to have me dead and buried. I don't want you to make a fuss. The surgery has gone as well as it could. I'll have an intensive course of radiotherapy in a couple of weeks, and then I'll prepare for Synod.'

'You'll never be well enough for Synod,' Ralph said, struggling to control his obvious disappointment.

'I'll say to you what I said to Tom. Wanna bet?'

Jenny shook her head and smiled.

'There's no keeping a good woman down, Ralph. Determination is what she's made of. We'll do everything we can to help you, sweetheart.'

That afternoon, with her usual impeccable timing, Bev Aldridge called the office to say she was in London, and could she pop in? Vicky was lying on the settee when Ann buzzed her. She sat up before her secretary could see her in her prone position. She was not as surprised as she ought to have been. Bev had always had a way of materialising unexpectedly, like the Cheshire Cat in *Alice in Wonderland* – with a grimace rather than a grin.

'I know you're not supposed to be seeing anyone,' Ann acknowledged, 'but as she is an old friend of yours . . .'

Some friend, Vicky said to herself, unsure that she was ready for such a reunion; but she agreed, somewhat against her better judgement, got up and made herself presentable.

Though Vicky had tried on several occasions to contact Bev, there had been no word from her since the last press debacle. The photograph on the front of the papers hadn't been recent, and Vicky wasn't sure that the press had even approached Bev directly at that point, though suspected that they had. Yet, despite everything, she had desperately wanted to see her again, even if it was just for the sake of all they had once been to each other. Friendship, however sorely tested, was too precious a commodity to throw away without giving it a seventy-times-seventh chance. So what brought Bev to her now, at last? She guessed that Mandy had told her about the cancer. Nothing like the possibility of one's decease to alert people to the things that really mattered in life.

Bev arrived shortly after and sat facing her, her back ram-rod straight, looking not just awkward but downright miserable, stalwartly refusing to catch Vicky's eye. Her hands remained folded tightly on her lap. Time had not been kind, Vicky thought, as she appraised her, looking into her face for some sign of the happy-go-lucky young woman she remembered.

The wonderful thick, shiny auburn hair had faded into grey-streaked ginger curtains that hung listlessly on either side of a papery, withered complexion. Her mouth turned down at the corners, and she chewed her bottom lip. It was not a mannerism Vicky remembered.

'How are you, Bev? Are you happy?' Vicky asked, never taking her eyes off her former friend's face. Bev didn't look up.

'I suppose so,' she said.

She took a sip from the tea Vicky had placed in front of her, then put the cup down awkwardly on the coffee table. The clatter made her wince. 'How does anyone know if they're happy? I've been in GP practice for around thirty years. It becomes depressing to see how little we can help the people who most need it. Sometimes I think we only have two weapons in our armoury – drugs, and referral to a consultant. And I wonder if that was really what I dedicated my life to.'

'And how's Celia?' Vicky asked her.

'Fine, thank you. Both the boys decided to live with their father when they were in their teens. We found that hard. But it was for the best. Boys need a father.'

'So do girls.'

It came out before Vicky had stopped to think, and she could have kicked herself. Bev threw her a swift, cool look.

'I'm sorry. I didn't mean . . .'

Bev's hands had returned to her lap.

Dear God, Vicky cried out in her head, help me get through to her. I don't think I can stand a whole afternoon of this. Then she saw that Bev appeared to be struggling to speak. She drew a deep breath and, with immense effort, managed to force out a formal, 'Vicky, I came here today because there is something I have to say to you.'

It sounded rehearsed, and Vicky waited, barely breathing. Bev looked up, studied the wall somewhere behind her shoulder, chewing her lip. Then her face crumpled. 'But now that I'm here, I don't know how to say it.'

She turned to look at Vicky for the first time, her face distorted in an agony of helplessness and despair.

'Will sorry do? So, so sorry.'

Tears welled up in her eyes, and began to spill down her face. Vicky longed to reach out to her. But also knew it was best to give her space.

'It sounds so feeble, but I don't know how to explain what I did. In the end I even convinced myself that it was true – that you had, well, loved me in a special way.'

The tears flowed freely now and she fumbled in her handbag for a tissue. Vicky got up and fetched her the box she kept on the dresser. Bev took one, and began to wrap it around her fingers.

'I can make excuses, put it down to the childhood abuse, say it caught up with me, as I am sure you knew it would if I didn't seek help. I have started therapy – better late than never. Nothing can justify what I tried to do to you. I suppose I felt rejected, and tried to wreak my revenge by hurting one of the people I had loved most in the world. A repugnant thing to do, and I am so deeply, deeply ashamed of it.'

She looked down at the fingers that had been knotting and unknotting the tissue as she spoke, then wiped her eyes with the shreds that remained. She looked so worn, so defeated that Vicky's heart went out to her. She couldn't just sit there a moment longer, but got up and went to her. Kneeling painfully in front of her, she placed her hands around Bev's, holding them still.

'I can't live with myself any more. Can you ever forgive me?' she whispered. 'What I did to you was so dreadful. It was awful, to try to destroy your reputation like that. And Tom, what about Tom?'

'Don't worry too much about Tom,' Vicky reassured her, holding her damp hair away from her face, and tucking loose strands behind an ear, 'he's fairly robust. He was blazing angry, of course, more for my sake than on his own account.'

'I was furious at the church, and at you, for what I perceived as a denial of everything I was.'

'I can imagine it must feel like that.'

'When you became the first woman bishop, I just saw red. You had achieved your dream and more. And I . . . I felt left out, left behind. But it's still no excuse for the damage I did.'

'I was devastated at the time – had to threaten the paper with legal action, as you're probably aware.'

Bev nodded, apologetically.

'But in the end it didn't matter much,' Vicky sighed, 'given the many others who have done a far better job of destroying my reputation. I am trying to learn to let people think of me what they will. The truth will out in the end, I hope.'

Bev nodded slowly.

'I was more angry at the cards God had dealt me, than with you. I know that now.'

'His shoulders are big enough to cope with all our anger.'

Vicky took Bev into her arms and held her until her weeping was spent. They stayed with their arms around each other for a long while, Vicky stroking Bev's hair until the sobs tailed off into tiny hiccups. And in those few, intense moments of quiet, a thousand joyous memories of the once-inseparable trio came flooding back to Vicky, and her heart filled with gratitude for the simple, heart-warming pleasure of relationship restored – an unexpected blessing when she most needed one.

'Vicky,' Bev said suddenly, pulling away from her, 'I want you to know that that last media frenzy just a couple of years ago had nothing whatsoever to do with me. I knew nothing about it until the press contacted me. I was appalled. I never spoke to them after you became Archbishop.'

'Worry not,' Vicky reassured her, 'I don't doubt that for one minute. But I think I know who did.'

TWENTY-SEVEN

*As long as hope does not embrace and transform the thought
and action of men, it remains topsy-turvy and ineffective.*

JÜRGEN MOLTMANN

FEBRUARY 2024

A few days later Vicky went into her study to begin preparing her defence in Synod. As she cleared her desk, sorting her way through letters, cards and files, Ralph charged in.

'So,' he said, holding out something tiny and shiny on the palm of his hand, 'the results are in, and I am afraid to say that you have been well and truly bugged, Archbishop.'

'What do you mean?'

'After our last discussion about the Archbishop of York, I had the room checked by a specialist, and he took your computer to inspect as well. You remember the police were sniffy about the likelihood of anything untoward, way back – well, they were wrong. This,' he said, holding up the pea-sized gadget to the light, 'is what comes of having friends in high places.'

'That was meant to be irony, I take it?'

'I checked your desk carefully, but they'd actually put it inside your laptop,' he said, with unveiled admiration. 'I'm afraid we're not really set up for that level of security.'

Her eyes travelled from his face to the device as she tried to imagine who had been listening in to her conversations. The thought of it made her shiver involuntarily.

'What have we said that could be used against us?'

'More to the point, where have we said it?'

'Mostly in your office, I think.'

'Thank the Lord for that. Except . . .'

Their eyes met in concern.

'The morning you showed me the printout. Ryan has certainly been playing hard to get. He doesn't return my calls.'

'This might be why he's been giving you a wide berth.'

'He knows?'

'Well – we don't know for sure. He may. Depends on who's listening in and whether they've told him. If he does know he won't be sleeping easily in his bed, that's for sure.'

They both chortled at the thought. But Ralph sobered up quickly.

'If Mark knows we suspect him of scheming and skulduggery, he may make a further, final attempt to discredit you on the basis that he's got nothing to lose.'

'Oh, let him do his worst,' Vicky said, feeling almost too fatigued to care any more. But Ralph was busy venerating the pea. Her irritation was re-energising.

'Why was I bugged, Ralph?' she insisted. 'Who would want to? It's not as if I'm a public risk.'

'Aren't you? All that criticism of its policies, and then the Wooten Grange success has made you an immense threat to the government. But I somehow doubt it was politically motivated.'

'Well, whoever was listening in to my conversations, all they'd have got was persecution, famine and distress with the overseas bishops, and cradle cap and cracked nipples with Alice, thanks to the new baby. I hope it was good for their souls.'

'Ah, but this little device hacks into your emails too. That's actually its main purpose.'

She looked at him in alarm for a second, sat down heavily at her keyboard and began to spin rapidly through past communications.

'All those leaks to the press,' she said, trying to stifle her sense of panic. 'I'm not paranoid, after all. What have they picked up?'

Ralph went behind her and studied the screen over her shoulder. She tapped in a search for BLEO.

'There,' she said, 'you mentioned pursuing them.'

'When?'

'When we were emailing about the job.'

Vicky turned round to face him. Ralph stood back, thought for a while, then his eyes opened wide as the truth slowly dawned on him.

'No wonder the assault on you has been so ferocious. They knew we were still interested almost from the start . . . I'm probably lucky not to have ended up dead in a hotel bedroom somewhere like the previous Archbishop.'

Vicky was both shocked and bewildered.

'How are you feeling, by the way?'

'Ralph, what on earth are you talking about? What is going on?'

He walked out from behind the desk and began to pace the floor.

'I need to tell you something else that will pain you. Are you up to it?'

'I don't think I can stand any more revelations,' she groaned.

'Sorry, but I didn't want to do it while you were out of action – but now I don't think it can wait.'

He pointed her to one of the settees, and sank into the other himself, one arm slung over the back, the other hand rubbing the day-old stubble on his chin.

She came and perched opposite him, her eyes never leaving his face, and noticed for the first time how exhausted he looked. It shook her. She had been so caught up in her own fight for survival that she hadn't been looking after her team. They deserved better.

'You need to know that I've gone over Sarah's head and been in touch with Helen Davis.'

Vicky's mouth fell open in astonishment.

'Ralph, I can't bear the woman, not after what she wrote about me.'

'I know. But we need a friendly journalist.'

'Friendly? Sure, if you can call a shark friendly.'

He ignored her and said, 'You'll understand when I explain. Which isn't going to be easy. Are you sitting comfortably?' he asked.

'I'm not a child,' she said, rearranging the cushions at her back. She folded her arms, and waited.

'I discovered something when you were away in Africa, and when you got back . . . I didn't want to upset you. Not until I needed to.'

She watched him, mystified.

'It's about Artemis, Athene, Lakshmi – and several other companies with similarly inspired names.'

'All called after goddesses?'

She leant back against the cushions.

'Ethan's digging finally came up trumps.'

'And?'

Ralph remained silent.

'He discovered something I might not want to know?' she asked.

Unsmiling, Ralph nodded slowly. Vicky felt herself tense and made a conscious effort to try and stay calm.

'You know who it is – the man behind these bogus companies?'

Ralph nodded again.

Vicky's brain began to accelerate. A host of characters raced their way through it, but none leapt into focus.

'General Synod?' Ralph prompted.

'Oh. Lord Kilmarton!' she said, relieved. 'Well, that's awful – but not much of a surprise.'

Ralph looked pained. He shook his head.

'Dominic? Not the Secretary General?'

Ralph shook his head again.

'Oh, stop playing twenty questions, Ralph, and put me out of my misery,' she begged.

He leant forward towards her, and looked into her face with such commiseration that her insides churned and her mouth felt suddenly parched.

'Vicky, I don't know how to tell you this. Tracking it all back to source, in the final analysis these rather less than divine entities are the playthings of your Lord Westburton. His is the ultimate controlling hand behind the Wooten Grange development, and a bunch of others we haven't really clocked, for that matter. I'm so, so sorry.'

Vicky sat motionless. She felt completely numb, her emotions refusing to deal with any more duplicity and devastation. Then she said, smiling reassuringly, 'No, no, no. There's some mistake. Ethan has this wrong. I've known Nick for years. He's been like a father to me. He's mentored and advised me, nurtured my career, never been anything other than encouraging and supportive.'

Ralph pulled his device out of his pocket.

'Nicholas Hamilton-Jones, 3rd Baron Westburton, OM, GBE, funded the recent Tory campaign to the highest amount allowable from a single donor. In the UK Rich List 2020 he was ranked number thirteen . . . with an estimated fortune of £6 billion.'

Vicky whistled despite herself.

'I never realised . . .'

'Has close business dealings with a number of countries that now dominate the global financial market. Brazil, for example. India. None of the goddess companies has an official UK offshoot, so it is fairly certain that most of his money is in an off-shore operations base and exempt from taxation. The Caribbean, in all probability, given the number of annual visits he makes there. Pure white sands, aquamarine ocean, and endless blue skies. He keeps a multi-million-pound ocean-going yacht. Nice life, if you can afford it.'

He stopped and sighed.

'You were never invited to join him?'

Vicky shook her head, perplexed by so much information that was new to her.

'I should take it as a compliment, a recognition of your integrity, because everyone else was, Archbishop Ryan foremost among them.'

Her mouth fell open. 'The . . .' she began, then couldn't think of anything derogatory enough to call him, and found herself groaning instead, 'Nick, oh Nick.'

'Need a drink of water?'

She nodded and he poured one for her.

She drank slowly, her free arm stretched protectively around her stomach. She had thought that the revelation of Ryan's betrayal was one of the most painful she would ever have. But this; no, this was worse.

'Why, oh why has he pursued me all these years, encouraged me?' she cried out eventually in sheer bewilderment, as the brain's natural anaesthetising effects to ward off such severe shocks began to wear off.

'I've thought about it a lot,' Ralph said gently. 'I suspect it was some kind of sting operation in reverse.'

She looked mystified.

'The bad guy setting out to ensnare the good, I mean. Oh, I suspect that in the early days he genuinely saw your potential and singled you out, enjoying the idea of having a protégée in a position of power in the church, and such an unexpected one.'

She rested her head on her hand, rubbed her forehead.

'I can't take this in. Can't believe it. He has always been so attentive, so considerate.'

'I'm sure he was only doing what came naturally,' Ralph said wryly. 'You do have a way with the opposite sex.'

'Go on,' she commanded.

'The C of E had invested in one of his companies, remember. I wonder whether he didn't use his influence to get you Larchester? Either he thought you'd be useful to him, that he could get you on his side. Or alternatively, that he could at least monitor your response to his precious Wooten Grange project, keep ahead of you, ensure any protests came to naught. How was he to know you'd become Archbishop one day and try and put a stop to the huge investment in his company?'

'He never came back to me on it, when I asked, though. Effectively side-lined me,' she said, reflectively.

'Friends at the Church Commissioners, I suspect,' Ralph said.

'So his grooming of me did pay off,' she admitted, sadly.

'Not when you led the negotiations at Wooten Grange that robbed him of a chunk of the profits. And there was always the danger you'd eventually go back to the ethics committee and demand an end to the investment. Worse, that we might discover who the goddesses were, and expose him.'

She had sensed in that first phone call that Nick hadn't been pleased with her appointment as Archbishop. Why hadn't she gone with that instinct, taken it further and seen through him? As she thought about their many lunch and dinner dates, it didn't seem possible that he could have been so thoughtful, so reassuring and empower her so effectively only for his own ends. She said so to Ralph.

'He probably saw it as a business thing. There was, after all, a great deal of money involved.'

'Thanks,' she murmured. 'I was an investment.'

Her darned vanity had let her down again. She had been flattered by the attention and adulation of such a charming, glamorous man. Genuinely believed it was for herself alone. How naive was that? But the more she thought about his treachery, the more the final pieces of the jigsaw puzzle began to slot together to form a more complete picture.

'I think I'm going slowly mad,' she said to Ralph.

He raised his eyebrows.

'It was Nick who knew about the diary piece that suggested an adolescent affair with Bev – because I told him about it. It wouldn't have been difficult to alert a keen young journalist to the existence of the relevant file. And Nick knew about the paedophile business, because I consulted him about that as well.'

Her brain was whirring.

'Meanwhile, Ryan knew which perfume I wore, and could alert the press to any "ecclesiastical difficulties" I might have. Mark must have accessed the dirt on Tom's affair, the intelligence services' photograph of the poll tax riot, and got his cronies to co-operate in placing that . . . device. Are the three of them really all in this together? I can't get over it – I've always resisted conspiracy theories as being too far out.'

'Just think, if you hadn't made an enemy of Lord W, you could be lying on that yacht slurping champagne even as we speak. What a coup for him that would have been.'

'But who actually put this thing in my computer?'

Ralph was engrossed once more, flicking through the file, and didn't hear the question.

'The so-called "Affluent" team at HM Revenue & Customs – the result of a Lib Dem initiative during the coalition some ten years ago, set up to investigate the 350,000 wealthiest taxpayers in the country – named Westburton as a tax exile. But the Tories never really had the will to pursue the major tax evaders, given that most of them were exceedingly generous to their party.'

'Keeping it all offshore, eh? I did tell you about the time I overheard Mark's family having a blazing row about an offshore account all those years ago, but you didn't want to know. Suddenly it's sounding like there might be something sinister about it after all.'

Ralph sighed and rubbed his bristles again.

'Back in the days when I handled his private affairs, more fool me, it wouldn't have been very professional of me to admit that I had my suspicions.'

'Are you getting enough sleep, by the way?' she interrupted, but he was still busily expanding on this theories.

'All roads lead to Westburton, it now transpires. The Hamilton-Joneses were very close to Mark's parents. Nick's father, Godfrey, and Mark's grandfather were in business together. When Mark's father inherited the shares, he allowed Godfrey Hamilton-Jones to manage them for him. Even before Godfrey died, Nicholas had taken over and was handling a large proportion of the Bradley-Hinds' financial affairs.'

A thought occurred to Vicky.

'So Mark must have a stake in the goddesses? It might be a more obvious, rational reason for his antagonism. But what did Ryan stand to gain from all of this?'

'I don't know Ryan's motive. Nor do I know for sure yet where the Bradley-Hinds' money is. That was why it was becoming so difficult to act as Mark's accountant. He kept me in the dark.'

Vicky's blood suddenly ran cold.

'Where are you keeping your findings, by the way? At your flat?'

'In various places. In case the flat's under surveillance.'

'Ah, okay. So what else is in the file so far?'

'Not as much as I'd like. But I do have a copy of a statement from a local government official responsible for Wooten Grange, claiming she was offered sweeteners to agree to the project and dishing the dirt on some of her colleagues. I put Ethan onto her after you got back and told me about her. But it isn't easy to get hard evidence. Westburton is as slippery as a snake. He has friends in high places. No one has managed to trap him yet. Once he has his fangs in your flesh, you're done for. The venom is lethal.'

'Ralph, you will be careful?'

'Not afraid, are you, my fearless Archbishop? The fact is, we're into this so deep without even knowing it, that there's no pulling back now. If we're not ahead of his game, he'll not stop until he's done for you.'

He looked up at her and smiled in a way she wasn't sure she liked.

'And that's why we need Helen Davis,' he said.

'It was Nick who recommended her to Sarah, I remember that now.'

'Thought she was another woman he had tamed. She had her suspicions about him, though; I picked up on a piece she'd done in a regional paper fairly recently that hinted at his involvement in something that smelled bad.'

'More astute than I am, then?'

'She's a journalist, trained to be suspicious. Anyway, I got in touch and she has been doing some more investigative stuff herself off the back of it. The *Mail* is interested, apparently.'

Ralph smiled at her reassuringly.

'She's very sorry for the piece she wrote, by the way. Claims she came under enormous pressure from the editor.'

'A friend of Nick's, I take it?'

'I think "friend" is probably too strong a word. In the pay of, more like.'

'A pity she gave in, then – and let's hope she's not so easily swayed now.'

'She says that she can't stomach the way you're being treated at the moment. I told her she owed us big time, and she agreed. So, I offered an exchange on what we had.'

Vicky was horrified.

'Ralph, that is such a dangerous game.'

'It's a huge risk, I admit, but worth it if we can unmask his lordship. We'll need the tabloids on our side.'

She looked into Ralph's face for a while and didn't know whether to express anxiety or appreciation, so simply nodded. There was so much to take in. She felt bewildered, bereft, sickened. Like the child who tried the spa water in Harrogate, she couldn't get rid of the bad taste in her mouth, or the smell that it left in her nostrils. She felt the need to rest a while, to be alone, to reflect on the morning's shocking revelations, and rose slowly to her feet. Ralph took the hint and got up too. Not before she had a chance to glance at the picture he had been examining so intently on his phone, and saw that it was the 'Naughty Nookie' photo.

'You know,' he said, turning round at the door, 'I was such a fool, all those years ago, not to take my chance when I had it.'

On the day before the vote, while she was taking a short after-lunch nap, there was a hesitant tap at the door. Jenny was standing there, waving her smart phone.

'A thought,' she said, following Vicky into the sitting room. 'I think we should go through the list of Synod members . . .'

'All 467 of them?' Vicky groaned.

'No, just the ones we know . . . to assess which way they might vote tomorrow.'

'Don't,' Vicky begged her.

'Why not?' she asked, finger hovering over her phone, where she already had the list on display.

'That thing is not a crystal ball.'

Jenny looked crestfallen.

'I can't say the thought hadn't occurred to me,' said Vicky, 'but a couple of days ago my morning reading was the story of Gideon, how his army had to be whittled away so that he trusted in God, not his own brute force. Trying to gauge who's for and who's against is a fatuous waste of time, not to mention a sad lack of faith. I don't know how most will vote. Some will be for the motion simply because I'm a woman.'

'That's misogyny for you. Only sees a pair of tits, not quality of character.'

Vicky couldn't help but laugh.

'Thank you, Chaplain. Laughter is just the medicine I needed.'

Jenny looked up and became aware of Vicky's white cassock alb hanging on the back of the door like a reproachful, faceless member of the Klu Klux Klan. She raised her eyebrows.

'Waiting to be ironed,' Vicky explained.

Jenny stood up. 'Iron?' she demanded. 'Board? And where's that magenta clerical shirt of yours? We can't have you looking like a bag lady.'

Vicky protested. 'You're a chaplain, not a lady's maid.'

'A chaplain who at this current moment is so angry that she needs something practical and diverting to do.'

She set to, her grey spikes bristling, her earrings jangling. Jenny had become more, not less adventurous with her appearance in later life – a tribute, she told Vicky, to the poem, 'When I am old I shall wear purple'.

'The role of geriatric delinquent was written with me in mind,' she confided. 'I was middle-aged and boring. To play the part, I needed to look it.'

So she had her grey hair cropped short and spiky, and started wearing enormous silver hoops in her ears.

'Your ear-lobes will end up at your shoulders if you're not careful,' Vicky said to her the first time she wore them.

'A tribute to the strong women of Africa,' she said, tossing her head until the hoops swung. She weilded the iron now with such force that Vicky feared she was going to burn a hole in the alb.

'You know,' she muttered, 'I could almost live with this opposition if it emanated from the open, honest, theological-problems-with-women-bishops brigade. What I can't stomach is magnanimous, egalitarian open-handedness twinned with the back-stabbing routine. The bastards.'

Vicky tried not to smile. Her chaplain was supposed to help her handle her emotions with equanimity and godliness. But today their roles were somewhat reversed. Jenny slipped the alb back onto its hanger, hung it on the back of the door, and stood, smoothing out its folds, still ranting against the 'scheming and conniving beggars'.

'Let's get things into perspective,' Vicky said. 'I suspect in reality we're talking about a tiny minority. Even if they might win the day on this occasion.'

There was a further knock at the door and Ralph marched past her, in buoyant mood, a buff-coloured file in his hands. She noticed that he had had a haircut specially and was wearing a crisp, freshly ironed shirt with his smartest suit. He stopped halfway to the sitting room, turned to her and asked, 'You okay?' the way people do when they don't want the truth.

'Fine,' she lied.

What did 'okay' mean when two of the people you had thought were your dearest friends were at the centre of a conspiracy to shaft you, and had indeed already done serious damage to your reputation? When you were battling, too, with a potentially terminal illness? Perhaps 'okay' in these circumstances was just this certainty, beyond the pain and loss, that whatever might come, she was ready to accept it. So, yes, she was okay, if not exactly fine.

Ralph, it seemed, had had a similar thought to Jenny, and said, excitedly, holding out his e-phone, 'I've followed up with my equivalents in at least thirty dioceses. Their bishops, by all accounts, are pretty bewildered by the motion, and appalled to see you treated in this way. I'm confident we'll see them all express their admiration for you, and their support.'

Vicky sighed and shook her head.

'Not you as well.'

He held out his hands in confusion. Jenny looked smug.

'Then why in heaven's name haven't they said so publicly?' Vicky asked.

'Come on, Vicky,' Jenny said, 'you know these guys and how difficult they find it to enthuse about a female colleague – if they're too positive it just sounds as if they're smitten.'

Reluctantly, she acknowledged the fact.

'And the state of play in the House of Laity and the House of Clergy?' she asked.

'No idea,' Ralph admitted. 'Those I've spoken to tell me there's been a huge amount of unpleasant tittle-tattle in corners. And they don't like it. Kilmarton has been back-pedalling, apparently. Having been Westburton's unwitting stooge for so long, he now seems a little uncomfortable with the hostility his actions have engendered.'

Vicky gave Ralph a warning look, and he looked across at Jenny.

'I doubt very much, when it comes to it,' he continued smoothly, 'that there would be anything like a majority for his precious motion.'

Jenny seemed reassured and Vicky asked her if she would mind taking a look through the draft of the talk she had prepared. Jenny scrolled through her emails to find it, and for a moment Vicky feared she was going to sit and read it there and then. But fortunately she said, 'I need some quiet for this,' and took herself back to her office.

As the door closed Vicky said to Ralph, 'What are we going to do about Ryan?'

'Still no word?'

She shook her head.

'He probably can't handle any communication with you, assuming, as we do, that he knows you know. Must be sweating over what you'll do with the information.'

'What if he hasn't found out?'

'I still don't think he would give you his whole-hearted support tomorrow – this has to be the point at which he turns against, otherwise what's it all been for?'

'And if I survive the vote?'

'He'll say he had to be neutral in this instance, but that he had been working on your behalf behind the scenes.'

'Why would he do this? I think I'm owed an explanation.'

'Maybe there isn't one. Or at least, not one he'd admit to. Perhaps it's the feeling that he can do a better job than you, and wants to have a go. Can you see him saying that?'

'What is he saying – behind the scenes?'

Ralph was reluctant to tell her, but she wouldn't let him off the hook.

'Actually, my sources tell me that he remains superficially supportive, but in the process of expressing that support he somehow manages to take as read your incompetence, high-handedness, your craving for popularity, your interventionism in ecclesiastical and political affairs; oh, and your doubtful morality. So – he's clever about it, but maybe not as clever as he thinks he is. Is that enough to be going on with?'

Vicky sank down onto the settee and began to massage her forehead with her fingers.

'Don't let him get to you, Vicky. He's not worth it. He wants Canterbury, so he breathes support and breeds criticism at the same time. It's certainly not the first time it's happened in the Church of England. Won't be the last, either.'

'I still can't take it in. I just see him popping up on my screen like Tigger in *Winnie the Pooh*, chirpy, encouraging, enthusiastic. So innocent-looking.'

She went back to rubbing her head.

'Anything else about him in your precious file?' she asked, looking up.

'Not on Ryan,' Ralph said, fiddling with his e-phone. 'But Ethan's been doing some more snooping. Gets into places I can't. I'm seeing him later this afternoon with Helen. I'm hoping we'll have enough to make Westburton sweat.'

He fished a tiny red button from his trouser pocket and handed it to her.

'I've made a copy of the file for you,' he said. 'Too confidential to send to your computer. Don't leave it lying around. Have a read, and after I've seen Ethan we'll decide how best to use it.'

She motioned to Ralph to join her on the settee.

'Have I been stupid, Ralph?' she asked him. 'I seem to have made so many enemies. Should I have been more accommodating?'

He looked down at the floor and shook his head.

'You know,' she added, 'Jürgen Moltmann said that a church with a real understanding of the cross led it to a "sacrificial enactment of the liberation of the world". I tried to lead both the government and the church into a more servant-hearted attitude, that was all.'

Ralph took a sharp intake of breath and looked up at her.

'That was all? Vicky, your sacrificial leadership has brought liberation to more people than you'll ever know. Including me.'

She looked into his face, so settled, strong and open now. He was such a different man from the cocksure individual she had known all those years ago in Durham, and from the broken version who had huddled in an armchair that night at Bishop's House in Larchester. It was only now that she recognised just how far he had travelled.

'Ralph, I'm so glad God brought you to my door all those years ago. For both our sakes. I couldn't have survived without you. I simply couldn't have.'

He held up his hands.

'It should be me thanking you, for taking me on and helping me find the faith and sense of self-worth that has brought so much good into my life, when it was all such a mess. I'll always be grateful for that.'

As he got up to go, she said, 'I'd like to see you settled with a good woman.'

He turned and gave her a wry, rather sad smile.

'So would I. But you can't have everything. And maybe my standards are just too high.'

PART FOUR

FEBRUARY–APRIL
2024

Encryptogram user z3qa | to user bx4sw

We have her. Finally. I love church politics. You chaps do vitriol even better than us. That sordid business of Mr Archbishop's a piece of luck.

Don't lose your nerve. Our position must be secured. Game almost won. Alternative unthinkable. Have kept back one card for an emergency.

Be assured, we will remember our promise. This time, the right man for the job.

PART FOUR

FEBRUARY–APRIL

2024

TWENTY-EIGHT

Resurrection is not a consoling opium, soothing us with the promise of a better world in the hereafter. It is the energy for a rebirth of this life. Hope doesn't point to another world. It is focused on the redemption of this one.

JÜRGEN MOLTMANN

FEBRUARY 2024

On Tuesday 14 February Vicky woke suddenly at 3.15 a.m. She had dozed off quickly, but dreamed that she was being chased by hounds. They could smell fear and were closing in, fangs bared, baying for the command to tear flesh from bone. Terror jolted her awake seconds away from being ripped into thousands of bleeding scraps. She reached out to Tom's warm form for comfort, but he never as much as stirred. 'How can you sleep so soundly, tonight of all nights?' she whispered, and quoted, 'Will you not wait with me one hour?' But he made no move and she hadn't the heart to wake him, so she got up before her tossing and turning disturbed him.

The flat was chilly at this hour of the night, the draughts having won their battle with fossil fuel – the penalty of living in a historic monument. Or perhaps it was just her metabolism protesting at being forced to function at such an unforgiving hour. She made herself a mug of cocoa and went into the sitting room, clutching it close for warmth, and there she sat, enveloped in a large, fleece rug, uttering prayers too deep to speak aloud and finding comfort in the psalms. Good old Roger Davidson, insisting she chant them at every Sunday service. 'I take back all the things I said about you, Roger. If you can hear me in heaven, thank you.'

Shortly after four she went back to the bedroom and checked on Tom. He was still snoring softly, oblivious to the cold space at his side. The peaceful blankness of his face and that rhythmic nasal rattle aggravated her. How did men manage to switch off so completely in the thick of a major crisis? She was too restless to sleep, but unsure of what else to do. She had put her affairs in order as best she could in case she needed to clear her desk quickly. She had jotted a last few thoughts onto her e-phone and sent them to Alice, needing to reassure her daughter that she would cope, whatever the outcome of the morrow's vote.

She couldn't face going back to the sitting room. It felt as if the walls were falling in on her, crowding her space, stifling her ability to breathe. So she fumbled in the wardrobe for her track-suit and trainers, put them on, then slipped out, cut across Lambeth Palace Road onto the Albert embankment and began to trot, carefully for her back's sake, towards Westminster Bridge. There she stopped, satisfyingly out of breath and as physically stretched as she was able. The London Eye, unnaturally, intrusively blue, filled one side of the night sky, casting a large, luminous patch of cobalt onto the glossy black of the water. Ahead of her, the floodlit Houses of Parliament illuminated the night sky, casting a shimmering, ochre glow onto the water. The entire river was a canvas, streaked with odd shapes and myriad, rainbow, reflected colours.

Vicky loved the uncanny stillness of the becalmed, pre-dawn city, its manic daytime activity impossible to imagine at this early hour. Intermittent sounds floated up to her, restrained voices from a tug or trawler, a clinking of cups, a bottle dropped in a bin. A couple passed her, laughing, carefree, his arm around her shoulders, on their way home from a night out. They did not see her. She was invisible in her Gethsemane. Alone. It could just as well have been that silent olive grove in Jerusalem.

She had read somewhere recently the words of the Holocaust survivor and psychiatrist, Viktor Frankl: 'Everything can be taken from a man or a woman but one thing: the last of human freedoms – to choose one's attitude in any given set of circumstances, to choose one's own way.' She might not know how today's events would work out, but her attitude to those events, to her cancer, to her detractors, to her future, was hers to choose and no one could take that choice away from her.

She suddenly became aware of a pair of disembodied legs protruding beyond the parapet, feet in socks that were so filthy that the sight of them almost made her gag. A vagrant had bedded down beneath the bridge. She leant over to take a look at him, and caught the sound of his even, gentle snoring. As she watched, a single spotlight chugged its way out of the night. A boat drew up down beneath the path, and a youngish man jumped across the deck and neatly flung a plastic bag up and over the parapet before disappearing back into the wheelhouse and shunting off down the river. The snoring dissolved into a snort, followed by a lengthy, rasping cough. The legs began to move, and then the hunched figure pulled himself up and helped himself to bits and pieces from the bag, munching contentedly as he sat watching the river. Breakfast – by boat. And obviously a regular occurrence.

She was deeply touched by this simple, yet considerate act of kindness. It was an immense privilege leading millions of Christians in their fight for freedom and social justice, engaged as they were in a massive struggle against every kind of imaginable human disaster – war, poverty, persecution and disease. But with the perspective illness grants us, the renewed awareness that each and every minute of life is a gift, she found herself yearning for the simple things that most people took for granted – to walk along the river with Tom's arm across her shoulders, to sit on a bench and watch life go by, to have her own front door that she could open at will – even if she was opening it to a 'gentleman of the road', who would share his skewed but interesting take on the world, as so many of them had when she was a plain parish priest.

Leaning over the side of a bridge, watching a homeless man tuck into his first meal of the day, she had an epiphany, her second 'Not my will, but yours' moment. The first was when she accepted the post. The second, now, was when she – what? Accepted it afresh? Or accepted defeat as guidance, as Bud had done, walking away with his hand in God's, and his head held high?

A proverb dropped into her mind: 'The lot is cast into the lap, but every decision is from the Lord.' All she could do was wait and see. Whatever the day's outcome, she would receive it from God, whose mighty hands encompassed the entire universe, and against which she, by comparison, was no more than a tiny fruit fly, balancing on one of the many creases on his palm. The thought of it filled her with an overwhelming sense of relief, and she felt an irrational fluttering in the pit of her stomach that she could only describe as joy.

It was extraordinary. Her career might be coming to its close, her life too, for all she knew, but at this moment all she wanted to do was sing and twirl her way around a lamp-post, like a young heroine in a West End musical. She looked around, assured herself she was alone and did exactly that – once, twice, several times. Then she stood, for who knows how long, quietly enjoying an overwhelming sense of deliverance from the pressure and pain that had blighted so much of her life in the past months, afraid that this vulnerable, new-born sense of liberation might dissipate with the passing of the night.

Dawn crept up on the city and she began to feel slightly chilled. Gold and crimson streaked the sky, painting the river a pale mauve that gradually dissolved into grey as the colourful lights of night were extinguished. London awoke, slowly, and stretched itself with a gathering belch of engine roar. She was shocked to hear Big Ben chime six.

Time to go back to the Palace, to shower, put on the war paint, and face whatever the day would bring.

She was about to make her way up to the flat when she heard a phone ringing in her study. She checked her watch. 6.10 a.m. Who could it be at this unearthly hour? Alice? Was all well with her new baby? She wouldn't use that number, though, would she? But no one is rational in distress. She might, in extremis. Vicky's heart was banging against her ribcage as she picked up the receiver.

A nasal voice with a strong Australian accent said, 'Good eve . . . g'day, Archbishop. This is Carol Robinson from the *Brisbane Daily Post*. Do you have a minute? We've had an incident here – a child that almost died on the operating table. Now, I've been doing a bit of digging, and I have a few questions I'd love to ask your husband about the Sophie Carpenter case.'

2005

It happened towards the end of Vicky's time as vicar of St Chad's; she had nipped home early from her parish duties in order to relieve the child minder and spend some quality time with her daughter. She was in the kitchen wiping down the counter after they had made a lasagne together, when Tom arrived home from work. The first thing she noticed was that there was no shouted hello, no arms around the waist and nuzzle from behind. No calling for Alice so that he could scoop her up and plant a huge kiss on her face. Today he simply walked into kitchen, sat down at the table and half-heartedly thumbed his way through the evening paper. His hands were shaking.

'Tom?' she asked, but he didn't respond. With a sinking feeling in the pit of her stomach, she rinsed out the dishcloth and dried her hands, went behind him and put her arms around his shoulders.

'What is it, Darling?' she whispered, leaning forward and kissing him on the cheek.

He folded the newspaper and threw it down, then resting his elbows on the table, covered his face with his hands. Vicky pulled up a chair and sat down next to him, keeping an arm stretched across his shoulders.

Alice ran in, and stopped dead when she saw him. She hadn't heard him come in, and he hadn't come to find her once he was in the house. How was that possible?

'Daddy?' she asked uncertainly. 'Are you crying?'

He looked up at her and shook his head. She ran to him and he lifted her up and hugged her tight, too tight. She pulled away, and Vicky saw that his eyes were glazed with tears.

'Alice, why don't you go into the sitting room and build Daddy the biggest ever castle from your blocks?'

'Can I do it in here?'

'Daddy and I just need to talk for a little while. Is that okay?'

She nodded, wearing her most serious, grown-up expression, and took herself off.

'Oh Vicky,' he groaned, when she was barely out of the door, 'we lost a child today. A little girl – six years old. It could have been Alice.'

'That's so hard, Tom,' she said, putting her hands over his in an attempt to steady the tremor.

Losing any patient was a personal affront, an attack on his professional competence. But a child . . .

'Hard?' He withdrew his hands and thumped the table with his fist. 'Hard? It wasn't just hard, Vicky. That comes with the territory. No, it was avoidable. That's what I can't come to terms with.'

Her stomach revolted and she was afraid to say any more. He rubbed his brow repeatedly with the palm of his hand, as if he were trying to erase the memory from his mind. She had never seen him like this before. So utterly desolate. She went on watching him, hardly daring to breathe, let alone speak. The only sound was the occasional crash from the next room, as Alice's tower collapsed and she presumably started all over again.

'All my fault,' he muttered eventually. 'All my blasted fault. I should never have given Jason another chance. I should have reported him the first time.'

It felt as if her stomach had gone into free-fall.

'Jason?' she whispered. 'Drinking again? Oh no, Tom. No. I thought you had reported him.'

Tom raised his head, but didn't look at her.

'We couldn't get him to respond to his bleep, and when he did, after half an hour or so, he stank of booze. We rang around frantically for another anaesthetist, but they were all in surgery. I called the management, told them Jason wasn't up to the job, but they insisted he was the duty anaesthetist and that I must learn to work with him, as if we'd had some kind of childish spat. What could I say? His wife and the Medical Director's wife are sisters. The two couples virtually live in each other's pockets. If I'd said he was half pickled, it would have been seen as a cheap shot from a prima-donna surgeon. I couldn't argue with them any longer. The child had an intestinal blockage. She was going to die if we didn't operate immediately.'

'Tom,' Vicky said carefully, 'how is any of this your fault?'

He looked up, but not at her, his eyes lost somewhere in the distance. Then he held out his palms in a gesture of total despair.

'Because six months ago, when I should have reported him, I believed him when he swore he'd never drink in his lunch hour again. We qualified together, for crying out loud. He was a friend. How could I ruin his career over one slip-up? So instead I've ruined the lives of a lovely young couple, by subjecting their little girl to a blundering anaesthetist who wasn't fit to practise and didn't act fast enough when her heart went into arrest. God, Vicky,' he whispered, rocking almost manically backwards and forwards, 'how do I live with this?'

Her immediate instinct was to reach out and restrain him, but she found she couldn't touch him. How would she have felt if it were Alice on that operating table? She sat helplessly at his side, appalled by the horrific catalogue of drunkenness, personal relationship and short-termism that had led to such a tragedy.

A report appeared in the paper three days later:

Thursday 24th February 2005

A heartbroken couple allege that their six-year-old daughter died unnecessarily when a doctor failed to operate in time, despite the urgency of the case.

Dave and Ros Carpenter claim that had swifter action been taken, their daughter Sophie would still be alive.

On 21 February, at 11 a.m., Sophie was rushed into hospital with severe stomach pains. After being diagnosed with an intestinal blockage, she was taken straight to the operating theatre for emergency surgery. But at 4 p.m. Sophie was transferred back to the hospital ward and her relatives were told that the operation could not start as the anaesthetist had been called away to another emergency. She was finally transferred to the operating room at 8:30 p.m. Complications ensued and the little girl died during surgery despite attempts to revive her.

A hospital spokesperson said, 'No formal complaint has been made. If we receive one we will of course conduct a full investigation into the matter. Meanwhile, our thoughts are very much with her parents as they grieve their tragic loss.'

In his evidence at the inquest, a few weeks later, Tom attributed the delay to an unusually large number of surgical emergencies and inadequate staffing. He claimed that there was no way of knowing to what degree it contributed to the arrest of Sophie' heart on the operating table. A verdict of misadventure was recorded.

'You still never told the hospital management about Jason then, Tom?' she asked, when he arrived home and poured himself a large whisky. He appeared relieved, more relaxed than he had been in a while. And it riled her.

'No – I have,' he said defensively. 'The theatre sister bore out my story. He'll never work again. They have promised me that.'

He took a large gulp of the whisky.

'But nothing was said about his drinking at the inquest? No real explanation for the parents? No closure?'

'She would have arrested anyway. We can't know it was Jason's fault. And what's better,' he demanded, directing all his frustration at her, 'that they believe their child's death was unavoidable, or that they were robbed of their beautiful little girl by an act of gross and unnecessary negligence?'

'The truth, Tom. The truth makes people free.'

'In this case, I beg to differ. It would destroy them.'

'Destroy them, or destroy your career?'

'Vicky,' he snapped, rubbing the bridge of his nose between his finger and his thumb, 'this is the best I could make of a thoroughly bad job. I'm not proud of myself, so spare me your self-righteousness for once.'

'How I wish you had never told me about Jason in the first place,' she yelled back at him, 'because now you've made me complicit in a cover-up.'

It was only then that she noticed the tiny figure standing at the open kitchen door, gripping Tracy the rag doll and sucking her thumb, eyes wide in alarm. Vicky rushed over to Alice, swept her up into her arms and stroked her hair.

'It's all right, Darling. Mummy and Daddy are just a bit upset. We'll be better tomorrow.'

But as Tom pushed past them, she saw a hardness in his taut, controlled features that she had never seen there before, and knew, with a sickening fear, that perpetuating the dishonesty wouldn't make the situation any better tomorrow. Little Sophie Carpenter would stand between them forever.

TWENTY-NINE

Passion is loving something enough to suffer for it.

JÜRGEN MOLTMANN

14 FEBRUARY 2024

One phone call, that was all it took for everything to click into place. She had the answer to all her prayers about what to do at Synod. 'If you seek for it, it shall find you,' Moltmann said. The certainty found her almost as soon as the journalist had started to speak.

'Yesterday,' said Carol Robinson, 'an anaesthetist at our hospital was sacked, following an inquiry into allegations that he regularly turned up at the operating theatre the worse for drink. Fortunately, there were no fatalities, but there was a near miss, which is why his colleagues shopped him. Now, I've been doing a bit of digging, and what do I find? It seems that this very anaesthetist was involved in the death of a child over in the UK some years ago, with your husband the operating surgeon. In his evidence at the inquest, your husband made no mention of his anaesthetist's competence to practise, and they were both exonerated. Strangely enough though, Jason Phillips chose to leave Britain immediately after that. He came to Brisbane and worked here instead. Did you know this man was working over here?'

'No, I certainly did not. And as far as I know, neither did my husband.'

'Did you know about his drink problem?'

'Look, Carol, I have a very full day today, in case the news hasn't filtered through to you just yet.'

There was a 'tsk' sound at the other end of the line.

'Oh, I think it has.'

'In that case, you'll not be surprised to hear that I have nothing to say to you just at this moment. But I'll get my press officer to send you a statement when she gets in.'

She interrupted the continued flow of words on the other end of the line by putting the phone down. Blasted woman, how did she get this number?

Vicky sank down onto her desk chair, shaken but sure. What we sow, we reap, she reflected.

Unusually, Tom appeared at the study door, barefoot and in his towelling robe, as if drawn by some strange premonition. He stood with his hands in his pockets, hair still bedtime ruffled, staring at her with wide, questioning eyes.

'Close the door behind you,' she said.

She got up, walked over to him, and put her hands on his shoulders.

'It's caught up with us?' he asked.

Strange how he'd guessed, she thought, as if he had been expecting it.

'It didn't have to. It never left us. That's the nature of such things.'

'What should we do?'

She marvelled at the extraordinary clarity of her mind.

'You know, it's such wonderful timing,' she said.

Tom thought she was resorting to irony and nodded apologetically.

'No, Darling, I mean it.'

She put her arms around Tom's neck and looked straight into his eyes.

'This is our moment of truth, Tom. All the other allegations and accusations – the misuse of funds, the relationship with Bev, the paedophile business, they are all fabricated and easy enough to disprove. Even your affair was a thing of the past till Mark found a way to resurrect it. We could have – we have – survived any and all of those. But this is different.'

He looked away from her, his face an agony of self-reproach. She took it in her hands and turned him so that they faced each other.

'No, Tom. Look at me. No more contrition. No more blame. Enough is enough. This is one of those "everything coming together for good" situations that you reminded me I believed in. This was Mark's last attempt to destroy us. But this time, he has overreached himself.'

At 8 a.m. the Palace awoke, as staff arrived to face the day that would decide their future as well as hers. There was none of the usual banter. The voices in the corridor were muted, more strained than usual. How she loved her team for their hard work and loyalty. It pained her that they should have to face such an ordeal. But there was nothing she could do to spare them.

She went into the office to ask Ann to ring Buckingham Palace as soon as she could, and find out if the Queen could see her as soon as possible. Immediately, in fact. A momentary flicker of concern registered on Ann's normally impassive face, but a few moments later, her usual inscrutable professionalism restored, she appeared on the screen in Vicky's study to inform her that though Her Majesty didn't normally rise quite so early

these days, as it happened, she hadn't slept well, had no diary engagements, and was always happy to see the Archbishop.

'She might not be quite so happy in a little while,' Vicky said to herself
as she quickly showered, dried her hair, and pinned it up on the top of her
head. She dressed in the freshly ironed clerical shirt that Jenny had left for
her, a long, sleek, pencil skirt and a short, sharply cut jacket with gathered shoulders, then applied just enough mascara and lipstick. She was at
Buckingham Palace by nine, and the Queen was waiting for her.

What passed between them that morning she would never recount to
anyone, not even in private. She owed her gracious monarch that one final
act of courtesy and discretion. But there was a wisdom, an understanding, an empathy that forced her to blink back tears, for fear of ruining her
mascara before the day's events had properly begun. The Queen took her
hand as she was about to leave, and Vicky said to her, 'We are one of the
most fortunate countries in the world to have been blessed with such a
remarkable figurehead, Ma'am.'

Back at Lambeth Palace she drank a strong coffee, spoke briefly to
the Prime Minister, who appeared awkward and embarrassed, then
rang for Jenny, who anointed her head with holy oil and prayed that she
would be given the words and wisdom she needed. After Jenny left, she
sat quietly for a few moments looking out over the garden, until its stillness settled upon her and she felt composed enough to face what lay
ahead. Then she went out to the car, where Noah was waiting to drive
her to Church House.

'Archbishop,' said her usually reserved young driver, as he held open
the car door, 'we're all behind you.'

She swallowed the lump that swelled in her throat and touched his arm
in thanks.

The entire Synod fell silent as she entered the Assembly Hall and took
her seat next to the Archbishop of York beside the Communion table. She
took a peep at him out of the corner of her eye, but he refused to connect
with her. The only sounds that broke into the unnatural hush were an
occasional cough, a clearing of the throat, a shuffle, a whisper, or the
squeak of a chair, all magnified as the vaulted glass dome sent the echo
back down. She gazed up at the gilded angels. What tales they could tell.
How she hoped that they were with her today.

Dominic Naylor appeared at her side, patted her on the arm. 'How are
you, Archbishop?'

Was he part of the conspiracy? She looked at the hand resting on her
arm, then up into his face and thought she detected a certain protective-
ness and pride in the fatherly concern. But she might be wrong.

'I'm fine, Dominic,' she said, covering his hand momentarily with her own.

It was strangely disconcerting to preside over a Eucharist, symbol of Synod's unity in Christ, on a day when they were so deeply divided. She tried not to catch Ryan's eye as she invited those who 'truly and earnestly repent of your sins, and are in love and charity with your neighbour' to participate. Love and charity, Ryan, she said to herself. Now where was that when you set out to finish me?

She didn't see Nick until he walked forward and held out his hand for the wafer. Placing it on his outstretched palm was one of the hardest things she ever had to do. She forced her own hand not to tremble, and looked up straight into Nick's eyes, but they were marbles in their sockets.

Still, his conscience was not her responsibility. The question for her was, did she have love and charity in her heart for these dear brothers of hers, who, without an ounce of mercy or compassion, had so ruthlessly planned to destroy her? She had examined her own conscience carefully that morning, looking, with Jenny, for any evidence of wilful malevolence. They had decided, whatever her feelings towards the two wretches, and the others who had brought Synod to this pass, and still stood before her to receive the element from her hand, it was her intention to forgive. And that would have to be enough.

During a short coffee break she took off her ecclesiastical robes and changed quickly back into her suit. By the time she returned to the Assembly Hall every seat was taken. In the press gallery dozens of cameras vied with a scrum of journalists for the best view. The visitors' gallery was packed to capacity. This was, after all, a first for General Synod.

As she waited for the chair to announce the motion, and invite her to speak, she breathed deeply and smiled at the blur of faces in front of her, trying to focus on those she knew were sympathetic, and was gratified by a large number of encouraging smiles in return. She was also aware of the one or two who couldn't raise their heads to look her in the face, and felt deeply sad for them. The overpowering joy she had experienced on Westminster Bridge some six hours ago, that she could have barely imagined at the same time yesterday, still calmed her, like a small sailing skiff at rest in the eye of the storm, and buoyed her up as she rose to her feet and addressed General Synod for the last time.

'Mr Chairman, my dear brothers and sisters, I have been a member of Synod for twenty-six years, which probably means I deserve some kind of long-service medal. It was never my intention to outlive so many of you, or indeed to outstay my welcome, like a cantankerous old aunt.'

There were a few feeble attempts at laughter.

'Sometimes, in the more turgid business that Synod must discuss, it does feel like a life sentence. At other times it has been the greatest privilege imaginable to be involved in so many decisions that have had a positive impact, not just on the life of the church, but dare I say it, on the global issues that affect this world that God loves so much.'

She was aware that her voice sounded a little high-pitched, and made a conscious effort to relax and lower it.

'In one of her most significant inaugural addresses over ten years ago, the Queen said, "Synod will have many issues to resolve to ensure that the Church of England remains equipped for the effective pursuit of its mission and ministry. Some will, no doubt, involve difficult, even painful, choices. But Christian history suggests that times of growth and spiritual vigour have often coincided with periods of challenge and testing. What matters is holding firmly to the need to communicate the Gospel with joy and conviction in our society."

'Those words have proved prophetic, time and time again, and especially today, as we face an unprecedented time of testing that is incredibly painful for so many, and not just for those of us gathered here today. We must, if we are to fulfil the essential task of mission that God has given us, grow through these temporary difficulties, stronger, more united than ever in courage and purpose.

'With that unity in mind, and after much prayerful consideration, I have felt it incumbent upon me to stand down as Archbishop of Canterbury.'

The heavy silence in the chamber that had seemed to cushion her words was ruptured by a large number of unreserved, dumbfounded gasps that expanded into an unruly hubbub of mutterings and murmurings as people turned to their neighbours or even the row behind to whisper their astonishment, anxiety and alarm. There was a commotion in the press gallery. With some difficulty the chairman managed to call the proceedings to order. Silence slowly settled over the Assembly Hall once more, and with every eye and every camera upon her, Vicky smiled around at her audience, then continued.

'I believe this decision is in the best interests, not only of my own family, but of the church family too. If you would just bear with me.

'Tonight the media will carry the story that, many years ago, my husband, for what he felt were the best professional reasons, made a difficult decision to protect a colleague who had contributed to the death of a child during surgery. He had done all he could before and after the event to highlight the problem internally, but accepted the urging of hospital management not to denounce this man openly. It was the wrong decision. I have his permission to say so. But before you rush to condemn, let me remind you of the old American Indian saying, "Never judge a man until you have walked two moons in his moccasins." We live in a society that apportions blame, not mercy, that makes no allowances for our common humanity. Never is that more so than in the press.

'A journalist rang me this morning and asked me if I knew of my husband's actions. What sort of a marriage would it be if a couple didn't share their deepest concerns and anxieties? Of course I knew. I knew that a couple who had lost their child had never had access to the truth. I knew that a doctor had been given the chance to repeat his disastrous mistake. On that basis, I cannot, in all integrity, go on crusading for honesty, justice, openness and truth, when I could not do so with a clear conscience.'

She allowed herself a moment to look round at the expressions on the faces in front of her, and saw a kaleidoscope of emotions – bewilderment, shock, disappointment, sorrow. Some sat with their mouths open or shook their heads. Others appeared unable to lift their gaze from their papers. One or two of the women chewed their fingers or held onto their stomachs as if they had been winded.

Desperate to take a quick peek at Ryan, she slid her eyes ninety degrees to the right. From the side his face appeared impassive, but there was something written on it that she couldn't quite put her finger on – a hint of defiance in the eyes, a slight smirk twitching the corner of his mouth? Carbury and Normington had both donned their self-righteous, vindicated masks. While Nick, whom she had kept in view once she had identified where he sat, returned her gaze, impassively. What was going on behind that inscrutable exterior? Could she detect a certain smug satisfaction?

Tell them all the truth, a voice said in her head. The truth makes people free. That's what you once told Tom, and you owe it to the majority here, who have quietly loved and supported you over the past four years, yet have been too modest to make a fuss. Good people, now reduced to a state of total confusion. Perhaps her real resistance to disclosure had been her pride, the unwillingness to admit that she, the first woman Archbishop, who needed to be tough enough to survive in a man's world, was as weak and dependent on others as any other human. And with that realisation she found herself saying, 'I have been helped in making this important decision by the discovery, a few weeks ago, that I have cancer secondaries in my spine. That, not stress, was the cause of my recent leave.'

The Bishop of Carbury, only a few yards away from her, looked startled, then shrivelled visibly like a burst balloon. She felt a frisson of gratification. Let him wangle his way out of that little *faux pas* with the media.

'With its many demands, the Archbishop's role is almost impossible for someone fully fit. Surgery and radiotherapy render it totally impossible. Forgive me for not making it public until now, but I had hoped to preserve some privacy and dignity while I fought a potentially life-threatening condition. Of course, life itself is a terminal condition, and like everyone here, I cannot put a time limit on mine. But cancer fine-tunes the mind and spirit, so that we re-focus on what really matters. No one on their deathbed wishes they had worked harder, only that they had spent more time with loved ones. So my plan is to spend more time with my husband, and with my family in the United States.

'For them, the personal cost of my work has been unfathomable. What marriage doesn't have its difficulties, its temporary estrangements, sometimes its betrayals of love and commitment, however small or great? I betrayed my husband with my devotion to my job as surely as if I had taken a lover. I owe it to him now to be there for him. Marriage and parenting are a sacred trust. And perhaps it takes a woman to say so.'

From the upper corner of her left eye she caught sight of Ralph. He had pushed his way to the front of the press gallery and was trying, surreptitiously, to direct her attention to the twin, glass-fronted doors that faced her on the other side of the chamber. Just inside them, with their backs to the glass, two striking and very obviously non-Synod representatives, in the apparently statutory poorly fitted dark trousers and navy overcoats of the plain-clothes policeman, stood surveying the room, largely unobserved by the members, who were too focused on Vicky's words to have noticed them slip in. One was Ethan. He nodded at her briefly, then stood watching and waiting, ready for her next move. She raised her eyes to the gallery, gave Ralph the slightest acknowledgement and took her cue, smiling.

'The pace and intensity of the Archbishop's job is unstoppable, as most of you can imagine. Virtually unsustainable. When the time for his retirement came, one of my predecessors said, "My liberation is at hand." My feelings entirely. I shall go to the theatre and the cinema, ride a bicycle again, whizz through the air on a water flume at the local swimming baths or sit on a swing in the park, without fear of criticism or comment from the press. I might try my hand at gardening – or even take up bowls.'

There was a gratifying chuckle from various quarters of the hall, dispelling some of the tension. Exactly as she hoped it would. She took several quick sips of water and stood for a moment, breathing slowly and deeply to steady her nerves.

'I want you all to be very clear today, however, that I am not resigning because I submit to pressure, intimidation or any other form of bullying unworthy of those who hold positions of responsibility and trust within the church. I could so easily defend myself against each of the allegations brought against me today. I won't. It would waste your time and mine.'

She held up the small red button on the palm of her hand and turned slowly around so that everyone could see it. And then she turned her gaze on Lord Westburton.

'I have here a dossier, prepared over the past months, that details the financial affairs and activities of one of our members, activities that are illegal in this country and most others. Though his name is not officially attached to today's motion, I have no doubt that he is behind it, and you may deduce from that what you will. What I can tell you for certain is that his actions and those of the companies he controls left hundreds of people in my former Diocese of Larchester, and indeed, throughout the country, without homes, or any adequate accommodation, and condemned others to penury, misery and virtual starvation. This dossier is an appalling catalogue of bribery, extortion, exploitation and tax evasion. I am about to hand it, and him, over to the custody of the police. In the normal run of things I would never have resorted to this kind of public exposure. In this case, however, since the government has consistently turned a blind eye to the corruptions of a man who helped them into power and is a key element in keeping them afloat, I fear he would otherwise go on evading the justice he must now face.'

As she was speaking, a whole gamut of expressions passed across Nick's face – disbelief, effrontery, antipathy, defiance and naked contempt – as if she were flicking the fast-forward button on an electronic photo-frame. In any other circumstances, it might have seemed comical. But not when it still seemed impossible that he could have been another person all along, and not the one she thought she knew. That knowledge made what she saw played out in front of her unbelievable, and wrenched at her insides. Only when the two detectives walked up to him from behind, tapped him on the shoulder and showed him their identity badges did he appear to have any awareness of the genuine seriousness of his own situation. At which point, bravado gave way to ashen-faced terror. Ethan and his colleague nodded at him courteously as if they were inviting him to play a round of golf, took him by the elbows and quietly escorted him out.

In the commotion that followed, she turned to the Archbishop of York and, picking up the jug, said, 'Water, Ryan? You don't look too good.'

He dismissed her with a cursory wave of his hand. She turned back to the microphone, and like a classroom teacher facing a roomful of children to whom she has just promised a trip to the circus, waited until her presence restored her control.

'My final reason for resigning today is to spare Synod a vote that would have torn us all apart. How could I allow the church I love and have tried so hard to serve to do that to itself? United, we are a tremendous force for good. Riven by tittle-tattle and gossip, plotting and scheming, jealousies and strife, we become indistinguishable from any other secular institution. What does that say to our nation about Christian belief? Whatever we admire in society, we should have in greater abundance – more integrity, more altruism, more joy, more hope, more life.

'I am so proud of what the church has already achieved, the thousands of initiatives, too many to mention, that make our country a better place, especially for the poor and the dispossessed. The church is the only institution, other than Alcoholics Anonymous, where the members come together to admit their fragility and failure. We, however, seek for personal character transformation that corporately should change the world. What better way is there to live than striving to treat others with the courtesy, respect and dignity you want for yourself? Even imagining the worst possible scenario, that the atheists are right and our hope is a grand deception, how can anyone regret having lived such a life? We, who know that we are not deceived, must demonstrate it by the quality of our lives. Evelyn Underhill, the great spiritual writer, said in the 1930s, "Every minute you are thinking of evil, you might have been thinking of good instead . . . Pick yourself up, be sorry, shake yourself, and go on again."

'So I beg you, let us not pick over the bones of today's shame, but rather bury them so deep that they can never be retrieved. Don't apportion blame. Be generous to yourselves and to one another. Welcome back those in need of restoration and healing, as our Lord himself is kind and forgiving with each of us. And address yourselves instead to the work of spreading the good news of his redemptive love.

'Those of you who know me well will understand that I could not let this one last chance to speak to you all pass without quoting from my beloved Jürgen Moltmann, who has been such a source of inspiration to me throughout the years of my ministry. Moltmann tells us that we cannot sit passively waiting for the day of the world's ultimate liberation and restoration. Instead we must actively pursue it by bringing healing, hope and forgiveness into our world now. Living such a radical lifestyle in an aggressive secular society that mocks and dismisses us, will inevitably bring us conflict and suffering. But what price the pain, when our guaranteed future is "the salvation of the whole enslaved creation".

'Go out from here and strive to bring the message of redemption to the whole enslaved creation. It is a massive task and there is no time to waste. I believe, when God's resurrection power is at work within us, anything is and will be possible.'

The chamber was deathly silent. Not a whisper disrupted the moment. Not a fidget or a cough. No one moved. Seconds passed. Five hundred people studied their laps, the carpet, the walls, or the dome, lost in a reverie of their own. And then there was the smallest sob. Merely a slight choking sound. The bubble burst. The room exploded. Synod rose to its feet, clapping, cheering, many openly weeping, as it said a last farewell and thank you to its first female Archbishop.

Uncertainly, Vicky reached for her seat, dizzy with exhaustion, irritated by the wound on her back. She had been aware of neither weakness nor discomfort as she spoke, such was the power of mind over matter. But now she was overcome by thirst and the longing to lie down and sleep.

She was barely aware that the Secretary General was standing at the microphone, until his deep, rasping tones resonated around the hall. 'Today's events are unprecedented, not just for Synod, but in the long and sacred tradition of Archbishops of Canterbury. They grieve me beyond measure. But as our dear Archbishop has urged, let us not dwell on our disgrace, but on the lessons that need to be learnt – with penitence, sobriety, charity and fear.

'I was, I confess, almost taken in by the lies that sought to destroy her reputation. But as I watched our Archbishop, none of them matched the integrity and luminosity I saw before me. I have no doubt that she has registered the appreciation that we have shown her just now. There will be opportunities in the future for fuller expressions of gratitude for all that she has meant to us. But I cannot let the moment go without paying tribute to her inspirational leadership, her warmth, approachability and vision. In these four stormy years she has shaken the church out of its apathy, inertia and complacency, and overseen a time of unprecedented growth, numerically, but more importantly, in spiritual depth and effectiveness. She has clarified our strategic focus, challenged us, united us, empowered us and galvanised us into action. We shall miss the smile that won our hearts, the gracious charm and humanity that earned her the affection of the people of this country and, yes, the determined fighter for justice who has held us to account when our own interests have obscured the right path. We lose today an outstanding leader and she goes with our heartfelt wishes and prayers for God's blessings of health, joy and peace, and many happy years with her husband and family.'

She nodded her thanks at Dominic as he left the microphone, and he acknowledged it, a sad smile lifting his rugged face. The Archbishop of York then leapt to his feet, and proposed that Synod take a short break before moving quickly on to its next business. Pilate washing his hands, Vicky said to herself, and signalling to Synod that they should do the same. But perhaps that was what it needed to do – continue as if the motion had never been.

Vicky stood up and went to respond to the cluster of faces homing in on her, ever closer, increasingly distorted, and the dozens of hands stretched out in commiseration, compassion and congratulation. But the floor seemed to rock and sway away from her. She was vaguely aware of Jenny and Ralph at her elbow, her chaplain a ferocious bull fending off all approaches, he almost plucking her up from the crowds and carrying her out through a side door.

'I couldn't have stayed upright another minute,' she whispered, falling into the rear of the waiting car, and resting her head against the back of the seat, just as the media descended in a vast, buzzing swarm of clicks and flashes, and a full-colour firework display burst in front of her closed eyes.

'I seem to have emptied my inexhaustible pot of nervous energy.'

'I know, I know, Darling,' Jenny said, covering her with a rug.

'I'm not an invalid,' she murmured, too weak even to push it away.

'No, but right at this moment you look as near to one as I've ever seen.'

'Where's Tom?' she murmured. And then remembered. He had wanted to be there, but she had told him that it would be better if he wasn't, that he kept himself well out of the media's way.

Slowly, Noah edged the car through the press.

'Kill a few of them if you have to, Noah,' Jenny called out, 'but let's get her home.'

'Hold on tight, then,' he shouted back.

'Do you know something?' Vicky said, smiling as the thought occurred to her, and Noah nosed the car finally out of the scrum towards Lambeth Palace. 'The press is going to get no more out of me. Let them do their worst with what they have. It's over.'

Later that afternoon, Tom arranged her on the settee, cushions under her back and knees, pillow plumped up behind her head.

He popped out to pick up her prescription and while he was gone Dalisay moved in and started vacuuming the carpet around the settee. She moved ever nearer to Vicky, then moved away again, then towards her and away once more.

'Dalisay,' Vicky called out, desperate for some peace so that she could get some sleep, 'switch that thing off. If you've something to say to me, just say it.'

Dalisay did as she was told, then came and stood in front of her, folding and unfolding her hands.

'I not tell tales, Archbishop.'

'I know, Dalisay.'

'But you been good to me.'

Vicky forced out a smile.

'What is it?'

'I am going home one day, and I see Ann outside the gates talking to Mr Clements. I think it strange. Not nice man, Mr Clements.' Dalisay looked at her anxiously.

'I do right to tell you, Archbishop?'

'You do Dalisay,' Vicky reassured her. 'Thank you. You couldn't go and give my study a clean now, could you?'

Vicky contacted Ralph the moment Dalisay staggered out of the room with the vacuum cleaner.

'What do you think was going on?' she asked him as she followed him on screen while he walked along the corridor to the office.

'We suspected we had a mole.'

'But Ann? Cosy, dependable Ann? Never forthcoming about her private life, but I trusted her implicitly. Why would she be involved in any of this?'

'She was never completely happy with the idea of a female Archbishop.'

'Come on, Ralph. There must be more to it than that.'

Ralph was in her office now.

'No sign of her,' he said.

Vicky saw that Ann's desk had been cleared.

Ralph said, 'Looks as if she's done a runner.'

'See if you can find out what's happened to her. Whatever she's been up to, I hate these loose ends.'

Tom joined her on the settee so that they could watch the evening news together. He plumped up her cushions, then handed her a sherry.

'Your medicine, Mrs Woods.'

'It worries me when you nurse me, doctor,' she said. 'It means I must be ill.'

But Tom simply smiled benignly, shoved himself in the space at her side and took hold of her hand.

'I don't suppose we'll have to vacate the Palace immediately,' she said to him, 'but we'll need to find somewhere to live. We could always move into your flat temporarily, I suppose?'

'I sold it.'

'You never told me,' she said, surprised. 'I thought we had decided on a new openness.'

'I wanted rid of it. It reminded me of so much I wanted to forget. My stupidity. Our separation. My lostness without you.'

Vicky decided not to pursue it, not to threaten Tom's fragile pride.

'So where shall we go? We have no roots.'

'There's nothing to stop us moving to Boston.'

'Now there's a thought.'

He switched on the television. The resignation story and its ramifications filled a good twenty minutes, and involved a number of reports and clips of her speech in Synod. There were shots of a thunderous-looking Westburton being escorted from Synod, then leaving the West End Central Police Station later in the day without charges, having helped the police with their enquiries. It was accurate enough reporting, unbiased, dispassionate. Until the cancer was referred to in a suddenly sober tone of voice.

'Strange,' she said to Tom, 'how the prospect of death makes saints of us.'

Sure enough, the assessment of her career was largely positive. A radical campaigner and moderniser, an irritant to the hierarchy, and yet again, the hackneyed 'breath of fresh air'. An Archbishop of the people and for the people, a maker of enemies in church and government. Brought down before her time. Unjustly and unfairly, many would say. 'The first woman Archbishop has rightly earned her place in the history of the church, despite spending only four short years in office.'

One advantage of providing the press with such a multiplicity of possible angles meant that the story of Tom's cover-up at the hospital was simply one of many. Relinquishment of one's role on a matter of conscience didn't make for sexy reporting. Vicky suspected that for most people it was barely comprehensible. Who resigns on moral principles these days, especially when it's a question of one's spouse's principles, not even one's own, that have been compromised? Ill health, criminal conspiracy and her desire to preserve the fragile unity of the church were far more accessible explanations for her resignation.

She commented on this to Tom as he switched off the television, then noticed in the gloom that his eyes were two glistening pools.

'What is it, Darling?'

She placed her hand over both of his, but he pulled them away and covered his face.

'All I ever wanted to do was look after you and keep you safe.'

She hadn't really realised until then how much her illness was an affront, not just to his professionalism, but to his very maleness.

'I don't plan to die, Tom – not for a while yet, at any rate.'

'I have let you down on every level. Destroyed your career. It's all my fault. I brought this upon you.'

'Oh, the cancer was your fault, was it?' she asked, putting her arms around his shoulders. But he shrugged her off.

'Don't joke, Vicky. You know what I mean. To be shafted by an oddball combination of episcopal and governmental bedfellows is one thing. To be shafted by your own husband is another. If I'd known I was handing them the ammunition . . . You were right all those years ago when you said I should never have told you about Jason.'

'No, Tom, I was wrong. I was a prig, putting my own conscience before your best interests. If you couldn't talk to me about it, who could you talk to?'

'Living with it all these years has been hell. It drove a wedge between us. It drove me to . . .'

She found herself saying urgently, 'No, Tom, don't go there. I love you so much, and I want us to forget, as well as forgive. As if it never happened.'

The words, as they flowed from her, felt like a healing, purifying stream. In the light of their potentially limited time together, why waste a minute more than they had to in regret or resentment?

'So you must live with yourself, forgive yourself, let go of the past.'

'But I as good as murdered that child.'

She took both his hands firmly in hers, determined that he wouldn't pull away from her, willing him to look at her, and eventually he did.

'That's completely untrue. You were not under the influence of drink. Your anaesthetist was. If you hadn't performed the surgery when you did, little Sophie would have died anyway. You did your best for her.'

'And now a couple will be forced to grieve all over again because I didn't listen to you and tell them the truth when I could have done.'

'But you're telling it now, and that matters.'

'I wish I could apologise in person. But I expect they wouldn't talk to me.'

'That sounds more like an attempt to assuage your own guilt than to be of any a real help to them. Your public admission must count for something. And think of all the other children whose lives you have saved

over the years. Accept absolution – for the sake of their parents if for
nothing else.'

He looked at her sadly for a while, then nodded. She took him into her
arms and he laid his head in the crook of her neck, like a child.

10:30 a.m., Tuesday 20 February 2024, filed by Helen Davis:

TOP TORY OFFERED
CASH FOR FAVOURS

One of the Conservative Party's foremost donors was re-arrested last
night at his luxury Mayfair home and taken to the West End Central
Police Station, where he was formally charged with tax evasion, money
laundering, extortion and the bribery of several high-ranking
government ministers and senior local government officers.

Wealthy businessman Lord Westburton, otherwise known as
Nicholas Hamilton-Jones, allegedly offered wealthy overseas
developers, seeking planning permission in the UK, special favours in
exchange for cash donations to the party. A number of businessmen
from South America, Asia and the Far East are currently being
interviewed by SIPT, the Special Investigation and Prosecution Team,
set up a few months ago to investigate business fraud and corruption.
Under new international legislation, SIPT also has a brief to seek out
tax evaders who sequester funds in secret offshore accounts. That their
first major case has led to the arrest of such a senior Tory figure can
only be a source of major embarrassment to the Prime Minister and
the party.

It is also alleged that Lord Westburton himself, who clandestinely
controlled a number of companies with overseas partners, including
Artemis Developments, the parent organisation of the Brazilian
Leisure and Entertainment Organisation, responsible for the 2019
Wooten Grange regeneration, offered sweeteners to government
ministers and local planners to ease the deal through. Local
councillors are claiming that threats, bullying and intimidation were
employed when bribery failed.

Despite a spend of more than £1 billion on the largest urban
regeneration project in the UK so far, Wooten Grange was opposed by
residents who claimed that landlords were offered highly inflated
prices for their properties, while local owners had no alternative but to
accept reduced prices as the estate was deliberately run down in
preparation for demolition. Their inability to afford the newly built
homes and lack of provision of social housing led to the setting up of a

'tent city', and a series of riots until the former Archbishop of Canterbury, Victoria Burnham-Woods, brokered a better deal for the protestors.

Lord Westburton has been released on police bail while investigations continue.

The following day, under the headline, 'Archbishop Shafted – A Conspiracy of Lies, Slander and Deception', Helen led with Bev's confession that no impropriety had ever passed between her and the Archbishop, and an apology for misleading the media. Helen went on to quote assurances from the Fraud Squad that no evidence had been found to support Lord Kilmarton's assertions of abuse of church monies. The Archbishop had evidently been the victim of a vicious smear campaign by 'certain individuals', intent on defamation and determined to oust her.

The article lauded her fearlessness in taking on both government and ecclesiastical hierarchies when integrity demanded it. It listed her political and ecclesiastical achievements – clinching a vital business deal in China, negotiating the peaceful resolution of the Wooten Grange riots, securing the abolition of the anti-proselytising laws that had limited the entrepreneurial and charitable work of faith groups, the establishment of The Well and its youth arm, that made the church the foremost provider of social welfare in the country, and the introducing of a modernisation programme that left a growing church more in touch with the people, and more financially secure to boot.

It's official, I am now the Archangel Gabriel in female form, Vicky said to herself. Then Mikey's open smile came to mind, as it so often had since she first saw it during the youth symposium, and she wished that society could come to grasp and appreciate a better measure of success – one where small gifts and sacrifices, acts of courage, thoughtfulness and consideration, were of the highest value. Like providing breakfast for a homeless man. Perhaps, on the day when the true and final judgement of her achievements would be made, Mikey would be top of the list.

Within days her involvement in Westburton's fall from grace became a minor consideration compared to the implications for the Conservative Party of the loss of one of its major funders and his alleged bribery of one or two of their senior members. The catalogue of Westburton's crimes grew by the hour as leading national and local figures either turned on him in an attempt to save their own skins, or scurried away into the shadows.

What followed next really did seem like the stuff of fiction.

THIRTY

In the end, the whole world will become God's home. Through the indwelling of the Spirit, people, and churches are already glorified in the body, now, in the present. But then the whole creation will be transfigured through the indwelling of God's glory. Everything ends with God being 'all in all'.

JÜRGEN MOLTMANN

FEBRUARY 2024

Westburtongate, as the press mockingly dubbed the affair, took on a life of its own. The peer's arrest had a swift domino effect. His massive international empire, built by his grandfather and father and developed by Nick into a web of interconnected enterprises worth mouth-watering millions, came crashing down. Caught in the debris were a motley band of politicians, investors, bankers, businessmen and churchmen.

On the second day after Synod, Toby Macdonald, the Bishop of Carbury, announced his early retirement. On day six, Westburton was charged with a raft of financial crimes. On day seven, Lord Kilmarton was taken in for questioning. He was subsequently released, though charged some weeks later with defamation of character

The Secretary of State for Health was arrested at his office on day eight. A week in which to sweat, cover his tracks and frantically seek the support of his party. All in vain. He protested his innocence loudly, of course. Vicky almost felt sorry for him. It transpired that he had heavily invested in the goddess projects, received bribes, misused public funds – the full gamut of offences. It was alleged that he had accepted sweeteners from Westburton to use his influence to secure planning permission for a host of new developments. A vast amount of undeclared earnings was stashed in an illegal offshore account in the Caribbean – following Westburton's advice, no doubt.

'The misuse of public funds?' Vicky mused, as she and Ralph studied the list of Mark's alleged crimes in the morning papers. 'Where did that come from?'

She was back in action, feeling stronger and fitter than she had in a long while, her radiotherapy set to begin later in the week. There were mounds of papers to sort through in her study. She was determined to help the staff come to terms with her imminent departure, and to find new employment, if that was what they chose to do.

'Yes, a nice little addendum, that particular one,' Ralph said, grinning with pleasure. 'Given that we suspect Mark got the Archbishop of York to convince Kilmarton you had misused the Church and Community Fund. But maybe it takes an embezzler to understand how to impute such actions to someone else.'

'What exactly is he supposed to have done?'

'You know only too well Mark's weakness for attractive women.'

She thought she detected a twinkle in his eye as he said it.

'Is that meant to be a compliment?'

'A compliment and a fact.'

'And look at what it did to me.'

Vicky made them both a coffee before beckoning him over to the armchairs, and encouraging him to continue.

'Our beloved minister, in his more junior days, used public funds to pay for one of his secretaries to have an abortion privately. I suspected that it was an oversight, an unthinking response to his initial panic, and that he intended to put the money back, but maybe I'm being too charitable, because when the crisis was over, it was . . . overlooked, shall we say?'

'He might have thought it was a perk that came with the job.'

They both smiled at the idea. Mark was capable of anything.

'But how did the police find out about it?' Vicky asked.

Ralph raised his eyebrows and made a gesture of feigned innocence.

'Do you know, that's the nearest thing to a smirk I have ever seen on your face, Ralph Cooper. You knew. You have always known.'

'Let's just say I thought it might be useful one day.'

He withered slightly under her look of disapproval.

'It was the only thing I could pin down at the time, and even then . . . well, it hardly seemed credible. Every now and then there'd be an unexplained transfer into his account, but I could never discover where they came from. When my questioning him about it destroyed our relationship I photocopied the evidence I had and kept it. Just in case. But as it happens, the connection with Westburton was there in my head all the time. I remembered where I first heard him mentioned. It was when we were still at school. I must have been about fifteen. Mark's father took us both out to some teashop. He said he was off to the Americas on business, and might manage a bit of holiday on a yacht out there.

'Mark and I talked about it later. He was so envious. The luxury yacht, called the *Aurora*, was moored off some magical, paradise island. In those days my family thought Brittany was exotic. A couple of days ago, when SIPT asked me if I knew what Mark's password might be, it was there on the tip of my tongue before I knew it.'

'What – Aurora?'

'*Aurora III* – the latest model, apparently. Goddess of the dawn, and the venue for Mark's regular holidays, it seems. Good old Mark, in love with a boat. Such a boy at heart. Ruthless as he could be, he was always too adolescent in his lusts and hatreds, just too transparent to get away with real villainy.'

'She did that to him,' Vicky said thoughtfully.

Ralph looked at her quizzically.

'Virginia, the mother. He was her golden boy who could do no wrong.'

'When Virginia died he was devastated.'

'The last restraint, gone.'

A vivid picture came, unbidden, to Vicky's mind. Mark as he was when she had first met him, blond, tanned, heart-meltingly handsome, and she felt a sudden pang of sorrow. Such wasted potential. Was there anything she might have said or done then that could have prevented all of this? But she had been so young, too young to articulate adequately her reasons for belief, or stand up to the power and influence of his parentage.

'By the way, you probably guessed that it was Mark who tipped off the Brisbane journalist. The Health Minister gets one of his minions to check Tom out. He picks up the gossip, not only surrounding the affair, but about the death of the child too. The anaesthetist's trail is followed to Brisbane, and Bob's your uncle.'

'And Mark bides his time. I always suspected he'd find out about the Sophie Carpenter case, and wondered how he would use it. And who else could have given the journalist my private office number?'

'We should have seen that one coming.'

'I'm glad you didn't. He did me a great service. What I can't understand is why anyone should be so bitter.'

'All those years ago . . . you really got under his skin, you know, in a way no one had ever done before, and I suspect no one has ever done since. Let's face it. You're completely unlike the other women he's consorted with. Your rejection really hurt him. No one ever said no to Mark. And I warned you then how dangerous he could be. I sometimes wondered whether he wasn't psychopathic. He appeared to have no sense of guilt or shame. That night you came to my flat . . . when he heard about that he must have thought all his Christmases had come at once.'

'How did he know?'

And then it dawned upon her.

'He was having you followed? How pathetic.'

'He knew from that email I sent you that we were on to him. Added to which, in his philandering little mind there was no way we weren't having a fling.'

'It was stupid to call on you so late at night. I played into his hands.'

'But you managed to survive the allegations. That must have rattled him. No wonder he became ever more devious – and desperate. Because the bottom line, Mark's real motivation in all this, wasn't sexual pique or your political manoeuvrings against him, however much they gnawed away at him. It was money.'

'Well, silly me for thinking it was personal,' she said with heavy irony.

'Don't underestimate your charms.'

'Never mind the flirting, Mr Cooper.'

'Politics, sex and filthy lucre. They really are a toxic mix. For someone as twisted as Mark.'

'Do you know, I used to tell myself he must have hidden depths. That one day I would dig down deep enough. But maybe there weren't any?'

As she tried to come to terms with where Mark's ambitions had led him, her mind kept taking her back to those halcyon days in Durham.

'Remember the three of us wandering down North Bailey, Ralph, our arms around each other's shoulders, with so many hopes and dreams, our whole lives ahead of us?'

Ralph laid back against the cushions with a wistful smile.

'And look at us now,' she said, shaking herself. 'Only one life on this earth – and there's more of it yet for thee and me. What will you do now? Will you stay on here?'

'No, I think I've probably had enough excitement for one lifetime. I shall find myself a nice, quiet, ordinary little management job, well away from all the shenanigans and skulduggery of the Church of England.'

They both laughed out loud.

'And,' he added coyly, 'I might even manage a social life at last.'

'Do I detect that there may be some rather special social life?'

'There might be, given half a chance.'

She waited. He fell into her trap almost at once.

'Helen Davis. She's . . . well, let's just say we've made up on more than a professional level.'

'Ah,' Vicky said knowingly, 'but that was no reason for giving her a scoop, of course?'

He smiled and shook his head vigorously.

'No, no, the scoop came first. I had to know if I could trust her properly.'

'I'm so glad for you, Ralph. You deserve someone of your own. I can't thank you enough for all you've done for me over these past few years. What would I have ever done without you?'

'Knowing you, you would have got by – of that I have no doubt. But maybe you wouldn't have had as much fun. It seems that we may have made more history than we ever imagined. You certainly won't be forgotten. The first woman Archbishop, conspired and schemed against, betrayed, double-crossed, driven out of office.'

'Prototypes often crash.'

'But you were not responsible for it, Vicky. You'll be remembered for creating a church that stood up to the government when the people had no other voice, for integrity at a time when it was a very undervalued commodity, and for the grace and courtesy you showed to all you met, even your most diehard opponents.'

'It would be nice to think so. Donald used to say, "When you're gone, no one will remember what you said or what you did, only who you were." It is a good guiding principle, but not an easy one to live by.'

Ralph stood up, took her hand and kissed it gently.

'If anyone has lived by it, you have,' he said.

On day ten Ryan Talbot received a visit from the SIPT at Bishopsthorpe Palace, the Archbishop of York's official residence. There were questions, according to the press, about the sports car in his garage, the glass-and-concrete retreat he'd just had built on the coast, and his own visits to Westburton's yacht. But criminal involvement proved hard to ascertain and no charges were brought. Moral compromise was another matter. For several days he bluffed his way out of suggestions of complicity very convincingly, appearing on the TV screen as the embodiment of wounded innocence. Until Helen Davis went public with Mark's inflammatory Encryptograms, as she had promised Ralph she would. They appeared in the *Mail* in full, with excerpts in every other media outlet. At which point the country's other Archbishop had no recourse but to resign.

Vicky tried hard to resist the ungracious smile that forced its way onto her face. Then she sat down and wrote him a card, in which she said that though she found his actions hard to comprehend, she bore him no ill will. It was tempting to chide him for bringing the church into such disrepute, but who was she to cast the first stone? Point a finger in judgement at another and there were always three pointing back at you. But she couldn't help but chortle as she paused and thought of the aggravation they had both caused, with two Crown Nominations Commissions delegated to find two new archbishops, again at an entirely unexpected moment. And who would blithely agree to accept these posts, after the recent debacle?

In the same week, the lovely Marilyn, bless her, made a second large sum from the tabloids by accusing the Secretary of State for Health of threatening her with the loss of her job unless she disclosed her affair with Tom. Why had no one ever told Mark that what goes around comes around? Marilyn, Tom and Vicky were now portrayed as a helpless triangle of victims in a dastardly plot hatched by a bullying government minister. That took the shine off the original revelation.

But the domino effect had not yet reached its finale. It gradually emerged that not only Kilmarton, the Tory chairman, but the Prime Minister himself must have known that certain associates of Westburton's had made a number of undeclared contributions to the Conservative Party on his behalf. According to certain 'senior sources', donations to this slush fund were kept secret because they came from lobbyists keen to influence key government decisions – a motley crowd, comprising not only property developers, but also drug and arms companies whose influence it would be highly destructive to reveal openly.

Even the most summary investigations revealed that any company in which Westburton had a hand appeared to acquire far more than its fair share of government contracts. Tightly controlled planning restrictions were miraculously lifted when the request came from Westburton's associates. The whole affair took on a farce-like tone when the press published stories of cash being handed to ministers in brown paper bags.

In an embarrassing interview on the BBC, the Prime Minister claimed that while his colleagues might have been a little 'perfunctory' in following the strict rules on political funding, he denied that he or his party were corrupt. He also refused to name the donors, on the grounds that they had been promised anonymity in exchange for their support. 'These people were public-hearted citizens who only wanted to do their best for the country and didn't want to make a song and dance about it. We're not talking huge amounts here.'

'More than £10 million, Prime Minister!'

'Peanuts, in the grand scheme of things.'

Goodness, the man's naive, Vicky said to herself.

She and Ralph had a very good idea who the party sneak might have been. Mahdi clearly hadn't reckoned on the Machiavellian tendencies of his Secretary of State for Health, who, they were sure, had turned Queen's evidence in order to secure leniency in his own sentence.

Before long it emerged that Mahdi had also received his own share of Westburton 'perks' – a major discount on building work carried out at his country home in Sussex, some rather expensive jewellery for Mrs Khan, and the inevitable luxury holidays. The *Aurora III* must have been crowded at times.

The Prime Minister was arrested and bailed on day forty-seven. One of his last gestures was to make Vicky a life peer – The Most Reverend and Right Honourable The Baroness Burnham-Woods of Larchester – a bitter-sweet end to an uneasy friendship.

'Take a look at this,' Ralph commanded her that evening, calling from his flat. She popped on the screen and saw Mahdi in 3D, a deflated, dishevelled figure, standing outside Number 10. He looked disoriented, bewildered by the flashes, as if he wasn't altogether sure what was happening to him, or why.

'How does that make you feel, my lady?' Ralph asked, sounding positively gleeful. She found the triumphalism in his voice hard to take.

'Sadder than I can say. All that wasted potential.'

'Vicky, the government will follow. There'll be a general election. That's what you have achieved.'

'It gives me no satisfaction, Ralph. I was never for or against any party. I just want the one we have to do the job honestly, justly and well.'

'I've never known anyone so dismissive of their successes.'

'You've earned yourself some Moltmann: "Success is no name of God. Righteousness is." Right relationships – open, honest, truthful, forgiving, redemptive. That's what our society needs.'

She didn't want Ralph or anyone else to think that she had acted out of political prejudice. The Labour Party had hardly been a friend to the church. It was the Conservative Party's misfortune that both Westburton and Bradley-Hind were on their side.

She sent Mahdi a quick line to express her sorrow at his situation, inviting him to come and see her. And to her surprise, he came. She suspected that few people had stood by him, and even fewer whose discretion he could trust.

'I was stupid, Vicky, so stupid, but not deliberately crooked. Believe me,' he said, in between taking several rapid sips of tea. Swallowed up in one of the large armchairs in her study, he seemed to have shrunk several inches. The recent stress had evidently cost him. She knew only too well how distressing such an experience could be, and felt deeply sorry for him. Whether she actually believed him was another matter. But she could hardly say so.

'I too made many mistakes, Mahdi.'

'We are alike, you and I. We both set a precedent – I as the first Muslim Prime Minister, you as the first woman Archbishop of Canterbury. And we got along, didn't we?'

'We did, Mahdi.'

'We had our differences, but ultimately, we both wanted the same thing – what was best for our country.'

She nodded and smiled in agreement.

'But in the end, you will be remembered for that, whereas I . . .'

He shook his head sadly.

'We're both alike in another way,' she reminded him, taking his cup and topping it up. 'We have both sought to serve God to the best of our ability. All we can do now is place ourselves in his hands, and let history be our judge.'

'Thank you for trying to make me feel better, Vicky,' he said with genuine appreciation. 'You remind me of the important things in life.'

Later, as he was leaving, he turned to her and said, 'You're not going to die, Vicky, are you?'

She was completely flummoxed, then realised it was his way of expressing his concern. She told him she would do her best not to.

'Good,' he said, gripping the hand she had proffered, and squeezing it for some time. 'I can't take any more sorrow just at this moment.'

He was only one of the many who came, one by one, bishops and bureaucrats, in a steady stream, the ashamed, the guilty and the conscience-stricken, to make full confession and find absolution from what they thought might be a dying woman. Dan Clements was one of the early ones, encouraged by gentle persuasion from Ralph, who had let him know that the Archbishop was aware that he was deeply compromised, but might be persuaded not to pursue the matter.

Sitting bolt upright in his chair, he admitted little at first, except to say that he was deeply sorry for any misunderstandings there had been between them, and had come to ask for her forgiveness.

'I know that you were involved in plotting against me,' Vicky said. 'I imagine that it was you who had Ann plant the bug in my computer?'

He went to protest, but she held up a hand to silence him.

'Tell me,' she continued, determined to have a full confession, 'why did you want rid of me so badly?'

He raised his chin, about to defend himself, then thought better of it, and gave a helpless little snort. 'I've lived with deception for far too long. It gets so tiring in the end.'

Vicky never took her eyes off him.

'Ann has been my mistress for years,' he said, refusing to return her gaze. 'He . . . saw us together, threatened to tell my wife – who is crippled with arthritis. It would have destroyed her.'

'He? Who's "he", Dan?'

He hung his head.

'The Arch . . . Ryan Talbot. You knew he told me that you were not the Crown Nominations Commission's first choice? Certain, I now realise, that I would use it one day. I presume he informed the minister. Around a year after we parted company, I was approached, out of the blue, and given the bug.'

'To give to Ann?'

He nodded, reluctantly.

'Will you forgive me, Archbishop, for what we tried to do to you? We're not proud of it.'

'So much duplicity, Dan. And for so long. I will forgive you both, but can't yet offer you absolution. Real repentance means doing whatever is in your power to put things right. You owe it to your wife to tell her the truth. She probably knows already. But the openness may grant all three of you some genuine peace at last.'

'We may face criminal charges.'

'You may indeed, and I can't say you don't deserve it, but it won't be my doing, and the grace to cope will be there when you need it. That I can promise you.'

He nodded reluctantly.

'Go in peace, Dan,' she said, and he got up to go. 'And God be with you.'

Toby Macdonald came next. He brought her a massive bouquet of flowers, and apologised for building too much on the information they had received about her supposed breakdown, as well as for telling the press that it indicated her lack of ability to do the job. He hoped the announcement of his early retirement would go some way to persuading her of the genuineness of his regret.

Repentance and reconciliation, in fact, were the surprise presents that cancer appeared to bestow with a wave of its magic wand. What her visitors did not know was that at her last appointment the oncologist had been far more upbeat than either she or Tom had dared to hope. The scan showed no further evidence of cancer in the spine, and while they shouldn't be too complacent, with the help of the expensive new wonder drug, she was in remission, for the time being at least.

She knew that few people had access to such medication on the NHS and felt an enormous pang of guilt. She told Tom she would fight for it to be universally prescribed. Her first retirement project.

'Blow your crusading spirit,' Tom had said. 'Will I ever have any peace?'

And so Ryan found her, fully clothed, flourishing, and very much alive. To his consternation, she suspected. It wasn't exactly the deathbed scene he had anticipated. He needed to re-think his lines. She watched him wipe the careful look of solicitude from his face, replacing it with something more like his usual bonhomie. He plonked himself down into her armchair and sat, one leg crossed over the other, drinking tea and eating the homemade flapjack Ann had left in her freezer a while back for occasions such as these.

She waited while he made pleasantries as if nothing had happened between them. It was almost surreal.

'I'm rabbiting on,' he said eventually, leaning forward to rest his cup and saucer on the coffee table. They rattled slightly. It was only then that she noticed that his hands were trembling. He folded them tightly and kept them on his lap.

'I feel I owe you an explanation, or at least, an apology.'

'The apology will do,' she said, curtly. 'I don't think any explanation will ever be satisfactory. "It is not my enemies who taunt me," she quoted; "I could bear that. But it is you, my equal, my companion, my familiar friend, with whom I kept pleasant company." That psalm seems to sum up the betrayal I felt.'

He nodded slowly and bit into his bottom lip, keeping his eyes firmly on the hands that continued to joggle slightly in his lap. She felt guilty for snapping at him. For not having appreciated just how much the cocksure, confident front covered a raft of insecurities. So much so that, despite his youth, an astute, well-informed committee had thought him competent enough to be a visionary archbishop. And the tragedy was that with his brilliance, his courage and his charisma he could have been.

What had happened to his spirituality, she could only wonder. But she had trusted him, relied on him so much that it had never occurred to her to find out whether all was well with his soul. And now he sat before her, vulnerable and frightened, like a boy about to report his crimes to the head teacher.

'I have thrown everything away,' he said, echoing her thoughts. 'And you're right. There can be no explanation, no justification for what I have done. Jealousy and ambition are forms of idolatry.'

'You were positioning yourself to take over my job?'

He looked up at her wearily.

'I always wanted Canterbury, from the moment I was ordained. It became a . . . blinding obsession. When I was invited to sit on the Crown Nominations Commission that appointed you, it was obvious, of course, that it meant I hadn't got the job, and I was bitterly disappointed. So I decided to do my utmost to steer things so we'd appoint someone who wouldn't last long, and then I'd have my chance. I thought the odds were good. But when I heard you speak, when I saw you in action and watched the impact you had on people, I couldn't help but admire you. I thought, I can never follow that, but still yearned for the chance to try. That meant I had to destroy the belief the people had in you.'

He rubbed his eyes with his fists.

'Shameful, isn't it?' he whispered. 'Eventually, when I tried to get free, I was in too deep. Westburton would have gone public with my part in the conspiracy.'

'What did they promise you – Mark and Nick?'

'That they would ensure my appointment as Archbishop of Canterbury this time round.'

She was puzzled.

'How?'

'Oh Vicky, don't be naive, these things can be arranged if the right people are in the know.'

'Ryan,' she said, gently, 'you were welcome to the job any time. I never wanted it.'

'And that's the irony, isn't it? You never wanted it and I never deserved it.'

He looked away from her, shaking his head.

'I hate what I see in the mirror these days.'

'What will you do now?' she prompted gently.

'Make restitution. If that's possible. There may yet be criminal charges. If so, I'll accept the just punishment for my greed. If not, I'll go back to being a parish priest, I think, and hopefully, re-learn what it means to serve – if any bishop, or parish, will have me. I may have to become one of the lay ministers you convinced us were so necessary to the future of the church. Clean the toilets, if I can't serve in any other capacity.'

She was aware that her jaw had dropped and that her mouth hung open, and struggled to regain her composure.

'I have done such terrible things,' he whispered. 'I deserve no mercy. I hardly dare ask for it. And if my plea for it is rejected, so be it.'

He leant forward suddenly, his elbows on his knees, covering his face in his hands, and began to rock backwards and forwards. She went over to him and laid a hand on his shoulder to still him. And as she did so she thought: to go to a parish, begging them to take you on, a failed archbishop – that willingness was a sign of real repentance and humility, if anything was. And if any organisation should accept such a man and be prepared to offer a second, even a third chance, it was the church.

'That's an enormous step back, Ryan.'

'But it is exactly what I need – if I'm not to sacrifice my treasure in heaven.'

She was seeing a side of Ryan she had never seen before and found it deeply moving. She handed him the box of tissues, and he took one and blew his nose loudly.

'Toby was here a while back. Perhaps I should ask him, before he disappears into retirement, whether he might have a vacancy for you in the Carbury diocese?'

Ryan finally managed one of those disarming, boyish grins of his.

'Who you know, not what you know. As ever in the Church of England. But yes, I'd be grateful if you would. I don't think he'd do it for me – but perhaps for you.'

They hugged at length as he left.

'Vicky, I'm so, so sorry for all of this.'

She dismissed him with a shake of the head.

'And I forgive you from the bottom of my heart. I have a chance to live again. And now, so do you.'

'Your determination to love and serve the church was always such an example to me, if I'm honest. So off I go, back to the drawing board.'

'You'll make a fine priest and pastor, Ryan. You always were – but not as you will be now.'

It was Bev who suggested a reunion of the trio. 'Somewhere expensive,' she exclaimed, her face animated as they watched her on the screen, 'and it's on me. I think I probably owe you,' she said, looking slightly sheepish.

'Really?' asked Mandy. 'I have no recollection of it. Do you, Vicky?'

'Absolutely not,' Vicky said.

And now here they were, three ladies in late middle age, assessing the damage time had wrought on each other's appearance as they took tea together at Fortnum's.

Mandy was every inch the company CEO, as slim and sophisticated as ever in designer jeans and a vivid fuchsia pullover, her dark, shoulder-length waves carefully streaked with flashes of ash and caramel. Her eyes glittered in a face so unlined that Vicky was convinced she must have had a little help. Being Mandy, it wasn't long before she admitted as much.

'Dermal filler, Darling,' she said, with a dazzling smile, the gold bangles on her wrist tinkling every time she raised the cup to her mouth. 'Marvellous, it's like pouring cement into all the cracks. Had the teeth done too. Expensive, but worth it.'

'If anyone is living proof that sixty is the new forty, you are,' Vicky said, intrigued by the smoothness of her skin.

'The new laser resurfacer,' Mandy said, following her stare and patting her cheek.

'Sounds like roadworks,' Bev said dismissively.

She too had made an effort, though, Vicky noticed. The greying curtains were gone, replaced by a new, shorter, shiny bob, and she was wearing a smattering of lipstick, which suggested that her fractured self-image might be on the mend.

'When I try and tell myself I look forty,' Vicky said, ruefully, 'I take one look in the mirror and say, "Who are you trying to kid?"'

'Yes, but I cheat,' Mandy admitted. 'And anyway, you look great, Vicky. Especially as the press made us all believe you were on your last legs.'

'I know. It's such fun to prove them wrong. The woman who just won't lie down and die.'

She went out to visit the Ladies, and when she came back, Mandy was saying, 'Chantal has a degree in business studies and is working for the company, of course. And Nathan is studying accountancy – a good profession for a Jewish boy, in third place only to medicine and dentistry.'

They all laughed.

'What about you, Vicky – how's the lovely Alice doing? And the grandsons?'

'I hate having them so far away. But I don't care how long the flight is, or how expensive. Now that I'm free to do it, I'll spend every penny I have on getting to see them. Thank you, cancer, for showing me what's important.'

'Don't joke about it, Vicky,' Bev said. 'It's a vile disease.'

'I know,' Vicky admitted, 'and it may well beat me in the end, but meanwhile, I plan to enjoy every moment I've got.'

'Everything we are is a gift. Everything we have is given,' Mandy murmured.

'Where does that come from?' she asked, turning to her.

'The Talmud.'

'I like it,' Vicky said. 'Every breath of life a gift.'

It was a balmy spring evening when they left Fortnum's and marched around the loud, bustling, garlic-smelling city, arm in arm, as they had in Harrogate so many years ago, laughing like the adolescents they once were, with nothing more to worry about than who they were going to meet at The Connexion. They shopped for a while, tried on shoes, sprayed themselves with perfume, held up pieces of jewellery to their ears, neck or wrists, and finally ended up hours later at a chic little restaurant in Mountpleasant Street. They settled into a corner window overlooking the river, the lamplight from their table casting a golden glow onto the gleaming ebony oil slick of the Thames as night fell.

Mandy ordered a vegetarian meal. Vicky raised her eyebrows.

'I eat kosher these days,' she said, fiddling with her fork. 'I've become more orthodox as I get older. The rituals seem more important to me. I suppose it's something to do with that feeling of becoming a tiny part of history.'

'That's what I miss most these days,' Bev admitted wistfully, 'a sense of belonging. There's a gaping hole where family and community should be. No faith to help me through. I feel disjointed, not part of anything. Perhaps if Celia and I had had a child together. But it never seemed right somehow.'

She looked at Vicky out of the corner of her eye, and Vicky smiled back affectionately.

'Don't you sometimes feel bitter towards the church, Vicky, after what it did to you?'

Vicky wanted to be honest and thought hard about what she really felt before she opened her mouth to speak. 'Not really. Most of the disenchantment was orchestrated. In the end, there were only a handful of adversaries and a large mass of predominantly well-meaning, wonderful people. I can't dismiss the whole church because of the few.'

'And every organisation has those types,' Mandy interjected. 'The great British workplace – where the mutterings and complaints of the few infect the entire workforce with a dry rot that stymies all creativity. Stop it and you'd solve the UK's manufacturing and economic problems in overnight. Why wouldn't the church be affected by it too?'

'Because the church is meant to be a living organism, not an institution?' Vicky suggested.

'In an ideal world,' Bev said, draining her glass.

'In your dreams,' Mandy added.

Vicky refilled their glasses with the last of the wine.

'Where will you live?' Bev asked her.

'No idea yet. Maybe Boston. It's a big step, but until we decide, we've found a little place to rent in the Larchester area.'

'Wooten Grange?' Mandy guffawed.

'Don't mock,' Vicky chastised. 'Not so far away. It's the nearest thing we have to home in this country.'

They ate enough food to floor the faint-hearted, put away a bottle or two of rosé, and passed another couple of hours, reminiscing, over coffee.

'Do you remember Bev in those tiny red hotpants? Have you still got the legs?' Vicky looked under the table. 'She has, too.'

'I remember carrying her home after a rough night at The Connexion,' Mandy said, stirring a sweetener into her cup. 'And bundling her into bed without her parents knowing.'

'And you,' Bev countered, grinning, 'grounded for seeing a DJ, after the parents found out he wasn't the nice Jewish boy they thought you were seeing.'

'Grief. They went ape,' Mandy said, her cup poised mid-air. 'You only understand why when you're a parent yourself. But my most vivid memory of Vicky is when she smacked that boy over the back of his head with her schoolbag, and sent him diving, head-first, down the stairs.'

'He had it coming,' Bev said.

'Even the Head thought so,' Mandy chuckled.

'She didn't say that to me,' Vicky remembered. 'Well, not exactly. She told me to put brain before brawn, and I've never forgotten it. Helped me win a few battles over the years.'

'Never one to shirk a fight, our Vicky,' Bev admitted, with a shake of her head, 'when it was a question of justice.'

'Oh, she was always something special,' Mandy said, laying her hand over Vicky's. 'You were a leader of men even way back then, Boudicca.'

'A toast,' Bev announced, raising her glass. 'To the Archbishop.'

'To the Archbishop,' Mandy joined in loudly, revelling in the stares from the other tables.

'We'll do this again,' they said to each other at the taxi rank, standing beneath a brilliant, starlit sky, huddled close against the night-time chill, their breath condensing and blending, as they yawned with drowsy contentment.

'Regularly,' Mandy added.

'I don't want to lose you ever again,' Bev said quietly, looking pointedly at Vicky.

'I shall do my very best to help you fulfil your wish,' Vicky replied, 'though I'm afraid separation must come one day, be it sooner or later.'

And then she saw Mandy's eyes glittering in the evening light.

'No tears, either of you,' she commanded. 'Not after such a lovely evening.'

'Till the next time then,' Mandy said, blinking furiously, squeezing Vicky tight.

'*Arrivederci*,' Vicky nodded, extricating herself gently as a taxi arrived. The other two clambered in and she waved them off. Till the next time.

A new government came to power, with a renewed commitment to work with the churches, not against them, and not to touch the legislation on gay marriage in the lifetime of the current monarch. Long live the Queen. The disestablishment of the Church of England might well follow her death, and then it would be for the church to decide how they would handle the matter of clergy conscience.

The new Home Secretary promised to tackle the problem of homelessness, and actively engaged The Well in seeking innovative and comprehensive solutions to the raft of social problems besetting the nation. The new Secretary of State for Education invited the Verity Trust to advise him in addressing youth issues, particularly internet addiction, and in setting up new schemes that made better use of young people's enthusiasm and ability in helping others. Schools would be encouraged to provide food for children's bodies as well as their minds, if hunger interfered with their ability to learn. The new Secretary of State for Health gave an undertaking to do all in her power to eradicate female genital mutilation.

Ah well, none of these things were her problem any longer, Vicky mused, as she and Tom said goodbye to Lambeth Palace and drove away for the last time. 'Lord, it is night after a long day. What has been done has been done; what has not been done has not been done. Let it be.' She turned around to look at the Palace, and had a sudden flashback to the first time they were driven through the gates, a mere four years ago. She had been nervous, fearful, excited. So gloriously, blissfully ignorant of what lay ahead. So many centuries of joy and sorrow, high hopes and anguish were buried deep in the very fabric and history of the building. And now her own were added to them. As well that walls cannot speak, she said to herself.

A lifetime had been crammed into the past forty-eight months. Enough activity for perhaps a dozen people. Few were given the opportunity to live at such intensity. Few would want it. But she might just miss it, from time to time. The dizzying buzz of feeling the universe revolve around her, the awesome responsibility of having the watching world waiting on her words, the satisfying yet frightening power to challenge and change some of the prejudices that kept human beings disempowered and downtrodden. Who could not be overwhelmed with gratitude for such a responsibility? All the same, she couldn't say she wasn't glad to be heading off to a future that held no palaces, just an ordinary home for the two of them, with enough room for a visiting couple, and of course the grandchildren.

'Just think, no staff,' she said to Tom, as he negotiated the London traffic and took the A1 north.

'No staff,' he conceded. 'No more London driving.'

'No endless visitors, no evening receptions, no more nightmare meetings, no tourists.'

'No goldfish bowl. No press. Just us.'

'How will we manage to live with just each other after all these years of living our separate lives?'

'I can't say I'm sorry to see the back of the Archbishop,' he said. 'Too thrusting. I'm not sure I always liked her.'

'You're right,' Vicky admitted. 'I'm not sure I liked her sometimes either.'

'We might even manage to have a marriage at last.'

'I just hope it's not too late,' she muttered, looking out of the passenger window.

'Don't, Vicky,' he commanded. 'We'll have years together yet.'

'We may not. And if . . . if we don't, if the cancer does come back, don't pretend it hasn't. Don't leave me alone in the dark. I don't think I could bear the loneliness.'

'Okay,' he said softly, putting his hand over hers. 'We're in it together.'

'No matter how long or short the time, let's have no regrets, Tom. These last months I've had a chance to test out what I've preached. Ruskin said, "There is no wealth but life." In the end, sooner or later, we all have to lay down even that. There have been times when I felt like Job, as if everything had been taken from me. But he finally managed to make his profession, "Before, I had heard of you, but now I have seen you." And now I can say, "Before, I preached about eternal hope. Now, it's a reality." Like Job, I *know* that my redeemer lives.'

Tom said nothing but his eyes filled. He reached across and held on to her hand.

'Both hands on the wheel,' she commanded. 'No pre-empting our destiny.'

'Yes, my lady.'

That night, their first in a new bed in a new home in a new life, Tom whispered in the darkness, 'Shall we have another wedding night? Remember how you laughed on our first?'

She chuckled at the thought of it.

'Grief, how it threw me,' Tom reflected. 'You always have, throughout our married life. I've been irritated, frustrated, aggravated, but not bored. That night, I should have guessed what was coming.'

'None of us ever knows what's coming, and just as well.'

He leant across and kissed her gently on the forehead.

'Now that the Archbishop has vanished from our lives, will you be okay with just being plain Mrs Woods?'

'Even though I'm a baroness?'

Tom guffawed loudly.

'Sorry, my lady.'

She dug him in the ribs.

'I'll have to think about it.'

'There's no time to think about it. "All we have is now, this beautiful, God-given moment. We must live it to the full." That's what she used to preach, the Archbishop.'

'Did she?'

'So, let's live hard, live fast, live like we mean it.'

'If it's going to be that much fun, I shall certainly take you to be my awfully wedded husband,' she said, drowsily. 'In sickness or in health?'

'For richer, for poorer.'

'For better, for worse?'

'Till death alone parts us,' he whispered into her ear.

'Until His kingdom comes,' she murmured back, as sleep slowly enfolded them both.

VICTORIA BURNHAM-WOODS – CV

Born:	12 May 1965
1976–83:	Harrogate Ladies' College
1983–6:	BA (1st) in Theology, University of Durham
1986–8:	RE teacher, Newcastle High School
1987:	*The Church of England ordains women as deacons*
1988:	Selected for ordination
1989–92:	St Christopher's Theological College
1992:	Marriage to Tom Woods
1992–6:	Curate of Killingdon
Nov 1992:	*The Church of England votes to ordain women as priests*
Nov 1993:	Daughter Alice born
March 1994:	Ordained as priest; Doctor of Theology
1996–2006:	Vicar of St Chad's, Potbury, East London
1998:	Elected to General Synod in a by-election
2002:	Appointed Diocesan Director of Women
2006–16:	Archdeacon of Westhampton
2014:	*The Church of England admits women to episcopacy*
2016–20:	First female Diocesan Bishop – of Larchester
2020–24:	Archbishop of Canterbury

SOURCES

The Jürgen Moltmann quotations were taken from the following works, and are used with permission:

A Theology of Hope: On the Ground and the Implications of a Christian Eschatology, SCM Press, London, 1967

The Crucified God: The Cross of Christ as the Foundation and Criticism of Christian Theology, SCM Press, London, 1973

The Trinity and the Kingdom: The Doctrine of God, Harper and Row, New York, 1981

On Human Dignity: Political Theology and Ethics, Augsburg Fortress, Philadelphia, 1984

The Way of Jesus Christ, SCM Press, London, 1990

Jesus Christ for Today's World, Augsburg Fortress, 1994

The Coming of God: Christian Eschatology, Augsburg Fortress, Minneapolis, 1996

In the End-the Beginning: The Life of Hope, SCM Press, London, 2004

And also from a talk given at the Garrett-Evangelical Theological Seminary, Evanston, Illinois, in September 2009

Other quotations are taken from the following sources:

Answers to Questions on Christianity: God in the Dock, C. S. Lewis, Eerdmans, 1970

The Prince, Niccolo Machiavelli

Os Guinness speaking at *The C.S. Lewis Lecture,* Trinity College, Dublin, 2012

Amy Carmichael of Dohnavur: The Story of a Lover and Her Beloved, Frank Houghton, CLC Publications, 1980

I'm also indebted to:

Robert Runcie: The Reluctant Archbishop, Humphrey Carpenter, Sphere, 1996

Know the Truth: A Memoir, George Carey, Harper Perennial, 2004

Do you wish this wasn't the end?
Are you hungry for more great teaching, inspiring
testimonies, ideas to challenge your faith?

Join us at www.hodderfaith.com, follow us on Twitter
or find us on Facebook to make sure you get the latest from
your favourite authors.

Including interviews, videos, articles, competitions
and opportunities to tell us just what you thought about
our latest releases.

www.hodderfaith.com

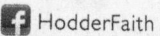 HodderFaith

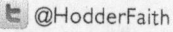 @HodderFaith

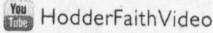 HodderFaithVideo

HODDER
WHERE FAITH IS INSPIRED